THE WARRIOR'S TALE

OTHER BOOKS BY
ALLAN COLE AND CHRIS BUNCH
Published by Ballantine Books:
THE STEN ADVENTURES:

Sten

The Wolf Worlds

The Court of a Thousand Suns

Fleet of the Damned

Revenge of the Damned

The Return of the Emperor

Vortex

Empire's End

A DAUGHTER OF LIBERTY

A RECKONING FOR KINGS

THE FAR KINGDOMS

for
Susan
and
Karen

BOOK ONE

THE
CHASE

❖

CHAPTER ONE

DEMON AT THE GATES

I am Captain Rali Emilie Antero, late of the Maranon Guard. I am a soldier, and a soldier I intend to remain until the Dark Seeker slips my guard. Like most soldiers, I praise firm ground under my boots, well-made and well-tended weapons, and a hot bath and a hot meal after a long, forced march. In short, I'm of practical mind and trust common sense over a wizard's blatherings.

For two years, however, I trod the wooden decks of a ship-of-the-line. I fought with rusted blades and was glad we had them. I bathed in cold seas and ate what I could, when I could. I was lost in the uncharted western ocean and doubted I'd ever see my home again. As for common sense, it was nearly my undoing; and it was trust in a wizard and magic that saved me.

My exploits—and those of my soldiers—have been praised by many. Mythmakers have already coined golden tales of our epic chase across thousands of miles to end history's greatest evil. The stake, they say, was destiny itself, with all civilization hanging in the balance. Truth has been sorely wounded in these myths, and with it, the lessons learned from so much bloodshed. Without those lessons, if someday darkness threatens again, we may find ourselves disarmed. Besides, I think you'll discover in this case the truth makes a more stirring tale than its prettier sister.

But before you enrich that thief at the bookstall for these adventures, I have a caution: I am a woman. If you object, keep your coin and depart.

I shall not miss your presence. All others are welcome to my hearth—this journal. If it's cold, stoke the fire and warm your bones. If you thirst, there's a hot jug of mulled wine just by the hearthstone. If you hunger, shout up the mess steward for that cold joint I had her put by. Your company is my pleasure.

My scribe warns me some beseeching of the gods and goddesses of journal writing is in order here. But I've my own deities to keep content and they're a jealous lot. I've told the old fool a sword beats a quill any day, so the gentle gods of ink are out of luck. My prayers are saved for those who keep my blood in my skin, and *that* tight and whole about my bones.

At the outset I gave the scribe one further order. The words he writes must be mine and mine alone. I do not give a dry wineskin if he objects to my choice of phrases. I *will* speak the truth—be it bald as his pate, or plain as that pale, chinless thing he calls a face. The truth doesn't need a scribe's garlands to sweeten its path. But this fellow is a stubborn, quarrelsome sort—not unlike the three I've already dismissed. I've told him if he persists, I'll cut off his head and mount it on a post outside my door as a warning to his successor. The scribe says he fears more for his reputation than his head. He keeps babbling about Scholarship and Art. This is a *history*, he insists, not a barracks' yarn.

I claim the opposite and see no shame. For in arms this story began and in arms it ended. In between there's many a fallen warrior to mourn and many a deed to honor.

It's bad luck to kill a scribe. Besides, he works for my brother, and I've promised Amalric to return him in good condition. In the interest of family peace I'll let him live. And I hereby warrant all blame for what follows is upon my head, and I so warn the reader.

This then, is my tale.

THERE ARE those who claim there were evil omens by the cartful on the morning my story begins: nursing mothers whose milk suddenly soured; a two-headed piglet born to a tavern keeper's sow; newly sharpened swords mysteriously gone dull at the armory; a witch whose bone-casting cup shattered in mid-toss. There's even a yarn about an Evocator who went mad and turned his wife and mother-in-law into a matched pair of oxen.

I couldn't say. On the day in question I woke with a blazing hangover. It took a long and agonizing moment to orient myself. In happier times I'd have been lying on the big soft bed in the charming home that was my due as commander of the Maranon Guard. Next to me would have been the beautiful Tries. Ahead would be a day that started with a bit of a tickle and a snuggle, a hearty breakfast, and a brisk hour of exercise with the steel-muscled women who make up the Guard. Instead, I found myself in a narrow, bachelors' quarters room, cramped on an iron cot . . . and very much alone. I'd fled my own home three weeks before following our final, angry row. And the previous evening I'd seen my former lover in the company of a fellow Guardswoman with a notorious reputation. She was considered darkly handsome by some, but to my mind she was greasy, wanted bathing, and had the shadow of a budding mustache on her upper lip. She was sure to be the ruin of my innocent Tries.

I'd treated my wounded feelings with first one jug of hot spiced wine then another, until evening became late night, a blur of loud song, alley stumblings, perhaps a fight, and finally the release of falling stuporous upon that hard bed.

I enjoy strong drink—but rarely to excess. The Goddess blessed me with a quick, powerful body, eyes that can count the lice in the feathers of a distant sparrow, and a clear, agile brain. This is no boast, but only the particulars of the gifts I was born with. I did nothing to earn these things, so have always seen it my duty to keep all in as fine a fighting order as the weapons I carry. Drink is as great an enemy to the body and mind as dirt and rust are to a sturdy blade.

All these things I told myself, as Madame Shame hounded me from the bed and I put my bare feet on the cold stone floor. As a thousand booted troops marched through my head and a thousand more squatted on my tongue, rebellion broke out in my belly, and I rushed for the chamber pot to surrender my innards. As I knelt there making a drunkard's penance, it suddenly came to me this was my mother's feast day. Each year, on the anniversary of her death, my family gathers at Amalric's villa to honor her memory. I retched again as Dame Guilt—that old fishwife—shrilled with joy at a new weakness revealed.

Drunk on *this* day, of *all* days, she tsked. I'm not drunk, damn you! I snarled back. I'm only *suffering* from drink. It was Tries' fault, the slut! Go ahead, blame that poor girl, Dame Guilt whined. Meanwhile, your mother's ghost will flee your foul breath and be forced into the company of strangers. She'll wander the earth mourning the low state her darling daughter has fallen into.

"Begone, damn you!" I bellowed. Then I groaned, for I'd shouted aloud and another angry mob charged about my belly. As I hunched over the chamber pot, the door swung open behind me.

"I see we're at prayer to the porcelain goddess," came a sarcastic voice. "You are an inspiration to us all, my captain."

I wiped my chin, came to my feet, and with as much dignity as I could muster, turned to confront my new challenger. It was Corais, one of my chief legates. She was slender and wiry and reminded me of a cat—especially the way she grinned and toyed with her game before she ate it. At the moment, I was her mouse, and she was hugely enjoying my misery.

"Leave off, Legate," I growled. "I'm in no mood for sarcasm."

Corais' grin only grew wider, sharp white teeth flashing behind sensuous lips, dark eyes sparkling with amusement. "I never would've guessed, Captain," she said. "You hide your troubles so well, I doubt there's a woman in the Guard who knows Tries has banned you from her bed . . . and taken up with another."

I slumped on the cot, defeated. "Don't tell me," I moaned. "I was shouting it from the rooftops, wasn't I?"

"Not shouting, exactly," Corais said. "But you certainly were in good voice. And although our fair city's roofs remained safe, Polillo *did* have to drag you down from the water tower on the parade ground."

As I picked at this new scab of humiliation, another voice joined us. It rumbled down the hallway like distant thunder:

"Who speaks my name?" The voice was followed by heavy boot steps, and an immense form filled the doorway. The speaker continued: "By the Goddess who made me, I swear if I catch someone talking behind my back, I'll cut off her left tit and have it tanned for my purse."

It was Polillo, who, with Corais, was my other chief legate. As she said the last words she ducked under the doorway and strode into the room. Polillo was well over seven feet tall, with amazingly long, shapely legs and a perfectly proportioned figure padded just enough to hide ropy muscles that became steely knots when she hefted her battle-ax. Her skin was nearly as fair as mine, and where my hair was golden, hers was closer to a light brown. If she'd been a courtesan instead of a warrior, Polillo would've soon made her fortune.

When she saw it was me sitting on the bed, she was instantly taken aback. "Oh . . . I'm sorry, Captain. I didn't know—"

I waved her to silence. "I'm the one who owes apologies all around," I said. "But if you really feel the need—the line starts behind the chamber pot."

Polillo boomed laughter and clapped me on the back, nearly breaking my shoulder with her good humor. "You just need a good fight to set you straight, Captain," she said. "And unless those sniveling Lycanthians turn coward, you'll get it soon enough."

The mention of Lycanth opened the door to responsibility. I groaned to my feet, stripped off my sleeping tunic and padded to the basin. A servant had crept in while I slept, and there was a pitcher of still-steaming water, perfumed with a cleansing aromatic, on a pedestal next to the basin.

I called over my shoulder to Corais, "What's the news?"

In the mirror I saw Corais shrug. "No news, really. Just a lot of rumors . . . some good . . . some bad. The only thing that's certain is we're still on the road to war."

Three weeks before, the Archons of Lycanth had tossed down the gauntlet—sending out a war fleet to sever our links with our allies and harass our trading ships. Their action had come the very day Tries and I'd gone our separate, stormy ways. And as I speak these words to the Scribe, I realize there was no coincidence. My profession was at the heart of our quarrel, and since my profession is war, the news from Lycanth fell like a sword between us.

"War might be certain," I said to Corais, gloomy, "but what's not is whether our exalted leadership will allow the Maranon Guard to serve."

Polillo sputtered. "But we're the finest soldiers in Orissa. I'd match any *one* of us against any ten men from any barracks or drill field in the city. Why, in the name of Maranon, wouldn't they let us fight?"

She was only exaggerating our abilities a little, but the answer to her question was in my mirror, as I saw the reflection of my body. Inside, I was a warrior. But in a world commanded by men, the outside made me something less in their view. I saw the tilt in my long neck and knew it to be dainty in appearance—never mind the cables that leaped up when I hefted my sword; my skin has always been my pride: it's pleasing to the eye and touch, but suffers little from heat, cold, or hard exercise. Although I'm past thirty summers, my breasts are firm and high, with nipples of virginal pink; the tuck of my waist is sharp; my hips, though narrow, flare like a bell; and finally, I saw the golden triangle between my thighs that marked my sex.

It was unlikely the Magistrates would let us fight for three very good— for them—reasons: (1) we were women; (2) we were women; and (3) we were women.

Everyone in Orissa knows *of* the Maranon Guard, but few know much about it—other than the obvious fact that it is composed solely of women. We are an elite unit whose beginnings stretch back into the city's dim history. Our usual force is five hundred souls, although in war it's reinforced to nearly twice that number. We all praise the name and pledge our lives to the service of Maranonia, the Goddess of War. We must forswear men upon entering the Guard—although, for most of us, this isn't much of a strain. I'm not unusual in my taste for a woman's company, and a woman's love. Besides, in this so-called civilized age we live in, the Maranon Guard is the only world a woman *can* escape to if she does not wish to be a wife, a mother, or a whore. Among those who still yearn for a man's bed, the trade-off is certainly not worth the price of a mounting.

My silence did nothing to stop Polillo's probing. As I finished washing and dressed, she kept worrying at the subject, like a gutter lizard with a pig bone.

"They're *sure* to let us march with the men," Polillo insisted. "Isn't that so, Corais?"

Corais gave another of her elegant shrugs. It was the kind that answered questions that hadn't been thought of yet. She was a small, slender woman, with beautiful dark features. Although she was no weakling, speed and cunning was her game. I alone in the Guard could best her with a sword—and I'm not boasting when I say that in all my years as a soldier, I've yet to meet my better with a blade.

"If we march, we march," I said. "If we don't, we'll accept whatever mission they give us. We must be ready—no matter what our orders."

My outward attitude was a lie. Inside I was burning with more than the effects of too much wine. The Maranon Guard had rarely been hurled into distant combat. Although we'd proven ourselves many times in our long and honorable history by fighting last-ditch stands at our city's gates, the Magistrates and Evocators consistently refused our pleas to join our brother warriors in battle on foreign shores. We were a force of last resort, we were told. Our holy mission was to guard Orissa. But there was not a woman among us who did not know the real reason, and that was our sex, which made us lowly beings—pretty pet things that must be protected—in our leaders' eyes.

Polillo stamped her foot in a fury. "I'll fight," she vowed. "And there's not a man in this city who can stop me!"

"You'll do as you're ordered," I snapped. "And if you wish to remain a legate, you'll keep your views to yourself. I'll not have the women riled up by a lot of hot talk."

"Yes, Captain," Polillo said. But her head drooped and her full lips trembled. "It's not fair."

Corais patted her, soothing. "Why don't we get in a little work with your axe?" she said. "We'll write the names of the Council of Magistrates on the practice dummies and you can lop off their heads."

Polillo wiped away a solitary tear and made a smile. She was a woman who was quick to anger—sometimes dangerously so—and wore her heart pinned to her tunic. But her saving grace was that her good humor was usually easy to restore.

"You're a good friend, Corais," she said. "You always know how to get me out of one of my moods."

But as they started toward the practice field, Polillo said: "Why don't you talk to your brother, Captain? Maybe he can tweak a few Magistrate noses on our behalf."

"I don't like to use my family connections," I replied. "The Guard will have to stand—or fall—on its own."

Polillo frowned, but Corais pulled her away. I finished dressing in solitude. I'd just enough time to make it to Amalric's villa for the rites honoring my mother. I wore my ceremonial uniform: gleaming boots, a short white tunic, polished harness bearing my sword and dagger, a golden, waist-length cloak, a half a dozen slender gold rings on each wrist; and to top the outfit off, a wide, gold band encircled my head. I sprinkled on some orange-blossom scent and got out my favorite earrings. They were also of gold: in the left ear I pinned a jeweled, miniature spear, fashioned after the one our goddess carried; in the other, a replica of Maranonia's torch, bejeweled as well.

I made one final check in the mirror. As I stared into it, I found myself fingering the dangling torch—the symbol for our goddess's vigilant search for wisdom. Perhaps Polillo was right. Maybe I was letting my pride stand in the way of the honor my Guard deserved.

Very well, then, I decided—I'd talk to Amalric. If anyone could kick those Magistrates' fat asses into motion, it was my youngest brother.

THE CITY WAS in the grips of war fever as I rode through it. Although war had not been officially declared, there was no mistaking that hot emotion had already outreached ceremony. At the Evocators' Palace on the hill, black smoke boiled from the chimneys of the conference rooms where our Magistrates huddled with the Evocators for wizardly advice. In the streets, people were buying goods at the market stalls at a furious pace, loading wagons and sacks with whatever they feared might soon be scarce. Young bravos dashed through the streets on horse and afoot, shouting war slogans and making silly boasts about what they intended to do when they met the enemy on the field. Pretty maids were ogling the boys from windows and doorways, and I didn't doubt they'd be slipping off to meet them before the day was through. Taverns were doing a booming trade, as were the witches' booths at the market, where many a crone was tossing bones, or peering into bloody animal organs for signs of what the future held. The armorers' shops were a racket of hammers against metal, and I knew that deep in the bowels of the Evocators' Palace, the spell casters were hard at work coming up with the latest in magical weapons. Why our superiors were still talking, instead of *doing*, was beyond me.

Like most soldiers, I am a fatalist—what will be, will be. I don't like politicians much because they tend to obscure the intentions of the fates. They rail on as if there really were choices, when it would be better to keep your peace and study what was sure to come. Show me a mountain pass with a thing of value at the end of it, and I promise you that by and by troops with greedy intentions will march along that path. Point out a good ambush site—no matter how empty the wilderness—and I'll give you a drunken corporal's odds that if blood hasn't already been spilled at that site, it's only a matter of time before it will.

In my mind the facts of the matter were that the Lycanthians were our natural enemies and should be quickly dispatched to the afterlife. We were as different as day and night. Orissa is a merchant city, filled with life, laughter, and a love of the arts. We're a river people, and like all river folk, we're dreamers. We see the worth of hard labor against a stiff current to achieve a thing, because we know how easy it'll soon be to lie back and bask in the sun and let that same current carry us swiftly home.

Lycanth, on the other hand, was a creature born on a hard coast from an unruly sea. Its citizens trusted no one and coveted all. They lived willingly under the yoke of two Archons, whose every word—no matter how evil— was strict law. The Lycanthians were dreamers as well, but they dreamed of conquests as they stirred in their sleep on that rocky coast. They dreamed of a vast kingdom, made up of our lands and beyond, where we would work as their happy slaves.

Over the years, we'd fought Lycanth many times—our talent as soldiers barely winning the day over their skills as seafaring warriors and their willingness to accept the most appalling casualties in massed frontal charges. The last time, we'd nearly hammered them into oblivion, but held back from a final obliterating blow. You may think that was wise, agreeing with the politicians who said a weakened Lycanth was better than no Lycanth at all; their presence kept other enemies from our borders. You may not be surprised I disagree. My reasons: (1) their Archons began conspiring against us from the first day of their defeat; (2) Amalric and the late—unlamented by me—Janos Greycloak were stalked and harried at every turn during their expeditions to find the Far Kingdoms; (3) when Amalric and Janos discovered the land we now know as Irayas, they also uncovered a conspiracy by the Archons and Prince Raveline to betray Orissa and Raveline's own brother, King Domas of Irayas.

Is that enough for you? This bloodless thing who poses as my scribe says no matter what the outcome, the original decision was humane, and therefore correct. Let me continue to number the facts that make up my case: (4) my brother returned from the Far Kingdoms with not only rich trading contracts, but tremendous magical knowledge, which King Domas had agreed to share with us; (5) the Archons of Lycanth were immediately seized with envy and especially fear that with this new knowledge in the hands of Orissa they would soon lose all hope of fulfilling their dreams of rising from the ashes to destroy us; (6) they went immediately to work speeding up their secret rearming. Facts (7) and (8) are less debatable, and had happened very recently and at almost the same time.

Secret patrols our leaders had been wise enough to post just beyond Lycanth's limits—near the neck of the peninsula the city was built on—returned with a shocking report: Lycanth's great wall stood again. It'd been built epochs earlier, even before the Lycanthians began their attempts in empire-building, and reinforced over the eons not only by slave work gangs, but by all the protective magics the Archons could cast. Then, during that last war—which my father, Paphos Antero, had fought in—all Orissa's Evocators combined to birth a great spell, and the wall was cast down in a single night. Now the wall stood once more, a barrier that served as mocking proof that the Archons had done more than merely conspire with Prince Raveline: some of his black secrets must have been imparted to the Lycanthian rulers, as well.

That would've been enough in itself for war, but the Archons—and this is the last of my reasons—broke every peace agreement between the two cities, and sent out their fleet to harry our merchant ships and those of our allies. It was a deliberate act of war, although I prefer to think of it as no more than piracy and the Lycanthians no better than any other bandit clan.

My scribe is giving me a grudging nod. If that little rodent has conceded defeat, I feel safe in assuming your added agreement. When Lycanth last fell, we should've razed their city, dispersed their people to the ends of the earth so the name Lycanth would be meaningless in a generation, and sowed salt in the ground their cursed city had been built on.

Where was I? Oh, yes: the politicians were politicking, the Evocators were wizarding, the lads were boasting, the maids were flirting, and Orissa was girding for war. And I was off to my brother's place to make peace with my dead mother.

The whole family, except Amalric, was gathered before her garden shrine by the time I arrived. It was during the Holy Hour of Silence, so I got some angry looks from my three other brothers and sniffs of superiority from their wives. But they're a mean-spirited lot and easy to ignore. Sometimes I doubt they're truly Anteros, and believe my father must've made them on the cot of some stingy whore. So, when Omerye waved for me to join her, I was grateful to slip through the ranks of brothers, cousins, and other chilly kin, to a seat by her side.

Omerye leaned close to whisper: "Amalric is at the Palace. He should return soon."

I nodded—it was no surprise my youngest brother would be at the heart of things. My mind buzzed with arguments I'd put to him later—but soon the silence of the others, and the peaceful scent and color of the garden, let all those busy thoughts slip away.

My mother, Emilie, was a modest woman, who thought decorated shrines and altars were unseemly. I was just entering womanhood when she died, and my father was too grief-stricken to properly tend her needs for the afterlife. Amalric was still a toddler then, and although my other brothers—especially Porcemus, the oldest—were intent on building an elaborate temple-like thing in her honor, I fought fiercely on her behalf and won. Instead of the temple, a simple stone shrine was set beneath a small rose tree. Instead of an elaborate simulacrum painting of her features—such as the one that graced the shrine to my dead brother, Halab—I demanded the stone remain blank. However, my mother had a love for the sound of gently running water, so I got an Evocator to cast a spell that made a small stream trickle continually down the face of the shrine, to run into a little pool now covered with fallen rose blossoms.

As I looked at the shrine I felt pride stir from more than twenty years past. It was my first real victory. I'd been a wild child who loved to run up trees, hurl stones at birds, and beat up little boys who, with sneering lips, called me a girl. Everyone was constantly complaining about the mischief I caused—except my father and mother. My father said I'd grow out of it and would soon be simpering about like any other pretty maid. My mother said nothing either way, but when I was in her company and did something ruffianlike, she only smiled and acted as if it was normal. She encouraged me to learn, and made father get me a tutor just like boys of wealthy families. And when I confessed to her one fateful hot night—when we were all alone in her room and the air was thick with mother-daughter secrets—that above all things I wanted to be a soldier, she did not gasp in shock, or weep from imagined failure. Instead she told me there were many things she'd wanted to accomplish in *her* life, but because of her sex, had never had the chance.

"Oh, why," I mourned in great youthful passion, "were we born women, Mother? Why couldn't we have been born men?"

Now, she expressed shock. "That's not what I meant," she said. "I've never wished to grow a man's parts. As far as I've been able to see, a penis does nothing but weaken the brain. No, my dear, don't pray to be a man. Only pray to have the same freedom as men, and if you get it, you will be content. I'll tell you a secret. I think someday our time will come, and when it does, women are much more capable of looking after the world than any man I've ever met."

"I can't wait that long," I cried. "I'll be old, and they don't let old people be soldiers."

My mother looked at me for long time, then nodded. "If that's what you want," she said, "then that's what you shall be."

A week later my father hired a retired sergeant to teach me to fight. He never said a word to me about it, but only smiled when I complained of bruises after a hard day of getting drubbed by a wooden sword. A year later that smile cut from ear to ear, as I'd bested the sergeant in every skill, and he had to trade him for someone more adept. By the time my mother died I was better than any youth in the city—or at least those willing to test themselves against a warrior girl. I was a young woman of sixteen when I entered the Maranon Guard. I've never looked back.

The sweet strings of a lyre coaxed me out of my reverie. It was Omerye, who'd left my side unnoticed and was now sitting on a stool by the shrine, playing that wonderful instrument of hers. She looked at me across the others as she played, and began to sing a gentle song I knew was meant for me. I saw the soft fall of her red hair—as bright red as Amalric's—and thought my brother a lucky man to find such a woman. I had a lover once, I thought, who'd touched me like Omerye must touch my brother. Not Tries, but Otara, she of the throaty laugh, soft arms, and fingers that could stroke the demons from my head. She was my lover for many years before she died, and I suppose in many ways she'd replaced my mother.

Forgive me if I weep, Scribe. But do not smirk, as if to say that is the nature of a woman. If you dare do such a thing—or even think it—I'll forget my vow and you'll not leave this room to smirk at another. Otara is close to my heart, and when I swore I'd speak only the truth, I knew very well I'd have to reveal things that are against my nature to uncover. There may be more weeping before this book is done—so beware, lest some of the tears that fall become yours. Now, let me wipe my eyes and gather my thoughts . . .

As Omerye sang, I mourned Otara—just as she'd meant. The song changed and I felt cleansed. The lyre took up a playful tune. It made me think of my mother's laugh, and I reflexively looked at the shrine. I watched the water running along the moss that clung to the stone and imagined the shape formed by moss, water, and rose petal shadows to be my mother's face. It seemed to come alive and I saw her eyes open and her lips move. There was the heady scent of sandalwood—my mother's favorite perfume. I felt a warm hand touch my neck and thought I heard a whisper—my mother's voice. It was so low I couldn't make out what she said, but I knew if I listened closer I could hear quite easily. I think I became afraid . . . Actually, I'm sure of it, for I suddenly thought—this is nonsense. It's the hangover still at work. Your mother was an ordinary mortal, like yourself. Certainly not the kind to play at ghosts. I snatched my head back, and the whisper broke off. The scent was gone, and when I looked at the shrine, so was the face. Omerye had stopped playing. I saw her frown and shake her head. I felt like I'd missed something very important—and the loss was painful.

Then all thoughts of loss, lovers, and ghosts vanished in a thundering of hooves outside the villa walls.

Amalric was back from the Evocators' Palace.

HE'D RETURNED with news that war had been declared. The remainder of my mother's feast day collapsed in a babble of fright and excitement. Every citizen of Orissa was expected to gather at the Great Amphitheater that night to hear the public announcement, undoubtedly to be accompanied by various morale-boosting displays.

My brother soothed everyone as best he could and tried to keep his temper as they deluged him with stupid questions: how long did he think the war would last; what kind of financial suffering did the family face; what goods did he think would become scarce, so they could begin their hoarding now with an eye to black-marketeering in the future. Although Amalric is the youngest of my father's children, he's the unquestioned head of the family. My father had wisely passed over my other brothers—all as weak and lazy as they were foolish—to bequeath his merchant empire to Amalric. Obviously, a lot of jealousy and hard feelings were stirred up, but my brother's force of personality, plus his fame as the discoverer of the Far Kingdoms, kept the weasels cowed in their dens. Eventually, he caught my eye and motioned to meet him in his study. Then he shooed them all home with reminders to attend the great meeting.

As I took a seat near his writing desk a few minutes later, I could see from the grim set of his mouth and high color of his skin that there was more news than just the declaration of war.

"What are you hiding, brother dear?" I asked. "Go ahead . . . tell me the worst."

He laughed, but the sound was harsh. "I can't ever keep anything from you, can I, big sister?"

"It comes from long practice, my dear," I replied. "Before you became a grown man and such a—dare I say it—*responsible* sort, I caught you with lizards in your pockets, and a little later, doxies in your bed."

My brother had been so young when our mother died, I'd practically raised him. We'd always been close, sharing secrets we'd never dream of mentioning even to our loved ones.

"So, out with it, Amalric," I said. "Tell your wise sister what those fools at the Palace are in such a panic about."

Amalric made a wry grin. "Even though we have had plenty of notice," he said, "our troops are hardly prepared for a real war."

"That goes without saying," I replied. "Although *my* women are ready enough. We've doubled our training schedule and have remained on full alert since we heard the first rattlings of Lycanthian swords. I've even, without orders, put extra recruiters out around the girls' lycées and marketplaces, paying their expenses from one of my discretionary funds, for which initiative I could probably be relieved."

My undisguised tone alerted him to my bitter feelings. He gave me an odd look, then moved on.

"Well, the rest of our troops will be doing the same now," he said. "Especially after the Magistrates were done spanking our incompetent commanders."

"They'll be up to the mark soon enough," I said, grudgingly admitting that my brother soldiers were not totally without worth. "Which means that problem will be quickly solved, and everyone knows it. So if the Magistrates and Evocators are still shitting their breeches, then the trouble must be *really* big."

Amalric sighed. "It's magical in nature," he said.

"I should have known," I replied. "But they're all panicky fools. Haven't they any faith in their own spells? Or have they been lazing about and ignoring the secrets you brought back from Irayas?"

"Of course not. But the Archons have been hard at work, too," Amalric said. "And it seems they got more dark knowledge from Prince Raveline than we suspected. Our Evocators fear they'll match us spell for spell. Look at that damned wall across the peninsula they restored. One of the Evocators told me no one in the Palace, even Gamelan, could cast a spell like that overnight."

"Who cares?" I scoffed. "In the end, hard steel always decides a fight. So their Archons have worked up some new spells to protect them from our weapons? That'll mean *our* wizards will find a counterspell, and so on and so forth, until finally it's up to us common soldiers to win the old-fashioned way—with blades, axes, clubs, and bows. Don't worry. We've always beaten them in the past. Magic isn't going to change anything."

"Normally, I'd agree," Amalric said. "For I learned as much about magic in battle from Janos Greycloak. He might have been a great sorcerer, but he was always a practical-minded warrior first."

He poured himself a goblet of wine. I waved him off when he offered me some and took some cold water instead.

"This time, however," he continued, "there are foul tales of some terrible weapon the Archons are working up. I know rumors are more plentiful than beetles in pig swill when war threatens. However, Gamelan reports strange disturbances in the magical ethers, which leads him to lend credence to the whispers."

I was silent. Gamelan was not only the chief Evocator—and our most powerful wizard—but an old man who had seen much and was noted for his cool appraisal. If Gamelan was worried, there was good cause to fear.

"What else?" I asked.

"The Archons are trying to win favor with King Domas," my brother said. "He is a cunning monarch, so I doubt they'll have much success. Unless . . . they convince him our cause is hopeless. Then he'll do the same as any sensible ruler—he'll support the apparent victor."

If that happened, we wouldn't stand a chance. The Far Kingdoms are superior to us all in the practice of magic. They were our allies, thanks to Amalric. But would they remain so?

"We'll just have to face that when it comes," I said, returning to the safety of fatalism. "If it comes at all."

"Preventing it will be my sole labor until the war is over," my brother said. "The Magistrates have ordered me to Irayas. I'm to keep King Domas sweet for the duration."

I didn't have to look at his gloomy face to know this was upsetting. He would not only miss the fight, but would be forced to live among strangers for as many years as the war took.

"When do you leave?" I asked.

"In a few days," he said. "As soon as I get my things together and a ship is readied."

Both of us considered what the future might hold. My own thinking was that there was little time for my brother to help me in my own task.

"Before you go," I said, "I want you to speak to the Magistrates. Every person is going to be needed for this fight. The Maranon Guard *must* not be kept home!"

Amalric shook his head. "I already brought the subject up," he said. "And despite all my arguments . . . it was rejected."

My heart plunged. I was stunned to have lost so quickly.

"But why?" I cried, although—as I said before—I knew the answer.

"The usual reasons," he said. "I listened to their tired old quarrel for hours."

"Let me list them," I said, my temper barely under control. "The gods made women gentle, and it's unnatural for them to be warriors; we aren't strong or hardy enough to take the field; our moods are controlled by our monthlies; we have no reasoning powers, but are victims of casual fancy; male soldiers wouldn't trust us to fight by their sides, or they'd be too protective, putting their own lives and the mission at risk; we, their daughters, would become whores, since it's a well-known fact women have no control over their base natures and will fuck every man in sight; and, if we are captured, the enemy will rape us, demeaning the Manhood of Orissa."

"I don't think you have missed one," my brother said drily. "The last reason drew the most heated comments."

"Oh, lizard shit!" I said.

"My feelings exactly," Amalric said. "Although my replies were not so colorful, or to the point. Plus, there is one thing I have not mentioned as yet. General Jinnah will be named to head the expeditionary force. It was he, in fact, who was the most vociferous in opposing the deployment of the Guard."

My anger found new heights. Jinnah as Supreme Commander! That surprised me, but shouldn't have. Jinnah was one of those soldiers a country at peace spawns like a compost heap breeds maggots. They're all of a type: coming from the proper family; educated in the proper lyceums; serving in exactly the right post at exactly the right time as they rise in rank; able to speak well to their superiors; calm yet resolute to politicians; almost always handsome and grave, the very image of what a leader should look like; and never touched by scandal. In time of war, all of these pluses become fatal defects: their families and teachers will not have allowed an original idea or person to cross the threshold for generations; their kowtowing to their overlords proves a mockery since they believe their superiors to be even stupider than they are; in frustration they take out their anger by treating their underlings with arrogance and disdain. Finally, they've avoided scandal by never doing *anything* unless they had to, and only then if there was a culpable subordinate to blame should things go awry. As for their cultured looks—I've never known a handsome face to turn aside a spearthrust.

In short, I felt General Jinnah to be an exact mirror of everything that was wrong with the Orissan army as it dreamed through the long years of peace.

I'd never run afoul of the man, although once in maneuvers, when we were detailed off as the mock enemy, I'd sent my Guard into "battle" using irregular tactics that not only "destroyed" his forward elements, but made a shambles of his most-precise, most-absurd timetables. Not that a direct confrontation would have been necessary for him to oppose me thus—Jinnah was well-known as a fanatic foe of anything that smacked of the new or original, not unlike our city fathers.

My anger fled and I was left with nothing but despair. Tears blurred my vision, although not one fell. I heard Amalric rise, and in a moment he had a comforting arm about me.

"Don't say you're sorry," I snarled. "Or I'll lose whatever dignity I have left."

My warning was unnecessary. Amalric knew me too well to say a word. But I didn't shake off his arm. I badly needed the steadiness of his loving touch.

I thought of that moment in the grove when I had seen my mother's face on the shrine, smelled the sandalwood perfume, and heard the indecipherable whisper. Why had I rejected her? Why had I turned away? Because, I chided myself, there *was* no ghost. You were only being weak—because of the hangover. You imagined it. But a part of me quarreled with that: imagination or not, it said, for a moment you *believed*. Whether it was a ghost or your imagination, you still rejected her. Why? I couldn't say. If there was an answer, it seemed to lie at the bottom of a great, black abyss.

As if reading my thoughts, Amalric said: "Mother would be proud of you, big sister."

"How do you know?" I said, my tone unwarrantedly harsh. "You barely remember her."

Amalric sank down on the thick carpet and leaned against my knee. It was the old, familiar position from long past when he was a little boy and I was the all-wise hero sister.

"You've told me enough about her," he said, "so I'm quite sure of it."

I snorted, but I liked his words just the same.

"What was she really like?" he asked, his voice as light as that long ago child's.

"You've heard it all," I said.

"Tell me again," he pleaded. "Was she beautiful?"

"Very beautiful," I said, remembering her fair skin, wide, deep eyes, and slender form.

"Was she gentle and wise?"

"She was the wisest and gentlest of mothers," I answered by rote.

"Tell me how she came to name you 'Rali,' " my brother asked.

"You've heard that tale as well," I said. But he gave my hand a squeeze and so I told it again, for I could never deny my brother anything he asked.

"In the village of her birth," I said, "there was an old idol by the well. It was the statue of a young girl, a heroine in ancient times. She was found in the wilderness—raised by animals, some say. When she came to the village, she had no knowledge of the right or wrong of things, and behaved as her nature moved her. She was as strong as any of the boys and could best them in any physical competition. But she was beautiful as well, so they also lusted after her. The village was scandalized by her behavior and the elders ordered her into exile. Soon after she'd gone, an enemy force attacked. There were so many and they were so fierce, it soon looked as if the village was lost. But out of the night the girl rode in on the shoulders of a great black cat. And there was more than just girl and panther, for every animal with fang and claw came roaring from the forest and fell upon the enemy soldiers. Soon they were saved and the animals—and the girl—vanished. The story goes that whenever there is trouble—overwhelming danger—that girl will return to rescue the villagers. So they put up a statue to remind themselves because someone might be strange, it does not mean they are necessarily evil."

"And then they named her," Amalric said.

"Yes. They named her Rali."

"Why?"

"Because . . ." And I remembered my mother telling me this story for the very first time. I'd sat on her lap and she'd cuddled me in her arms. I'd asked the same question, and she'd told me the same answer I was about to relate.

"Mother said it's an old word . . . from her village. 'Rali' means hope. And that name came to her the first instant she held me to her breast."

We sat in silence for a long time. Finally, Amalric patted me and rose. "Thanks for the story," he said.

I grinned. "I should be the one doing the thanking, brother dear. Although nothing has changed . . . your little trick has made me feel better."

Amalric didn't bother denying his intent. Instead, he took my hand, saying: "I'll ask the Magistrates again."

I only nodded. But in my breast, I'll admit, there was a small stir of . . . hope.

THAT NIGHT the whole city gathered at the Great Amphitheater. Rich were jammed against poor; fishmonger next to fat merchant; market witch beside thin-nosed lady. On the huge platform in the center of the vast arena were our leaders: the Magistrates; Gamelan and his chief Evocators; the military commanders; the merchant princes; and—just to the side, but in a place of honor—my brother, Lord Antero. Spells cast their images large so all could see, and made their voices loud so all could hear.

I knew that Amalric—as promised—had once again urged the Magistrates to change their minds about the Maranon Guard. He hadn't had time to report their answer, but I knew what the decision was when the runner rushed to our barracks an hour before the meeting. The Council of Magistrates was kindly asking us to play a special role that night. Fifty of us were asked to serve as the honor guard. To symbolize our important role as Orissa's protectors, we were to bring our idol of Maranonia, and special prayers, as well as rich sacrifices, would be made to her.

In other words, they'd said no, and were throwing us a bone to bolster our pride.

I didn't breathe a word of this to my soldiers, and as we formed up just inside the amphitheater's big gates—arranging ourselves around the idol—every woman's face shone with pride. Polillo's beam was enough to light the night, and Corais was so thrilled she forgot to berate one of the soldiers for a spot on her golden cloak. I myself felt proud of my soldiers, their spirit, their professionalism, their confidence, despite my certainty that disappointment was but an hour or so away. I looked at Maranonia's face and whispered my own private prayer of thanks for being blessed in leading such fine troops. The Goddess made no answer, but I liked to think there was a gleam in her jeweled eyes. She seemed to stand straighter than ever before—torch outstretched, golden spear raised high.

I lowered my eyes as Gamelan advanced to the center of the stage to ask our gods to bless the meeting. He was a tall scarecrow of a figure, with long white locks and beard. He threw up his arms, the sleeves of his black Evocator's cloak falling back to reveal long, bony limbs.

"All hail Te-Date," he cried.

"All hail Te-Date," the crowd roared back, hot blood stirring in our veins.

"O Great Lord Te-Date," Gamelan intoned, "your humble people are gathered before you to beg your assistance in this, our greatest hour of need. Evil wizards are conspiring against us. They covet our lands—your lands—and desire to enslave us, your faithful servants. Orissa is in grave danger, O Lord Te-Date. Orissa is—"

A terrible howl of fury ripped the night. The clear and star-filled sky was blackened by an immense cloud, with lightning cackling about it. The howl became two great voices—chanting in unison:

"Demon come,
Demon eat.
'The Trap is closed,
Rats in the nest.
Demon come,
Demon eat!"

Not one among the thousands there had to ask who the speakers were. Not a babe, not a maid, or warrior or lord, needed to wonder. It was the Archons of Lycanth, striking the first blow of the war. It might be the final blow as well, for the whole city was trapped in the amphitheater, at the mercy of the Archons' sorcery.

buried our dead, tended our wounded, and mended the tools of our trade. It's good to be praised and admired. But any warrior who thinks the cheers of a grateful and worshiping public will stick longer than a too early snowfall is in for a sad and bitter reckoning.

On the fourth day, Amalric sent a message, asking me to meet him at the main port. I hurried to the docks, knowing he was about to leave for Irayas and his mission with King Domas.

The ship was in its final loading stages when I arrived, and I found Amalric pacing back and forth on the dock. As soon as he spotted me he shouted like a boy and ran to hug me. We clung together—brother and sister—for a long moment, then drew apart for the farewell. But instead of a sad frown, his smile was as white as any glad smile of greetings.

"I have good news for you, big sister."

I waited. Rali means hope, I thought. Rali means hope.

And Amalric said: "The Magistrates have had a change of heart. And since I have a special interest, I wanted to tell you before the official announcement. You have won. The Maranon Guard will march out with the others."

I laughed. He hugged me again.

Then: "That was quite a thing you did the other night."

I shrugged. "I had help. Besides, that was just a skirmish."

"Then I won't bother lying and claim it will get easier as it goes," he said.

"Did it ever get easier," I asked, "when you and Janos went after the Far Kingdoms?"

"No," Amalric said. "There was always another, bigger hill to climb, horde to dodge, and desert to cross. I learned it never gets easier. In fact, it gets harder, but you just keep going . . . until it's done."

"I hope more people than you and I know that," I said.

"A few might," he said. "Some of the Evocators, in fact, thought the demon was the Archons' rumored secret weapon. They were ecstatic you'd destroyed it. But Gamelan set them straight. It *was* powerful magic, he said. But—"

"It was just a demon," I broke in.

"Yes," Amalric said. "It was *just* a demon."

The ship's bell rang a warning. We embraced and kissed a final time. Amalric boarded and the crew cast off. I stood on the dock until the ship tacked at the bend in the river and sailed out of sight. The last thing I saw was Amalric's scarlet hair, blazing in the sunlight.

And it was many a year before I saw my brother again.

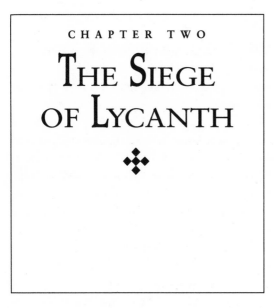

CHAPTER TWO

The Siege of Lycanth

❖

Not two months ago I was invited to the Citadel of the Magistrates for the blessing of a great frieze. There, I wielded the holy knife and sacrificed a white bullock to dedicate the ornate carving, which runs the full circumference of the central dome. It was a rare honor, especially for a woman. But each time I looked at that frieze—which claims to be a history of the Second Lycanthian War—I had to alternately hide either a smile or a flash of anger. The ceremony was actually a rededication, since it'd been necessary to drastically alter the sculptor's first version after I finally returned home from my adventures—and certain tales could no longer be told as before.

My little scribe, who I'm now seeing as less a wharf rat than a sometimes-annoying chipmunk chattering for more nut meats, is alarmed, frightened I'll ruin my tale by detailing just how, and why, the first frieze became so embarrassing to the Magistrates and Evocators. You may rest easy, chipmunk. I'm too experienced at bellowing war ballads and telling lies of battle, beer, and bed to equally deceitful comrades-in-drink to reveal anything in my story before its proper time.

I thought of the frieze because the sculptor's vision—like most tales of war, whether pictured, sung, read, or told—is still as big a lie as any hasty stammer a parent fumbles up when her child first wonders how babies came to be. The carving begins with a few panels showing the horrible outrages of the Lycanthians, ending with that demonic attack in the amphitheater. The next panel shows the Orissan army, proudly arrayed, marching off to war. Then we see the assault on Lycanth's peninsular wall, followed by a boring series of scenes showing Orissans cutting, shooting, spearing, and otherwise bashing our enemies—ending with the last battle. I suppose I ought to be more polite about this molding, since it now prominently features my women of the Maranon Guard—including an impossibly beautiful warrior woman intended to be me. But I swore I'd tell the truth in this tale, and that truth must include my thoughts and opinions. Else I'm no different than any drunken old soldier whose creaking boasts serve only to send the tavern's drinkers rushing eagerly out into the heart of a winter storm.

I remember well when we set off on that sharp spring morning, splendid in our ceremonial armor and marching in perfect unison like we were hung from strings controlled by a master puppeteer. As we marched we sang some thankfully forgotten ballad about how we were going to fuddle ourselves on Lycanthian blood and banquet on their guts. I've noticed that such gory hymns never last beyond the first fighting; and then the old songs of home, the past, plenty, and peace are called for.

I won't suggest the frieze should next show the army as we halted an hour after the last well-wisher turned back to Orissa, hastily changed out of our heavy, blister-causing, eye-blinding, but glamorous dress uniforms—hurling them into the quartermasters' carts, not to see them again until the campaign ended or we were slid into them for burial—and then shambled off in easy route step and field garb. What I am objecting to is the jump to the breaching of the wall—as if nothing happened in between. We did break through—but only after we'd fought for a full year. And when we first marched up, our enemy was waiting on the parapets to fire a deadly stream of missiles—from catapults to crossbows.

During that year, all too many Orissans died. Almost a third of my Guardswomen became casualties, and I learned a duty never mentioned in the epics—constantly begging my superiors and anyone who seemed to have a speck of authority for more: more weapons to replace those lost; more supplies to replace those consumed or spoiled; but most of all, replacements for my poor wounded, crippled, invalided, or slain comrades. New recruits arrived, but they never seemed to be as good as the sisters we'd marched out with—no matter how thoroughly we tried to train them before they were awarded the crested helmet of a Guardswoman. I also became skilled at writing letters to the bereaved—letters in which I invariably assured the mother, father, or lover their beloved had been struck down in the midst of some heroic act, dying instantly and without pain. Those lies didn't bother me then nor do they now. The only reason to show a civilian the bloody mask of real

war would be if that might somehow put an end to solving problems with
a sword, but no one but a fool or a romantic can dwell on her people's history for more than a moment and keep *that* dream alive.

Once we'd formed battle lines in front of the Lycanthian wall, the killing
began. We attacked and were driven back. We assaulted once more, with the
same result. We cut down the forests on the mainland behind us to build
siege engines, then attacked again. Again we were sent reeling away from
that scarred stone face as impervious as any mountain cliff. Sometimes we
would reach the parapets, but be unable to hold them; and men and women
were butchered or hurled to their deaths if they could not retreat in time.
Still, we kept up the pressure, and the Lycanthians were thoroughly trapped.

When they first erected their city, time before memory, it was cleverly
conceived as a fortress. They built at the tip of a narrow peninsula, where a
volcano had bellowed fire at the heavens and then the sea had breached its
crater—creating an enormous high-walled harbor. The Lycanthians mounted
an immense chain across the harbor's mouth to guard it from enemies such
as ourselves. Just at the tip of that crater was the Archons' monstrous sea
castle, where my brother had been imprisoned. Around the crater and down
the peninsula, the city itself was built. The Lycanthians preferred to build upward in great street-long tenements, rather than sprawl outward, like Orissa.
At the narrowest part of that peninsula was the wall. Beyond it began the
wilderness, with not even a Lycanthian hovel to mark the forest.

Our army had them sealed by land, but Lycanth's huge fleet was still a
threat. We river dwellers had only recently realized the necessity for Orissa
to be strong on the sea, so our warships were few and their reinforcements
were still a-building—many of them in the Antero yards Amalric had constructed when he returned from the Far Kingdoms. We could not allow
Lycanthian warships the freedom of the seas, for fear they might attack
Orissa, or land soldiers behind our lines. At the very least, their ships might
bring in enough supplies and reinforcements to lift the siege. Once they realized the Lycanthian navy must be confronted, our Magistrates and Evocators
made a hard decision—they hired seaborne mercenaries: by the sailor, by the
ship, by the squadron, by the fleet. No one was under any illusion that a
mercenary fights for other than immediate loot; and not very fiercely even
then, if his opponent is battleworthy or offers payment for the gallowglass to
change sides. But no one saw other options, and so the Orissan banner was
hoisted on craft that a few weeks earlier had been privateers and freebooters
sailing under anarchy's black flag. They were commanded, after a riotously
drunken "election," by "Admiral" Cholla Yi, a great hulk who—from his os-
tentatiously waxed hair worn in a double row of spikes, to his al-

ways spotless silks, to the three, some said four, daggers he kept secreted about his body, to his laced, tightly fitting rainbow-colored boots—was the very image of a merchant-eating corsair. I'll admit, grudgingly because of later events, Cholla Yi at least seemed to keep his rogues under control. He began his reign by erecting gibbets on either side of the beach encampment, and saw to it those gibbets were always creaking with the fresh bodies of miscreants. He also struck fast and bloodily, driving the Lycanthian ships back into their harbor—sinking or capturing those who were slow in their flight. That huge chain—which hung from the Archons' sea castle across the harbor entrance to a watchtower on the far promontory—served its purpose well and kept our warships from attacking the harbor, or sending in fire ships or cutting-out parties. It was a stalemate, but the Lycanthians were now sealed by sea as well as by land.

The battles for the wall went on. Sorcery rebuilt that great wall before the war began, but as I'd promised Amalric, it finally fell to hard steel, only slightly assisted by magic. A particularly alert subaltern with the Frontier Scouts, a unit that'd become nearly as elite a fighting force as my Guards, noted that a section of the wall was lightly manned. For a week thereafter our heaviest trebuchets hurled boulders in the sector, only occasionally loosing a "wild shot" that happened to strike just at that nearly deserted section. When the stonework was deemed sufficiently weakened, but not so obviously that one of the Archons or their underlings cast a reinforcing spell, the assault troops were told off.

General Jinnah assigned the Scouts the honor of being first up the ropes, although I argued long and hard for my Guardswomen.

Gamelan was in Jinnah's tent during my protest, which grew quite heated. He'd chosen to leave Orissa's comforts to lead the expedition's Evocators. At the time, his decision was praised as a great patriotic deed—or, murmured by the cynical, that our Evocators were most worried about the rumored secret weaponry the Archons might be developing from Prince Raveline's knowledge. As I learned, and you shall in time, there were other reasons for Gamelan's seeming selflessness.

He stepped in when the argument became loud enough to alert the sentries outside, and calmed us both. I didn't appreciate it at the time, but he probably kept me from being relieved and sent home in disgrace, since I was about to call Jinnah an incompetent lizard fart whose only ability in war stopped at the sand table. He offered a compromise: once the parapets were taken by the Scouts, my Guard would make up the second wave. I grudged agreement, forced myself to knuckle my brow in respect, and stamped out, angrily pulling my helmet on. Gamelan followed, and once beyond earshot of the sentries, touched my sleeve. I almost snapped at him as well, before remembering not only my politeness, but that this sorcerer was quite capable of casting a spell of, say, invisible pubic lice to suggest the virtues of courtesy.

Since we'd arrived at the wall, Gamelan had visited the Guard and my own tent several times. No one knew why, and not even Corais chanced a bawdy theory. Personally, I thought it might be an odd sort of apology for his having taken so long to openly support Amalric in his struggle against the corruption in the Evocators' Guild; or even, perhaps, because he remembered my long-dead brother, Halab, who'd been destroyed by the guild working as the unknowing cat's-paw to Prince Raveline. But these theories, thoroughly considered, made as little sense as a Guardswoman explaining the real injustice of why *she* was chosen to dig a privy.

In the light from a nearby fire I saw Gamelan had a bit of a smile on his facé. "I understand your disappointment, Captain Antero," he said. "But have you considered that, because of General Jinnah's obstinacy, it's not unlikely more of your Guardswomen shall be alive to see tomorrow's sunrise than would be otherwise?"

I must have blinked in astonishment, but before I could formulate a more politic response, I blurted, "What of it? A soldier's final duty is to die. Why else would she serve if she didn't understand that?"

I heard a ghost of a chuckle. "Most straightforward, Captain. Just the answer I would prize from a brave soldier. But . . . perhaps I might have expected more from an Antero. After all, a mirror need not reflect a single image."

"I don't understand."

There was no response, and Gamelan was gone, having slipped away into the darkness as silently as if he'd used magic. I puzzled briefly, then put the matter away. Evocators always behaved like that, I thought. As much of their powers came from deliberate confusion and fumadiddle as from magic itself. Another thought caught me and this deserved more attention: Gamelan, that severe brooding eagle, had not only smiled, but actually laughed—unless I'd been listening to the wind. Perhaps, sometime in the distant past, back in the days when fish had legs, Gamelan had known human concerns? Had laughed, had loved, had joked, had even, perhaps, drunk a flagon too many or even winked at a pretty girl or boy? Impossible, I thought, and hurried to issue orders for the after-midnight attack.

The attack went perfectly, to the surprise of all veterans, since war's characteristic is as much confusion as blood. The Evocators, under Gamelan's direction, cast a subtle spell that merely covered the sky with black clouds and sent a wind from the sea whistling across the peninsula, a wind gusty enough to mask a soldier's clumsiness if he happened to slip noisily as he crept forward. Padded grapnels were cast and the Scouts went up the wall handily and silenced the Lycanthians on the parapet with their favored weapon, a leather-bound, sand-padded slung shot. They signaled for the next wave. Ladders were rushed forward and steadied, and my Guard went up and over. Torches flared and the shouting and slaying began, but there was no more need for silence, as below us the sappers brought forward their rams and the rhythmic crashing began. Before the Lycanthians could do more than rush in the closest reinforcements, the wall was breached and the army poured through, into the peninsula and then Lycanth itself—first the low buildings on the outskirts, then through the city streets and the towering stone tenements.

Gamelan was wrong about how many Guardswomen were to die that day, because we pressed the Lycanthians hard, knowing if we stopped for food, for water, for even a breath, they'd have time to counterattack. We gave them no succor and battered them back and back through their city. I'd read war in a city is the worst of all, that an attacker can lose control of his entire force and have it butchered to the last warrior before he realizes what has happened. That is correct. Of all the fighting I did before, and even afterward, on land or shore, I cannot remember any time as dreadful as that gore-soaked day when we drove the Lycanthians through their home city to the sea.

If the fighting had been bloody before, now it became awful. Soldiers and demons poured out of those strange tall buildings, slashing through their own panic-stricken populace to get at us. More than soldiers died in this swirling madness. I saw Lycanthian women, not in armor, using flails and butcher knives lashed to poles as well as swords and javelins from downed warriors, fighting in the front ranks, and saw them killed. I saw old men, other women and children, unarmed, screaming in fear, trying to run, trying to hide, trying to surrender. I saw them cut down by battle-maddened soldiers—even by my own Guardswomen. My officers and sergeants shouted against this blood lust, and in moments it was gone. The fighting went on all that night and the next day, and suddenly we were in front of another great wall.

This was the sea castle of the Archons. There they stopped us. Again the siege was mounted, and again almost a year passed. The sea castle's walls withstood assault after assault. Our blood and theirs stained the black, smoking stone. The gates were buckled and blasted, but still held firm. At any moment they could swing open and unleash a surprise attack by warriors made mad by the Archons' spells. Inside those walls we could hear the screams of the wounded and the pitiful moans of the starving. Outside, our army suffered as well. War had denuded the countryside for many miles. Our supply ships were simply not enough to support our land forces, and we had, through common humanity, to try to feed those poor Lycanthian civilians who'd not been able to flee into the sea castle in time: civilians the Archons refused to admit to the castle in the one brief truce we were able to call. Our soldiers were exhausted and plagued by hunger and disease, overflowing the hospital tents with their numbers. Sleep was no release: the air was so festerous with the stink of magic that nightmares constantly stalked our dreams.

But it was the will of the Archons, not the defenders of those walls, that had ground our advance to a halt. The two wizard kings of Lycanth were fighting for their lives with a fury. Our Evocators, though bolstered mightily by spells my brother had brought back from the Far Kingdoms, were blocked by the Archons' counterspells at every turn.

I said the bloodbath of the assault through Lycanth was the worst fighting I've ever known. I wish I had another set of words to describe what a siege is like, because, in some ways, it is more terrible. There is constant boredom, but you must never let yourself relax. One momentary pause in the open, and a sharp-eyed archer sends a shaft through your guts. You must never speak too loudly, nor shout, or else the enemy might use that sound to catapult a boulder onto your position. You must keep your ears sharp, or a raiding party might slit your weasand before you see the glint of his steel. You must never leave your shit unburied, or flies will walk first on that, then on your food, and the curse of diarrhea or worse shall be passed. You must try to keep yourself clean, because if you are wounded and dirt from your filthy rags enters the wound, it will fester—although how you're to be so sanitary living in a hole pickaxed through the city's cobbled streets, no one can say. You must try to be cheerful, because a woman who constantly complains will weaken herself and those around her. You must . . .

. . . and so forth. I could go on, but I was reminded by my beady-eyed collaborator this is not a manual intended to instruct soldiers.

As the siege continued, matters became worse between General Jinnah and myself and therefore the Guard. We were denied what little glory was to be gained being the first to attempt an assault, or even on what we call a "futile hope," which is a small party seizing a sudden opportunity—a small-scale version of the Scouts' attack on the wall, which now seemed to have happened so long ago it might've been an exploit told our grandmothers. We were sent into every action: the more bloody, the more likely the Maranon Guards would be at the forefront. We were slowly whittled away to less than two hundred, and it seemed as if no more replacements would ever arrive. At times it seemed Jinnah wished the Guard to die to the last woman. This I refused to let myself believe, attributing it to the heartsickness any leader feels, seeing her best die and others replace them and die as well—and to what end? So I said nothing of my thoughts to anyone, not even Corais or Polillo.

There were tales claiming that Jinnah was enriching himself at the army and Orissa's expense, that he had special teams assigned to comb through the city's apartments for gold and riches and secretly take them to his estates outside Orissa. No one had actually seen these looters-by-command, so I spoke harshly to anyone incautious enough to repeat the rumors in my presence. But when I was in conference with the general, I couldn't help but study him closely for some sign of avarice. All I saw on his face, however, was despair that the siege could not be maintained much longer. There was also real fear in his eyes when he heard tales from our spies that the Archons had nearly mastered a death spell that would be the end of Orissa.

Finally the day of reckoning arrived; although like all such days I have experienced, there were none of the Signs and Symbols I hear are supposed to accompany these events.

General Jinnah gathered us for yet another dawn attack on those impenetrable walls. There was a weary desperation about the whole thing. The sergeants shouted and lashed the men into formation. Bellowed orders followed, and the soldiers cursed their officers and their fates as they were driven into battle lines. Half-starved oxen dragged heavy war machines through the muck. There were rams and wheeled towers and great catapults. Men with scaling ladders were rushed to the jumping-off points, where they nervously eyed the walls. Meanwhile, our enemy prepared as well. Pots of hot oil and molten lead steamed and smoked on the ramparts; rubble was perched to tumble; crossbowmen cranked their bows taut; archers chose their straightest shafts and pikemen made a deadly, sharp-edged forest along the breastworks. We were a motley army of twenty thousand. Only a few thousand were professional soldiers now, including my two hundred. The rest were shopkeepers, butchers, laborers, and former slaves. As for the enemy, we did not know how many opposed us—perhaps ten thousand, perhaps more.

As the horns sounded and soldiers on both sides tiredly pounded their shields and croaked jeers at the enemy in what had become a routine prelude to battle, I led ten women away from the field, on a special mission given us by Jinnah—although he swore Gamelan had as much to do with it as he did, which I doubted.

The diversion we were about to launch bordered on the suicidal. This was why I led the mission that day, with a handpicked force that included my two top legates. I was determined to bring them all back alive or, if my hopes were dashed, at least I would have the thin comfort that I'd not given the duty to someone I might think less capable or experienced. Besides, no soldier is fit for command if she will not herself go where she proposes to send her charges.

All of us had blackened our faces and any exposed skin with burnt cork, and a spell of nonreflection had been cast on our blades. We wore no armor, since its weight could slow us enough to become a target. We wore only dark short tunics, caps, and tight-fitting breeches.

We darted from cover to cover, moving easily, by hand signals, feeling as if we were all one flesh. Our first goal, which we reached without being observed from that curtain wall that loomed closer and closer, was the ruin of an outer guard tower that neither side could hold for long. We crouched beside its high wall and Polillo stirruped her hands. I thrust my foot into that brace and she catapulted me upward, to where timbering protruded from the wall that'd floored the upper story. I caught a broken beam in both hands, pulled myself onto its narrowness and flattened—trying not to send debris showering down on my companions. A sharp rock dug into my breast as I turned on my side and unhitched the long rope slung over one shoulder. I double-hitched it around the beam and dropped its end back down, and a moment later Corais swarmed up. She had no trouble finding a steady perch; and while I belayed the rope for the others, she steadied them in the last few feet of their climb. The only sound we made during all this was the creak of our leather harness, the scrape of our boots, and the occasional dull thud of a rag-wrapped weapon.

The last woman up was Polillo. I strained against her weight—she was easily twice the weight of any two of us—and a few agonizing seconds later she was on the shelf of rotting wood. She unslung the heavy leather bag that was her charge and dumped it on the stones. She grinned.

"Now, for a little sip of Lycanthian blood," she said. She patted the beaked axe at her side. "Precious is hungry, poor thing."

"We are supposed to create a diversion, Legate," I reminded her. "Killing Lycanthians rates way down the ladder of our duties."

Polillo sulked, those lovely full lips of hers making a childish pout.

Corais gave her a slap on the back to boost her suddenly sour mood. "I'll catch one for you," she promised. "So you can break his little neck." She made a snapping gesture with her two hands and clicked her small sharp teeth to approximate the sound of broken bone.

Polillo started to boom laughter, then caught herself, with a guilty glance at the castle walls now very high and close beside. "Oh, Corais, what would I do without your cheer?"

"If that cheers you, my sweet, I'll catch two of them and really put the shine in your eyes."

I paid no attention to this prebattle jawing, but peered carefully first at the sea castle's main wall—I could see no signs that we'd been spotted—then back at the battlefield from whence we'd come. Our Evocators had mounted a small platform near the center of our lines. On it I could see half a dozen of them, busy chanting and casting spells with great and meaningful gestures. In their center was Gamelan. Suddenly he flung up his hands. His shout, magically amplified, thundered across the field.

From behind the castle walls I heard an equally loud roar from the brazenly magnified throats of the Archons. The air crackled with the roar and then shattered. Then came a chorus of howls so piercing we all ducked our heads, eyes forced shut and ears clamped to avoid the pain.

As we realized we were behaving as foolishly as any raw recruit seeing the first flight of arrows arching toward the battle line—knowing each is aimed directly at her heart—and recovered, the spectral part of the battle commenced. The morning sky was night, and magical fires raged overhead and demon legions howled and clashed. On the ground all too human men lurched forward.

This was our cue—we slid through a narrow port, and now we were inside the ruin. I tossed our rope into what'd been the guard tower's central room and slid down. There was no far wall standing that'd keep us from being seen by an alert soldier atop the castle's curtain wall. I shivered. This was closer than I'd ever been to this dreadful haunt. Here Amalric had been imprisoned, he and Janos Greycloak, first in an apartment high in the castle's battlements in an attempt to break them with magic, then deep underground in its dripping dungeons. I collected myself—my purpose, the purpose for us all, was to destroy this evil, from its huge, nitrous stones to the Archons who ruled from within. Mooning about, feeling evil emanations as if I were a market wife scared out of her girdle by a fortune-teller's cant, accomplished nothing.

The ruined guard tower had blocked our way to a narrow lava ledge that began a few dozen yards away and ran around the perimeter of the castle wall. The shelf was no more than a spear length at its narrowest and twice that at its widest, or so my observations had suggested in the two days I'd spent reconnoitering the mission from afar. Do not think this shelf was in any way a weak point our army could exploit. To one side, as I've said, was the castle wall, going straight up, with not a place to spike or lash an assault ladder to be seen. On the other, it fell away, a vertical glasslike cliff two hundred feet or more to the harbor and bottled-up ships rotting at anchor below.

I motioned and Corais and three others slipped away onto the ledge itself. I heard a muffled cry and the remaining six of us had our weapons bared—there must've been a sentry or even a roving patrol. Polillo dropped the sack and reached for her axe. I held her back with an angry frown—Corais would chance a shout if she needed us. Polillo muttered as we heard the clash of weapons, and I knew her hot blood was rising. There was silence. A few breaths later Corais rushed into view and beckoned us forward. Polillo growled with jealousy, seeing her bloody sword. Corais made a small smile, then shrugged: what could she do? Duty and all. I hissed at them: Quit the byplay, pay attention. Then we hitched up our harness and ran out onto the shelf, around the castle.

We crept almost halfway around the castle before reaching the spot I'd picked for the diversion. Here the shelf widened briefly, room enough for perhaps half a company to assemble on and then be crushed from above—since there'd be no way a full assault could be mounted from this position, nor any troops reinforced once the defenders on the walls realized their presence. But the shelf's width was not the reason I'd picked this place for the diversion: I thought I'd seen, and a minor vision-enhancing spell had confirmed the sight, that gates had once been cut into the curtain wall here, at a corner tower. I'd wondered for what purpose at the time, and considered the thought once more. I thought I saw, just at the cliff edge, a splintered stone foundation where a derrick might've been set a long time ago. Possibly this would have been a secret entry to deliver items to the Archons, hoisting them straight up the cliff and hurrying them into hiding. I shuddered, not able to conceive anything so awful that the Archons would fear discovery by their completely subjugated people.

After I'd seen these gates and told Polillo and Corais of their existence, fire had sparked in their eyes. Perhaps we could somehow break those gates down? Perhaps we could lead a party into the castle itself? I cut off such speculation. I knew the Archons and their military commanders were hardly fools, and such a weak spot in their defenses, even one as hard to reach as these, would've been sealed long before. Now, close to these gates, I saw I'd been right. They were cemented firmly closed, and the lightness of the mortar showed they'd been sealed for years. If it were possible to break down these gates, it'd take an enormous ram to do it—and how could such a device be transported to this cliff edge? But the gates had inspired a bit of modification to Gamelan's diversion.

Below us was the harbor mouth, and I saw the catenary arch of the colossal chain that blocked it. Each of the chain's links was the size of a river yawl. The chain was green with age, dripped seaweed and slime. I had spent hours staring at that chain as I planned this mission, wondering if we could work our way along the shelf to where it ended against the castle walls, held by a huge staple. But I'd suspected the shelf petered out before reaching the chain, and now my impression was confirmed. Even if we had been able to reach it, what good would that have done? However the chain was raised and lowered—I knew as much by magic as by levers, pulleys, and human engineering—that was done from the tower on the promontory across, a tower as fiercely defended as the sea castle itself.

I brought myself back to the business at hand and felt ashamed. I was behaving as bloody-minded as any young subaltern, always with an eye out for that single stroke, that single charge that'd not only win a war, but cover its architect with glory. Our duty today was more prosaic, since at most it would be an assist to the main attack now being mounted far behind us.

Cold fingers eeled up my spine. I had the eerie feeling of being observed by unfriendly eyes. I let my own eyes scour the battlements above and saw nothing. But that feeling is something I've learned to prize highly, so I next scanned the walls themselves, looking for a window or even an arrow slit from which someone might observe us. But there was nothing.

For a moment I wondered if this corner tower was where Amalric had been imprisoned—he'd said he had a clear view of the harbor and the chain from the window of his prison apartment. No. These walls were blank; except for the barred gate, there was no feature to mar those smooth stones. Amalric's cell must've been at a different point. Still, the feeling of being watched persisted.

I heard something then. It was a voice, but yet not a voice, and I thought it whispered a warning, although I couldn't make out any words, nor the speaker's sex. It was vaguely familiar, and I shivered, wondering in a mad moment if it might be Halab, my long-dead brother. Amalric had said Halab's ghost had come to his aid on the expeditions to the Far Kingdoms. Although I've found Amalric to mostly be a man of sense, at that time I personally believed his imagination had been stoked by that rascal Janos Greycloak. Either that, or they made an especially heady wine in the Far Kingdoms.

I steeled myself and gave the signal. Polillo threw the sack over her shoulder and leaped forward. I ran behind her across the open ground. The big woman moved easily, toting a weight that would've foundered two strong men. We stopped on the ledge's widest point and my legate upended the sack. Out tumbled three massive crystal spheres, along with an odd mounting apparatus designed by our wizards in their weapons shops. It consisted of a three-foot cylinder, knobbed on one end, and a wheeled tripod base. The cylinder telescoped to twice its length, as did the legs. As I struggled to set it up, a beam of sunlight speared through the magical haze, bathing us in light. I cursed my clumsy fingers, knowing at any moment we could be spotted. But finally it was done and Polillo had the cylinders arranged into a triangle. At my signal, Corais led the others out. They took the formation Gamelan had drilled into us for half the night.

Polillo frowned, as distrusting of sorcery as I. An Evocator should've been assigned to perform these functions. Gamelan had urged Jinnah to let him go, but the general had refused—without explanation—not even allowing the presence of a junior and therefore more expendable wizard. Polillo unhitched her axe and spread her long legs into a comfortable striking stance. I pulled a small bag from my waist pouch and sprinkled gray dust on first one sphere, then the others. The dust was the ground bones of fallen warriors. Feeling more than a bit of a fool, I chanted the spell Gamelan had hammered into my head.

"We are few.
We are many.
We are bone.
We are flesh.
We are ten.
We are one thousand."

I stepped back and drew my sword. Then I threw back my head, opened my lungs and hurled the battle cry of the Maranon Guard. My sisters echoed my challenge. Our voices ululated up and up until the keening pierced the roar of the battlefield we'd left. Then we waited—an army of ten, certain we were about to die. I saw figures running along the castle walls above us and braced for what would follow.

Suddenly I felt a tingling all over my body. My hair rose, my nipples became hard as stones. The tingling turned to warmth and centered itself at my belly. It plunged into my womb, where it gathered strength and flared into a hot fire. I howled with the joy and strength of that blaze, and I heard my sisters joining in until our ten voices were that of a multitude. I felt I was no longer one warrior, but ten. That ten became ten times that number, and I was one hundred women, with one hundred swords slashing the air in defiance. And about me were nine hundred warrior sisters raging at our enemy.

Gamelan had promised we'd appear to our enemy as an army of a thousand that had suddenly leaped up from the very earth to confront them. I heard shouts of surprise come from the castle walls and knew he hadn't lied. Battle lust clutched at my throat and I wanted to order the attack, but sanity held sway over my magically charged imagination and instead I shouted to Corais. She and another woman raced to the wheeled apparatus and ran it forward. The knobbed end slammed into the gates, and although I knew it was too small to leave even a mark, the sound it made was that of a mighty ram—and that is how it seemed to our enemies. A shimmer in the air gave me a glimpse of their view: the odd apparatus had become a huge war machine, towering above the two hundred women warriors who operated it, an engine easily big enough to shatter those gates and their reinforcing. The rest of us—eight hundred plus—were dressed in sparkling armor, and we displayed all manner of weapons besides that great ram: axes and bows, lances and crossbows, grappling hooks and scaling ladders. We made a terrifying sight.

The shouts of warning were many now, but I could see they offered no threat; panic was the commander of those walls. I heard Polillo laugh and mock their manhood. I laughed with her, imagining their balls shriveling against their thighs. Soon the enemy would strip his defenses from the front gates and rush back to oppose this new threat. Jinnah had held a great force in reserve that would then burst through those weakened defenses, and for the second time in Orissa's history the Archons' sea castle would fall.

I heard one of my soldiers cry in alarm. Huge black clouds rushed through the sky. They hovered above us, boiling and whirling. My marrow froze as ghostly laughter roiled from within them. The clouds parted and I saw a man's gigantic face. His eyes were the black of graves, his fleshy lips bloodred, and his great beard a desolate forest. The lips peeled back to expose long filed teeth. The Archon laughed again, and that laughter was so powerful it broke Gamelan's spell and my strength fled. I was swiftly diminished, until I was not a hundred soldiers, but ten; then but one—and such a small one at that, to dare the Archons of Lycanth.

The Archon's lips compressed to form a word, and when he hissed it, his breath was foul, so cold it froze us in place. "Antero," he said. I thought I heard a note of surprise. His gaze became worms crawling out of black mud to sniff at me, leaving trails of slime on my soul. More laughter. "A *woman!*" His mockery was thunder. He drew in his breath—a howling in the air—and spat.

His spittle rained from the cloud, drenching us in unimaginable filth. We were humbled and humiliated by that fetid storm. The face vanished into the cloud mass, which swirled furiously for a moment, then funneled down and down into the sea castle . . . until it was gone.

The ten of us stood on that naked shelf, helpless against our enemies. Before we died, it was our turn to suffer jeers. The men on the walls shouted, mocking our sex, taunting us with threats of the obscene acts they'd perform on our corpses. But the jeers had an opposite effect—instead of fear, they roused anger.

Polillo roared: "Come down and fight, Lycanthian scum! I'll cut off your arms and legs and send your heads back to your women with your balls stuffed down your throats."

She hurled her great axe upward. But she was so angry she loosed too soon and the axe fell short of the parapets—if any of the rest of us had tried a similar throw, we could not even have reached half the distance. The blade struck the blank stone with a crash—but instead of falling back, it stuck! I gaped: the axe had not penetrated the stone, but seemed to hang there in midair. Why didn't it fall?

There was a knot of archers on the parapets, and a thick flight of arrows rained. Training overtook fear and we dove for the ground, rolling over and over until we lay close along the castle wall itself. I sprawled next to Polillo, hugging the stone to make as difficult a target as possible. But the safety was illusory; soon the archers would crane over and pick us off, or other soldiers would fry us with boiling oil.

I peered up and realized I was just beneath Polillo's axe. To my amazement I saw it wasn't stuck in a crevice or joining at all, but hung from the ledge of a shuttered, not even barred, window. I turned my head this way and that, examining what I had believed to be blank walls. Instead I saw other windows pocking the face. As I puzzled over the trick that'd made the walls seem blank from a distance, someone gave a cry of pain. Jolted, I saw one of my soldiers plucking an arrow from her thigh. Our doom was moments away. I saw those crystal spheres, still out in the open, and an idea struck. I gave quick orders to Polillo. She nodded, her face lighting up.

I came to my feet and darted out—back along the shelf—as if trying to flee, zigzagging and dodging as arrows fell around me. Then I wheeled and doubled back. Polillo had followed me out, but took a different course. While the archers concentrated on me, she raced to the spheres. She plucked one up and hurled it at the knot of archers. It whistled toward them like a shot from a siege catapult. The magical sphere struck just below the parapet, where it exploded with a huge flash and roar. I had guessed, or perhaps just hoped, that all of the spells the Evocators had muttered over the device must have given it a mighty charge—one as likely to be unleashed by physical strength as sorcery; just as a perfectly blown crystal may shatter when tapped with a fingernail at the correct point.

As stones showered down, Polillo scooped up another and flung it. This sailed entirely over the walls to explode, unseen, in the courtyard within. The final sphere found its mark, and I heard screams of pain and terror follow its blast.

Before our enemy could recover, we were serpenting back the way we had come. Corais led the race and Polillo took the rear, the wounded woman slung over her shoulder. We didn't bother dodging, but sprinted straight as swallows for their nest. But even in that mad flight, shame stung at me; and despite my improvisation, defeat was sour on my tongue.

We doubled along the shelf toward that shattered guard tower, the ropes and safety. A flight of arrows whipped after us. Time was running out.

But as the first swarm struck at our heels, a thought pierced my desperation. I suddenly knew how to solve the riddle of the Archons' sea castle. I prayed to Maranonia to speed my feet and blind my enemy. If the Goddess smiled on her daughter, I would return.

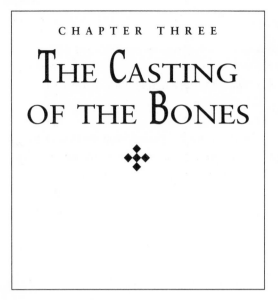

CHAPTER THREE

THE CASTING
OF THE BONES

❖

D o you know what it is to hate, Scribe? Have you ever looked a fellow in the eyes and felt a loathing so fierce you wanted to pluck them out? No need to answer—your guilty flush betrays you. Good. It's comforting to know there's marrow in your bones. It'll help you understand how it was between Jinnah and me.

At first I thought it was merely a mutual dislike. That wasn't so shocking. It's perfectly natural for two people to find each other offensive on first meeting. I've already underscored the faults I found in Jinnah and his breed. As for Jinnah's bitterness toward me, this also seemed natural. The patricians of Orissa disapprove of the merchant clans such as the Anteros. Money earned by toil and trade is unseemly to them. They see themselves as the kings and queens of our society. But in Orissa a peasant with pluck and skill can work his way into the glittering chambers that Jinnah entered merely by being born. What's more, it was the Anteros—thanks to my brother—who freed the slaves, to the immense displeasure of the old families.

So there was foundation for dislike. He was the commander, so I did my best to hide my feelings. He, however, made little effort to conceal his. Never mind. I'm a soldier who prides herself on being able to serve under *any* circumstances—even the displeasure of my superior. However, the night before that final battle, as I sat in Jinnah's tent and laid out my plan, I caught a glimpse of how deep his feelings ran. But I was in such a fever of inspiration, I failed to look closer. There is much blood on my hands for that failure—the blood of my sisters and friends. Their ghosts are too sweet to haunt me. But I do not sleep well, Scribe. And when I do, I *never* dream.

THE MEN made no comment as I told them what I'd seen from that stony shelf. General Jinnah stared down his handsome nose at me, his pale, haughty features cast into a mask of polite attention, his thin lips stretched into what could be mistaken for a smile. But as I spoke his fingers drummed impatiently against the top of his ornately carved field table. His aides, taking the cue from their master, sat in cross-armed boredom. The tent was dank and reeked of spoiled musk, which was the manly perfume Jinnah, and therefore his aides, favored. The dark bulk that was Admiral Cholla Yi amused himself by undressing me with his eyes. He stroked his lace cuffs while he stared and occasionally fingered the stiff spikes that were his hair. Wonderful, I thought. Another fellow who thinks I need only a good bedding by a *real* man to change my sexual preferences. Normally I'd have challenged him to a ball-kicking contest, but I was so caught up in laying out my plan, I ignored his attempt to humiliate. In the far corner Gamelan sat as quiet as the rest. I couldn't read his feelings, but I sensed no hostility from the wizard.

Jinnah had yawned when I'd first told him about Polillo's axe hanging from the spell-shrouded window, but one of Gamelan's bushy brows had arched high over his hawklike features. When I told my commander the use I intended to make of that discovery—along with several others—he yawned wider still. But I saw Gamelan tense and stroke his long white beard.

Captain Hux, Jinnah's chief aide, made an elaborate pretense of scrawling a note. "Shall I send a scouting party around to confirm Captain Antero's . . . unusual observations, sir?" His voice was languid, moist with mockery.

Jinnah roused himself enough to put on a mild show of careful thought.

I jumped in. "That might give it away, sir," I said. "Only Te-Date knows if we'll have another chance like this."

Jinnah frowned. "Assuming I found favor with your . . . *notion*, I'd certainly insist on professional confirmation."

I bit off an angry retort. I pointed at the copy of my report—complete with detailed sketches drawn by Polillo. "You have not only my word, sir," I said. "My officers have signed on as well."

Hux made no comment, only shook his head.

Taking the cue, Jinnah said: "I don't like to insult my command team *unnecessarily*, Captain. So there's no need for me to comment further on that point." He picked up my report and riffled the pages. Then he sneered and let it fall. "This plan of yours, however, gives me much distress. It is the work of—how shall I say it?—an unstable mind." He turned to Hux. "This is the sort of thing I warned the council about."

Anger almost brought me to my feet. But I held back. "I won't speak for myself, sir," I gritted. "But I will not have my soldiers maligned. They've served as ably and have suffered as much as anyone and more than some in this war. Sir."

Jinnah's eyes burned, but he remained outwardly calm—that sneer of his tilting upward. "What you have said is mostly true, Captain," he said. "I emphasize the 'mostly.' " His head swiveled to Hux again. "It's the inconsistencies that concern me," he said. He turned back to me, his face taking on a look of kindly superiority. "But I suppose we must make allowances for *nature.*"

Cholla Yi laughed, quick and mean. I'd had enough. I patted my sheathed knife. "Beware, Admiral," I said, quite low. "Didn't you hear our general? My nature can't be trusted."

His features darkened, but his anger tangled in nets of confusion. How should he respond to my challenge? No woman had ever spoken to him so. I moved on before he could recover. As I shifted my attention to Jinnah I noted Hux and the other aides had been chastened. It was as I intended. They knew my reputation as a fighter. Some had even seen me at my work. They squirmed in their seats like small, naughty boys. But Jinnah met my gaze full on.

"I respectfully protest your reaction to my plan, sir," I said, making sure there was no hint of insubordination. "I believe it deserves more thoughtful study. If I'm right, by this time tomorrow this war could be over—our enemy defeated."

"I *have* given it careful study, Captain," Jinnah said. "And I've made my decision."

"Then I must insist, sir, my protest be noted."

Jinnah gave a sly grin. "So noted, Captain Antero." He started to rise, as if our business were concluded.

"I want it *officially* recorded, sir," I demanded. "It is my right to have it drawn up and witnessed by every person in this tent. There is a courier leaving for Orissa tomorrow. It is my intention, sir, for my protest to accompany him."

Jinnah exploded. "How dare you challenge me!" he shouted.

"I'm not challenging you, sir," I said. "I'm only asking what is my right, if you please."

"Well, I don't please," Jinnah snarled.

"Are you refusing, sir?" I asked. I added an edge to my voice.

Jinnah's fury grew, but before it could spill out, I saw Hux give a tug at his cloak. The general, as I'd hoped, was being warned that he was treading very close indeed to the edges of his authority. If the war continued to go badly, my protest would be made much of by politicians looking for someone to blame.

He sighed deeply, then slumped into his camp chair. "What do you want of me, Captain?" he pleaded, trying his best to sound like a tired but reasonable man.

"I want you to make many mothers happy, sir," I said. "I want you to end this bloodshed and be the hero of all Orissa. I want you to give the orders that put my plan into action."

He drew in a long, shuddering breath. "I can't do that," he said.

"Why not, sir?"

"Your plan is without merit."

"If this is so," I answered, "then tell me why. Let me learn from your wisdom, sir, and I'll withdraw my protest. Tell me, sir, where did I err?"

Jinnah looked about for support, but before any of his aides could weight in, Gamelan broke his long silence.

"Yes, General," he said. "I should like to hear those reasons myself." Jinnah turned to him, startled. The Evocator toyed with his beard. "I've gone over her report, and I see no flaws. Of course, I'm not a professional, but . . ."

Despite his calm manner, the old man was a powerful presence now that he had spoken up. His eyes were mild, but Jinnah visibly shrank under their gaze.

"Perhaps I *should* give it further study," Jinnah said nervously. He tossed my report over to Hux. "I want a staff team on this," he said, his manner brusque. "Tell them I need an answer within a week."

"A week?" I shouted, forgetting myself as I saw everything about to vanish down that familiar paper shufflers' tunnel. "There'll be another thousand dead within that time!" My outburst was a mistake. I'd given Jinnah the avenue he needed. His thin lips drew back in a wide smear of satisfaction.

But before he could strike, Gamelan stepped in again. "Yes, yes," he said, rather absently, as if I'd spoken in reasonable tones. "I fear this must be done now, or not at all."

He fumbled in a pocket of his black wizard's cloak, and as he drew out his hand, the acrid stench of sulfur filled the room. Jinnah's eyes widened as the Evocator opened his palm, exposing five ivory knucklebones with mysterious red symbols etched on them. The room crackled with energy. We were looking at the casting bones of a Master Evocator. I heard Cholla Yi whisper a prayer to whatever pirate god he worshiped. Hux and the other aides were so frightened they looked as if they were about to bolt. On the other hand, I was so swept up with my challenge that I felt nothing, not even a tinge of awe.

Gamelan's eyes were now a glowing yellow. He held the bones out to Jinnah. "Cast them, General," he said.

Jinnah averted his gaze from the yellow lion's glare. He licked dry lips. "But I thought you . . ."

Gamelan shook his head. "It is upon *you*, my general, that our fates rest."

After a long hesitation, Jinnah reached with a trembling hand. Gamelan let the bones fall into it. Jinnah reflexively clasped them tight. And Gamelan began to chant:

"Bones of Fate
Reveal thy tally:
Who shall win?
Who shall lose?
Who shall greet thee
In the Demon's Pyre?"

Jinnah shrieked in pain and flung the casting bones onto the field table. The smell of his burnt flesh fouled our nostrils.

Jinnah sucked on his injured hand. "I . . . I . . . can't," he croaked.

I heard fearful whispers from the other men. I kept my own feelings frozen in heart and brain. The only comfort I allowed myself was a hand firmly clasping the hilt of my sword. It did my nerve no good, however, when I saw the look of shock on the Master Evocator's face.

"It's *happened*!" he hissed.

"What?" Jinnah said. Fear made it a whisper.

Gamelan shook his head, commanding silence. He turned this way and that, sniffing and listening to every small sound of the night. I felt my skin prickle as his senses ferreted about. Somewhere far off we heard a direwolf pack howl over a fresh kill.

Gamelan whirled to confront Jinnah. "The Archons have made some kind of breakthrough," he said. "We must act quickly, or all will be lost."

"But what . . ." Jinnah was confounded.

Gamelan ignored him. He grabbed up the bones and thrust them at me. "Toss them, Captain," he said.

I only stared at him. Why was I being asked to do this? If the gods were suddenly deserting us, how could I alter their flight?

"Do it, Rali," Gamelan snarled. "Before it's too late!"

Numb, I obeyed. I opened my hand and steeled it as Gamelan once again let the bones fall. And I swear by all that we hold true and holy, time seemed to stand still. It was as if a shadow fell between me and the others. I smelled my mother's sandalwood perfume. My skin seemed to take on a sweet glow, as if I'd just stepped out of a bath of warm milk and honeyed wine. Everything just seemed so . . . right in this shadow world. The bones nestled in my palm as if they had been specially carved for the fit. They were cool to the touch, and for some reason it troubled me that their feeling was quite pleasing.

Once again Gamelan chanted. Once again he prayed for a tally of our common fates. The bones remained cool in my palm; the only change was an increased feeling of tingling pleasure. As he chanted, another voice—a woman's voice—whispered in my ear: "Rali means hope. Rali means hope."

"Cast them," Gamelan said.

Awkwardly, I threw the bones. The shadow world feeling—and those are the only words I can think of to describe it—left me as the bones bounced and rolled across the table.

As they struck, the tent was lit by a lightning bolt striking close by. Thunder followed—so loud we clutched our ears in pain. Gamelan didn't seem to notice. Instead he gave a gleeful cackle and jumped forward like a cat to peer at the knuckles. Another cackle and he swept them up. But as he returned them to his cloak pocket he gave me an odd look. I made no effort to read the look. To be quite honest, I consciously avoided any reflection on what the wizard might be thinking.

He turned to Jinnah, who stood staring, gaping like a pond fish. "She is our only hope, General," he said. "I don't know the why of it. I just know it is so."

Still, Jinnah hesitated. He looked at me, and in that brief moment the veil was lifted and I saw the hatred in his eyes. It was cold and black and deep. I was rocked back. At first, wonder leaped into my mind. Why should I be the object of such hatred? Then my wonder grew deeper still as I saw that beneath his look was fear. Before I could reflect further, I felt my own hatred stir. It became an intense flame, and I was so caught in it I nearly leaped the table to kill him where he stood.

Then the tent glowed as another spear of lightning pierced the night. We all jumped as a second volley of thunder blasted us to our boots.

Jinnah grabbed a tumbler of brandy and drank it down to steady his nerves.

"Well, General?" Gamelan pressed.

Jinnah nodded weakly. His voice rasped through the tension when he answered, "We attack tomorrow. At dusk."

AT DAWN we made sacrifice, or rather three sacrifices, which suggested not just how important, but how dangerous that coming night's mission might be. First we sent Maranonia a sheep. It should have been a fat ram, but as I've said, the land around us was combed bare and the poor scrawny ewe we found would have to suffice. After the battle was won, proper homage could be made. Maranonia was a soldier's goddess and would understand that sometimes the idea must satisfy more than the reality. Someone suggested a Lycanthian prisoner should be given to Maranonia, but that idea was quickly rejected since it doesn't make much sense to seek a goddess's approval by sending someone whose blood-drenched soul would make the strongest argument against what we desired. Next we made a smaller sacrifice of fish to Orissa's gods, and each of us made a private offering to her own hearth god. I hoped those gifts in particular would be found satisfying and a few of us would have to make personal obeisance by the next dawn.

The rest of the morning was spent in final preparation. Just as the ballads of battle seldom mention the sweating smiths ensuring the cavalry mounts are well-shod before the charge, or the armorers and spark-shooting grindstones putting the final edges to the killing blades, no one ever realizes that soldiers—at least soldiers who succeed—almost never spy an objective and, bellowing mightily, rush to attack.

Our camp was a haze of activity from dawn until midday. Each woman's kit was checked by her sergeant, double-checked by her section officer, and then finally inspected by Polillo and Corais. At noon we ate heartily—a traditional before-battle meal of roast beef and eggs. I'd had to send a victualing mission composed of my most skilled thieves far out into the countryside to procure it.

A sudden shower—invoked by two medium-level Evocators—sent us scurrying in mock surprise for our tents. Out of sight, we changed into battle gear—drab clothing and blackened armor. The rain whipped a breeze through the open door of my tent and I shivered. But it was not from the chill wind.

I'd cast too much of my capital on this single spin of the top. The cold logic of war dictated that a complete unit should never be committed to a single battle, particularly if the odds were high. Soldiers could, and did, shrug when only a handful returned form battle; but when a unit was completely destroyed, death fingers went down all our backbones.

But only a handful of my Guardswomen were to remain behind. A few of them were sick or injured, and the rest were a fresh draft of untrained recruits from Orissa who'd arrived under an eager young ensign the day before. She was the only officer left, besides Corais, Polillo, and myself. Since the Guards' officers led from the front and by example, the death rate had been catastrophic, and there'd been no time for officer's boards or field promotions.

The new woman's name was Dica, and she seemed even younger than I'd been when I enlisted. I took her aside and told her if I didn't return on the morrow, she was the new commander of the Maranon Guard. She paled, but her lips firmed. I made note: such resolve indicated a worthy soldier in embryo.

"Should we fall," I ordered, "it will be your task to return to Orissa and rebuild the Guard. Maranonia requires no less of you, and there are enough pensioners of the Guard left in Orissa to assist you. Your first duty, however, will be to recover the colors—which we'll be carrying tonight. If we don't return, the colors will be where all the Maranon Guard lie—inside the citadel of the Archons."

I dismissed her and turned to Corais, who'd waited until Dica left the tent before smiling wryly, knowing full well why I'd spoken as dramatically as I had. "Very good, my captain," she said. "If we must die this night, your words will help build our legend. Polillo, were she present, would be in tears." The she sighed. "Isn't it a pity this legend business can be so damned *painful*?"

While the storm still continued, our tents were taken over by a small detachment of men. It'd been arranged for them to light cooking fires, move from tent to tent, mount guard, and in short suggest to any observer, magical or physical, that the Maranon Guard was still being held in reserve.

We girded for battle and moved quickly along the rear of the Orissan encampment to the bluffs that led to the shore beyond Lycanth, where Cholla Yi had his galleys beached on rollers. The night before, I'd attempted, in my stumbling, landswoman's way, to suggest what craft we might need for our attack. Cholla Yi had snickered in a pretended friendly manner, as if our near duel hadn't occurred, and said I needn't continue.

"It isn't uncommon, Captain Antero," he'd said, "that we sailors also prefer silence and secrecy on occasion. Each of my galleys carries one or two boats of a design so perfect, you yourself might have worked with the builders. I'd hoped to use them for cutting out expeditions against the Lycanthian merchantmen bottled up in the harbor—once we'd found a way to cut that great damned locket chain keeping us out. But none of us should dream, for the gods love disappointment."

He went on briskly. "Each boat can carry ten men, and is crewed by a cox'n, with four seamen to work the paddles. You might have your *soldiers*"—and he couldn't but put sarcastic emphasis on that word—"told off in teams accordingly, so our debarkation won't sound like a goosegirl calling her flock."

I'd merely nodded. The admiral was what he was, and we were what we were. I thought then, one way or another, that the night's purpose would be the last I'd see of him, so his behavior was unimportant. So much for my talents as a seer!

Once we reached the mercenaries' camp, I dispersed my Guard under cover and put them under the charge of Flag Sergeant Ismet, who was one of the great oddities in the already strange group of women who made up the Guard. Soon as I saw her, my confidence rose. With women like this, how could we fail?

Ismet, you see, was an example for us all: from the green recruit to her fellow noncommissioned officers and finally to the officers themselves. She was a constant reminder—to use the hackneyed phrase—of the spirit of the Guard we served. Some whispered Ismet might be an incarnate of Maranonia herself, especially since she hadn't seemed to age in all the years she'd served. Ismet's dark complexion—darker even than the tropical natives of the North—added to her mystery. Where she came from, no one knew. She'd merely appeared one day and announced her intent to enlist. When questioned about her background, she made no answer—only vowed she'd become a Guardswoman or else starve herself to death. There was a hubbub, but not one doubted her determination. The tale is a bit foggy about the details—perhaps my predecessor of long ago was softhearted, perhaps there hadn't been enough recruits to fill the ranks. More likely someone looked into the woman's eyes and simply *knew*. Ismet showed familiarity with all forms of arms. She was sworn in as a recruit, but spent less than a month in the rear ranks. She was promoted again and again, until she reached the highest rank of noncommissioned officer. She refused further promotion, in spite of wheedlings, blandishments, and threats. That was two generations ago. Ismet never took a leave, but only passes. She never sought to live outside the barracks, nor made a pairing that lasted beyond a week or so. She often said that a soldier should concern herself with but three entities—herself, her squad, and the Guard.

After my women were sited, I went with my legates and a squad of four to the admiral's tent. Gamelan was waiting. He told Cholla Yi he wanted to speak to us alone. Cholla Yi grumbled menacingly, but Gamelan only gazed steadily at him. The Evocator's eyes changed from placid, deep pools of wisdom to the yellow stare of a great cat about to pounce. Cholla Yi's mouth snapped closed and without another word he bulked out toward the beached ships, shouting pointless orders to his men.

Gamelan had the materials for his spell ready. He'd quizzed Polillo closely about her axe left buried in the sill of that sea tower window. Now he held up a small model of her weapon. He lit a brazier and said we should kneel in front of it. Herbs long known to be good for the eyes were cast onto the embers: rosemary, hyssop, rock rose, white willow. He whispered as he scattered the herbs and plumes of sweet smoke rose, split in three and blew across our faces. Instead of burning our eyes, the smoke felt soothing, comforting. I saw a fourth plume move back toward his open palms, where he held the tiny axe exactly as if it were the full-size murderer's tool cast by Polillo. He softly chanted:

"The axe that was blind
Could still see to find
Let the gift of the blade
Pass on to the maid
And sharpen, not fade
The eyes they shall see
All that can be."

As he chanted he moved around the brazier, gently touching the tiny axe to each of our eyelids. Polillo flinched involuntarily—she was as leery of magic as anyone I'd ever met. Once she confessed to me that she'd dreamed that sorcery, somehow, some way, would be the death of her.

"There," Gamelan announced. "You should feel nothing at present, except perhaps that the world looks a bit ... sharper." And he smiled at his mild jest. "This is a nice, simple spell," he explained. "It should be of use at the proper time, but is not strong enough to attract ... shall we say, attention from the wrong quarters at an inappropriate moment."

My legates rose and saluted, and I dismissed them. Gamelan stretched. "Now, all we have to do, my good captain, is wait. I will allow myself a single glass of Admiral Cholla Yi's wine while we wait. Perhaps you might join me?"

"I don't usually drink before a fight," I said. "However ... I'll gladly keep you company, especially since I wish to ask a favor."

"You have only to request," he said. "I could prattle on about how our hopes are with you and how much rides on this, but I believe speeches are best suited for those who can be stirred by them. After the signals of the bones last night, any words would be redundant. I only wish that I could go with you, at the point of the spear. But my age, and ..." He gestured down at his robes. I nodded in understanding. The presence of such a powerful Evocator on our hopefully silent assault might well send magical signals to the Archons as clearly as if we wore full parade armor and were attacking at midday with pipes blaring.

That led naturally into my request, which startled him. He stroked his beard. "I am very surprised, Captain, or Rali, if I may. I don't know if you're being extraordinarily cynical about your own tactics, or what."

"I'd like to think I'm merely planning for all eventualities," I said. I was not telling the truth at that moment. "Could it damage my main plan in any way?"

"Possibly, possibly," he said. "Yet another piece of magic riding with your soldiers does increase the likelihood of the Archons or their minions scenting you. But . . . wait. I know of a spell. Very old. Very simple. It was used by witch smellers in my father's father's time. Such a primitive conjuration might be beneath the senses of sophisticated wizards such as the Archons. I can cast it in a few minutes. If you were an Evocator, I could teach you the spell for your own use. But since you are not . . . hmm. An amulet, perhaps?" He nodded, finding favor with his idea. "Very good, indeed. And I could scrape my casting bones for a bit of detritus. What they sensed last night from the Archons' own magic . . . that could serve as a trigger for you. Hmm. Not at all improbable or difficult.

"Yes, yes," he went on, becoming excited. "I think there *is* merit. I must set aside what has become, if you will forgive the confession, a growing sense of friendship for you, Rali. I must now consider you as nothing more—nor less—that the best hope of Orissa; a warrior, not a friend, without considering if I am sending you further into harm's way."

"If risk wasn't my chosen companion," I said, "I'd be in Orissa surrounded by husband fools and babes, worried about the next meal and a new gown."

Gamelan half smiled. "If I give you that amulet, not only might it lead to those you desire . . . but also to the center of their power."

I said: "If you're right, and they are plotting some great stroke of magic against Orissa, won't that have to be destroyed, as well?"

"Destroyed, perhaps, or possibly, if the taint is not monstrous, the knowledge brought back to Orissa to be put to better use." Gamelan shook his head. "Although I am reminded of what Janos Greycloak once told your brother about magic—that sorcery is only dark or light depending on the observer, a cynical thought I am still not sure I understand completely." He drank his wine. Then: "Very well, Captain. I shall give you something that can turn you into a little ferret seeking evil—and, if you choose to use it, you shall be pulled inexorably down those dark shafts after your prey."

At this, I managed a smile. "Ferrets," I said, "have always been lucky for my family. My brother swears the ghost of such a creature he owned as a boy saved him in his fight with Raveline."

"That is an omen indeed," Gamelan said, brightening. "I feel less like I am sending someone out on a mission they will not return from."

A smile was on his lips, but it didn't light his eyes. And I knew he was merely trying to reassure himself as well as me.

AS THE sun dipped toward the horizon, the galleys were pushed down rollers into the low surf break and, once launched, rowed to a crude floating dock leading out from the beach to deeper water, where we boarded. Since we wouldn't be journeying far or long, we crammed into three of Cholla Yi's ships. The eighteen small boats he'd spoken of, seventeen plus one spare, were towed close to the stern of the ships so they couldn't be spotted from the Archons' castle. We sailed east—as if setting course to Orissa. The oarsmen, twenty-five to a side, rowed easily—as if for a long journey that required no haste—and our sails held firm in the wind.

I was on the lead ship—Cholla Yi's own craft—and as we slipped through the waves, I tried to relax with Corais and Polillo on the quarterdeck. The sea was calm, and glittered gold and red in the dying sun. I tried to think about the calm waters and the sharp cry of a gull hanging in the calm air beside the ship rather than what lay ahead of us. A dolphin sported in our bow wave, then was gone. Cholla Yi joined us. I'm afraid I didn't try very hard to disguise my distaste for him when I asked why he'd decided to accompany this expedition. Wasn't it beneath the dignity of an admiral?

Cholla Yi's gaze flickered—he'd caught my tone—then he became a jovial patriarch. "Ah, Captain, you don't understand the problems we poor souls face who choose to soldier for a more material goal than glory. If we don't make certain to be at the final triumph of the war we enlisted for, all too often our employers attempt to economize in the settling of accounts. Which leads to all sorts of unpleasantness." Then he became serious. "Besides, with sailors like mine, a leader is only allowed the quarterdeck so long as he remains in the battle's van. By accompanying you, I therefore accomplish a double task."

He bowed and walked down the companionway, to the main deck, where the rowers sat along the bulwarks on their slightly raised benches.

"If he happens to get too near the railing," Polillo said, "I might accidentally bump into him. I've heard many sailors never learn how to swim."

Corais showed her sharp fox's teeth. "Afterward, dear woman, afterward. When we're safe on dry land we'll invite him to a cliff, promising to indulge his most horrid fantasies in private, and I'll kneel down behind him and then you can bump to your heart's desire."

When the sun was down, sails were furled and masts and yards struck, as if we'd disappeared over the horizon. In the gathering dark, with little to see above the deck line, the ships were almost invisible. The small boats were let out on their tow lines so as not to impede the oarsmen, and the galleys turned back toward Lycanth, the rowers stroking as if racing. I'd wondered how men could accept such a fate, endlessly pulling a length of wood to and fro, and thought they might be slaves. But Corais, who was insatiably curious about everything and had asked, said no, they were free. In fact, galleys were only rowed when speed was vital. Under normal circumstances, they'd be driven by sail alone.

Two hours before midnight we closed on the entrance to Lycanth's harbor. I could see, bulking huge against the night, the sides of the crater that was the city's harbor—and even the mass of the sea castle, which was our goal. The night was peaceful, balmy, exactly the weather Gamelan had ordered spells to be cast for. It bespoke of spring's arrival, warm and just a bit sleepy. Nothing could happen on such a peaceful night: sentries would dream of an end to their pacings; their watch commanders wouldn't find it necessary to make rounds more often that the regulations required; men off watch would sleep soundly, and so forth.

We disembarked into the boats. In spite of what Cholla Yi had implied about my women's probable incompetence on the water, not a sound was made in the loading, not a weapon was lost, not a Guardswoman fell into the dark, heaving ocean. We moved off toward the harbor entrance. Indeed, these boats were perfect for what I intended. Instead of oars, each had two wheels on either side near amidships. Each wheel was fitted with paddles, like the fins of a sea turtle. The "oarsmen," if that was the correct name for them, sat in the center of the boat next to the wheels, working a circular crank that sent the wheels spinning and the boat slipping silently toward the shore, with nary an oar splash or needed command from the man at the rudder. I could see, however, that maneuvering these boats wasn't for simpletons, since all four oarsmen must work in close unison, or else we'd have zigged across the ocean like crazed water beetles.

As we moved toward our goal, I reconsidered my plan. Its greatest virtue, I believed, was its simplicity. Elaborate tactics seldom survive the first shower of arrows. I planned to have my Guardswomen climb the chain blocking Lycanth's harbor from the water all the way to the top of the cliff, where it fastened to the castle. After we reached the top of the chain, we'd look for a window large enough to enter. Once inside, we were to move as rapidly and quietly as possible to the castle's main gates. General Jinnah would have assault battalions waiting just outside. When we swung the gates open, the main attack would be mounted.

It wasn't as impossible as it might seem—more than one great fortification had fallen to a handful of soldiers with steel in their hands and hearts. If we failed, as all were predicting—what of it? My women would leave their bodies inside the sea castle. More than ten times their number had died just in that one hopeless attack we provided the diversion for earlier. And from what Jinnah felt about the use of women in battle, wouldn't it please him to no longer have the "cloven sex," as I heard him call us, insisting on such annoyances as logic and forethought instead of mindless brawn and battle planning worthy of a bull in must?

Now it was time to test the edge of the sword I'd hammered out, to see whether it cut clean or bent or shattered uselessly. There was also a second, very private goal, which was the one I'd asked Gamelan for help with, even though I hadn't fully explained exactly what I intended.

The harbor opened before us like some fabulous monster's gaping jaws. Then we were drawing close to the chain rising from just below the water's surface up to the sea castle high above, and there was no longer time for reflection. Training, muscles, and, yes, familiarity took over.

My scribe lifted an eyebrow as I said the last, thinking perhaps that a basic part of the Guards' training was swarming up and down great chains, and wondering why he'd seen no such training devices on our parade ground. Actually, there's little difference between climbing from chain link to chain link—a woman bracing herself, a second woman stepping on her to reach the next link, at which time she became the top rung in the ladder, and so on—and what all Orissa has seen us do in holiday demonstrations of our athletic prowess, scrambling over obstacles at great speed. With the minor exceptions that now there were several thousand enemy soldiers above, and our "obstacles" were big pieces of slimy, rusting iron, dripping seaweed, barnacles, and other sea creatures that would no doubt be revolting in daylight. Polillo and other Guardswomen known for their strength were in charge of the maneuver, and I became nothing more than one more climbing, and bracing, soldier.

Link by link, woman by woman, we went up the chain. Finally, Corais, Polillo, Ismet, and I reached the last link, where it was fastened to a huge staple set in the sea castle's vertical wall. There were four of us clinging to this final link—the others waiting below—and I had a momentary image of us as tiny charms on some giantess's bracelet. I shook my head. For some reason, perhaps the proximity of so much sorcery, my imagination was rioting like a drunken civilian's this night.

Three of us sent our eyes scanning the sheer blank tower above and to the side, while Ismet kept a sharp watch—an arrow nocked on its string—on the battlement above, in case a sentry should peer over.

Gamelan's spell was running through all our minds. *Let the gift of the blade . . . Pass on to the maid . . . The eyes they shall see . . .*

Our eyes saw past the ensorcellment around the tower. Here were arrow slits; there, slots that were to illuminate dark stairs. Then we saw windows that gaped open with nary a bar or shutter. The Archons, like many people with a single strength, put too much trust in their main weapon of magic. Far above I saw half a dozen wide openings and guessed they marked the luxurious prison Amalric had been held in. But we wouldn't need to further test our climbing skills, because not twenty feet to the seaward side, and about fifteen feet above, was a portal nearly as wide.

Polillo chuckled low as Corais unbuckled the pack on her back and took out the heavy grapnel and ropes. I knew what she was thinking—all this time, all this blood, and now we find we can enter this castle with no more effort than if we were spending a lazy afternoon climbing one of the steeper faces of Mount Aephens in Orissa.

Polillo cast the grapnel easily, and two of its prongs hooked on the windowsill. She tugged to make certain the padded hooks were secure, then busied herself with the only complicated part of the task—making sure the ropes were unsnarled. This grapnel was designed for use in a major assault. Before the incantation was laid, it looked as if the hook carried a rope ladder instead of a single knotted line. When the various ropes were straight, Polillo leaned back until they were taut. She slid the bitter end around one of the chain's links, then whispered—and all of us knew the words, having been given them in our command training. Years ago, before Amalric and Janos Greycloak forced Orissa's Evocators to loosen their stranglehold on the most minor spell, an Evocator would have been teetering up here, re-evoking the grapnel's built-in spell. But that was no longer the policy, and so any high-ranking sergeant or any officer of the army, once blessed by an Evocator, could do as Polillo was doing: "My words are those of another, but he has blessed my cause. Make hard, make strong, make straight, hold firm. Hold fast, like steel, like hook, for need . . ."

The ropes obediently became rigid. Now we had a solid bridge between us and the window, a bridge wide enough for a beldame to stumble across. Polillo looked back, sneered and whispered: "I could walk this on my hands."

Before either of my legates could move, I slipped past Polillo, sword ready, onto that bridge. I moved fast, not wanting to give an enemy, if there was one waiting, any more time than I must. I went through the window like a leaping cat, landing on solid stone, going away from the window to the in-

terior dimness, then I crouched. I was in a bare chamber. There was a door
at the far side. It was unbolted. By the time I had it opened, revealing a narrow landing and stairs, my Guardswomen were pouring into the chamber.
Without commands, not even hand signals, we formed into attack teams and
went out.

It was near pitch-black, and gloom and fear must have hung close
about. But none of us felt dread; all of us had the hard taste of blood in our
mouths and the shrilling joy that finally, by Maranonia, we were through!
Just as our fathers had broken into this great castle in the first war against
Lycanth, so too we'd proven ourselves worthy of their heritage. This time we
would ensure there would never be a Third Lycanthian War.

We went down the winding steps toward the main floors of the castle
like fluid death. We met Lycanthians once, twice, four times. Each time, a
sword glittered and a body sagged, surprised into doom before it could cry
out. Perhaps they were soldiers, perhaps servitors. It didn't matter. We came
into a wide room, high-ceilinged and hung with tapestries. Fires still glowed
on either side of the room. I thought it some sort of audience chamber. But
now, in the hours past midnight, it was deserted. From the castle around
came the normal sounds of a still-garrisoned battlefield: I could hear sentries
on their watch and dull shouts of alarm from somewhere. Few people think
of a battle as being anything other than hellishly noisy, and such is mostly the
case. But a siege can be different. It was very silent to me, although a civilian's ears would probably hear more—would hear that low constant growl
that we no longer noted, a sound like great carrion beasts: the sound of armies waiting for battle.

I signaled for stillness. All of us held for a moment. If anyone had seen
us, they might've thought we were praying. We were not. Maranonia is a
good and sensible god, who knows the time for prayer is before and after a
battle, not during. What all of us, from the lowest Guardswoman to myself,
were doing was recollecting our "map"—the mental image of the models and
drawings General Jinnah's staff had drawn up of the sea castle, taken from
every conceivable source, from prewar visitors to captured prisoners. Yes.
Yes. It was most likely we were here . . . or possibly over there . . . so there
should be some sort of passageway out into the huge courtyard, and, from
there, through the castle's inner defenses to the gates themselves. At worst we
might be a floor too high. But now we were oriented.

Corais and Polillo were waiting for me to lead the charge. Their eyes
bulged as I signed . . . a touch on my helmet crest, a touch on each of theirs
. . . *you are now in command* . . . a point . . . *as your mind tells you* . . . as
you were ordered . . . as we practiced . . . and a gesture with the sword.
Attack!

But no one needed that final gesture. My legates—and my women—may have been astonished by this unexpected change, but they were soldiers and so they obeyed, just as I'd trained them. There was a scuffle of boot heels that sounded as if but one person was moving, and I was alone in the great chamber. Alone except for Flag Sergeant Ismet. I started to glower . . . but she moved first. Two fingers were held up in the gloom. I was reminded that we always, *always*, fought in pairs. One hand extended, palm up. *I await your orders.*

I grinned. Even here in this house made for nightmares, I found a moment of amusement. *You*, you poor idiot of an officer with only fifteen years or so of service, you are actually thinking of countermanding one of the flag sergeant's wishes? Not a chance, I thought. We were a team and we would die as a team.

It was time for Gamelan's other spell. I took the amulet—nothing but a stitched-together twist of leather that held the scrapings from his divining bones—from my pouch and touched it to my nose, then to the flagstones I stood on. I sniffed. There was no change.

No. Perhaps there was a new odor, sweet, distasteful, and my mind compared it to a battlefield with unburied corpses. But it told me nothing. I considered, then remembered Gamelan had said the amulet might need to be reinforced. I looked about. If I was right, and this was an audience chamber, and the Archons had used it, they'd most likely have stood . . . over there. On that low stone dais. I went to it, stepped up, and again touched the amulet to the stones. For further strength I pressed it against one of the tapestries against the wall.

Again I sniffed. Again came the odor, but now very strong, very heavy. I fought back a reflexive gag. Now I had a direction. I turned to gesture to Ismet, and of course she was just where she should have been, three paces behind, three to the side, sword ready, paying no attention to my doings, but eyes scanning the darkness for an attacker.

We went out of the chamber at a dogtrot. Our path led up four floors, but we didn't use the stairs we'd come down. Now we trod wide, stone-balustraded ramps that were richly carpeted. I stopped every now and then, but the amulet guided me onward and the stench grew stronger.

Outside I heard shouts, screams, and the clash of steel. Battle was joined. I wondered how far my Guardswomen had gotten before being discovered. The castle was coming alive as soldiers were bellowed awake and to battle. I heard cries of "Betrayal!" "They're inside!" and screams of panicked women and children.

The corridor opened onto a balcony, and I could see the courtyard. It was huge. An entire army could've marched in review across were it not for the guard towers and newly improvised breastworks. This was where the Archons held their monstrous sacrifices, where a victim first chose and then slowly butchered himself, spell-tied by their magic. Here was where they had sought my brother, but another counterspell had saved him. But now it was a battleground. Torches flared as Lycanthian soldiers ran out, buckling on armor and brandishing their arms. Far across the courtyard I heard the shouts of my women fighting. I could barely hold back a cheer as I saw the knot of struggling warriors. My Guardswomen had nearly reached their goal. They were fighting just before the castle's great gates. If they could but fight on and unbar them, our army could pour in.

But they'd been discovered at the most perilous stage. Naturally, the Lycanthians had their strongest defense at the weakest point. The outer gates were protected by an inner, open passageway, the tops of its high walls fitted with fighting decks. The inner gate had been burst open by Guardswomen, but before they could pour down the passageway, the counterattack had been mounted. Now they fought for their lives just outside the passage's entrance—soldiers blocking their way and others waiting atop those passageway walls to send spear showers and arrow flights down. My Guardswomen were between that anvil of the gatehouse and the onrushing hammer that was the reinforcing soldiers.

Still worse, I heard from just above a loud hiss—like a giant serpent awakening. Across the parade ground two cyclones spun up—black against the torch flare and three or four times taller than a man. They whirled into the melee, and Lycanthians and Guardswomen alike were picked up and smashed into the stone walls. My amulet gave off a last wave of scent—the stench of Archons' magic—and I turned and raced up another ramp toward the chamber above, Ismet close at my heels. I couldn't help by standing and watching. Either my Guardswomen could hold back the physical threat or they would die. I had to strike against the greater jeopardy now building.

This was my secret purpose. I'd made two plans. The first called for my Guardswomen. The second was for myself—and now for Sergeant Ismet. My intent—and I realize it sounds insane—was to personally attack the Archons. I'd told no one because they would've refused me, damning my plan as that of an eager fool. I believed otherwise, knowing very well just how great an effect a determined warrior, who's willing to make the last sacrifice, can have. But of course, in these modern times when men talk of great battalions and scores of Evocators and battles that stretch on for leagues and days, such an idea is romantic nonsense. Nonsense it may have been, but I'd commended my soul to Maranonia, my effects to my friends and family, and abandoned all thought of seeing the morrow.

The hissing grew louder as I reached the entrance to the chamber. There were no guards, which surprised me at first, but why should there be? Who would dare disturb the Archons?

I heard voices from inside—"brother" . . . "strike" . . . "just women!"—wishing I had a moment to collect my mind, my force, and my breath, but I couldn't chance it, even now thinking I heard, perhaps I did hear, "from behind!" "from within!" "Danger!" and I stormed into the Private Chamber of the Archons.

I saw in a blur glass and gold, alembics and scrolls, burning tapers and incense, bones and horrid creatures, but had no time, realizing there could be but one chance for a mortal to confront such sorcerers, and that was with blinding speed and surprise.

Two tall, bearded, vulture-faced men whose malignity marked them clear, spun, hands coming up to tear, one stretching a finger like a lance, and something gray-black began to build; it darted at me, striking the sword from my hand, and I hurled my shield sideways, spinning through the air into his guts, leaping after, and there was a great cloud of smoke as I heard a very human screech of pain and a shout from the other. Then I touched flesh, flesh became scales, became flesh, and the Archon and I smashed to the floor, rolling about and I could feel huge muscles contort, as if I were in the ring against the strongest man I'd ever wrestled, and great hands came up, forcing mine to the side, and I was rolled over onto my back as those hands came around my throat, gripping, thank the gods not knowing enough to press the arteries but squeezing my windpipe . . . The world was turning black, and I struck straight up with my free hand, fingers clawed, stiff like a hawk's talons into the Archon's eyes. He screamed, and I felt wetness and kickspun him off, both of us on our feet, but blood and fluid seeping through the fingers held to his face . . . but no time for that, and I stepped into him, both fists together, swinging sideways like a morning star's ball and smashing into his temple, and the Archon flipped back in a convulsion and fell, body thrashing, dead but not realizing it.

My eyes sought and found my sword, and I scooped it up. I smashed one foot down on the Archon's chest, just as you would immobilize a snake, and struck once, cleanly. My sword severed his head from his shoulders and splintered on the stones. Dead, yes, for a moment at least, but now for the other one—and I came back on guard.

There was no need. The only other person in the room was Sergeant Ismet. "He fled," she said. "He was turning toward you, hands moving to build a spell, and I cast my dagger. It struck him full on the chest but fell away as if he were wearing armor."

"Which way? Where did he go?"

Ismet pointed to where a small doorway yawned. It was dark, black, just like the burrow Gamelan had promised I'd go down. "Follow me," I ordered.

"Aye, ma'am. After we cover our rear."

Before I could snap a "Now!" Ismet had found her dagger, strode to the Archons' headless corpse, knelt, and made the cut of the eagle. When she stood, she held up his dripping heart. Then we were running into that tunnel, after the last Archon.

The tunnel was their final escape route. Here there were alcoves where someone could wait in ambush. But no one lurked. There were cunning devices, mantraps, but they were not cocked. My mind kept wondering: Why had the other Archon not remained to help his brother? Fear? Panic? Not likely from men, or once-men, who'd ruled so long and so bloodily. I didn't know the answer, but kept the pursuit, trying to move fast enough so we wouldn't lose our quarry, but not so fast we'd stumble into a trap.

The tunnel went on and on, growing narrower and smaller as it burrowed deeper. The tunnel was no longer masonry, but hewn from the living stone. I prayed it wouldn't grow narrower still so we'd be forced to our knees and bellies, only to find the tunnel taper down to nothingness and a magical escape—a nothingness that'd hold us in a vise in this castle's bowels.

Then the tunnel ended and there was a moon and starlight. I peered out. We were about ten feet above the surface of the harbor. Above us was a cliff, and above that the sea castle we'd left to slip through the rock of the old volcano itself. I saw no sign of the Archon. I flinched, hearing an enormous smashing. I saw that huge chain blocking the harbor snap as if invisible hands had parted it. It came crashing down into the water. Now the harbor mouth was unblocked.

Sergeant Ismet shouted, "Look there!" and I saw flags snap to the masthead of some of the Lycanthian ships we thought had lain unmanned. I knew both flags. The lower banner was long, split, with a sinuous panther in red. The house flag of my family's feudal enemy, Nisou Symeon! Still worse, the upper banner was the royal flag of Lycanth, a black twin-headed lion holding in its paws a crossed sword and wand. Somehow the Archon had made it aboard that ship. There were other ships—I heard Ismet mutter "Nine"—but I paid little attention, watching the small fleet sail directly toward me . . . and the harbor mouth. I groaned as I saw the last Archon was making his escape.

It was as if my eyes had been given a magical glass at that moment, and I could see, as if they were only yards away, the two men beside the lead ship's helmsman. The first was Nisou Symeon. I'd never seen him before, but knew him by his fire-scarred face, which had once been as fair as any woman—wounds made by my brother and Janos Greycloak. Behind him was the Archon!

I heard a roar like a hurricane wind coming from that ship, and I knew they'd seen me, as well. A flight of arrows arced toward the tunnel mouth. Ismet pulled me back, and the arrows clattered harmlessly against the stone. I saw the ships sail past and was drawn back to watch. There was no one waiting to stop their escape. Perhaps, if we'd guessed, we could have had Cholla Yi's ships in position, blocking the harbor, but who would have expected such an eventuality?

The roaring sound grew louder, and then from out of the depths snapped a long tentacle. It lashed around my waist. I lost balance, tottered, then found a grip on a rock outcropping and held on as I heard the roaring turn to a bellow of glee. I fought with all my strength, but I was being pulled loose as if I were a limpet being plucked for a seaside picnic. I looked down at the filthy harbor water and saw other tentacles thrash, then curl up to take me in their embrace. I heard the clack from a yellow beak and saw the gleam of a cold eye.

A dagger flashed past, down toward the water, and the air was a spray of black ink and I was free and the sea was a roil of scum, and then there was nothing.

"I never miss more than once," came Ismet's voice.

Both of us were ink-stained from the spray from that cuttlefish, which the Archon's last, parting spell must have called up.

"One escaped," I said. I saw Symeon's nine ships as an offshore wind caught them and their sails filled.

Ismet said nothing, but pointed upward.

I looked at the sea castle's battlements just as Orissa's golden banner floated forth.

So one of them had escaped, I thought. But what was a magician, even one such as the Archon, without his base, without his charms, without his scrolls?

The war was over. Orissa had triumphed. Lycanth had fallen.

The Archons' rule had been destroyed.

CHAPTER FOUR

THE WIZARD'S HEART

❖

There has never been a victory feast as great as the one that came after the fall of Lycanth. It didn't matter that one of the Archons and Nisou Symeon had escaped. It was enough, when the new day dawned, that soldiers saw the Orissan banner flying from the highest point of the Lycanthian sea castle. Now they could creep out from their tunnels and walk freely about under the looming battlements that'd spat death at them for so many months. The soldiers were drunk with joy, shouting, singing, whirling about in mad dances. All of our gods were hauled out and bedecked with garlands, looted finery, and jewels. The sea castle was plundered and real drink found, and the celebration grew wilder still. Beeves, fowls, pigs, and pups were sacrificed to the gods.

Just knowing there'd be life the next day and the day after that was so soul-filling that all discipline was swept away in that joyous storm. Wisely, we officers made no attempt to stem their antics, other than making sure no civilians or prisoners suffered.

My women celebrated as wildly as any of the others. Polillo tromped into our encampment with a keg of looted brandy on each shoulder. She broached them with her axe, and the amber liquor flowed into my sisters' throats. Corais and Ismet stayed reasonably sober, keeping watch on their comrades' tempers. Such extreme happiness, mixed with brandy, can be a powerful elixir for the unwary, and the demons of anger are always ready to pounce on the smallest insult. Many a lovers' quarrel has been settled with a blade after a battle. We had blood enough on our hands.

As for me, I suddenly found I'd become that oddest of creatures—a hero. The young recruit dreams of such a thing, weary muscles trembling as she sleeps after a day of shouting sergeants lashing her from one absurd task to the next: dreams of one day standing tall but humble as thousands of voices shout her name, while old soldiers speak in hushed tones when she passes. I dreamed such dreams when I was young. But when a hero's garland really was bestowed on me that day, I did not find it so pleasant. The fast ship that carried news of our victory to Orissa also bore flowery descriptions of my deeds and the deeds of the Maranon Guard. The battle-blasted landscape echoed with my praises. Wherever I walked, crowds of soldiers parted before me. Some reached to touch my tunic as if it were sacred cloth, instead of a rough soldier's weave. Gifts were heaped before my tent, and the mound grew so quickly I had to post a guard to politely turn their bearers away. There were marriage proposals by the scores. Men begged to father a child with me. Women—even those who'd once turned their noses up at me—left intimate things in my path, and whispered hot entreaties from the shadows to share my cot. It was said a day would be named in my honor, with all the special sacrifices and ceremonies that sort of thing entails.

I did not find it pleasant, Scribe. I still do not. It is a false thing, a deadly thing, that can turn a happily common mortal into a demon of vanity. Heroes belong in the grave. It is the only place they can be safe from themselves—and their worshipers.

The worst thing about my sudden leap to sanctity was Jinnah's deepening hatred as he saw himself being robbed of the hero's crown *he'd* coveted. Somehow word leaked that Jinnah had been forced by Gamelan into carrying out my plan. Within hours after the last Lycanthian surrendered, there were jokes being made at his expense. The long, bloody siege was being dubbed "Jinnah's Folly," and there were those who cursed him bitterly for letting the fight go on so long, and for so many addlebrained decisions which, they charged, had cost thousands their lives.

To be fair, the Lycanthians had been the toughest of foes, and the Archons so powerful they nearly bested our own Evocators. Still, there were many things Jinnah would have to answer for, not here, but when he returned to Orissa and stood before the Council of Magistrates. It was apparent that some god would have to take a sudden and very great liking for Jinnah if he were to save himself from a shame that would last into the ages. Jinnah's luck, however, changed that very night. It rode in on a furious storm that sank our encampment in a sea of mud. The rain was blinding. The seas raged high, crashing over the rocky shore in waves three times the height of a tall woman. Then Jinnah sent word that I was to come to him—immediately. Not to his tent, but to the sea castle and to the Private Chamber where I'd killed the Archon's brother.

As I entered the vast room I couldn't help but grip the little amulet Gamelan had given me. I took comfort in the fact that the awful odor that had betrayed the Archons' presence was gone. As I looked about, shielding my eyes from the white-hot glare of sorcerous torches rekindled with Orissan magic, I saw with much surprise that there was no sign of the struggle that'd taken place just hours before. Everything seemed to have been put back into pristine order by Gamelan and his Evocators. I saw white-sashed novices sweeping up the last bits of broken glass. They were given to yellow-sashed apprentices who shook sweet-smelling smoke on them and whispered enchantments; the bits reformed themselves into jars, or vials, or crystal bowls, etched with sorcerous symbols. Other wizards and their helpers were moving quietly about, replacing things on tables and benches and hand-carved shelves. The whole thing was being directed by several red-sashed senior wizards, who seemed to be working from parchment maps of the room that Gamelan, or an assistant, had used spells to re-create. To one side, near a large golden urn, I saw Jinnah and a knot of aides. They were watching Gamelan, who had set up an odd apparatus on a portable altar. He was making some adjustments, but no sooner had I entered than he looked up, his yellow eyes darting about until they found me. He made a signal, as if in warning. Before I could make clear his intent, Jinnah saw me.

"Ah, Captain Antero," he said. "The hero of the hour." There was venom in his tone. "Come here, if you please. We have need of your assistance."

I knew jealousy and hatred had mated in Jinnah's breast, but as I joined the group I was startled to see a look of pure delight in his eyes. I wasn't sure what to make of it, but the look reminded me of our old kitchen cat when she had a rat at her mercy.

"General," I said. "What is the trouble?"

"It seems we may have won the battle," Jinnah said, with odd relish, "but not the war."

"Well put, sir," his toady, Captain Hux, said. Then to me: "We fear all your bold actions may have been for naught."

I looked at Gamelan. "The Archon?" I asked.

Gamelan nodded gravely. "The general sent Admiral Cholla Yi after him," he said. "But the Archon raised the storm we are now experiencing, and forced him to give up the chase."

He continued making adjustments to the apparatus, which was a complicated thing, with spidery tubes and wires and glass retorts filled with multicolored liquids set to a boil by some magical force. Colored steam issued from them, but there was no odor.

I shrugged. "It can't storm forever," I said. "We'll catch him soon enough. No land will take him in, now that he's lost his armies and his homeland. Our spies will soon ferret him out."

But as I said this, I felt a chill at my spine, and involuntarily touched Gamelan's amulet. The old wizard caught my motion and nodded. "We can't risk our future to chance and spies," he said. He made a wide gesture, taking in the vaulted room. "We've re-created every detail of this chamber at the moment before you so boldly entered, down to a cockroach that had just investigated the contents of a wizard's pouch."

Gamelan lifted up a small leather bag. The leather was rich and scored with symbols. He undid a gold tie and pinched out a bit of dust, which he held over one of the glass retorts. "This was one of the ingredients for a spell. It's made of ground bone and the stalk of some vegetation. But it is bone and plant life that none of us have ever encountered." He dropped the dust into boiling liquid. Then he corked the retort and pushed a piece of copper tubing through a hole. The tubing ran into the maze of tubes and glass that made up his apparatus. Gamelan spun the blades of a small prayer wheel set up next to the device. We heard the faint sound of bells, as the wheel began its automatic chant. I knew little of magic then, but had no doubt the machine, linked somehow to the prayer wheel, was born from my brother's and Janos Greycloak's discoveries in the Far Kingdoms.

Gamelan made no explanation. He turned back to us as if the apparatus had nothing to do with our conversation.

"Tell her the rest," Jinnah urged. "Tell her what you have learned."

Without preface, Gamelan said: "We have found unmistakable evidence that the Archon and his brother were only days away from creating that weapon we all so feared. What's worse, the Archons had prepared for possible defeat by making duplicates of all their equipment and notes. Those things were placed in special trunks that cannot be penetrated by any natural or sorcerous force. When our friend fled on Lord Symeon's ships, those trunks went with him."

My innards gave a lurch. I turned angrily to Jinnah. "Storm or no storm, we should be out there right now hunting him down. What possessed Cholla Yi to turn back? Symeon didn't have much of a start on him. And I've no doubt that pirate has faced worse tempests before."

"Admiral Cholla Yi did his best," Jinnah said. "But he did not have the means to press the chase."

"He wanted more money, I suppose." I did nothing to disguise my disgust.

Jinnah nodded. "Naturally. We fight for ideals. He fights for coin. Besides, he needs more ships, supplies, and a greater force, so that when we catch the Archon, we can finish the job."

It suddenly came to me that the general was being altogether too casual. What was the purpose of this meeting? Why was he wasting time telling me all this? I was but one of his officers. Instead of telling *me* his plans, Jinnah should have been issuing the pertinent orders. An expedition needed to be mounted immediately. The greater the distance the Archon and Symeon put between us and their ships, the more difficult it would be to capture and defeat them. As we spoke, an Orissan commander of sea-experienced soldiers should have been readying his men to board Cholla Yi's ships to resume the chase, just as I should be putting my women in motion for a quick march home to take up guard in case the Archon somehow found the means to threaten Orissa. All the talk of doomsday weapons and slippery wizards reminded me of the Maranon Guard's historic duty to keep Orissa safe. Then it began to dawn what Jinnah had in mind.

Before the realization was fully formed, he said, in the most oily manner imaginable: "You'll be pleased to know, Captain, that I've decided the Maranon Guard should have the *honor* of this most vital mission."

"That's foolishness, sir," I retorted. "My soldiers are more battle-weary than any others in our army. Or are you forgetting today's battle?"

"Of course I haven't, dear captain," he oozed. "It was your courage and theirs I had uppermost in my mind when I made my decision."

I knew instantly what he was about. He was as transparent as any courtesan's dancing veil. With me out of the way, Jinnah would be able to shift the glory my Guard had won onto his own shoulders. As well as a jackal pack's worth of the booty from our defeated enemy.

"Yes, indeed," Jinnah continued. "This is a mission of such importance that only one *woman* is suitable for it. The Hero of Lycanth. Captain Rali Emilie Antero."

I knew I was lost, but I tried one more sally. "I'd be glad to oblige, General," I said as smoothly as I could. "And we all thank you for the singular honor, but the Maranon Guard's duty is at home. As a matter of fact, I was going to come by in the morning, and ask you for my orders."

"You can have them now," Jinnah said. "But you won't be going home. As I said, this is a task for a hero. And a hero it shall have. As, no doubt, the Magistrates shall agree when I toast you at the victory feast in Orissa a few weeks hence."

Hux and the other aides sniggered.

Jinnah's next words came in a growl of command. "You and your women *will* join Admiral Yi at first light. Your orders are to pursue the Archon. You will find him and kill him. You will spare no effort, no cost, no life, until you find him and kill him. What's more, I order you to not return until that goal has been accomplished. Do I make myself clear?"

It was like a banishment, as if my women and I were being punished for our success—which we were.

You seem as stunned as I was, Scribe. The histories that've been written of those events make no mention of Jinnah's motives, do they? Welcome to the side of the world that women dwell in, my friend. It's quite cramped, for men require—and command—a great deal more room than me and my sisters. It's quite cold over here, as well, Scribe. The fuel for our fires have been rationed, you see. It has been deemed that we only need enough to warm childish pride in our looks, the ability to win a bedmate, and to keep hearth, children, and kitchen clean. And it's quite gloomy. You don't need much light when you're a mere reflection of a man.

I stared long and hard at Jinnah after he had spoken. I tried to will him to call back his words. But I wouldn't, and perhaps from his view couldn't, retreat. I wanted to shout that the Guard was a land force and had been so since its inception. We had no experience with the sea. I wanted to curse him for trying to steal the glory that only an hour before I'd disdained. I wanted to plead with him—not for my life, but for my sisters' lives. How many now had a hope of returning to Orissa's blessed shores? But I couldn't do any of those things. Orders had been clearly given, no matter how insane.

But I didn't give him the least satisfaction in seeing my turmoil, my fears. Nor did I click my boot heels and fire off my crispest salute. For he did not deserve this respect. And respect was all I could deny him.

So I merely nodded. "Very well, sir. But if I am to do this, I must insist on one thing."

"What is that, Captain Antero?" Jinnah sneered. He did not dare retort that I could insist on nothing. After all, the general himself had called me the Hero of Lycanth. How can one deny a hero?

"I want complete command of this expedition, sir. Cholla Yi is to be told in no uncertain terms that my every whim is to be instantly obeyed. Obviously, I will not misuse this, sir. I will leave to him matters of the sea. But in the hunt itself, and in any conflict, it is my word that must rule."

Jinnah laughed unpleasantly. "The admiral and I have already discussed these things, Captain," he said. "I made quite clear what role he is to play."

More sniggering from Hux and the other aides.

"Sir, I request that you repeat all that I have said in a formal conference with the admiral."

"If you think it's necessary, Captain," Jinnah replied, "I shall be glad to do so." He turned to take leave. "I'll call a meeting within the hour."

Then I heard Gamelan croak. "One moment, General."

Jinnah stopped. He looked at the old wizard, a frown of worry creasing his too handsome features. Was Gamelan going to somehow interfere? I had such wild hopes myself, but Gamelan quickly dashed them.

"An Evocator will need to be assigned to this expedition," he said.

"Choose whom you please," the general replied.

"Oh, I *shall*," Gamelan snapped, making certain Jinnah realized the Chief Evocator's choices were his and his alone to make. "And I choose myself."

Jinnah gaped. "But that's—but you're—"

"Too old?" Gamelan snorted. "That's the very reason why I shall go. The work that remains to be done here would best be dealt with by younger wizards. And I dare say I am more of a match for my sorcerous cousin, the Archon, that any of my fellows. No, I believe this expedition will have a better chance if I am along."

I saw delight in Jinnah's eyes: two enemies with one blow. He could not have hoped for more. "May the blessings of Te-Date be upon you," he intoned.

Gamelan didn't answer. He was fussing with his apparatus again—acting as if he'd already forgotten the general's presence. After a long, somewhat embarrassing moment, Jinnah shook his head and departed, his aides crowding around his heels like rock lizards just out of the egg scurry after their mother, in case father comes home to make an early dinner.

I remained behind. I was beginning to get an inkling of the old man's ways.

"Thank you," I said.

"For what, my dear Rali? For burdening you with someone with years as long as his beard?" He stroked the unkempt mass at his chin. Gamelan's eyes were a warm yellow, like a cheery hearth. Crooked teeth laughed through the gray thicket.

"Just the same," I said, "until you spoke up, I thought this whole thing hopeless."

"You doubt your ability to carry it off?"

"Not really," I said. "If the odds were even. But I do not think my commander intends for me to return. I believe he's more worried about his own reputation—and fortunes—than the safety of Orissa."

The yellow hearth of his eyes burned hotter. "That was my opinion as well, Rali," he said.

For the first time I took note at how familiarly the wizard had begun to address me. As if he saw friendship in his future. At that instant, I welcomed that offer. Although, as an Antero, I was nervous about it. My family has not had good fortune with wizards. But we did not speak of such things then.

"My distrust," Gamelan continued, "was the reason why I insisted I go along. We can give the Archon no peace, or he will complete that weapon. It will take him longer than if he were allowed to remain untroubled in his chambers. Also, he does not have his brother to assist him. But we dare not let him rest in one place, or the victory here will be hollow indeed."

As I pondered that danger, Gamelan laughed. It is an odd thing to hear a wizard laugh. I have met many in my travels, and that human thing we all do so naturally does not come easy to them. Some shriek like a witch. Some croak like a mating frog. Some howl like direwolves greeting the moon. When he was happy, which I later learned was a rare thing in Gamelan's life, Gamelan hooted—like a great hunting owl. For the first time since we had met, I rather enjoyed that sound.

"I have another reason," Gamelan said. "I must confess that it is quite selfish."

"And what is that?" I asked.

"I remember the day when I gave permission for your brother and that rogue Greycloak to seek the Far Kingdoms. I sat on my throne of office, feeling like a little boy, instead of a wise old Evocator of much responsibility and power. I tell you, I would have traded that throne and every speck of knowledge and authority, if only I could have gone along."

Now it was my turn to laugh. "Adventure? Is that your poison, wizard?"

Another hoot from Gamelan. "I was born to it, Rali," he said. "But fate intervened. I was unlucky enough to be cursed with sorcerous talent. But that is another story, which I shall be delighted to bore you with on our voyage."

He shook his head and twisted his beard in great delight. "Imagine. To speak of such things . . . storytelling, and voyages, and adventures. Why even now I feel quite like a youth again."

Indeed, he seemed to have dropped years in the few minutes that'd passed since our conversation had begun. His cheeks above his beard had a rosy hue. His eyes were brighter. His form straighter. Why, he almost looked handsome. If my women were of a different bent, I dare say several of them would have been ready to come to blows for a chance to trip that old man up on a hearth rug. I swore to myself that sometime during our journey, if the moment presented itself, along with a comely woman who liked the company of men, that I would guide her to the wizard's cot.

Gamelan gave a start. "See, I *am* too old," he said. "I'd almost forgotten the work I was at." He hurried back to his apparatus, sniffing the odorless steam, turning little petcocks to let one liquid drip into another, talking as he went about his tasks. "Thanks to you," he said, "I have the means to arm ourselves against the Archon with a secret weapon of our own. It may not be enough to defeat him in the end, but it will certainly weaken him. And it will make our job easier to hunt him down."

He put an ornate box on the table. It was ebony black, with rich inlayed colors. There were no seams, no sign of a means for entry. Gamelan passed his hands over it, whispered a few words, and pressed the sides with the thumb and forefinger of each hand. It sprang open. I looked inside, and nearly retched at what I saw there. It was a large hunk of flesh with the brownish-purple hue of an internal organ a few hours from rot.

"It's the heart of the Archon you slew," Gamelan said. He lifted it out with the ease of a man comfortable with offal. He placed it under a large copper spigot that protruded from the machine. He turned the petcock. Thick, oily drops of liquid—a glowing green in color—dripped onto the heart. The liquid flowed over the organ, coating it with a thin sheen of green. Gamelan chanted:

"Heart of stone,
Brother to fear:
No love
No tears
No pity!
Heart of stone,
Brother to hate:
No joy
No warmth
No beauty!
Hate to hate,
Fear to fear,
Stone to stone:
Brother find brother!"

The heart began to shrink, and change form and color. It got smaller and smaller, slowly at first, then I blinked and it had gone from the size of a fist to that of a bird's egg. Then it was as smooth and black as the ebony box. Gamelan lifted it gingerly with crystalline tongs and placed it in the box. Once again he pressed the sides and whispered a chant. The box snapped shut.

Gamelan picked it up, holding it between flattened palms. He bowed his head, squinting in concentration. Then he nodded and looked up, those gnarly teeth gleaming thorough his beard.

"It works," he said, quite pleased, as if he had been in some doubt.

He offered me the box. I drew back.

"I don't want to *touch* that thing," I said, as skittish as a new blooming maid.

"I don't blame you," Gamelan answered. "After all, we *do* know *where* it's been. Still . . . to please me, if nothing else."

I took the box and held it as he had. Instantly I felt a tingle. A vibration, like a stringed instrument that had recently been strummed.

"What's happening?" I asked.

Gamelan made that hunting owl hoot of his. "Why, it's telling us that its brother is still quite near. And now we only have to follow it, and—"

Then excitement at his victory caught the wizard. Gamelan threw back his head and gave a shout that rolled and echoed across the great Chamber of the Archons:

"I've got you, you bastard! I've got you!"

CHAPTER FIVE

CHASE TO THE ENDS OF THE WORLD

❖

We set sail on the First Candleday of the Harvest Month in the Year of the Hart. For the blessing, Gamelan chose two soldiers convicted of raping several Lycanthian women. They were crushed between two millstones in the manner prescribed; but instead of sprinkling their blood across the fields, Gamelan anointed the ships' prows, then cast the remains into the sea, as an offering to its gods. Everyone agreed it was a lucky way to begin the voyage, and on a most auspicious day.

That's as may be. But at the risk of singeing your shell-likes with my blasphemies, Scribe, I think that old devil of an Evocator made cunning use of coincidence to rattle Admiral Cholla Yi and his pirates. The entire army was turned out to see us off with as much panoply as Gamelan and several friendly senior officers could squeeze out of Jinnah's jealous fists. It was so elaborate that we missed the morning tide, but Gamelan whispered for me not to worry, for he had a trick or two to make it up.

Our fleet consisted of fifteen of Cholla Yi's galleys, long sea wolves that looked deadly, even drawn up on their rollers on the sand, thus giving us more than even odds against the fleeing armed merchant ships of the Archon. I'd detailed a platoon of my Guardswomen to ten of the ships, plus the command group on my own ship. Four others would be manned only by Cholla Yi's armed sailors. I'd wanted to put a detail on each ship, since I had little trust in Cholla Yi's honesty, and less in that of his men, but even with the new recruits brought out by Officer Aspirant Dica, the Guard was still woefully short.

After much spell-casting and speechmaking—Jinnah even managed a little languid praise of me and my women—we paraded through the ranks of cheering soldiers. They shouted good wishes and prayers for our safe return, and as I passed by our comrades of the long siege, I saw men whose emotions were so overflowing, they openly wept. Drums pounded and horns brayed as we drew up before our ships. Cholla Yi was there to greet me. He was wearing his best—meaning his most gaudy—uniform, with enough medals to nearly cover even his broad chest. As I returned his salute I made the reflexive soldier's survey of his honors. I recognized a few of his self-awarded gold and silver medallions. They were from fleets Cholla Yi never could have commanded, for valor I doubted any amount of coin could have purchased from the mercenary. But it made a good show—especially since it was a show meant to impress me. His rogue's grin was nearly as dazzling as his medals, and about as honestly meant.

But I ignored that and let the moment of new experience wash over me. After days of little sleep I felt faint-headed and everything came to me in a dazzling confusion of sights and sounds.

"Guard!" I shouted, and Polillo and Corais echoed my call to attention. "In files . . . board ship!" Weapons clattered as my women doubled up the gangplanks to their new duties.

I heard shouted orders from the master of my own ship, another rogue named Stryker, echoed by other captains' voices. There was an eerie shrill of pipes as we mounted the gangway of my own galley. The officers and crew shambled to a seaman's crooked attention. Stale sweat mingled with the sharp salt tang of the harbor air. The rowers, who all seemed to have massive arms and chests and spindly legs, stood by their benches and racked oars. The sailors among them—and there was a *marked* difference, I was later told in no uncertain terms—stood in motley groups. Other than the officers, the men were mostly barefoot; but they were turned out in their best, a bizarre mixture of rags and looted finery. Women's scarves and colorful tunics were mixed with canvas breeches, or even loincloths. Jewelry of every variety glinted around their necks, or dangled from ears, noses, and lips. I even saw several bare-chested fellows with rings that hung through pierced nipples.

As I viewed this savage lot, all the usual doubts and half-formed ideas leaped into my already buzzing brain, but then my color guard unfurled our standard. They clipped it to a halyard, then waited as Gamelan chanted traditional blessings and prayers to Maranonia. Before he gave the signal for the banner to be hauled aloft, he plucked a small gourd from his sleeve and dashed it to the deck. Sweet-smelling smoke boiled up, foggy tendrils of red and green and blue waving this way and that. As the color guard raised the banner, the smoke climbed with it, ascending higher and higher until the banner reached the very top. It hung limp for a moment, then I heard Gamelan shout and a wind swooped up from the shore. The colorful cloud of smoke scudded westward and the banner snapped taut—revealing our goddess in her glory. She was every inch a warrior woman, from her golden boots to outstretched spear and torch. Light mail draped her pure-white tunic, and black tresses flowed out from under her peaked helmet.

I was never so proud as that moment, with the flag of our goddess hoisted over a ship for the first time in anyone's memory. I heard Polillo stifle a sob and saw Corais knuckle wetness from the corner of her eye. I had to cough, as something suddenly appeared to be caught in my throat.

The launching parties put their shoulders into it, and our galleys slid over the rollers until they floated free, rolling in the gentle beach swell.

Stryker whispered, in that strange penetrating tone that carried for many yards: "Shall I give th' orders t' put t' sea, Cap'n Antero?"

I could only nod agreement. Another shrill of pipes and shouts from the shore and the crew scrambled about in the mad farewell ballet of every ship about to depart the land that has held it too long captive. There was a blur of orders, bewildering sounds, and the clatter and drum of oars as the other galleys went through identical motions.

Gamelan motioned to me and I stumbled forward. He handed me a golden spear, identical to the one carried by our goddess. He pointed at the distant horizon and bade me to cast the spear. I was so numb from the weariness that had descended on me, I was afraid I'd end up playing the fool, but Gamelan squeezed the muscles of my right arm and I was suddenly very strong. My right side was like a steel spring ready to be unleashed. I set my feet and reached back for the cast. Gamelan chanted:

"Spear fly swift
And far
As Te-Date
Commands
Our spirits to follow."

I loosed with all my power. I felt the sweetness of perfect motion. The cast was with such force that I came off my feet, but I landed back on the deck as agilely as any acrobat, or dancer. I saw the golden spear pierce the air, hurtling toward the distant west. Its arc carried it higher and farther than any mortal could have cast it. The spear flew like a hunting eagle, until it disappeared from sight.

There was a jolt as fifty great oars bit deeply into the sea and our galley shot after the spear. We moved with amazing speed, as did the other ships as they cut through the water after us.

The huzzahs from the shore drowned all else out, and I turned to watch first my shorebound comrades and then the land itself grow small before my eyes.

I swayed, but felt Polillo take my elbow. I mumbled protests that there were things to be done, orders to be issued, but she shushed me as if I were a child and led me below to tuck me into a hammock. My eyes grew heavier than my will to hold them open. And I slept.

I DREAMED I was in Tries' arms again. It was the eve of my departure for Lycanth, and we'd forgiven one another and had made wild, almost violent love. Now the dawn was near breaking and my head was pillowed on her soft breasts. I knew it was a dream, and that dream lied about the real events—we did not meet, much less embrace, those long months ago. But it was a delicious lie and I let it take me where it chose. I kissed her rosebud nipples and caressed those slender thighs until they opened to my hands and lips. I thought I heard Omerye's music playing very faintly in the distance, telling me this was right. This was where I belonged. This was real life, a place of love and music and scented sighs.

I heard the crack of a whip, the thunder of hooves and rumble of an iron-wheeled chariot. The wall of our chamber crashed away and I leaped naked from the bed as the Archon rode a black chariot into the room. The chariot was edged with sharp-steel spikes and blades, and it was drawn by a matched pair of black horses with the broad wings of giant eagles. The shattered room became the deck of our ship, and the Archon mocked me from his chariot. Cholla Yi and the crew laughed with him, pointing at my bare flesh and scorning me for being a woman who loved another woman. Somehow Tries was the Archon's captive, and he shook the reins, shouted to the horses and gripped Tries tight by the manacles that bound her hands. I leaped for them, but it was too late, as the horses took flight, carrying the Archon and his chariot high into the sky. I heard Tries scream and a final boom of laughter from the Archon. Then nothing. I was awake. Eyes closed. Muscles trembling with the ghost traces of my violent dream. The sound of sea and oars and wind outside. The rough hammock swaying under me. I felt a presence. Danger? Slowly, I opened my eyes.

Tries stood over me. She was draped in a filmy, billowing white gown. She smiled at me, then her eyes glowed with hatred and I saw she held a slender, silver dagger. She plunged it down at me. I rolled to the side, clumsy in the hammock, and felt the sting of the blade in my arm. Somehow I freed myself from the hammock and plunged to the wooden deck. I heard Tries scrabbling after me. I tried to get up, but I was weary, so weary, I could not move a limb. Then—

Nothing. Eyes closed. Muscles trembling. Sounds of sea and wind. Hammock swaying under me. I felt a presence. Danger?

Once again I opened my eyes. Corais grinned. "Sweet dreams, Captain?"

Groaning, I got up, swinging my legs over the edge of the hammock. "It was more like a dog's dream of a bad hunt," I said.

I felt a stinging sensation on my arm. I saw a single drop of blood oozing from a small wound. Dazed, I wiped it away.

"Some sailor must have lost his sewing needle," Corais said. She ran a hand along the edge of the hammock, searching for it.

"Yes," I said, with visible relief. "That must be it."

Corais stared at me, concerned. "What else could it be?" she asked.

Exactly. It could be nothing else. Otherwise, the dream was no dream at all. And that wasn't possible—was it?

I rose to greet the new day, and within the hour was so consumed by my strange surroundings that I forgot the dream and the wound.

THE FIRST ORDER of business was to pick up the spoor of the Archon. I called a meeting aboard Cholla Yi's flagship. I set it there for two reasons: (1) It had been put to him in plain terms that *I* was in command. I'd made certain this had been ground into him, almost to the point of humiliation. So, this was a dab of honey to make the aftertaste less bitter. (2) He had a large cabin. If words became heated enough to go to arms, I wanted room to swing my sword. Not that I thought anything like that would happen, but if I needed to put fear into him with a gesture—like gripping the handle of the blade—he'd know there was nothing to impede me, or trip me up.

As soon as I entered the stateroom it was plain Cholla Yi made his living as a pirate as well as a mercenary. It was as gaudy and bawdy as a courtesan's chamber; actually, more like a street whore's who'd found a rich benefactor. There were wall hangings and rugs so colorful they hurt the eye. It was crammed with all sorts of jewel-encrusted objects whose purpose ranged from pots to squat on to what I swore appeared to be some sort of feathered sex machine, with a handle inlaid with rare stones. Everywhere, veils and lace of the highest quality material, and lowest taste in obscene decoration, draped shelves, bulkheads, and figurines—many depicting rather gross sexual acts. There were enormous pillows thrown about, also lewdly decorated. There was one particularly good one, showing two women in an embrace; one of the lovers looked remarkably like Tries. In the center of the cabin was a broad table of dark polished oak. There were leather chairs around the table, with an exceptionally high one at the head of the table. Obviously, it was the admiral's. I made my way to it and sat down. There was no sense in making that honey *too* sweet. Cholla Yi frowned, but I turned this way and that, examining his possessions with complete boredom and superiority. I am my father's daughter, and although I took up the soldier's trade, there is enough of a merchant's wiles in me to turn any ground into my own. The admiral veered to the seat to my right. The ornately carved gallery window of his cabin was behind it, and he'd be favorably framed by the late afternoon sunlight. Gamelan, however, gave a little hop like a boy, and slid into the seat first. He winked at me, then with much gravity peered at Cholla Yi's more lurid figurines, shook his head, then turned his attention to Phocas, the sailing master of Cholla Yi's flagship, who was unrolling a large map. Rank, as with everything else afloat, was damnably different from what I was used to. For instance, Cholla Yi was an admiral and in charge of all ships. But technically he was the honored guest of Phocas, who held command of the ship itself. Similarly, on our own ship, Stryker was the captain, and under him was Klisura, our own sailing master, and Duban, in charge of the rowers. What Stryker's duties consisted of beyond posturing nobly on his quarterdeck and making my life difficult, I wasn't sure.

When I saw Phocas' chart, I immediately forgot the little battle of wills. The quest we were upon seemed unreal when you noted the map's scale. From Orissa and the Lycanthian peninsula, the map sprawled west more miles than I could have imagined. At the moment it seemed like the kind of distances star seekers must attempt to fathom when they ponder our fates. I'd seen maps like this before in my father's and Amalric's studies. But I'd never had to actually place myself on one of them, if you understand my meaning. I saw the familiar ports and cities where my family and others traded. But those ports and cities became smaller marks, until they disappeared into cartographer's speculation—little pictures of fiends to warn of savages, or demons to mark places of supposed ill luck and black magic. But it was the sea itself that took my breath away. It was so enormous that it seemed as if it were ready to swallow the slim slices of land that dared mar its majesty, or the islands that perched so precariously on its brow. The sea stretched west to the edge of the map. There was no land to show the end of it. This was merely as far as anyone—even in handed-down traveler tales—had sailed. The distance was frightening.

Phocas scratched a mark on the linen—only a finger or so west of Lycanth. No one had to tell me this is where we were—near the easternmost edge of the map.

"They've had nearly two days start on us," Cholla Yi said, "and favorable seas and wind. But still, they can't have gone much more than this . . ."

He laid two fingers against our position. Phocas marked it, then the admiral stepped aside as he inscribed a circle. Somewhere inside that circle was our enemy. But we didn't know if we were sailing in exactly the right direction. If we weren't, the Archon could have changed course and be pulling away from us with every minute that passed.

"I believe we are safe to say that he's still fleeing westward, for the moment," Gamelan said. "All the spells I've cast to increase our speed, or slow his, have been countered by spells that can only come from our old friend. And it is from that direction that the ethers are troubled."

"Then it's only logical we continue west," I said.

Phocas laughed. "West takes in a lot," he said snidely. He gestured across the map. "Most everything you're lookin' at's west."

"Mind your manners," Cholla Yi snapped.

Phocas paled. The admiral was in an angry mood. In the meeting with Jinnah, I'd made certain—with the support of Gamelan and the officers sympathetic to me—that Jinnah laid the blame for the Archon's escape squarely on Cholla Yi. He should have had the harbor mouth blockaded. What's more, Jinnah had informed him the agreed victory bonus would not be paid until the expedition was completed. Even worse, he and his crew would not be eligible for any shares of the loot from Lycanth until our return. I'd expected him to explode when he heard the last, but he and Jinnah exchanged odd glances, and it seemed Cholla Yi had bit back his temper. I wondered if some private arrangement had been made. The most likely, it seemed at the time, was that Jinnah had said he'd compensate him for shouldering the full blame of the failure to capture the Archon. By rights, Jinnah—as the commander of us all—deserved the greatest black mark for the failure.

Gamelan broke through the tension. "We shall let our enemy resolve our dilemma," he said.

He took out the black box that contained the talisman of the Archon's heart.

Cholla Yi and Phocas stared nervously at the box. They'd heard rumors of the talisman, but actually seeing a thing of such magical power was more intimidating than whispered speculation.

"I'll only require a compass from you," Gamelan said.

"Pardon?" Cholla Yi gaped like he was just rising from deep waters.

"A compass, if you please," Gamelan repeated.

Hastily, one was found. Gamelan placed the box on the circle Phocas had inscribed, and the compass on top of that. Then he waved for silence—as if there was a need of warning for these dumb stricken pirates. There was no prelude to the spell. No chanting, at least not aloud; no calling on the gods for assistance.

Gamelan stared at the box, his concentration total. His yellow eyes glowed like the sun, and the whole room seemed to be lit by the inner light spilling out. I heard gasps as a low, humming noise began to vibrate the box. Then the box itself glowed. The compass needle jolted. It spun wildly about, once, twice, then as it whirled for the third time, it froze in mid-gyration, as if a hand had stopped it.

Gamelan drew back. The light faded from his eyes until they were merely that odd yellow. He wiped sweat from his brow, then pointed at the compass's arrow. It was quivering, as if ready to move on.

"Follow that," Gamelan said, "and we will find our enemy."

The compass pointed due west.

I'm not certain what transpired next. Cholla Yi spoke to me, and I answered whatever question he asked. But everything seemed very dim to me— far away. I found myself staring at the compass needle and vast expanse of the map.

I could see all the familiar places. Here was Tros, a rich city my family had traded with for generations; then Savia, renowned for its wines; Thurgan, masters of fine blades; and Luangu, with its famous cattle pens that ladder the shore for miles. Beyond was Jeypur, a barbaric, coastal port, where caravans spill in daily, carrying silks and spices and magical rarities from places that would only exist in legend if we did not know them from their goods; next was Laosia, where the J'hana family controls the market in ivory and that beautiful black wood that's so hard it can turn aside steel.

On the opposite coast I saw Redond, and then the nearly impassable mountains of the Kingdom of Valaroi, which girdle the shore; across those mountains is the great desert where wild tribes of horsemen rage. We know them only for their rich carpets and sweet-smelling oils that we burn in our lamps on festive occasions. Still farther west was Tiger Bay, named not for the beasts, but for the color and markings of the gems of the shellfish that dwell there and are collected to make the finest fire beads. I knew all those places well, as does any Orissan schoolchild. But past that point, beyond the Jasmine Islands, the Coral Sea, the Ginger River, and the Lemon Coast—all was unknown.

There is an exhilarating moment, my brother has often said, when all journeys begin in earnest. Before that moment all is foolish speculation; afterward, the journey lapses into mere progress to be marked each day. My brother is a man to be listened to about such things, for there is no one in our history who has traveled farther; although now I may rival him.

It was that day in Cholla Yi's stateroom when my adventures truly began. At that instant I knew for certain that before I was through, I would see for myself the places on that map. My eyes were drawn to the edge, where all beyond was unknown. And it came to me I would see *those* places as well. I was not frightened by this vision, Scribe. And as I have promised absolute truth, I must confess that for a short time I had no thought of the Archon and the threat he represented. Instead, I was filled with a great yearning. I wanted to know, I *had* to know, the answer to the riddle the map posed—which was: *What lies beyond?*

For the first time I understood the blessing—and the curse—of seekers like Janos Greycloak, and yes, my brother, although he will not as yet admit it.

Confused by the realization of a new side of me—a side I had never expected to exist—I looked at Gamelan. I could not see him clearly for a moment: a shadow seemed to fall between us. It was a familiar shadow, and I smelled a familiar scent. I thought I heard a woman whisper. I shook my head and my vision cleared as the shadow was swept away. I saw that Cholla Yi and Phocas were absorbed in planning. But the old wizard was watching me intently.

"You had a vision?" Gamelan asked.

I shook my head no. But there was a smell of sandalwood in the room, and I knew I'd lied.

WE SAILED after the Archon, always keeping close watch on the magical compass. When it veered, we changed course. When it came back to the heading, we aped the motion. We didn't know if the changes were made because our enemy knew we were on his heel, or if it was only the vagaries of his flight. But none doubted the chase was for real. The Archon was out there—that was certain; a few leagues or a few days ahead.

The excitement of the chase waned as one day bled into the next, and we got down to the routine of our new lives at sea.

As time passed, I slowly realized these ships were to be our new battlefield, and I knew as little about them as I would, say, about fighting on ice. I set out to become expert, then to see to it my women became the same. Any hour or day—if Te-Date please—we might sight the Archon's ships. I found the most boring man aboard ship, who carried the title of master's mate, which I soon found meant he was a seagoing version of a quartermaster. Except where a quartermaster could send you to sleep prattling about tent ropes and kettles, this man had the opportunity to natter about anything, from ropes to cutlasses, everything in fact except the saltwater around us.

For those who wish to know a bit about the world we found ourselves in, the world we would spend far too long on, some of us the remainder of our lives, in fact, here are some details:

Our galleys were of the type known as "long runners," and were intended, the mate told me pridefully, for anything from going up a river to harrying and conquering a merchant vessel to raiding a seaport to making long sea passages out of sight of land. "'Course," he confessed, which we'd already found out, "bein' shallow draft, the ship rolls a bit in any sort of wind or seaway. Matter of fact, a long runner'll pitch some tied up to a dock, which is why any good galleyman had best have a solid-cast stomach. Or else not need to hold vittles down longer'n the next wave." For some reason, men seem to find the cramps of seasickness hilariously funny, but only if it's shown by someone else. Corais wondered if they'd find the sensation so risesome if they underwent something much the same every twenty-eight days, as we did. But I made no response to the mate's chortles.

Each galley was about a hundred feet long and twenty feet wide. It drew only about three feet of water, which accounted for what the mate called its liveliness. There were three officers to each ship: the master, sailing master, and rowing master. Under them were other men, also called mates, but they were not considered officers, but rather like our sergeants. "Mate" was also the title given the ship's artisans, such as carpenter, sailmaker, and so on. Each galley was crewed by fifty rowers, who also doubled as seamen when the captain shouted for all hands to turn to. There were, in addition, fifteen able seamen, who considered themselves elite and wouldn't touch an oar if the ship was being driven onto the rocks. Almost any number of soldiers could be carried for a day or so, but under normal peacetime conditions (which I knew meant for Cholla Yi piracy), some twenty-five marines—soldiers with a modicum of sailor's training—would be on board as a shock force.

Each galley had a weather, or main deck, which was open, and a deck below for sleeping and for bad weather. It took *very* rough seas to go below, since this deck was dark and cramped. Anyone over five feet walked in a stoop, or rang her skull against the deck overhead like it was a bell. We slept in hammocks, which were taken down each day and stowed, then hung each night wherever we chose, which was on deck for the most part. The upper deck could be shaded in hot weather under canvas awnings, and it was most pleasant to loll under such a brightly striped tent when the sea breezes blew and required real effort to get up and go through yet another set of exercises or sword or spear drill.

Up forward, above the knife bow, was a raised deck, from which an attack would be launched in battle. In the stowage spaces under it were weapons, spare sails, ropes, barrels of water and rations, and the like.

At the stern was another raised deck, the quarterdeck. From here the galley was commanded and steered with a long tiller, connected to the rudder along one side. Under this deck was the one bit of luxury the galley had—separate cabins for the ship's officers.

A long, narrow deck about three feet wide ran just above the weather deck fore and aft and connected the two raised decks. This was called a storming bridge, and served not only as a passageway when seas broke over the main deck, but to strengthen the hull.

Each galley had two masts with a lateen sail on each, which was how the ship normally was moved. In the face of a wind, or when speed was required, the sails would be lowered and the oars manned.

For cooking there was a sanded, built-up area on the lower deck. One man cooked, in great kettles, whatever was to be eaten, then these roughly cooked viands were handed out to "messes," for further distribution. Each mess was ten sailors, whose utensils and plates were kept in a chest, along with whatever condiments they'd chosen to purchase from their own pockets. A sailor was free to join—or quit—a mess, just as his messmates had equal freedom to accept or reject him.

For a jakes, there was a framework pushed out over the stern when someone had the need. For bathing—well, as the mate said, "a sharp bow means speed, but you'll think you're swimming half the time."

That was all. Each galley was exactly as it appeared—a machine dedicated for only two purposes, speed and war. Everything else had been discarded. I spent time walking and then drawing the ship, until I knew its every dimension without thinking. Then I began studying another aspect—how this ship was sailed and brought into battle. And that was a study that lasted until the end of the voyage.

I ASSEMBLED my officers and we began discussing how battle should be joined from these galleys. Cholla Yi and one of his marine officers gave a speech, not that there was much to be learned. A sea battle was fought as if each ship was a wagon full of infantry, attacking other wagons, or perhaps a better image would be a group of small enemy forts, each surrounded by a swamp. First we would wreak as much damage as possible while we closed with our enemy, using spears, catapults, magic if there were Evocators aboard, and other weapons. Then we would close with our opponent and, at a signal, our Guardswomen would leap onto his ship and attempt to slay all his soldiers. One side or another would triumph; the winners would have the ship if it were undamaged enough to be afloat, and the losers would be dinner for the sharks that even now trailed in our wake.

There were subtleties, from ramming to the crow's beak to boarding nets, all of which I'll explain when necessary. But basically there was not much difference between storming a castle and storming a ship. Infantry was infantry, whether on land or sea.

Corais and I quietly discussed what we had learned afterward. To both of us, it seemed there was something missing, something wrong. This style of battle had all the subtlety of two blindfolded drunkards with clubs in a small room. There must be something more, or another way. But neither of us had any ideas then.

We were right, but that, too, is part of my story, to learn in the telling.

IF IT WEREN'T for the piratical looks of the crew, and my soldiers at constant hard practice with their arms, our voyage would have appeared as a pleasure jaunt to any outside observer. The seas were sparkling, the air alternately bracing and languid, the days all clear blue skies, and the nights as starlit as the most romantic dream. Fast winds made the rowing easy and the days pleasantly long. We neither gained nor lost ground to our foe, and it soon became apparent the fight was a duel of wills between the pursuer and the pursued. And whoever made the first mistake would lose. Even Gamelan and the Archon had lapsed into a truce in their magical fight. It had proved pointless, with every spell cast being countered by the other—and at such distances no one even had the diversion of watching a magical show. Both wizards had apparently decided to save their energies for a close-up battle. Gamelan, however, stayed alert for a surprise attack—and he assured me the Archon was doing the same. We believed, however, we held the edge, because not only did we outnumber Symeon and the Archon in both ships and soldiers, we knew were much better supplied; and that the day would soon come when they would be forced to stop for water, or food.

Among my women, morale was better than I could have hoped. Those who longed for home, and lovers and family, were caught up by all the new things they saw and the new skills they learned. Friends became faster friends, new lovers were found for those who were seeking it, and beds remained chaste and untroubled for those who could make love's memory suffice. Among the most trusted members of my staff, Ismet continued to keep her own company, which she preferred; Corais played the field in the smooth way she had of keeping dalliances to nothing more than a lovely tickle, no harm done, no promises expected or made; while Polillo fell in huge sighing love with a little blond legate, Neustria, who stirred her to white heat by playing coy, then satisfying her in a memorable two-day tryst filled with much mooning and thrashing about wherever they could find privacy, and finally a glorious fight where each swore they had never been such a fool as to fall for the other. Polillo was as happy as I'd seen her since she cut two

Lycanthian throats in the space of five minutes. As for me, I do not dally where I command. And even if I did, Tries would have come between me and any woman of my fascination.

So the seas remained friendly for many a day. Each morning brought an empty horizon that beckoned us onward, and each night fell to a gloriously red sun the sailors claimed was the gods' promise of an equally pleasant to-morrow.

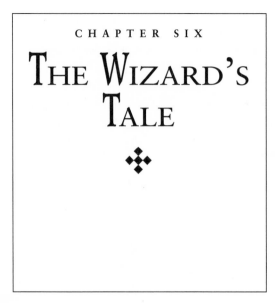

CHAPTER SIX

THE WIZARD'S TALE

A s the days drew on, I found myself more and more in the company
of Gamelan. At first I was quite uncomfortable, for I still harbored
bitterness against the Evocators for their part in the murder of my
brother, Halab. True, Amalric made peace with the wizards of Orissa, and
freed us all from the tyranny of magic with the gift of knowledge he brought
back from the Far Kingdoms. But I had not, and doubt I ever would have if
it hadn't been for Gamelan. I am not one who easily forgives, especially
when blood has been shed.

But that began to change the day we sighted the floating field of ice. It's
rare to see such things in the western ocean, but sometimes, travelers say,
currents pull them from their home in the frozen south and turn them into
these seas. It was an enormous thing, perhaps the size of a farm village. It
was peaked and jagged, with a great pink cavern bored in one side by the
warm waters. We all marveled, and a party ventured to it in a small boat and
returned with a big chunk of pink ice. I put some of it in a cup of wine and
it fizzled and bubbled most pleasantly.

As our ship passed, I strolled along the deck, to study the ice field. I was
so absorbed I almost bowled over Gamelan, who was busy doing something
at the rail. After we'd made apologies for mutual clumsiness, I saw two large
buckets of seawater with several fat fish inside. In his hand Gamelan had a

strong line with several nasty hooks attached. The wizard ducked his head when I saw them, but continued baiting the hooks.

I laughed. "You, a fisherman? And a fair one at that! I'd have thought that when wizards fished—and it never occurred to me they might—they'd cast a spell on the sea. Or dump some evil potion in the water to kill the fish."

"As an acolyte," Gamelan replied, "I was taught the first rule of magic is to never use it unnecessarily."

"*Eating* is necessary," I pointed out.

Gamelan actually blushed. Even with his long white beard and gnarly features, he looked definitely boyish. And if I had any inclination of mothering—which I definitely do not, to Tries' great anger—I'd have clutched him to my bosom. Then he shrugged. "I wouldn't want this generally known," he said, "but I enjoy fishing. If truth be known, I was once a fisherman. My family always said that when I grew, I would be the finest fisherman in all Orissa."

I was as astounded as if he'd plucked a demon from his sleeve and called it sister, dear. "A fisherman? You?"

He smiled and cast his line. "Is it really so strange?" he asked. "I come from a place, like anyone else—complete with both a set of parents and a family."

"But how does a fisherman become a wizard? Much less Chief Evocator of all Orissa?"

He was silent for a long time. I watched him let his line play near the ice field. Then he said: "My watery friends have taken refuge under there. As soon as I saw it, I knew the fishing would be good."

I let him shift the subject. It was apparent he had become uncomfortable. I said: "I'd have thought the cold would have driven them away."

"I've no experience with ice," Gamelan answered. "But when I saw the ice field, it came to me that a fish would be happy under there. Not only for hiding, but for eating. Don't ask me how I knew this. I just did."

"Magic?" I pressed.

"Oh, no. It's just that I . . . suddenly thought like a fish. And I knew I liked it under there."

His line jerked, once, twice. In less time than it takes to draw a breath, he was fighting to pull it in. I almost reached in to help him, but he looked so capable, his hands sure and strong as he played the line, that I held back. A few minutes later there was an enormous fish gasping its last on the deck.

"You see?" Gamelan said.

"I never argue with dinner," I answered.

"In that case," he said, "why don't you join me this evening. I promise you will dine well."

I accepted, knowing there was more to the invitation than eating.

Later that night I crowded into the little space the ship's carpenter had abandoned to make way for the Evocator's necessities. The cabin was full of all kinds of strange devices, illuminated books, vials, jars, and pouches of mysterious things. But the smell of the fish cooking over a small brazier overpowered my curiosity. I was ravenous. We tucked into the food with no preamble.

When we were done, I loosened my belt and sighed. "If you were to tell me in a previous life you were the head cook for the richest family in Orissa, I'd not doubt it for a minute." I picked a final bit of meat from the backbone. "I'm learning you are a man of many talents, wizard."

Gamelan laughed. "The cooking *was* by magic," he confessed. "I have a little demon I lured from some magician's kitchen. A copper pincher, apparently. My bargain with the demon is to provide him with as much as he can hold, and he cooks in return."

"I thought magic was supposed to be used only for important things," I teased.

Gamelan grinned through his beard. "Eating *is* important," he said.

I hoisted a bottle of brandy I'd brought along. "If you fetch me two cups," I said, "we'll partake of another kind of spirits. After a drink or two, perhaps you won't be so shy about your fishermen's beginnings."

"I wasn't being shy," he said, but he got the cups just the same and I filled them up. We drank. "Actually," Gamelan said after the first jolt had settled and he'd mated it with another sip, "I thought my tale would best be told in a quieter moment. For I believe it has some bearing on your own circumstances."

I was surprised. "Me? In what way?"

"You have the Gift," he said flatly.

"That's nonsense," I said, a bit angry. I didn't have to ask what he meant. "My gifts are physical, and hard won at that."

"Deny it all you like, Rali," Gamelan answered. "I know it to be true. Remember casting the bones in Jinnah's tent? Also, it was more than fighting skills and good fortune that allowed you to kill one Archon and put another to flight. I tell you, no ordinary person could have accomplished it."

"I don't even *like* wizards," I said, still hot. "Present company included, if the talk keeps shifting this way."

Gamelan took no offense. "Your brother, Halab, had the Gift. Do you deny that?"

I couldn't. According to Amalric, if Halab had been allowed to live, he might have been one of the greatest Evocators in our people's history. But the Evocators, before Amalric tamed them, were jealous of his power and made certain he failed a deadly test of his skills.

"He was the only one in my family," I said.

"Really?" Gamelan pressed. "I sensed a small talent in Amalric himself. So there's another."

I gave a violent shake of my head. "I don't believe it. Besides, if it's so common in the Antero family, why haven't there been others in the past? Others as strong as Halab?"

"Are you certain there haven't?"

"Of course I am. No one in my father's—"

Gamelan broke in. "I know that. But what of your mother and her family?"

I was silent. There had always been something about my mother. Sometimes she seemed as if she lived slightly apart from us all. Almost as if she were on a . . . higher level? As for her family, she rarely spoke of the folk she came from in that small village where she'd met and been wooed by my father.

"I don't know," I finally admitted. But my voice was so low, I could hardly hear it myself.

"But I do," Gamelan said. "That's why my brother wizards were so wary of your family. I cast spells once, and learned your grandmother was a famous witch, well-known in the villages around her, as was her mother before her."

I accepted his statement as truth. Why would he lie? But I didn't like it.

"Still," I said. "That doesn't mean I was so cursed."

"It *will* be a curse," Gamelan answered. "If you continue to fight it. Only tragedy can come from your present course. And I do not mean only for yourself. But for others around you."

I did not answer. My temper was a blade's breadth from snapping, and I was full of confusion and dread. I drained my cup and filled it with brandy again.

"Now, you shall hear my story," Gamelan said. "For you should know the man you see is not the man I desired with all my heart to be."

I drank . . . and listened.

"I was born on a fishing boat," he began. "All my family were fisher-folk. They'd fished our blessed river from the time when Orissa was only a village."

I knew the kind of people he meant. They spent all their lives on the river, coming in only to repair their boats, sell their fish, and take on supplies. At night they tied their boats close so they were like small towns, going from one to another as easy as from house to house. Sometimes, late, I'd heard them laughing, and the strains of the music they favored. They always seemed so free of care that on certain evenings I longed to join them, to abandon the city for the river.

"The river is in our blood," Gamelan continued. "No. It *is* our blood. The river bears us up and carries us away from our troubles. It is our food, our drink. Our . . . everything. And a river is always so full of mysteries—dangerous mysteries at times—that one can never be bored. What is in its depths can never be completely known. It was that life I was born to. It was that life I desired above all else. And do so to this day."

He drank, reflecting. "But I had the Talent," he said. "No one really noticed at first. But from the time when I was very small, if I touched the most hideously fouled net, the tangles would fall away, and the net would be as good as if it were newly made. There were other signs, small at first. My family and friends learned if they lost an object, they only had to ask, and I could instantly go to it. Sometimes, when I had a childish tantrum, the fire in the hearth would rise most frighteningly. Objects would be hurled about, with no visible hand to throw them. Glass would shatter for no reason. And there might be pounding—knocking—on the bottom of the hull, as if there were a man there, signaling."

"There, you see!" I blurted. "Nothing like that has ever happened to me! So, I'm an ordinary mortal after all."

Gamelan paid no mind, but went on. At first his family was proud—especially when they found he could heal small wounds with a touch. His odd gift, plus his budding skills as a fisherman who always returned with a catch and could lead others to rich grounds during difficult times, made them the envy of their friends and relations. At eighteen summers his future was assured. His father was about to give him his first boat, and everyone agreed Gamelan would someday be their leader. Then he fell in love.

"I remember Riana as the most beautiful young woman who had ever graced a man's dreams. We believed there never could have been such lovers as us, and swore to all who would listen that the gods, when they made us, had decreed neither of us would be whole unless we were joined forever."

I refilled our cups as he reflected. Then he said: "I suppose most people would say we were only suffering the symptoms of our fevered age. But I do not think so. I do not think so. However, it soon became plain the gods lied. They had other plans."

I thought of my long dead Otara, and almost wept when I remembered what it was like to love and be loved so completely.

"One day we witnessed an accident. A young city woman, pleasure-boating with her family, let her arm dangle in the water while the fool who steered their craft ran too close to a merchant ship. Her arm was ripped away. My boat was the first to answer her screams. I recall the horror and pain in her face as the blood gushed. She cried out to me: 'But I'm only sixteen.' I saw the severed arm lying next to her and I snatched it up and pressed it against the stump. Then I prayed, oh, how I prayed. I don't know to whom, but all I could think was of that poor girl whose life was ebbing away. I heard a shout, then a cry from her, and I opened my eyes and saw she was whole again. The arm had been reattached and was as good as it'd been moments before. Her family and companions praised me and tried to get my name. I was so shaken by the miracle, I became frightened and leaped into my boat and fled as fast as the sail would take me."

A few days later Gamelan met his first wizard.

"For a boy with his head full of silly notions, he was quite disappointing," Gamelan said. "I'd expected a fellow who looks much as I do now. Old. Bearded. With eyes that would freeze an oxen in his path."

I glanced at Gamelan's strange, yellow eyes. Just now they were as kindly and warm as a kitchen fire.

Gamelan caught my look. "They get meaner," he said.

I laughed, then eased back. The tale he spun was so intriguing, I forgot my own worries.

"But back to my first Evocator," Gamelan went on. "He was quite young, handsome. And rich. He was the brother of the young woman I had saved. His name was Yuloor, and he was a wizard of small talent but enormous ambition. He wanted to reward me for helping his sister by sponsoring me to the Council of Evocators. Soon I would wear a wizard's robes and would be respected by everyone in the city. But I wanted nothing of this. For I knew once I left the river, I would never be able to return.

"Yuloor admitted this, but said it was a small sacrifice and my family would greatly benefit. More importantly, it was my sacred duty to the people of Orissa not to waste a talent given to so few. He wooed me and my family for many a day, until finally I believed I had no other choice. To do otherwise would doom me and my family to a wretched existence, caused by that magical spirit inside me gnawing and clawing to get out. Finally I agreed."

"I suspect Yuloor actually saw his chance in you," I said. "The real reward was to be his."

"Quite right," Gamelan said. "He became my mentor, and as I rose through the levels of knowledge and power, he rose with me. He died not long ago. He was quite a happy man."

"But what of Riana?" I asked.

"She was lost to me," he answered. "Our marriage was forbidden. After all, how can an Evocator marry a fisherwoman?"

"Didn't you argue?" I blurted. "Didn't you fight?"

Gamelan sighed. "Yes. But it was hopeless. I was told quite plainly what would happen to her if I continued to defy them. I suppose my loss is one reason I achieved the powers that I now call my own. I've never loved another. So there was nothing to keep me from my studies, until they finally consumed me and there was nothing left of the fisherman. Only a wizard."

I said: "And this is the life you want me to take up? I'm happy as I am."

"Are you, Rali?" he asked.

I thought of the dream I had of Tries' betrayal. I could not answer yes.

"Anyway, happiness is beside the point," Gamelan said. "You must follow your weird, or suffer the consequences."

"Consequences?" I snapped. "That's what your lying friend Yuloor said."

And Gamelan answered: "Ah. But that part was no lie at all."

"I'm a soldier," I muttered. "Nothing more." My words were slurred. I was drunk. It wasn't the brandy that made me so.

"Will you think on it?" Gamelan asked.

"That's all I'll do," I said. My mood was evil, hating.

"We'll talk again tomorrow," Gamelan said.

I said nothing. But I thought, if I had *real* magical power, tomorrow would never come.

Well, it did come, Scribe; but the day wasn't spent as either of us had expected.

Each day after the noontide sighting, the wizard was rowed over to the admiral's galley to confer on the course they believed the Archon fleet was on. Navigational tools were matched against Gamelan's magical skills, and the bearing was set. Signal flags announced the course, and each ship made any corrections necessary.

On this particular day, however, the routine changed. Corais and I were discussing the progress of our recruits' training when we heard the lookout shout. I glanced around and saw with mild surprise that Gamelan's visit with Cholla Yi had been cut short and his little boat put out for our ship. Corais and I idly strolled to the rail to see what was happening. There seemed to be much excitement—Gamelan was pointing impatiently at our ship and urging his rowers to make haste.

"A wizard in a hurry," Corais said drily, "rarely bodes well."

I heard Polillo shout and I looked to see some fifty yards off the bow of Gamelan's boat a huge bird with leathery wings struggling with a sea lizard over a large fish. There was no danger to Gamelan, so I was quickly caught up in the fight between two such unlikely adversaries, as was the rest of the ship.

The lizard was twice my size, but the bird was not intimidated. It'd caught the fish in its heavy tooth-lined beak, and had been about to swoop up with its prize when the lizard had struck. Both creatures had strong holds on either end of the fish, one dragging down, the other up.

"A silver piece on the bird," Polillo cried.

But there were no takers, for everyone seemed to find favor with the strange creature from the sky, shouting and cheering its efforts. We groaned as the bird suddenly let loose.

"Two silver pieces against one!" Polillo jumped the odds as the lizard rolled back, the fish gripped in its jaws. She was deluged with shouted offers. I could see from her wide grin she believed the bird was as clever as bold. Sure enough, as the lizard lay there, stunned by its sudden victory, the bird swooped back and slashed its white belly with its hooked talons. The lizard screamed, curling and flopping in agony. Instantly, the bird grabbed the fish and shot for the skies, to cheers, and some groans from those who'd taken Polillo's bet.

"I know a fighter when I see one," Polillo gloated, diving in amongst her new debtors. "Let's see the color of your coin, my friends. White metal only. There's no room for copper in my chest."

We were all exhilarated by the struggle, as if we'd been in on the fight ourselves.

"Now, that's a good omen if I ever saw one," Corais said.

I wanted to agree. But my natural caution—some brand it cynicism— crowded in. Perhaps it was a good omen. On the other hand, from the point of view of the sea lizard, it could be a warning.

A swish of robes brought me back, and I turned to find Gamelan hobbling toward us as fast as his old legs could carry him. He'd reached our galley during the middle of the fight and had boarded with little or no help.

"I'm sorry—" I started to say, but the wizard brushed my apology aside with an impatient gesture.

"The Archon's fleet has stopped," he said.

I goggled and made the usual silly noises of an officer who's become so used to routine that she's forgotten her profession is founded on surprise.

"I don't know how long his fleet will tarry, or what his trouble is," Gamelan said, "but all signs show he's lying as if becalmed or anchored."

"Perhaps he's taking on water, or food from somewhere," I ventured. "They had little time to prepare before they fled."

Gamelan nodded; his beard bristled with energy and his yellow eyes danced like twin suns. "That is what the admiral and I surmised," he said.

He unrolled a small, crude chart I'd never seen before. "Master Phocas found this among his other charts. It's supposed to show what lies beyond our master chart, although he gave it to me saying he had many doubts as to its truth, since he was given it in a wine shop rather than buying it from a chandlery."

Corais and I bent close to see. Gamelan jabbed a finger at a small group of islands near the westernmost edge of the map. "This is where his fleet appears to be at this moment. Whether or not the islands can provision him, no one knows. Cholla Yi says that even the existence of those islands is speculative."

I saw a small symbol next to the islands warning that the mapmaker was relying on rumor rather than fact about those tiny dots. Still, blood began to hammer at my ears. "If there are no islands, why else would he stop in the middle of the ocean?"

The wizard twisted his beard in delight. "Why else, indeed?" he asked.

Corais laughed. "The next time I see a wizard in a hurry, I won't be so quick to fear for our luck."

"Don't dare the gods," I warned, only half in jest. "First we have to catch him. Then we have to fight him."

Polillo, who'd come up behind us, broke in. "Did I hear someone say fight? Or was it my imagination?"

"No, my friend," I answered. "It was not your imagination. And yes, you finally get to fight."

"Good," she answered. "For a while I'd been wondering if I'd fallen into the company of cravens. My axe is thirsty."

THE FIGHT did not come that quickly. As I'd warned Corais, first we had to catch the Archon. We rowed with a will, the drums around our fleet hammering in constant double time, the oarsmen digging in so deeply with each pull that their oars could be seen to bend. The fleet skimmed through the seas so swiftly that sometimes it seemed the hulls barely had time to get wet. We rowed like that for two days, then after only a few hours rest, for two more.

The tension hung so close that no one remarked when we passed the westernmost edge of our master chart and crossed into unmapped seas.

On the fifth day we sighted the Archon.

CHAPTER SEVEN

THE SEA ON FIRE

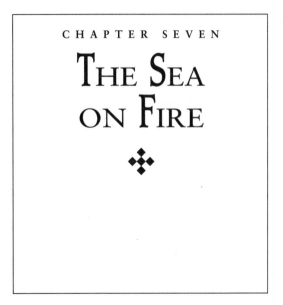

A s hard as we pressed before, we pressed harder still, and within two hours the fleeing Lycanthians could now be glimpsed from the fore-deck. I even thought I could distinguish sails of individual ships. The deck was crowded—there was myself, Corais, and Polillo, as well as Captain Stryker and Gamelan. Then Cholla Yi arrived, unbidden, for an impromptu conference. The air crackled with excitement and tension.

"Will they have sighted us yet?"

Corais' question was intended for Stryker, but Gamelan answered: "They have. If not by sight, by castings. I have already felt the fingers of the Archon stretching out toward us."

Cholla Yi frowned when he saw a nearby sailor shiver—and the reaction wasn't from the breeze. Gamelan nodded understanding and we moved back along the storming bridge out of earshot.

"How long until we're on them?" Polillo asked.

Cholla Yi eyed the full mainsail and estimated the time from the distance the foremast's shadow had traveled on the deck since we'd gathered to watch the ships.

"If the wind holds fair," he said, "and from the same quarter . . . and they keep their current course . . . two, perhaps three days."

"If I was runnin' that fleet," Stryker said, "and knowin' a fight's for certain 'cause they can't outrun us, I'd be formin' my battle line now—and maneuverin' for the weather gauge."

"As would I," Cholla Yi said. "But once a man starts running, it's hard to stop. Fear makes us all do strange things."

"Are you certain, Admiral," Gamelan said, "they are afraid? That they're running from—rather than to—something?"

Cholla Yi began to snap a retort, then considered. He looked slightly worried and ran his fingers over his spikes. "They *are* holding the same course, aren't they?" he said. "And have been for some time."

"That was what I thought," Gamelan said. "Though I'm hardly a seaman."

"Do you sense anything, Lord Gamelan?" Stryker asked.

"Not as yet," the wizard said. "But I am spending most of my energy attempting to determine what battle spell or spells the Archon may be intending; and casting counterspells against them. I shall attempt, though, to see if there are any porous spaces I could slip an inquiry through."

He went back down the storming bridge, then to the maindeck and below to his cramped cabin.

Polillo shook her head. "I don't like warring against sorcerers, and I wouldn't want to be Gamelan. Imagine an enemy you can't see, can't hear, can't slay with steel."

Corais put her arm around Polillo. "Don't fret, sister. There's an Archon roasting away in some black hell who thought like that until Rali taught him different." Polillo's mood changed and she grinned.

Then words ran out and all of our eyes were held by those tiny dots, far out against the horizon.

THAT NIGHT we entered strange seas. The sun sank, but the sky was still alight. As twilight died we could see that the glow was coming from beyond the Archon's fleet. The light was red, as if there were some fire raging just over the horizon. I'd heard of phosphorescent seas and asked Stryker if this was the case.

"I ain't ever heard of sea fire bright enough to light the whole sky," he said.

"What do you think it could be, then?" I asked.

Stryker spit over the rail. "I left off thinkin' when we started this voyage, Captain," he said. "Else, when we catch that black wizard, I'll be a foul hand on the tiller."

As the hours progressed, the light in the sky grew stronger, and by midnight, when I forced myself to my hammock, I could see four distinct blazes in the sky.

* * *

I SHUDDERED awake before dawn, brought up by an awful stench and shouts from the deck. At first I thought we were under some sort of magical attack and rolled out of my hammock scrabbling for a sword. But it wasn't that at all. The air, the sea, the entire world stank like the mud and sulfur baths outside of Orissa that my father used to take us to when I was a girl. I hurried on deck, once again nearly skulling myself on that damnably low hatchway as I came up. I must have been the last to awake, because most of the ship's company was already there, crowding the ship's railing.

The sun hadn't risen yet, but there was a thick, drowned yellowish light that let us see clearly. A brown haze covered the sea, and even though we must've sailed leagues closer to the Lycanthians, their ships were still dots, half hidden in the murk. But that wasn't the signal attraction everyone was gaping at. Land was in sight. Land of a sort, anyway; land that explained the stink and also that eerie glow in the night. I counted low mountaintops, seemingly rising out of the sea itself—three, no five, volcanoes a-borning. From each of them rose a column of smoke, and now and again, sparks and a dull flame. Corais and Polillo joined me but said nothing.

I saw Gamelan and Stryker on the quarterdeck and climbed up to them. Both men looked drawn.

"It looks," I said to Gamelan, "as if your thoughts were right about the Archon running for something."

Stryker chose to answer. " 'Pears, so, Captain. Do yer 'spose they thinks there be shelter ahead? Or, mebbe friends to help them?" He scratched his head. "Yer'd have to have skin made out of iron to live in these parts. So that don't make sense."

Gamelan broke in. "But this region surely looks to be their goal," he said. "Our friends aren't blind, and would have changed course earlier if they thought they were sailing into a trap."

I remembered something Amalric had told me. "My brother once said," I offered, "that the Symeon clan had voyaged into the west, but no one knew to what distance."

Gamelan stroked his beard. "This far? With no navigational aides? I would think it more likely the seas remain as unknown to Nisou Symeon as us, but the Archon has used his magic to peer ahead."

"I wish yer'd done the same with *yer* own arts," Stryker half whispered, "and warned us of this gods-forsaken ocean."

Gamelan looked at the mercenary, his yellow eyes glowing. His tone was cold, cold. "As I said before, I have needed all my powers just to keep magical sight of the Archon and his ships. There have been many spells cast and sent wafting back on their wake, intended to delude us onto another course, or even to give up in hopelessness. As for these eruptions . . . the greatest danger we face is being built right now, in the flagship that holds the Archon. Even now, as Symeon and his sailors are polishing their weapons for the battle, so the Archon is readying his spells." Then his teeth gleamed through his beard as he said: "Concentrate on your duties, Captain, and I shall attend to mine."

Stryker quailed under the wizard's scorn. Then he recovered. "Sorry to be speakin' out of turn, Lord Gamelan," he said. He spun and went down the companionway to the main deck.

Gamelan said nothing, but only stared after him.

"What spells do you sense we'll face?" Corais asked, breaking the tension.

"I don't know precisely," Gamelan said. "But we can all take a hint by looking about us. Not only are we sailing strange seas, but the weather itself is worsening."

Indeed, we'd been so engrossed in watching the bellow and boil as these new mountains were a-borning from the depths of the sea that we'd paid small attention to anything else. The sun must've risen, but the sky was overcast and the clouds were gray, becoming black. The wind whipped against our helmet crests and armor. The seas themselves were long rollers, with great intervals between the waves, such as I had seen building on beaches at the mouth of Orissa's river during winter storms. We were occasionally taking water over the bow, and the lookouts were crouched under the rails.

"We should expect *any* sort of magic to be cast at us—confusion, despair, anything whatsoever," Gamelan said. "The Archon must either destroy us or so weaken us his flight can continue. Otherwise, he will die this day."

"There won't be any otherwise about it," Polillo said firmly.

Gamelan smiled approval. "We should all curry such firmness as you have, Legate. Bear in mind that we have a great advantage—the Archon's soldiery are those soldiers and sailors who happened to be aboard Symeon's ships when they fled. Against them, the Guard is as keen as the blade you carry sheathed at your side."

Corais and Polillo acknowledged the compliment as no more than the Guards' due and left on their duties. Gamelan and I exchanged glances. I realized he spoke truth about our readiness for battle, but I also realized he'd not mentioned two greater truths—first, about what might be in the Archon's trunks loaded from the sea castle in Lycanth, and secondly, that the Archon now appeared trapped. No warrior knows of an enemy more dangerous than one with his back against the wall.

TWO HOURS LATER the lookouts shouted alarm—we were sailing directly toward a reef line. Stryker issued orders to change course and for signal pennants to be hoisted to the rest of the ships. Then he shouted other orders, countermanding the first.

"It ain't rocks," he said. "Or leastwise, not the sort that can sink yer."

He gave no further explanation, and again the rails were crowded as we cut directly toward roiling seas. As we neared the "reef," I jolted as I saw the rocks seemed to be rising and falling with the waves.

Stryker ordered a sailor to fetch a dip net, lowered it and brought up one of the rocks. It was near as big as his torso, and Polillo was about to exclaim at the officer's great strength, which he'd never before shown. Before she could speak, Stryker took the rock from the net, turned and pitched it, one-handed, to her.

Polillo gaped and ducked aside. The rock struck the deck with no more force than a cat jumping from its lady's lap. She picked up the stone and brought it to me. It weighed no more than a pillow.

Stryker explained: "Pumice, it's called. Comes from one of them volcanoes. I've seen it before—sailed through whole beds of it." His expression turned wry. " 'Course, that'd been just afore the volcano the stuff come from burst like a boil."

He looked ahead. Now the volcanic islands were closer and I could make out half a dozen of them. I wondered what would happen if one of those volcanoes did erupt before we closed with the Archon's ships. I decided that would be in the hands of the Goddess, and I made a brief prayer to Maranonia, hoping her reach extended to these burning seas.

LATER THAT DAY we sighted more debris: first trees drifting aimlessly, then clumps of brush that appeared to have been cast far from the land we still could see but the peaks of. It appeared that each peak belonged to a separate island. Then we saw signs of life—or what'd once been life. We sighted a small boat being carried toward us on the current. I ordered a squad into armor and to the forepeak, with their bows strung. As we drew closer I saw that the boat appeared to be a fishing craft, and I determined to capture the men on board and quiz them as to these strange seas. There were four of them and all were seated. I found it odd that none of them stood and waved, or attempted to steer away from our fleet; nor did they change course toward us, so we altered our own.

We were within a spear's cast of the craft when I realized why these fisherman were so complacent—nothing on this earth would ever disturb them again. They half sat, half lay in the bottom of the boat, their heads turned to the heavens. They were dead, but I could see no mark of violence on them as we drew closer. The bodies appeared fresh, as if the men had died but recently—there was no sign of corruption or mummification.

Just as their boat came under our bow, I did see one thing: their eyes were gone. Hollow, blood-caked sockets peered up, trying to pierce through the overcast to see toward the sun.

"Gulls," I heard a sailor say. "That's the first thing the bastards go after. Sometimes . . . sometimes when a man's not even dead, but just too weak to fight them away."

I shuddered.

THE STENCH grew worse as we sailed on, still holding our course toward the volcanoes—as were the Archon's ships. At twilight I estimated we'd close with them the next day. I allowed myself the luxury of hoping I would have the honor of slaying Nisou Symeon myself. That would be the end of the Symeons, and my family would be revenged for many wrongs—not the least of which was the imprisonment and torture of Amalric and later his attempted murder.

The seas continued rough, their interval closer, and the wind had risen to a near gale, so Cholla Yi signaled the fleet to reef sail.

"Heavy seas're a boon to ships like the Archon's," Stryker told me. "Galleys like ours can ride out most any storm. But they don't make a damn bit a headway. With no keel and shallow draft, we'll be sailin' as far sideways as for'ard with the wind blowin' like she is." When he saw my concern, he added: "Never fear, Captain. Tempest or calm, when tomorrow comes, we'll have our chance at him for certain."

I ordered the Guard to quarter alert for the night and posted a ready squad with the lookouts in the bow. I didn't think the Archon would turn and sail down on us for a night attack, but we would've been foolish not to be ready just the same.

I WAS BELOWDECKS, going over my battle plans for a tenth or one hundredth time—a futile exercise every commander does until the first bowshot—when a cabin boy said Gamelan wanted me on deck. As I came up the companionway I saw two sailors in quiet conversation at the rail, their backs toward me. I paused a minute, listening.

"I'm damned," the first was saying, "if I'm not thinkin' I should've stayed in Jeypur and let the Watch take me. It would've been five years in the quarries . . . I've known men who lived through that! Instead . . ." He spat out to sea. "First we're cheated of rights t' loot Lycanth t' go runnin' off on some bootless errand with naught but these sluts who pleasure themselves with spear butts and each other. And we're chasin' a magician who'll likely send us all screamin' to the fires on the morrow . . . an' even if we take him

. . . even if we take him, I tell you, there's a long voyage back and those bastard Orissans'll *still* try to weasel out've our blood price."

"Now don't you think," his mate said, "th' admiral's not thought of that? Once th' bitches kill the Archon, an' we have our hands on the gold his ships must be carryin' . . . don't you think there'll be some changes in th' plans? Also, don't be forgettin' there's supposedly some magic he's carryin' that'll surely be worth the sellin' to somebody . . . hell, mebbe those wizards in th' Far Kingdoms'd be interested, if f'r no other reason than to make sure nobody else'll get ahold of it. Don't start your deathsong now, shipmate. By t'morrow, we'll all be fartin' through silk."

The first sailor grunted, but before he could respond, I clattered my sword sheath against the companionway rail, as if I were just coming on deck. Both men spun, saw me, and ducked aside. I said nothing, but thought there could well be two battles tomorrow, and vowed to have my soldiers ready for betrayal. Perhaps the sailors' words were just the wishful thinking of rogues, but I didn't doubt Cholla Yi indeed had alternate plans in his black heart if he could see a greater profit.

It was easy to find Gamelan. He had a small tent set up on the deck, just ahead of the mainmast. Even above the sulfurous air I could smell incense from the four braziers, screened against the spray, set on either corner of the tent. He was in a dark mood when I entered. He sat cross-legged on a carpet spread on the bare deck. In front of him was his wand, some small vials, and the five red-charactered knuckles that were his casting bones. Four perfumed tapers hung from silk ropes tied to the tent's roof. But what held my eye was the now-open ebony case, and the black jewel that'd been the heart of an Archon.

"I cast," he announced without preamble, "in an attempt to determine what the Archon plans for tomorrow. I can sense a spell using the same strange arts I felt before the final assault on Lycanth. But I have not the craft to determine just what it might be."

"Obviously it's directed against us," I said.

"Oddly, it isn't as yet. It *is* building, just as the storm is building. But it lacks focus. I do not know how to make an analogy to things of this world, but . . . perhaps it might be compared to a cyclone, gathering strength in the air, invisible, before it touches the earth. I wish I could look into the Archon's mind as easily as a village witch claims to peep into a suitor's heart."

"You wondered yesterday," I said, "if perhaps the Archon had deliberately chosen this region for his last stand. Do you sense anything about that now?"

"Yes . . . and no. I feel a black purpose, but I am not sure if this was his plan all along, or if he's merely seizing an opportunity. In either event, I can feel no sense of menace from whatever lies ahead, which would be the case if we were sailing into some sort of sorcerous ambush." He shook his head in frustration. Then: "But the reason I sent for you is I have learned the Archon sees you as his greatest enemy. He fears you."

I made no protestations of false modesty. He damned well should have!

"I suspect he intends to destroy you at the battle's onset," Gamelan said. "You and the sergeant who actually cut his brother's heart out. I have already summoned Sergeant Ismet and given her as much protection as possible. I think she will be under no greater jeopardy in the battle than any of us—which will be extreme, of course. You'll need a bit more of a shield. Here. Sit across from me."

I unslung my sword and slipped into a cross-legged stance as he'd ordered. Gamelan stretched out his bony hand and recited quietly:

"The hawk hunts high
His prey is still
The ferret moves not
Her spoor is gone."

When he was done, he said: "I suspect the Archon might have divined that ferret spell I gave you before the last battle to make you my hunting beast, so I have lifted it."

I nodded thanks, although, in my heart, I felt loss—Gamelan still didn't understand my family's affinity for those small determined hunters and how their spirits have aided us. Once this was over, I thought I'd ask him to cast another spell, one giving me blood kinship to the breed, perhaps.

"One other thing might be of help," he said. He took up a tiny golden sickle and laid it against the relict that had been the Archon's heart. "Hold out your hands, palm up." He touched the sickle to each wrist, just where my pulse beat blue. "I have already prepared the herbs and cast the spells on this device." Then he chanted:

"There are no songs to be sung,
There are no words to be given.
Blood to blood,
Blood to blood.
Let the blood of the man now slain
Be a red mist,
So the eyes of the man who yet lives

Are clouded.
Let his eye see,
But pass on,
Without seeing."

Then he said, in a normal tone: "That is all, my friend. I'm afraid that most of the protection you'll have tomorrow will be provided by your sword and your sisters."

"More than that," I said, "no warrior could wish, except the blessing of Maranonia and Te-Date." I began to rise, and then an idea struck and I re-seated myself. "Gamelan . . . I am hardly an Evocator. But . . . you said a few minutes ago the Archon most likely wasn't headed for these seas when he fled, but now hopes to take advantage of something. Would that—*could that*—be these volcanoes we're closing on?"

I could see Gamelan's face pale, even in the flickering light from the ta-pers. "Earth magic," he whispered, more to himself than me. "Here, where it reaches up from the heart of the world?" He thought long, then shook his head, regaining his calm. "No, Rali. Even with the arts gained from the Far Kingdoms and from Janos Greycloak, I do not think the Archon capable of that. To touch *that* power would require not merely a great Evocator, work-ing at the height of his powers, but some sort of sacrifice, a great sacrifice I cannot even imagine . . . But for a moment I was worried. Thank you, Rali. You've given me something tonight. Not only the reminder that my brain is getting as old as my bones, but that I spent too much time delving into my own thoughts and not enough asking others theirs. Please, Rali, bring any other such notions to me, no matter how farfetched you may think them. The Archon may be almost brought to bay, but there is a considerable ways between tracking the bear to his den and lying on his skin in front of a roar-ing winter fire."

"You're telling me?" I laughed, remembering my first time with a spear against a great brown bear, and how it'd ended with me up a tree fortunately thick enough to bear a young girl's weight, but not enough to support that of the animal who'd suddenly become the hunter. "And I will need all the rest I can snatch." I stood. "Good luck on the morrow, Gamelan. Good luck to us all."

I went out into the reeking night, knowing there would be no sleep for me or anyone else until the Archon was dead.

DEEP IN THE NIGHT we altered course. Just ahead was the first of the great vol-canic cones, rising sheer from the ocean bottom. In the red light from its peak we'd seen breakers crashing against the base of the mountain. There appeared to be no more land other than the volcano, as the man sent forward to sound the depths found no bottom to his castings.

The night sky was light enough to easily track the nine ships of the Archon. They, too, had changed course, sailing close along the mountain's base. By the time that cone lay to our stern, it was just dawn, and we could see clearly.

Ahead, spaced evenly in the ocean, were three more volcanoes, these neither as high nor as threatening as the one we'd just sailed past. These were not isolated peaks, but were connected by low shoals and bars that ran across the horizon as far as we could see. Finally the Archon was well and truly trapped.

BY FULL LIGHT the Archon and Symeon had their ships into a line of battle and lowered their sails—either waiting for a signal to attack or for us to come to them. Full light is hardly a fitting description—the air was as murky and thick as that in the midst of a burning forest. I thought I heard a rumble from the volcano to our rear, but it was most likely the seas on the reefs ahead.

The seas were gray, tossing, nearly a full storm. The wind had changed once more, no longer coming from abeam, but blowing in our teeth. We'd lowered the masts on our ships, a standard practice when galleys went into combat. It was done both to keep the oarsmen from being injured if a mast toppled during the fray, and to ensure we had full advantage from our oars. The benches were fully manned and the war drums were sounding, the heavy thuds sounding from ship to ship above the wind's keening. The rhythm not only set the stroke for the rowers, but also was meant to stir the blood for the coming battle. It might well stiffen the sinews of Cholla Yi's seamen and marines on their ships, but my women hardly needed encouragement—the long pursuit had indeed proven a stern chase is a drear one, on land or sea. Now, at last the long struggle between Lycanth and Orissa would be ended within the day, no matter how mighty a wizard the last Archon was.

It was hard to make out the other fourteen ships in our squadron; with their masts sent down, the only protrusion above the fighting decks were the small jackstaffs on the stern used to send battle signals from ship to ship. Not that there were any signals being sent now—our tactics had been worked out long beforehand. Each galley was to take a target as it presented itself, close with that ship, and seize it by boarding. Yi's captains and my own sergeants and warrants in charge of the Guard detachments on the eleven ships so honored, were to keep close watch for any Orissan in danger and sail to their assistance when possible. If they saw an opportunity to strike at a distressed Lycanthian trying to flee, they were to attack and show no mercy.

The Lycanthian ships were considerably bigger and different than our own. They were sailing ships rather than sailing galleys, and each vessel bulked two or three decks above the waterline, and had three masts and a sail-equipped bowsprit. They were, I'd been told, the pride of Symeon's fleet—fast armed merchantmen, little different than warships except in the luxury of their quarters. Now, with the wind at their backs, they held the weather gauge.

I saw a great flag dip once, then again, on the tiny pulpit atop one ship's bowsprit, and, in a ragged display, the Lycanthian ships hoisted their sails. I heard a cheer roll across the waters from our fleet.

"Now," Stryker said, "the bastards'll try to ram us, and good luck to them. 'Cause we're too good at bein' Cholla Yi's sharks than to hang in the waters waitin' to be struck by a dolphin."

I saw oars dip and our galleys gathered headway. I also saw, but did not say anything, those ships containing my Guardswomen moved to the fore, eager to close with the enemy; but some others, the ones with Cholla Yi's marines, appeared willing to hang back and let others win the glory—and shed the blood—of first encounter.

"Captain Stryker," I shouted. "That ship that was signaling. That will be the Archon's. Strike for it!"

Stryker barked orders and our galley sped across the waters toward our target. We weren't the only ones to have seen the signals, and other Orissan ships joined in the attack. First in the fray was Cholla Yi's own galley. Knowing what I do now, and what Cholla Yi became, I'm tempted to ascribe his mettle to what he'd said to me before we made the attack on Lycanth, about how a mercenary chief must lead from the front or he'll be pulled down by the rest of the pack. But though I hope Cholla Yi's soul is being slowly ripped apart by demons now, I won't diminish his courage. Bravery, I must never forget, is not the exclusive property of heroes.

I saw two Lycanthian ships cut in front of the Archon's ship, attempting to protect their wizard king. The ships seemed able to sail at an unnatural rate of speed. Even though the wind was fierce, blowing directly from their sterns, I knew wind-magic was their real benefactor.

I was struck by a wave of fear. I knew at that moment I would die—and not nobly, but as a failure, my guts cut out to leave me writhing, while the Archon made good his escape. I heard other women and men cry aloud as the same spell struck them. I struggled to fight it down, looking for reassuring words, but found none as the Archon's second war spell hit—and confusion sent my mind reeling. I no longer knew what orders to give, nor what I should do once we closed with the enemy.

Then, from our bows boiled a great green cloud, and both the panic and the mind-tangle vanished and I saw Gamelan, his hands moving in an arabesque as he cast the counterspell. Normally magic does not work well in battle, since both sides spend a vast amount of time spinning spells from personal protection to invincible armor to tactical ones such as the Archon had cast—but it's very seldom Evocators as truly powerful as Gamelan or the Archon are physically present on a battlefield. Without a doubt, this was an historic magical duel.

I sucked in air, and sulfurous as it was, it felt good to my lungs. I looked to the side at the rest of our ships just as one of the galleys attempted to skitter out of the path of an onrushing Lycanthian. But either the confusion spell still lingered, or else the oarsmen were not skillful enough, because the Lycanthian ship's ram struck the galley squarely amidships, crushing its bulwarks and spitting it like a game fish speared by a hunter. I heard screams as the galley came clear of the water and hung for a moment; and then the wood ripped free and the galley rolled sideways, back into the water. The Lycanthian ship's bow smashed into it, and the ship rode up and over the galley, sending it down into the depths—seamen and Guardswomen alike trying to find something to keep them afloat, but being dragged down by their clothes and armor, or dashed down by the frothing waves.

I had time for no more, and ran toward the bow, shouting for my women to make themselves ready. Sergeant Ismet was close behind me. As I ran I heard another rumble, and this time knew it was neither the seas nor the rocks, but the volcano behind us. Erupt and be damned, I thought. There's a sword closer in my future than any lava flow.

Corais and Polillo were waiting at the heads of their elements. Corais had the tight grin she always wore, a rictus empty of humor. Polillo was humming a tune, which was one of her characteristics. I'd asked her once, after a fight, what song she found so inspiring, and she looked at me in bewilderment and asked if I were feeling poorly, since she had no ear for music and only sang when she was comfortably drunk and buried in a chorus of other sponges.

The two protective Lycanthian ships were only about three bowshots away now. Behind them was the Archon's vessel, and I could clearly distinguish the banner of Symeon and, above it, the twin-headed lion of the Archon. I couldn't see Cholla Yi's ship.

Three galleys struck from out of the gloom and breaking seas, straight for the Archon's escorts. I saw well-aimed spears and arrows shower the farthest Lycanthian ship's quarterdeck, and she veered aside, her helmsman struck down. Two galleys went alongside the second ship, and I saw my Guardswomen swarm up and onto their decks, swords lifting and coming down.

The first galley was about to do the same to its now-drifting enemy, and then the Archon pounced. From nowhere, a line of fire ran straight from his ship, on the water itself, as if shot by an invisible archer. The galley's bow burst into flame as if it were dry kindling. Gamelan began shouting a spell, and the flames died as rapidly as they'd been born—but the Orissan ship lay dead in the water as crewmen and Guardswomen fought to regain control of the craft. Slowly it took on headway once more, and I found myself holding back a cheer as the galley, undaunted by the burst of flame, hurled itself once more at the heart of the Lycanthian fleet!

And now the way was clear for our own attack.

"Your orders?" Polillo waited.

I considered. The Archon's ship had great, sagging nets hung from the mast's lower yards to the bulwarks. There were spearsmen poised along the railings, waiting a chance to drive their weapons through the body of any Guardswoman trapped in the nets. I saw archers lining the sides, and there were two trebuchets on the foredeck and a derrick rigged from the mizzen-mast, the rear mast's sail struck for battle. I thought I could distinguish, far back on the quarterdeck, the figures of Nisou Symeon—and the Archon.

One of our other ships had come alongside a Lycanthian, bow to stern, and had cast grapnels across. But the thrust of the magic wind was pulling our galley backward and it was wallowing out of control. One of the Lycanthian ship's derricks swung out over the side, a huge stone held in its net. The net released, and the boulder crashed down through the hull of the Orissan galley. There were screams and a gout of water as the impact crushed the ship. Instantly the grapnels were cut away and the Lycanthian bore on, leaving our galley sinking in its wake.

The Archon's ship loomed close. They'd seen us, realized their danger, and cast a rock from a trebuchet. It splashed down close on us, sending a cascade of water over the soldiers in our bows.

An idea came, and I shouted to Gamelan: "Wizard! Stop me that wind!" He heard, and I saw him begin to weave a new spell. I cupped both hands and cried to Stryker on the quarterdeck: "Put us under her bows!" I seized a bow and quiver from one of my women and slung them over my shoulder.

I don't know if he thought me mad, as if I was ordering him to ram the Archon's ship, but Stryker never wavered, and bellowed orders, his voice now coming as a high whine, like the sea wind. The man at the helm muscled the tiller, and Duban—the rowing master—issued his orders . . . and the wind died, Gamelan's counterspell working . . . and the Archon's ship's sails sagged and then flapped in a lull, and the Lycanthian ship began to lose way.

Our ship arced close alongside the Lycanthian, its side looming high over us, and then we were at its bows, our ship's oars on that side feathering and lifting. I saw Lycanthian heads above us and spears and arrows arcing down, and we were just under the ship's bows, and I leaped, seeing nothing except one of the ship's anchors hanging from its cathead; and then I had the corroded metal in my arms, and, nails tearing, brought myself up onto it. I stood on one fluke, the anchor swaying on its chain, and reached down, had Ismet's arm locked in mine—and then she, too, was on the Lycanthian ship as I saw, beyond her grim, helmeted face, our galley fall away, oars thrashing as Stryker fought to bring it alongside once more.

We were a boarding party of two and there were shouts above, and an archer in the bowsprit's pulpit loosed a shaft that went wild; I had my own bow in hand, an arrow nocked, and it hummed away; and the archer flung back his hands as the arrow buried itself in his chest and he fell into the sea. There were two other archers beside him, each aiming more carefully than his dead brother, but time was something they'd run out of, as Ismet dropped one, and I, moving in that dream-time underwater battle sense, had no need to hurry, found a shaft, saw as I nocked it the fletchings were perfect, drew, and as I had learned, felt the moment when the arrow and bow whispered "loose me" to my soul, and that arrow buried itself in the Lycanthian's throat, and there was no one left in the pulpit and for a moment we were safe—until the Lycanthians on the deck above us found a way to wiggle onto the bulwarks through the netting that now gave us a moment's cover.

Stryker's galley was coming up on us now, and then I saw Cholla Yi's ship coming in at full speed. We'd need all the reinforcements we could get to seize this flagship. I slung the bow, went hand over hand up the cable, found a solid wooden hold and pulled myself up onto the bowsprit.

Scribe, I will take a moment and mention that here is yet another part of real battle that's not found in the sagas. The handhold was one of those ports cut in the bow to serve as a jakes. I will make a wager—one of your tunic buttons against all the Antero estates that I stand to inherit—that none of the heroic paintings that have been or will be done of that moment will depict me as I stood, hands covered in shit, Ismet beside me.

But that didn't matter, then or later, because leading up from the bowsprit was a heavy cable, the forestay running up about halfway on the forward mast. I had but seconds, as I saw through the boarding net's meshes soldiers swarming toward me, spears ready.

I shouted down to our galley for fire support, but my voice was lost in the wind as it came up once more, Gamelan's counterspell broken against the Archon's wind-casting; but there'd been no need, as arrows spat from both Cholla Yi's and Stryker's galleys and the soldiers wailed and fell back, their attention diverted.

We were climbing again, upside down and monkeying up that huge rope toward the mast. The forestay ended just at a tiny platform on the mast which I later learned was called a top, just above the foreyard, and Maranonia was aiding us, for the platform was empty of enemy soldiers. Our swords were out and we spotted the lines holding that boarding net aloft. We edged out on the yard, the great beam that held up the sail, and slashed and slashed again, and the net collapsed on the deck, burying in its folds a handful of archers who'd been aiming up at us. Now the way was open for boarders.

Stryker's galley was nosing alongside, tossing in the stormy seas, and grapnels were coming up and my women swarming onto the Lycanthian ship. Behind it was Cholla Yi's galley, its bow full of archers firing into the Archon's ship.

Ismet and I took a moment to catch our breath and an arrow whipped past, missing my head by a whisper—its broadhead slashed Ismet's arm as it buried itself in the mast we clung to. She started to jump, but caught herself even before I could grab her.

"This is no more a safe haven," she managed, wiping blood from the shallow gash on her arm, then forgetting her wound. "Yet I can't see the archer who fired this. Let's move! We'll settle his account later."

Yes, I thought, but where? Below, the foredeck was a swarm of fighting men and women and I heard screams and battle cries. I spotted Polillo by the flash of her axe as she parried a spearthrust and, with her immense strength, sent the axe back on a counterstroke, its beak burying in the side of the spearman. No one flinched on either side, nor did anyone cry for nor give quarter. The Lycanthians may have been evil, but by the gods they were brave. I felt in my bones that this day's fighting, even if it were not for the ultimate fate of our city, would live long in legend. There is no glory in battle if your enemy is craven.

Over the battle sounds I heard that terrible rumbling once more from the nearby volcanoes.

We could have gone down the shroud lines into the battle, but there was more that should be done. There was a solid wall of soldiery across the deck, just back of the mainmast, keeping our boarders from reaching the ultimate target. On the quarterdeck the last Archon stood in plain view, just behind the Lycanthian helmsman. Until he was taken, we were but killing cubs and leaving the wolf unharmed.

In front of the Archon were two open, dull black chests, and he was taking things from them and casting them to the winds, sending a frenzy of spells against us. It hurt my eyes to look at him and I forced them away, to see Nisou Symeon. I knew him well, even though we'd never met before, from his slender form to the blond hair that fell in waves to his shoulders to the slender blade in his hand to the scars with which Janos Greycloak's sorcery had marked his once-beautiful face for the monster's countenance it truly was.

I became something other than Captain Rali Antero of the Maranon Guard. My blade flicked, and a line that led from where we stood to the main mast was cut free and in my hand as my sword snaked back into its sheath—and I was off, swinging across, seeing the main yard coming up and hitting it with my feet, about to rebound, and then dropping the rope to find haven, all a-scramble, on the yard. I could not allow myself even a moment to consider the stupidity of what I was doing, or the awful fall that would await if I slipped to crash down either on the deck below or, worse, to fall and be ground between Stryker's galley and the Archon's ship. I chanced a glance below. No one, including Nisou Symeon, was heeding us, concentrating instead on the battle on the foredeck.

Then I saw, and I froze just like a rabbit, pinned by the gaze of the hawk, the Archon look up, scanning the masts. A line of Gamelan's spell crossed my mind, *The hawk hunts high . . . the ferret moves not . . .* but I dared not even mouth the words. Once, twice, that icy stare crossed me, but passed on, and I hoped Gamelan's protection still reached me. But I couldn't rely on magic.

I saw Ismet cutting free a line for herself, back on the foremast—but my business with Nisou Symeon and his master could not wait for support. Again I found a bracing line that led from this main mast to the mizzenmast, and swarmed across it.

Now, just below me, were the Archon and Symeon. There were only two soldiers guarding them, plus a couple of ship's officers and the helmsmen.

I realize the telling of the events from the time we jumped from our galley until I stood above Orissa's most deadly enemy makes it sound as if it was a leisurely undertaking and much time passed. So it seemed to my mind, but in fact there could have been no more than four turnings of the minute glass.

The way down couldn't have been easier—the lines to the rigged derrick dangled and I went down them as quickly and easily as if I were on a training ground. I let go the line when I was ten feet above the men and free-fell, landing just behind Nisou Symeon.

He spun, his mouth gaping, but his muscles responding as they should, his blade coming up into guard position. I saw one soldier dart forward, spear lunging, and my blade brushed it aside and spitted him. I yanked it free just as Nisou lunged, hoping my own steel would be cumbered. I sidestepped and slashed at him, a clumsy stroke but one that sent him scuttling back. Behind him I heard the Archon shout and knew I'd have but a moment. But we were in the realm of steel, and magic was a slow second.

Symeon lunged once more and I tried a blade beat, in the hope my stronger sword could shatter his duelist's blade. But he turned my stroke aside cleverly, and I recognized he was not far from a master swordsman himself.

I managed to flick my point across his chest, but heard it skitter on steel and knew he wore mail under his black tunic. Now came a brief moment as our blades touched . . . touched . . . touched, then I let my point sag, as if I were not experienced; before he could take advantage, I struck his blade again with the flat of my own, this time just above the hilt; a tap really, enough to turn his guard—and I struck. My sword dug a furrow into his thigh, and I saw his mouth twist in pain. He recovered, and lunged in his own turn, and I stopped him with a stop-thrust to the wrist.

Neither of us spoke—in real fights, when blood is the object, there is no time for tongue prattlings.

His next attack was for my face, no doubt thinking a woman would be more defensive of that area. I but moved my head and his blade missed. I did not let him recover, but struck, point going for where I could see a pulse—in the hollow of his throat. I, too, went wide, and for a moment we were breast to breast and I could smell the sweetness of cardamom on his breath. He tried a head butt, and I jerked mine away and spat in his face as I back-leaped clear.

I remember nodding involuntarily as I returned to guard—Nisou Symeon was a fighter, by the gods. I would remember long the moment of his death, and this was truly it. Both of us knew; his eyes flashed wide, then clenched involuntarily at the expected pain as I jump-lunged, coming up, and my blade drove under the edge of his mail and deep into his belly.

Symeon staggered back, and I jerked my sword out and slashed at him before he fell, the keen edge cutting across his throat, nearly severing his head as blood gouted across the deck and I smelt the reek as his guts spilled.

He collapsed, no longer a man, no longer of concern—and I was turning, back on guard, hearing the cheering of women and realizing they must've broken through the Lycanthian line down on the main deck as the sailors saw Symeon die, but my mind paid little heed of that.

In front of me was the last Archon. Behind him stood the last soldier on the quarterdeck, but he mattered not.

The Archon was the world entire.

Now the underwater battle time became real, not an illusion of the senses. It was as if I were buried in some thick treacle, or wading in quicksand, the stuff of nightmares.

"The ferret!" the Archon snarled. And then he hurled his curse at me: "The bitch ferret! Slayer of my brother, draped in deceitful magic not her own. Antero! This time, your line must die, as must all of your works! Die for impiety, die for your arrogance, die for the destruction you carry!

"Now you will stand, stand you must, and wait your death, and then I shall sweep this ship and these seas clean of all Orissans. But for you, Antero, the manner of your death shall be most awful, awful as only those who have died as my Chosen Ones can know, to die at your own hand, yet in a manner of my choosing.

"Do not look for help, bitch ferret. There is none, none from your sorcerer, none from the sluts you serve with."

I knew he spoke truth, and everyone else on this ship was as immobile as I.

"You will meet my gaze now and listen to the orders of my soul," he commanded.

Slowly, slowly, my eyes crept up, over his bony chest, seeing the wild tangle of his beard and his filed teeth, and I could not stop myself and looked deep into the maelstroms of eyes.

"Yes the eyes," the Archon said, almost musingly, as if the two of us were in some safe, secluded chamber. "Your eyes. They shall be first. Drop your sword and pluck them out, bitch ferret. You have claws that dig deep. Dig deep, bitch ferret, and I grant you permission to scream as you do."

I felt my grip loosen on my sword and my hand obediently form talons. But as my hand crept reluctantly toward my face, I *felt* something, and then I was my own woman again . . . and for just a breath was free of that quicksand spell. I had firm hold on my sword again, and my clawed hand unclenched. It was Gamelan! Or rather his magic.

"Your ally is better than I thought, but not near enough to stand against me," the Archon said, and as he spoke he bent, eyes not leaving mine, and his hand dug into an open bag in his chest and cast a handful of dust across the deck toward me.

Dust became solid became tiny slashing darts. I tried to leap aside, but was mired once more. A thought raced through my mind as I readied myself to die, a thought that made no sense:

Turn away
Turn away
With the wind
With the storm

It was as if I'd cast a spell, but it must have been Gamelan's doing, because the cloud parted and its tiny killing bits sped past on either side.

The Archon's gaze flickered, then he recovered. "Die you will, die you must," he said, his voice rising to a near shriek as his hand snaked out and plucked the sword from the hand of the Lycanthian soldier who stood, mazed in horror, beside him.

"My power becomes the steel, becomes the sword, and reaches for your heart, just as you took my brother's." He stepped forward, sword ready to strike, moving swiftly and lithely, not at all an old man, but a young warrior.

I stood still like a stalled ox waiting for the butcher's hammer, but just then something came between us.

All I can name it is: a presence, one that changed as I half saw it. First I thought it was the helmeted, armored body of Maranonia, but then it changed, becoming the form of my long-dead, long-mourned Otara, and changed again, and I thought I saw Tries, but it was my mother's face, and then it was the form of a woman I did not know, one wearing the ancient costume of Orissa's villages ... but it was nothing but sea mist from the storm around us as the binding spell freed my arms and I hurled my sword as if it were a spear; the Archon in mid-attack, almost on me.

The blade struck him point first, just in the side, below the curve of his ribs on the right side, in the lung.

The Archon screamed, his muscles spasmed and he sent his own sword spinning high, high, to fall into the sea. He stumbled back, nearly falling, but somehow—and I knew it was the power of his will—he kept his feet, and my sword fell from his body.

There was red, red foam on his lips, and he spat, and spat again, and his beard reddened.

He stumbled once more and caught himself on the open lid of one of his magic chests. "Very well, very well. I feared this ... and made the castings. There are worlds and yet other worlds.

"Bitch ferret, you struck me, but your blow shall give you nothing. You will still die now, or mayhap in a day or a month. And what days you have will be spent in pain and confusion. But they are numbered, Antero, and the number is but few."

He looked up at the dark stormy skies and his voice steadied and rose to a shriek, as loud as when he had railed at me from the clouds outside his sea castle, shouting in some language I knew not, casting some dark spell that I did not understand, but his voice sent ice through my soul. Then I understood his last few words:

"The price I paid
The debt I'm owed
I claim the debt
The blood is paid."

Then it was as if I had never struck him a deathblow, and he was strong and virile, growing to a height much greater than mine. A wizard dies hard, I thought, and my hands found my dagger and unsheathed it.

But before I could attack, the Archon bent, picked up one of his chests—a chest that three strong men would have strained to lift—and went in three great strides to the rail.

"The blood is paid, and the battle yet joined," he howled, and leapt straight out into the storming seas, his magic clutched in his arms.

I rushed to the rail, peering over, but there was nothing but the rolling waves and scud and foam.

I had just a moment to realize the last Archon was truly dead.

Then the seas went mad and I knew what he meant by his blood price, and even understood Gamelan's words in his tent last night: "To touch that power . . . some sort of sacrifice . . . a great sacrifice I cannot even imagine."

The Archon had paid that price, and the earth granted his greatest spell, as fire smashed up into the skies, driving away gray and rain, and two volcanoes exploded. Lava sprayed from the nearest one's mouth, and smoke and fire blasted to the heavens.

I stood gaping, and then Corais was beside me and had me by the arm.

"Rali! We must flee!"

My memory is not exact for the next few minutes and hours, but I do remember being half dragged along the deck, clumsily going across to our own galley, half carried by my women. I do not remember any Lycanthian soldiers still fighting. Perhaps they were all dead, or perhaps they were like me, staring at fiery death. I remember hearing Stryker shouting orders for everyone to man the oars, and I remember seeing through the gray haze, Cholla Yi's ship skittering away at full speed, oars digging deeply as it fled the wrath to come.

I remember seeing some of the Lycanthian ships wallowing in the swell, as if their helms had been abandoned by panicked sailors.

Great boulders, hurled by the gods' own trebuchets, boulders far larger than even the biggest ship, were crashing down into the seas around us, and there was a steady rain of searing dustlike particles.

I remember seeing other Orissan ships following our lead, rowing desperately away from the volcanoes' eruption.

But there was no safety, for we were caught in the same snare as the Archon and his ships had been. Behind us were the volcanoes. Ahead of us were reefs, savage rock fingers sticking up from the crashing waves, long sand spits waiting to embrace our keels, stone islets with never a beach for a merciful landing. All of these closed off the safety of the open sea to us.

I was on the quarterdeck, Stryker having taken over the helm, assisted by two of his strongest, most skilled seamen.

"Get your women below," he ordered.

I wondered why. If one of those boulders struck our ship, we were all doomed, and I for one would rather die here in the open air, even though it stank of sulfur and ozone, than below in the reeking bilges of the ship. Then one of the soldiers looked back, at the volcano, and screamed.

I turned to see something that still haunts my dreams, that sends me shouting awake in panic. A monstrous wave, no, not a wave but truly a wall of water, was rushing down upon us. It was gray, struck with white, and a line of dirty foam frothed along its crest. It came faster than a tiger at full charge, faster than a spearcast, faster than an arrow, faster than doom itself.

My eyes told me it dwarfed even the volcano that gave it birth, although I knew that to be impossible. How tall was it? I do not know, I cannot even guess. Taller than our masthead by far. Perhaps twice or even three times that height—over a hundred feet. It had been birthed near the land, because as it closed on us I could see that it bore trees ripped from the earth and even what I thought to be huts and small boats tumbling in its core.

It roared—louder than the wind, louder than the volcanoes. Perhaps I screamed. Certainly I heard others scream, and there would be no shame in that. I dove for shelter, as Stryker, a man harder than anyone had a right to be, shouted final orders for the oars to be brought inboard, and found myself clinging for life to a grating.

Then the sea took us.

It lifted us by the stern, up and up, and canting us forward, and I was looking down at the foredeck and the oarsmen, flattening themselves and grabbing their benches for a hold, and on beyond the deck, *down* at the wave-tossed sea below.

We rose and rose, being lifted to the top of the wave, and I felt a moment of hope and then the crest broke and the sea buried our deck. I didn't know what happened—which way was up and which way was the sky; feeling water pummel me as if I were being beaten in the square ring and my lungs were gasping, shouting for air, no air, no air; my lungs couldn't stand another moment, but I forbade them the weakness of giving in, and then there *was* air, and we were sliding out of control down the far side of the wave.

I pulled myself up, had time to see most of my Guardswomen had found holds and few had been washed overboard; and Stryker was alive and shouting orders once more; and Duban as well; and the oars were manned, just as I heard a man scream there were breakers ahead.

We were about to crash into the reefs. Their claws rose, grasping, just ahead of our bows. And there could be no turning, no evading, as another wave was upon us.

Again we were lifted, lifted, and then buried in the depths, and yet again we lived through it, spinning down into the swirling oceans in the wake of these hell waves, and we yet lived.

I remembered the reef, the reef we were about to impale ourselves on, and searched ahead for that new death. But there was nothing, and I realized what had happened and looked *behind* and saw the wave had lifted us up and over those knife-rocks.

But there were more rocks around us and Stryker was giving commands and the oarsmen were trying to obey but there was no time for anything, as yet a third wave bore down on us.

This time, as we rose, I saw two other ships in the grip of the wave— both Orissan.

Again we survived.

The waves came four more times that grim day, each time lifting us and taking us farther to the west, farther into unknown seas, farther from that solid line of reefs that blocked our only known path home to Orissa.

But finally the last wave had taken us and passed on, and we were tossing in a "normal" storm, able to take stock. Through the murk I saw other ships. One of them was Cholla Yi's.

We were not the only survivors.

I saw no sign of the Lycanthian ships. I think, being less quick at the helm, they must have been destroyed by the volcanoes' waves. But perhaps some survived, to be driven against the reefs or even to live on, to die on barbaric shores. It mattered not to me. Lycanth was ended.

But at an awful price.

We were lost on unknown seas, our charts useless. Men and women were dead and wounded. The only salvation I could see would be in magic. Just as sorcery had brought us to these straits, so our own magic was the only hope we had.

But lying bloodied, just where his tent had been set just before the battle, was Gamelan. He moved not at all, and there was a great bruise at his forehead.

He appeared quite dead.

BOOK TWO

ON
STRANGE
SEAS

❖

CHAPTER EIGHT

CRY OF THE LIZARD

❖

At heart, all gods are malign thugs. I say this without fear, for I have been both favored and damned by the gods, and I'm still uncertain whether we are better off blessed or cursed. I think we are all part of a game of theirs, overseen by a master jester, and the board he designed is so littered with pig shit that no mortal can cross without fouling her boots. I've also never seen a treasure that didn't have a serpent hidden in it—nor encountered a person, no matter how gifted, who at some point did not have just cause to bemoan her fate.

As I think back on the day of that sea battle, I strongly suspect the halls of the gods were ringing with laughter at our plight. Once again they granted Orissa victory. But once again that banner was hoisted on a fouled stick.

Our losses were frightening: many were dead, and the cries of our wounded echoed across the hissing seas; our original fleet of fifteen was reduced to nine, of which two were so damaged they would soon follow the others into the depths if not repaired. The only real luck that day was that nearly all of my women had survived the fight unscathed. But those I lost I mourned deeply, and their absence, as well as Gamelan's, weighed heavily. But there was no time for mourning or for the dead, not yet.

In spite of the still-heaving seas, I had a longboat lowered and told Stryker to detail his best seamen to row me across to the flagship. I needed to talk to Cholla Yi, and not by signal flag or speaking trumpet. I also took Corais and Polillo with me.

The mercenary was somber when I entered his cabin, but after I'd assured him Orissa would bear the cost of replacing his lost ships, his mood lightened greatly. When I offered condolences for his own dead, he shrugged them off.

"Don't let them trouble your sleep, Captain," he said. "They certainly won't trouble mine. They knew the odds when they signed the papers. Besides, they're nothing but kelp scum and easily replaced when we return to friendlier seas, and our own share of the spoils will be greater."

Polillo growled at such disrespect. She'd despised them all, and had even broken the head of one man who'd ogled her too openly. Still, by Polillo's code, they were fellow warriors just the same and deserved more from their master. My own thoughts ran along similar lines, so I did not admonish her.

I was also vaguely uneasy because I felt Cholla Yi had reacted with barely hidden displeasure when I first boarded his galley. It was as if he was surprised that I'd survived the battle. I reminded myself not to be foolish and let my dislike for the man read emotions onto his scarred face. Of course Cholla Yi would've held a banquet if I fell and broke my neck when we were safely back in Orissa, but on these strange seas every sword counted as ten, and he was no more likely to indulge his petty hatreds than I.

Corais filled the gap: "You talk of our return as if it were as easy as polishing new steel." She pointed at the chart unrolled on the table. "We don't even know where we are. We've sailed off the great chart, and even that rough map Gamelan had, in case you haven't noticed."

"It's not so difficult as all that," he replied, giving Phocas a wink at the foolish question. "We'll sort it out once we're back on the other side of the reef."

Corais smiled back, but it was a thin smile, and I saw a glint in her eye hard enough to sharpen a dirk.

I looked through Cholla Yi's big stern window at the black reefs studded with growling volcanoes. From the deck they'd seemed to stretch forever both to our north and south.

"I suppose they *must* end at some point," I said. "The question is, which direction will get us there the quickest?"

"Too bad the wizard's not with us," Phocas said. "We could get him to cast the bones."

I wished Gamelan was at our side for more reason than that. When I'd seen him lying on the deck, blood streaming down his still face, I'd suffered a deep hurt, almost as if I'd lost one of my own. He'd become a good friend in a very brief time, and I knew I'd miss his company, even if he had nagged me about my supposed magical birthright. The sailors responsible for gathering the dead for burial had refused to touch his body. They feared the wizard even in death. I'd ordered him placed in his little cabin until we had time to prepare his corpse for proper purification and funeral ceremonies worthy of the greatest of Orissa's Evocators.

His death rites should've lasted for weeks, with an entire city in mourning and the Palace of the Evocators darkened and the skies themselves cast with a magical darkness. Whomever the Evocators' Guild named as his replacement, after long and solemn conclave, would've officiated at the ceremonies, and eulogies would've been given by all the Magistrates and leading citizens. His name would've been bestowed upon a square or a boulevard; herds of cattle and perhaps even a human soul or two, possibly a grief-stricken volunteer, would've been sacrificed. But out here, many unknown leagues from Orissa, we would do the best we could, when there was time. I planned to slip him over the side myself.

Cholla Yi's scoffing reply broke through: "We don't need a wizard to choose," he said. "Either will do. What's a few days, one way or the other?"

He fished a gold coin out of his pocket. It was from Irayas, with the head of King Domas engraved on one side, and the serpent and sun symbol on the other. I wondered how the thief had come by such a rare coin.

"Let's let the tavern gods decide," he said. "If it falls kings, we go north. Snakes is south."

I merely nodded. But as he tossed the coin and it spun upward, King Domas' image leaped into my mind. North. We should strike north. The coin rang against the table and I looked to see the serpent side lying faceup.

"South it is, then," Cholla Yi said.

I almost told him: No! We *must* strike north. I prickled all over with the need for the telling.

Then the prickling vanished, leaving me feeling confused and foolish.

"Very well," I said.

With that, I sealed our fate.

So we sailed south. The chain of reefs was unrelenting, mile after mile of jagged rock ridged with endless volcanoes. Many of them were active, spewing smoke and lava that poured down the sides and set the seas to boiling. At one place, dead fish by the thousands floated belly up. Swarms of birds circled and cried out in delight at the fresh meat. The wind shifted, carrying with it a dense cloud of smoke from one of the volcanoes. As the birds passed through it, I was shocked to see them plummet from the sky. Then the acrid fumes washed over us. The stench was so poisonous that many of us fell retching to the deck. Gasped orders sent us pulling away, but I tell you, Scribe, the rowers were so overcome that we barely moved. And if the wind hadn't shifted at that moment, I doubt I'd be here at this moment boring you with my adventures.

When we reached what we thought to be a safe distance, we hove to, so we could recover. My skull was pounding, and every bone in my body felt as if I had been wrung out by a giant. I gulped sweet, tangy air until my head spun, and it soon did its job and I felt cleansed.

As I turned to see how the others fared, I heard a voice cry out: "Get away from me, you fool!"

It was Gamelan! But wasn't he dead?

"By Te-Date, I swear I'll turn you into a frog! And your mother and father will be frogs as well!"

I rushed below in time to see a wizened little fellow with a scar the size of my palm dash out of Gamelan's quarters. I ignored him and ran inside.

Gamelan was sitting up, ripping at the white cotton cloth that had been wound about him. He looked up when he heard me enter.

"Another thief!" he cried. "Good. I'll make you a heron and you can eat that other man and his kin. Then I'll conjure a demon to strip your feathers for arrows and flay your skin for his quiver."

"You're alive!" I cried.

"Of course, I'm alive," the wizard grumbled, tugging at the burial cloth. "Now, if you'll be so good as to light a lamp so I can see whom I'm cursing, I'll reward you by putting you out of your misery as quickly as possible."

I didn't answer. I could only stare at those great wide eyes. Instead of fiery yellow, they were washed-out and vacant. He turned his head this way and that, but his eyes would not focus on anything. I knelt by his side.

Gamelan sniffed the air. "Rali?" He reached out a hand, quite tentatively, and it touched my breast. I did not push it away.

"Yes, my friend," I said. "It's Rali."

He blushed, realizing where his hand had fallen, and snatched it away. "I'm sorry," he said. "But it's so dark in here. Get them to light a few lamps, will you Rali? There's a good woman."

"It's midday," I said, as softly as I could.

Gamelan grew still. A wrinkled hand lifted slowly to his brow. He shuddered. I gripped his bony shoulder. His face grew stony. Then he smiled and patted my hand.

"I'm blind," he said matter-of-factly.

"Yes," I said.

"Then I'm no good for you," he said. "I've only known one blind wizard, and he was stricken quite young. And he had his whole life to learn to cast spells without sight to aid him."

"It won't take so long," I said. "You're a master wizard, after all."

The silence was very long this time. I could sense Gamelan pulling himself together, reaching deep for strength. When he finally spoke, his tone was almost normal, as if he'd accepted his terrible mutilation of body, soul, and Talent as fatalistically as the bravest soldier. He sighed. "No, I'm just an ordinary old man now. And please don't think I'm wading in self-pity. I know my limitations. I pushed them as far as I could many years ago."

"We'll be home soon," I said. "You'll have acolytes by the scores to assist you."

The wizard shifted his head this way and that. His tongue flickered out—surprisingly youthful and pink—and tasted the air. "We're lost," he said.

"Nothing to fear," I said. "We've only to get around that confounded reef. We'll find our way in no time."

Gamelan shook his head. "I may be blind," he said, "but my wits are keen enough to know it won't be so easy."

"The gods only make things easy," I said, "when they are preparing the way for your fall."

Gamelan laughed. It was good to hear. It almost made him seem whole again. He said: "Then we'll take my misfortune—and the misfortune of all the others—as a good omen."

He yawned. Gently, I pushed him back into his bed. He did not resist. I found a cover for him and tucked it around him and under his chin.

"Don't let me sleep too long," he said. "We have much to talk about."

"I won't," I promised, dreading the prospect of what I knew he was going to ask of me.

As I was about to go out he said: "Rali?"

"Yes?"

Gamelan turned his blind face toward me. "You must have made your father proud."

I didn't know how to answer, so I just shut the door.

THAT NIGHT I dreamed of Tries. It was the same dream as before. We made love, but this time my passion was hot, spiced with fear of what I knew the dream demon would bring next. The Archon came again. My nakedness was mocked. I awoke to the dream within the dream and found Tries ready to betray me once more. We struggled. I felt the pinprick of her silver dirk. Then I found myself trembling in my hammock, eyes shut against new dreams, praying the nightmare was done.

There came a hammering. I heard Polillo curse, and the creak of ropes as Corais rolled out of her hammock and went to see what was happening. Still, I did not open my eyes, because I did not trust what they might find.

I felt the burn of scored flesh where Tries' dirk had entered. I heard a tumble of confusion and then Gamelan's voice.

"Rali!" he shouted. "Rali!"

I opened my eyes. The wizard stood over me. His flesh was scratched and bleeding from finding his way across the deck from his cabin.

I swung up from the hammock.

"Yes, my friend? What is it?"

"It's the Archon!" Gamelan said. "He's still with us!"

"I know," I said.

I felt cold, empty.

"Do you hear me, Rali?" Gamelan cried. "It's not over yet!"

"I hear you, wizard," I answered. "I hear you."

Far out in the night I heard a young sea lizard bellow for its mother.

CHAPTER NINE

THE TATTOOED CHIEFTAIN

❖

W e limped south for days, our supplies dwindling, our water brackish, but the reefs were unrelenting, never offering a channel toward home. Gamelan's health improved, although there was no sign that his blindness was anything but permanent. We spoke rarely, and certainly did not bring up our conversation about the Archon. I think both of us believed it an aberration caused by exhaustion. My practical nature reasserted itself: the Archon was dead, by Te-Date! I'd seen him die myself, and even if he had cursed me with his last breath, I'd much rather be cursed by a dead man than a live one who might actually be able to do something about it.

My women's attitude was that we had won a great victory and sooner or later we'd find our way around the reef and return home to many honors. Cholla Yi's men, however, muttered and cast dark looks whenever I was about. Neither Stryker, the sailing master Klisura, nor the rowing master Duban made any attempt to stop the muttering, or to cheer the men up. Instead, anything anyone said that was in any way positive, or hopeful, drew an immediate and quite negative response.

I was beginning to wonder how to deal with this, when we awoke one morning to air rich with the moist smell of fertile soil, strange blossoms, and the familiar tang of hearthsmoke. A hazy blue shape on the horizon hinted an island was ahead. We saw a tree floating in our path and hauled it aboard. Its leaves were trumpet-shaped, its buds purple and cream, knots growing close on the limbs, and its branches covered with fleshy, rose-colored gourds filled with a thick, sweet-tasting fluid that put sparkle to the eye and a lightness to the feet.

"There *must* be people about," Polillo said. "Nothing so good could exist without people to eat it."

Corais laughed at her reasoning. "You always think with your stomach, my friend."

Polillo blushed, but her shy smile showed she'd taken no offense. She didn't answer, but pierced another gourd and held it out to me, her wrist curved like a serving maid's.

Despite her size and manner, there was something so feminine about Polillo—sometimes even dainty, if you can imagine daintiness in a near giant—that it has become the trait I remember most about her. I should tell you Polillo and I were nearly lovers when we were girls. We sighed and mooned over one another for nearly a week. It would have gone further, but before our tender feelings were consummated, we met at the bitts with our practice swords, and after I'd disarmed her twice, she called it quits with some embarrassment. Later that night we agreed we should be friends for always, and not lovers, although that word was never mentioned. It was I who broached the subject, knowing Polillo would have difficulty being in the arms of a woman who was her superior in any feat of arms. Polillo agreed in obvious relief. But as the years passed, in rare moments we would look at one another with a tinge of regret. It would have been lust, pure and simple—not love—had we ever come together. But it would have made a stormy night.

I took the gourd from my girlhood crush, gave her a wink to let her know *I* remembered as well, and drank. The heady liquid lit hope in my belly. Perhaps Polillo was right. Perhaps there *was* a hint of human life in the elixir's taste.

Gamelan hobbled up beside me. I'd detailed two Guardswomen to take care of him, and ignored his grumbles about being treated as if he were a cripple. Even blind, he was too valuable to us to chance losing through any accident.

I offered him the gourd, and he, too, drank deeply. "Why is it," he wondered as he passed it back, "fruit this sweet never seems to grow in our own gardens, but always on the far side of strange seas, and is guarded by demons?"

I was about to say so far we hadn't seen any particularly interesting monsters when the lookout in the bow shouted we were closing on land and the sea was shallowing.

I noted a green isthmus extending out from one side of the island, almost like an arm reaching to embrace us. We entered a small, marshy bay and I saw the smoke columns of cooking fires. The blossom smell grew stronger, as well as the smells—both pleasant and foul—that said the island was inhabited. Marsh birds swept up from thick rushes along the peninsula, and we heard heavy drums. That brought me back, and I shouted to Stryker to halt the ship and signal Cholla Yi's flagship for a conference.

Canoes skimmed out of the reeds. They were long and low to the water, with reeds painted on their sides, which had camouflaged their presence until they were on us. I shouted the alert, and in less than a long breath Ismet sounded the Guard to battle positions. My women leaped to their predetermined places, swords bared, spears at ready, bows drawn. The rowers backed water, and we quickly came to a stop. I heard the signal echoed from other ships' trumpeters as the fleet sprang to readiness.

The canoes drew into a long line and halted. One of the canoes sped out toward us. I've called them canoes, and so they were, but far unlike what a swain paddles his lover across a calm lake on. This craft, like its sisters, carried at least a hundred warriors, and I could make out, first the glint of their weapons, then the wild-colored smears that striped their bodies, naked except for a pouch containing their sexual parts. A tall man stood in the bows. He carried a long, thick staff—decorated with red and green plumes of some forest bird and shaped like an engorged penis. His flesh was decorated with such glorious, swirling color, it was impossible to imagine anyone other than a man of high rank with many slaves at his beck and call could have worn them.

The war canoe sped to our side and stopped. The tall man shouted up in a language none of us understood. His tone was imperious: his words, although indecipherable, were unmistakably a command. I chanced an answer in trader's cant, but although he turned to me, surprise on his face for being addressed by a woman, he shook his head to show he did not grasp my meaning. He grew angry, shouting at me and shaking his staff.

I felt a nudge. It was Gamelan. "Do as I say," he said. "Quickly."

Praying to Maranonia that our wizard had his magic back despite his blindness, I said, "What would you have me do?"

"Is there any more of that odd fruit about?" he asked. "The gourdlike fruit, with the sweet-tasting milk?"

I still held the one Polillo gave me in my hand. I nodded, forgetting Gamelan was blind.

"Answer me," he snapped. "I cannot read your motions."

"Yes," I said, too worried about the angry chieftain to be embarrassed. "I have one right here."

"Drink it," he said.

"But how—"

"Just drink it. Then repeat the words I give you."

"Gladly," I said. I drank deeply, then lowered the gourd. "I've done it," I said. "Now what shall I say?"

Gamelan gripped my arm. I was surprised at the strength in his wizened fist. "You're going to have to do this yourself, Rali," he hissed. "I don't have my magic back, if that's what you're thinking. The Spell of the Tongues must be performed by *you*."

I was taken aback. "But I told you I have no Talent."

"Then we're all lost, Rali," he said. "For there is no one else in this fleet who can do it."

I wanted to argue. I wanted to tell this wizard to begone! Instead, I said: "Very well."

Gamelan abruptly began: "*Words beget wisdom . . .*" he intoned.

"*Words beget wisdom . . .*" I echoed.

"*Words beget fools . . .*"

Although it was all nonsense to me, I repeated all he said. Then he commanded: "Drink again, Rali. But this time, look inside and . . . *see* . . ."

I drank again. But I didn't have the slightest notion what he wanted me to see that wasn't plainly in view.

"Look, Rali!" he hissed. "Do you see the tree that bore that fruit?" I shook my head, forgetting his condition once again. "The tree, Rali," he pressed. "Think of that tree." Suddenly, I saw it, saw it floating in the water, saw the odd-shaped limbs, the blossoms, and the long, trumpetlike leaves. "Look deeper, Rali," Gamelan said. "Deeper, still!"

I tried with all my might. A door opened in my mind and a light flickered on and I saw the leaves move. They became tongues and the tongues began to speak: "*. . . Words beget fools. Hear thy brother, hear thy sister, hear the stranger on the darkest night.*"

The spell took a grip on me, harder than even Gamelan's grasp. My head swirled, fear quickened my heart, and with a great effort I pulled away to find myself gasping as if I'd just risen from a great depth. A humorless smile peered through Gamelan's white beard. "You can talk to him now," he said.

He took the gourd from my hand and drank. I saw him pass the gourd to Polillo and the others for them to drink as well.

Numb, I turned to the chieftain, who'd grown silent during the quiet struggle between Gamelan and I. He looked up at me, interest in his eyes, as if he sensed a bit of what had been going on.

"I am Captain Antero of Orissa, my lord," I tried.

The chief's eyes widened, and I could see he understood. "You are in command?" he asked, barely hiding amazement.

"Yes. I command here. And I speak for all when I tell you that we come with peaceful purpose. We come as friends."

The chieftain laughed. "I already have friends," he said. "Why should I want more?"

"Come aboard and meet us, my lord," I said. "You'll see at once that we can be good friends to add to the others."

I didn't think he'd agree, at least not immediately. To my surprise, he called to his men to wait and leaped for the side. In a moment he was pacing the deck, looking all the taller from so much naked, painted skin. His outward appearance was as barbaric as any I'd ever seen. He wore his hair in plaited ropes, each daubed with a different color, each decorated with rough gems, odd, gold figurines, and bits of ivory, feathers, and beads. The body of a great, taloned lizard was painted on his chest. It coiled about his neck and emerged at his right cheek, its mouth open and angry, hissing flames that were actually his braided, red-painted beard. A naked woman curled up his right thigh, a beautiful boy his left; each had their hands outstretched as if to enclose his sex pouch, which bulged with thick muscle. He stopped in front of me and looked me up and down. Despite his barbaric appearance, I saw cold intelligence in his eyes. I stared back, refusing to be cowed by his heavy, male posturing.

He frowned, then rapped his staff against the deck. "I am Keehat," he said. "I am king."

"We are honored, King Keehat," I replied, careful to mix authority along with my respect. "But you must forgive our ignorance, for we are strangers here. What is the name of your realm?"

"These are the Isles of Lonquin," he said. He looked about our galley, then peered beyond us at the others. "The shaman didn't tell me you would have such fine ships." His eyes glittered with greed.

"You knew we were coming?" It was not possible to mask my surprise.

"I knew," he replied grimly. "All of us knew."

"Then I hope you will welcome us," I said, not daring to question more. "We have rich gifts to please a king. All we ask is to buy a little food, some water, and perhaps a small area to beach and repair our galleys. I'm certain your shaman told you we do not intrude upon you by choice, Your Highness. We are victims of the sea, and want only to return to our homes as quickly as possible."

He ignored this, saying: "You are from the other side of the reef?"

"Yes, Your Highness. And we planned to go no farther, but the sea lifted us up and carried us across."

"You were unlucky," Keehat said.

"Yes," I said. "Unlucky."

"We are a lucky people," the king said. "At least we were until a few days past. Then the sea gods grew angry and cursed us. They sent large waves that burst upon our shores. Villages were lost. Fields were destroyed. And now many of our children have no fathers and no mothers, and many of our fathers and mothers no longer have children."

"Then we are kin to the same misfortune, Your Highness," I said. "For we have lost loved ones and comrades as well."

King Keehat only stared at me. His face was expressionless, but I did not sense welcome. Then he said: "The shaman claims you are the cause of our bad luck."

"That can't be," I said. "We are also normally a lucky people. If truth be known, when the sea struck us, we had only just defeated a terrible enemy in a battle so great that only those favored by the gods could survive, much less win."

The king glanced at the galleys and saw the scars of battle. "Perhaps so," he said at last. "My shaman was also ignorant of the quality of your ships. But he's young, and before I had his father killed, he promised his son would serve me ably."

I did not answer—there was none called for—but only bowed to show respect.

"Where is your shaman?" the king asked.

I pointed to Gamelan. "Here is our wizard. In our land he is the master of all our Evocators, and a very wise and powerful man."

Gamelan stepped forward to greet him, but he seemed to lose his footing and stumble; catching himself on Keehat's staff. The king snatched it away, insulted. As he did so, I saw Gamelan clutch a feather, which ripped free. He hid it in his robes, then bowed in the wrong direction.

"My apologies, Your Highness," he said, his eyes wide and blank and staring. "My wounds have made me clumsy."

Keehat's anger turned to disgust. "More bad luck," he scoffed. "Your wizard is plainly blind."

"And yours is too young, my lord," I said. "Both conditions are temporary, so we meet on equal ground."

"Not so equal," he said. "It is you who beg my charity."

"Perhaps you misunderstood, Your Highness," I said. "We do not ask charity. We have offered to pay for whatever kindness you offer."

Keehat was silent. He was clearly taking our measure. As he thought, he scratched the bulging pouch.

After a moment he nodded: "We'll see," he said. "Wait. I must confer with my advisers."

He whirled and plunged into the sea. He tossed his phallic staff to one of his men, and he hoisted himself into the canoe with little effort, and much grace. The war canoe shot back to join the others.

I heard Stryker call to me. "The admiral is signaling us for instructions, Captain."

I studied the line of canoes, trying to read Keehat's intent. My gut squirmed with worms of suspicion. Was Keehat conferring with his men as he'd said? Or was he giving them orders for battle? He didn't seem the type of leader who confers with anyone but himself. But was he willing to risk a fight to revenge his kingdom for the misfortune he imagined we had brought? Probably not. But what of his plain desire to have our galleys for himself?

Herons cried from among the reeds to the west. I saw one pair circling a clump of rushes, diving close and then away, hooting threats, as if something were after its nest.

"We'll have to fight," I told Corais. Then I shouted to Stryker: "Signal the admiral. He is to withdraw at once. We'll guard the rear."

No sooner had the flags been hoisted than I heard the high-pitched wail of a thousand voices crying for battle. The canoes speared toward us, King Keehat's war canoe in front.

"To the west, Captain," Polillo shouted, and as I feared, a score or more enemy craft skimmed out of hiding to flank us.

A black cloud of arrows lifted from Keehat's group, but the range was too great and only a few fell among us, and none struck their mark. We came about and pulled hard away, the rowing master's drum pounding for full speed. But fast as our galleys were, the canoes were faster, and they were quickly closing the gap. There were hard bumps all along the side as the first of the flanking party reached us.

"Repel boarders," I shouted, and Polillo leaped forward with a squad of pikewomen.

One man was already coming over the side, but Polillo got to him first, her axe swinging down, severing his fingers, and he fell away with a terrible scream. There were more cries of pain as her pikewomen thrust and clubbed away.

I sent archers to the rail just as the second swarm of arrows struck. Once again none of us fell, and I had the satisfaction of seeing our own shafts plunge into Keehat's forces. At least nine were hit, one fatally. Ismet led a group of slingwomen back to the quarterdeck, and a hail of lead stones smashed among the attackers. The galley shuddered as we ground across a sandbar, and I stumbled. When I came up, we'd broken out of the bay, but the canoes were all around us and men were swarming over the sides, swinging swords and clubs. I had time to see the other galleys speeding for the open sea, then I drew my sword and plunged into the fight. I cut my way to Polillo's side, then together we charged a knot of boarders, Polillo bellowing her war cry. Her axe swept a man away from my back, and I parried a sword thrust, then cut back to spill its owner's guts, spun left to hack another man down, then right to catch an attacker under his chin, then left again to kick one man in the groin and thrust my sword into another's chest. Blood sprayed to blind me, and I cut instinctively until I could clear my sight. I saw Gamelan with a heavy staff, swinging wildly all around him, clubbing anyone who came into his reach. Not far from him one of the oarsmen swung his own monstrous club with deadly effect. Polillo hooted laughter as blood lust overcame her and she plowed into half a dozen naked swordsmen. She left them flopping on the deck, with severed limbs and burst skulls.

Then a stiff breeze caught our sails and the galley surged forward. In a few minutes we were clear, chopping down the last of our attackers and hurling their dead and wounded over the side.

I ran back to the helmsman's post and saw the war canoes falling behind us. In the prow of one I could make out Keehat, shaking his staff and urging his men on. There seemed to be hundreds of canoes, with hundreds more pouring out of the bay. Keehat was not going to give up merely because we were outpacing him.

I exchanged hasty signals with Cholla Yi. The wind was pressing us west, but we feared to divert too much from our search for a southern route around the reef. Cholla Yi attempted a feint. We sped west, putting as much distance between us and the war canoes as we could, then tried a dash south, but as soon as we neared one of the islands, a huge group of war canoes leapt out at us, forcing us west again. Again and again we attempted the same ruse, but each time we were turned back.

I could sense that Keehat's shamans were magically passing the word from island to island, giving each tribe a chance to ready themselves to attack us.

As we pushed past one island, we entered a sea of debris. Countless trees, timbers, and entire houses bobbed in the current. There were bloated corpses everywhere, farm animals, wild creatures, and hundreds of people— men, women, and children. It was the aftermath of the great sea quake that had nearly destroyed us and wrecked much of Keehat's kingdom. The devastation was an awful answer to any fool who might ask why the king hated us, and why he would go to any lengths to revenge his kingdom.

As we tried to pick our way through the horror, one of the damaged galleys was hulled by a log lurking just beneath the surface of the water. As it sank, we hauled the crew off. But we weren't quick enough, because the war canoes were on us again, dodging easily through the flotsam. Once again we were showered with arrows. Once again a galley was boarded. It was one of the damaged ships, and it was not so lucky as we had been—none of my women were aboard to fight off the attackers.

We heard the sailors' screams for mercy, but couldn't stop to help as we eluded Keehat's hordes and fought our way out of the trap.

After we had made good our escape, I wearily called for Stryker. I told him to signal Cholla Yi and the rest of the fleet. As I spoke I could see Keehat and his forces churning steadily along in our wake. Another group was spearing off to one side in case we attempted another dash south.

We had only one choice: flee west into the open sea, and deeper into the unknown.

KING KEEHAT pursued us as relentlessly as we had hunted the Archon. For a week we drove onward, sailing, or rowing as fast and as hard as we could. But as soon as we slowed, or came to a stop to rest, or to fish to restore our rapidly dwindling supplies, the war canoes would appear on the horizon. The weather was inconsistent, alternating between foggy calms and sudden squalls, so we could never depend on wind-driven speed to carry us far enough and long enough to shake him. Once we thought we had, after nearly two days of nonstop rowing and sailing. We anchored late the second night in a dead calm, too exhausted to go on, but fairly certain we'd escaped. We awoke the next morning as his canoes burst out of a fog bank, with Keehat bellowing for our blood. We barely got away in time; even then, one galley was within bowshot and several rowers were killed by the king's strongest archers.

Finally, I had enough. I was tired of running, tired of the dark looks my Guardswomen were giving me—all our training and tradition was to confront, not to retreat—and tired of feeling like a small fish trembling in fear of a larger one. Besides, the farther we got from the volcano reefs, the more certain we were of becoming hopelessly lost.

I called a meeting: my staff, Cholla Yi and his, and Gamelan. I opened by asking the wizard how he thought Keehat had managed to stay at our heels so long, without ever seeming to tire.

"Is it his shaman?" I asked. "Has he cast some spell to continuously replenish their strength?"

Gamelan shook his head. "It is not magic," he said. "Spells for such things sap a wizard's powers. They only work so long as the magician is fresh."

"Then what is it?"

"I suspect it is the milk of those gourds we found," Gamelan said.

"Even a small sip, if you recall, seems to stoke the furnaces of both body and mind."

I did, indeed. We had shared all we had gotten from the floating tree. Reluctantly, still wanting little of magic, I'd duplicated the speaking spell, so that at least some of the others could understand and communicate with any people we might encounter in these waters. And even with so little for each to drink, everyone had remarked how giddy and . . . *well* they'd felt.

"I'm certain that with a good supply of that wondrous fruit, the king and his men can keep up this pace," Gamelan continued. "It also has the side benefit of staving off hunger pangs, so their canoes will be burdened only with their weapons, and water. They can easily keep their bellies from feeling pinched with a little fishing on the run."

"This is stupid," Polillo growled. "I say we stand and fight. There can't be more than a few thousand of them."

Corais had a similar view, although much cooler and reasoned: "We can play the fog trick on them," she said. "We can charge out, pick off as many as we can, then slip away again. It won't be long before he shouts 'Enough!' "

"It'd never work," Phocas said. "The men are too tired."

"Whiners," Polillo snarled.

"The smallest mistake could bring disaster," the admiral said. "There's too many of them."

"Cowards," was Polillo's reply.

Phocas and the admiral's other men were angered by her taunts. "You should be more careful with that mouth," Phocas warned. Others growled their assent.

Polillo bulled her head forward and made a wide, mirthless smile. She pointed at her mouth. "There it is. Stop it from flapping, if you dare."

There were mutters, but no one was foolish enough to test her. Phocas turned away and pretended to be busy with some charts.

I said: "I think Legate Corais is on to something. We can fight them like direwolves against a herd of boar. We hide in the fog, leap out to harry them—hamstring a few if we're lucky—then back into hiding. There's other tricks . . . like pretending that one of us is falling back, letting them close, then strike and run, strike and run, until he's sick of so many dying, or becomes so weak we can finish him off."

Cholla Yi shook his head. "It's too risky. My men would refuse."

I raised an eyebrow. "Aren't you their *admiral*? Who commands—you or their livers?"

Cholla Yi shrugged. "I command, of course. But that'll end the moment the men lose faith in me."

His tone was so sanctimonious and oily that I didn't believe a word he was saying.

"My women are ready to fight," I said.

"By the gods, we *are* ready," Polillo hissed. "And if you put me alone with your men for a day, they'll be ready, too. I'll put some steel in their spines, or they'll curse their mothers for bearing them."

Instead of taking offense, the admiral sighed. "If you want my men to fight," he said to me, "you'll have to turn the expedition over to me. To be frank, they're tired of getting orders they know come from a woman."

So that's it, I thought. Cholla Yi was playing as much of a waiting game as King Keehat. And he would drag his heels until I stepped aside.

"They blame our bad luck on you and your women," the admiral continued. "And who can say they're wrong? Every sailor knows women and ships don't mix. For some reason, the gods of the sea don't like women, and the goddesses become jealous of your presence."

Gamelan laughed—a mocking sound that turned Cholla Yi's words into a fool's song. The big man flushed, twisted his hands into fists, but still managed outward calm. He gave me a bland smile.

"Are you refusing to fight, Admiral?" I asked. It was time for bluntness.

"Not at all," he answered, but the bland smile vanished. "I'm only warning you that if you order it, the men may not follow."

"And if the orders came from you?"

Cholla Yi smiled. "Then they'd fight."

Abruptly, I rose from the chair, ending the meeting before Polillo's temper got the better of her. That was my excuse, at any rate. I'll admit mine was beginning to blow foul.

"We'll talk again?" Cholla Yi asked as we took our leave. He sounded anxious.

"Oh, yes," I answered. "We'll talk again, Admiral. You can be sure of it."

I gave him my most carnivorous grin and exited.

THERE IS a barracks' game young soldiers played in my time. It was called Loser's Win, or Hobble. Hobble was played between two young women. Each had to be barefooted, and each was provided with a sharp throwing knife. You faced your opponent from a distance of two paces. The object was to throw the knife as close to the other's foot as you could, without cutting it. There were three tries each. Each throw had to be closer than the last, and if any thrower faltered, she lost. We played for money, watch and duty sharing, and once to settle a love triangle. The winner in that contest lost part of her big toe, which brought the game to the attention of our superiors, and to its end.

It was that sort of game I found myself engaged in with Cholla Yi. With a seaborne horde at our heels, he was betting I would be the first to falter, and relinquish command. The stakes were our lives.

So, I must admit, Scribe, when I left him that night, displaying my most evil, knowing smile, I was bluffing. But you should also know that I always back my bluff. You see, it was *I* who was one of the combatants in that final game of Hobble I told you about. No need to sneak a look at my feet. I have *all* my toes.

But the conclusion of that test of wills was delayed for a long time. And it was Gamelan who delayed it.

Two nights after the meeting, a heavy fog settled over us. It was so dense we dared not continue, or the fleet might have been separated for good. I ordered a halt, using horns to signal, and we lay becalmed to wait until the fog lifted. We could only pray that Keehat was doing the same.

Gamelan called me to his cabin. There was a cheery light glowing in his magical brazier when I entered.

"Come sit and share a little brandy with an old man," he said.

"I should be on deck, keeping watch," I replied.

"Nonsense," he said. "There's nothing to see. If there were, it would be too late and those savages would be on us. Come and sit and I shall tell you how to end this chase in our favor."

I had reason to be nervous as I obeyed, and better reason to empty the first tumbler of brandy with one swallow and pour another. The first spell he'd made me cast had left me shaken from the strange world I had encountered. When I'd duplicated the Spell of the Tongues for the others—again, at his insistence—I'd become more fearful still. The feeling of being drawn down, as if by a water devil, had been even stronger. To my horror, I realized I was reluctant to withdraw. There seemed to be so many promises beneath the surface of that magical meniscus; promises that drew me as much as when I'd first seen that map of the western seas, and ached to know what was beyond.

Gamelan fumbled in his robe and came out with the scrap of feather he'd stolen from Keehat's staff. Blindly, he held it out to me. "We have something that belongs to that barbarian king," he said. "Something he prizes above all else . . ." I took the feather, knowing what he was going to say next: "His manhood."

I took the feather, my fingers trembling. "I know what you want, wizard," I said. "And I cannot—will not—do it."

"What is it about magic that you fear so much, Rali?" he asked.

"You know," I said.

"I don't know! Tell me!" he snapped.

"Get someone else!"

"There is no one. Tell me!"

And so I told him. It is a tale that has nothing to do with Halab's tragic ending. And I have told it to no other person in my life, with exception of Otara, and she is dead. So, write carefully, Scribe. I only tell it now because of my promise to speak the truth.

I became a woman at an early age: my monthlies began at ten; by eleven I had the breasts, hips, and feminine beard below my belly of a full-grown woman. But although my body had blossomed, my mind was still in early bud, and I went about my days in tormented confusion. I thought about sex a great deal, which disgusted me, because I didn't yet know my inclinations and connected all such yearnings with men. I'd become all hot and sticky for no apparent reason, but whenever I saw a man when I was in such a state, my stomach turned when I contemplated their rough beards, hard forms, and sour smells.

It was in my twelfth summer, and we were visiting one of my uncle's estates. He had vast olive orchards, a good kitchen garden, and kept several herds of goats as well, so summers at his estate were always filled with plump black olives, good white cheese, my aunt's rich black bread, and tomatoes and onions as sweet as any confection. One day my cousin, Veraen, and I made up a lunch of such things and took a long hike into the hills to watch the young goats play. Veraen was fifteen, and although he had grown since I'd seen him last, I was taller than he, and stronger as well, so our time together had been uneasy and conflict-ridden. Normally, we were the best of summer friends. This was one of those afternoons, however, that was so blissful that all thoughts of such things had disappeared along with the dandelion fluff that flew over the green hills on scented winds.

That day, we ate our fill, drank from a small spring that sprang out from under an old oak tree, and lay down to enjoy the shade of the tree. It was a hot, quiet afternoon. The cicadas buzzed among the wood, a few birds twittered and hopped about, and a solitary wasp hunted for mud to daub her nest. The air was thick with the smell of wild rosemary, oregano, and thyme that had gone to blossom.

Veraen began to tell silly stories, which made me laugh, and then he started to tickle me, and I tickled him back. We reverted to childhood, becoming nearly hysterical with laughter—rolling about and wrestling and tickling.

Then childhood ended, and before I knew it my hem was up, my undergarments were down, my legs apart, and Veraen was clambering on top of me. Then my senses returned and I pushed him up with a hard forearm. Veraen was on his knees, his breeches open, and I saw his penis—not a boy's, but a man's organ, thick and hard, rising up like a drawbridge. The sight soured my stomach.

"Get away!" I said.

Instead he fell back on me, pinning my arms and driving blindly at me, trying to force entry. I bucked and fought and finally managed to get one hand free. I hit him as hard as I could, got my other one loose and was about to hurl him off when I felt a heavy blow against my head.

"Stop fighting," he shouted, and I saw he had a rock in his fist.

Instead, I screamed in anger and pain. My strength surged and somehow I rose up and somehow he struck me with the rock again and somehow I killed him.

Yes, Scribe, I slew my cousin. And yes, I am speaking of Veraen Antero, and I know what you are thinking, and I am telling you to speak not one word to me, but write all I say, exactly as I say it.

One moment Veraen was on top of me, hitting me with a rock, and the next I was standing and Veraen was motionless on the ground—his neck twisted, his dead eyes fixed in terror and pain.

I stood there, too shocked to feel anything but the sharp knowledge that my life had just plunged from a cliff. Now only evil could follow.

A woman's voice came from behind me. It was a sweet, lilting voice that drew me around as if I were a compass head, drawn to the will of Sirens of the South, who command all direction.

"Rali," she called. "Raaaleee."

She was under the oak, just by the spring. She was beautiful; other-worldly beautiful; goddess beautiful. Her hair was black as night and spilled like water across skin of fresh cream. Her eyes were smoky black, with lashes like a dancer's fan, and they were so striking that for a moment I did not realize she was naked. But she wore her nudity like clothing, as if this were her natural state.

She motioned to me with a long, slender arm. "Come to me, Rali," she said.

So I went. I felt as if I were floating slowly across the ground. She took me in her arms, and I wept for me and what I had done, and I wept for Veraen, for what he had done. Then she raised my head up from those soft, mother's breasts and looked me deep in the eyes. I looked back and lost myself in the welcome darkness I found there. All else vanished from my mind.

"I love you, Rali," she said.

Instead of surprising, her words seemed natural—right. I knew that she loved me.

"I have been waiting for you, Rali," she said. And that seemed right, too.

She took me by the hand and led me to the place where the spring leaped from beneath the oak's great roots. We walked into the little pool, and a gate opened just where the spring came out and then we walked into her garden, the gate swung shut behind us, and we were standing before a house made of green forest bowers.

"This is your home now, Rali," she said.

And that is what it became. I lived there with Basana for one month short of a year. We were lovers. Basana said she was the goddess of the spring and had fallen in love with me when Veraen had first showed me the spring two years before. It did not occur to me to wonder why. Youth accepts such things blindly—as its due. Except, perhaps, with Otara—and that only once—I never felt such passion as Basana fired in me. I say this as a woman of much passionate nature, which is a trait all Anteros share. It is our greatest weakness. She enveloped me in love: gave me gifts, sang me songs, fed me delicacies, praised my beauty, my wisdom, my nature, my all. I forgot my home and family—indeed, all the world I came from. Until one day when I tried to rise from the bed of blossoms she made fresh for me each night, and found I could not. I was so weak, I could barely lift a hand, or voice a call for help. And when Basana came into the room, her loving smile became a hungry snarl.

She came to the bed and pinched my flesh all over, saying: "So sweet, so sweet."

I tried to weep, for I knew I had been betrayed, but could only shed a single tear. Basana giggled when she saw it, and kissed it away. Her mouth lingered, but not from love.

Then she rose and said, "Don't cry, Rali. I've fed you on love for nearly a year, and now that you're ripe, you mustn't complain, because it's my turn now."

I tried to move, and she gave me a soothing pat. "There, there, dear," she said. "It's my nature that's at fault, not you. I have no soul of my own, and require a young girl's every ten years for nourishment. It's true, I didn't really love you, dear Rali, but I had to make you believe I did, or that withered little thing I found by that boy's body would have been no good at all. The best soul, I've learned, is full of happy, love-fed sweetness. Not just flavor, mind. You have no idea, my dear, what wonders it does for my mood. To be so *young*, and so . . . *alive* year after year!"

She told me she'd leave my room for a small while to prepare. While she was gone I could take comfort in the fact that although she did not really love me, of all the girls she'd pretended to love, she'd come closest to not pretending with me.

As she was turning away I smelled sandalwood, and then my mother entered. She was naked, like Basana, and more beautiful, I think. She moved like a panther and fire sheeted from her eyes. The only thing she carried was a sharpened willow switch.

Basana shouted and sprang to meet her—great talons reaching where hands and feet had been before. Her teeth became long fangs snapping for my mother's throat. Before she could reach her, my mother thrust with that willow stick and it pierced Basana through the heart. Blood spurted from her breast, and she fell dead to the floor.

My mother didn't look at her, but came to me and took me in her arms.

"I've come to take you home, Rali," was all she said.

I struggled to rise, but she pushed me back on the bed. She sang me a song, whose words are always at the edge of my memory, but I can never call them up. And she stroked my brow until I closed my eyes . . . and slept.

Veraen's voice awakened me. I opened my eyes, and found myself lying beside him, beneath the oak. It was just as before. The same warm, summer afternoon. The smells and sounds. He said something silly and I laughed. Then he tickled me, and I tickled back.

I heard my mother's voice calling me. Veraen jumped away, with a guilty flush. I stood and answered her, and she came over the hill. My mother was dressed in a simple short tunic of blue, with blue walking breeches below, stuffed into high boots. As she came near us, I smelled her sandalwood perfume.

She looked at me with her gentle eyes and said, "I've come to take you home, Rali."

And that is what she did.

I told Gamelan that I didn't know if what happened was real or a dream. Mostly, I believed it a dream, Scribe, just as you do. You were going to call me mad when I began this tale, for as all know, my cousin, Veraen Antero, is very much alive, with good family and good fortune of his own. Now, you'll say it was just a dream. A dream of a young, confused girl.

But sometimes, I told Gamelan, I thought it no dream at all. I thought that I really had been stolen by a wood sprite, if that's what Basana was, and that my mother had rescued me. One thing—my mother was never the same again. She became weaker, day by day. Until, nearly a year later, she died. On my weaker nights, I wonder if she made a bargain with god or demon—my life for hers.

"And that," I said to Gamelan, "is why I not only fear what you ask, but refuse it."

"I understand your reasons now, Rali," the wizard replied. "And I'm very sorry. But have you told me all? Is your mother truly gone to you? Does she come to you sometimes? Is her ghost still near her child?"

I didn't answer—which for Gamelan was answer enough.

He said: "It doesn't matter just now. You've confessed your reasons and your fears. But that doesn't change our circumstance. If we continue like this, King Keehat will catch us and kill us. Between the two of us, however, we can stop him. We can stop him now, and the only blood that will be shed is his."

Once again he offered me the feather. This time I took it.

Gamelan smiled. "Drag this over my chest," he said. "There's a special oil we'll need, and some other things."

I fetched the chest, found the proper bottle of oil and some dried-up, foul-smelling powders he said were necessary. Then he told me what to do. I imagined myself going into battle, dousing all emotion, pushing everything from me, except what he was saying.

At his direction, I chalked a pentagram about the brazier and sprinkled in the powder and oil. Purple smoke gushed up and a demon hopped out. It was small, with leathery green skin, a fanged toad's face, but the wizened legs and arms of a man—if men had talons and claws. It hissed and snapped at me. Numbly, I handed him the feather. He plucked it from my fingers and leaped back into the brazier.

Gamelan told me what would happen, but still I had to steel myself as the flames exploded up and out. I closed my eyes as the fire engulfed my face, then my whole body—but instead of burning, the flames were cold on my flesh. I opened my eyes and felt the icy flames lick me. All about me were swirling colors, and below me—at the bottom of the brazier—was smoke. I blew . . . and the smoke swept away.

I found myself looking down from a great height at the war canoes. They were still partially hidden by fog, so I blew again and the fog wisped away across the gray seas.

King Keehat lolled in the largest of the canoes. He was being fed by a slender youth who wore not even a loincloth. The youth had the breasts of a woman and the private parts of a man. As I watched, the youth dipped food out of a bowl and offered it to Keehat. The king opened his mouth and ate from the woman/man's fingers, then licked them clean. The youth giggled and dipped out some more. From far away I heard Gamelan urge me on.

"Keehat!" I called. My voice seemed to echo as if I were in a large cavern.

The king jolted up, pushing the youth aside. He looked all about for the source of the voice.

"Who addresses the king?" he demanded.

"Keehat!" I called again.

The king's head snapped back and forth, blazing eyes jumping from one of his warriors to the next.

"Who speaks?" he shouted.

His men were clearly terrified, thinking their king had gone mad.

"Keehat!" I said.

This time the king leaped up, and as he did so, the youth suddenly became that obscene staff Keehat carried. Keehat gripped it, then shook it at his men.

"Answer," he shouted, "or you will know my wrath!"

They were all too terrified to speak. Keehat struck the man nearest him with the staff. The warrior screamed and shrunk back as if he had been burned by an intense heat.

"It wasn't me, my lord!" the man shrieked.

"Who, then?" the king shouted. "I know you all speak of me behind my back! Calling me mad or a fool for this pursuit!"

The warriors were silent.

Keehat struck another man with the staff. The victim howled in agony like the first and begged his king to please believe him and spare him. But the king pushed him down with his foot and ground the staff into his belly. The man cried out and writhed in pain as the searing hot staff burnt into him.

"Slave like master," I intoned, and my words rolled out like a wave.

Keehat whirled, looking up, realizing the voice came from the skies. For a moment I thought he was looking at me.

He shook his staff at the heavens. "I am Keehat!" he roared. "Who dares defy the king?"

Lightning speared from the tip of the staff, and I nearly ducked as it crashed up. Then I felt the reassuring touch of Gamelan's hand on my arm. The lightning bolt crackled harmlessly beneath me.

"Master like slave," I continued, piling phrase upon magical phrase. I felt a shock of power as I spoke. But it was a power that sickened me and made my head swim as if I were gripped by fever. I dared not stop, for Gamelan had warned that to do so would be fatal. I pushed on: "Like to like . . . Hate to hate. Slave find thy master! Master find thy slave!"

Near the canoe, the water roiled and then Keehat shouted in alarm as the toadfaced demon I'd sent shot up from the spume. The king lashed out with his staff and the demon shrieked in anger as Keehat's totem charred his flesh. The king laughed and struck again. But this time the demon vanished just before the staff connected.

Keehat whirled this way and that, looking for where the next attack would come from. His men were silent . . . unmoving.

Suddenly, he shouted in fear as the staff writhed in his grasp. Another cry as the head of the staff transformed itself into the demon's sharp-fanged face. Keehat moaned in pain as the staff seared his flesh. He tried to fling it away.

But the staff transformed itself into Keehat's lover. The king screamed when he saw that his woman/boy lover bore the head of the demon.

"Master!" the demon hissed in an ugly parody of passion. "Come into my embrace!"

And Keehat screamed again as his lover-slave leaped on him—burying his teeth in his throat.

Not one warrior rose to help as the youth wrapped both arms around Keehat and jumped over the side.

The men watched silently as the water boiled violently. Then there was stillness. Blood floated up to pool around the war canoe.

I heard one of the men say: "Good riddance."

And another said: "Let us call the others, my brothers. Our loved ones await us at home."

I felt a lurch, my vision clouded, and the next thing I knew, I found myself kneeling on the deck of Gamelan's cabin, retching into a bowl as he held my head and whispered soothing words.

When I was done, he groped about and found a cloth dampened with some sweet herb. I wiped my face.

"An excellent first effort," the wizard said with much satisfaction.

I didn't answer or protest. It did not make me happy, but there was no denying that Gamelan had just made a wizard of me.

I felt a bit like I imagined one of my sisters might feel if she had just become a whore.

The next day I sent out several boats to scout the area in every direction. There was no sign of the war canoes.

No one cheered. Because it was apparent to everyone in the fleet we were completely and hopelessly lost.

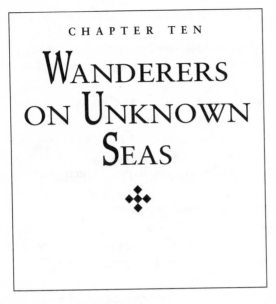

CHAPTER TEN

WANDERERS ON UNKNOWN SEAS

❖

Our disaster struck like a storm demon's hammer. It numbed all feeling, paralyzed all thought. I doubt there are few alive who know the true meaning of the world lost—or certainly who have known the despair. For most, to be lost means standing on a small circle of the Unknown, surrounded by an enormous Known. The correct path only awaits the aid of patience and luck. My brother once asked Janos Greycloak—who had experienced just about everything any traveler could encounter—if he'd ever been lost before. Greycloak, after some consideration, finally said: "No. But I admit to being bewildered for a month or two."

We were more than bewildered. Our very sanity was being shaken. The circle we sailed in was nothing but a vast Unknown. True, the creatures of the sea were mostly familiar. The ocean tasted just as brackish. The winds blew as they had before. The sun rose and set on the same schedule and from the same directions. Even a few of the stars were familiar, although so oddly placed, no navigator could use them to set a home course. These things did not soothe our guts, calm our lurching hearts, or offer even the most wispy of hopes.

For a time we were all frozen in that nightmare—although even that word is weak. Even nightmares offer the comfort of having visited their drear landscapes before. We did not look, much less think, of our fellows—but only stared out at the empty sea, knowing it was impossible for any wave that crossed under our bows to break on a familiar shore.

Numbing fear swept through the fleet like the plague. At first the sailors—and even my Guardswomen—were listless at their posts; barely hearing orders from their equally demoralized superiors, and what duties they did perform were perfunctory, halfhearted. Accidents and injuries increased, caused by lack of attention; petty squabbles erupted; friendships were tested; and lovers parted, seeking no others to fill the void.

It was Gamelan, our poor, blind wizard, who was the first to shake off the dread.

One day, just at dusk, Polillo, Corais, and I were slumped against the weather rail, not seeing, much less enjoying, a spectacular sunset. I was thinking bleak thoughts of Tries and home, while they carried on a desultory conversation.

"What happens when we die?" Polillo moaned. "Our bones won't know the ground they're buried in. And what of our ghosts? Will they be as lost as we are?"

Corais shook her head, her normally fiery eyes dull as poor steel. "I don't know," she said. "But I've heard that a soul can never find rest if it takes flight in such a place."

Gamelan's voice rasped at our backs. "Who told you that?" We turned, startled that he'd come on us unawares. He jabbed his blindman's stick in Corais' direction. "What fool has been lecturing you on the preferences of ghosts and souls?"

Corais sputtered: "I, uh . . . I don't, uh . . ."

"Speak up, woman," Gamelan snapped. "Name the jape."

"It was Master Klisura, if you must know," Corais shot back, recovering some of her missing spark. "He has an aunt who was washerwoman to a witch. Practically raised him—the aunt, I mean, not the witch. So, he's quite knowledgeable about such things."

Gamelan was disgusted. "Washerwoman to a witch, you say? Servant to a dog's mother, more likely." He rapped his stick on the deck. "It simply amazes me that where the spirit world is concerned, normally rock-solid people will listen to any nonsense from anyone. As long as the wisdom is purportedly from a creature with a warty nose and an addled manner, why, it *must* be so!" A sneer creased his beard. "What if I told you my father was fishmonger to an armorer's grocer? Does that make me expert on the soundness of shields and blades? Would you trust your life on my wisdom?"

Corais turned as scarlet as my brother's hair. She is not a woman who is easily rattled, and it pained me to see her so embarrassed.

"Leave her be, my friend," I broke in. "Corais didn't mean anything by it. She was only making conversation."

Gamelan was not calmed. "Conversation is just about all that has been made around here for some time," he snorted. "That and whimperings over our supposed fate. I wish we had let that savage catch us. At least I'd have some peace from all this mewling."

Polillo was caught by the same barrage fired at Corais. She slumped so much, she seemed to have lost a head in height.

I came to their rescue. "Don't you two have some armor that needs burnishing, or some blades that require sharpening?"

They leaped on this like kitchen mice on overripe cheese, babbled excuses and scurried away. I turned to the wizard, braced to become the sole object of his wrath.

Instead, he said, quite mildly: "What's to be done, Rali?"

I sighed. "What can be done? I'm not a navigator, much less a sailor—thank the good Maranonia, who has sense enough to leave the seas to gods who like to be wet, and actually prefer a smelly old fish over a nice charred calf's haunch."

My attempt at levity was met with an impatient rapping of Gamelan's stick against the deck. "You are the leader of this expedition, woman. Speak as such."

Stung, I lashed back: "How can I lead, when I don't know where we're going? If the admiral and his officers are mired, what can I do to get us unstuck?"

Gamelan laughed. "Why, lie, of course! All good leaders have a trunkful of untruths. It's time you started rummaging in yours. True, our problems are many. But as I see it, they can all wait until we tackle the most important two. And of these, the least important at this juncture is the route home."

"If we knew that," I snapped, "we wouldn't even be having this discussion."

"Agreed. However, if everyone gives up hope of finding our way, then it becomes a fact for lack of trying. And we are doomed to making a poor life among strangers who have so far proved to be most unfriendly. We'll either be killed, enslaved, or—for your Guardswomen—forced to be concubines or wives."

"I can't quarrel with that," I said. "But what lie could I possibly tell that would put steel back in their spines? And why would they believe the lie? I'm a soldier, not a miracle maker."

Gamelan made no reply. He only rapped on the deck with that damned stick of his.

I groaned. "Not again, wizard. You can't make me something I'm not.

And don't say that I've already proven my talents. And don't shine any of that grandfatherly charm on me, so I start spilling deep dark secrets all over the floor like a trooper on a wine binge. I've had enough, you hear?"

A flying fish broke the surface. It skimmed across the sea a startling distance. Where its flight began, I saw the dark shape of its enemy. The wizard asked me what was happening, and I told him of the remarkable fish.

"Now, there is a creature," Gamelan said, "who made good use of its fear. It grew wings."

He turned away and started rapping his way back across the deck.

"All right," I called after him. "I take your point. If only to stop your nagging, I'll do as you ask. What trick would you have me perform this time?"

Gamelan turned back. "I'll want more than just a trick or two, my dear Rali. We can't feed the fleet with a single baited hook. You're going to have to set out the entire net."

It was on that day I truly began the practice of magic. Because for the first time, I learned to treat it as it really is—a grand entertainment, and no more. And I tell you this, there is little difference between the greatest Evocator and the meanest bacchanal faker. It's all smoke and mirrors, Scribe. Don't stretch a long, disapproving face at me. As you shall see, Gamelan was the first to admit it.

What the old wizard had in mind was a lavish ceremony, with as much splendor and excitement as someone of my limited knowledge could muster. The ceremony must be staged at just the right moment—when we could make some poor scrap of luck seem a banquet.

First, we began a grinding, daily routine of magical lessons. The first thing I learned was that sorcery is hard work. The second thing I learned was, although Gamelan insisted I had much natural talent, I certainly didn't have any natural enthusiasm to go with it. I'm afraid I grumbled more than a little—so much so that Polillo and the others made excuses to sail clear of my course whenever I'd completed a lesson.

"I'm trying to teach you as much as I can, as fast as I can," Gamelan said one day. "But we're going to have to jump past all the rules and spell-memorizing that apprentices normally have to go through. It's probably just as well, for I fear that after Janos Greycloak's discoveries, all of those things will soon be considered old-fashioned at the best, and unnecessary and even harmful at the worst."

We were sitting in his cramped cabin, fiddling with the small details of our preparations for the ceremony. At his bidding, I'd conjured up Gamelan's kitchen demon and set him to work mixing powders, sewing magical cloth, and grinding little mirrors to specifications Gamelan had me find in a fat old book with a cracked black cover that felt warm when you touched it, as if it were a living thing. It was, of course, no ordinary book. When you opened the covers, the pages were a swirl of color and letters and phrases that didn't seem to stick to one place but leaped all over, and scurried to the next leaf when you turned it. They only took form of a sort when you spoke a word, indicating what you were looking for. Say "demon," for instance, and the pages would flip madly in first one direction, then another, and little green creatures—bearing what appeared to be miniature fire beads—would leap out, squealing to be recognized. "Look here for conjuring ardor in your lover, great lady," one might squeak. Or, "Cursing enemies, our specialty, mistress." Or even, "Housebreaking your Favorite guaranteed." When you settled on the category, the creature whose wares you'd chosen would snarl at his fellows to cow them, then crawl onto the page you wanted. He'd lift the fire beads and you'd see letters scurrying all about like ants gone mad from dry thunder. At his squeaked orders, they'd form up and reveal their message. Give the order—"speak"—and they'd even read themselves aloud.

When Gamelan reminded me of Greycloak, I was trying for the tenth time to follow the book's directions for snatching ribbon out of empty air. It's done like this, Scribe. Watch. First I crook my fingers so. Then I make a motion as if tying a knot. Then I push my fingers together like this, and . . . See. Ribbon. Bright red ribbon. Here's some more. You take one end and pull. Keep pulling. Sorry, I know you can't write and pull at the same time. But you see how easy it seems. And there's at least a mile of the stuff in whatever place it exists, so you could pull for a long time before it comes to an end. But even such a simple trick isn't easy when you're starting out. So I was all fumble-fingered, turning out only knotted twine, and that of the cheapest sort. Since that trick was failing me, I thought I'd try the old ploy of the lazy student—engaging your teacher in a subject dear to his heart, thereby escaping an hour or so of work.

"As you know," I said, "I am not among those who admire Janos Greycloak. He betrayed my brother, after all, and nearly slew him. But Amalric claims that the magical secrets he's bequeathed to us outweigh his failings, and all Orissa is obligated to sing his praises on his death day."

"That is certainly the view of my fellow Evocators," the wizard answered, but his tone was bitter.

Interested, I forgot this was only a conversational trick—idle talk to win me idle time. "You don't share that view?" I pressed.

"Oh, certainly I do," he answered. "Greycloak's gift was greater than any in history. Equal, at least, to the first man who made fire and shared it with his fellows. From Janos we know there are laws to magic. And with that knowledge there is little we cannot accomplish, given time and experimentation."

"I hear words of praise, my friend," I said. "But I sense you don't really believe them."

"Oh, I do," Gamelan said. "If you hear otherwise, you are mistaken."

I remained silent.

Finally, he sighed. "Very well. I'll admit that in weak moments—especially since I lost my powers—I hate Janos Greycloak for his gift. But it is only envy. When I was young, and denied the life I was born to and the woman I loved, I traded ambition for the contentment I would never have. I was determined to be the greatest Evocator in Orissa."

"And this you became," I said.

"Yes," he said. "Except for Greycloak. But the distance between his achievement and mine is as vast as the watery wilderness we find ourselves in. I am a mewling babe compared to Janos."

"Come, now," I said. "All know the extent of your powers. Without you, we never would have defeated the Archons."

"Even if that were true," he said, "it would be no comfort. You see, before Greycloak, we practiced magic as it had been done since the first spell was cast in the days when even fire was new. Successful spells were memorized and passed on to acolytes. When writing was learned, we put them in books, such as the one you have before you. Not once did anyone ask *why* a thing worked. We believed the results were the doings of the gods in the spirit world, and that was answer enough.

"Knowledge can never grow in a field absent of questions. I know that now. But I did not know it before. All that could be accomplished in those times were better twists on an old trick. Or, refinement of a trick. Power was limited to native-born ability. Which I had in plenty—more so than my fellows, at least."

"But what of the wizards of Irayas?" I asked. "The magic of the Far Kingdoms, as all know, is much greater than ours. They progressed mightily—without Janos Greycloak's laws."

Gamelan snorted. "That's only because they found old scrolls and books from the Ancients. The things they have accomplished do not come from wisdom, but tricks lost to us over the ages."

"I don't call changing common metal to gold a trick," I said. "They can do that in the Far Kingdoms."

The wizard tugged hard at his beard. "According to Greycloak—or at least the musings your brother returned with—it's no less a trick than conjuring up that ribbon which at the moment is giving you so much difficulty. If you know the law for how one is accomplished, you can do the other with equal ease. Janos claimed there is a single *natural* force—and not gods—that controls magic, and indeed, all else in our everyday world . . . heat from a fire, the flow of water, the stuff that makes up gold—particles, he called it—is the same as conjuring a wart off a nose, or commanding the rain to fall or cease."

"I don't understand," I said.

"But you will," Gamelan answered. "The more I teach you, the more apparent it will become."

"Then why are you envious?" I asked. "Seems to me that what you're saying is Greycloak freed everyone from rote, and much greater things can be done—things even *he* never dreamed of—with that freedom."

"Quite true," Gamelan said. "But consider this. Consider a young wizard who in the rebellious years of his youth glimpsed for a moment what Greycloak saw clear. But then he thought he was a fool for even thinking that. How could he know more than his teachers, his masters, or the ancient Evocators who had passed down their wisdom?"

"Are you saying that you could have unraveled the same mysteries as Greycloak?" I asked.

"No. Even I am not that conceited. A genius like Janos comes only once in many lifetimes, if at all. But still, it haunts me that such could be so."

"Other discoveries await," I said. "Even Greycloak's most enthusiastic admirers say what he found is only a beginning."

"Yes," Gamelan said. "Which just makes me more envious. All the discoveries that follow will be made by young men and women who will not be burdened by a lifetime of wrong thinking. I'm too old, Rali. And now I'm blind as well. What's worse, to an ancient like myself, is that when Janos made the Gift—no matter how involuntarily—he took away my gods. For that is at the heart of his teachings. The gods—if even they exist—are bound by the same laws as the most common beggar at the door of the meanest tavern keeper in the land."

Shocked, I said: "What do you mean *if* the gods exist? Do you doubt it?"

The wizard shrugged. "They have appeared too many times in our history to actually doubt them," he said. "And not just to fools and liars, but men and women whose word cannot be doubted. However, if what Janos Greycloak suspects is true, they aren't gods, at least by what we mean by the word—which implies reverence, and worship."

I looked wildly about for a place to hide when the lighting bolt struck—a bit like you are this moment, Scribe. But none fell. I calmed myself.

"If they aren't gods," I said, "then what in whoever's name I ought to evoke just now is our purpose? Whose will, whose plan, are we following?"

And the wizard answered: "According to Greycloak, there is no purpose. Our will is our own. And there is no plan, save what we make for our own lives."

"But what of good and evil?" I sputtered.

"No difference," Gamelan said.

"Then what's the use? Why not just give up?"

"Do you want to?" Gamelan asked. "Greycloak believed it doesn't matter one way or the other."

But it mattered to my Guardswomen, I thought. It mattered even to the slippery Cholla Yi and his crew of pirates. Most importantly, it mattered to me.

I shook my head. Then, remembering he couldn't see, I said, quite loud. "No. And be damned to Janos Greycloak."

Gamelan laughed harshly. "He very well might be . . . if he was wrong."

He lifted up his stick and rapped the deck. "Now, back to work. And put your *mind* to it, woman. If you were as lazy in your sword practice as you are with simple ribbon pulling, your head would have been hoisted on a pike long ago!"

SEVERAL WEEKS PASSED before we were ready. Even then, both of us would have preferred more time; but the mood in the fleet remained so draped in miasma that any spark we might light would be smothered if we waited much longer. Gamelan had me practice casting the bones each morning. I'd describe their pattern, and he would tell me if they boded good or ill. Mainly, they seemed to fall in a shape that Gamelan said predicted neither, but urged us to wait instead. I found the whole bone-casting thing vaguely humiliating.

"It's all very well for you," I told Gamelan. "You're an Evocator. You even *look* like an Evocator. Dignified, gray-bearded, the very image of stern wisdom. No one would dare think you were silly, dropping a bunch of smelly old bones on the deck, then kneeling over the filthy things, staring, and mumbling and twisting your beard. But I look like—well, *me*, dammit! Not particularly wise, certainly not dignified, and the last time I checked, my body is free of hair every place but one, and that makes a very short beard, indeed."

"If you're saying a woman lacks the necessary demeanor to be an Evocator," Gamelan said, "then I suppose we had best give up the whole thing."

"I didn't say that!"

"That's what I *heard*. And now that I think on it, perhaps this whole thing is ridiculous. Perhaps the women haters are correct. Perhaps it *is* true that your sex lacks the same mental powers as men, and, I must admit . . . without a beard, you probably—"

"Give me those damned bones," I snarled. I grabbed them from his hand and tossed. "I still think this is stupid. From what you were saying about Greycloak and his laws of magic, bone-throwing makes no sense at all. How can a future be predicted, if there is no godlike plan to spy out? In fact, this whole exercise seems like one big—"

"What is it, Rali?" Gamelan asked.

"The bones," I said.

"What about the bones?"

"I don't know, they . . . look *good*. I can't explain why. They just do!"

I described the pattern. Gamelan laughed. "You are exactly right! Bright dawns are ahead, my friend. Bright dawns, indeed."

And that is how I became a bone caster. One moment I was an ignorant, the next a sage.

An hour later I heard the lookout halloo—an island had been sighted. Excitement fired the fleet. The island was a poor, rocky-shored thing with a slender pebbled beach hugging a few tired peaks. But any land at all stirred thoughts of home and hope. A scouting party was quickly sent out, and it reported the island was uninhabited, but seemed to offer some food and drink. We went ashore, leaving only a skeleton crew on the ships.

The gleeful mood, however, was short-lived. Within moments of landing, a cold, sticky mist enveloped us. There was little vegetation, and all of that sickly. What trees there were, bore only a few bitter-tasting nuts. Stringy birds mocked us from the peaks with cries as harsh as a fishmonger. The water was drinkable, but barely. It came from a half-dozen steaming pools circling a small geyser that sat at the base of one of the squat peaks. The geyser fountained intermittently and weakly—rising only as far as my head.

I stood near the geyser, alone save for my blind wizard friend, thinking dark thoughts of magic and bone-casting in general. If this was the new luck that had been foretold, it was a mean-spirited thing. I heard cursing from a large knot of sailors who had gathered at one of the pools to fill casks with the foul-smelling water. I didn't blame them for the cursing—they were only voicing my own thoughts—but I became alarmed when I saw Cholla Yi and some of his officers standing nearby. The admiral was normally such a harsh master, no one would dare complain in his presence.

One of the sailors—a big burly fellow with a bloated, pillow of a nose—dipped up water, drank, then spit it out with an oath. "Whore's piss," he said in a voice so loud that only a crop-eared thief could have missed it. He flung the dipper down. "They got us drinking whore's piss now, mates. And if that ain't enough, they're making us fill our holds wi' it so's we'll know what fine lads they think we be f'r weeks t' come."

One of his companions, a tall, skeletal villain with a chin as sharp as a dagger, spoke up just as loudly. "It ain't gonna change 'long as that big bitch is givin' th' orders."

He turned and looked directly at me, as did the others. Cholla Yi and his officers strolled away as if they'd heard nothing. I heard him laugh at something Phocas said, and then they disappeared behind a jumble of rock. All the men were looking at me now, bold as you please. Without another word being exchanged between them, their hands went to the knives at their belts.

Sensing danger, Gamelan tugged at my sleeve and whispered: "We had best go."

I knew we'd never take ten steps before those knives were in our backs. I was ready to draw my sword and make a fight of it, and even went so far as to shift my stance, when my boot glanced against a hard object. I looked down, meaning to kick away anything that might tangle my feet, and saw an empty conch shell—the size of a child's head. A feeling of great calm descended. My blood was hot—not with the fighting rage I'd bent to my will long ago, but with a kind of power that was more like a river charging through a narrow course.

Instead of drawing my blade, I bent and picked up the shell.

I spoke to Gamelan, but made my voice loud enough for all to hear. "Here's another conch, my friend. I'll bet a fat purse of gold against a thin copper coin that its flesh is as sweet as its brother's."

Gamelan's brow wrinkled. "What are you—" He stopped abruptly. "Oh." I pressed the shell into his hands, and he quickly felt its shape. Then, raising his voice as well: "Yes, it is another. I'm sure it'll be just as good as that last one we found not an hour ago." He smacked his lips. "Delicious. And do you know, its flavor quite reminds me of a rare shellfish our cooks used to serve up on feast days in Orissa. Food fit for the gods themselves."

I looked at the men, widening my eyes as if I'd just noted their presence. Then I made my features stern and called out to them in my best commander's voice.

"You there. Stop what you're doing and come here at once."

They were so startled their hands fell away from their knives. I motioned to them, impatient. "Be quick about it, men. We've a hungry crew to feed."

They stumbled forward, stiff as a rich child's mechanical toy. But before they reached me, Pillow Nose had begun to swagger and he and his skinny companion moved to the front.

I gestured at the shell. "Start collecting these," I ordered. "You can use some empty water casks to put them in for now." The men gaped at me. "Don't dally. Do as I said. I'll make it right with your officers, so you needn't worry about that."

Pillow Nose sneered. "Why'd anyone want a cask of old shells?" he said. He turned to his friends. "She'll be havin' us stewin' rocks next." The men laughed, but there was a deadly edge to it.

"Don't talk foolishness, man," I retorted. "These are delicious."

I plucked his knife from his belt quicker than he could blink. I plunged the knife into the shell, willing it to find life. I imagined a tidal pool, teaming with all sorts of swimming and crawling things. I felt something flinch under the blade. I dug in and scooped up, and out came a fat animal—thick and squirming on the knife.

"Wait a moment, and you'll see for yourself," I said.

I knelt by the edge of the geyser and plunged the speared flesh into the steaming water. I thought of a pungent fish stew my mother used to make. And in my mind the sulfurous water was that rich stew, which I was using as a broth to cook the shellfish. I had no doubt at all when, after a few seconds, I rose again and dumped the meat on a flat rock. Quickly I sliced it into many pieces. An enticing odor filled the air.

I speared a piece with the knife and took a bite. "Mmm," I sighed in real delight. "Just like my mother's best dish." I wasn't lying. It really did taste that good. I speared another hunk and held out to Pillow Nose. "Try it," I said.

The sneer was gone as he took his knife. The others crowded about him. "Go on, Santh," his skinny friend urged. "Give it a try."

Pillow Nose—or Santh—popped the flesh into his mouth and chewed. Instantly a look of delight widened that great nose across his face. "Why, it's good," he exclaimed.

"Looks like enough for everyone to have a bite," I said, indicating the sliced-up morsels.

They all jostled forward, grabbing what they could, and practically licked the rock clean.

"You say there're more of these about, Captain?" Pillow Nose asked. There was grudging respect in his tone.

"We've only found one other," I lied. "But there's certain to be many more. I was just consulting with Lord Gamelan, on how best to find where they breed."

As soon as I said this, my confidence weakened. How could I possibly accomplish what I'd just all but promised?

Sensing my distress, Gamelan stroked his beard, looking wise. "Give me the shell, Captain," he said.

I handed it to him, and the men stood in respectful silence as the old wizard turned it this way and that. He gave it back to me.

"Put it to your ear, Captain Antero," he said, "and *listen*."

I covered my puzzlement, and—wishing all the while I had a beard to stroke so I could at least look as if I knew what I was doing—I put the shell to my ear. I only heard the familiar sea noises we all hear from the first time we try this trick as children.

"I didn't know fish talked," I heard Pillow Nose's skinny friend say in some awe.

I wanted very badly to reply: Neither did I, brother. Neither did I.

Then I remembered one of Gamelan's first lessons on spell-casting.

"I can't teach you all the spells in so short a time," he'd said. "The best ones fill many volumes on many shelves. Instead, I'll tell you what the young wizards—the followers of the late Janos Greycloak—advise. They claim that the words used to form a spell are not important. That they only serve to focus your energies. And I must admit there is truth to what they say. At my great age, I couldn't swear that the words I say are memorized spells or created by me on the spot. They just come to me when I need them."

"That's no help to the likes of me," I replied. "Words are *your* profession, wizard. Not mine."

"If you listen closely, Rali," he said, "the words you require will come."

"Listen?" I asked. "Listen to whom?"

"To yourself, my friend. To yourself."

So I held the shell to my ear, and listened. At first there was only the sea noises, and the slow hammer of my heart. Then a chill fingered my spine as I heard a voice. It came from within. Words rose like hot ash, and I opened my lips and let them spew out:

"Sand and spume,
Rock and sea flower;
I bear my shield
As I bear my home:
In the tidal bower
Where the sun last touches."

I raised my head to see the sun's position. I pointed. "There," I said. "Just beyond those rocks you'll find a small beach, and just off it, the place where our briny cousins make their homes."

There was no doubt in the men's minds as they cheered, grabbed the water casks and trooped off in the direction I pointed. Gamelan and I followed. Sure enough, there was a beach and tidal pool with hundreds of shellfish. I bade the men to call the others, and soon the beach was crowded with hungry men and women, scooping, scraping, and netting until the whole shore was covered with food.

Someone started a big driftwood fire and heaped it with seaweed. Clams and mussels and conches and even a few score crabs were tossed onto the weed, and the delicious steaming smell made our cares seem small.

Gamelan tapped his way to me. I thought he was going to congratulate me on my spell-casting. Instead he tugged at my sleeve and said: "Tonight, Rali. You must speak to them tonight. There may not be a better time."

And so that night I gave my maiden performance as an Evocator.

I ordered the crew and my Guardswomen to gather at the place where I'd found the conch shell. The site was Gamelan's idea, saying the atmosphere of steaming pools and bubbling geyser would help make the audience vulnerable.

It was a sullen group that gathered before me. The high spirits I'd invoked with my conjuring had been short-lived. The food I'd found had only been enough for that one meal—the tide pools had been scraped clean. There would be nothing to carry away from the island except the foul-tasting water. Cholla Yi had been opposed to the ceremony, saying there was little to cheer about and it would only make his crew angry. But Gamelan quelled him by saying, quite sternly, was he refusing to honor the gods?

I stood on a large boulder next to the geyser so all could see. Gamelan was at my side to coax me and whisper directions if I should need them. I quickly cast the spell he'd taught that magnified my voice, then I began. I opened with a short and highly dramatic account of our adventures thus far, stressing our accomplishments. I spoke of our defeat of Lycanth, and our holy mission to hunt down the escaped Archon. I praised them for the heroism they'd shown in the sea battle, which had ended in the defeat of our dark enemy. Finally, I talked of the great gift the gods had bestowed upon us by allowing us to escape the terrible upheaval of the sea. Some of the men grew angry, shouting that it was no blessing, but bad luck. Ill luck, they said, that was my fault for bringing the curse of the Archon upon them.

"How dare you offend the gods so?" I thundered. My voice echoed and resounded against the rocks, startling even me. "You are alive, aren't you? Is not that fact alone gift enough? And as for lost, why, that is a temporary condition. We have all been given a chance of a lifetime by the great god of seekers everywhere—Te-Date! Do you dare question our mighty Lord?"

Fear of blasphemy silenced them.

"No one in all our history has sailed these seas," I went on. "For countless generations our people have wondered what mysteries and riches awaited in the vast regions beyond the western edges of our world. You all know that my brother, Amalric Antero, along with the mighty and wise Janos Greycloak, unraveled the secrets of the East by finding the legendary Far Kingdoms. Many adventurers have wept since that time, crying there was nothing new to be discovered. Well, here is your chance. Here is the opportunity of a hundred lifetimes. What we learn here shall be carried back to our hearths and homes. Our names will be written on the Stones of Greatness for all to see and marvel over in the eons to come. And others will weep, my friends. Weep in helpless jealousy that they were not here to share our great adventure!"

I saw smiles and heard cheery mutterings for the first time in many a mournful day. And now that I'd hooked them, as Gamelan said, it was time to gaff them into the creel.

Calling on Te-Date and Maranonia, I commenced the show the wizard and I had planned. I threw a small pouch on the ground, causing a loud explosion to erupt. My audience gasped in wonder as colorful smoke swirled. I tossed small mirrors into the smoke and they burst upward, shattering into more pieces than there were stars in the night sky. Another explosion, and they shattered again, then rained gently down, glittering with color, then melting into small droplets as they touched any surface, creating the most wonderful perfume. Then I performed the ribbon trick, and this time there was no fumbling or twine-making. Ribbons red and green and gold shot out from my fingers, wove themselves into filmy veils that caught the wind and swirled all around us like magical kites.

Gamelan and I had decided the next trick would be an even greater blast than the first, causing an enormous pillar of red smoke to rise up. Then I would call upon the gods to bless us in our adventures, and to stay by our sides until they came to a happy and fruitful end. I took out the pouch of ingredients I'd mixed at the wizard's direction. It was fatter than the first, so as to make a larger display. But as I was about to hurl it down, something stopped me. I felt a ghostlike hand on my arm nudging me to turn. When I saw the bubbling geyser, a voice whispered in my ear, directing me. I threw the pouch into the steaming pool.

Instead of an explosion, a horn larger and louder than any mortal has ever seen trumpeted. The geyser shot up twice a tall woman's height and whirled like a desert dervish. It was a cacophony of vivid colors. Other music joined the trumpet; drums and strings and pipes all blended into a wondrous sound. The pools surrounding the geyser burst up like their mother, whirling about in a wild dance to the music of the ghostly players.

As quickly as they'd erupted they fell and became calm pools of blue. I looked and saw that the geyser had taken on a similar hue, except it reflected our forms as well as any palace mirror. The music stopped. Not even a hiss from the geyser marred the perfect silence.

A voice welled up in me. And this I swear on my mother's ghost was a voice that was not directed by me, or any wizardly tricks. I listened, as if I was another, as the words boomed from my lips. "O Great Te-Date. Protector of the wanderer. Lord of horizons yet breached, all mysteries yet revealed. Grant us this boon. Wither do we sail, O Lord? In which direction is our destiny, our weir?"

The whirling geyser took solid form, and a vision appeared on its mirrored surface. It was our fleet sailing across smooth seas. At its lead was my ship, the flag of Maranonia fluttering in the breeze. And we were sailing west, chasing the setting sun.

The vision vanished and the geyser collapsed into a hissing pool.

I turned back to my audience, overflowing with joy. I spoke again, except this time the words were my own.

"There is our answer, my friends. Te-Date has pointed the way home. We sail west! And praise be Te-Date, we will be lost no more!"

Cheering erupted. The rocky glen echoed with their cries. Some laughed and pounded the backs of their fellows. Other were so overcome they wept. My women, caught by the truth of the moment, cheered more loudly than any.

But as for me, a great weariness shook my knees. I collapsed on the rock and all was blackness.

When I awoke, I was aboard the ship and we were at full sail, skimming across the seas under a brisk wind. I was in Gamelan's small cabin, and when I opened my eyes, he was dusting my brow with a cloth dipped in a sweet-smelling healing powder.

He smiled when he sensed my eyes fluttering open. "Ah, you are with us again, my friend," he said. "How do you feel?"

I started to rise, but my limbs were so weak I gave it up. "I feel like I just lost three falls out of three," I said. "But that's to be expected, I suppose. Being new to the conjuring arts and all. A few more hours rest will put me right."

"I should hope so," the wizard chortled. "You've already slept for nearly a week."

Stunned, I groaned up to a sitting position. "A week? How could you let me stay here so long? By Te-Date, there's things to do. Plans to be laid. Training to—"

Gamelan's continuing laughter made me cut short my babbling. "They just don't make Evocators like they used to," he said. "Why, in my youth we acolytes were expected to preside over a blessing before breakfast, and heal half a hundred before the bell rang us to tenth hour abasements."

"Stuff a batskin muff in it, wizard," I growled.

Gamelan turned serious. "I must admit you frightened me with your extemporaneous bit of future-casting. Calling on oracles can be quite dangerous, especially for an ignorant beginner."

I shrugged. "It worked, didn't it? The gods were kind enough to point our way home. We sail west, to find Orissa."

Gamelan shook his head. "Not necessarily," he said.

"Listen here," I said, a little hot. "The vision clearly showed us sailing west."

"Obviously, I couldn't see the vision you conjured up," Gamelan answered. "But although I'm blind, my hearing is quite sound, thank you very much. And I clearly *heard* you ask in which direction our *destinies* lay. You said nothing at all about finding Orissa. In fact, I know of no spell that would accomplish such a thing. If there were, I would have had you conjuring up a map or two long ago."

In a weaker voice I asked: "Then west is not the way home?"

"Who can say?" Gamelan answered. "Perhaps our fates and our wishes coincide. Perhaps by sailing west—which we know, broadly speaking, is the opposite direction from Orissa—we'll meet someone who knows the way. Or perhaps we'll encounter some swift current, or passage, that will carry us home."

"Then I accomplished nothing," I said, feeling a total dolt and failure.

"Oh, but that is certainly not so," Gamelan protested. "The others made the same mistake you did. Or at least believed your interpretation of the vision. Everyone is convinced you showed them the way. No sooner had I ordered you carried back to my cabin than your legates gathered with Cholla Yi and his officers and it was decided to strike west at once."

Hastily, I rose up from the bunk. They'd stripped me when they'd put me in bed, and I was wearing nothing but a frown. "Where are my clothes?" I demanded. "I must stop the fleet at once! We could very well be going the wrong way!"

Gamelan grabbed my arm and pulled me back. "Don't be foolish," he hissed. "You have succeeded more than we could have ever dreamed. The fleet is overflowing with confidence, a commodity in short supply these last days. You've put steel in their spines, Rali, and hope in their hearts."

"But it's a lie!" I protested.

"Only you and I know that," the wizard said. "And perhaps it isn't a lie after all. Only the gods know our true course. It may end happily after all. One thing I know for certain—if you tell them the truth, they'll hate you for it. Things will be even worse than before. And if that should happen, there's no chance at all that we'll ever find our way home again."

I sank back on the bunk, pulling a blanket about me, for I suddenly felt very cold. "What should I do?" I moaned.

"Do nothing," Gamelan said. "Just keep a smile on your lips, and if asked, lie again. And keep on lying. If fortune blesses us, the lie may yet meet the truth."

I WAS WELL ENOUGH to leave my sickbed the following day. Everyone greeted me with such huge enthusiasm, fawning, making sure I had the best morsel of whatever food we had, or rushing to do my slightest bidding, that I felt a complete scoundrel. But I did as Gamelan advised, and only smiled and choked out modest remarks regarding my renewed status as heroine to all. Whenever necessary, I shored up the falsehood I'd created back on the dismal isle.

It got easier as the days went by, because we were the sudden recipients of good luck. Every day was sunny and the winds fair. Our little fleet leaped over the waves, chasing the sun into the most marvelous sunsets anyone had seen in their lifetimes. The sea teemed with more fish than we could eat. And the day I arose, we encountered an island entirely populated by enormous birds—nearly half again as tall as Polillo—that were not only wingless, but so dumb they let you approach and club them down without protest. Their drumsticks were enormous and tasty, and the white meat of their breasts better than any delicate fowl I'd ever nibbled. We filled our meat casks with their flesh—both smoked and brined. We found sweet water on that island that rivaled any liquor we'd ever drunk. We emptied the sulfurous stuff we'd collected on the geyser island, scrubbed the barrels, and filled them all to the brim.

So good was our luck during those days that it became the norm—the expected. I guess childishness is at the heart of all our natures. Set the most sumptuous banquet before us, and we will marvel at it, revel in the myriad tastes in almost sexual ecstasy. But serve that same banquet every day, and soon we'll begin whining: "What's this? Honeyed hummingbird tongue—again?" And so it was with my fellow adventurers. The wind was the best any sailor could hope for, but Captain Stryker complained it was so constant he never had time to repair the sails. Duban the rowing master griped that his charges were getting soft. The quartermasters were upset that the rat population had increased because our holds were full of fresh food; Ismet worried the soldiers were exercising with such enthusiasm they might become overtrained; and my officers fretted that something must be amiss because it was not possible for morale to be as good as it seemed.

I did not fall prey to this weakness—not because I am any less petty than my sisters and brothers, but because I knew all was false to begin with.

Then the winds died; and with them our luck.

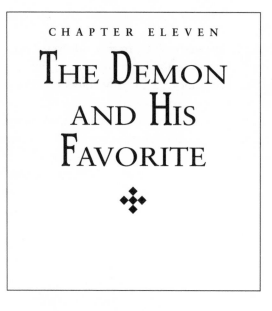

CHAPTER ELEVEN

THE DEMON AND HIS FAVORITE

❖

O n the day our luck vanished, I awoke just after dawn with a blinding headache. It was hot for such an early hour and I felt short of breath. The air was thick, syrupy. It had an odor of damp things, old things, and things long in death or slow in dying. I heard the sails being lowered and stowed. Duban cursed his rowers onto their benches. The drum sounded— increasing the pressure on my throbbing temples—and there was a shudder as the ship pulled slowly forward. It moved with difficulty, as if the water had turned to mud, and I heard things rasping along the sides. I groaned up and stumbled into my clothes. As I passed Polillo's hammock to go up on deck, I heard a piteous moan—I was not the only sufferer that dreaded morning.

A bizarre scene awaited me above decks. The light was a murky yellow that blurred detail; our shadows seemed bloated and indistinct. The rowers, working to a slow drumbeat, grunted at their task, rising completely off their benches with each stroke, then digging in hard with their heels as they mus-cled the oars through the water. Despite their labors, the ship only inched along.

The trouble was apparent. The ship—nay, the entire fleet—was mired in a vast waste of kelp. On other ships I could see men dangling from the sides on ropes, cutting away fleshy vines that'd snared them. Captain Stryker was gathering a similar work party as I approached to ask what had gone amiss.

"It's not my fault," he growled, surprising me that he thought there was anything to defend. "I said there was gonna to be a squall last night, an' Klisura agreed, but would th' admiral listen to th' likes of us? Me, who's got so many years in th' salt you could stuff me in a brine barrel and sell me for provisions? Why, I was a sailin' master before that damned Phocas was a wet spot on his father's prong, if you'll be beggin' my pardon, Captain Antero. But th' admiral, he just listens to that ignorant son of a Lycanthian whore. Pays no mind when I says we oughta heave to, drop our sea anchors and wait'll she's done."

The squall had awakened me during the night, but it hadn't seemed too fierce. Actually, it soothed me and I'd been easily coaxed back to sleep by the slow rolling of the ship, while listening to the sounds of the falling rain and hissing seas. As I listened to Stryker I remembered earlier days when the smallest chop sent the landlubbers among us running to spew our guts over the rail. I nearly laughed, covered with a cough, then put on my best Concern for My Fellow Officer visage.

"You saw danger in the storm, I gather?" I asked.

"Any fool coulda seen it," Stryker said. "Wasn't th' strength of th' winds that troubled me, but th' visibility. Rain was fallin' thicker'n my oldest wife's curses when I'm late from th' tavern. An' it was th' blackest night I'd seen since I was a lad just gone raidin' off th' Pepper Coast. I was fearful we'd lose each other in th' blow, or worse, come up against some reef in th' dark. Best thing to do, I signaled th' admiral, was wait it out and take new bearings in th' morning. But Phocas was all for makin' time, an' Cholla Yi agreed. Time to get where? I ask you. Don't even know where we're goin'! Anyways, we stuck together, although I had to practically mutiny to get 'em to hang out lanterns so's we could see each other. Then th' wind quit quicker'n a whore hauls in her tits when she sees you got an empty purse. Ain't been a breath of wind since. But that's not so bad. What's bad is what we got ourselves tangled into."

He waved at the kelp forest, so thick that in places you couldn't see water, but only a slow rising and falling as waves passed underneath.

"Never seen a thing like it," he said. "Not this size and this thick! But I've heard tales. Oh, yes, I've heard things that'd get your heart movin' right sprightly."

"I'm sure you have, Captain Stryker," I said. "But I hope you keep those tales to yourself until we're out of this. No sense frightening people unnecessarily."

"If we *do* get out," Stryker said darkly.

I paid no mind to his gloomy words. He was only trying to add drama to the wrong that'd been done him and what had come of Cholla Yi ignoring his sensible advice.

"We'll be all right," he said, relenting to reveal his true thoughts. "Just need us another good blow and we'll be out and smellin' sweet."

But we didn't get another good blow. Not a breath of air stirred that day, or the next, or for many a day to follow. And it was *hot*! By the gods who forsook us yet again, it was hot. The yellow haze that cloaked us only seemed to intensify that heat, making us feel we were simmering at the bottom of a soup kettle. Meanwhile, the kelp prison tightened about us. We found what seemed to be a channel leading out, cut our way to it, then muscled each ship into the passage. But that channel, instead of carrying us out, led us into a maze of dead ends and narrows that curved back on themselves, and others that went deeper and deeper into that tangle. We had no choice but to go on, for no sooner had we hacked a passage and rowed through it, then it closed behind us, with the kelp quickly tangling itself again.

I cast the bones each day, but they had returned to the stultifying sameness as before. No matter how hard I tried, no matter how I cast them, the identical pattern showed up again and again. And that pattern, Gamelan had taught, showed no change in our near future. As the crew labored in the awful heat, dragging us foot by foot through the watery forest, Gamelan and I tried every trick the old wizard knew to raise a wind.

We got out the magical wind bags that'd been brought along for just this purpose. They were the best Gamelan and his assistant Evocators could create before we left Lycanth. Much magical talent had gone into them, but all for naught. Each time I performed the ceremony and recited the words to call forth the winds, when the bag was opened, only a hot, foul-smelling gas escaped. Gamelan worried over this, saying a spell must have been cast over this immense sargasso to assure no wind could ever disturb its horrible symmetry.

The deeper we drew into it, however, the more it changed. What had first appeared like a gently rolling plain soon proved a false perception. Once in the canals, the seaweed piled higher and higher, in places forming banks that reached half the height of a ship's mast. The kelp branches were tumbled into all kinds of odd shapes. Some appeared to be the turrets of a fleshy, brown-toned castle. Others took on the images of people, or beasts. I passed one I swore looked like a woman's torso growing out of a rearing mare's body. Astride that mare was a young woman, breasts heaving, tresses flying, as if she and her steed were moving at speed. Polillo said I was only seeing such things because I'd been too long without a lover. I laughed, but secretly worried she was right.

A week into our struggle we broke into a channel whose current moved more swiftly. It was still a leisurely pace, to be sure, but to see any motion at all in this swamp was a cheery sight. The joy, however, was short-lived. It was Santh—old Pillow Nose himself—who ended it. One minute I was conversing with Stryker, the next we were running forward, beckoned by Santh's hoarse cry. We had to push our way through a knot of crewmen to reach him at the bow, where he stood pale and jabbering nonsense.

"What is it, man?" Stryker said.

But Santh was too hysterical to respond. "May th' gods forgive me," he wailed. "I've been such a villain all me life, but no man deserves t' die like this!"

Stryker grabbed him roughly by the shirtfront. "Quit blubberin', you fool," he barked. "You ain't dead. And you ain't got no cause to fear it."

Santh recovered enough to jab a shaking finger to his right. "Look, Captain," he cried. "Look!"

We peered in the direction he pointed. I saw something grayish-white poking through the kelp forest. As I recognized it with a jolt, I heard Stryker suck in a fearful breath.

"By Te-Date, we're in for it now," he harshed.

We were looking at the clean-picked bones of a human skeleton. A small crab scuttled out of an empty eye socket, waved its claws about, then scurried back inside. I looked closer and saw the rotting rags of the man's clothing scattered about. Just to one side was what appeared to be a belaying pin.

"Th' poor whore's son," Stryker muttered, pitying his fellow mariner. He turned back to Santh and the others. "Get your arses back to your duties, lads," he snarled. "There's no lesson to be learned here, 'cept what's plain as that sack of puddin' Santh calls a nose." He pointed at the skeleton. "There's a lad that didn't listen to his cap'n's orders. And his ship had to sail without him, leavin' his bones for th' crabs to sup on."

He harangued them some more to get some spleen into them, and they went back to work—looking nervously over their shoulders as they went about their business.

"Well dealt with," I said in praise.

Stryker shook his head. "I'm a lyin' shit, and they knows it," he said. "Weren't for th' conjurin' you did back on that island, there'd be no talkin' to 'em." He shuddered. "We knows th' gods be with us. We seen that right plain. But they ain't makin' it easy on us, Captain Antero. Not one bit, they ain't."

He moved on to keep watch on his men, leaving me to gnaw on my guilty knowledge that my vision had promised nothing. Our future might lie west, but only the gods knew how it would end—or when. At the moment that future might well be to have our bones picked by the low forms that scuttled about in our prison, just like the mariner we'd just seen. I was about to seek out Gamelan for counsel when the uneasy peace was destroyed again. There was a shout from our lookout. I didn't need to be told what he'd seen, because no sooner had the cry burst from his lips than I saw for myself.

Both banks had become an enormous charnel house. Countless skeletons—both of men and animals—littered the scene. Some were whole and still carried the remnants of clothes, others were hurled about, with their large bones burst open, as if cracked by scavengers for the marrow. Some of the crew wept, others spewed their guts over the sides, while the rest stood pale and mumbling prayers to whatever gods they hoped might rescue them from such an end. As that horror burned itself into our dreams, the channel turned, spreading into a small lagoon, and an even greater terror was unveiled.

The rotted hulks of ships of every age and nation spread out before us. Some were caught in the tangle by the edge of the lagoon, others jutted out of the kelp as far as the eye could see across the slow-rolling plain. Some of the ships were of recent design, but others were—even to my untutored eye—of great age and scabbed with centuries of time. The whole thing was a great graveyard of all the ships that had been lost without a trace since history's beginnings.

Something made me duck, and as I did so, a shadow passed over me. I heard the squeal of startled pain as an object struck a sailor behind me. I dropped to the deck and tuck-rolled back to my feet, drawing my sword as I rose, and dodging once again as a missile hurled past. A shrill chorus of battle cries rent the air and scores of heavy objects crashed down. I saw skinny, naked figures swinging from the banks on kelp vines, brandishing all manner of weapons. A rusted spear was thrust at me. I brushed it aside and cut my attacker down, roaring for my Guardswomen to repel boarders.

The deck swarmed with small brown figures with limbs so slender they looked as if you could snap them with two fingers. But they made up for size with fierceness and surprise. Many sailors went down under the first rush, but as my women smashed into our attackers, the crew rallied, clubbing with anything in their reach. I saw Corais and Gerasa—a superb bow woman—shielded by an axe-swinging Polillo, fire arrow after arrow into our attackers. Three rushed at me. My left hand found my knife and I put my back against the mast as the three crowded in. The one on my left jabbed with a trident. With a quick blow of my sword I cut it off at the haft, ducked forward and came up to slip my dagger between his ribs. It stuck as he fell, so I left it there and pivoted—making a two-handed slice at the axeman beside him. My blade bit deep, nearly cutting him in two. Blood gouted from his wound, blinding me. As I desperately yanked on my sword to pull it free, I felt the presence of the third man rushing forward. I dropped to my knees and he tripped over me. Before he could recover, I'd ripped my blade free and chopped blindly at him. It was a lucky stroke—lucky for me, at any rate— and it sliced through his kidney as he tried to roll away. He shrieked, and before I'd clawed the gore from my eyes, he was choking a death rattle.

Somewhere a horn trumpeted, and by the time I'd reached my feet again, our enemies were scuttling away. But as they ran, many were carrying grisly burdens—arms and legs and huge pieces of flesh hacked from the bodies of our fallen comrades. And it was no rout—they were retreating in an orderly fashion, with flying squads to protect those burdened with meat.

I rallied my women and we charged into those remaining on the deck, but we'd only managed to kill a few before the rest scampered off jeering as they scuttled along kelp vines thicker than a large man's trunk. I heard sounds of fighting on the other ships, but that too faded, to be replaced by the shrill ridicule of our attackers. I could see lines of naked bodies moving along like ants. They converged into a single column and headed off. I sheathed my sword and swarmed up the foremast to see where they were going.

I found Santh's tall skinny friend cowering on the foretop. He was blubbering something, but I paid no attention as I peered this way and that until I spied the line of men. In the distance I saw an enormous mound shaped like a ship. I looked closer and saw it *was* a ship—like no other that I'd ever seen. It was so huge it could have housed our whole fleet. The top consisted of a crazy scrap-wood edifice that formed three turretlike structures—the one in the center towering twice as high over the others, smoke curling out its peaked roof. The line of men curled toward the strange ship, and in a few minutes I saw them disappear into a huge maw of a hole that pierced the side.

I shinnied down, ordering my officers to set guards and see to the needs of my troops, and sent for Cholla Yi. As I waited I learned that I'd only suffered a few wounded, and those were minor. Poor Stryker, however, had lost ten men—and all of their corpses had been carried away.

"But we gave better'n we took," he said with grim satisfaction.

Our attackers had left thirty-six bodies behind, but I saw no cause for celebration. They were hardly in mourning when they'd fled with their booty of limbs and flesh hacked from our comrades. That they were cannibals was no great revelation. What puzzled me more was why they all looked like such starvelings, with arms and legs like twigs, and swollen bellies. Water was a problem in these plant-choked seas, but not food. There was much edible life among the kelp vines, and a plenitude of fish to be gotten out of the channels. But all of the corpses sported the orange-tinted hair and swollen bellies of malnutrition, and the running sores pocking their skin would've never healed if they'd lived.

Admiral Cholla Yi arrived shaken by the encounter, but spoiling for a fight.

"They're nothing but bags of bones," he scoffed. "They caught us by surprise, is all. Who'd expect anything human to be living in this perdition? They're probably nothing more than survivors off those wrecks. And they aren't trained fighters. Most of those hulks look like merchantmen."

I agreed. "It's not likely they've ever encountered a war fleet before. If we try to work our way back out, they'll pick us off a few at a time. But if we put the fear of the gods in them now, they'll cower in their bolt holes until we're well gone."

"One thing to take note of," Gamelan broke in, "is they seem to act in concert, and with purpose. Which means they have leaders—perhaps even a master."

I nodded. "Probably makes his headquarters in that big ship I saw them parading into. Maybe that's where we strike."

"It would seem so," Gamelan said. "But that's not what I was getting at. What occurs to me is this might be the opportunity we've been hoping for. There's no doubt in my mind there's some kind of magical force at work in this place—the permanent lack of wind, this maze of vegetation. It was created, not formed by nature."

"A wizard?" I asked.

"Perhaps," Gamelan replied. "It could be other things, of course, but I'd really prefer it to be someone we can bargain with to find a means to escape this place."

"Far as I can see," Stryker said, "we got nothin' they want but th' skin we're walkin' around in. So there's nothin' to bargain. I'm with th' admiral. I say we fight."

But I had a glimmer of what Gamelan was getting at. A plan began to form in my mind. "I'm in complete agreement, gentlemen," I said. "But perhaps there's also something in what Lord Gamelan says. I propose we try to accomplish both. Cow our enemy, and find passage out at the same time,"

I laid out my plan. There was some grumbling, but gradually agreement was reached: we would attack that night.

I took eight of my best soldiers, including Polillo, Ismet, and Jacena, a swift, sure-footed runner. I left Corais in charge of the others and had her post archers to watch for our return, making sure Gerasa was among them.

We wore only what was needed for modesty, darkened our skin—except for Ismet, who had no need—and blackened our weapons. Gamelan helped me conjure up a tarlike substance that we painted on our bare feet, and when we went over the side onto the immense ropes of kelp, our footing was as secure as it could be on the pitching, slippery terrain. We had a full moon to contend with, but fortunately the mist rising up from the cooling vegetation nearly obscured it. Jacena took the lead. I followed, with Ismet close behind, and Polillo—her big axe strapped to her back—protected the rear.

I knew if we were successful, our return trip would be at a dead run. To help, Gamelan had me mix special oil, which Polillo carried in a leather flask. She sprinkled drops on the vines as she went. They were nearly invisible, and Polillo groused about what seemed to be a pointless task, but I assured her at the right time the purpose would be quite clear. I'd also ordered scores of fire beads hung from the mast of our ship so it would be easy to find our way. As for our target—that monstrous ship—getting to it would not be difficult. At dusk the high center tower had lit like a huge beacon. Strange raucous music trumpeted out, interspersed with wild, bloodchilling howls. Some kind of victory feast, we surmised. Or perhaps our skinny friends were working themselves up for another attack on the morrow. In either case, I fully intended to spoil their celebration.

It took time to get used to clambering across the odd terrain. The whole mass was in constant motion, rolling with the seas. In places where the growth was thinner, the water would geyser up without warning, and it was all we could do to keep our balance. To make things more difficult, a foot might go through a space between the vines, threatening to pitch us on our faces, or smaller tendrils might tangle in our harness. There were also weak places where you could plunge down into the depths below. I had to be hauled out once, and Polillo, with her greater weight, went in three times. It was not a pleasant experience. The water was warm and viscous and filled with scuttling little things that nipped at me with sharp claws and teeth. Instead of a pool, the hole was more like a watery nest, choked with barnacled vines that rasped on the flesh. As I fell through and the water rose above my head, I was overcome by fear that something was watching. As my head emerged, I sensed it was slithering for me. It was all I could do to force myself to remain calm so my companions could haul me out. As I lay panting by the side of the break, bubbles rose on the surface, and when they burst, there was a smell of rotting things. I shivered and nearly retched as my imagination supplied several unpleasant sources of the bubbles and the smell. The loathsome sensation of being in that nest troubles my sleep to this day. The whole time, I had the disgusting notion that not only was I about to become something's dinner, but that I'd first be humiliated in the foulest way possible before I was fit for it to eat. Each time Polillo went in, I knew what she suffered and nearly lost my rations as I worked frantically with the others to get her out.

Eventually we discovered the easiest method to make our way was to trust to instinct and go full force. With the agile Jacena at the lead, we ran along the vines, hesitating only when we'd reach the top of a rolling mass of kelp, then leaping forward to the next and running until another wave caught up to us. It took us over an hour to learn this method of locomotion, and in that time we made only a short distance. But once we abandoned clumsy caution, it took us less than fifteen minutes to reach the hulk.

We dropped to our bellies and crept cautiously toward the gaping entrance. Jacena hand-signaled an absence of guards, but that didn't ease my worry. I was heeding Gamelan's warning before we left that traps can take many more forms than nature and the ugly side of human ingenuity can create. I motioned a halt and slipped up to where Jacena waited. I made signs for her to stay and crept onward, moving only a foot or so at a time, then stopped, pushing out with all my senses.

I felt dusty threads touch my cheek and adhere like a spiderweb. I nearly brushed them away, then froze. I backed up slightly, then slowly reached a hand forward—closing my eyes and concentrating. It was difficult because the strange music had grown even louder, hurting my ears and scratching at my bones. Finally my fingers touched the sorcerous web. I stopped. My fingers began to tingle. Very slowly I drew them back, feeling the magical threads cling, then fall gently away.

Gamelan had instructed me what to do before we left the ship. "Since I have no powers," he'd said, "I cannot tell you what kind of sorcery awaits. You will need to adapt yourself to what you encounter. To elude our enemies, you will have to wear their skin."

I signaled the others to join me. Making motions, I alerted them to the trap, then had them huddle around me in a tight knot. I pulled a small balloon of spun glass from my belt pouch and shattered it in my palm with my knife haft. A speckled powder spilled out. It smelled of fish bone and insect parts. The bone, Gamelan said, was actually the ground beaks of cuttlefish, mixed with a bit of their dried ink. The insects were the similarly treated husks of a beetle that lives in great colonies on flowering plants. To feed and live in safety, they'd learned to form themselves into green twigs and leaves and the multicolored flowers of their host. I stretched my palm flat and blew the dust into my companion's faces. Then I sprinkled the residue—glass and all—on my head, and whispered the spell:

"Form and Shadow,
Shadow and Form—
Paired wings that
Carry the nightbird."

In my mind I became small and weak and without pride. Hunger burned in my gut. A voice wept inside: *I am dying! Poor me. Poor dying me.* The weeping turned into a wailing plea: *Help me, Great Master. Oh, please, Master, if only I could . . . eat.*

I heard low groans from the others as they sank into misery. Instinctively, I fought the weakness, but knew that until the right moment, I must give way. I let myself go, struggling only to keep a kernel of reason alive. I became pitifully fragile again, and hungry—*so* hungry. I babbled to my Master, my good, kind Master for food. Something dark and ugly stirred and said I must obey Him in all things. My thoughts shrilled agreement and abasement, and the ugliness chortled acceptance. I became glad as hatred flooded in, numbing the hunger. The hatred gave me strength, and it was directed at—my fleet! They must die, all of them must die. Then and only then could I feed! I almost broke under that hot outpouring of anger. It was time to act, but I didn't have the will. I searched frantically for that seed of self I'd planted. Just as I was about to give up hope, abandoning myself to my Master, I found it. I gripped it hard in my mind. Tighter and tighter still, until I could feel my hands reflexing into fists and my nails biting deep into my palms. Sweat burst from my pores, and then I felt a coolness. Strength returned and I rose and one by one took my weeping companions by the hand and led them through the magical web. It parted, accepting us—sensing no danger. We rested on the other side, quite whole again, with only a ravening thirst to mark the ordeal. I made no protest as each of my women emptied the flasks of watered wine we carried. This would be the last chance we had to drink.

There was no one to stop us or give the alarm as we went through the cavernous entrance into what appeared to have once been an enormous ship's hold. We almost bolted as soon as we entered. It was filled with men. But they seemed asleep, or spellbound, as they twisted and groaned on the deck. I suspected the latter because the sound of the celebration echoed even louder than before, but did not seem to disturb them—at least not as much as their dreams. We crept through the men, stepping over or dodging as they thrashed about in some nightmare's grip. I stopped at a massive wooden pillar in the center, pulled out a long piece of red thread and wrapped it about the post. We went on, stopping now and again for me to tie other bits of thread around likely timbers and supports.

We climbed ladders to a higher deck; went along passages and climbed again. The only people we saw were asleep, and all of them were men. Everywhere we went I found dry timbers for my thread. At last we came out into the open on the main deck. Towering above us was the central turret. Stairs spiraled up. At the top, circular windows spilled light and sound. The light was so intense our shadows were cast huge across the empty deck. I left Ismet and five others behind to guard our retreat, and sprinted to the tower—Jacena and Polillo at my heels. Once there, the two of them split off in opposite directions to scout the circumference of the turret, while I got out my last spool of thread. There was just enough to complete the job. We tied it around the turret—circling it twice. I made the final knot. Now it was time to spring the trap. But before I did, I wanted to see whom we faced.

I motioned for Jacena to wait, and Polillo and I went up the staircase. At the top it joined a circular deck. There was an open door to one side. I could see figures prancing about. On the other side was one of the windows. Polillo and I moved to it, crouching low. Then we came cautiously up to look. Polillo sucked in her breath in shock. I don't know what either of us expected, but what we witnessed in that turret chamber is not a tale to tell to children, or even hardened companions over a jug of wine and a tavern roast.

It was an immense room, containing all the goods looted from the ships that had been caught in the sargasso net. There were great piles of finery and trunks of gems and golden plate. Stacked all around were sacks of what appeared to be grain and rare spices. The walls were cluttered with all manner of tapestries, draped brocades and silk. Old weapons and shields and armor also hung from the walls, as well as odd, rusted machines whose original purpose I could not decipher. In the center of the room a pot large enough to feed an army bubbled and smoked over leaping flames. The fire shot out so many different hot colors that I knew it must be magical. Hunks of flesh roiled about inside the pot. It gave off a smell I do not care to dwell on. The music the men danced to blared out from everywhere and nowhere. At intervals a man would dart from the pack, jam his bare hand in the boiling liquid, screaming in pain as he fished about until he caught a hunk of meat and pulled it out. Then he'd gobble at it madly, sobbing all the while. But no sooner would he choke down a few bites than several others would claw and fight to grab a morsel away.

I was so shaken it was a moment before I saw who presided over the insanity. But there was no mistaking who the master was. The demon was sprawled across a raised platform, carpeted with thick tapestries. From his yellow-taloned feet to the single barbed horn that curled from his forehead, he was at least two javelin lengths long. The horn was mottled white and shot with red, like fat from a butchered pig. His arms were long, like an ape's, and his hands were taloned, as were his feet. He had death-white scales for skin and a long, barbed tail that lashed about in pleasure each time a man made the painful trip to the boiling pot. Although he was long in length, his body carried no extra weight. He was all heavy bone, big knotted joints, ribs like ship's staves, and long cabled muscles. His horned head was flat and shovel-shaped, with two red-rimmed holes for a nose and sharp-ribbed bone for lips. As we watched, another fight erupted. In the struggle for food, one of them mistakenly ripped the flesh away from another man's arm with his teeth, but gobbled it down without hesitation. The beast I knew to be the master howled in delight. It was the same unearthly sound we'd heard shrieking over the music since we began our journey. His teeth were pointed and as long as a finger, his tongue a quick-flickering ribbon of grayish pink.

It is unfair of me to brand the demon "him." For I cannot say with certainty he was not actually a she. I have been fortunate to know more good men than evil and have always been well-treated by those men most important to me. So I must apologize for this description, but it's how I think of that demon to this day. Although he was naked, I could not tell what manner of sexual organ was between the demon's legs. I saw only a bulbous white lump, ringed with red. I did not care to let my gaze linger to see if a penis emerged when he became most amused at the painful antics of his slaves.

Polillo nudged me and pointed. On a broad, carpeted step just below the platform, I saw the source of the music. It was a woman—the only woman we'd seen among the demon's slaves. She was also the only person we'd seen who was fat. Naked as the others, she had immense breasts that drooped over a bulging middle, legs and arms so obese they looked nearly useless, and she sat on huge hams wreathed with roll after roll of fat. She was short— even seated you could see she wouldn't stand much higher than a normal person's belt buckle. Her hair hung in greasy strings from a head so small in all that obesity that it looked like a doll's. Her eyes were mere dots and she had a little bow of a mouth that she kept pursed as she played on an odd lyrelike instrument. It had a deep black frame and was strung with strands of a gray, fleshy-looking material that gleamed with moisture that oozed down along the strings as she played. Her hands moved smoothly over the lyre, stroking rather than plucking the strings. All sorts of sounds screeched out to the rhythm of the whirling men. Beside her was a wooden trencher the size of a small table, and on it were heaped masses of food—mounds of grain mush, lumps of boiled meat clotted with fat, and heaps of crabs and other shellfish.

The master seemed to tire of his amusements. His tail flicked out to stroke the woman. She turned to him and drooled what I think was a smile. She nodded as if he'd spoken and stopped playing. In the silence, the men immediately fell to the floor, abasing themselves to the demon.

"We love you, Master," they chorused. "You are all that is love and all that is beauty and all that is good."

The demon opened his mouth and spoke: "I give you eat." His voice rasped out dry and rattling like a serpent's warning.

"Yes, Master," the men cried. "You give us eat."

"Others not eat," the demon said.

"They are unworthy, Master," the men responded.

"I give them sleep," the demon said.

"Sleep, yes, sleep. You give them the gift of sleep."

As he spoke, the woman was stuffing herself with food from the trencher. She ate with both hands and food spilled from her mouth and ran in streams down her chin to drip on her pendulous breasts.

"Tomorrow, more eat," the demon said. "Tomorrow all eat!"

The men became so excited their chorus shattered into all manner of wild praises.

"Tomorrow," the demon continued, "you go ships. Bring more eat for all."

I felt Polillo shudder. He was speaking of us. The men screamed promises to kill us all. But they grew suddenly quiet as the demon rose to his full height, towering over them.

"Not kill all," he roared. "Kill some. Keep some. Slaves for Master. Eat for Master." The men groaned agreement, vowing obedience in all things.

The demon turned to the woman. She was scooping food into her mouth, but seemed to sense that he wanted her and stopped in mid-shovel.

She said: "Master eat, now, yes?" Her voice was gentle, little girl sweet.

"Yes. Bring good eat," the demon said.

The woman shook the food off her hands—almost daintily—and rose. She waddled among the kneeling men, poking them, pinching their arms and haunches and groins. After she had gone among them all, she circled once again, making sure. Four men were tapped on the shoulder.

They shrieked in false joy. "Thank you, Master. Thank you for finding me worthy."

The demon gestured, and they scuttled forward on their knees.

His tail whipped out and plucked one of the men off the floor. The barbed end drove into the man's flesh and he was lifted up, babbling in terror and pain. Then the demon plunged the man into the boiling pot, howling with glee as the man screamed and writhed. Then he drew the man out, still alive and struggling, dangled him over his mouth and began to eat. He started on the toes and crunched upward, all the more to enjoy the man's agony.

I turned away from the window, gut roiling. I could bear no more. I looked at Polillo, ghastly pale with sickness. Neither of us could speak. We put our arms around one another, finding sanity and warmth in the embrace. Polillo sniffled back tears and drew away.

"I would like very much to kill that . . . thing," she said.

"I promise him to you," I said, "if we get the chance."

We fled back down the stairs, gathered Jacena and the others and retreated the way we had come. In a few minutes we were slipping through the heaps of spellbound men, and then we were outside, catching our breath in the moist night air. When we were ready, I ordered everyone to take up position just outside the yawning entrance. Polillo grinned evilly, unsheathed her axe and began slicing this way and that to limber up. The others drew their various weapons and stretched stiff muscles while I knelt and began my preparations. I unrolled a thin sheet of leather, marked with symbols Gamelan had had me copy out of his book. I used a few sticks of magical incense for tinder, sprinkled on a bit of powdered charcoal Gamelan said came from a holy tree, and struck a long spark with flint and steel. The spark ignited the tinder, and I blew gently into the small pile until a steady glow burned on the leather parchment. I'd saved a small bit of the red thread. This I dipped into a vial of oil and dangled over the glowing particles while I chanted:

"He who dwells
In fire . . .
She who sleeps
In flame . . .
I release you!"

There was a small flash of heat and light as I dropped the thread onto the parchment. Quickly I rolled it up into a tube. I rose, swinging the tube about my head until it burst into flames. Although my whole hand seemed alight, I felt no heat or pain. I rushed to the entrance and hurled the burning mass inside. It fell near a knot of sleeping men. No one stirred as the parchment tube began to hiss and throw off a shower of sparks. I stood there watching, cold with guilt, as the flames grew higher and brighter. In the center of the hold I saw the thread I'd tied about the big post begin to glow. Then the post exploded into flame. Still, not one man stirred. I backed out, looking up to see other places where I had tied the thread glow into hot life, then burst into hungry, licking flames.

We heard the first screams as the center turret caught and became a roaring wall of fire. I saw naked men run out onto the landing, but it caught as well, enveloping them, turning them into charred, writhing flesh. Then the landing collapsed, spreading fire across the big main deck.

I heard a bellow of enraged pain and looked up to see the demon break through one of the windows. He clung there for a moment, then reached in to pull out the woman. He put her on his shoulders, then climbed to the top of the turret. He stood there, flames all around him, head swiveling this way and that. Then he seemed to look directly at us. His taloned hand shot out, stabbing at us, and he roared in fury.

"Awake!" he shouted. "Awake!"

In the hold I heard screams of agony as the spellbound men came to and found themselves on fire or surrounded by flame.

"Kill them!" the demon shouted. "Kill them!"

Men came stumbling out of the smoke, some on fire, some coughing blackness, but they were not fleeing, but charging us, clawing with their nails, or stabbing with swords they'd scrabbled up when the demon awoke them. But they were helpless before my women. Polillo howled her battle cry and leaped in, chopping about with her axe. Ismet and the others called for Maranonia to give them strength and cut down anyone within reach. Within a few short minutes the rolling kelp ground around them was heaped with bodies and slick with flowing blood. The men were hurled back into the in-ferno to die. Some tried to break free, but each time, my women fought so furiously that the only escape was a fiery death.

I held back, watching to see what the demon would do next. He was howling with helpless fury, screaming for his slaves to attack. A sheet of flame burst through the roof of the turret and he leaped back. The woman lost her grip and fell from her perch, screaming as she plummeted down-ward. She hit, seeming to bounce as the kelp absorbed the shock, and then I saw her rise up, screaming with fear.

"Polillo," I shouted. She turned her blood-spattered face toward me and I pointed at the woman, who was only a few feet away. "I want her!"

Polillo bounded over, and as the woman tried to scramble away, Polillo clubbed her down with the flat of her axe, scooped her up and threw her over her shoulders.

The demon howled in fury. More flames exploded through the roof of the turret. But instead of destroying him, they seemed to only make him stronger. His body glowed with energy and he seemed to be growing longer. The glow became an armored carapace, and as I watched, six insectlike legs shot out from his sides, pivoting in muscular sockets. He came scuttling down the sides of the turret, straight through the fire. His jaws gouted snapping mandibles as he ran, and his long barbed tail dripped with venom.

I shouted for the others to retreat, and we all turned and ran. I sent Jacena speeding ahead to alert the ship. The path was plain before us. The oil Polillo had dribbled behind us was now a luminescent path straight to my ship and safety.

I chanced a look over my shoulder as I ran and saw the demon drop to the ground. He screamed for his slaves, and I saw the survivors boiling out, gnashing their teeth and crying for our blood.

Then the demon called my name. "Antero! I kill you, Antero!"

I only ran harder, leaping over the nests where Polillo and I had fallen through. As I neared the last one, a tentacle curled out. It was huge and ringed with gaping suckers. It snaked around Ismet and she cried out in pain. But before the beast could tighten its grasp I was there, my sword slicing through the tentacle. The kelp erupted under us as the beast reacted to the pain. Ismet stripped away the still writhing stump, and I saw bloody scars where the suckers had bit. We ran on, but the time lost was enough for our enemy to gain. They were right on our heels now, and behind them the demon was cursing and hissing and urging them on.

I saw our ship, and at the same moment heard a great rushing as our archers fired their volley. Behind me men cried out as the arrows found their marks. When Polillo reached the ship, she flung our captive on board, then turned to unlimber her axe.

"Come on, you swine lovers," she shouted. "I've got something sweet for you." She whirled the axe above her head.

Some of the men cut in to flank us, and she hammered them down as Ismet and the others were helped aboard. From the deck another flight of arrows was sent a-hunting. Finally, I reached the ship. I turned to join Polillo, but saw the demon was calling his slaves back. Scores of bodies heaped the rolling plain, all eerily lit by the fire that was consuming the demon's lair. As for the demon, I saw him transform back to his original shape, then snarling and hissing, lead his men deep into the darkness, until I could see them no more.

"They gave up too easily," Polillo grumbled. "I was just getting warmed up."

"Don't worry," I gasped. "He'll be back."

Exhausted, I climbed on board into the welcoming arms of my Guardswomen. They all cheered and pounded our backs and passed around wineskins to slake our thirst.

I upended a bag and drank mightily, letting the cool wine overflow and spill down my body. Tiredness fled the boozy river. I felt very well, indeed. It hadn't been a great victory, but it was good enough for now.

I slept for a few hours and rose early, quite refreshed, to prepare for our next encounter with the demon. I had no doubt he'd come, especially since we had his favorite slave for bait. Her name was Chahar, and she was quite nonplussed at being a captive. I had a tent made of cheerful material erected on the main deck and had her brought to me for interrogation.

"You'll be sorry," she said as soon as she entered. "My Master Elam loves me. He'll make you pay."

I didn't tell her I was counting on her dear Elam trying that very thing. I merely indicated some soft pillows I'd had installed for her to plant her naked haunches on. Polillo hovered over her, anxious to apply whatever pain was necessary to learn what we needed to know. The image of the demon's chamber of horrors haunted her, as it did me, and it was not unnatural for her to want revenge for all those poor souls.

"Give me the fat little bitch for half an hour," she growled. "She'll spill her guts, or I'll cut them out to make sausage for our supper."

Chahar shrank back in fear. I gave Polillo a wink, saying, "We shouldn't be too hasty. Perhaps we have been wrong about Lord Elam."

Gamelan, who was also in attendance for the questioning, took up my theme. "You are quite right, Captain Antero," he said. "We could have misjudged the good Lord Elam. Perhaps he really is a kind master who will treat us handsomely if we serve him well."

"Oh, he *would*," Chahar said. "He can really be very kind. He just acts angry sometimes because he's so sad."

"Sad?" Gamelan asked. "Why would such a powerful lord be sad?"

"He's lonely 'cause he can't go home," she answered.

"Oh, *really*," I said. "Tell us more, my dear. And while you're at it, Lieutenant Polillo will bring you something to eat. This has all been such a trial, I'm sure you're famished."

"Well, I could eat just a little bit," she said, holding two fingers lightly apart for illustration. "It wouldn't be polite for me to refuse."

Polillo glowered, but I tipped her another wink, and the glower stretched into the best smile she could make under the circumstance—more a curling sneer than anything. She went off to do my bidding. I sat down on the deck next to Chahar and chatted idly about this and that until Polillo returned. She'd caught on to what I intended, and enlisted some help to bring huge platters of every variety of food we could manage. Chahar plunged in with both fists, and was soon a greasy mess.

When I thought her lulled enough by bloat, I resumed my questioning. "You said your master couldn't return home. Why is that?"

Chahar daintily wiped away a gob of food dangling from her lower lip. " 'Cause he's lost," she said. "See, he's not from here. He's from . . ." She waved her hands, searching for words. They didn't come. "Not from this place. Not from any place. Sort of."

"You mean, another world?" Gamelan asked.

"Yes," Chahar said. "Not our world. But another one. That's where he's from. That's where his home is."

"How did that come to be?" I asked.

"Well. He 'splained it to me once, and it's kind of hard to remember everything. And I'm not too smart. I'm not too good at most anything. Except making my Master happy. I know what he wants, even if he doesn't ask me out loud. I can make him happy. That's what I'm good at."

Gamelan's bushy eyebrows rose over blind eyes. "She is his Favorite," he said to me.

"Oh, I am!" Chahar said brightly. "I'm his favorite over everybody else."

I knew that's not what Gamelan meant. He meant her role was the same one minor demons played to some wizards in our world, such as the little fellow who cooked Gamelan's meals and now did my bidding when I needed small tasks performed. But I didn't say this. I patted her hand.

"I'm sure you are, my dear," I said. "Now, tell me, how did Lord Elam find himself in this terrible predicament?"

"As near as I remember, he said he was brought here by an evil wizard. He was . . . uh, summoned . . . that's the word. And this bad wizard was so powerful that my Master couldn't help himself. So he came. And the wizard made him do things. And then the wizard was killed in some kind of fight, and now my Master doesn't know how to get back home. He's lost, you see. And he's been lost for maybe two hundred years."

She made a broad gesture with one hand, indicating the great sargasso we were trapped in. "It's taken him all this time to make this. So he has a place to live, and can eat, and get servants and everything. He says it's sort of like a big spiderweb. Except it's not really that big. That's what he says, at least. He's making it bigger all the time."

I pretended to scoff at this. "Come now! No one could have made something like this. Even your master isn't powerful enough for that!"

Chahar was indignant. "He certainly did! And he keeps on doing it. He makes the winds stop. And he makes the kelp grow and stick together. And he makes the others happy, even when he hurts them. He doesn't do that 'cause he's mean or anything. It just makes his food taste better. 'Sides, he never hurts me. Well, maybe a teensy bit when he needs some of my blood for his magic. And that's not very bad. I make a little cut and drip some of my blood in his cup, which he mixes some other stuff in. It only stings a little, and he's so kind, he lets me eat extra whenever he does, so I don't mind so much."

"Why did he choose you for this, my dear?" Gamelan asked. "What makes your blood so special?"

Chahar scooped up more food. "My father was a witch," she said matter-of-factly. She ate. We waited until she swallowed. "I'm not a witch. But my father was. Then he died. And the new witch made a big ceremony for the funeral. My people built a long boat and put all his stuff in it. Also me and my mother and all my brothers and sisters. Ten of us, there were. 'Sides my mother. Then they pulled the boat out and let the current get it and it took us away. Far away. Finally, I got here. And my Master found me."

"Just you?" I asked. "What happened to the others?"

Chahar shrugged. "They got dead," she said. "We didn't have any food. So we had to eat the ones that died all by themselves. Then they started looking at me, 'cause I'm kinda fat, I guess. So one night I killed the ones who're left. With a knife. While they were asleep. Then I had plenty of food." She gnawed on a bird haunch. Then she said: "I ate my mother last. She was pretty skinny. Anyway, that's how I got here. And I guess my blood is special because even though I'm not a witch, I got enough of my father in me to make my blood just right for my Master's magic."

We were all struck dumb by her adventures.

Gamelan was the first to recover. "That makes you very—" He coughed. "—special, indeed, my dear. But tell us, don't you ever miss your home? Your people?"

Chahar gave a vigorous shake of her head, quaking her fat from jowl to thigh. "Never," she said. "They weren't nice to me. Ever. Not even when I made the stick charts for them. The hunters would just grab them out of my hands and say mean things."

"Stick charts?" I said, trying to hide my excitement. "What stick charts?"

"The ones my father had me make, silly," she said. "Sometimes the hunters have to go a long ways in their boats, so my father would give them stick charts so they could find their way to the places they had to go where there was game, and then get back."

"Why did he have *you* make them?"

Chahar gave me a look like I was dunce. " 'Cause we had to have lots of them. And they'd get lost or broken. So we'd have to make more. My father didn't have time to do all that, and my brothers and sisters were always busy working. I wasn't good at it, but since I used to get sick a lot and couldn't work, my father had me do it. Then he'd bless them and that was that!"

"Could you make one now?" I asked.

Chahar snorted. " 'Course I could. I'm not smart, but I did so many of them I could never forget. Sometimes I even dream about it." She shuddered. "When I have bad dreams. About home."

"Would you make one for us?" I pressed.

Chahar shook her head. "I don't think my Master Elam would like that," she said.

"He wouldn't mind," I said, "if in return we let you go."

Chahar stared at me, hard. "What do you need it for? You're never going to get out of here."

"Just the same," I said. "If you make one for us, I'll release you."

I got another long, hard look. Chahar gobbled more food while she weighed my proposal. Finally: "You promise?" she asked.

"I promise," I lied.

So she had us fetch some sticks and whatever shells and small rocks and yarn we could find. It took her about an hour. Her fingers moved swiftly for such a lazy, obese creature, but the primitive map that formed seemed well-made—although I had never seen such a thing before, but had only heard traders' tales of the extremely accurate maps that savages made.

When it was done, she handed it to me. As I held it, she pointed out its main features. "We're sort of here," she said, indicating a shell near the top of the chart. "I'm not exactly sure, but that's the way the current was going when they put us on the boat." Her finger traced a blue strand of yarn woven through the stick frame.

She showed us important islands, but said the people who lived there didn't take kindly to strangers. And finally she indicated a whole scatter of large islands near the bottom.

"That's Konya," she said. "Lots of people live there. It's so far, only a few of my people have ever visited, and that was a long time ago. They said there was hundreds of big islands, all crowded with people. And they had all kinds of wonderful things, and never got hungry, because their wizards are the most powerful in the whole world. They have a king, and big buildings instead of huts, with fireplaces that don't smoke. They've also got things they look at for hours, called books, and ships that go almost everyplace." She shrugged. "I guess they don't come to visit us because we're all pretty stupid."

Polillo smiled for the first time since the interrogation had begun. "Civilization!" she said.

Chahar shook her head. "No. I said it was Konya. Not ciliviz— whatever it was you called it." She sneered at Polillo. "You must be pretty stupid, too."

But Polillo only laughed. Gamelan was practically squirming with glee. Her chart was like finding the key to a fabled treasure house—except in this case the value of that treasure was our very lives.

Chahar was looking at us, suddenly alarmed. "I did what you told me," she said, indicating the stick chart. "Now it's your turn. You really are going to let me go when my Master Elam comes, aren't you?"

"Absolutely," I said as heartily as possible. "I wouldn't dream of doing otherwise."

Gamelan rapped his stick to catch my attention. "I think you and I should have a little chat about that very thing, Captain Antero," he said. "Privately, if you please."

I left Polillo to guard her, whispering stern instructions about not harming the bitch, and led Gamelan from the tent.

When we were out of earshot, he said: "I hope you intend to keep that promise."

I was startled. "By all the gods hold sacred, why would I ever do such a thing? She's trading fodder. The only thing we've got that the demon wants."

"Oh, I don't oppose some bargaining. Obviously, you don't expect him to keep his side of it. But a bit of bargaining for appearance's sake might be wise so he doesn't become suspicious that we're giving her up too easily."

"Wizard," I said, "I sense a plan budding in that white-fringed noggin of yours."

Gamelan's teeth shone through his beard. "Not a plan," he scoffed. "But an outright plot."

"Tell me more, my wise friend," I said.

He did. It was brilliant, it was simple, and it was evil. In short, it contained all the key ingredients that go into the best of plots. The magic required took only a few stale sweetmeats I scrounged from the bottom of Corais' seabag—she has a weakness for such things, which she does her best to control. I freshened them with a potion any market crone could make and chanted a few words I will not repeat. Murder is easy enough as it is. We returned to the tent and made casual conversation. When I presented the sweetmeats to Chahar, she purely blubbered with joy. And yes, the wordplay *was* intended.

By the time the sun reached its highest point, she was growing sleepy. A few minutes later the demon returned.

Gerasa was the first to see him. I'd set her to watch with half a dozen of our best archers, in case Elam tried a surprise attack. When her warning came, at first all I could see was what appeared to be a large wave rolling under the thick kelp. It was moving at great speed and coming straight for us. About ten yards out it stopped abruptly. A hole gaped and a thick black column of smoke boiled out. We all braced, not knowing what to expect. The smoke whirled, hurling off hot sparks. Gradually the smoke formed and we saw Elam. He was twice as big as when I'd first seen him. His eyes were pools of fury and his tail lashed angrily. Knowing he wouldn't have come alone, much less so close, if he hadn't cast protective spells, I whispered to Gerasa and the others to hold their fire.

As calmly as I could I approached the ship's rail and addressed him. "Good day, Lord Elam," I said. "We are all deeply honored you've graced us with your presence."

He ignored my pleasantries. "Where she be?" he hissed, and his breath was so foul that even from that distance I nearly gagged.

"I expect you mean the good Chahar," I answered. "And she's quite well, as you will shortly see for yourself."

I motioned, and Polillo fetched Chahar from the tent. She was yawning and rubbing her eyes, but soon as she saw Elam, she cried out in joy and waddled to my side.

"You've come for me, Master," she said. She began to weep in relief.

"As you can see," I told Elam, "she's quite well. And although she's had a lovely time with us, the poor dear is tired from all the excitement and is anxious to return home."

One of the demon's taloned hands shot out. "Give to me," he roared. "Give to me, or I kill you all."

I shook my head, as if my feelings were injured. "Why all this talk of killing, Lord Elam? We've only had her to supper."

I patted Chahar's head. "We treated you well, did we not?" I asked.

Still weeping, she nodded. "They didn't hurt me," she called to Elam. "And they promised to let me go."

I gripped her shoulder tight enough to make her wince. "In a moment, dear one," I said. "First, your master and I must talk."

I looked back up at Elam. "You can have her," I said. "But first you'll have to free us from this place."

The demon laughed. At least I think it was a laugh. It sounded more like a pack of baying direwolves. "No," he said. "You give. I not kill. Let you be slaves. I need slaves. Too many die in fire."

I shook my head. "Much as we'd like to have a nice long visit with you," I said, "it's quite impossible to stay longer. I'm afraid you'll have to make some sort of concession, or . . ."

I grabbed Chahar's hair, unsheathed my knife and placed it against her throat. "Your fat little Favorite will be the one who dies this day."

Chahar screamed. "Don't let her hurt me, Master! Please!"

Instead of becoming angry, the demon adopted my pose of a trader trying to be reasonable against a tough bargainer. His talons brushed away a nonexistent speck on his scaled chest.

"Why I let you go? She's only slave."

"Perhaps so," I answered. "But we've had a little chat with Chahar and we know all about you now. You don't belong in this world, and you need the magic in her blood, or someone like her, to live."

I gave him my most pitying look. "Why, you're probably growing weaker already. If we wait long enough, maybe we won't need to trade."

The demon's frighteningly wide shoulders shrugged. "I find other," he said. His flat nostrils flared and he began to sniff. Ghostly fingers seemed to move over my body. I repressed a shudder, but only smiled wider to show he didn't affect me. His lipless mouth parted to show fanged amusement.

"You have witch's blood," he said. "Maybe I wait. Let you kill Chahar. Then you be Elam's Favorite."

"Are you sure you have time?" I asked. "Before you lose your powers, I mean? We have much food and water. And all of us are warriors. More than a match for your puny slaves. I wonder . . . who can wait the longest?"

Elam's tail lashed in renewed anger. "Give me Chahar," he roared. "Give me! I want!"

"And you'll let us go if I do?" I asked.

His eyes squinted, crafty. "Yes," he said. "You let Chahar go. Then I free you. Is trade?"

I put on a worried frown and pretended I was thinking this over. Finally, I said, "You swear that if I free her now, you'll keep your end of the bargain?"

Again the demon bayed laughter. "Elam swears. Let Chahar go now, yes?"

I pretended to hesitate, then—with seeming reluctance—I pushed Chahar forward. "You're free to go," I said.

Chahar squealed in delight, and with a grace that seemed odd in all that blubber, she went over the side into the water. Strong strokes took her swiftly to the bank, and Elam scooped her up and put her on his shoulder. She hugged his neck and pounded her fat heels against him in joy.

"We've done our part," I called to him. "Now it's your turn."

If his laughter was like a pack of direwolves before, now it seemed like a thousand of them had gathered to feast. I acted as if I were stunned.

"You *are* going to let us go, aren't you?" I said, my voice all a-tremble.

"I lie to you, little fool," he brayed. "Now I make you slave. Or maybe kill. Not decide yet."

He turned and started striding away. "I leave now. Make magic with Chahar. Be too strong for you. Then I come back."

I railed at his retreating form, hurling curses for his betrayal. Soon as he disappeared, I stopped. As I turned, a large smile of pleasure pasted on my face, I saw Polillo looking at me in awe.

"If you'd been a merchant instead of a soldier," she said, "you'd be richer than your brother."

I laughed, protesting I was an amateur compared to Amalric. But her words pleased me. Not that I'd want such a thing—remembering, of course, that no woman would be allowed to join the ranks of merchants in Orissa. I liked being a soldier. It was nice, however, to think that maybe Amalric wasn't the only crafty bargainer in our family.

"What do we do now?" Stryker asked.

"Signal the admiral to make ready," I answered. "If the gods remain with us, we'll sail within the hour." Shaking his head in open disbelief, Stryker left to do my bidding.

Gamelan tapped up to my side. "That was well-done, Rali," he said. "I'll make a wizard of you yet."

His words soured any satisfaction I felt. I wanted to snarl at him, tell him once this voyage was over, I'd never lift a conjuring finger again. But he looked so proud to be my mentor that I bit my tongue and patted him instead.

As I searched for a kind response, a shriek of awful pain shattered the air. I whirled to see the demon stumbling from behind the charred remains of his ship. He gave another shriek, doubling over as the poison burned his guts. Then he struggled up and charged toward us, his long legs eating up the distance. Behind him I saw his remaining slaves pour out of hiding and run after him.

I barked orders as he came. My troops unsheathed their weapons and nocked their bows in readiness. I could see Elam gathering all of his strength, shooting up in size as he neared us. He was rattling his talons and gnashing his teeth. He stopped at the bank's edge.

"You lie to me!" he screamed.

"Why, Lord Elam," I replied most mildly. "How can you say such a thing?"

"You kill Chahar," he gritted out, as another wave of pain took him.

"And I'm very sorry about that," I said. "But it was necessary to poison her, so I could poison you. Now, what can I do for you, my lord? I'm a busy woman."

His men were massed behind him now, waiting for his orders to attack. He raised himself up to his full height to scream our death warrants. Then pain gripped him and he fell to his knees. His slaves moaned in fear.

"I see you are in some discomfort, my lord," I said. "Perhaps I can assist you . . . if you free us, that is. And this time, if you want to live, you'll have to keep your side of the bargain."

The demon shuddered and nodded his head. "Yes. Elam agrees."

I motioned for Polillo to hand me a leather flask Gamelan and I had prepared. I uncorked it, took out my knife, and nicked my arm. I let the blood drip into the flask, mixing with the elixir. I recorked it and handed it back to Polillo.

"If you'll do the honors, Lieutenant," I said.

Polillo hurled the flask across the distance. It fell in front of the kneeling demon. He struggled up, opened the flask and sniffed the contents suspiciously.

"How I know you not lie?" he asked.

"You don't," I said. "But let me tell you this. That potion will not only cure you, but it binds us both to our solemn oaths. Cheat us, and you will die most painfully in a few hours. Honor your word, and you will live to go about your filthy business. To be perfectly frank, if I had my choice, I'd let you die. And then I'd skin you and hang your hide on a tavern wall so all could mock you when I told the tale of the demon, Elam, and all the evil that he'd done. But I have no choice. For me and my companions to live, you must live as well. It's to be regretted. But there's nothing else I can do. So drink, my lord. Drink deep and thank the foul gods you worship that they did not permit the woman who defeated you to do worse."

Elam glowered at me, then another wave of pain racked his body. Hastily, he drank.

"Quickly now," I urged him. "If you do not act this instant, the potion will not work."

He hesitated for a long moment, turning his head as if he were about to unleash his slaves. They leaned toward him, moaning for the pleasure of the anticipated kill. Instead, he whirled back, rose up to his fullest height and opened his mouth. Air rushed in with such force that it sounded like all the ghosts of all time were crying out for release. Then he blew.

A great foul wind washed over us, our ship heeling over from the force. It was so strong many were hurled to the deck. The wind roared through us, hammering over the fleet and across the rolling kelp plain. Then it stopped as abruptly as it began. The hot moist air turned chill and I saw huge black clouds scudding across the sky. Stryker barely had time to shout orders, when a new gale swooped in from above. The seas burst up above the kelp and we were surging forward, sails cracking in the wind. The banks of kelp were ripped away and the floating beds pushed aside, and a wide, straight passage yawned, a path to the open seas beyond. I heard faint cheers echo over the wind as the rest of the fleet saw what was happening.

I pulled myself to the rail and looked back. I saw Elam's black form standing where we had left him. We were moving swiftly and his figure got smaller and smaller as the distance grew.

Just before he vanished all together, he gave a great shout that boomed over the howling winds: "Did you lie, Antero? Did you lie?"

Then we were on the open seas again, freed from our strange prison. And that was the last I saw of him, thanks be the gods.

What was that, Scribe? You want to know if I told the demon the truth? Was my potion really a cure? I'm hurt. How could you doubt me? Very well. I'll only say this. If you should ever sail beyond the fiery reefs, and find yourself becalmed in some seaweed . . . don't speak my name to the gods there when you pray to raise a breeze.

THE MAGICAL gale soon died, but was replaced by brisk, natural winds that raised our spirits and our hopes. Even Cholla Yi and Phocas seemed cheerful when we gathered to examine Chahar's stick chart, which Phocas declared to be accurate, at least as far as the features he'd marked before we came upon Elam's lair. We agreed to sail for the distant Kingdom of Konya and throw ourselves on the mercy of the civilized people Chahar had assured us dwelt there.

"They're sure to have detailed charts of these seas," Cholla Yi said. "With their help, all we need to do is to add it to our knowledge and we'll soon be sailing home."

I had some doubts of my own—Chahar was too stupid to dissemble, but was she also stupid in her estimation of the kindly Konyans? But what other course did we have? I shrugged off the worry and joined the celebration. The wine flowed quite freely that night.

We sailed for many weeks, our confidence in the stick chart growing as more landmarks were sighted. One day I arose in spirits that were brighter than any time before or since. I bounded up on the deck, full of cheer and goodwill to all. I found Polillo exercising, heaving an immense cask about to stretch her muscles. When she saw me, she let it down. The deck groaned with its weight.

She drew in a long, joyous breath, swelling her bosom to such size the crewmen's eyes were popping from their heads.

"What a great day," she exclaimed. "I'm no wizard, Captain, but I have this feeling that something marvelous is about to happen to us."

I laughed in agreement, then went to Gamelan for our daily ritual of casting the bones. He was as cheery as I, combing his beard and teasing me about what a great wizard I was going to make when he was done. For a change, I took no offense. We got out the bones and I threw them. Gamelan chortled over the pattern I described, saying nothing but the best was in store for us. To me, the bones looked no different than any other day, but I thought I must be wrong.

An hour later I returned to the deck and strolled along the rail, enjoying the sun and fresh air. Then the lookout shouted "Land," and I craned to see what lay ahead across the dancing seas.

I saw a pale blue mist, edged with a dark line below. The mist lifted, and my heart leaped as I saw the most glorious island. It was deep emerald and beckoned us with sweet promises and even sweeter dreams.

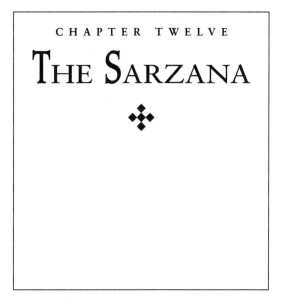

CHAPTER TWELVE

THE SARZANA

❖

A s we closed on the island our happiness grew, almost as if we were returning home. There wasn't any reason for it, but after the past few
weeks of gloom and disaster, all of us welcomed that peacefulness.
The sea mirrored our feelings—the waves near calm, a warm, gentle early
morning breeze off the land ruffling the placid waters, the sails, and our hair.
I found myself smiling inadvertently at Stryker, as if he were an acceptable
excuse for a human, then grinned more broadly at my sappiness.

My women and even some of the sailors, who I thought would've seen
everything, lined the railings. A curious seal broke water ahead of our prow,
then dove and swam past underwater—so close to the surface we could see
the muscles rippling beneath her smooth brown hide.

"It might not be bad," Corais said dreamily, "if the fools who believe in
rebirth happened to be right. I wouldn't mind returning as a seal."

I thought of saying something sarcastic, such as it'd be best to be reborn
in waters that seal hunters hadn't found yet, but thought better. Corais seldom relaxed as much as she had on this day.

For the first time since his blinding, Gamelan also looked content. I
chanced ruining the moment and asked if he could sense anything that might
portend danger from the approaching land. He smiled and just shook his
head no.

The island looked like a curled hand, with fingered headlands enclosing the bay, and in the center the land rose to a plateau. I guessed the island to be about ten miles long by six wide. Everything was green, so green it hurt the eyes. I thought I spied a bit of white atop the plateau, but when I searched again, I decided my eyes had been deceived.

The water shallowed as we entered the bay, and the ocean became a crystal-blue like the finest diamond. One Guardswoman pointed, and I saw first a dolphin, then its mate, below our keel. They were swimming about thirty feet apart, and it looked as if they had something clenched in their jaws. I thought I saw glints from their foreheads, a reflection such as that which would come from a prince's diadem. Ahead of them I saw the flash of a school of silvery fish trying to escape their fate as the dolphins' midday meal. Then our ship passed over them and our wake obscured the scene.

I heard a shout from across the waters. It was Cholla Yi, calling for the fleet to assemble on him. Oddly, he gave his orders without an obscenity or a curse. The day must've worked its charms on him as well. Within minutes our ramshackle ships gathered, sails lowered, each rocking gently in the low waves. I could see long strands of weed and barnacles along the waterline and below. Shrouds were frayed and the ships' sides stained; the planking was battered, splintering. I took a moment to pray this new island would fulfill its promise of peace. We desperately needed not only supplies and water, but to beach and career our ships for repair.

Cholla Yi's orders were brief—take arrow formation, half the ships as the point of the arrow, the others in line to the rear. No ship was to anchor or land without orders from the flagship. Then something most unusual occurred—he called to me, asking if I had any comments or additions. Perhaps the voyage and its travails had made even a man as stubborn as he was realize there was no room for conflict among ourselves. I had only one suggestion—perhaps one galley should remain outside the bay for a few hours, close to the headlands, to make sure no hostile ships were lying in wait to bottle us in this beautiful trap. Cholla Yi grinned broadly and bellowed, "A good idea. This one will be a sailor yet. Captain Meduduth . . . you're the watchman. We'll try to save any wenches or wine we find for you."

My section sergeants had already ordered the Guard into armor, and the rowers outed oars and crept into the great lagoon. At first it appeared we were the first people to encounter this paradise, which was not improbable, considering how isolated it was in these uncharted seas.

Klisura told Stryker the bay would make a perfect base for a war fleet. Stryker's lips twisted into a grin and he said, "Aye, but for the small problem that yer'd have to sail for two small forevers before yer came upon anythin' worth thievin'."

A few minutes later one of the lookouts posted in the chains shouted, and we hurried to the rails. " 'Pears some admiral shared yer view," Stryker said.

Across the center of the bay were buoys, studded at measured intervals. Those buoys would have been meant for mooring in even rows, rather than to chance chaos and damage by haphazard anchoring. I counted . . . ten, twenty, perhaps more. A fleet, indeed, could have harbored here. Our ship closed on them, and there was no sound except the whisper of the wind and the splashing of the oar blades as they lifted and feathered. The buoys were large wooden barrels, each connected to a cable that ran down to a greater one laid across the ocean floor. The buoys had not been in place long—the cable anchoring them was spotted with rust, but not yet covered with sea growth. It was strange, though, to see gaps in the line where buoys had broken away or sunk, with no one making repairs. It looked as if whoever laid out this anchoring had sailed away just after completing the task.

We rounded a point and saw what we all knew had to be there. White stone buildings climbed up from the water on cobbled streets, to end at a high stone wall laid against the mountain face rearing up toward the plateau.

"Naval port," Klisura said, and I asked how he could tell.

"Merchant ships need docks, or a mole at any rate, to unload cargo. Warships lie out to harbor when they anchor. Makes 'em feel safer, and they can get under way faster. But if it weren't for those buoys, I'd call this port a fishing village." I knew what he meant. There was no sign of either defensive fortifications or war machines along the waterfront.

That feeling of content lessened as I realized I heard nothing coming across the water from the town. There were no cries of hawkers or children, no creaking of wagon wheels, no bawling noises from draft animals. All was still, all was silent. I saw no signs of life whatsoever. There was but one boat in the harbor, a small smack that lay half submerged along the single dock.

"Captain Stryker," I ordered. "Signal the other ships to heave to where they lie. The admiral will remain in command. We'll send an armed landing party ashore first."

After our earlier experiences, Stryker didn't argue. I ordered Polillo to assemble a landing party—two boats, fifteen women.

I wasn't surprised, soldiers being what they are, fearing boredom far more than the most grisly death, to see all my best milling in an excited knot; and there were twice as many Guardswomen as I needed, including Polillo, Corais, Ismet, and Aspirant Dica, who I suspected was going to become a fire breather like the worst of us. They—and the others—were looking at me like so many puppies, eyes pleading not to be left aboard.

I muttered a curse at always having to be the villain, but also found an inward smile—command may be a lonely task, but at least the commander has some sway in being able to choose who leads an expedition. I left both Polillo and Corais and put Sergeant Ismet as my second, taking Dica with me.

We clambered into the boats, encumbered with battle gear, and the sailors rowed toward the beach. No one came to greet us, no one came to warn us off. One of the oarsmen muttered, "It's like some wizard whisked 'em up into the skies. A phantom village." Sergeant Ismet glowered him to silence.

The sound of the boats' keels scraping on the sand was loud. We jumped overside hastily, not intending to present any lush target if there was an ambush. The thigh-deep water was warm and inviting, as was the sand stretching up to a cobbled esplanade that ran along the front of the village. There were fishing nets hung from racks, but they'd been hanging for some time, I noted. The beach sand was blown smooth and showed no footsteps, its only markings those of birds and where water animals had beached themselves to sun.

I sent Sergeant Ismet and seven women to scout the eastern stretch of the waterfront, and I patrolled down the western section. Again we heard nothing but the cry of gulls, and saw nothing, except the occasional rat scuttling across the cobbles. There was a scattering of roof tiles in the streets, blown off by storms. *Winter* storms? I wondered. We were now in spring, so the village might have been abandoned some time ago.

The village appeared unremarkable, except for its inhabitants' disappearance. I chanced entering one small shop, sword ready. It was just what one would expect in a fishing village, a bit of a chandlery, a bit of a grocery. There was a faint, disagreeable smell I traced to some long-spoiled bait in a wooden bucket. There were still items on the shelves, but not many. I guessed the shop would have been barely making money for its owner, who probably had another job, either farming somewhere behind the village or working the fishing boats. That made me wonder where the boats themselves had gone to. Had all the inhabitants sailed off, fearing some doom that never came?

I went into the back of the shop, where the owner had his living quarters—and the peacefulness was gone. There'd been a great struggle here. Blood, dried to black, spattered the bed, its blankets, the floor and walls. Someone had died here, fighting desperately before they did. I looked out the back door, which hung ajar, but saw nothing. I shivered, then retraced my steps through the shop to where my patrol waited. This was more than strange. But what made it eerie was that I didn't feel any sense of danger. All this was most unusual, but there didn't seem to be any special reason to keep my sword ready, my eyes darting from side to side. I forced wariness on myself—looking here and there for any threat. But nothing happened and we continued on.

We checked the rest of the waterfront without learning anything more. We trotted back to the boats, where Sergeant Ismet waited. Her end of the village was equally desolate, and she, too, had found evidence of a fight. Yet there were no bodies, no bones. Whoever had attacked this village had either taken the corpses with them or, singularly neat butchers, performed funeral services after the massacre. I thought it might be seaborne slavers—but slavers never destroy a village utterly. Rather, they take the young, the comely, and the talented, and leave the rest to breed another generation to harvest. But what did I know about customs in these far lands?

I sent Sergeant Ismet out to the ship to report and to give my orders to Captain Stryker and to Cholla Yi. There appeared to be no immediate danger, so the ships could be brought in to anchor, although a fighting watch should be kept until I ordered differently. As an added caution, I wanted another galley to join Captain Meduduth, out beyond the headland. I ordered the Guard to land in full strength. We would explore and secure the island. I told Sergeant Ismet I also thought it'd be safe for the ships to send watering parties ashore—there was a small creek with sweet water just at the west end of the village—although the parties should not skylark about, and should be accompanied by armed sailors.

Within the hour my Guard was ashore. Cholla Yi's marines could provide safety along the waterfront, and we did not plan to venture far inland, for fear of an ambush from the sea. The village was no more than a few blocks deep. For the moment we would ignore whatever lay on the plateau and the rest of the island. If we found no reason for alarm, Cholla Yi could send work parties inland to cut and shape trees for keel blocks, warp his ships two at a time close inshore, and wait for the tide to strand them. Then work could begin on cleaning, caulking, and retarring the bottoms, while my Guardswomen, with great relief, could become hunters to resupply our victuals.

Then Gamelan, who'd come ashore without my noticing, came tapping up with his blindman's stick to ask if he could come with us. I thought several things, but said none of them.

"Perhaps," he explained, "I might still have a small bit of my power left and could at least offer a warning of any magical danger."

I couldn't see any reason to deny him, and detailed two Guardswomen to help. We had no intention of racing through the village, and if we were attacked . . . well, Gamelan had said enough times that he hated the idea of being thought an anchor to the expedition.

We moved into the village, weapons ready. I was in the front, and once again I kept Dica beside me. Corais was just behind me, and Polillo and Flag Sergeant Ismet commanded the rear. We passed shops, homes, all the things that made up a prosperous village. I entered several homes, trying to figure out how much warning the people would've had. Contrary to what I knew our barracks tales would say later, when and if we returned to Orissa, there were no meals left unfinished on tables or tasks abandoned in mid-stroke.

There was one exception—the main taproom of a large tavern was the remnants of chaos itself. There were wineskins ripped asunder, bottles and casks shattered, goblets scattered across the floor, and tables overturned. Here also were several large bloodstains. I estimated that at least six drinkers, perhaps ten, had been surprised and slain in their cups. Remembering the shambles of the bedroom I'd been in earlier, I thought death came in the night, without warning. We moved on, ready for anything. But again there was no sense of danger. It was as if we were exploring ruins of a civilization that died in our mother's mother's time.

One of the flankers doubled back to report a large building ahead, just on the outskirts against the mountain face. She thought it might be a barracks, the first sign of a military presence beyond the anchorage. We moved toward it.

It almost certainly was a barracks—a long, two-story building, and, outside, a guard shack. For the first time I felt a whisper of danger, or of something untoward.

"Sergeant Ismet up!"

In a moment she was beside me, and I chose six others, all exceptional swordswomen, to accompany us inside. I sent Polillo with the rear element around the side. I put archers out as a screen, with orders to guard in all directions.

We entered the building and found a charnel hell. The barracks had sheltered at least two hundred soldiers—I knew because the building was filled with their bodies. Even my hardened soldiery was taken aback; I heard one or two gasps of horror and muttered curses.

The ghastly scene reminded me of something, and before I could close my mind, the memory came: once, when very young, I'd been in one of my father's barns, playing with three half-grown kittens. They'd found a nest of field mice that had moved into what they thought was a sanctuary of unbaled hay. The kittens, so friendly and lovable a moment before, hewed true to their duties and, with a great yowling and shrieking, slaughtered the entire nest before any of the mice could flee. Not content with killing them, they played with the dead and dying. Some they devoured, some they merely mutilated. Just as someone—or something—had done to these soldiers. Some had been asleep, some awake and on duty. It didn't matter. I saw shattered javelins, broken swords, fine plate armor that lay burst like potsherds.

Time had passed since that murderous night, but the horror was not lessened. Some of the bodies had rotted to skeletons, but others had dried and mummified, brown lips pulled back over yellowed teeth in horrid mirth. Not one body, though, was whole. Perhaps scavengers or rodents had fed, or carried the bones away for their own usage. Perhaps.

It was just then I heard the music. Flute music. It came from outside. Without orders, we ran out of the barracks, toward the sound.

It came from beyond the barracks, where a large semicircular wall reared. I started to rush toward it, then caught myself. I motioned, and my Guardswomen spread into a hedgehog semicircle and advanced. We rounded the end of the wall and stopped in our tracks. The wall became a high stone balustrade. A matching wall curved toward us on the other side. In the center, stone steps had been carved, a colossal staircase up the side of the plateau. On either side of the stairs luxuriant vines grew down, their flowers rich with a rainbow of colors.

The music came from the base of those stairs. It came, indeed, from a flute. The flute was being played by a strange creature. He was certainly not a man, for not even the barbarians of the icy south are that hairy, or so I've been told. Nor was he an ape, at least not from any species I've ever seen in the wild or a menagerie. Its face was neither ape- nor manlike. The best I could compare it to was that of a lion, with great fangs but without whiskers. Around his neck he wore a ribbon with a small jewel on it.

The creature looked at us with calm interest, showing no fear whatsoever, and its flute-playing never stopped, a melody that sang of birds over a stormy sea, birds wheeling in search of a home the winds had driven them from, a home they could never hope to find again.

I caught my breath, realizing what the flute had been made from. It was a human femur that had been lovingly pierced and polished. I saw a blur from the corner of my eye. It was Gerasa, my best archer, bringing her bow up, right hand drawing smoothly until the broadhead just touched the arrow rest.

"Stop," I snapped, and such was the discipline I'd worked into my women that the shaft never flew. But neither was the bow lowered. "We aren't starting a war here. We don't know who those soldiers were, nor why they were killed. Let alone whether our friend was the killer."

Gerasa's eyes flicked to the side at me, and I could tell her thoughts: No trooper should be slaughtered in such a manner, nor his or her memory mocked by an ape. But she lowered her bow.

Gamelan was beside me, his two guides just behind. Since the musician showed no sign of tiring, I briefly told him what we were looking at, and what I'd seen in the barracks not far away. Gamelan was silent for a long moment. His head turned back and forth, sweeping the wide base of the staircase as if he were sighted or, better yet, a hunting hound keen on the scent. A smile came and went on his lips.

"I do not know how to describe this. My powers are not returning," he said, and I could see he was forcing calmness. "There is *something* here. It is . . . it is like when you have had your eyes shut in absolute dark for a long time and then your thoughts claim you are seeing something. I can sense sorcery all about us . . . good or ill, I do not know. But it is something we must meet and face."

The creature's fluting broke off as if it were waiting for those words. It sprang to the railing of the stairs, took hold of a vine, swarmed up and was gone.

I listened within myself, to see if *I* sensed anything. There *was* something here, I realized—just as Gamelan had said. It was stirring; I felt as if I were a minnow near the surface of a pond and a great pike was moving below me in the mud and the reeds. Yet still, I felt no menace, no threat.

"We climb those stairs," I decided. I sent a runner and escort back to the beach to inform Cholla Yi of our intent. We started up, keeping six steps between us so if archers or spearmen lay in wait, they could find no target more inviting than a single woman. The steps were carved perfectly out of the rock, as if masons by the multitude had all eternity for their task. We reached a landing and turned—the steps becoming a tunnel into the cliff itself, windows cleverly carved to appear like fault lines to anyone below. The stone walls were also carved with bas-reliefs. They told a story, a story of bloody battles and strange cities on even stranger islands. I tried to follow the story, just as one studies a tapestry, but could make no sense of it. The carvings grew more elaborate, and stranger and more violent—and I took my eyes away.

We reached a second landing, and now the stairs were in the open once more, going straight into the rock wall's face. There was blue sky overhead, and the rock stretched high above us on either side.

I stopped and looked back to check the progress of my Guard. The climb was winding some of us, and I swore under my breath, realizing again how much a voyage saps one's strength, no matter how many calisthenics you do, or how many times you're chased around a deck by a leather-lunged training sergeant. Gamelan passed me. His escorts were panting a little, but the old Evocator was tapping along with the speed of a man a third his age. I hurried back to the head of the column and we continued up.

"I think I liked it better," Polillo said, from where she climbed not far behind me, "when we were in that damn tunnel with some overhead cover. That clifftop would sure be suggesting things to somebody who doesn't think I'd make a boon drinking companion . . . and who had a rock or six handy."

I fell in beside her and we climbed on in silence, trying not to count the steps, and then we were at the top and in the open.

The plateau was one great meadow. Low, rolling hillocks carried the eye from side to side. There were groves of trees set here and there among them, and I could see the blue of ponds and creeks. But this wasn't any natural paradise—in the middle of this plateau sat a great villa, with outbuildings scattered around. It was marble, and must have been that flash of white I saw while yet outside the island's bay. The building itself was multiple-storied. There were two polyhedron domes at the building's center, connected by an enclosed archway. This was an estate as grand as the finest Antero horse farm—and more.

I saw movement coming from the house. My Guardswomen deployed out into a vee formation at the head of the stairs, archers on the flanks, spearwomen guarding them, and swordswomen in the center.

The movement became a horse with rider. But the sight became more fabulous the closer it got. The horse was no common domestic, but a black-and-white-striped zebra, such as I had seen but once, when a ship laden with exotic animals bound for a king's court had docked in Orissa. Riding bareback on it was yet another of the beast-men. This one was even more grotesque than the musician, because it wore red knee breeches and a green jacket. The zebra stopped without command and its rider slid off.

The creature looked around curiously, then came directly to me. Then I saw that it, too, wore a jewel hung around its neck. The beast-man bowed, took an ivory tablet from inside its jacket and handed it to me. There was but one word on the tablet:

WELCOME.

The greeting was written in Orissan.

The beast-man did not wait for a response, but vaulted back onto the zebra. Again without command, the animal galloped away, not toward the great villa, but to a large barn I saw in the distance.

I told Gamelan what the tablet said and asked if his feelings had grown any stronger.

"No," he said. "All I know is that we must go on."

And so we did. I put my soldiery out in extended formation, with strong skirmishers on the flanks, and we marched toward the villa. It was even larger than I'd thought and not nearly as close. In fact, it was almost two miles away. As we came closer, I could make out gardens, a maze to one side, fish ponds, and other lavish outworks. But I saw not one of the vast company of gardeners that'd be necessary to keep these grounds so perfect.

There was a curving drive, wide enough for half a dozen formal carriages, paved with broken white oyster shell. Our boots crunched as we walked toward the villa's entrance—double doors thirty feet high and set in the center of a colonnaded terrace.

I brought my troops to a halt, and without any orders they automatically formed up in column, as if awaiting inspection by a great prince, never fearing an attack.

After a moment the doors opened and a man walked out.

"I greet you, and welcome you to Tristan," he said in Orissan, and his voice sang like a great gong, as welcoming as spiced cider on a winter's night. "I am The Sarzana, and I have waited long for your coming."

A DAY has passed since I dismissed the scribe, telling him I wasn't angered, but needed time to reflect on what words I would choose before continuing my story. I needed the time not because I was afraid to say what happened. We all err, and the only sin is committing the same stupidity twice.

It was rather that when you first meet someone great, someone who rocks the earth in his passage, memory has been known to shake a false ivory. Certainly The Sarzana must be considered great, for that word describes both good and evil. I do not want my knowledge of what came later to color what I saw and felt there on that island, seeing this man for the first time. But now my words are ready.

The Sarzana might have been taken for a merchant prince. He was richly dressed in a wide-sleeved tunic that came close about his neck. He wore pantaloons whose legs flared as fully as his sleeves. Both garments were purple, and he appeared born to that imperial color. I guessed them to be made of heavy silk. He wore a belt of twisted turquoise thongs; and I saw the glossy toes of ebony boots peeping from under his pantaloons.

The Sarzana was a bit under medium height and was full-bodied. It didn't appear as if he'd missed many meals, but neither did he appear to be a piggish feeder like Cholla Yi. He was clean-shaven and his cheeks were powdered. His pomaded hair hung in waves to just above his shoulders and looked to have had the attention of an artist with the curling iron minutes before he stepped out to greet us. His face was roundish, marked by very dark eyebrows and a straight mustache. If you passed him on an Orissan street, you might have thought him a visiting magnate, no more. A man of dignity and wealth.

At that moment I looked into his eyes. I swear this is not my jade of a memory adding something I didn't notice at the time. His eyes were a deep well of expression. They were dark—I can't say whether they were the deepest of greens, blues, or black snow—and they shone with the memory of power. The best I can compare them to is those of a caged eagle, who sits in the mews remembering how his talons ripped all that came before him; or perhaps the glow that comes to the goshawk's yellow eyes when she's un-hooded and sees the woodcock in the field.

No. Even on a busy street, in a rich district, the Sarzana would not be casually dismissed—not once you saw those eyes.

The Sarzana stopped when he came off the last step and bowed.

"You are safe," he said, and I *knew* absolutely that he spoke the truth. "You may summon the ships you have on guard beyond the headlands to en-ter the harbor and anchor, and may allow as many as you wish of your sail-ors to come ashore. There is no harm here. I do not expect you to take me at my word. I sense there are two among you who have the Talent. One has been badly hurt, I can feel . . ." I could sense Gamelan stirring from where he stood just behind me. ". . . the other is young, still feeling her way to power."

I removed my helmet and bowed. "I greet you in the name of Orissa," I said, but made no response to his statement about sorcerers. "I see you have the powers of magic and are what we call an Evocator. Can you sense aught of our history?"

"Some," he said. "And what I cannot, I am sure you will tell me. But we need not go into that now. I know you are not long from a great voyage and a greater battle, and since your victory, which nearly brought you down, you have been harried and sore-struck. But now you are safe. You may re-main here as long as you wish and refit. What tools and equipment you find, you are welcome to use as you wish. You may find housing below in the vil-lage, or up here, on the plateau. There are more than enough barracks to ac-commodate regiments far greater than your own.

"The fresh water, the grains that grow wild, the fruits of the trees, are yours for the taking. You may hunt, you may fish where you will. I ask only that you hunt no creatures who walk upright. Nor should you take any crea-tures who wear my sign, a jewel set in their forehead or on a band around their neck. They are my servants and my friends and I have sworn to let them come to no harm. This I must insist on, and anyone who breaks that law will be punished, and the manner of his punishment shall be most dire." Now all of us could see that sheen of authority in his eyes.

I broke the hold he had on us. "We come in peace, and none of us are fools or children. We hold to the laws of the country we visit"—I allowed a bit of steel into my voice—"so *long as we are honored as guests*. If that agreement is broken . . ." I did not finish my sentence, nor need to.

"Good," The Sarzana said. "I have already sent one of my . . . servants down to welcome the rest of your party, and to invite the officers of the ships, particularly the one you call Cholla Yi, to my villa. Captain Antero, you may, if you choose, allow your soldiers to break ranks and relax. There will be an opportunity to fresh yourselves before we dine."

I thought a moment. It would have been absurd to have listened to his honeyed words, but once more I felt nothing but calm and welcome. I looked at Gamelan, and he had a slight smile on his face, lifted as if to the warm afternoon sun.

"Thank you, Sarzana," I said. "We thank you deeply for welcoming us to your kingdom."

The Sarzana's expression changed, darkened. "Kingdom?" he said, and his voice, too, altered. It was as if a sudden storm cloud had rolled across the clear sky. "I who once ruled lands that stretched so wide no man could see them all in a lifetime? *This* is not my kingdom.

"This is my doom, Captain. This is my exile. This is where I was sent to die!"

BY MID-AFTERNOON all of our ships were moored in the harbor and most of the men ashore. The Sarzana said he'd have his minions clean out the death barracks in the village and our people could quarter there. Those of us who heard the offer shuddered collectively at spending even one night in that morgue. The Sarzana saw our response and said we were more than welcome to sleep up on the plateau if we wished—his enemies had built more than enough rooms when they exiled him to this island.

Corais boldly chanced a question, and asked what had happened below.

The Sarzana smiled, and his smile wasn't humorous. He said we'd learn in time, but that was near the end of his tale, and he preferred to tell it later. Unless, he added, the legate was worried that somehow what happened to those scoundrels bore on her fate? Even though his words were a taste harsh, no one took offense. Corais shrugged and said it was his island. All of us were still feeling that odd contentment, as if our troubles had come to an end.

The Sarzana's offer was generous, but neither Cholla Yi nor I wanted to be that far from our ships. Also, it would've taken too long for the working parties to go up and down that staircase, and as long as our ships were near-derelicts, we felt naked, unprotected.

We decided a small party of my Guardswomen, headed by Corais, would be quartered on the plateau, more to keep an eye on The Sarzana than anything else. The rest of us would use the abandoned houses along the waterfront, and cleaning them would be our first task. Two taprooms would be used for Cholla Yi's and my headquarters. The tavern I'd chosen also had good-sized rooms abovestairs, so these became quarters for Polillo, Aspirant

Dica, and myself. I'd determined to make her a legate if she survived our next battle, and to blazes with the official policy of not making promotions without a higher officer—which meant a man—approving. The long voyage had given me time to think about many things I'd taken for granted in Orissa, and there would be changes when we got back.

The Sarzana informed us he'd planned a feast to celebrate our arrival. We accepted, but told him some of my Guardswomen and a small watch aboard each ship would be unable to attend. They would mess off ship's rations. Tomorrow, if none of us fell ill from the food we'd eaten, they could have their own feast. This was common practice when dealing with foreign lords for whom poison might be an ordinary tool of state.

The Sarzana frowned when I told him we wouldn't all be able to take advantage of his hospitality, and I said, perhaps a little sharply, that we, too, had our customs. He smiled, not taking offense, and I felt whatever bit of suspicion I might have felt melt in his warmth. He said custom was a most good thing and that one of his own personal beliefs was that the commoner was as deserving a banquet for his or her deeds as any lord. It had been his way, he said, from the very beginning, that nobility and peasants should sit intermingled.

"If nothing else," he said, his smile becoming jovial, but never touching his eyes, "I've found that the man or woman of the soil or sea has far more interesting things to say than the latest court prattlings."

I was most impressed, as were my women. This was the way we ate and lived in battle, but in barracks even the Maranon Guard had separate messes for sergeants, officers, and privates. I made a note to think about this way of The Sarzana's. Perhaps when we returned home, this would be another idea worth introducing to the cobwebbed customs of the army, at least for the Guard. Only Cholla Yi and some of his officers appeared to resent the planned seating arrangement, but none of them said anything within my hearing.

We toileted in shifts and did our best to smarten up to our best full dress. But it was pretty pathetic. Our dress tunics were salt-spotted and our armor had discolored, in spite of constant polishing. Our brass was a beautiful greenish tint that took much cursing and ashes to remove. We whitened our leather as best we could, although it needed more than oiling and blanco—I hoped we could find time to cut and tan new hides before we sailed on. Our beautiful plumed helms had not taken the passage well and looked like seabirds who'd been tumbled about in a winter's gale. Only our weapons gleamed with never a stain.

We ourselves were so many harridans. Polillo took one look in a pier glass set between the two windows that looked out onto the harbor and moaned. "This isn't hair, this is a dust mop," she said, waving a handful of her brown locks at me.

I tried to be polite, but she was right. My own hair was in even worse shape, since a blonde's hair and skin is always the weather's first choice for destruction. We'd combed and washed, and when we could, oiled. But the sea and salt air had laughed at our efforts. Somehow, it hadn't seemed important aboard ship, when we all looked equally good or bad and who gave a damn what any sailor thought. But now, with the promise of this banquet, even though there was no one to impress but The Sarzana and his half-men, we felt shamed.

But we did what we could with the time and materials we had. And from this came another tale my women would be telling as long as I led them and beyond.

The villagers of Tristan had evidently been cleanly sorts, because there were more than enough tubs, wooden or metal, for bathing. Two of Cholla Yi's sailors decided to amuse themselves by peeping on our pastime. One earned himself a broken arm courtesy of a hurled stave by Polillo, the other bruised or broken ribs from a blunt-headed arrow fired by Gerasa.

Those of us who preferred our limbs hairless stropped our razors or smallknives and shaved. I wondered, as I cut myself and swore, why no Evocator had ever provided a depilatory spell, until I realized that men set great store by their own bodily hair and of course paid little heed to a woman's desires. I did remember having heard tales that some of Orissa's finer courtesans had their bodies completely ridden of hair below the neck, and realized that perhaps such a spell did exist and I'd never considered magic as being intended for daily use, until Gamelan began tutoring me.

And from there came my disaster. Just as I opened my small personal case and groaned, I heard other women complaining. The few cosmetic items we'd carried in our war bags had seen even worse treatment than our bodies. Our powders were caked, our oils were dried and thick, our creams were clotted, our rouges were cracked. This, and the way I'd been thinking a few minutes earlier, brought inspiration. I would save the day. I called for my sergeants and had them collect these dried-up items, each marked as to its owner. I thought for a moment and set my own kit in front of the others. I collected a bit of clean rainwater from a nearby cistern, some sweet-smelling flowers from a bush, a bit of oil from the tavern's kitchen, and finally a gaily colored scarf that'd been abandoned in a closet. I touched the scarf to each of my other ingredients and was ready.

All I needed was some species of goddess. I thought of Maranonia, but instantly put her aside. If she heard my prayer, she was as likely to turn me into a warthog for bothering her with something so trivial as face powder as grant my wishes.

I tried to remember another god, but unfortunately, being a true and skeptical Orissan, I grew up paying little attention to any gods except my own hearth god, Maranonia, the gods of the city, and any other beings it might have been politic to pray to in a public place. Having a god or godlet for each and every function—why, that was for superstitious peasants and outlanders. I asked if anyone knew of a goddess that might help us, and there was a long moment of silence.

Finally Polillo brightened and said that when she was but a mite of a youth, she remembered a friend of hers, "she was like a young deer," Polillo mooned, "but she preferred only men, the hairier the better, so she had no time for me. But I remember she used to pray to . . . to some goddess named . . . let me think . . . I have it! Helthoth. No, Heloth. Yes, that's it. I'm sure of it."

By this time about half my Guardswomen had gathered around and I knew I had better pull this one off most handily.

So I began my spell:

"As you were
So shall you be
Listen Heloth
And grant my plea.
Turn back
Turn back
Turn back again
Now you are
What you were."

As I chanted I touched my scarf to each of the cases, willing the properties of the oil, the flower, the sweet water, to rejuvenate our powders. I thought I saw a bit of a flicker and looked down at my own case. It looked as if it were brand new, and the nicks and scratches from a hundred hundred campaigns in my war bag were gone.

I'm afraid I got a little overexcited, this being my first real spell from intent to end. In fact, I yelped, "I did it!"

Corais was the first to pick up her case and open it, even before I opened mine. She gaped . . . and then she started laughing, laughing like a vixen in the spring watching her kits play. I had just time to realize something had gone very wrong and then my fingers fumbled my own case open.

My spell had worked very well. In fact, it'd worked too well. My cosmetics had grown young—inside the case was a disgusting mess of ingredients: almonds, before they'd been crushed for their oil, rose petals, metallic powder, butter, olive oil, and all the rest of the things skilled chemists ground and mashed to make unguents from.

As the laughter grew into hoots, I glumly knew it would be a *very* long time before the Guard forgot the tale of how Captain Antero Turned Back Time.

BEFORE WE ASSEMBLED and went back up those stairs to the plateau to meet The Sarzana, I drew Gamelan aside. He, too, was dressed in his best. I'd detailed two of my women off to help him get ready, and told them if he gave any sign that they were treating him like a cripple, they would not have to wonder who was assigned to the jakes detail for a long, long time.

Just as I had before we landed, I asked Gamelan if he sensed any magics being constructed against us.

He said he did not.

"But I can tell you one thing for certain, which you certainly will have realized already. This Sarzana is a mighty sorcerer, as mighty, I can *feel*, even though stripped of my powers, as any I have heard of or encountered. Further, I sense that he held power in a temporal sense."

"Like the Archons?" I said.

Gamelan thought for a while. "In a way. It is hard to describe exactly, but with a difference. The Archons learned magic, and with that magic seized the throne, true to the tradition of the rulers of Lycanth. This man is different. I feel that this Sarzana—and I wish I knew what that word meant, whether name or title—seized wand and scepter at the same time, and used one to give the other greater strength and then return the favor before he fell.

"I wonder what brought him down?" I said.

"All my senses tell me he was a great ruler, which from what I have heard of his palace, is obvious. My senses also say he ruled wisely, if firmly. So I wonder why he was overthrown. How and why?"

"Perhaps he'll tell us." I said.

"Perhaps he shall. Before he lets us know what he wants. Because no ruler, no matter how godlike, no matter how long since he lost or gave up his throne, is ever content with his lot. All we can do, though, is let the wind carry us, just as we have had to do since we fought the Archon."

"And do you sense any sign of *him*?"

"No," Gamelan said. "At least that's a relief. Not since . . . since I woke blind but still feeling his presence. I have almost managed to convince myself that was a hallucination."

"Almost," I said. "I wish you were certain."

Gamelan's lips quirked, but he didn't answer me. Instead, he took me by the arm. "Young Rali, we have a banquet to attend. Sit close beside me, to make sure I don't put my fish on the meat plate. You can be my eyes."

"I'm sure," I said, my tone very dry, "you want me to be your eyes just for etiquette's sake."

"Why, Captain," he said archly, "what other reason could there be?"

We laughed, and then I shouted for my troops. It was time for the banquet.

THE MEAL was maybe not the oddest I've ever eaten, but it was well up on the list. The dining room was a wide marble hall, hung with tapestries showing deeds as heroic and grotesque as those on the bas-reliefs on the passages leading up to the plateau. There was room and to spare for all of us—in fact, the entire expedition as we set out in pursuit of the Archon could have fit comfortably into the great chamber. The dining room was as splendid as any I'd ever seen, as rich as the great Banquet Room in the Citadel of the Magistrates, back in Orissa. The chamber was brightly but not harshly lit, yet no one could see any sign of taper or torch. Similarly, there was music playing, but there was no orchestra in view, nor curtained anteroom where one might have been hidden, at least not that I could see.

As The Sarzana promised, we were seated sailor next to officer, slinger next to legate, and, indeed, the conversation was more interesting than most court banquets I'd been forced to attend in Orissa. This *was* a custom worth adopting.

I've just noticed my scribe frowning, wondering why I said the banquet was so strange, yet haven't given him any reasons for saying that. I could remind him of our circumstances, how but a day earlier we'd been storm-tossed waifs on deadly seas, or how this man, sitting at the head of the table between Gamelan and myself, with Cholla Yi and Stryker on the other side, seemed the only human living on this island. But such knowledge wasn't necessary to make the night bizarre.

The servitors accomplished that all by themselves. All of them were the beast-men like the flutist or the rider who'd presented The Sarzana's welcome. They were dressed even more oddly than the rider, however. They wore various costumes, all expensive, some in jeweled women's gowns, some in rich robes such as a Magistrate might wear, others in gold-laid armor that a general might envy.

The Sarzana noted my interest. "This is my conceit," he explained. "Or, rather, one of them. Each of my servants is dressed like a member of my court. So I am surrounded by the same lords and ladies I was in the past. Except," he added, and his light tone grew bitter, "I do not have to await betrayal, as I did in another palace, in another time."

I nodded, realizing that, like any storyteller, The Sarzana was preparing the way for his tale, and I wondered when he would choose to tell it.

In spite of their clumsy regalia, the beast-men were most efficient, never allowing a plate to remain in front of a diner when she was finished, nor a goblet to be empty for longer than it took to be refilled from a golden pitcher.

I remember each course of that meal very well, each accompanied by a different, perfectly chosen wine. We began with various dishes intended to whet our appetite: richly seasoned liver pastes on bits of bread; shellfish raw in their shells or baked with bits of pork or vegetable; spiced vegetables. Next were ortolans, baked in a wine jelly, each one but an instant, vanishing mouthful. Then there was salmon, a great fish to every few diners, served smoking hot, the grill marking its flesh, and a dill and butter sauce to complement it for those who wished more seasoning; for myself, a dash of fresh lemon was enough. Then came a wild mushroom soup, with as many varieties of mushrooms in each cup as I have ever seen, each having its own unique savor, as if cooked alone.

The main course came next—great haunches of a game animal, served with a jelly of tart crab apples and berries, and larded with salt pork. I asked The Sarzana what the animal was, and he told me a species of single-horned antelope that lived on the north of the island. "A huntsman's challenge," he said, "since they never congregate in herds, but live solitary lives. I know nothing about how or when they mate."

"You yourself hunt?" Polillo asked from her seat down the table.

"I do not," The Sarzana said. "I would find myself puffing and panting, looking like a portly fool who's trying to become an imbecile, dashing through the woods chasing something he'd just as soon first meet on a platter at dinner. My servants hunt for me. Hunt and fish."

"We saw no signs of boats," Polillo said. "Do your . . . servants hunt from the shore?"

The Sarzana smiled. "These"—he gestured around at the beast-men—"are not the only ones who've chosen to serve me. There are dolphins . . . seals . . . hawks . . . others who have chosen to serve me."

I suddenly remembered the two dolphins, swimming abreast under our ship as we approached the island. Was that a net I'd seen them hold in their mouth, and the emblem a diadem such as the beast-men wore?

"Chosen?" Gamelan said gently.

"I admit," The Sarzana said, "to having prepared the ground with a spell or two. But what of that? These creatures live far better lives than they did before. Then they hunted and were hunted, lives no longer than an instant. If they sickened, or if storms tossed them, they were helpless. Now, in exchange for performing small favors for me—most of which, such as fishing, were already part of their bestial habits—their lives are happier and gentler."

I wondered if any beast, taken from the wild, is happier, but said nothing. This was an argument I'd heard from zookeepers as well. Gamelan, too, had no comment.

The meal continued. Almost everyone was on his or her best behavior. All of my Guardswomen had been cautioned to remain sober, and I noticed that none of them, not even Cliges, my most notorious drunkard, did more than sip at their wines. Three or four of the sailors, however, being sailors, decided to seize the moment. One of them got so rapidly in his cups I heard the beginnings of a song coming from that table. The Sarzana appeared not to notice, nor did his casual, clever dinner conversation change. But I saw him glance at the budding drunkards, and as soon as he did, they became quiet.

One of my women said later the sailors did, indeed, grow instantly sober, but shuddered and shook, as if they underwent the throes of a seconds-long hangover before they did. It was obvious The Sarzana controlled his dining with more than courtesy.

Our meal finished with various tarts—fruits, berries, and such—accompanied by an assortment of cheeses such as I'd never tasted.

Just as I finished, there came a babble. My Guardswomen and the sailors were getting up and, most politely, taking their leave, just as if we were at the end of a barracks meal and the last of the wine had been drunk. Outside, I heard the shouts of the sergeants forming them up. Before I could do more than gape, I heard them marching away, across the plateau.

The only ones remaining in that vast chamber were Cholla Yi, Gamelan, Corais, and myself. I felt alarmed for a moment, then noted, just in the entranceway, Sergeant Bodilon, whom I'd assigned with Corais to stay up here with The Sarzana. On either side of the doorway were two guards, each with her spear butt braced beside her, looking most alert.

The Sarzana looked at me. "Captain Antero. Forgive me for overstepping my bounds. But I rather assumed your women would be happier returning to their quarters. They've had a most long day, as have had your sailors, Admiral Yi."

For some reason, neither of us objected, nor were we alarmed by The Sarzana's magics. That warm, rich feeling that had marked the day sat about our shoulders, like a welcome wool cloak on a winter's night.

"Now," he went on, "if we can adjourn to another room, we can continue our conversation. I know almost everything about you. I know you, and your homelands. I know of your pursuit of your great enemy, and his destruction. I know the perils you have overcome crossing these seas. And I know what lies ahead . . . But you know nothing of me."

He smiled. "Now, that shall change . . . Now I shall tell you my story, of how I came to be The Sarzana, and of the evil that brought me and the great civilization of Konya down."

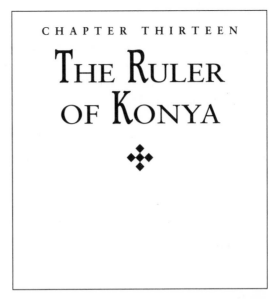

CHAPTER THIRTEEN

THE RULER OF KONYA

❖

The Sarzana turned and walked away through the banquet hall. He gave neither command nor invitation, but the four of us knew we were to follow. Corais took Gamelan by the elbow, and we threaded our way through the tables. The beast-men were busily cleaning up and paid us no attention.

We walked down a long hallway that reminded me of a museum—there must've been a hundred items, from paintings to sculpture to colorful costumes on the wall, each coming from a different culture.

We went through an archway into a circular room with a round fireplace in the center. In spite of the evening's balm, a fire blazed, but I felt no unpleasant warmth coming from it. Comfortable couches sat around the fire, and there were small tables near each couch set with glasses and bottles.

"I used a small bit of divination to determine what each of your favorite tipples is," The Sarzana said, trying to assume the casual gaiety of his earlier conversations. "I trust you will forgive my intrusion."

We seated ourselves, and I recognized the flask in front of me—it appeared to be an exact duplicate of Talya, the sweet dessert wine the Antero estates has produced for some generations only for their most honored guests. We make it from grapes allowed to shrivel on the vine, then picked at the height of their ripeness; the grapes are carefully taken from their stems and placed into a vat, where they are crushed by their own weight. For an instant I forgot where I was, and my eyes blurred, remembering what was so far away and, I was beginning to fear, unattainable. The last time I'd had this wine had been years ago, when the harvest had been plentiful enough to justify the making of Talya, since it was incredibly wasteful. I'd shared the flask with Tries in the days when there was nothing but silken love between us.

I turned my face away so The Sarzana wouldn't see tears touch my face. Cholla Yi harrumphed and said something gruffly about how pleased he was Lord Sarzana could produce the finest drink of his homeland, a distilled concoction of cherry pits it seemed not many had the palate to appreciate.

"Not Lord," The Sarzana said, "if you please. My title, to all Konyans, needs no further embellishment."

I nodded to myself. One of Gamelan's questions had been answered. I used the tip of my dagger to peel the wax sealant off, pulled the cork, poured a bit of the wine and tasted. I hid a smile. The Sarzana's magic wasn't quite perfect—there was a hidden tartness to this vintage our own grapes never held. But I had to admit the effect had been startling, and the wine's taste was quite pleasant.

"This room," The Sarzana said, "I use as a reminder of what once was. Look about you." Two of us turned, but I did not, keeping my eyes fixed on The Sarzana's hands, as Gamelan had taught me to do when watching a sorcerer—right crossed over left, turned palm up, and fingers beckoning. I had the gesture, but thought it would give me nothing, since I saw his lips move in the incantation, but I couldn't make out the words he spoke. Then I turned to see.

The spectacle he'd evoked took me. We were in the midst of the sacking of a great palace. The walls were hung with tapestries, roaring in flames. I saw beautiful women, screaming and being dragged off by drunken men. I saw looters carrying away finery, or tearing or shattering it for the sheer love of destruction. I saw soldiers in armor: some sprawled in death, having fulfilled their last duty; others had turned their coats, and become looters. I saw men, and women, too, dressed in the finery of the ruling class, ordering the mob in its destruction. Then there was nothing but marble walls, the marble worked with threads of exotic minerals.

"That was the day of my downfall," The Sarzana said. "That was the day my beloved Konya lost its last chance of greatness, freedom, and peace." I saw his lips tighten as he fought for and regained control. "I keep this memory fresh," he continued, "because I do not want to soften, here in my long exile."

"Perhaps," Gamelan said in his low but commanding voice, "you should begin by telling us what you ruled."

The Sarzana's lips curved. "Thank you, Lord Gamelan. I shall. I am not accustomed to tale-telling, and I forget that not all the world knows of Konya and its once greatness."

He sat down on a couch and poured a goblet of what appeared to be water from a clear pitcher.

"My kingdom," he said, "is far to the south of us, and if you will forgive me for waxing poetic, I think of it as jewels spilled across the seas, since it is composed of many thousands of beautiful islands—whose center is Isolde, the most lovely gem of all. It is from here that the kingdom has been ruled since time began. The islands have every climate imaginable, from desert to coral atolls to high glacial mountains in their reaches to the farthest south, which remain unexplored. Isolde itself is about three weeks sail under strong winds."

"So many islands," Cholla Yi said. "Are they all peopled?"

"Most of them," The Sarzana replied. "And this is the great tragedy of Konya. It sometimes seems as if each island is its own nation, a nation entirely different from its nearest neighbor. Worse, each island is perpetually at war with the other."

I saw Cholla Yi smile, and knew what he was thinking—if each man's hand is turned against his fellow, there are rich takings for a pirate.

"We Konyans," The Sarzana went on, "have only one thing in common: we are hot-blooded and fiery, quick to judge, love or hate. There's a proverb: 'With a Konyan beside you, you shall lack neither friends nor enemies.' I fear it is true."

"A hard land to rule," Corais said.

"It is . . . was, indeed."

"Were you born to the throne?" Cholla Yi asked.

"I was not. Like your Evocator, I was a fisherman." I glanced quickly over at Gamelan and saw him suppress a start. "Perhaps," The Sarzana continued, "I misspoke. My family was less masters of the net and line than expert with our boats and, just as importantly, the marketplace. My family owned five smacks, and another ten families owed us fealty."

"You outreach me," Gamelan put in. "We had but a single boat to fish the river, not the sea, and we owed money on that one to our lender."

"Perhaps," The Sarzana said, "I would have been happier if that had been my position as well, for I never would've ended up there on this forsaken rock. But I'm probably being naive—a man is, I believe, born to the throne, no matter if he is birthed in a ditch. Ruling is a destiny, not a profession."

Cholla Yi looked approving, and Gamelan frowned slightly, but none of us interrupted.

"As I said, I was no different than a dozen other shipowners on my island, with but one exception: early on, my family recognized I had a talent for magic. On our island, unlike some other places, a witch or village wizard was respected, particularly if he had any of what we called the Weather Art. But what knowledge I gained was here and there. There was no formal schooling to be gotten that I was aware of, unlike what I have divined your home of Orissa to have. Perhaps, if there had been more money, or if my family was higher in the social order, although we had no aristocrats to speak of on the island, I might have been able to go to Konya itself to perfect my art. But this wasn't to be. Perhaps it was for the best, when I think about what happened to many of the lords and ladies a few years later. I reached my young manhood not much different from any of the others in my class. I did everything in my family's trade, from fish-gutter to helmsman to harpooner to using my small Talent to feel where we might have the best luck casting our nets.

"The misfortune of our island was that it lay in rich waters on a main trade route leading to Konya itself. Rich waters with fish beyond count for the taking—but our seas were traveled by other sharks. Pirates, slavers, warships, even merchants who were nothing loath to waylay one of our boats if they were short a hand or two. Everyone knew the men of the Island of the Shark were, they said, birthed with webbed feet and hands curved to fit an oar's handle.

"Every year five, ten, sometimes more islanders would vanish. Some would find their way back after a single voyage, others . . ." The Sarzana shrugged. "I, myself, barely escaped being forced into servitude half a dozen times, either by weather luck or being able to feign disease or feeblemindedness when one of my boats would be stopped. Of course, I never showed any sign that I might have a bit of the Talent to these raiders, or I would have been a great prize."

"Couldn't your government help?" Gamelan asked.

"Government?" The Sarzana sneered. "Our rulers were far away and cared little what happened to us, except when they sent a tax ship to levy a toll. That was as great a burden, some thought, as any pirate. Konya was ruled, or I should say mis-ruled, by a single family and its septs, whose blood had gone thin over the centuries. No, we could look for nothing except harshness from those who thought themselves fit to wear a crown."

"The gods gave man steel," Corais said, "so he would not have to suffer unjust kings forever."

The Sarzana looked at Corais strangely, then said, "Perhaps that is the legend in your land, Legate. But not in mine. In Konya there is a belief that he who kills a king will die a million deaths, and his soul shall never be permitted peace, but be tormented by demons through all the worlds that exist, forever. But we have veered from the subject at hand, and what happened to my poor island that began all this.

"One day pirates surrounded ten boats in the middle of a great haul, and took all of our men off, sinking the boats in callous glee as they did. That day marked the end, and the beginning. All of us shipowners assembled, determined we must do something. That was the day the gods touched me, because I *knew* what we must do. Perhaps this was the first time my Gift really showed what it could become. We must fight back, I said, and fight back hard. We were becoming a joke, not men, not women, but eunuchs, and if we stood for this treatment, we deserved to be wiped out, our island to be a desolation and our women transported to port towns to whore for their bread. We might as well rename our island Jellyfish Isle, instead of calling ourselves after the ruler of the seas. Honey was given to my tongue, because all at once my fellow villagers were shouting their approval and hoisting me to their shoulders."

The Sarzana stopped for a moment, then went on. "That was the first time I heard cheering and my name being cried aloud, and it was very sweet." I thought he was speaking to himself as much as us.

"We formed a defense league. No longer did each fisherman flee his fellows to work a secret reef or hole. Now we sailed in groups of at least five boats, and would work common waters, always with one man in each boat keeping his eye on the horizon for a hostile sail. Each of our boats now had weaponry under the nets. At first it was little more than sharpened gaffs, tridents, and gutting knives, but after the first raider made the mistake of attacking us, we had swords, spears, and bows." He smiled tightly at the memory. "Very quickly, we learned to use them well, against others who were foolish enough to take on the men of our island. The word spread—the waters around the Isle of the Shark were safe for all, except those who sought blood. Those pirates and raiders found the death they thought they were bringing to us."

The Sarzana's eyes flashed. "There were other islands who sent representatives to marvel at our accomplishments. To each of them we made the same offer—join us, and have peace. It took little persuasion once they saw the benefits of cooperation."

Cholla Yi appeared as excited at the story as The Sarzana was. "And they chose you as their leader?"

"Of course," The Sarzana said. "Who else *was* there? Within a year, our entire archipelago was at peace. The islanders found my ideas and ways to be convenient, and so they asked me to rule them in their daily life, not just as a defender. We were able to choose certain men, our most valiant, and pay them to do nothing but stand guard. We regulated the markets so a fisherman could go to sea knowing he wouldn't return home with his holds full to find the prices so low he wouldn't even have paid for the twine to repair his nets or the scrap fish to bait his hooks. Disputes between villages could be handled by a traveling court, rather than settled with feuds as before. We made our own flag. In honor of where our movement began, we chose the Shark . . . Once again, we had peace. But not for long."

"I don't think your rulers would have thought very much of this new kingdom in their midst," I said.

"True. But that is not the way it happened, exactly. We found there is a worse despotism than an aging, senile family. It is the people themselves. The old king died. And that gave the opportunity. There can be no regicide when no one has been crowned. On Konya, and on other islands, the populace rose spontaneously. Mobs formed, and attacked the rulers' palaces. By the time word reached our islands, what government of old there had been had disappeared in a welter of blood and flame, and noble heads paraded through the streets atop pikes."

The Sarzana shivered. "Now came true terror. Let me tell you, gentle people, if you have never been misfortunate enough to know tyranny, you should know there is none worse than that wielded by the people. Let the slightest man or woman of ability, thought, or genius rise up, and he will be cut down, just as the scythe first slashes the ripest grains of wheat that have grown above the rest. That is when I learned that if the first principle of monarchy is to rule with justice, the second is that those whom the gods meant to be governed must never be allowed to influence the scepter."

I glanced at Corais, keeping my face blank, and saw her own expression as closed as it was when she heard an order she knew to be wrong. But Cholla Yi was nodding, enthralled. I could tell nothing at all from Gamelan's expression. The Sarzana continued:

"Once they'd overthrown the government, then they met in solemn enclave, what they called a People's Parliament." He snorted disgust. "Imagine all those shopkeeper's wives, bloody-handed soldiery, dirt-caked peasants and their like, milling about the palaces they'd sacked, each shouting he knew the best way to rule. Eventually, they settled on a form of government in which each man or woman was to be no better than the worst, and anyone who deemed himself better than the others was evil and must be destroyed, a horrible reminder of the days of kings, which were gone, never to return.

"What was worse," he went on grimly, "was that these peasant-rulers had sycophants of the worst sort, yea-sayers who kept those poor fools from realizing their stupidity. Early on, when the people had first begun their revolt, the lowest class of the nobility, the barons, those who'd never done anything to help Konya except sit on their estates and exploit all who came near them, saw the straws in the wind and cast their lot with the usurpers. These petty lordlings were held up by the rulers of Konya as proof positive they didn't desire to turn all mankind into a swarm of ants. So, of course, these noblemen and women danced constant attendance to their real rulers."

"I gather," Gamelan said, "that about this time your Shark Islands must have come into conflict with the Konyans."

"Just so." The Sarzana nodded excitedly. "When they realized there was another way to live, a way in which each man freely paid the debt owed to his superior, and his better gave even more of himself—why, a great expedition had to be mounted to extirpate this heresy from Konya.

"Also," The Sarzana went on, and this comment was the second that seemed inwardly intended, "I have learned that a ruler's task is easier if the masses always have an external enemy to arouse their anger.

"They sent out a great fleet, with orders to lay waste to our lands. Perhaps the old regime might have mounted an expedition successfully. But not this new rabble. It took them months to raise and half train an army, find ships and educate their merchant captains to be naval officers, and then longer still to victual and outfit the men. All this took great time—time they no longer had. Because something had happened to me. One day—and if I were telling anything other than the raw truth, it would have been a day of thundering and lightnings—I . . . I *understood*. I do not know how else to put it. Gamelan?"

"I *do* know what you mean," the Evocator said. "It's not unknown for a particularly gifted sorcerer to suddenly be enlightened, and see the elements of his craft open before him."

"Just so," The Sarzana said excitedly. "This part of my life I do not discuss with others, and it is a relief to find that I am not alone. Because once I held this power, I knew I must not confide in any magician who could become dangerous to me. I could feel my enemies—the enemies of my people—building their strength. But my own strength was growing fast. I felt at times that the very spirit of my islanders, and those who'd chosen me as their ruler, was giving me power."

The Sarzana stopped and poured his glass full. He drained it, set it down, and smiled, his mind in the past.

"When their fleet arrived off the Island of the Shark, it was met with a great storm. A storm my powers had helped raise. There were two hundred or more ships that sailed to the islands. But the rocks and the tides and the winds took them and scattered them and sank them! When the winds died, and the sun came out once more, then we put out in our small ships against their great galleys with many-rowed oars. My men swarmed against their ships like barracuda striking a sunfish. And then it was over, and the men of the Island of the Sharks held the day. Now we were the strongest force in all of the Konyan lands. We knew what we had to do. We could not discard the sword and return to our nets and our lands—the mob would try once more, never satisfied until they dragged us down.

"So we assembled our own battle fleet, but it didn't come just from our archipelago. There were others in Konya who loathed this new order, and saw it could bring nothing but doom to all mankind. There were nearly a thousand ships that assembled off Isolde. We expected a great battle—but there was none to be fought. The rabble had broken. Some fled, some recanted, some chose death by their own hand rather than see order return to the world.

"They carried me from the docks where my flagship had docked straight into the Palace of the Monarchs, where I was crowned by the trembling hand of one of the survivors of the great family that had once ruled. That was nearly thirty years ago."

The Sarzana sat silent, his eyes hooded, recalling that long ago triumph. None of us broke the silence.

Then he said: "At first, things went well. No one seemed displeased at seeing mob rule discarded. I punished as little as I could, wanting peace with no one having blood to revenge. I tried to rule mercifully, and that spawned my downfall."

"How," Corais wanted to know, "can mercy ever be a base act?"

"Legate, that is hardly a question I'd expect of a warrior. Let me offer an example to clarify things. Would you fell an enemy, then turn your back on him if he still had a dagger at his belt?"

"Ah," Corais said.

"Exactly. Some of those who'd sent that fleet out, or who conspired to murder the lords and ladies of the old regime, I merely exiled to distant lands or even their own estates. Others, more culpable, I imprisoned for a fixed time. There were only a few who had to meet the most severe penalty. And what was the result? The exiles were able to plot beyond my eyes on their lands. Those I'd executed became martyrs. Those in prison wrote passionate documents to stir up another rebellion, which were secretly passed from hand to hand."

"But all this," Cholla Yi put in cynically, "is no more than any strong man must face who seizes power. Although I quite agree with you when you said you were too merciful. In my own land, when a man takes the throne, his first act is to slay his brothers and uncles, so there can be none of his blood to rise against him."

All this was too much for me. "Sarzana. With all respect, my own city has gone through great changes in the past few years. But there is no hidden conspiracy against the new Magistrates or those Evocators who now speak for the people—at least not one I'm aware of."

"I suspect, Captain, you come from a more phlegmatic race," The Sarzana said. "You remember, I said that we Konyans are hot-blooded, and quick to any extreme? People such as we can be ruled in only one way—and that is firmly. Konyans will not cry out against their rulers unless they see the laws enforced without an even hand. But I had an additional problem, one that became the hub of the conspiracy."

"The nobility you spoke of," I guessed.

"Just so. At first, the barons could not sing my praises too loudly. But then, I found it necessary to examine their position, and realized they still held all too many of the unjust powers that had been the greatest evil of the old rulers, powers that went back for hundreds of years. Some collected rents on lands they'd never seen, others had entire islands or even the seas around them as their private fiefs. A slave was a slave, until the last generation, with no way to free himself."

I flinched a little at that, since it was only recently that Orissa had righted *that* great wrong herself, a doing of my brother, Amalric.

"Even more, some of them held writs that enabled them to circumvent common law and imprison or otherwise punish anyone who offended them, with no recourse whatsoever. Great areas of land were held by them, and rack rents charged, when most Konyans had but a tiny parcel of land to raise their crops. Perhaps I should have moved more slowly. But raw injustice brings rage to my heart, and a sword to my hand. I announced all of those baronial privileges would be examined, and a fresh wind of change would blow across the land.

"That was the spark. It fell on dry tinder because the gods had turned away from Konya. We had had several seasons of great storms, and then hot dry winds sweeping across our fertile lands. The schools of fish that were once so common seemed to find other seas to live in, and there was starvation for the first time in memory. The spark grew into flame. Some of the outlying islands rose against me, and I found it necessary to send out soldiers to suppress the risings. Unfortunately, the captains I chose were brutal men, men who thought the most profound peace was that of the graveyard. My advisers kept the tales of these misdeeds from me, so I thought all was well with my people and my crown.

"Finally, the darkest of sorcery was used. Somehow my enemies tapped into a greater power than mine. I do not know where it came from—whether it was a natural force, some demon-lord or imported full-blown from a dark world, or what. But all that I turned my hand to, trying as best I could, failed. A screen was drawn between me and the future. No longer did I have any sense of what the morrow would bring.

"Then the revolt came. Men and women rose up in blind rage and panic. The mob ruled Konya yet again. But this time, there were cunning hands behind it. The barons guided this senseless rage against the one who loved them best. And they brought me down, me and those around me, those I'd brought up from many parts of Konya and given power to because of their talents and their love of their fellow Konyans. It was the greatest destruction our poor shattered lands have ever seen."

Again there was a long silence.

"They should have killed me," The Sarzana said finally. "But they were too cruel for that. In secrecy, they sentenced me to death. Even the barons knew most Konyans still held the truth within them, and would quickly remember I was their salvation, not downfall. They sentenced me to die, but in the delight and savoring of their cruelty, they said they would carry out the sentence at a time of their choosing."

"What of that curse you mentioned?"

"I was secretly told the soldiers assigned to me had been promised a great counterspell would be laid over them, when my death was ordered. Also, if many hands held the sword, there was no way the death-demons could determine who the actual asssassin was. Besides, great amounts of gold and rich estates were promised. I have noticed rewards such as those make men forget about the distant gods and their threats," The Sarzana said cynically.

"What did the people of this island, Tristan, think, when you were exiled here?" I wanted to know. "And . . . what happened to them?"

"At first," he said, "they didn't know what to think, since they'd been removed from the bloodbath on Konya. They were pleased at all the new building that was required. Oddly enough, this palace was already half built. It had been ordered by an eccentric lord, who retired from the world with great riches. But the mansion was but half finished when he fell off a cliff, while shouting poetry to the gods in a drunken ecstasy. Since the barons who now ruled Konya had ordered my exile to be luxurious until the moment of death, there was a great deal of further gold spent here, in addition to completing this estate. Also, those great warships moored in the harbor kept off slavers or pirates.

"The villagers welcomed the soldiers at first. They had money, and new stories and songs, and the island women were tired of their old swains. That brought the first troubles. The garrison's officers should have stepped in, but they did not, most of them having already commenced their own tawdry affairs. I didn't know what do to, but knew I would not pace my cage, no matter how silken they made it, until they sent in the slaughterer with his maul.

"Fortunately, my Talent was returning. I sensed that whatever had blocked my sight was gone, where I knew not, although I was still handicapped by the long months without my powers." Gamelan winced at this last. "I needed allies. And constant use of my Art would restore it to its former strength."

"The animals," I said.

"Yes. Untouched by man's evil in their souls, but always and forever man's victim. I cast general spells of benevolence. When the soldiers held one of their hunts, I sent a knowledge-spell with it, so all the creatures of the island knew what evil their enemy, man, was doing to them."

"And the beast-men?"

"Those are mine own. Are not they fabulous creatures?"

"It takes a mighty spell to create life itself," Gamelan said. "There are those who call it a Dark work."

"When one is fighting for one's life, and for the lives of one's people, there is no place for moral judgments. Let those who write the history books make them, from the peaceful libraries the bloody-handed ruler has created. I hold no truck with those who constantly second-guess from some lofty position, what the man who is down in the arena must do in the blood and heat of the moment."

I, too, felt about to argue the point, and then thought better of it. Why, in the name of whatever god ruled the mouth of fools, were we sitting debating morality in the middle of this man's realm, small though it was? It was hardly politic, nor did what this man had done in the past matter now. Perhaps he had ruled more harshly than I would've, if anyone were stupid enough to offer me a crown and I imbecile enough to accept it. But I *felt*, with every sense, The Sarzana had intended the best for the Konyans, and been betrayed unjustly. As that thought came, along with it came warmth, that I had just gained a great truth—those who wear the crown must not be judged with us commoners.

"These creatures," The Sarzana said, "who are better friends than any of the butter-tongued fools who danced attendance on me at court, came from many places. I used the ... There is no word for it in Konyan nor Orissan nor any speech I know—'souls' would be the approximation if they had been men, but they were but the spiritual presence of animals, killed at sea or on land. I gave them new flesh, and animated them, with powers and strengths they'd never known before. They know it, too, and their gratitude never ceases. One day, when—or should I say if—I can flee this island, I will set them free, and they will be the rulers of this land, ruling more mercifully than man ever could, keeping common cause with the other creatures on the land and sea.

"But again I've turned from my story. I could feel the moment coming when a ship would slip into harbor, carrying orders for my death. It seemed like the villagers also felt something, because when I was allowed to go down the great stone steps, I heard mutterings against the soldiers, and the fishermen went out of their way to show me small kindnesses. It touched me to my depths, as it has always touched me when those who are under the iron boot do what they can to preserve their humanity. And it reminded me of my own village, so many miles and years gone.

"One day, a courier *did* arrive. I braced for the moment of death, but nothing happened. Life seemed to continue as before, except now I was forbidden to visit the village. One night, I was roughly seized, and held in a locked chamber under this mansion, guarded by a full squad of soldiers. This was the end, I thought. But the sun rose the next day, and I yet lived, and I was set free. Now I could go wherever I wished on the island—because the villagers were gone!"

"How?" Corais asked.

"At nightfall, the soldiers commanded them to collect at the waterfront. They were ordered into their boats, taking nothing with them. Their crowded boats were taken under tow by warships. This I discovered from discreet questioning of the soldiers. It took divination to learn the rest. The boats were towed well out to sea, out of sight of land. The soldiers had been ordered that there must be no witnesses to my coming death, and they gladly obeyed this order, feeling perhaps the doom that pursues king-slayers might be fooled. The villagers' boats were rammed by warships, and the poor floundering men, women, and children let drown or made sport of by archers and spearmen. Not one soul was allowed to survive.

"I knew then my life's cord was measured in finger spans. I was desperate. I thought long, and then realized blood is a lever in magic, a great weapon. The villagers—I thought of them as *my* villagers—would not have died in vain. I cast the first of my great spells. It swept in that night, like a sudden winter storm. The soldiers knew nothing, felt nothing. But my animals, my friends and servitors, felt the weight of all the generations they'd been prey to men. And that compact with the gods that frighten animals when they see man was broken. They were given free rein to revenge themselves.

"They did just that, in one long night of gore. I must say, I listened to the screams with satisfaction. My spell required my beasts to show no more mercy to the soldiers than they gave the fishermen. Some died easily, in their sleep, some fought back and were butchered, some tried to flee to the ships and were drowned by the seals or my dolphins. By dawn, I was the only human on Tristan.

"I ordered the bodies brought to the end of the plateau, beyond this mansion, and tossed over the cliff, to be carried away by the strong currents. Then, and it was a savage chore, my servants and I went from ship to ship in the harbor, cutting free the moorings, setting full sail so the ship sped out beyond the headlands, to sail and sail with no hand at the helm through desolate seas until the sea grasses and monsters took it down into the depths. Then the next ship, and the next, until the outer harbor was as bare as the inner one had been after the villagers were killed."

The Sarzana stopped. None of us said anything. This tale of blood and murder was as ghastly as any I'd ever heard. Indeed, the Konyans were a hard race, from rulers to ruled.

Then he said: "I left the barracks and the corpses inside alone, deliberately, as a warning to anyone who arrived intending harm."

"That doesn't seem like much," Cholla Yi said. "You must've known the barons would send more assassins."

"I knew they would, and they did. But they ran into my second great spell. This is one of confusion. It's a simple one, correct, Evocator?"

"It is," Gamelan said. "But to conceal an entire island requires great power."

"Oh, I hardly went to that amount of trouble," The Sarzana said, a note of pride in his voice. "All that was needed was a slight miasma at four or five days distance from the island. Enough for a navigator to doubt his charts or astrolabe, a captain to have suspicions about his underlings, and so forth. That was enough to guarantee I'd never be found unless I wanted. Besides, why would anyone want that hard to discover what happened? That tale of doom for anyone who murdered me lingers on, and who would chance the wrath of the gods if they did not have to?"

The Sarzana rose, stretched, and went from couch to couch, ceremoniously refilling our glasses. None of us had drunk heavily, so taken were we by his saga.

"It is late," he said. "Or, it is early, and you have much to do to make your ships seaworthy. Perhaps we should find our beds."

We stood and lifted our drinks in a strange sort of toast. We then started out of the room. I stopped. A thought had taken me, and I had the boldness to ask. "Sarzana? You said you could see a bit into the future. What, then, lies ahead for you? Will you spend the rest of your days here alone?"

"Prognostication comes hard when one is trying to use it for your own good," he said. "So it is with me. I know what I think I see, but perhaps it is just a wish: I see myself returning to Konya. I know that if I land any-where, the people will remember me. Time enough has passed, and the bar-ons' evil has grown, so there would be a great and final rising. Perhaps I'm foolish, and just a dreamer, but I still hope that my native islands will find true peace again, a peace that shall linger until time itself has a stop. And I know how to bring this to them. But as I said, perhaps it is just an illusion, a happy mirage."

"Why didn't you use one of the ships, crewed by your animal friends, to return to Konya?" Corais said, ever the practical one. "You said you came from a seafaring family."

"I said the power that blurred my powers is gone, but there still seems to be some remnant, or perhaps I'm still ensorcelled by a conjuration laid on me when I was first dethroned. I can't think of sailing without my mind fall-ing into confusion. A mental version of the common fumble-finger spell, I suspect. No. I must be saved from my exile by someone else, someone who is willing to trust my words and believe he shall be rewarded greatly when I return to power."

CORAIS WENT to her quarters in the mansion, and the three of us went down the steps. There was a soft moon out, and we could see clearly. I waited until Cholla Yi had gone on to where the sailors of his gig drowsed on the beach, then asked Gamelan what he felt.

"He is a king," the Evocator said. "And kings don't have the same views I do. I think he intends well, that he truly wishes the best for his peo-ple. I didn't sense any waves of hatred for them, which he might well have felt after they overthrew him. I also perceived, behind his words, a truth that these barons are more savage than The Sarzana or even those bloody-handed captains he spoke of. But these are only feelings, with no facts or magic be-hind them. If my powers would return, even a bit of them, I would know better. What did you perceive?"

"No more than you did," I said. "In fact, less. There was nothing about the barons that came to me. But yes, The Sarzana does appear to intend be-nevolence." I smiled. "If it's possible *any* king is of that nature."

Gamelan chuckled and turned toward the small cottage I'd assigned to him. He walked toward it as if sighted, and I marveled how quickly we can learn to overcome frailty if we are strong enough. At the door, he turned back.

"It was ... interesting," he said, "to speak to another Evocator, one with Talents nearly equal to mine. Or, rather, what mine were. Meaning no disrespect to your own Talent, Rali. But it felt, when he referred to our com-mon Art, almost as if I was back at the Palace in Orissa, sharing trade secrets with another." He sighed. "It seems to me," he said, "what we must do is ride with the current, much as we have done. Perhaps The Sarzana can give us aid to set our course home. He *is* a great sorcerer. Perhaps he might choose to help us, although it's easy to tell what debt we would be incurring. Certainly he hinted strongly enough at the end of his tale. And just possibly the reward would be worth the price."

Then he said good night and went inside.

It was only an hour or so before dawn when we parted. I thought that if I tried to sleep, in all likelihood I'd just toss and turn, thinking of The Sarzana's tale, and a single hour's nap would do no more than turn me into a growling lioness at my duties. Besides, it was better I walk off the dying fumes of the evening's wine.

I walked to the waterfront and along the beach. I returned the salute of two sentries, but didn't bother them with idle chat. The night was as calm and mild as a summer's evening. I waded into the blood-warm water and kicked at the surf, seeing it spray in the moonlight, which made me giggle as if I was still a child. That feeling of happiness that had come upon me off the island still hung on. All I could wish for was . . . and I shut off the thought before it could complete.

I went all the way down to where the creek mouth entered the water, and saw one of the ship's boats landed there. I thought I'd sit down and wait for the sun to come up. But the romantic spot was taken. Dica and Ismet lay asleep on a cloak, naked in each others' arms. The sight made me feel glad and sad at the same time.

I heard footsteps and turned. It was Polillo, evidently taking, as was her frequent custom, the last watch before dawn.

We looked at each other and the two women sleeping in the sand.

I bent and pulled the cloak up over the two. A small smile touched Dica's lips, but she didn't stir.

Then I walked away back down the beach.

Alone.

CHAPTER FOURTEEN

SOUTH TO KONYA

❖

The next day we set to. By the gods, it was wearisome. By the time we were done and our galleys rode at anchor looking as if they'd just been launched with the blood of the sacrifices fresh on their prows, any of us who'd dreamed of buying a small boat to play with in our twilight years had discarded the notion. Amalric always had little use for ships, except as a necessary way to move his goods from one port to the next, but my feelings became stronger: I wished I could become the Greatest of Evocators, and pave the damned seas so no one save those who were demented, and I include *all* sailors in that lot, would need water for any other purpose than bathing.

It might seem I'm railing on, and I suppose I am. But let me tell you just what we had to do to make just one galley seaworthy once more:

First the ship would be stripped of anything removable, so it rode high in the water, and then it was rowed close inshore, until it grounded on a rock-free bottom. Then it would be dragged farther in to shore, and when the tide fell, heavy logs, padded at the end, kept the ship from rolling onto its side.

Next we started scraping the hull free of the barnacles and seaweed. In the process we scraped enough skin off our hides to make belts for any army. Then all those shellfish we scraped off died and began to rot. By midday our brave warship smelled like a dockside latrine. This task, I'd been told by

Klisura, required no shipwright's ability beyond having a large neck and small helmet, so the Guard would be perfectly suitable. I growled, then saw he was attempting a joke, and regained my good humor. That lasted until I realized I'd have to set the proper example for my women and be the first to wade out and begin scouring away.

"I thought," Sergeant Ismet said, from where she labored a few yards away, "we were going to be noble huntresses and all that, instead of scullery wenches to these tubs."

"Pleasure," I managed, "comes after business."

It wasn't that we were being taken advantage of—Cholla Yi had Klisura and the other shipmasters driving the sailors even harder. Nor were we doing the worst job conceivable, which came after the ship's bottom was sufficiently clean. This job was for the fleet's various petty offenders, both the handful from my Guardswomen who needed more severe punishment than a boot or backhand from her sergeant or a week jakes-cleaning, and the much greater number of sailors who'd fallen afoul of their masters-at-arms. All rotten ropes had been stripped off the ships and tossed in a great pile on the foreshore, and the punishment parties were assigned to pick the tarry ropes apart, strand by strand. These threads were then driven into the space between the ship's planking, using a tool like a narrow chisel and a mallet. Since this served to reseal any leaks, even the laziest sailor worked with a will on this task, but to make sure, a particularly vicious master-at-arms with a knotted rope end paced back and forth behind the workers. He was forbidden, however, to strike any of my women.

Polillo had explained it to him simply: "Only the Guard touches the Guard." The brute considered Polillo's muscles, looked into her icy eyes, and nodded understanding.

Once the hull was caulked, it was painted. The paint was a reeking mixture of tar, oil, and some vegetable poisons from the island. The poison would hopefully help keep new barnacles and weed from clamping onto our hull for a while. Each one that did would slow the ship and make it more unwieldy to row and steer; plus it'd eventually eat through the planking. While all this was being done outside the ship, more was being done above us. All rotted wood was replaced—we were lucky and found a yard full of seasoned timber we could use. This included already-shaped tree trunks that replaced masts that'd split or had rot in their core. The decking and timbers were oiled. We found enough rope in and around the village to replace our old rigging.

Also, the holds and cabins had to be fumigated. In an Orissan yard, I was told, an apprentice or journeyman Evocator would have cast a spell on the ship, so that all the rats, roaches, and other vermin would have been blighted. But we had no such recourse, at least not at first. I determined, after a sailor nearly died from breathing the fumes from his sulfured torches, something must be done. With Gamelan's help we produced a spell that worked very well, thank you. It consisted of rat's blood, the remains of a few ship insects, the blossoms of a night flower whose scent carried many yards, clay from the village's burying ground, and a few simple words in ancient Orissan. Soon the galleys were relatively pest-free.

Everything on the ship was carefully checked, replaced if possible or strengthened if not. Finally, the refit would be complete, and on the high tide the braces would be struck away and the ship dragged back into deeper water, its anchors having been rowed out and all hands pushing handsomely on the capstan.

That was one ship. Then another was beached—and the task begun anew.

It was exhausting, but there were still some of us who had energy for other things, some for good, some not. I noted Dica spent most of her evenings in Sergeant Ismet's company, the two of them carrying light bedding off into the country beyond the village if they were not on duty. I heartily approved—pillow talk is one of the best ways to learn, and my flag sergeant had been the first shield lover for more than one aspirant in the past. Somehow, Ismet also knew how to painlessly let her affairs come to an end, with neither discipline nor her young lovers' hearts being hurt.

Others began, renewed, or continued affairs. I'd always thought being aboard ship would make one romantic. But not on a warship, and not when the most privacy obtainable is a few minutes in a canvas-cloaked jakes in the bows of a ship, or having the nearest hammock hung no further than two feet.

Once again the old problem with the men roused itself. Regularly one or another of my Guardswomen would be importuned for her favors, some politely, some crudely, some demandingly, as if the sailor had certain rights given by the gods to sow all the furrows he could reach. I don't know why men seem to share a common fantasy—that a woman who chooses to find love among her own is deluded, and never has known a "real lover." It isn't just men with equipment grotesque enough to grace a stallion in rut. I've heard a pip-squeak clerk promise a great strapping corporal "such a night of love that you'll forget all this foolishness." Pah! Let those who think like that spend their time drilling soft sand with their never-to-be-sufficiently-lauded tools, since they seem to match love with post-hole digging! It isn't just sailors who act like this—it was a constant problem in barracks in Orissa, everytime certain young lords came a-wooing the Maranon Guard.

Enough of that. Suffice it to say the would-be lovers were rejected in much the same manner as they proposed—some with a smile and a laugh, others with a well-driven blow to just below where their mother's cord was cut off and above where their souls seemed to live.

I allowed my women to be used as common laborers until half the galleys were completed, then stepped in and told Cholla Yi firmly his sailors and marines could finish the task. We had another job—to make sure the fleet would be well fed when we sailed on.

I REMEMBER CLEARLY our first great hunt. I remember my women hallooing and rattling their spears against shields as the great boar snorted and broke out of the thicket . . . It pelted toward me, tusks gleaming dirty yellow in the late afternoon sunlight, blood glinting from the spear wound in its shoulder. There were no other two-legs in the world but me, and for me nothing but those huge curved swords flashing as the boar squealed, put its head down for the charge, and ran onto the head of my spear. The shock sent me stumbling back, and I went to one knee, bracing the spear butt on the ground as the animal ran itself up onto the spear and against the cross bit halfway down the shaft. It roared its soul to the heavens, stumbled sideways, and fell before it knew it was dead.

My women broke their spear wall and ran toward me, shouting congratulations. For a moment I paid no mind, but sent up a prayer thanking Maranonia, and begging her to treat the spirit of the animal kindly. It had led us a hard chase on the steep slopes along the far side of the island, turning often to charge and try to break through the tightening cordon. Brought to bay, it'd fought hard and died bravely. Polillo was loud in the beast's praise, as were some of the other Guardswomen.

For them, hunting was the noblest of pastimes, second only to war. For some of my women who came from the wilder provinces beyond Orissa, it was, in fact, a religious ceremony. For me, it was a task I enjoyed, since it was outside, it tested my muscles and ability to read the ground, and put food on my table that I myself had harvested. But there were other sports I enjoyed more—a cross-country paper chase, crag-climbing, or, without a weapon, tracking an animal to its lair to see her kits or just to watch how she passed her time. When I hunted, I preferred to take my game as simply as possible, to stalk it without it being aware, and to grant the gift of death before fear came on it.

It was interesting to see, though, how others felt, and how their feelings affected the way they performed this necessary task of supplying the fleet with meat for salting and smoking. Polillo, as I said, thought hunting the finest sport known. For her, that meant the chase itself. She loved to hunt by herself, or with one or two equally agile Guardswomen. She would start game and then run it down, killing it with a short spear, or sometimes even with a hatchet, thrown with deadly accuracy on the run, and then giving the final grace with her gutting knife.

Corais, on the other hand, said she found hunting not only too much like work, but boring. She hunted alone, and *always* made a kill. Her method was simple, but difficult. Before she armed herself, she'd walk through an area two or three times, generally at first light and again at twilight. When she knew the habits of the animal she wished to take, she'd creep out and find a place to hide either in the middle of the night or at midday, when the animals slept. When her prey came to feed or water, Corais would strike. She preferred a short, heavy bow, and seldom needed but a single shaft to bring the animal down.

To others, hunting was more social. Ismet dearly loved to organize a hunt, with beaters driving the prey toward positioned killers, a hunt she'd laid out on a sand table, making sure each hunter understood exactly what she was or was not to do. Sometimes I thought the hunt itself, with its precise moves and strikes, not unlike a running-ball match, was an end for her, and the kill no more than a trophy to award a well-played match.

We heeded The Sarzana's cautions and didn't take any of his beast-men, not that any of us would've considered killing them, either for sport or food; nor did we hunt those animals who wore the diadem of his servitude. We also held to the code of the huntswoman, and took no animal with cubs or who was about to bear young, and no unbred yearling. All the game we slew, or fish we hooked or speared, was for the pot. We paid no heed to brilliantly plumaged birds whose feathers might have graced our helmets, or exotically furred animals whose skin might have decorated shields or hauberk. After gutting and skinning, animals were either smoke-dried, brine-cured, or potted. Game birds we netted or quick-limed, and then gutted and salted their bodies before packing them tightly into barrels.

We didn't need to spend any time fishing—that task was handled by working parties of seamen and The Sarzana's dolphins. It was eerie to watch. All that was needed was for sailors to wade out on a beach. Then the dolphins would drive the fish toward them, just exactly as I'd seen dogs drive sheep into their pens in the highlands above Orissa. Suddenly there'd come a threshing and splashing out in the bay, rapidly moving toward us. Then we'd see the fish, forced into schools, trying to escape the diligent dolphins. Once the fish were close inshore and within the net's killing circle, the sailors would be ordered to drag out, and yet another bulging net of flashing silver would be beached, ready for cleaning and smoking.

I noted The Sarzana always took part in these fishing "expeditions," and made sure, when the nets were dragged ashore, that a portion was taken for him. He'd wade out into the low surf, moving awkwardly for a man whose trade had at one time been the sea, and toss a fish or two to each dolphin.

I told Gamelan about this reward, and he smiled. "Didn't I tell you once before that magic held more than its share of flummery? The Sarzana, not being a stupid man, doesn't waste his strength with spells when a well-thrown tunny can keep a servant bonded to him as strongly."

As for vegetables, these were either dried or kept fresh with a rejuvenating spell The Sarzana cast for us. They would last at least a month, perhaps two. Eggs were dipped in hot tallow, and would be good for three or four months.

Finally all the galleys were nearly ready for sea, and we wanted to be on our way. Orissa lay many, many leagues away, and we still needed help in finding a course home. I think all of us knew that our time here on Tristan was at an end. Now it was time to sail on.

THE SARZANA'S ISLAND gave us more than just a place to refit. It also let us relax, and let the long tension of pursuit, battle, and blood ooze away, even though all of us knew we were half a world from home, and the seas between us were most unlikely to be peaceful ponds.

There was one strange and ugly incident that marred the calm.

I had the night duty and had just finished changing my guard at the second glass after midnight, when two Guardswomen pelted into the guardroom. One was Jacena, the other Ebbo, a spearwoman. Both of them had been assigned to Corais' detachment on the plateau above with The Sarzana. They brought themselves to attention and took several deep breaths before reporting. There'd been an attack on Corais.

"What happened, exactly?"

"We were not told the full details, Captain," Jacena said. "We heard shouts, turned to, and Legate Corais and Sergeant Bodilon were outside the building we're barracked in. Legate Corais ordered us to arm ourselves and make good haste to you and report. She said she hadn't been injured, but requested your presence. She said there was no need to turn out the Guard."

"Anything else?"

Jacena looked to either side, ensuring no one might overhear her, and even as my anger grew that someone or something had dared to attack one of my people, I noted Jacena's professionalism. "The legate wore no armor, but was naked, except for her sword."

I decided Corais might or might not have been right. I told the sergeant of the guard to wake all the watch and post two sentries at each post. Then she was to wake the Guard, but without causing alarm or disturbing any of the sailors. I turned command over to Polillo, and, taking five of my steadiest women from the night watch, went back up those long flights of stairs with Ebbo and Jacena.

Corais' detachment was quartered in a small domed pavilion made of stone that might've been intended as a trysting place. It not only gave luxurious living quarters to Corais' squad, but sat separate from the other buildings on a low rise, and was the most easily defensible structure on the plateau. Torches blazed around the pavilion, and as I trotted toward it, I saw The Sarzana's mansion come to life as well.

Corais' women were ready for battle, swords unsheathed, bows strung, and broadheads tucked into archers' belts. Corais, now wearing full battle array, sat grim-faced behind a table just inside the entrance.

She stood as I entered, and saluted. Before I could say anything, she said, "Captain. May I report privately?"

I dismissed the others. Corais looked about her, and evidently decided she might still be overheard. She led me outside. I could see, just at the edges of the torchlight, the gleam of armor where she'd put out sentries in the darkness. I waited, but some seconds passed before she spoke. I could see Corais' face, and it was pale and shaken, far more than I'd ever seen her look even after a battle where we'd both lost friends. I realized something was very wrong, softened my voice and told her to report, from the beginning.

Since the weather was so pleasant, she said, she'd taken to sleeping on a cot just outside the pavilion's entrance. Perhaps it was wrong, but there were guards set at the four compass points around her, and she "felt" no threat could come to her. "Evidently," she said, "I was overconfident."

She'd gone to sleep wearing what she normally did when on standby, as all of us were—light, quilted underclothing of silk that would serve as padding under her armor if she were called out.

"I was dreaming," she said. She fell silent for a long time. I was about to prod her, but something said not to. "I dreamed of . . . men," she eventually continued. "A man, actually. I thought my mind painted him clearly, giving me every detail, but I guess I was wrong. All that I can remember is that he was tall, broadly muscled, black hair—close-cropped, I think—clean-shaven, and with a smile that spoke of dark sins and their pleasures. He was naked.

"His—his member stood erect, and he came toward me." Corais shuddered. "I knew what he intended, and—and I *wanted* it! I wanted him to take me!"

She turned to the side and was rackingly sick, vomiting again and again, trying to purge not only her body, but her mind. I shouted for Bodilon to bring a rag, a washbasin, and wine. Corais started to say more, but I motioned silence until the sergeant had left. I sponged Corais' face and made her rinse her mouth with wine, then drink a full cup.

"How in the name of Maranonia could I have wanted *that*?" she said. "The idea of—of being with a man has *always* sickened me. You know that."

I did. Corais, like myself, was fortunate in that we'd never thought of the embrace of men as desirable, nor had either of our parents forced the notion on us.

"He was about to . . . about to touch me," Corais went on, "and then, for just one moment, I came back to myself, and it was as if I were struggling upward for air, through some pool of slime, and I would never wake in time.

"But I did, and the spell broke, and I saw that loathsome body for what it was. I was awake, and I was naked, and Rali, as I love you, as I love the Guard, as I love Maranonia, I swear that creature was still there, bending over me, one knee trying to force my thighs apart! I shouted and rolled to the side and came up with my sword in hand, ready to strike. But—"

"But there wasn't anybody there," I finished for her. "And your sentries were fully alert and said no one had come between them."

I could see what Corais was about to say next, and put out a hand to touch her lips into silence.

"You weren't dreaming," I said.

"*I* know that. But how can you?"

I didn't have an answer, but I spoke the truth. I did know. Something or someone had tried to rape Corais, rape or more, and it was not a nightmare, but something that stalked this island, and lived, either through sorcery or in the real world. Scribe, don't ask me where this truth came from. From my own ghosts, from the power I was learning from Gamelan, from the Goddess herself, from my faith in Corais, who had told me once her only dreams were of sylvan glades with gamboling animals.

Corais' eyes were wet. She stared long into my face and then nodded once. "Thank you," she whispered, "for believing me."

I was about to say something more, then noticed, standing beyond the sentries, one of The Sarzana's grotesquely costumed beast-men. I went to him. He held out one of the ivory tablets. I paid no mind.

"Take my greetings to your master," I said. "I wish an audience with him in one hour. Go!"

The creature looked at me, and I saw fear in its eyes. It bounded away into darkness.

I turned back to Corais.

AN HOUR LATER I tramped up the long path to The Sarzana's mansion. Flanking me were two squads of Guardswomen, weapons ready. There were two beast-men waiting at the steps. I paid them no mind, but strode past them into the mansion's hall, without removing my helm.

The Sarzana was waiting. He wore gaily colored robes, as if he'd only recently risen from sleep.

"Someone," I began, without preamble or polite greeting, "tried to attack one of my officers. It was Legate Corais."

The Sarzana's eyes widened in shock. "Up *here*? On my plateau?"

I nodded.

"Gods. What did she do? What happened?"

"That doesn't matter," I said. "*She* did nothing, and is safe. I know it wasn't one of our men. She described the person, but I'm not sure her memory is exact."

"May I ask what you're thinking?" The Sarzana began, and I could see his brows furrow, that fire-ice gaze start to burn at me and his lips form into that thin line.

"I am not accusing you, Sarzana," I said. "I hardly think a lord of your powers would stoop to rape. But what of your creations? Your man-beasts?"

The Sarzana shook his head rapidly from side to side. "Impossible. Quite impossible. When I created them, I gave them the power to lust, and to breed. But I held it back, as a final gift for when I leave this island. No, my friends are as safe as the castrated ones who once guarded my seraglio. Safer even, since even the knife can err. Captain Antero . . . I vow that none of mine had anything to do with this. When I heard the outcries, I was in deep slumber. I tried to use sorcery to determine what had happened, but there is—was—something out there in the night that clouded my vision."

"You think Corais' attacker was magical?"

"I don't know," he said. "A demon? An incubus? I had no time to learn from the villagers before they were murdered what spirits might haunt this island. Nor did I perform any thaumaturgics to find out. Evidently I should have.

"Captain, I cannot say how horrified I am. I take this as an affront. I promised you safety, and I failed to provide it. I am deeply ashamed. But I promise you for the rest of the time you remain on this island, nothing shall happen. I'll begin casting spells this very hour to keep your women—and Cholla Yi's men, as well—from the slightest jeopardy. More, I'll send my own demons, and there are some who owe me fell deeds, to cast about for whatever tried to commit this terrible thing. And when I find it, him, or them, their tortures shall be beyond your most hateful dreams."

I looked deeply into The Sarzana's eyes, and I *believed* him. I saluted formally and stalked out.

There were no other incidents until we left the island. In fact, even the sexual attempts from the sailors stopped quite suddenly. But I no longer let any of my women go anywhere except in pairs, and at night no one, from Corais to myself to Dica and Ismet, was permitted to sleep beyond the sentry ring.

THE SARZANA was a constant presence, although he never intruded nor forced his company when it might not be wanted. But he was always there. The lowliest spearwoman might be walking her post at the loneliest end of the village, and The Sarzana would stroll past with a word of cheer; or a sailor might be concentrating on a splice, and find The Sarzana holding the line's end away from his knotting so it wouldn't snag. We officers ate with him often, although never so sumptuously as that first banquet.

He never asked directly if he could accompany us when we left Tristan. But it was an idea that grew and grew, until at last we somehow all knew he'd joined the expedition, and we felt stronger and safer in that knowledge.

Just how he would help us, and just how much assistance we, in turn, were supposed to provide, was also never discussed. Not that The Sarzana was mute about his dreams, nor how one of us or all of us might be included. He systematically wooed each officer. I first saw his seduction at work one afternoon in his mansion. I'd gone looking for him at Gamelan's request, to see if he had power over wind spirits, such as seaport witches had. I found him in deep conversation with Cholla Yi, sitting in that alcove where he'd told us the story of his rise and fall.

As I approached he said, "There's much wisdom in what you say, Admiral. Perhaps if I would have had a small cadre of loyal and skilled seamen with their own ships always at my beck, things might've gone differently, and I could have summoned aid from my home isles and not been driven from my throne. You've given me much to think on, sir, much indeed."

I cleared my throat before I entered. The Sarzana stood and greeted me. I made my request, and he said such a matter was quite simple and he'd begin preparing the proper spells at once. After he left, I looked at Cholla Yi and lifted an eyebrow. I realized he'd heard me approach.

"So?" he said without embarrassment. "So I'm looking for gold? What's the sin in that, because you choose to fight for a flag? I'm a mercenary, and we must always be looking for a new master. Certainly when we return to Orissa your Magistrates will be only too glad to see us sail away. Not that I've any great love for them anyway, to be honest. My men and I still think we were given an unfair casting of the die when we were compelled to carry you and your women over the seas chasing that damned Archon, instead of getting our pay and our loot as promised. Besides, do you care, Captain, *what* I do once my duty to you and Orissa is honestly fulfilled?"

"I do not, Admiral," I said. *"Once your duty is complete!* And not before!"

"Then we are friends once more," he said, and emitted that great boom of noise he meant to pass for jovial laughter.

That was but one instance. The Sarzana also spent a great deal of time with Gamelan. It seemed if I saw one, I saw the other. I found myself resenting it, oddly, then caught myself short. What was I thinking? Was I being basely jealous? Of course a great Evocator such as Gamelan would find more to talk about in the company of an equally gifted sorcerer, rather than a beginner like myself, who had less than a village soothsayer's knowledge. But there was a very real concern after I'd overheard The Sarzana's offer to Cholla Yi. I knew what The Sarzana must be dangling in front of Gamelan.

At last I asked Gamelan directly. As always, the Evocator was straightforward.

"Of course The Sarzana has been trying to win my support," he said. "He's offering, once he's restored to the throne and given full access to his former demons and alembics, to force a great spell against the other worlds, so that my blindness, both physical and sorcerous, will be ended."

Another question occurred: "All of us seem as if we've conferred on The Sarzana's fate and agreed we are to help him, even though no such discussion's occurred. That smacks of wizardry, and I'm not at all sure I like the thought of a spell touching any part of my thinking," I said frankly.

"I, too, sensed that. He admitted his subconscious powers have perhaps sent a projection, if that's what it is. But what of it? I doubt if the man has sufficient strength to force such an opinion on all of us. My powers may be in abeyance, but I *know* our minds would rail if we sensed evil intent from him."

A thought came and went, one that I didn't analyze until later: *Here it was again . . . again we knew something, without any firm foundation to that belief.* But before I could say anything, something more important came to me: "What do you think he wants us to do, specifically, besides taking him off this island he's exiled to?"

"I've asked him that. He said very little, other than take him to an island group some distance to the south and west. These islands were among his earliest supporters, and he can use them as his base and rallying point. We'll have to sail secretly through two others first, however, since those Konyan outer islands are not only peopled by rude barbarians, but garrisoned with strong ships of the Konyan barons, minions of his fiercest enemies. Once we reach the lands of his friends, we'll be free to sail on our way if we wish. As payment, he'll summon a conclave of the group's most skilled navigators and ship captains. Since these people are famous explorers, or so he tells me, he hopes that at least one of them will be able to help us set a true course for our home, and give us such magical aids as he can. He also vowed to help us see if the Archon still lives, and if so, to gather his wizards together to aid us in our fight."

I thought hard. It didn't seem we had much of a choice, actually, and the longer I considered, the more sure I became. We could either continue wandering these strange and deadly seas until we died, or else provide this small favor for The Sarzana. And what evil, my mind ran, would be caused by our doing this? Very little, I thought, again remembering the great respect I'd first felt for The Sarzana. If there must be kings, and from all he'd said, Konya needed to be ruled firmly, there could be no better being than him. Of course he'd be far more just and merciful than any conspiracy of greedy petty lordlings, trying to force all these peoples into the wretched near-slavery of the past.

"Thank you, Gamelan," I said finally. "Again, your wisdom has opened my mind further."

A day later, while taking a predinner stroll along the waterfront, I encountered The Sarzana. I knew it was no accidental meeting, so after we exchanged courtesies and he asked if he could accompany me, I was most gracious. Besides, I was most curious to see what he would offer, which might indicate how well he'd gauged me. The answer was very well, indeed.

"You know, Captain, I have been speaking to others in your expedition."

"I know," I said.

"Then you also know I've been making some of them offers of employment, or discussing other ways I might be able to help. I wish I could do the same for you."

I said nothing.

"But I'm hardly that much of a fool," he went on. "I feel I know you quite well, Rali Antero, and consider you one of the most remarkable people I've ever met. Ruling is a harsh and cynical sport, and I've always believed that all men, and women, have a price. But you prove I must always allow for the exception."

"I don't know about that," I said, a bit tartly. "But I do know flattery has never struck a chord in my guts."

"I'm not flattering anyone," he said, his voice ringing sincere. "Although I know it sounds it. No, what I'm saying, evidently quite badly, is that there's nothing I could offer you that you do not already have."

I stopped and looked at him closely. I'm sure my eyebrows were lifted high. What, in fact, did I have? I slept alone, and felt that weight. The woman I once loved was lost and unknown leagues away, as were the handful of people I called family, Amalric being the only real one I cared about. Riches? I supposed I was wealthy, with my share of the Antero lands and holdings. But here all I possessed were my weapons, my armor, a few clothes, and what was in my war bag.

A thought struck. No, even here I was rich, at least by my own thinking. I had the respect, the obedience, and, in a manner of speaking, love of all my soldiers. What more did I want, save to serve them well and keep that love?

"Just so," The Sarzana said gently. "If you have a price, gentle captain, it is beyond anything I can pay. Which is why I wish to incur a debt from *you*. If I regain my throne, I propose to establish a Guard much like the Maranon women. Its oath will not be to me, nor my descendants, if I indeed chose to have any. Instead, it will serve Konya. I would want such a force above all small concerns of men and the day-to-day rule. I think such a unit might be a great force for stability. I wonder if its greatest strength might be that it cleaves to its own, as does your Guard."

"What do you mean?"

"I mean men who prefer their own, or women like your Guardswomen, or perhaps even those who belong to a single clan."

I was instantly seething. "Do you think, Sarzana, that we are what we are because of who we fuck?"

"No, no, of course not," he said hurriedly. "I've offended, but don't mean to. What I'm trying to say is that I do not know *what* makes you and your Guardswomen what they are. But something deep inside says I must find out. Not just for me, but for all of Konya. We need to learn how to serve something greater than ourselves. And that is my request. When you and your women have returned to Orissa, and returned to your duties, would it be possible for me to send two or three of my most skilled ministers and one or two high-ranking soldiers I have in mind, if the barons haven't murdered them, to spend time with your Guard? I warn you, they will ask the most penetrating questions, trying to understand what you are and bring that knowledge back to me."

My anger subsided. The Sarzana smiled wryly. "You see? Just because someone is—or has been—a ruler, doesn't mean he can't offend by accident. Perhaps that is why we kings know enough to surround ourselves with silk-tongued agents, so we don't say the wrong thing and end up starting a war. Again, my apologies, Rali, or rather, Captain Antero. I shall say no more. But when the time is right, would you at least consider my request?"

My anger was gone, and I found myself feeling quite warm. I didn't say yes, nor did I say no, and after a few more minutes one of The Sarzana's beast-men appeared with a summons and the lord left.

I stood looking after him. A most unusual man, especially for a king. A ruler of great nations, but a man who was still capable of making mistakes, and being embarrassed for making them.

THAT NIGHT, deep in the dogwatches, I snapped awake. Nothing had happened to wake me, but I was as alert as if I'd had more than the normal four or five hours I require, and a sharp round of calisthenics and a mile run, as well. I dressed quietly and went out into the village street. I stood indecisively for a moment, then started away from the waterfront toward the long stairs that led to the plateau. I came to the picket line and easily slipped past the sentry. She was alert, but the day I, or any of my sergeants or officers, can't be more cunning than our soldiers is the day we'd best consider sheathing our blades and retiring to a room lined with thick batting. I was breaking my own orders, but felt quite safe with my sword on my hip and my dagger sheathed at the small of my back.

I went up the vast stairs leading to The Sarzana's plateau as far as the second landing, where the stairs opened again to the sky. The landing's railing faced south, and I went to it and gazed out into the night. The moon was only quartered, but there was more than enough starlight to see clearly. Down there, to the left, was the harbor, and the black dots of our ships. Over there were the headlands we'd sail beyond in the next few days, headed away from the pole star. My gaze turned in that direction. At first there was nothing but the darkness of the ocean, and perhaps a line where the horizon marked the sky and the stars began.

Perhaps what I saw was nothing more than night fires or phosphorescent seas. Perhaps it was a vision. I don't know to this day, and think it best to let the reader, or even you, Scribe, judge what it meant, and I'll restrict myself to what I witnessed with my own eyes. Fires began, low and spattered across the horizon, as if we were traveling across a desert and brightly lit cities were no more than a journey of a day or so farther on. But then there were more and more of them, and I imagined them to be the lights of the Konyan islands, and knew the archipelago was vaster than I could imagine. Bright and even brighter they shone, until it was as if I was on a height far greater than I was, looking over a valley.

The lights flamed, and then, from behind me, from above the plateau, came a darkness, far more stygian than the night, swooping like a monstrous bat toward those sea fires. It swirled and dove, and then—and this was the strangest of all—that darkness was joined by an even more greater gloom, one coming from above. The two joined and dropped, and it was as if a water-soaked cloak was cast across spattered kindling, because all went quite black. No, my memory plays me false, for three or four lights flared, as if fighting that darkness, and then they, too, were gone.

I stood there for long moments, but saw nothing else. Then I noticed a sea breeze. It was chill, and I wondered why I'd not felt it before.

I went back down the stairs, past the guard, and to my bed, but slept no more, thinking about what I'd seen, without knowing what made it to be marked. I thought of asking Gamelan what he thought, but didn't. Perhaps my mind whispered that something, once spoken, is known to all, but what is in your heart can remain safely a mystery.

CHOLLA YI DECIDED we were ready to sail. The ships were fully provisioned, and both the sailors and my Guardswomen as fit as they'd ever be. Finally we did hold a conference about The Sarzana, if something so short can be called that. Mostly the discussion was about which ship he'd sail on. Cholla Yi, naturally, wanted the honors. It didn't matter to me, other than I felt a slight niggling discomfort at the idea of this great lord—whom honestly I could hardly say I knew well, even though my guts told me I was a worrywart—and the mercenary admiral being partnered. When the meeting was over, we went to The Sarzana's mansion and formally offered ourselves as his escort, volunteering to return him to his homelands.

He was effusive to the point of tears, and behaved as if he were surprised. He swore we'd made a magnificent decision and would be known in history as the saviors of Konya. As for he himself, he could hardly find the words, and he knew that his descendants, and indeed, people who loved freedom everywhere . . .

At this point my ears closed and I exchanged looks with Corais. At least there was one thing familiar about these lands—rulers still emoted noble speeches, full of grand words and magnificent gestures, speeches that went on and on and on. There were many ideas of what brave deeds qualified one for the Guard. Not the least was my own private one—an ability to listen to the biggest fool drone on for hours about the most empty things, while never moving a muscle from rigid attention and keeping your face bright and interested.

But at last he ran out of kingly things to say, and made a most surprising request: Would it be possible for him to sail on the same vessel as Gamelan? A look of anger flashed over Cholla Yi's face, and The Sarzana hastened to explain that he felt it his duty to attempt to restore Gamelan's powers, and wished to be close to him, so their hearts could feel as one. Also, he felt it best if Gamelan were also on familiar grounds, the ship he'd been traveling aboard since leaving his homeland. After that, there wasn't anything Cholla Yi could say, and so it was agreed.

I expected The Sarzana to enship trunks and bales and cases full of everything from jewels to furs to magical volumes. There were but five boxes, and each of those could be lifted by one not terribly strong boy.

Evidently The Sarzana noted my surprise, because he smiled and said, "When all the world's been yours, and taken away, you learn what matters and what does not. A man travels best who travels lightest."

The night before we were to sail, Gamelan approached The Sarzana and inquired when he planned to fulfill his promise to free his subjects. I thought I saw a momentary frown, but knew I must be wrong. The Sarzana smiled and said, "On the morrow. From the ship."

And so it was. Our ships had upped anchor and sat rolling in the slight harbor swell. The Sarzana had insisted the foredeck of our ship be set aside for him, and on it he'd put up eight torches, forming an octagon. He stood in the center of them and held his hands cupped, as if carrying something weighty. But there was nothing to be seen. He began chanting, but I couldn't make out his words, nor, when I asked later, could Gamelan or any of the oarsmen or sailors forward distinguish what he said.

I gasped as I saw a torrent of creatures coming down the village streets from the plateau. At first I thought he'd invoked the ghosts of those slaughtered villagers, but then realized I was looking at his beast-men. None of us had realized how many of them he'd created, although we should've been able to, knowing how many servitors any palace requires. I couldn't say how many there were—Corais estimated five hundred, Polillo thought more, Ismet less. Most of them still wore the odd court clothing The Sarzana had made them wear.

The Sarzana kept chanting, and his arms moved farther and farther apart, as if what he held was growing. His chanting grew to a shout, and the torches flared and flashed myriad colors. Overhead, hawks, eagles, and other birds swooped, and the calm sea frothed and dolphins and fish leapt high. He cast his invisible burden, the "gift" of freedom, up and out, and the torches flashed and died without ever a wisp of smoke. Above us the formations of birds shattered, and the sea in front of the village was calm and empty.

But there wasn't any calm in the village—the beast-men had gone into a frenzy. They were ripping, tearing, shredding their clothing, until they were naked, if beasts can ever be naked.

Polillo stood next to me and said, under her breath, "It looks as if Sarzana's servants maybe weren't the cheerful volunteers we thought, hmm? They look pretty damn ungrateful, if you ask me."

I heard a snicker from Corais. "Worse than a mustering–out party after a war," she said.

I suppose I should've reprimanded them, but certainly didn't. I still remembered The Sarzana telling us about the spells he'd used to "prepare the ground," and again when he'd told us how grateful these creatures were.

No one, beast or man, is grateful for chains, no matter how silken they are.

THE WIND came fresh from astern, and we had no need to row beyond the headlands. As our ships caught the first ocean rollers and bowed obeisance to the sea gods, and I smelt the clean salt air, we spied something odd: Sailing across our course, from headland to headland, was a flight of swans. They swam swiftly, white curving amid whitecaps.

"Now, there's an omen a good," I heard a sailor say. "Th' voyage's bound to bring us luck an' send us home."

I found my fingers crossing, and felt some dark hesitations that'd been growing the past few days vanish.

WE SAILED under fair skies with favoring winds for almost two weeks, bearing south by southwest. Not only were sailing conditions good, but all of us, freshened by our time on land, were more cheerful and willing to work together, sailor as well as Guardswoman.

On the fifteenth day after leaving Tristan, we sighted the first land. I was shouted on deck just after I'd finished dinner, and was teaching some of the newer soldiers how to redo the serving on crossbow strings, and heard the halloo. Without waiting on ceremony, all of us pelted on deck, eager to see what lands awaited us. I'd made sure all of my Guardswomen were quietly told what Gamelan had been told by The Sarzana—we were sailing into hostile seas and must be prepared for anything.

An island rose from the water ahead of us. There'd been heavy mist all that day, and we'd sailed close before the fog lifted and we saw it. The Sarzana was already on deck, on the quarterdeck with Stryker. I joined him there.

"This is one of three islands," he told me. "I'm not sure which, precisely, but it doesn't matter. All of them are garrisoned by the barons' forces, and their own natives are evil-natured. Our course is just as I wished."

Then he said, "Captain Stryker, if you will send signals to the other ships for them to assemble?"

Flags fluttered, and the other ships pulled close to hear The Sarzana's wishes. His voice was magnified magically, but it didn't have the echoing, trumpet sound to it that such sorcery usually produces. Instead it was calm and soothing and as personal as if he stood near every man and woman. His instructions were, we must bend on all sail, and pray we were not seen by anyone, least of all another ship.

I went to the taffrail and watched that humped island sink out of sight as we sailed on. Gray-green, ominous, and jungled, it did indeed look menacing.

For the next three days we sailed as if we were pursued. The Sarzana had cast wind spells to help our passage, but, or so I was told by Captain Stryker, he was afraid of casting a foul weather incantation to cover our passage for fear his sorcery would be "heard" by some of the barons' magicians.

The Sarzana had changed his habits. Now he kept to himself in the cabin Stryker had given up, and when he appeared on deck, made it very clear by his manners that he wished no company that wasn't most important.

Islands rose in front of us and fell away. Some were mountainous, like that first. Others were bare rocks jutting out of the crashing surf. Still others were the brightest green, and at night we could see the sparkle of lights from villages. I wondered how long it would be before we were discovered. But we weren't.

I attempted to distract myself by studying the notes I'd taken of Gamelan's teachings. But whenever I tried to concentrate on magic, my attention seemed to wane and I'd find myself yawning and losing interest. Similarly, when I tried to continue our lessons, it always seemed inconvenient either for me or for Gamelan.

I kept myself busy with exercise, and with not letting my women get slack. I'd ordered the sergeants and officers on the other ships to keep a similar regime. The problem was finding a way to keep exercise from becoming screamingly monotonous. I set up for myself, and for anyone else interested, a midday workout that climaxed with swarming up a line, knotted at intervals, that led from the deck all the way up to where the yard crossed the foremast. From there you were supposed to swing over to a different line leading back to the deck, this one with loops every two feet, and come down it, using only your hands. Five times around that circuit and you hurt too much to be bored.

I was slumped against the mast, panting, after my second turn on this horrible invention of mine, watching a party of sailors just below me, on the main deck. They had a harpoon tied to a line and were hoping to spear one of the fish that frequently surfaced just off our bows.

I noted that The Sarzana was on deck, and also had become curious and walked forward.

Sailors, I've noted, don't have much respect for anything other than each other, particularly not for landsmen, and most particularly not for landsmen of great rank, no matter how powerful they may be.

One such sailor tapped his forehead with a knuckle in as casual a salute as I'd ever seen and said, "Lord, we're a-fishin', an' th' beasties aren't cooperatin'. They say you were a fisherman, oncet. Or anyways a fishin' lord an' magic-man. Would y' mind spinnin' y'r hands some and sayin' some words that'd send a few finny ones our way?"

The Sarzana looked at the sailor, and his expression was hard and cold. "I have no time for such as that. Nor you." Then he walked back toward the stern.

The sailors watched him go. The one who'd spoken spat over the side. "Well now, ain't *we* been told, boys. Guess t' him we're 'bout lower'n squid shit, an' we all know that's spread thin at th' bottom a' th' deeps."

"Wonder if he forgot his fishing spells," another man said. "Or, maybe, if he knew any ever. Wouldn't be the first one I've known who claimed sea-magic, but made his way with fast words and a faster way when somebody's back was turned."

They noticed me and fell silent. I thought about it, then put it aside. Even someone who claimed to be as interested in the common folk as The Sarzana might be entitled to an off day when he figured the only ones who ought to be able to speak to him were heavenly beings. But still, this was a man who'd gone out of his way on Tristan to be uncommonly civil and interested in everyone's doings.

Two days later an even odder thing occurred, although I didn't realize it at the time. I'd been standing at the taffrail after we'd eaten, wondering how in the blazes our cook had managed to turn a simple stew of salt cod, shrimp netted from the stern, limes, and a scattering of vegetables, into something that tasted like oceangoing paste. I heard boot steps on the companionway rail and saw The Sarzana come onto the quarterdeck. The man at the rudder paid him no mind, eyes intent on the star he'd been ordered to keep the ship's prow aimed toward during his watch.

We spoke idly of various things for a while. Then his expression became serious. "Captain Antero, may I bring up something that is somewhat unpleasant, even though, the gods be praised, nothing serious came of it?" I nodded. "You remember that attack on your legate?"

How could I forget?

"You recall, I said at the time I had no knowledge of what could have happened, whether there was some demon of the island who'd lusted after your officer? Well, I spoke too soon, because this afternoon I was remembering my first few days when I landed, when the villagers were still permitted to speak to me freely.

"I remember there was a young maid who'd decided to be my personal bed-servant. Perhaps she was thinking of other things to come. I don't know, but certainly she would have been disappointed. A man who has had his entire world stripped away has little interest in things of the flesh. At any rate, she lingered late one evening, making sure my bedclothes had been properly folded and put away. I was in another part of the building, and wasn't aware she was still there.

"The Konyan officer who was my close guard came to me and said there was a distraught man outside, looking for his daughter. It was the young girl's father. We quickly found the girl, and I thought the villager would burst into tears. Instead, he slapped his daughter and told her never, ever to be up here after night fell. She ran, sobbing, from the mansion. Before her father could go after her, I stopped him, and told him she was in no danger from me, certainly. I doubted any of the Konyan solders needed to think of rape—there were already more than enough willing maids to serve them. He said he cared neither about me nor the soldiers. If she chose to bed one of them, that was her business. Or me, if she'd set her eyes on a great lord, he said, and I felt he would have actively encouraged such an act.

"It was the Old Man, he said. I asked him to tell me more. He said any island maiden, particularly if she was virgin, who was out by night or, even worse, feckless enough to sleep alone outdoors, might be approached by him. He would come to her at first in a dream, then, waking, in horrid reality. The woman he attacked would invite his embrace at first, but then, as the coupling grew fiercer and bloodier, try to fight against this monster. But there would be no hope. It would be too late. When dawn rose, all that would remain was a torn body. That was what he'd feared had happened to his daughter.

"I told the man he needn't worry—my magic was more than strong enough to protect anyone serving me. Evidently, from what almost happened to your legate, the Old Man was more than a legend." The Sarzana's expression became rueful. "Also, my web of spells cast around my mansion wasn't as powerful as I'd thought, especially against such elementals as that demon."

I waited, but The Sarzana had evidently said all he'd meant to. "Thank you. But why," I wondered, "did you tell me about it now? The incident is past, and I hope Legate Corais has been able to forget about it, or at least force it to the back of her mind."

The Sarzana looked at me queerly, then said, "To be frank, I wished to make sure that none of my servants were still thought of as capable of such a misdeed, even though they are free now, and many leagues behind us."

I began to say something, but thought it wiser to merely thank him for recollecting the story again, and assured him that what happened in the past would stay there.

After some more inconsequentials, he said good night and went below.

TWO NIGHTS LATER we encountered the second island cluster The Sarzana said were his irrevocable enemies. This time the islands were bigger, and the dark green of jungle replaced by the light green of fields and orchards. From now on, he said, until we reached the open seas once more, we should travel only by night, the fleet finding deserted islets for shelter during the day, and he would chance a spell for fog banks whenever he could. We obeyed his wishes. As we sailed deeper into the cluster by night, it became obvious these islands were much more civilized than the first. Each island glowed from tip to tip, and often we could see solid strands of light marking lit streets.

Perhaps we should have been afraid, but I think most of the men and women on our ships shared my melancholy. Were we doomed to sail forever in furtive darkness past settled lands like these, where men and women spent their lives in peace and plenty, no matter what lord or lords held fealty over them? When would we ever see Orissa?

The Sarzana promised we would reach his islands within a week, perhaps less if the winds blew stronger. Then we'd see an end to this slinking around, as if we were so many seagoing thieves.

We prayed he was right.

MOST PEOPLE KNOW what it is like to lie awake in the hours before dawn, when there is nothing but utter darkness within the soul and without. This is a time when we believe no one has ever loved us, our lives are futile struggles against nothing, and our end will be unpleasant and all we were quickly forgotten.

Such a time came to me. I've never known how to overcome such thoughts, other than to realize I've gone through this before, and shall again.

The dreary panoply passed again—I was an incompetent woman and officer, those who claimed to follow me gladly were secretly laughing, nothing I would turn my hand to would ever prosper—the normal ghastliness. I forced myself to try to think of other things: My family. My brother, Amalric. My mother, Emilie. Even the panther-woman I'd been named after. I felt the sordid images swirl and start to vanish. I sighed, knowing the depression was passing and I'd soon be asleep.

My mind became clear, as clear as any crystal spring, as clear as any rouged gem. I thought of what The Sarzana had said the other night, and then remembered one of the best ways I had of telling which of my women might be guilty of a minor peccadillo: suspect most the one who explains the most. Then confusion dropped her cloak over me again, but I struggled against it. I remembered that sudden clarity and fought to bring it back. And gradually I won the fight. And I remembered.

I remembered the Old Man. I remembered something I'd heard, or read. Perhaps my mother might've told it to me, although I doubt I was old enough to have heard it.

Maybe it was a tale another soldier had passed along . . . that was it. I'd heard it, but oddly, more than once; once from a fellow soldier, then again from an old village witch who'd assisted a patrol of mine when we'd been after bandits in the hills. Two legends, from people who came from very different places and could never have known each other. It came clearly—the legends were *not* an Old Man, but a woman. She was called the Old Hag, and would come to a man and drain him of all his strength, and leave only a husk in the morning. No one was invulnerable, unless . . . he had a sword. Bare steel would keep away or drive away the Hag.

I remembered Corais saying she came awake with a sword in her hand, and knew anywhere but in barracks she slept with one beside her bed.

I wondered about the legend The Sarzana had told me so conveniently, and, more darkly, why he'd told it to me.

My mind flashed into another channel—The Sarzana's snarl when asked for a simple fishing spell, and the sailor saying perhaps he didn't know any. I thought of Gamelan's eagerness and pleasure at being able to hook a fish from under the ice, and how clumsy The Sarzana had looked wading in the surf when his dolphins were fishing for us, most unlike a man who'd grown up close to the sea.

All these thoughts were unborn foundlings compared to the next ones: from the time we'd come in sight of Tristan until we'd left, all of us had felt queerly safe and contented. Yet we'd seen: an empty village; houses that were blood-soaked; a barracks charnel house; beast-men playing on human bones; and more.

What fools we were!

Worse, we'd met a wizard king, who told us he'd been exiled by evil men, and all of us had instantly believed him. Of course. That made perfect sense. We *all* knew of wizards who had power enough to create beings from the dead and who always used the power unselfishly. We all were familiar with kings who needed to answer to no one, and how generally benevolent they were. How could anyone dream such a sorcerer king as we met could be anything other than a saint? Of course The Sarzana would never be the same as the Archons.

Fools, fools and worse.

So we'd blithely agreed to become involved, to take this man, who an entire group of island nations had driven out, and help him return to his throne.

No. We *knew* . . . we *felt* . . . we *thought* . . . we *knew*, by the gods how we *knew*.

I understood why The Sarzana had chosen to sail on our ship—it was the only one carrying an Evocator, no matter that he was temporarily helpless, and his apprentice. That was also why my attempts to study my magic or further study with Gamelan since we set sail from Tristan had come to nothing—The Sarzana didn't wish any petty magics to ruin his own great spell.

The night was red around me now, from anger as well as shame at my stupidity, at all of our imbecility.

I rolled out of my hammock and pulled on clothing. I started toward the companionway, not sure what I intended. I set a course in my mind—I must quietly wake Gamelan and tell him what I was thinking. Maybe I was being a damned fool, maybe these were nothing but dark thoughts. No! This was real, not those pink happy clouds we'd been drifting through since coming on The Sarzana's island. I came back for my sword. I don't know why, but felt I might well need it before the dawn. Just then I heard a soft cry from abovedecks, a thud, ropes creaking, and a splash.

I went up the companionway like a bolt, blade in hand, and burst on deck. All was still, all was silent once more. Up forward I could see the two lookouts, peering out into the night. Amidships, my two Guards paced their rounds back and forth, fully alert, around the area where some of my women had chosen to sleep on deck. None of them noticed me, and I realized they'd been ensorcelled.

I could see no sign of movement on the quarterdeck. No sign of the helmsman, no sign of the master's mate who should have the watch. We'd lost way, and I could tell by the S-curving of the wake, no one was at the rudder.

I ran up the ladder. The man who should've been steering the ship sat against the rudder brace. His legs were splayed and he lolled as if drunk. I smelled no wine on his breath, but he babbled in a stentorious whisper, and his eyes were glazed, as if he'd drunk strong wine or gazed on horror. Sprawled just behind him, facedown, was the heavy bulk of Klisura, the ship's sailing master. His own dagger, a long sliver of steel he'd loved, was driven deeply into his back, pinning him to the deck. Behind him dangled the falls where Captain Stryker's gig should have been, just overside. They now hung to the water, and the boat was gone. I swore, then shouted loud for the Guard and the watch below.

I had a clear picture of what'd happened: Klisura and the helmsman had been forced by magic to lower the boat. Somehow Klisura had found the strength to fight back, and been slain. And the killer had escaped in the boat.

I looked out, astern and on either side, where I could see the bulk of more islands, but saw no sign of the gig.

Men and women were boiling out of their sleep, both on deck and below. I went back down the ladder, paying no mind to the babble, and went straight to one cabin.

It was empty. The Sarzana was gone.

It was just then the spell broke for all of us.

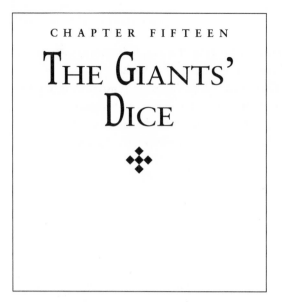

CHAPTER FIFTEEN

THE GIANTS' DICE

❖

A s you might imagine, the meeting that followed was grim. We'd signaled by lantern what had happened to Cholla Yi's flagship and the
others and called a captain's meeting at first light. It was purely by fortune that predawn light showed a low sand spit about a quarter mile distant.
That would be ideal—the conference had to be for officers only, with no possibility of eavesdropping, since the meeting would almost certainly be acri-
monious. And so it was.

Each ship sent her captain and sailing master. We had to use one of the
longboats, not only because of the theft of our gig, but because I thought it
necessary for both Corais and Polillo to be present, in addition to Gamelan,
Stryker, and Duban, who'd been promoted from rowing master to Klisura's
position. Duban, who I liked no better now than when he was bellowing at
the oarsmen as if they were slaves, immediately had to wonder why it was
necessary for *three* women to go, especially when two of them ranked no
higher than his mates. I didn't answer, since any explanation would've been
insulting—I wanted at least two people I could trust at my back at a council
with these pirates.

Stryker kept muttering aloud that he couldn't believe what'd happened.
How in all the wet hells could every damned one of us be bound by The
Sarzana's spell? Gamelan reminded Stryker he'd already seen greater

sorceries—the wall that'd been quickly rebuilt around Lycanth, or the Archon's last spell, which had cast us into these strange seas.

"Th't be different," Stryker said. "Volcanoes ... walls ... but not somethin' like this. One of us should've seen, dammit! Seems t' me there should've been a moment somebody, anybody, could've know'd better!"

"There was such a moment," Gamelan said quietly. "Captain Antero was graced with it."

Stryker nodded somberly. "Guess that's better'n nothin'. Sure makes yer wonder what would've happened if'n nobody'd caught on, and we'd a just sailed right into whatever th' devil intended fer the likes of us. And I wish t' hell she'd seen the light back on th't damned island."

On the islet, the meeting broke into the predicted storm, after I'd given the details on The Sarzana's flight. Cholla Yi alternated between rage and bluster at how Gamelan and I had failed. I pointed out no one had exactly shown much second sight concerning The Sarzana, which made Cholla Yi's bellowing louder:

"What of it? None of *us* have pretended magical abilities! None of *us* spent nearly as much time in the company of that damned pretender as you two. None of *us*—"

Gamelan interrupted. "What you say is true, Admiral. But the past is sealed in amber. What happened, happened. It seems our time should be best spent trying to figure out what comes next."

"Next? How can we be plannin' anythin'," Stryker said in his near whisper, "here on strange seas, knowin' we've loosed a demon? How does we know what Th' Sarzana's got in his noggin fer us, once he lands on friendly shores? Won't he cast some kinda spell so's no one'll know he escaped? Dead men have still tongues."

"I don't think he'll bother," Gamelan said.

"Worse yet, then," Duban growled. "Wonder how long it'll take before somebody figures out how he got off Tristan and go looking to scupper who-ever cut him free?"

There were mutters from the other captains. One of them, Meduduth, burst into blind rage: "This gods-cursed expedition is dooming us all! We should've never sailed on this booby's task in the first place! We should've held firm at Lycanth and demanded our gold, and the hell with what the friggin' Orissans and their damned pervert bitches wanted!"

Steel whispered from its sheath and Corais blurred across the sand. Meduduth yelped and leaped back, but the point of her sword was at his throat. Other hands went for their blades, and both Polillo and I had ours half drawn.

"One more word," Corais said tightly, "one more, shitheel, and that shall be your last."

"Stop!" I shouted, and Corais came to herself and stepped back, but didn't lower her blade. "We don't have time for any of this! The Sarzana is loose, and we loosed him. As Gamelan said, what now? Admiral? What are your suggestions?"

Corais calmed, resheathed her sword and stepped back beside me. But her eyes stayed on the ship captain.

I'd deliberately turned the discussion to Cholla Yi. If he had any ability to lead, beyond his talent at chicanery and brutality, he'd best show it now. Finally, he forced composure, breathing deeply. I knew he was more angry than any of us, not just because all rogues fancy themselves perfect judges of character, even though they're mostly the quickest fooled, but also because he must've been counting on The Sarzana's invitation to join his banner for loot and gold. Cholla Yi growled and plucked at his beard, but the ruddiness faded some from his cheeks as he thought.

"I see nothing good," he finally confessed. "No shining strategies open before me, save one, and that I won't mention, since it's barely worth laughing at."

"No one will laugh," I said. "We are all equally fools, it appears."

"Very well," the admiral said. "My only thoughts are these: What are the chances of The Sarzana making it safely ashore to a friendly isle? If what you said is right, Captain Antero, and your suspicions sent signals to him—although I must wonder how in the hell you, of all people, managed to slip free from his incantation—he must've fled before he planned, which suggests he might not have ended at his planned destination. Perhaps he fell on a lee shore or, better, in the company of cannibals." Cholla Yi tried, and failed, to look hopeful.

"Damned doubtful," one of the other captains, Kidai, put in. "I've never known a scoundrel to do anything convenient."

Cholla Yi nodded soberly. "Maybe, Captain Antero, you could prepare a spell with Gamelan's help, and confirm whether or not . . ." His voice trailed off. "No. I wasn't thinking. Even I know that'd be like lighting a beacon in a mist. Forget I spoke of that. Let's do nothing that might attract that demon's sorcerous eye." He thought again, then brightened. "Maybe I've put too harsh a face on things," he said. "Perhaps no one'll find out we loosed this scourge until we've somehow found our course back toward home."

Gamelan shook his head. "I wish I could sustain your hope, Admiral. But that's not very likely. We've got to assume Konya has wizards as powerful as The Sarzana, since they were able to topple him. When someone with his power suddenly reappears, there'll be many conjurations made, and all of them will be trying to find out how he broke his bonds. No, we can't assume we'll not be netted with the blame, at least not for very long."

"Suppose we turn back now," Polillo tried. "Could we resupply at Tristan, and then sail due east, toward familiar seas? Maybe sail a little to the south, in the hopes we can avoid those reefs and volcanoes that blocked us, in the hopes of striking familiar land, Jeypur or even Laosia, whose coast we could follow back to Orissa?"

Both Stryker and Gamelan started to say something, and Gamelan indicated the captain should speak first.

"I sure don't want t' throw them dice," he said. "You can figger it'll be a long damned sail. On seas we don't know more about th'n a half a copper whore knows gold when she sees it. If we had charts, maybe. But th' way she lays, I susp'ct the men won't hold firm fer long."

I knew what he was thinking, and agreed—these officers held their commands by force, luck, and consensus. Mutiny could never be further away than one order that rang false to these disgruntled seamen. These rootless freebooters might easily overthrow their officers, murder us, and hoist the black flag. They might think they were as likely to find fortune as pirates here as back in more familiar waters around Orissa. Besides:

"Even if they would," I said, "would we be able to find Tristan again? Wouldn't the same spell The Sarzana laid to keep the Konyans from finding the island, assuming he spoke the truth, work against us, since we're surely now his enemies?"

"It would," Gamelan said. "That was just what I was about to say. No. We can't turn back."

"We sure as hell can't just sail on blindly," Phocas, Cholla Yi's sailing master, snapped.

"Of course not," I said. "We have the stick map, and now we know, since we've seen other islands, it's a true model. If we could manage to decipher it fully, we wouldn't be sailing blind."

"Still ain't good enough," Stryker said.

"No," I agreed. "But I don't see anyone having a better plan. I suggest this—we sail on, south and west. We should look for the most civilized island we can find. We sail in, boldly, and tell the truth—or at least a bit of it. We claim to be an exploratory expedition that lost its way. We come from a great mercantile empire and seek to open trading routes with the West. It would be of great benefit for someone to aid us and give us directions back toward our own lands. Also we can hint it'd be dangerous to obstruct us, since our country has powerful magicians who'll seek revenge if harm comes to us. Maybe we can get a spell from one of their wizards, or better yet, since there'll be less possibility of our part in The Sarzana's escape being discovered by magic, sailing directions from a navigator or ship's captain. Perhaps they've got guilds for deep-water seamen, as Redond does."

There were mutters of approval. Stryker hissed, a noise that I thought signified support. Cholla Yi looked at the other sailors and nodded his great head.

"Possibly," he said. "Possibly. At least your plan is a bold one, and we won't have to slink around until we're found out. Not at all bad, for a woman, and not dissimilar from what I myself had been about to suggest."

Corais and Polillo stiffened, but showed no other sign of resentment. It didn't matter at all to me if Cholla Yi wanted to hog credit for this plan—if my vague idea could even be given that much of a name. I also chose to ignore the jab about it coming from a woman. Cholla Yi would never change.

"The most important thing," I went on, "is we'll have to move quickly. I sense Gamelan's right—sooner or later our role in unloosing The Sarzana will be discovered. It'd be best if we were long gone from these islands they call Konya before that."

So it was agreed. We'd sail on. Any landfall would be compared to the stick map, to see if we could begin triangulating our location and start drawing our own map of these seas and islands.

When we returned to the ship, Gamelan drew me aside. "I think you did come up with the best idea, Rali, even though it's far from perfect, as you said. There's but one problem we haven't considered."

"The Sarzana," I said.

"Of course. I don't need any magic to know he'll begin working to regain his throne as rapidly as possible, by blood and spells, which is another reason for us to be out of this region quickly. Also, there is the blood debt we've incurred in unleashing him."

"I know." That weighed heavily on me. There was a stain on us all, even though we committed our crime unknowingly, under the influence of sorcery. "How'll we make recompense? Or, at least, be shriven?"

"I don't know," Gamelan said heavily. "I don't know. But I do know it will have to be paid."

AS OUR SHIPS set full sail once more, Corais joined me on the quarterdeck. I noticed she had a strip of brightly patterned silk tied around her biceps.

"You've sworn an oath?"

Corais nodded. "I tore this from one of the robes The Sarzana left behind. It'll remind me how I was shamed by that bastard. I vow, Rali, to you, to Maranonia, to Te-Date, and to my own hearthgod, that when next we meet—and I sense we aren't free of him yet—I'll pay him back in blood for what he did to me!"

* * *

FOR SEVERAL days we saw little civilization. The isles we passed were small and rocky, and the few villages we saw clinging to their sides would hardly give us either the magician or navigator we sought. A few times we chanced hailing fishing boats, and bought fish for our supper with a gold coin. Of course a few coppers would've been sufficient, but we wanted information as well. I invited the fishermen on board and casually chatted about their lives, to lead into questions about what we really sought.

There was little to be learned. Each island was independent and had little contact with another, or with what one fisherman called "the men of the lights" farther south and deeper into the archipelago. Sailing was hazardous beyond this island group where the sea was open, with little land except the reefs and ship-rending stacks known as the Giants' Dice, where the ocean currents pulled your vessel into their embrace.

They explained why they never dealt with the Konyans farther south. Neither had anything the other wanted. No, they knew of no noted sorcerer, and were most grateful they didn't. One fisherman said he'd heard stories of a great war between lords and magicians some time gone, one that'd ended in the defeat of the wizards. He told us, and swore it was true, that sea demons had been raised to bring them down. I guessed he'd heard tales of The Sarzana's defeat. The only diviners he knew about were the village witches, which were all they needed to call the fish, and maybe provide a bagged wind to drive a boat safely home or, failing that, a little weather luck to keep boats from getting caught in the storms.

As for navigators skilled with map, astrolabe, and compass, they had no place here with these fishermen. A man didn't need to sail far beyond his own village. Half a day out, half a day back, at most, and any boy knew how to read the sea close to home long before he was permitted to stand behind the rudder. If a boat was caught by a storm and driven out to sea, well, the fisherman shrugged, if the gods were good, he might find his way home. Otherwise . . .

We were told we'd likely find what we were seeking farther south. Beyond the Giants' Dice, which had been cast there by monstrous beings ages before, after they'd gambled and lost with men—the stakes being these fishing islands. But we'd best sail carefully, and perhaps wait some weeks, until the summer storms that were brewing blew past.

But we had no time to spare. We sailed on, and as the tiny dots of land grew fewer and fewer, the seas became stronger, green rollers that seemed to have traveled through many waters, building strength as they went.

The way was rough and wet for our small galleys, but I'd learned by now a small light boat like these could ride out almost any tempest. Besides, we'd survived the storm of the Archon, and those great waves that came with it. And so, unworried if a bit queasy, we bore away from all land, still questing toward the heart of Konya.

One morning, just after dawn, a lookout sighted a sail far ahead, just on the horizon. One, then three more, as we overhauled them. We conferred hastily. Should we avoid them? Should we close? Cholla Yi said we should proceed boldly. We outnumbered them more than two to one, probably had speed on them, and if they were hostile, well, *his* men at least were eager to wash the salt from their swords in blood, particularly if there was loot in the offing. Perhaps this might be a way to test the situation rather than sail blindly into some harbor where we could be trapped.

We altered course toward the four ships. When we did, our ships began rolling even more. Now we were sailing almost due east, with the wind on our starboard beam. The seas grew heavier as we sailed on, the wind rose in ferocity, and rain began sheeting down in intermittent squalls. It was midmorning, but it might just as well have been a gray, dark twilight.

"I'm thinkin' we'll be comin' to a blow," Stryker said. " 'Pears to me them fishermen weren't tale-tellin' when they said th' summer storms be damned fierce."

Duban drew him over to the staff our long weather glass was stapled to. I followed. Stryker tapped the glass, eyed the level the liquid within had sunk to, and whistled.

"Aye," Duban said, having to nearly shout to make himself understood over the wind's roar. "Dropped 'most a finger width in less'n three turnings of the hourglass. We're in for it, Cap'n."

"That we be," Stryker agreed. "Turn out the watch below. Make certain all's lashed down. 'N' have th' galley fire quenched. Double-lash th' boats, and secure th' oars." He turned to me. "Cap'n Antero, if you please. Could I have a work detail of yer Guardswomen to help secure th' cargo below? I'll detail mates to supervise."

I shouted for Corais, and told her to follow Stryker's orders. She nodded, then looked over my shoulder, and her eyes widened in amazement.

I turned, and I, too, gaped. As the storm built, I'd momentarily forgotten the Konyan ships. Now we were within a few hundred yards, and even through the rain, could see them clearly. Three of them were smaller, about twice the size of our galleys. Each had three masts, with lateen sails, and were high-decked, with a single poop deck running from amidships to the stern. It was the fourth ship that made us marvel.

It was a galley, but one such as I could never have imagined. I thought it about ten times the length of our ships, and as wide as it was long. It had but a single row of oars, but those oars stuck far out into the water. They disappeared into oar holes on a lower deck, so I couldn't see how many men it took to work each of them, but thought there must've been at least five or six to each bench. Above the main deck was a shelter deck that wasn't much smaller than the main, and above that, the top deck. Perhaps it was this that gave the ship its amazing appearance, since it was set with three cabins that were roofed like houses on land, with each roof uptilted like so many sunbonnets at the corners. I could see the ship's timbers were covered with elaborate carvings. All of the cabins had huge round portholes, as did the main structure on the deck below. Heavy railings lined the decks, and the ladders leading to each level were more like stairs. It looked, in short, like a two-story villa, or a small country temple had been magically given a hull and sent to sea. There was a single mast set in the middle of the ship, and one square sail, now with a double goose-wing reef, hung from a yard that must've been turned from a huge tree.

"Damned thing's a wooden water beetle," Stryker said, and so it appeared as the long oars flailed at the seas, sending up nearly as much spume as the wind.

"Surely hell to navigate in a storm like this," Duban said. "Look at how it's bein' driven downwind, an' the full storm ain't struck yet. Must be near flat-bottomed like a barge."

It didn't take any expertise on my part to know he was right—I could see ten, no, fourteen men bending mightily at twin tillers that led to the monstrous rudder I saw for a flash when the ship pitched into a swell, burying its bow in a wave and sending its stern pointed skyward. More sailors swarmed around the shrouds.

"What is it?" Polillo asked.

"Can't tell," Stryker said. "Unhandy vessel like that, I'd say she might be some kinda inshore merchantman. But look at them workin' parties they got crawlin' all over th' pig. Too damned many sailors fer a merchantman's profit. Maybe she's a warship. But how does she fight, dammit? If'n she's got a ram—'n' she's wallowin' like she do—I can't see how it'd do any damage, 'less she was a'ter somebody at anchor. Hell, maybe these Konyans get cross-eyed drunk 'fore they go to battle and try to run down anythin' they spy. Probably, though, they just pull up alongside each other and go at it till they run out of heads to chop off, and there be the winner, by damn." He grew thoughtful. "It'd surely be interestin'," he said, "t' see what we could do against such a ship, considerin' the amount of prize cargo she might bear."

I, too, was thinking in those terms, but caught myself. Was I becoming as great a freebooter as Cholla Yi's men? There was a purpose for ships, after all, besides war and booty. But still . . . I thought of four or so swift galleys harrying such a behemoth, like direwolves taking down a giant bear. I set the thought aside, to ponder and develop at a more placid time.

The three smaller ships were obviously escorting the fourth. When we approached, they'd been in a vee formation in front of the galley. Now they'd changed course, and all three were between us and their charge.

"Damn protective, ain't they," Duban said. "I'd surely give a year out've my life to root around in them holds for an hour or so, playin' keepsies. Pity we've got other business with 'em."

Signal bunting fluttered to the tops of the escorts' masts, which we couldn't read, but were, no doubt, challenging us—what waters these ships of an unknown type hailed from and what was our intent? I looked at the flagship to see what reply Cholla Yi was making. He'd bet on a single large white banner, evidently figuring that would be taken for peaceful intent even in these foreign waters. I told Stryker to do the same.

Perhaps it meant something else here, or perhaps we weren't being believed, for I saw armored men fight their way out on deck into positions by the rail, and two light catapults on each of their foredecks were cleared for action.

"Stryker," I ordered. "Signal Cholla Yi to stand off. They think we're attacking."

"Not in this weather we ain't," he said, but shouted for the mate on watch.

"We'll try to stay within eyesight of them," I decided. "When the storm's over, we'll approach them again with a single ship."

"Signal from Admiral Yi, sir," the watch mate ordered. "All ships . . . proceed independently. Run south-southeast before wind. Will reassemble . . . That's all I can make out, sir."

Now there was no time to worry about these foreign ships, as the storm closed around us. The air was heavy with spume. The wind had grown into a steady scream. I counted one, two, only three of our ships visible through the murk, then lost them. The Konyans had already vanished into the storm.

"How's the glass?" Stryker asked.

"Still dropping!"

Stryker swore. He snapped a stream of orders, and working parties fought their way forward along the storming bridge and put a double reef on the foresail, leaving only a scrap of canvas to steady us. The main mast and yard were lowered, and I heard Stryker cursing Duban for not bringing it down an hour earlier. I had a moment to wonder whether Klisura's murder might not punish us further, since it was evident from Stryker's treatment of the new master, he had nowhere near the regard for Duban as he'd had for Klisura.

I ordered my Guard below. Polillo, who was looking distinctly pale, pulled me aside and swore she'd rather be washed overside than be stifled in her sickness below. I took pity and ordered her to tie herself to the port rail, and stand by to help the steersman. Stryker had already detailed two men to the tiller, but even they were fighting to hold the ship on its course. I went below and told off Dica and two others to take care of Gamelan in his cabin, and also quietly gave them the harsh order that in the event of complete disaster, their lives were less vital than the wizard's, and they should act accordingly. They understood and took no offense.

Back on deck I tied a line around my waist and to the staff, with about ten feet of slack so I could move around the small quarterdeck. Stryker and Duban did the same.

The winds grew louder still, rising to a howl. The rigging screeched like a cornered bear. Stryker ordered the lookouts in the forepeak below, and we began taking green water over the rails. We had barely gotten the mast down in time—now, anyone venturing down onto the weather deck wouldn't stand a chance. It didn't look as if we were on a ship at all, but rather on two square rafts, the foredeck and the quarterdeck, invisibly tied together, drifting through this tempest.

The strangest thing, though, was something you would never hear from an old sailor's dockside yarn about great storms—the weather was tropical, muddy. The waves that dashed over us were warm as blood.

We were running due south, the wind behind us, unable to hold the south-southeast heading Cholla Yi had ordered. A cross swell hit us from the east, and our ship was pitching, slamming from side to side. Polillo was now at the tiller, and I saw her muscles bulge as she and the tillermen fought to hold our course. The ocean was slate-gray, the shrieking wind blowing the tops off the waves and streaking the sea itself. It was hard to tell where air stopped and the water began. The winds paused for a moment, and I saw, astern of us, another Orissan galley, and then the typhoon closed in.

The cross swell was making our ship yaw, and Stryker shouted, close in my ear, we were in peril—we could broach. It was more than the wind, he thought. We were in the grip of an ocean current that drove us along as fast as if we were riding the spring flood down Orissa's river. We needed to put out a sea anchor. Stryker told me what was needed. I knew where the bosun's stores were, up forward, and worked my way to a hatchway, waited until there was a space between waves, jerked the hatch open and dropped down the companionway.

If the deck was hellish, it was worse below. The world, lit only by the dim glow from a handful of small glass deadlights set in the deck above, pitched and rolled. The air was thick and reeked of fear-sweat, dirty bodies, stale bread, mold, vomit, and shit. Not everything had been lashed down in time—a mess chest skittered across the deck, and a sailor barely rolled out of its way. Bronze dishes clattered their way from side to side as we rolled, and I felt the crunch of shattered pottery under my boot heels.

Stryker's sailors were in every posture imaginable. Some tried yarning with their shipmates, and I wondered if the stories made sense, and if so, who could tell. Some were praying. Some just waited, staring blankly, having tied themselves to a deck stanchion. Some pretended unconcern and cast lots on a blanket, although I noted no one seemed quite sure of the stakes. But one sailor, an old gray-bearded man whose name I remembered as Bertulf, topped everyone. He'd slung his hammock from its beams, crawled in, and gone to sleep. He wasn't shamming. I bent over and heard him snore, and his breath would've made a whale's spout smell sweet.

My Guardswomen were holding in as good an order as could be expected. Even though I'd never trained them for such a time, there were no signs of panic or disorder. Again, the truth of the old saw that to fight easy you must train hard came. I took Cliges and Ebbo, both nearly as strong as Polillo, and we worked our way forward.

We were just to the main-mast step when I smelt something. Smoke! A wooden, tarred ship could explode in seconds if fire broke out, and I'd heard tales of ships that'd ironically been destroyed in storms by runaway fire, not water. I saw, or maybe thought I saw, a tiny wisp of smoke. It was near a chest mounted solidly to the deck, and I remembered it contained the cook's pots. I rushed to it, jerked the catch away, and the door opened. Smoke billowed out. Someone shouted fire, and I heard a rush of feet and a blow, and a shout of "Stop" as panic spread, but I paid no attention. I looked about wildly for water, saw nothing, had a moment to realize the irony, then spotted a bucket lashed to a beam, ripped it from its stays and cast its contents into the chest. Steam billowed, and I heard a hiss over the roar of the wind outside. I nearly vomited. But the jakes bucket did its work, and the smoke was gone, the fire out.

I spun, looking for the culprit, and spotted him. The cook cowered against a bulkhead. I stepped toward him, and he moved away, holding his hands up as if to ward off a blow. "It was . . . just a bit of punk . . . I didn't mean . . . I thought it was safe . . . It was so I could start the fire when the wind died . . ." And then both his hands jerked up in the air, as if he were praying, and he collapsed.

The pillow-nosed sailor named Santh bent and wiped the wet blade of his dagger on the corpse's smock. He straightened, sheathed his knife, and looked at me. "Someone's intent on killin' me, I think it's on'y fair I do them first." Santh laughed. " 'Sides, th' bastard couldn' cook worth fish shit, anyway."

I didn't say anything, but pushed past. We had an entire ship to worry about. Punishing him was Stryker or Duban's duty, anyway, since I tried to stay clear of disciplining the sailors, if he'd even committed a crime in their eyes.

We found our way to the bosun's storeroom, and cumbered with the coil of heavy line, went back the way we came and out on deck.

I didn't think it was possible for the storm to worsen, but it had. There was nothing in the universe except our ship and the storm. I could barely make out the forepeak through the streaming rain. Following Stryker's orders, we tied the great line in a bight and lashed it securely to the sternpost. Then we let it stream astern. I could feel the difference almost immediately, as our ship slowed its wild yawing. It did, however, have a nasty snap as each wave rolled past under us and the sea anchor came taut.

A great wave loomed up from astern. I had time to grab Cliges, scrabble for a handhold, and saw Ebbo go flat, both hands clinging for life itself to the taffrail, and the wave came down on us. I felt that same swirl and water pulling as I'd known when the volcanoes' sea waves took us. But this lasted only for half an eternity and then was gone. I stumbled to my feet, gave Cliges a hand up, and then shuddered, as I saw four full feet of the taffrail had been ripped away by the wave. The taffrail . . . and Ebbo! I pulled my way to the side and peered out. Perhaps, just for a moment, far astern, I saw the white flash of an arm flailing, or else I imagined it. But then there was nothing.

Duban was beside me. "Mebbe," he growled, "that'll give th' tempest a sacrifice it wants."

I almost struck him, but what good would it do? Perhaps he was right. I said a short prayer for my spearwoman Ebbo to Maranonia, and resolved to make sacrifice for her when we returned to Orissa, as I must do for all too many of my women. But there wasn't time for mourning, as the storm took us again in its grip, shaking us, shaking us, shaking us, as one of my brother's warehouse terriers worries a rat.

The storm roared on. The sea anchor helped, but it still wasn't enough. The ship shuddered as wave after wave cascaded over the main deck, and I wondered how long the hull could take the punishment. I asked Stryker, and he shrugged—who knew?

We needed something to flatten the seas. I wished yet again Gamelan hadn't lost his powers—perhaps he could've cast a spell to help, maybe surrounding the ship with calm, a placid moon pool. I knew it would take a sorcerer of mighty powers to produce a conjuration that'd stand against this hurricane. I thought, and then it came. Oil. Stryker said we only had a few containers of cooking oil below, and one or two jugs of mineral oil to keep the weaponry from rusting.

I grinned—this might be easy. One container could easily become many. Just then, in the height of the storm, it came together, if only for a moment. I had a flashing memory from my childhood, of puzzling over strange squiggles that meant something to others but were meaningless ciphers to me, until one day there was a snap, and I could read. Now I had a vision of what Gamelan had been saying about Janos Greycloak's "single natural force." If that was true, and I knew it so, there must be many, many ways to the same end, as many as the mind of man or demon could produce. Now, as to what I needed . . .

It was as if there was some bearded pedant in my mind, perhaps one of my brother's boyhood tutors, except one with *real* knowledge, saying, "Oil, harrumph, yes. Oil is a liquid, and all liquids share common qualities, do they not? The trick then must be . . ."

The trick was easy, and I didn't need to go below. I grabbed the pannikin that hung next to the scuttlebutt for the steersman and held it out. In an instant the pouring rain filled it to overflowing. I opened the door to the storage cabinet under the binnacle and found the small vial that held oil to replenish the compass needle's bath. Holding myself steady against the ship's pitching, I uncorked the vial and let a single drop fall into the pannikin.

The words came swiftly:

"Water listen
Water hear
Feel your cousin
Hold her close
Let her body be yours
Breathe together
You are one
You are her."

. . . and the pannikin was full of oil.

It was equally simple to dump the sand out of the fire buckets, let them fill with water, drop a bit of the oil from the pannikin into the bucket, and then heave the full bucket of oil over the stern. Polillo exerted all of her great strength and held the tiller steady, and the other four of us emptied bucket after bucket overside.

Emboldened by success, I chanced another spell, telling the men to touch each bucket against the sternpost before dumping it. Again, I chanted:

"From the ship you were born
Follow your mother
Follow her close
Follow her near
Let none come between."

I couldn't tell if this incantation worked. The oil did seem to hang close to the ship's stern, and follow us as if we were leaking from a great tank, but maybe our suction was just drawing it along. I didn't think the spell was a complete success, certainly—it wasn't what I'd envisioned, intending to produce that huge moon pool with us sitting in the middle.

The second spell's partial success didn't matter much. The oil held the seas down, and not nearly as many waves came crashing aboard, especially from astern. Not that we'd suddenly entered some kind of magical safe harbor. The winds still screeched and the ship snapped back and forth, back and forth.

There was another problem: When we rolled, the ship hesitated for long moments before coming back to normal. Maybe we were taking water in the bilges, maybe we were rolling farther than the craftsman who first carved a model of this galley to build from could dream of. On one such roll I found myself hanging from the port rail, looking almost straight down at Polillo at the tiller. We stayed like that nearly forever, then, reluctantly, the ship groaned and started back. Even with the sea anchor and the oil, we were hard-pressed.

Time passed. It must've been only hours, because I don't remember darkness. I remember water, and wind, and being slammed back and forth, bruise growing upon bruise. I remember only two things clearly from those long hours: I relieved Polillo at the tiller, as two other sailors took over for the steersmen. Her face was bright red. I thought at first it was merely flushed, but then realized she was bleeding. The wind was strong enough to cut skin like a knife. I ordered her below. She peered blearily, then nodded and made no protest. The other was when a wave lifted us, almost broaching us and rolling us under, and I thanked Te-Date for the sea anchor. We rolled almost on our beams, and I looked out and nearly screamed. In the trough below was that monstrous Konyan galley, its sail ripped to shreds, mast broken halfway up, and no sign of life on its decks, its tiller lashed hard and unmanned. For a moment I thought we were going to be cast down on top of it, shattering both ships, but then it was away, invisible in the gale.

There wasn't anything then, except the wind and the water and the fear.

Then we broke into clear, sunny skies.

"We're in th' eye of it now," I heard Duban shout.

It should've been a calm summer sea, fit for dabbling with a lover in a canoe from the blue sky and bright sun. But it was a maelstrom, as waves battered us from all directions and the wind whipped through all points of the compass. A flock of gulls were hurled past by the wind and then were gone.

I saw the Konyan galley once more, rolling and pitching in the seas. Just ahead were the rearing reefs and rocks I knew to be the Giants' Dice. The current was pulling both of us down to doom. Huge rocks, reefs, and stacks jutted from the tossing ocean. Nowhere was there a bit of green or even brown earth to be seen, nothing but bare stone.

Duban and Stryker shouted for all hands, and the oars were manned, the oarsmen lashed to their benches. Gamelan wanted to come on deck, but I refused to let him, and told Dica to make sure he stayed below. Even with eyes, it was all too easy to let your attention slip and the sea take you. Gamelan grumbled but obeyed.

Somehow, the main mast and yard were hoisted, and a small amount of canvas unfurled. It was enough to give us way against the current, and slowly we beat out of harm's way.

But there was no salvation for the Konyan ship. It was carried relentlessly toward its fate. Of all the islets and reefs that made up the Giants' Dice, the ones the galley was being drawn to must've been the deadliest. Sheer pillars stuck straight up, curved across the ocean like a cupped hand, or better, fangs set in open jaws. There were spaces between these rocks, but certainly not wide enough for even the most skilled captain to pilot a ship through in calm seas. We saw no sign of the three escort vessels, either then or ever, and I guess they must've been driven down in the storm.

Even through the spume-thick air I could see Konyan sailors on the decks of the galley, trying to jury-rig some sort of storm sail on the mast stub. Brown canvas showed, and I felt a bit of hope, but seconds later the wind ripped it away. The galley's oars were manned, but it looked as if the oarsmen were panicked, each oar sweeping to its own rhythm. The ship pitched sideways, nearly broaching, nearly smashing against a rock as large as it was, but it cleared, brushing past but smashing all of the oars on that side like toothpicks. Now the Konyan ship was completely out of control.

Polillo, her seasickness forgotten, was beside me. "What can we do?"

I didn't know.

"We can't just . . . let them die," she said.

I looked to Stryker. "Captain?"

He shook his head. "If that bastard was smaller, and the seas calmer, and this gods-cursed current weren't runnin' at full ebb, maybe we could work closer, pass them a line and try to tow them out. But . . . hell! There's nothing!" His eyes moved past me, onto the ship. Now it was very close to the rocks. "Anchor it, you stupid bastards! Get some iron down!"

It was as if they heard, because I saw tiny figures fighting to derrick out the only anchor I could see that was still on the ship. It dropped, and line ran out, and I had a few seconds to pray for these unknowns before it came taut. The current paid no mind to man's thread, sending the galley closer to destruction, and I saw the ship give a jerk as the anchor line snapped and whipped across the ship's deck.

Then the galley struck. A wave lifted it and sent it slamming toward that semicircle of rocky teeth. But there were other rocks before them, and the Konyan ship smashed down. They must've been just below the waterline, because when the wave receded, the ship sat stranded, almost completely out of water, and I could see its bottom planking and ram up forward, carved like some fabulous beast. Then the seas swirled up and over its main deck.

"She won't hang there long," Stryker said. "That blasted ram'll break her back in a few minutes."

I looked at him, and he stared at me. He began to say something once, then again, then shook his head from side to side.

On the galley someone saw us, and then I saw faces turning and arms waving frantically, pleading for something, anything.

"If you can get enough sailors to man the boat, I'll try to take it in," I said.

"Not a chance," Stryker said. "Not in these seas."

"What about through there?" I pointed to beyond the awful curve of the rocks. The current swept around them on either side and on, and it looked to me as if there was smooth water, just as a gale splits around a wall and there's calm in its lee. "If we take the galley downwind, then back up, couldn't we put a boat through the teeth and come up from the rear?"

Duban was listening. "I'd sure not be the one to cox'n it! And damned if I'll order any of my men out, either."

Stryker turned and looked at Duban. The ex-rowing master shifted his gaze. Maybe that was what made up Stryker's mind, because he turned back to me and nodded.

"You're right. We gots to do somethin'. Else the sea gods sniff our fear, 'n' mark their slates fer us to share th' same fate. 'Sides," he added, "there might be somebody aboard who'll pay red gold to a lifesaver, or a family who'll be grateful for a body recovered and given proper burial. Master Duban, we'll do as she wants!"

Of course, there wasn't any way the mercenary sailor would permit anyone to think he was capable of feeling another's pain, or of doing good without gain. Even now I remember that, and hope the gods give him a moment of respite from whatever horrors his sins have sent him to.

Duban scowled, but shouted orders. Oars swept, and we inched our way past the reefs. Arms waved once more on the Konyan ship, but this time in rage. I fancied I could hear screams that we were abandoning them, but that would've been impossible over the wind's roar.

We sailed free of the rocks' embrace and let the current take us past them. Then we rowed up by main force to their rear. I'd been right—there were still tremendous swells, but it was far calmer than before. Not that I had much time to look—I was busy sorcelling water into oil and pitching it overside again. Stryker shouted for me when we were in position.

There was a knot of crewmen below the quarterdeck. Stryker called for volunteers for the boat. No one moved. I hadn't really expected any. But then the second surprise came. That skeleton-looking villain with the dagger chin who was Santh's partner scowled, said "Shit!" spat on the deck, rubbed it out with a bare heel and stepped out, saying nothing more.

"You'll have your rating back, Fyn," Stryker said, which was when I learned his name.

"Hell I will," the skeleton growled. "I don't need nothin' from you, Cap'n." He turned around, ran his eyes over the other seamen, and spat out six names, including Santh's. "Least I can do is drown wi' drinkin' partners," he said. "An' least you cocks know how to pull an oar." He looked over at a longboat. "We'll need four—no, eight—empty water casks. Lash four of 'em under the thwarts, so as we don't sink when you frog spawn go 'n' stove th' plankin' against th' rocks. Tie th' other four up in hammocks, an' run a hunnerd yards a line out t' use f'r floats. One cask fulla water, dry rations for two days, case we get swept out t' sea an' you dicks sit wi' your thumbs up your arse before rescuin' us, an' a pair of spare oars."

He looked at me. "We gonna have any of the bitches along? I could use four, ones that got some heft to 'em an' mebbe can swim, when we go over."

"You'll have them," I said, not taking offense—Fyn was a complete bastard, without question. I turned to the women on deck.

"Volunteers?"

Of course all of the Guard stepped forward. I didn't bother looking to see if any of Stryker's men had the grace to appear ashamed—no doubt they felt we'd proved the point that no woman should ever be allowed aboard ship, if for no other reason than they were total fools. I chose four—Cliges once more, then Locris the archer, and was about to name Dacis the slinger, who was even brawnier than Cliges, when I saw the look in Polillo's eyes.

Again I weakened, knowing it was utterly foolish to allow two officers out onto those seas.

All this takes longer to tell you about, Scribe, than it did to happen, and the boat was ready. We boarded, the boat was swung out and the falls manned. I sat in the sternsheets with Fyn. He calculated the swells, then snapped, "Awright!" and that was the inspirational cry we heard as the boat dropped into the storm-ripped seas.

The minute we splashed down, oars came out and the men pulled frantically away from the side of our ship. Our home was now a death trap, as dangerous to close in on as any of the rocks we pulled toward. It was very different being in the boat—we couldn't see very far, not much farther than the next wave, and our boat rose and fell alarmingly, or so it must've looked from our ship. But down here the sun glared and the tossing sent us from side to side, but it was almost pleasant.

I found a grin on my face, and Fyn noted it. "Wanted you 'cause you got magic on your bones. Prolly you'll end up dragged down by a demon f'r black wizardry, but not drownded, so you'll be our luck," he said, and spat overside, evidently the way he put a period to any sentence.

We couldn't see the Konyan galley at first, our view blocked by that rock ring ahead. The seas crashed and rose around their bases, and my idea looked utterly foolish. Fyn appeared unperturbed. "Lift oars . . . awright, on my count . . . pull! Pull! Pull!" And we shot between two rocks as if we were in a canoe pulling past bridge pilings in a summer race on a river.

We spun crazily on the other side, in a rip of currents. Now I saw the Konyan ship, and swore. It was actually *bending*, bowing in the middle as the rocks and the waves and the weight of that ram forward twisted the ship's keel. Waves were washing over the decks, and those uptilted roofs of the cabins were splintered and torn. The hulk moved on the rocks it was embedded on, and I heard the scream of timbers over the wind.

But I could still see life crawling over the decks and clinging to spars and rails. There was wreckage in the waves around the ship, and I could see bodies thrown up as well. I heard a great ripping, and the galley split in two. Instantly the bows were torn off the reef they'd been impaled on and swept spinning against one of the sheer stacks, splintering into fragments.

Only the stern was left, hanging precariously on the reef, but still with sailors clinging to it.

"We'll take off what we can," Fyn ordered, and we pulled closer. They saw us, and again people were waving, shouting, pleading, although we couldn't hear anything. Somebody jumped on a railing, poised, and even as we signaled frantically, jumped into the surf. I saw his head appear, his arms flail, and then he sank and I never saw him again.

"Gods-damned fool!" Fyn snarled. "We'll go in close, an' then they can jump, or mebbe slide down ropes. We'll float the casks down to 'em . . . Pity there ain't no ladders aboard," he said, and his voice was as calm as if he were tale-telling in a wharfside bar. "Ladders 'bout th' best thing t' pass through breakers an' all."

I wondered where the Konyan ship's boats were. I didn't see any at first, and guessed either they'd been lowered when the ship first hit the rocks, or else had been swept away earlier in the typhoon. Then I saw one, dangling from far aft.

Now we were very close, and I could make out faces. I don't know how many were left aboard the ship. Ten, twenty, maybe thirty. But each time a wave smashed over the ship, I saw fewer. I managed to stand, braced against Polillo's back, cupped my hands and shouted, "Now! Now!" and swept my arms toward the boat.

First one sailor then another went overside. Some tossed wooden pallets into the water for rafts, others had what looked like small buoys, and others just jumped, hoping they could swim to the boat or else they'd find some floating flotsam to cling to until we pulled to them.

Polillo hurled one of the empty casks far out, almost landing against the galley's hull, and the rope between the cask and the boat would be a lifeline. The other three followed. I felt a savage wave of exultation—the damned sea might have taken the ship, and many lives with it. But by Maranonia, we weren't standing by and watching it happen, and the gods were blessing us, helping us save at least a few. The hulk grated again on the rocks, and I knew it'd be washed off into deep water in seconds. We were very close—it loomed almost above us. I glanced up and thought the last man had jumped and the wreck was completely abandoned.

Then I saw her. I don't know how I knew it was a woman—it could've just as easily been a very long-haired man. But I knew. She was dressed completely in white, and her soaked garments draped her body. It was good that it was warm, or else she would've frozen in seconds. The woman had come from the ruins of the deckhouse, and now stood near the rail, holding onto it, looking about. She seemed not to see us. It looked as if she was in shock, or perhaps she'd been injured.

We shouted, we screamed, but for the longest time she took no notice. Then she looked down and spotted our boat. I swear I saw her smile. Moving very slowly, very deliberately, she climbed to the top of the railing, poised as if she were making an exhibition dive into a favorite swimming place, and then the wind caught her clothing and sent her tumbling out, spinning crazily before she struck the water and sank.

Without thought, without decision, I flat-dove into the roiling current. I came up, swimming strongly to where I'd seen her go under, feeling the current try to take me and smash me against the rocks so close, so deadly. Salt stung my eyes, but I could still see most clearly, see the brown and black and gray of the rocks so close, see the looming overhang of the galley's barnacle-dotted bottom, and then I spotted a swirl of white.

It was on the surface but a moment, then disappeared as the woman went under again, and I vee'd my body down at the waist and kicked under, stroking down, down, hands reaching, and I felt cloth, silk, in my fingers, and I clutched it and pulled it to me, and I could feel arms flailing weakly, and then I was kicking for the surface.

We broke water, and I gasped air even as I was pushing her arms away, arms that were trying to drag me back down, and I had a tight grip around her neck and under her arm, forcing her onto her back, and I was swimming hard, lungs pounding, and then I felt strong arms, arms that could only be Polillo's, grab me and lift me and the one I'd saved from the deadly seas.

T he next thing I remember is staring up at Corais' dark, sardonic face. She was trying to hold up my head with one hand, while juggling a tumbler with the other. The cabin smelled like a dirty tavern floor.

"Quit fighting me, Captain," she said. "You're spilling good brandy."

I realized I was struggling and stopped. I opened my lips and obediently gulped the contents of the tumbler. The brandy flared in my gut and the fumes swirled up to clear my head.

"Thanks," I gasped. "I'm feeling like a new woman already . . . I think."

I plucked at the front of my sleeping tunic, which was sopping with the brandy I'd spilled. My breasts were sticky with the stuff. "Looks like I'm leaking spirits instead of milk." I laughed. "If so, I'm certain to cause a fuss with the Wet Nurses' Guild."

Corais chortled. "First time I've had to force drink on you, Captain. Have you given the stuff up, perchance? Now that you're on a higher plane than the rest of us, cavorting with wizards and all?"

"Watch your manners," I mock snarled. "Gamelan's halfway through a lesson on turning sharp-tongued legates into the afterbirth of a shrew."

"As long as it's *legate afterbirth*, that's fine with me," Corais replied, filling the tumbler again.

Outside, calmness reigned. A peaceful sun peeped through the cabin door; the smell of balmy seas wafted in after it. Memory flooded back and I shot up.

"What happened to the—" I was cut off in mid-panic as Corais pressed the tumbler against my lips.

"Everything's been taken care of," she soothed. "Now, drink. Those are Lord Gamelan's orders. Two brandies, sweetened with some sort of wit restorer he had Ismet grind up."

I drank. While I sipped the elixir, she filled me in. She said the orders I'd spewed when I'd been hauled back to our ship had been carried out. I didn't remember issuing any orders—I recalled nothing beyond Polillo's cold, wet embrace—but I didn't mention this to Corais; she'd only use it as fuel for her sarcasms. She told me we'd ridden out the storm without further incident and it appeared our losses were minimal. We'd rescued thirteen Konyans in all, several of whom had suffered minor injuries. They and the others were being well cared for.

"Once again," she said, "you've proven you may not be the *best* commander the Maranon Guard has ever had, but you certainly are the *luckiest*!"

"I'll discuss my leadership merits with you later," I growled, barely suppressing a laugh. Corais' sharp humor was a refreshing reminder that we'd all come up together. We'd taken the same drubbing on the practice field, suffered under the same foul-mouthed drill instructors, and performed the same senseless duties ordered by less than enlightened superiors. In short, we were sisters of a time, as well as the sword.

"So that's how it's going to be," Corais fired back. "The bad news later, the good news now. Very well, O Great Captain Antero, beautiful as she is wise, wise as she is—"

"Stuff a dirty loincloth in it, Legate," I said. "Tell me about the good luck."

"Why, you've rescued a princess, Captain," she said. "A Konyan princess to boot."

I gawked. "You mean that woman . . ."

Corais nodded. "That's right. That sweet young thing you fished out of the brine is as royal as a tavernkeep's behind the day before payday. She is none other than the Princess Xia, daughter of one of the members of Konya's ruling council! Why, when we sail into their waters, we'll be heroes! They'll give us anything we want!"

I looked into the empty tumbler. Whatever Gamelan had laced the brandy with was doing a better job of wit-sharpening than I liked just now.

Where Corais saw luck, I saw glimmerings of trouble. Exactly what the trouble might be, I wasn't certain. I hid my doubts from Corais. No sense spoiling someone else's good mood with my cynical second-guessing.

"May the gods be smitten with your every word, Corais," I said. I swung out onto my feet. "I'd better see to our royal catch before the day grows much longer."

I stripped off the brandy-soaked tunic and began to wash up, mentally upgrading my intended dress to something more fitting to greet a princess.

"One other thing, Captain," Corais said. "Cholla Yi's flagman has been flapping away like a constipated gull all morning. The admiral wants a meeting. Urgently."

"And he shall have it," I said. "Send him my compliments, and say I'd be pleased if he would attend me within the hour."

Corais hurried off. I paused in my washing to examine myself in the mirror. It had been a long time since I had consulted it. Our adventures thus far might have been hard on my nerves, but they'd done nothing to injure my looks. My skin glowed with dark health, my hair was bleached nearly white by the sun, but was softer and more manageable than any time in my life, and my figure was as tight as hard exercise could make it. My cheekbones seemed set higher, the cheeks themselves pinched deeper into shadow, and the whole effect was one that made my lips appear fuller than before. My eyes were clear blue, with small tight lines of authority fanning out that I had to admit were not unattractive, and only added seasoning.

If you think it was vanity that made me take stock, Scribe, you're mistaken. Ever since I'd accepted Gamelan's tutelage, I'd remembered with some dread my brother's description of the effect the intense practice of magic had on Janos Greycloak. Amalric said Janos' body had been ravaged by it and he'd visibly aged many years. To be certain, Amalric had been speaking of Greycloak's obsession with black magic, but that'd done little to allay my fears. So it was with more relief than satisfaction that I took inventory.

Very well, I'll admit one bit of vanity—my skin, which I've always thought my best feature. As I said, it positively glowed with health, which pleased me to no end. And I thought: Nothing like a little power to put a blush in a woman's cheeks.

I daubed myself with my favorite orange-blossom perfume and donned my best dress uniform. I strapped on my sword, pinned on a gold brooch of rank, and hooked my spear and torch earrings into my lobes. I gave the mirror one last look, feeling a bit like a child playing dress-up.

"They'll never know, Rali," I assured myself, and went off to meet the princess.

The ship's carpenter—a miracle worker in his own right—had conjured enough space next to Gamelan's cabin to create comfortable, if minuscule, quarters for her. At the door I raised my hand to knock, but paused when I heard voices.

The first crackled like an old, scolding hen: "Come, come, my lady. I know you despise the taste of spirits, but you really must drink this. That old wizard may be blind, bless his soul, but he knows how to brew a nice restorer. My dear departed granny couldn't have done better herself, and she was a favorite of all the great ladies in her time when they felt frail."

The answering voice was young, and remarkably sweet: "Oh, very well, Aztarte. Not that I need it. I'm only a little tired. But you'll nag me without mercy if I don't."

There was a rustling, sounds of dainty gulping, and then a gasp. "Oh, dear. That's strong enough to take one's breath away. But not so awful as I feared." More rustling and gulping as she drank more. "Mmm. That's almost quite good. The taste improves the more you take. And I must say, the day looks cheerier already. I believe I'll change my view of spirited drink. It's obvious I've only been offered brandy of lesser quality before."

"You see, Princess Xia," the crone admonished, "you should listen to your poor Aztarte. I only want what's best for you. And hasn't that always been the case since the day your dear mother, bless her bones, had me brought from the village to nurse you?"

The princess giggled. It had a marvelous tone, like a lyre. "And to this day you still think I'm that infant you cuddled," she said. "Did you say that wizard prescribed two tumblers of his elixir? I'm quite looking forward to the other."

Sounds of liquid pouring and drinking. Then: "Tell me, Aztarte, whom do I have to thank for our good fortune? We'd be at the bottom of the sea with the others—poor things—if these very brave people hadn't risked their lives."

"It was Captain Antero who ordered the rescue," the crone said. "And it was Captain Antero who personally saved you."

"A captain?" the princess asked, sounding puzzled. "I distinctly recall that it was a woman who fished me out! I thought it odd at the time, but I was drowning, you see, so I didn't question her too closely." Her voice dropped a note, sounding disappointed.

"Oh, well. I can see now that such a thing is not possible. Perhaps I dreamed her. It was such a wondrous dream, Aztarte. She was simply the most beautiful woman I have ever seen. Her arms and legs so shapely, but muscular, as well. Her hair streaming behind her like the mane of a golden horse fairly flying through the seas. A most remarkable vision, you must admit. But alas, it seems it was only that . . . a dream. What a world it would be if women such as us could aspire to such brave actions."

"But my lady," the crone broke in, "that was no—" I knocked, cutting her off.

Silence, then Xia said: "You may enter."

I did, bowing low as I cleared the door. "Captain Antero, Your Highness," I said. "At your service."

Princess Xia was agog, staring up at me from her pillows quite speechless. I was stricken dumb for a moment myself. She was exquisite—dark as Corais and as slender, but even though she was in bed I could see she was nearly as tall as me. She wore a borrowed rough white robe, but with her regal bearing, it seemed a much richer garment. Her hair fell in long black waves that glistened where the light struck the brightest. Her eyes were wide pools of blackness, bubbling with all the energy and youth of someone eighteen summers old. Dark brows arched over those eyes, setting off high cheekbones and a patrician nose. Her lips were naturally rose-colored, and perhaps a bit too full, if you prefer the ice maiden look over ripe sensuality.

Xia flushed prettily at my too close inspection. Then she recovered and clapped her hands with glee. "You see, Aztarte, I wasn't dreaming. It *was* a woman who rescued me."

The gray-head who was her servant shook her head at this, setting many dowager's chins in motion. "But I've been trying to tell you, Your Highness . . . Captain Antero *is* a woman. A woman soldier, bless her heart. Thank the gods she came along when she did, instead of those pirates I see in this crew. Why, our virtue wouldn't last a second with the likes of them."

The princess leaped to her feet, and in her excitement her robe fell open and I was treated to a glimpse of high, full breasts with nipples like fresh berries, and the pink tender lips of her sex, which were plucked as smooth as a young girl's. I thought for a moment she was going to hug me, then she blushed again when she saw my hungry look and pulled the robe closed. But not *that* tight, I noted.

Then she said, quite formally: "I owe you my life, Captain Antero. And more importantly, I owe you the lives of twelve of my countrymen, including Aztarte, who is dearer to me than any other—except for my father, of course."

Aztarte smacked her gums loudly in pleasure at this. "You're too kind, Princess." Then she looked at me, her brown eyes startlingly young in such an old face. "But I must tell you, Captain, I thought I was done for when that big soldier of yours—Polillo, I think her name be—grabbed me by the hair and hoisted me up like I was a flounder that just took the bait."

I bowed low again. "We did nothing more than any civilized person would do," I said. "If we had been in the same fix, your people would have done the same."

"I'm not so certain of that, Captain," Xia said. "We are a suspicious people, and you appear to be strangers."

"That we are, my lady," I said. "Our leaders sent us on a vital mission, which we accomplished, but in the process we became lost. When we met, I was sailing to your land to beg for assistance in finding our way home."

Princess Xia laughed. It was a most delightful sound. "And you shall have it," she said. "I'll speak to my father—Lord Kanara. I promise you he'll be happy to use his influence. After all, you've just rescued his only child."

I was about to thank her, when a knock came on the door. It was Corais.

"Excuse me, Captain," she said. "The admiral's boat is on the way." As she spoke her eyes were moving to the princess, then to me, then back to the princess again.

"I'll be with you in a minute, Legate," I said, and Corais shot me a salute—it was quite crisp, and meant, I'm sure, to impress Xia with my importance. Then she ducked out again.

"If you'll forgive me, Princess," I said. "Duty calls."

Her look was not quite as bright as before. "Of course," she said, "you must attend to your admiral."

I laughed. "Actually, my lady," I said, "he's attending to me. In this fleet the admiral takes *my* orders."

Xia glowed. "Fancy that," she said. "A woman in command! We must speak again soon, Captain."

She extended her hand. I bowed over it, brushing her soft flesh with my lips. She shivered. I rose, troubled by the heat rising in me, and made a stiff farewell.

Cholla Yi was pacing my cabin. I'd had my bunkmates clear away their gear and ordered a table and chairs brought in along with a few refreshments. Besides his angry pacing, the first thing I noted was he was alone. Which meant he didn't want witnesses to our conversation.

He whirled to confront me. "You've landed us into a mess of trouble, Captain Antero," he snapped. "And if we don't act fast, we're all doomed for a flaying, or worse."

I was rocked by his accusation. "What have I done?"

"Saved those Konyan bastards, is what you've done." he said. "I'll be the first to admit it was a brave act, but it was also a damned foolish one."

"Since when has rescuing people been foolish?" I asked. "I thought it was one of the unwritten laws of the sea to come to the aid of your fellow mariner."

"Your seas, maybe," he said. "Not mine. And especially not these waters."

I had no immediate reply—I had an inkling of what was troubling him. Cholla Yi looked at me, then he let his anger whoosh out in a long breath and got himself under control.

"Look, Captain, we've been through a lot together. I still don't like you much—I'm honest enough to admit that. And I expect the feeling's mutual. But I've got a lot of respect for you now that I've seen you in action. But we've got a big problem here, and me pointing fingers is no help, and I'm sorry for that. We haven't had time to talk since that Sarzana business, and that's the root of our trouble."

The germ of worry that I'd had since Corais awakened me had become a full-blown plague. As full understanding hit me, I sank into a chair and poured us both tumblers of strong wine. Cholla Yi nodded when he saw my look of realization and sat across from me. We both emptied the tumblers and refilled them.

"The way I see it," Cholla Yi finally said, "is everything The Sarzana told us was a lie. Not only that, the opposite of everything he said was the real truth. He was a right bastard, he was, and the Konyans hated him for it. They couldn't kill him—because of the curse. *That* was truth. Any Konyan who kills the leader is doomed. So they did the next best thing, which was to stick him on an island. Then they gathered up every wizard and witch in the kingdom and cast a spell on that island so strong that he could never escape."

"And then we came along," I said, "and freed him. But it wasn't our fault! With Gamelan out of action, how were we to know The Sarzana pulled the magical fleece over our eyes?"

"You think the old wizard would've picked up on it?" Cholla Yi asked.

"Sure, he would," I said. "That may have been one mountain of a blissfulness spell The Sarzana smothered us with, but it would have been nothing to Lord Gamelan before he was hurt. As Captain Stryker commented before, I belatedly sensed it myself, but my talents are too new to stand up to an experienced wizard like The Sarzana. Regardless, that's past. We were fooled, but by powerful magic. There's no shame in that."

"I don't give a piss hole about shame," Cholla Yi said. "Getting rich and dying old is all I care about. And right now, you can keep the coin, because I don't see much hope of growing a gray beard if word of what happened leaks out to the wrong people."

"Which brings us back to the Konyans we rescued," I said.

"Which brings us back to the Konyans," Cholla Yi agreed. "Before they came along, we were going to bluff it out. Slip into a port in a hurry, boast about how important we were in Orissa, then cozen some help out of them and get the blazes out before they learned we were the ones who set that devil loose. But that plan—weak as it was—is wrecked now that you rescued those people.

"You can't keep secrets in a fleet. We all live too close. The Konyans will find out, and soon as we drop anchor at one of their ports, they'll let the rat out of the barrel. And then we're done for. Looking at it from their lights, we deserve the worst that can be handed out."

"Maybe The Sarzana drowned," I said, knowing it was a weak prayer. "That was a pretty small boat he escaped in."

Cholla Yi shook his head. "He's too mean to drown," he said. "The fish would spit him back. No, my guess is that as we speak he's hauling into his home port and rousing the rabble to his cause."

"We *did* rescue a Konyan princess," I said. "That should count for something!"

"So they don't gouge out our eyes after they flay us," Cholla Yi said. "Which is about all *that's* going to produce."

I lapsed into silence, drinking my wine as I pounded at mental doors for a way out.

"There's only one course I can see," Cholla Yi said.

"What's that?"

Cholla Yi shrugged. "Toss them back. They drown, just like they would have in the storm. And we sail innocently into Konya and make our plea. No one will be the wiser, as long as we keep the mouths of the crew shut tight."

I shook my head. "I won't do that," I said.

Cholla Yi went from reasonableness to instant fury. "By the gods, I'll drown them myself, if you don't have the stomach for it."

"I don't make war on civilians," I said. "These people have done nothing to harm us."

"But they would have been dead anyway, if you hadn't of interfered," Cholla Yi shouted. His hand hovered over his sword. I came up, kicking the chair back and out of the way.

"But I did. And that's that. As long as I command here, they will not be touched."

Cholla Yi looked as if he were about to draw his sword and have at it. I was more than ready to accommodate him. Then he fought for control again and won. I heard leather harness creak and shot a look over my shoulder to see Polillo's bulk filling the door. Just behind her was Corais. Our argument had been so hot and loud they'd come running to see if I needed help. I didn't. On the other hand, killing Cholla Yi was no solution. I'd only have a mutiny of his men for a reward.

"We shouldn't fight amongst ourselves," Cholla Yi said. "Perhaps there's another way. I'll return to my ship and think on it."

"I'll rack my own brains," I said.

"Shall we confer again tomorrow, Captain?" Cholla Yi said, cold and formal.

"If you please, Admiral," I replied.

After he left, I looked at my two legates. "How much did you hear?" I asked.

"Enough to know we're in for it," Polillo said.

"Half the ship knows now, Captain," Corais said. "You two weren't exactly speaking in whispers."

"There has to be some way out of this," I said. "Let's go talk to Lord Gamelan."

Some hours later, after attacking the problem from every angle we could think of, even the wizard admitted defeat.

"There's a spell I know of that causes forgetfulness," he said. "But it's quite unreliable, and dangerous as well. If it went wrong, it would be more merciful to simply kill them. Besides, I don't think it would be within your powers as yet, Captain Antero."

"But you all agree with me that it would be wrong to harm these people?" I asked.

"That would be a cowardly act, Captain," Polillo growled. "I'm more than willing to spill blood, as you all know. But I won't be a party to injuring innocents."

"I had my fill of that kind of fighting on the streets of Lycanth," Corais said, shuddering at the memory of the civilians who were hurled against us by the Archons.

I looked at Gamelan. As if sensing my gaze, he shook his head. "I have enough to account for on the other side when the Seeker comes for me," he said. "My vote is no."

"The only path I can see," I said, "is to confess our error to the princess and pray to the gods that she'll not only forgive us, but champion us."

No one could see any other course, so I sent for her. When she entered, the room lit with her presence. She wore a short, borrowed tunic that displayed her long legs, and hugged her narrow waist and high breasts. When she looked at me, her eyes were full of admiration. I hated to kill that look. But I did.

They widened in shock when I told her about our encounter with The Sarzana, then they hardened into dark mirrors when I revealed what we had done.

"I wish you had never rescued us," Xia said. "I'd rather be dead than to witness what is going to happen to my people with The Sarzana loosed."

"At least they will have warning," Gamelan said.

Xia made a bitter laugh. When she spoke, her words were much beyond her eighteen summers. "You cannot realize the full extent of what you have done," she said. "The Sarzana is the most evil man in all our history. He enslaved us, he robbed us of all dignity. Whole seas of blood flowed from our islands while he reigned. It was a miracle, a once in a lifetime blessing from the gods that we were able to rid ourselves of him.

"He will not be so easy to defeat again. In fact, it may not even be possible. He is a wizard of tremendous powers and is certain to have been practicing, planning, when he was in exile all those years. And only awaiting the day when he would be freed by fools such as you."

She looked at me, angry tears coursing down her cheeks. "When I told you my father would be grateful for rescuing me, his only child, I did not explain that I was his only *surviving* child. I once had four older brothers. They were slaughtered by The Sarzana during his purges."

Xia wiped her eyes and composed herself. Her features became cold, distant. "My family, you see, is cursed with royal blood. Through my mother, who died when I was a child, we spring from an ancient line of Konyan monarchs. The Sarzana slew all the male children of every family with royal ancestors."

Her head fell and she wept again. There was nothing I could say. Sorry seemed such a mewling word. The weeping stopped and the princess raised her head. I saw puzzlement in her eyes.

"Why did you tell me?" she asked. "Now that I know . . . it isn't safe for you."

I told her about Cholla Yi, studying her closely as I did. I saw no fear, even when I explained that although I commanded the fleet, Cholla Yi and his pirates held the upper hand in numbers.

"Are your women better warriors?" she asked.

I said they were, but it would be a mistake to underestimate the admiral's men. They were good fighters, fearless fighters, with much experience in slaughter.

"And you still refuse him?" she asked.

"Yes."

"Why?" she pressed.

I answered, but with difficulty. "I am a soldier. But above that, I command the Maranon Guard. We are sworn to protect hearth and home. It has been thus for hundreds of years. All of us here would rather suffer the most humiliating of deaths than to defile that tradition."

The princess thought a moment, and once again I marveled that one so young could display such depths. Then she said: "I will help you . . . if I can. There is a small, lightly populated place near Isolde, which is my home and the chief island in the Konyas. Drop me and my kinsmen there secretly at night and then wait. I will talk to my father and explain you were as much of a victim of The Sarzana as we have been."

"Do you think he'll listen?"

Xia shrugged. "I don't know. And even if he does, he is only one of nine lords who make up the Council of Purity that rules us."

She made a face when she named the council, as if she found the group distasteful. "I don't know what they'll say. If they agree, I'll send word to you. If they don't, then you must flee. Sail as far and as fast as you can. And although you have harmed me and my people most dreadfully, the gods forgive, but I pray that you will someday find yourselves safe and at home again."

It was a generous offer and we accepted.

"What will the admiral say?" the princess asked.

"I don't know," I said. "But I'll do my best to persuade him."

"And if he refuses?"

I looked at my companions. They nodded, firm.

"Then we fight," I answered.

The next day came too soon. I slept little, but arose early to prepare. I passed the word to my troops to be ready for the worst, but to be quiet about their preparations.

Gamelan and I took a morning stroll. The atmosphere among the crew was so chilly and the looks so hateful that even the blind wizard could sense the trouble brewing. Captain Stryker stayed well clear of us, and I could tell he had communicated with Cholla Yi, because rather than urging the crew to work with a will, he passed among them, pausing to speak low and casting quick glances in my direction. Gamelan kept a smile on his face as if nothing was amiss, but all the while he whispered instructions to me, filling my head with an arsenal of small, defensive spells.

Two hours before the sun reached its highest point, Cholla Yi sent word that he was coming. I waited on the deck and saw several boats leave the admiral's ship. They were all bristling with armed men. Cholla Yi did not make the mistake of trying to board with all of them. Ordering the others to stand off, his boat skimmed up to us and he swarmed aboard, followed by several of his key officers.

He strode toward me along an aisle created by crewmen on one side and my troops on the other. He stopped within sword range, his hair fresh-greased and bristling.

"Well, Captain Antero," he said, "have you considered my words of yesterday?"

"That I have, Admiral," I said. "And I've spoken to Princess Xia as well, and she has pledged to assist us."

Cholla Yi goggled at me, then threw back his head and laughed. "You take the word of a girl? You're an even greater fool than I thought."

Some of the crew barked harsh laughter. In return, my women cursed them under their breath.

I smiled at Cholla Yi and raised an eyebrow at his crew's behavior, as if to say, at least I do not command rabble.

"Perhaps I *am* a fool," I said. "But I'm not so foolish that I'll stop my ears to whatever it is you have to say. When you departed yesterday, you pledged to think of some alternative."

"And I have so," Cholla Yi said.

"You have a plan that will spare the lives of the Konyans?" I asked.

"Indeed I do," he said. "I propose we find an island. Something out of the way, so no one will ever find them. We'll maroon them there, with all the food and water we can spare, and then sail to Konya as if nothing had happened. Then we proceed with our plan to seek help, and once that is granted, we sail for home." He rolled back on the balls of his feet. "What do you think of that, Captain?"

I shook my head. "It would be kinder to kill them then to abandon them to starvation or worse," I said. "I'm sorry, Admiral, but that's not a satisfactory solution."

Cholla Yi's face purpled with anger. His hand dropped to his sword.

"You would rather fight me, then?" he shouted. His men growled like dogs ready to be loosed.

"I'd rather settle this peaceably," I said. "But failing that, I'll fight."

"All I have to do is give the signal," Cholla Yi said. "And the whole fleet will be on you."

Blood sang in my ears. I laughed at him. "Not the whole fleet, my friend. My troops are with me. And some of your own men as well, I'll wager. But if it's steel you have a taste for, have at it."

Our swords flashed out, and all over the ship I heard fighting metal rasp its greeting to the day.

But the lookout barked alarm and we all froze as his warning was echoed from every mast in our fleet. We turned to see a mighty warship bearing down on us. Its decks were black with soldiers, and in the heights of its forest of masts and sails were scores of archers, bows bent and ready to fire.

There were more cries from our lookouts, and we swiveled to find yet another huge ship, then another and another, until we were entirely surrounded.

I shouted orders to my troops and they turned to face the new enemy. Cholla Yi thundered commands to his men and they did the same.

He stepped up beside me, a grin twisting his lips. "Funny how quickly the game changes," he said, "when you're playing dice with death."

Princess Xia sprinted out of her cabin. "They're Konyan ships," she cried. "My people!"

Cholla Yi made way as she came up to us, his pirate's wit quickly sniffing out a small hope of survival.

"Let me speak to them," she said. "I'll tell them you rescued us. I won't say a word about The Sarzana. I'll feel like a traitor, but as my father says, sometimes honor requires a lie."

I looked at Cholla Yi. "We don't seem to have any other choice," he said. "At least not one that involves a chance at living."

So we put down our arms and signaled the rest of our shipmates to surrender as well. A few minutes later Konyan soldiers were swarming on board. At their head was a tall, silver-haired man with the uniform and bearing of a commander. To our relief, he instantly recognized Princess Xia and was quite surprised to see her with us.

"Your ladyship!" he exclaimed. "Thank the gods you're safe."

"I do thank the gods, Admiral Bhazana," she said. "I thank them for sending these strangers to my side. They saved our lives."

Bhazana's features mottled. "You owe them curses, not thanks, Princess," he barked. "These scum freed The Sarzana. He's already mounted his first attacks. And I was sent out to hunt these dogs down!"

He motioned to his soldiers and they were on us, kicking and hammering us to the deck, despite cries of protest from Xia.

In minutes all of us were beaten into submission and chained. Actually, we were all too surprised to put up much of a struggle.

"How did they find out?" Cholla Yi muttered to me as they lined us up to be hurled into the waiting boats.

My mouth was too full of blood from the beating I'd taken to answer. Even if I could have, I was bewildered as he.

I was thrown headlong into a boat, my knees and elbows taking all the shock, so it was a wonder nothing was broken. I looked up in time to see Gamelan being tossed over the side. I did my best to roll under him to soften his fall. It must've worked, because when he hit, my ribs were nearly stove in and my breath whooshed out. I fought to draw in air and kept getting his beard in my mouth.

"Get off me, wizard," I finally managed to grit out.

"Is that you, Rali?" he said. He rolled off me and I shuddered in a long breath. "I feared they'd already killed you."

"I think they're saving the honors for the torturers," I said.

Gamelan nodded. "I suppose so," he said, remarkably mild. "Still, we're alive. When you get to be my age, you'll marvel at that simple fact when you awaken each morning. A good day is when you don't hurt someplace new."

"Wizard," I said.

"Yes, Rali?"

"If you please . . . just shut up!"

CHAPTER SEVENTEEN

THE DUNGEONS OF KONYA

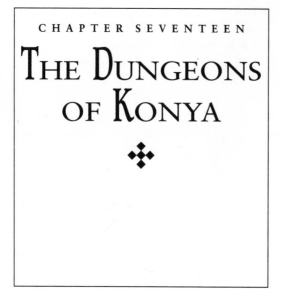

I solde claims to be the most beautiful and gracious of all the hundreds of islands that make up the Kingdom of Konya. Mythmakers say the islands were born from the gardens of the gods when a magical wind scattered flower seeds across the western seas—and Isolde, they say, is the daughter of the loveliest flower of all. Konyans wax most lyrical in praising the charms of the island. Haunting farewells have been created, telling many a tale of Isolde heroes and lovers who've been forced from the land and struggle mightily to return. They sing of perfumed air, bees that make honey headier than any wine, birds whose voices rival the very lyres of the gods, and warm suns and balmy winds that forever bless those shores. Even the seas, whose bounty never ends, according to the balladeers, produce fish whose flesh is sweeter than any milk-fed calf that ever graced a royal table.

There was a fellow four dank cells down from mine who sang those songs whenever melancholy overtook him—which was frequent, since he was madder than a lead maker's apprentice. After listening to him for more days than I care to number, I was ready to cut out his tongue. On really bad nights, as we listened to his warblings echo along the dungeon corridors, I would've traded a chance for freedom if they'd only let me wring his neck.

"It'll almost be a relief when the torturers come and get us," I told Gamelan. "There's nothing they can do worse than being forced to listen to that son of a poxed alley whore."

"I must admit," Gamelan said, "when we were first shown to our . . . guest quarters . . . I thought his voice a delight. And I wondered what manner of men could these Konyans be to punish such talent. So, he was fool enough and drunk enough to compose a song comparing the Council of Purity to nine warts on a crone's behind. In civilized lands they make allowances for artists. We say the gods must, by necessity, leave out common sense from the holy clay they use to form such a person. But I've changed my view. If I ever get my powers back, the first thing I swear I'll do is turn that croaker into a fat toad whose curse it shall be to dwell among eternally hungry cranes who will slowly pick him to pieces each day, and shit him whole again on the morrow so he can make another meal for them."

I brightened at the vision he painted and went back to sucking the marrow out of the rat bone I'd saved from the watery stew we'd cooked up the night before. Gamelan always had a way of cheering a woman up, no matter how low her circumstances.

Oddly enough, we owed our lives to the very man who'd put them in jeopardy—The Sarzana. He'd broken out of the Cevennes—the large island group that had the misfortune to be his birthplace—and with thousands of berserkers and a steadily growing fleet of warships, was laying waste to everything in his path.

"The Council of Purity is too busy to deal with the likes of you just now," Admiral Bhazana'd said as we were led away in chains. "But do not fear—they will not forget you. When the time comes, you will suffer most horribly for what you have done."

The dungeon they put us in was carved out of a small mountain. The main city crawled up that mountain on crowded terraces that narrowed to a sharp pinnacle where the old, red-domed Palace of the Monarchs sat. The palace, we learned, housed the offices of the Council of Purity and their legion of clerks, tax collectors, wardens, and petty officials. Over much time the city's sewers had leached through what soil can cling to those rocky slopes, and seeped between countless cracks and other deformities until the filth made its way to us in the form of ever drizzling walls and ceilings.

A prisoner—who through stealth and a willingness to engage in any crime or obscenity had managed to live more than forty years in that odoriferous tomb—said the dungeon had been dug by the first men and women sentenced there. New populations had enlarged it to its present great size over the centuries.

"Mark my words, there'll be more rock crackin' soon," he chortled. "Al'as happens like that wh'n there's a war on. Gotter make room, room, room for alla traitors that get sniffed out. They's th' good times for old Oolumph, they is. 'Cause wi' a traitor, you gots your families that's gotter be locked up 's well. 'N' old Oolumph gotter show 'em th' ropes, 'n' fetch 'em treats, 'n' do 'em all sorts of favors, he does. 'Course, I gets me price, but I sees it me duty to alla poor misfortunates what comes down here to get their bones stretched and skin took off." He exposed stumps of rotted teeth. I suppose it was a smile. "Last time things was this good, The Sarzana was runnin' things. Pickin's been slim since then. I s'pose old Oolumph's th' only feller in Konya what's got cause to thank you Orissans."

Then he eyed my earrings speculatively. "So, when th' time comes, sister," he said, "I kin put in a word wit th' sergeant what runs th' rack. Price a one a those get yer neck snapped first go. Won't feel a thing a'ter that."

I'd been alone in the heavily barred cell for four days by the time Oolumph had come scuttling along the corridor. The guttering torch he held was the first light I'd seen in all that time. I'd also been without food, and the only water I'd been brought was a rusty bucket with more scum than drink. The cell was bare wet stone, with a hole cut in one corner for me to do my business. So, Oolumph was a welcome sight, indeed.

I didn't turn away from his ruined face, which looked like it'd been melted on the bone. He wore filthy rags, but the cloth had once formed a fine garment, and his toes curled out of the rotted boots of a long gone nobleman. Other than my weapons, I'd been allowed to keep whatever I had on me at the time of our surrender, including my jewelry and wide leather belt, which was studded with gold coins struck with Maranonia's face. Oolumph's watery red eyes traveled a slow path to that belt, starting with the earrings, then my breasts, skipping down to my feet, and then lingering up my bare legs until the tunic hem blocked further view, and finally to the belt at my waist. I made no protest as he examined me, but only smiled so he'd believe I was no threat.

His eyes widened when he saw the belt, and he forgot his foulest thoughts. I plucked a coin off the belt and held it high for him to see.

Licking his lips, he came closer to the bars. "So, what kin old Oolumph do fer th' pretty lady?"

My other hand shot out and grabbed him by the hair. He howled in pain as I crushed his face through the bars. I bared my teeth and snarled: "If old Oolumph wants to live to draw another breath of this filthy air, he'll mind his manners."

"Sorry, your ladyship," he groaned. "So sorry. Please!"

I abruptly let loose, and he nearly fell to the floor. He straightened as much as his rack-hunched spine would let him, watery red eyes simmering in that ruined mask. Before he could speak, I tossed the coin through the bars. He snatched it from the air with the reflexes of a market thief. The anger turned to interest.

"Do I have your attention now?" I said.

"Oh, yes indeedy yer does, your ladyship," he said.

"That's Captain," I corrected. "Captain Antero, if you please."

"Well, Cap'n Antero it is, then. Or General, if yer like. Makes no never mind to th' likes a me."

"To start with," I said, "I'm not too fond of these quarters."

Oolumph nodded, eager. "Better kin be had, your—I mean, Cap'n."

"I also want company," I said. "I have a friend. An old blind man. Goes by the name of Gamelan."

More nods from Oolumph. "I knows where they keeps him, I does," he said.

"Then get about your business," I said. "I want quarters large enough for the two of us, and blankets, lots of blankets. Food, of course. And—"

"Old Oolumph knows what th' Cap'n needs," he broke in. He held up the coin. "Yer needn't worry I'll cheat yer. This'll buy a lot. 'N' I'll let's yer know when more'll be due." He gave my belt another long look. "From what I hears," he said, "you Orissans ain't long for this life. So that belt'll more'n last yer." And he scuttled away.

I don't know how much time passed before the guards came. It was impossible to count the hours, much less the days, in that foul blackness. The new cell was a royal chamber compared to the last. It was fairly large, not quite so damp, and had two stone shelves on either side for beds. There was a musty straw mattress on each shelf, and—thanks be the gods—a large pile of moldy blankets that were nearly vermin free. And to add to these delights, there was even a supply of fuel to burn to keep warm—with a nearly rat-free hole above to carry away the smoke—and material to make torches.

I was busy smoking the vermin from the blankets when they brought Gamelan. His hair was stringy, his flesh gray, but he had a spring to his walk that let me know he was as well as could be expected.

"Welcome to your new home, wizard," I said. "Come warm yourself by the fire."

Gamelan whooshed relief. "Thank the gods it's you, Rali," he said. "I thought I was being taken to have my bones bent, or worse."

He carefully made his way to the fire—he'd have taken offense if I'd led him there—and squatted down. He sniffed at the bubbling stew Oolumph had provided. "Is that meat I detect? Real meat?"

"It's rat," I said, ladling out a bowl with a nice plump thigh in it.

"I could learn to like rat," he said. He sipped the weak broth. "Not bad." The thigh bumped against his lips. Gamelan fished it out and gnawed on it with vigor.

"There's more where that came from," I said. "I know the innkeeper."

I shook out the blanket and put it around his thin shoulders. He hugged it close, a smile of great bliss gleaming through his dirty beard.

"Oh, to be warm again," he said. "I didn't mind the thought of dying. As for the pain our hosts promised, I'm too old to pleasure them long. But the idea of going to my grave half starved and chilled through to my back-bone did not please me."

"You've been speaking of death too much, wizard," I said. "Eat your fill. And warm those old bones to the marrow. I need your wisdom to get us out of here, my friend."

"I doubt escape is possible, Rali," he answered. "We're so deep in the bowels of these dungeons, you'd need a full year's production of a pipe maker just to get the sunlight to us. And magic is no good. The Konyan wizards have so many layers of spells on this place that even the great Janos Greycloak would've had trouble raising a boil on a pox victim's hide."

I didn't quarrel with him. I'd encountered the block with the very first spell I'd tried when I was dumped into that Konyan hole.

"Still, there must be some way," I said. "I've no intention of giving up without an effort. My brother escaped from a place much worse than this, and he was up against the Archons, to boot. Besides, I have my soldiers to think of. I got them into this mess. It's up to me to get them out."

It was then that the singing started. A plaintive ballad in a remarkably sweet voice echoed along the dungeon corridors. It was a love story—the tale of a young woman who died tragically, and her lover who slew himself so they could be joined together as ghosts.

I was about to remark on its beauty when another voice rang out: "Shut yer gob, Ajmer!"

I was shocked at the crass treatment the singer drew, as was Gamelan. But the song continued without interruption.

"You heard 'im, Ajmer!" rang out still another critic. "I swear I'll kills yer if'n yer don't stop."

Ajmer paid them no mind. He finished the song and began another—An ode to a tree that stood alone on a riverbank for a thousand years. The tree, it seemed, had once been a maiden who was so beautiful, a god fell in love with her. He spurned the attentions of a goddess to woo this maiden, making the goddess so jealous she turned her into that tree.

Soon the whole corridor rang with raucous threats. Through it all Ajmer sang on.

"What barbarians," I said to Gamelan.

"I was thinking the same thing myself," he said. "There's no accounting for taste."

Much time passed. Another coin found its way into Oolumph's pockets.

Gamelan and I racked our skulls every waking moment, but no solution presented itself. Meanwhile, Ajmer kept singing, stopping only to sleep and eat. And all the songs were of the same sweet love-lost theme. His voice evoked bitter memories of my own lost loves: Tries, who left me for another; Otara, from whose death I'd never fully recovered; and—more maddeningly still—the Princess Xia, who was not my lover, but in my captivity the memory of her haunted me most fiercely.

I began to hate Ajmer as much as the others. To keep ourselves from going mad, Gamelan and I would rate the curses hurled at him. "I'll rip your heart out if you don't stop," someone would shout. The wizard and I agreed this was poor and lacked imagination. On the other hand, the fellow who screamed, "I'll get a poxed whore to piss in your soup!" rated the highest mark of all. We rewarded him with a bowl of rat's stew. So much for our amusements, which, as you can tell, were few.

Through Oolumph we learned the others were doing as well as could be expected. My Guardswomen were being held in the same area and seemed to have enough valuables to trade to ease the hardships of the dungeon, and I sent word to Corais and Polillo to keep them exercised as much as possible and added a few hopeful lies to boost their spirits. Cholla Yi and his pirates were having little difficulty—none of them, after all, were exactly inexperienced when it came to incarceration.

Meanwhile, Gamelan and I were having no luck coming up with an escape plan. The more we investigated, the less likely it seemed such an opportunity would arise. Hovering over all our musings and many debates was the mystery of how the Konyans had learned of the part we'd played in freeing The Sarzana.

"The more I keep circling the question," Gamelan said one day, "the more it seems to me only The Sarzana himself could have been responsible. Other than him, the only people who knew were with our fleet, and none of them had contact with the Konyans until their ships surprised us."

"But that doesn't make sense," I said. "What did he have to gain? It would've been better for him if his enemies believed he was so powerful he could escape without assistance. It'd make them fear him more when he suddenly showed up in the Cevennes."

"That's true," Gamelan said. "Only a fool would not see such a claim was to his advantage. And The Sarzana, we've sadly learned, is no fool. Still . . . there is no other possibility. And if what I suspect is true, The Sarzana—or someone close to him—believed it was more important to have us killed than to reap the benefits of secrecy."

The wizard's logic was flawless, but no matter how hard I pounded my noggin, I couldn't make out what The Sarzana hoped to gain.

The routine of dungeon life moved as slowly and as agonizingly as one of Ajmer's songs. We arose each day—if day it was, since there was no sun to mark it—to the sound of Oolumph bringing the fixings for our meals. By necessity, these always involved some sort of stew. There were a few pitiful vegetables, a few unskinned rat carcasses, and sometimes a lump of an unrecognizable meat—with more fat then flesh. If there were rice, or beans, I'd pick out the stones before putting them in the pot. Any crumbs left over from our daily bread ration went in with them. Then I'd skin the rats, preserving the blood for the pot, scrape all the nourishment I could from the hides, and set the whole thing to simmer in a broth of boiled bones and hide.

We'd make fresh torches when necessary, breaking down the remnants of the others for fire kindling, and then wash as best we could. I exercised constantly, bending and stretching and fighting my shadow on the dungeon wall. I ran in place hour after hour, and dangled from the bars of our cell door, raising and lowering myself until my muscles screamed. This way, instead of weakening, I grew stronger each day.

Even with all the exercise, sleep was difficult. It seemed each time I was about to fall into a deep sleep, some force would suck me down with such fearful strength I sensed I'd suffer some great evil if I surrendered. I dozed in snatches—always an easy thing for a soldier—and in this manner remained fresh. Once a week we'd smoke our blankets, mattresses, and clothing to rid them of any fleas or lice that'd found their way into the seams.

There was no privacy possible between us, but we made do by meditating on other things while the other performed the human necessities.

Gamelan was such an amiable companion that our bonds only grew stronger. He became father, brother, and friend to me. I confessed my most secret thoughts, detailed my weaknesses and failings, which he always managed to point out some good in. One night I told him about Otara and her death and how ever since then I could never let myself go completely; even I could see this was the source of my troubles with Tries. I told him how she desperately wanted to adopt a child, which I for some reason opposed. Gamelan said he thought it was because I was frightened of the bond that would be formed—a bond that I might secretly believe was a betrayal of my love for Otara. I wept at this, because I could see he was right, and he embraced me and soothed me as if he were my own father.

"I think Otara was as much a mother as lover to you, Rali," he said. "So your grief is all tangled with your feelings for your mother, whom you admire above all others."

I told him I thought she sometimes came to me, such as that day in the garden—which seemed so many years ago—when Omerye sang, and the smell of my mother's sandalwood perfume infused the air, and how I'd turned away and refused to accept her presence.

"Let me tell you what I think, Rali," Gamelan said. "Do you remember the story you told about the dream you had in which you slew your cousin?" I nodded, wiping my eyes. "That was no dream, my dear. You know this, or it would not haunt you so. I concluded then your magical talents came from your mother. She passed them to your brother, Halab, and in a very small way to Amalric. But it is in you that the greatest ability dwells—coming directly from mother to daughter."

"Are you saying my mother was a witch?" I asked.

"Yes."

"How can that be? She never practiced magic, or seemed to pay much attention to spell casters or their kind."

"I think she gave it up," Gamelan said. "For the love of your father."

I thought of the sacrifice Gamelan had been forced to make, how bitter about it he was to this day, and could see the sense in what he said. Then I recalled the myth of my namesake in the small village that was my mother's birthplace. I told Gamelan about it.

He thought for a long time, then said: "It was no myth, Rali. It happened."

Understanding flooded in. "Then the Rali of the tale was—"

"Your ancestor," Gamelan broke in. "Now I know myself why I've pressed you so hard. I've sensed from the moment we met that a heavy duty awaited that only you could perform."

I'll confess, Scribe, that I was crying again. "My mother always said," I burbled, "that Rali means hope."

"Yes, my friend," the old wizard said. "You *are* hope. Our *only* hope."

HOPE, HOWEVER, seemed in short supply as the days progressed. The war with The Sarzana was going badly for the Council of Purity. All their efforts to stop his depredations were as naught, and only Oolumph seemed happy as the admirals and generals who commanded the forces they threw at him failed in one battle after another. Those who survived joined us in the dungeon, and Oolumph's purse grew fatter as he tended their needs.

From them we heard reports of The Sarzana's atrocities. He would besiege an island, hammer it with magically raised storms, terrify it with hordes of demons who committed the most unspeakable acts, and when the island finally bowed to the inevitable and surrendered, blood flowed in rivers as his forces moved in for the slaughter, killing and raping and burning. As he advanced, his powers seemed to grow stronger, as if all the souls he'd sent to the reaper were fuel for an evil conflagration. The Konyan wizards seemed as helpless as the military forces sent against him. A jailed general told us his defeat came after six of the greatest wizards in the land worked in concert to conjure up a shield for his advancing troops.

"They worked for days on it," he said, "and when all was ready, I was assured no force known by our gods could penetrate that shield. I led a flanking attack myself. At first all went well. They came at us, but we beat them back, and were even making some progress. I saw The Sarzana—mounted on a large black steed—directing the battle from the hill we were advancing on. I sent word for our archers to shower the hill with arrows, thinking even if they failed to kill him, they might drive him from his command post. But as soon as the arrows were launched, a black wind blew up that darkened the sky, and the arrows meant for The Sarzana fell on us instead. Then my archers, instead of easing fire, acted as if they were possessed, firing volley after volley. Every arrow was deflected. And every arrow found a mark—except it was my own soldiers who were slain."

The battle ended in a rout as the general's troops turned and ran. As they fled, the general said, huge direwolves leaped out of the very ground in pursuit, hamstringing them one after the other and leaving them where they fell.

"I only survived myself," the general said, "because my horse was killed, toppling on me as it died. I was trapped under it all night."

The general—whose legs were crushed—wept as he told us of how the direwolves came back to feed on the men they'd hamstrung. He listened to his solders' screams until dawn.

"A few of my bravest officers returned to rescue me," the general said. "But I wish to the gods they'd cut my throat instead."

The general proved to be a brave man himself. He made no protest when they came for him—in fact, he seemed glad. We heard the torturers working on him, and he only cried out a little; but not once did he beg for mercy.

A FEW DAYS LATER Oolumph brought word of an even greater disaster.

"I'll be needin' another coin sooner'n usual, Cap'n," he told me as he doled out our day's rations. "Thing's are gettin' right dear on th' outside, they is."

I made some sarcastic reply about the greedy farmers and merchants who afflict people whenever any crisis arises.

"Oh, that's been goin' on from the beginnin'," he said quite cheerfully. "Way old Oolumph sees it, they's doin' folks a favor, they is. Why, everythin'd disappear right outer the stalls from all th' hoarders if'n they didn't bump up th' prices high 'nough. But when food 'n' stuff's real dear, like, there'll al'as be plenty for them that's got the price. It's almos' a duty, if'n yer looks at her right. 'N' it's not so bad, really. Th' poor's used to starvin', so they ain't too worst off. 'N' it makes th' folks wit' coin to spare spread it around for those of us who're lackin', if'n you sees what ol' Oolumph means."

I started to get angry, but he was such an unabashed rogue, it seemed pointless. I flipped him a coin instead.

"Are you saying things are worse then before?" I asked.

"Indeedy, they is," Oolumph said. "Week 'r so ago, I hear tell, a hot wind started blowin'. Blew day 'n' night, it did. Sucked th' juice right outer th' crops, it was so hot. 'N' it's still blowin'. Even th' old folks say they never seen nothin' like. We don't feel it none down here 'cause we's so deep."

I nodded, reflexively pulling my blanket coat closer. In the dungeons of Konya it was always winter.

"But it ain't just th' wind," he continued. "Folks started gettin' sick. Real sick. Some kinder plague, I guess. They tells me there's gettin' to be so many dead folks, there soon won't be enough of the livin' left to bury 'em."

"The Sarzana!" Gamelan rasped.

" 'At's a way they figger," Oolumph chortled. "Looks likes he's a conjurin' fool. Hittin' Isolde wit' ever'thin' he's got!"

"It doesn't seem to make any difference to you, who wins?" I said.

Oolumph cackled louder. "I tol' yer afore," he said, "these be good times for old Oolumph. But not near so good when Th' Sarzana was on top. Why, last time they added to th' dungeons was durin' his day. You'd brand me a liar if'n I tol' yer I was sorry that it looks like he's comin' back for good!" He popped the coin I'd given him in his purse, gave it a good, loud rattling, then hobbled off on his dirty business.

"No wonder they haven't come for us yet," I said. "They're too busy for revenge."

Gamelan didn't answer. I looked at him and saw his brow was beetled in concentration. His fingers were curling around and around in his beard.

"It's not possible," I heard him mutter.

"What isn't possible?" I asked.

He gave a querulous hiss and so I left him alone. We didn't speak the rest of the day. That night as I prepared for bed, he was still sitting on the edge of the mattress, toying endlessly with his beard. I started to ask him what was amiss, but thought better of it.

I no sooner closed my eyes than I plummeted into sleep. This time there was no warning sensation of being pulled at by some dark force. I felt as if I was falling at great speed from a mountainous height. I wanted to scream, to sit bolt upright and break the grip of the dream, but I couldn't. I heard a voice calling my name. It was deep, and harsh and full of evil. I thought I recognized the voice, but couldn't recall who it might be. Rocky ground rushed up at me, but just before my fall ended, a hot wind gusted, carrying me up again, and then I was sailing through stark, cloudless skies.

I flew like that for what seemed to be a long time. An endless sea, devoid of life, rushed under me. Then up ahead I saw an island. Flame and smoke gouted from it and I saw villages on fire and hordes of soldiers making sport with its inhabitants. Men and young boys were being speared, or ripped to pieces. Women and girls were suffering all sorts of degradation. A long line of horse-drawn carts were coming down a hillside road that led to the summit.

I willed myself to move in that direction, and a moment later I found myself hovering over the hill. Beneath me was a splendid temple. It had a large golden dome, and its vast gardens were decorated with the statues of what were obviously important deities. Soldiers, laden with booty, were pouring out of the temple. I saw others with the temple's priestesses, forcing them to perform all sorts of obscene acts. Then, atop a small knoll at the edge of the garden, I saw The Sarzana. He was seated on a black war-horse. He was laughing and urging the despoilers on. They began to topple the idols, stripping them of any rare metals that might decorate them. Some of the priestesses were dragged to those fallen idols, thrown across them and raped. When the soldiers were done with them, the women were killed. I was too numb for anger, or even horror.

The Sarzana raised his head and looked up toward me. He laughed, and the sound of his laughter boomed out as if he were a giant. Then I heard someone laugh in return. It rolled and buffeted me like thunder. It came from above, and I craned my head back to see a thick black cloud knuckling under the sky. The cloud swirled and whip-cracked with lightning. Laughter seemed to pour from a hideous, mouthlike hole. A face began to take shape in the cloud—fiery eyes, beaked nose, and yellowed fangs. It was the Archon!

He saw me and hissed: "It's Antero. The bitch ferret!"

He formed his lips into a funnel and began to draw in his breath. I shouted in fear as I was sucked toward him. I was falling upward, hurtling for the foulness of his mouth.

The nightmare shattered and I bolted up in my bed. Sweat was flooding from every pore and I was shaken and weak. I looked over at Gamelan and saw by the light of the guttering torch the wizard was still asleep. I swung off the shelf, gasping with effort. I lit a new torch, then strode to the water pail and scrubbed my skin until it was raw. Then I sat on the edge of my mattress, waiting for morning.

Finally, a rattle of food buckets and a shuffle of feet announced Oolumph's approach. A new day had begun. Gamelan groaned awake.

"Here yer be, Cap'n," Oolumph said as he passed the pails through the food hole.

Usually Oolumph was full of cheer and foul jests. Today he was glum, withdrawn.

"What's the matter, Oolumph?" I said. "Are you ill?"

He shook his head. "I'm well enough," he said. "But it's best not to speak. Today's an unlucky day."

"I'd call a city besieged by the plague about as unlucky as it can get," I said. "Why is this day any worse than the others?"

Oolumph was quiet for a moment. Then he looked this way and that to see if anyone was near. He came close to the bars. "Somethin' terrible's happened," he said. "The Sarzana's finally gone too far. He wrecked th' temple at Chalcidice yestiddy. Desecrated it, they says. Looted it of ever' stone and raped the priestesses to boot."

I just stared at him, gaping, as he rambled on describing the things The Sarzana had done at Chalcidice. All of it was identical to my nightmare. And if even Oolumph was shocked by what I now realized I had somehow witnessed, then The Sarzana had gone quite mad. Or worse.

When Oolumph left us, I told Gamelan about my vision.

Gamelan's features darkened. "The Sarzana we knew would never do such a thing," he said. "He would not foul his own gods. He'd know that no matter how great his victory, the people he'd once again rule would never forgive him." The fire cracked and I jumped. "It's as I feared, Rali," the old wizard continued. "Somehow the Archon has returned. And he has made a bargain with The Sarzana. And he is in control."

MORE THAN OUR OWN puny lives were now at stake. With the Archon loose, Orissa itself was threatened.

"His ghost has followed us from the reefs," Gamelan said. "He's been looking for a path that would allow him to return, and he has found it in The Sarzana. Except, it is no mortal wizard we face, but a demigod whose powers are growing mightily from all the blood being shed."

When we first pursued the Archon, we had known he was on the verge of discovering a great spell that would destroy our homeland. With his new powers, that spell was more than ever within his grasp.

"We must foil him here," Gamelan said.

"That's all very well, wizard," I said. "But what makes escape any more possible now than before?"

"We know who our enemy really is," Gamelan said. "If the gods are with us, that knowledge alone may be all we need."

He told me his plan. Four coins from my belt put the first part in motion.

TWO DAYS LATER the soldiers came for me. I was manacled with heavy chains, and they led up along twisting dungeon corridors that wound up, up, up, until the cold was gone, to be replaced by stifling heat. Outside, I could hear wind howling like tormented spirits. I smelled rancid vinegar and the sulfur of plague fires, and when we went past the guards' barracks room, I saw mottled sunlight through barred windows. We stopped in front of a large iron door framed in heavy timber. One of the soldiers rapped on the door.

"Enter," came a voice.

We went in. The soldiers bowed low before a cowled figure.

"Remove her chains," the figure ordered. The soldiers did not argue, but quickly struck them off. Then, one last command: "You may leave us."

The soldiers left, muscling the door shut behind them. I heard a large bolt shoot across, barring the door. The figure swept away the cowl and black hair spilled out. It was Princess Xia, so achingly beautiful after all my days in ugly gloom that I nearly swooned. A cool, spiced perfume swirled around and through me as she ran to my side to steady me.

"My poor captain," she said, her voice so sweet after all the harshness that my heart lurched in its moorings.

She led me to a bench and helped me sit. A silver flask was thrust into my hands and I smelled strong wine. I drank deeply. Fire blossomed in my veins.

I looked at her and time stood still. It was as if I had suddenly entered a world where only Xia and I existed. All convention, all reason, was swept away as I gazed on that exquisite face, skin as pale as new milk, lips red and bursting for a kiss. So I did.

She fed me life through those lips, her tongue honeyed and swirling. Her breasts were crushed to mine and I could feel the swollen fruit of her sex pressing against my thigh. We drew back for air, both of us shuddering with passion.

"I thought I'd never see you again," I said, nearly weeping.

"Oh, Rali," Xia said, tears flowing down her cheeks. "I've thought of nothing else. I've dreamed of you every night. I feel as if I've known you all my life."

"And I, you, Princess," I said.

We embraced again. She fell back on the broad, hard bench and I fell with her. My hands ached to feel her flesh, and I dragged up the hem of her robe, exposing snowy white limbs. She lifted her hips and helped me pull the hem up to her waist. The lips of her sex were smooth and tender, with a sweet pink bud peeping out. She cried my name as I nibbled my way to it.

Princess Xia and I became lovers in that dismal dungeon where nothing but foul night spores and mosses could ever grow. The bench was our bridal bower. The gray stone room, our chamber of first passion. And nothing before, or since, could ever match it. She was hauntingly familiar—Otara and Tries and all my other lovers combined. But at the same time she was new and teasingly strange and fresh. I poured all my longing into the kisses, and she responded in kind. When we were sated, we held one another, whispering idiocies like two moonstruck girls. In a way, we were. We'd gone from strangers to lovers so quickly that only the goddess who rules the moon could understand. Outside the door there was a chink of chain mail as one of the soldiers shifted at his post. We slowly drew apart.

"I must go soon, my love," she said. "Tell me quickly what you want of me. I shall do all in my powers to help."

"I want to be called before the Council of Purity," I said.

Xia paled. "That is beyond me," she said. She shed a few tears. "I'd so hoped you had a plan I could help you accomplish. But that is not possible. Who would listen to one such as me?"

"More than you think," I said. "As girls we're taught we have no power, so we never test it. But you'd be surprised what can happen when the womanly strength you possess is aimed single-mindedly and with force."

"But why should the Council—"

"I can help them," I broke in. "I can end the plague."

Xia's eyes widened. But instead of speaking, she only nodded—go on.

I told her about the Archon and our mission, which we'd mistakenly believed we'd accomplished. I told her what a great danger he was to both our peoples and what I had to do to stop him.

"Do you really think you can succeed where our wizards have failed?" she asked.

"Yes," I said. "And not because I think little of your sorcerers. But because the Archon and I have a bond. A bond in hatred, to be sure, but sometimes hatred can be an even stronger glue than love."

One of the soldiers rapped on the door. It was time for her to go.

"Will you see your father for me?" I begged.

"As soon as I return home," she promised.

We kissed again, then dragged ourselves apart before passion overtook us again. She called out to the soldiers, the bolt shot back and the door swung open. Xia pulled the cowl forward, and after a fleeting glance at the soldiers putting the chains back on, she fled.

* * *

I DON'T know what Xia said to her father, but the spell she cast with her words must have been as good as any sorcerer's, because only a few days lapsed before I found myself standing in front of nine pitiless men.

The guardians of the public good were a motley lot of nobles. Two were so old they drooled; four had less hair among them than it takes to make up one healthy head; and the remaining three—including Lord Kanara, Xia's father—were hammering hard on the last gates of middle age. If I had been a young soldier in this land, it was not a group that would inspire me with devotion. Even the drooly-lipped ones remembered enough to despise any mere creature who stood before them. I nearly despaired when I swept their faces, looking for a friend, and found none—not even in Lord Kanara. He may have pressed for my appearance to appease his daughter, but he was not going to be an easy wheel to turn when I pleaded our case. In every gaze I saw an ambush waiting. So I took the soldier's way—I attacked.

"My lords," I said, "as I was led up the hill to these chambers, I racked my brain for a pretty speech. I was going to fling my life—and the lives of my brave companions—at your feet and beseech you for mercy. I was going to tell you that we were peaceful strangers who came to these shores by misadventure. Just as it was misadventure that led us to injure you. But all those words were swept away when I saw the horror in your once great city. Your streets are despoiled by the corpses of your subjects. The marketplace is barred and empty. The doors and windows of your homes are shuttered against the plague that stalks the avenues, and the hot wind The Sarzana sent has sucked the very life from the trees in your gardens.

"It was a city near defeat, that I saw, my lords. And if you do not grant me my request now, I fear we will soon both be at the mercy of our mutual enemy."

Beside me, Xia quailed. Behind me, I heard Gamelan mutter for me to beware.

One of the droolers spoke first—his voice high-pitched and squeaky, like a boy's nearing manhood. "You're just a woman," he said. "Why should I believe you can do what our own wizards can't?"

"If I am such a puny thing," I answered, "how is it I stand here at all? I have traveled farther than any man or woman in my homeland to reach these shores. I have fought and defeated great armies, crushed a mighty fleet, and it was I who slew the brother of your real enemy—the Archon of Lycanth. I doubt any of your own subjects—men or women—could claim the same."

The old lord cupped a hand around his ear. "What's that, you say? The

Archon? I've never heard of such a fellow. It's The Sarzana who's the cause of all our ills."

I shifted my attention to Lord Kanara. "Ask your own wizards why they are helpless before The Sarzana. To be certain, he is a powerful sorcerer. But how can he stand against all of them? He's not *that* powerful."

A black-robed sorcerer leaned close to Lord Kanara and whispered in his ear. Kanara nodded. He turned to his companions of authority.

"Our chief wizard agrees," he said. "It is a mystery that has been puzzling them mightily."

"Ask him," I said, "if he and the others have wondered if perhaps The Sarzana has made an alliance with some other dark force."

The sorcerer bent low again to whisper fiercely. When he was done, Kanara said: "Yes, it is true, Captain. They have speculated on such a possibility."

"Your wizards' suspicions hit the mark," I said. "It is the Archon he made his bargain with."

"What do you propose?" Lord Kanara asked.

"First, I urge you to allow me to attack this cursed plague. Once I have ended it, you will know whether I am woman enough to carry out the rest."

"Pure foolishness," the drooler said. "It might even be heresy, to allow a foreign woman to practice magic in Isolde."

"Is it heresy?" I said, aiming my question directly at the chief wizard.

He looked at me, then shook his head—no.

"Then what do you have to lose, my lords?" I said. "If I fail, back in the dungeon I go and good luck to you. But if I don't, the plague is ended. It can't be the worst gamble you've ever been asked to make."

The nine men conferred, voices too low to hear. They'd had long practice with secrecy. Finally, they turned back to me. Princess Xia gripped my hand hard.

"Very well," Lord Kanara said. "You shall have your chance."

The drooling lord broke in. "Do not fail, Captain," he warned. "Our torturers have no match when it comes to ways of making and prolonging pain."

MY WORDS TO THE Council of Purity may have been bold, but inside I quaked with doubt. Gamelan said the plague spell could be lifted. I was certain *he* could have done so before he was blinded, but I had serious reservations about my own abilities. I was no more than a green apprentice. What chance did I have against the Archon? Gamelan's continued assurances did not soothe me; but what choice did I have but to carry on with the bluff?

They put us in a guarded stone hut at the edge of the palace grounds. Gamelan's captured implements were brought to us, and we began. I did not see Princess Xia in the two days it took us to prepare, but her seamstress came to measure me for the costume I required—a simple red, sleeveless tunic cut at mid-thigh, so my arms and legs would have freedom of movement. It would be tied with a golden sash. Gamelan warned me not to wear jewelry of any kind, especially metal, and he said my feet must be bare. Using Gamelan's magical book, with many annotations from my wizard friend, which he'd learned over his many years, I ground up disgusting powders and mixed evil-smelling and highly volatile oils. We worked without stop, the eerie wind howling outside and buffeting the stone hut. Finally, we were nearly ready.

There was no visible audience—other than a few nervous guards—awaiting us in the small park that'd been set aside for our efforts. There was a pool in the center of the park. Placed about it—forming a square—were four pyres of rare wood. As we entered the park, a wagon thundered across the cobblestone path. The driver was terror-stricken, lashing at his horses. He nearly wrecked the wagon stopping it. He leaped off, cut the wagon loose, took one last horrified look at the contents, and ran off, driving the horses before him.

I shuddered at the task awaiting me, steeled myself, and dragged off the first corpse. It was a child, covered with putrefying plague boils. The three other bodies in the cart were his family—father, mother, and sister. I'd smeared my body with the silver ointment Gamelan said would protect me from the disease, but it did not ease my fears as I lifted the small boy's body in my arms, carried him to the pyre, and placed him on it. The other three corpses followed.

Gamelan was silent as I worked, angry with himself that he could not help. I dressed each body in rich garments, then I thoroughly doused each pyre with magical oil. Other then the wind, all was silent; but I could feel scores of eyes watching me from the palace windows. When I was done with the bodies, I went to Gamelan. He handed me the ebony box that held the heart of the Archon's brother.

"Be very careful, Rali," he whispered. "Say and do only what I taught you. Otherwise . . ."

He didn't have to finish. I'd already been warned that if I failed, the Konyan torturers would be cheated of their pleasure; the Archon would make a meal of my soul.

I walked to the pool and gingerly placed the box in a toy sailboat. I opened the box, exposing the hard gem that was the talisman heart. Next to it I placed a single fire bead, chanted the spell which made it glow into life, then set the boat in the water and gently pushed it forward.

I whispered:

"Sail swiftly, sister
To Dawn's portals,
Where the gods play,
And demons are denied!"

Defying the winds that pebbled the surface of the water, the boat moved smoothly—its sails moving this way and that as if commanded by a skilled navigator. It stopped in the center. The black heart began to glow a fiery red. I stared at it, transfixed.

Gamelan hissed at me: "Quickly, Rali!"

I leaped to my feet, threw up arms and shouted: "Arise! Arise!"

There was a clap of thunder, and flame gouted up from the boat. Another clap and I leaped back as the entire pool sheeted with flame.

"Now, Rali!" Gamelan cried. "Do not hesitate!"

The fire was growing hotter, but I had to put aside mortal reason. I stepped forward, felt searing heat, but pressed on to the edge of the flaming pool. I put one bare foot out, marveling that the skin did not peel away and blacken as fire licked over it. I gulped and stepped forward onto the surface of the burning water. I felt intense heat, but no pain, as I walked across the unyielding surface to the boat. I picked the boat up, lifting it high, flames pouring over and around me. I shouted the spell, my voice booming over the winds and hammering at the skies.

"Come Father, come Mother,
Come Sister and Brother—
The one who slew you awaits.
Take thy hate to him,
Take thy suffering
And demon pain.
Foul winds blow sweet,
Sweet winds, blow cool.
Awake!
Awake!"

I took out the glowing heart, placed it in my palm and blew across it into the boat's sails.

The boat stirred, then jolted forward, leaping away like a bird. As it cleared the flames, the fire suddenly died and I was standing up to my knees in bloodred water. The small ship sailed over each pyre, and as it did so, they exploded into black smoke and flame. The smoke rising above each of them twined together like snakes and formed a single thick column of foulness, geysering upward. The sky mottled, then clotted, and I saw a black brow with fierce red eyes beetling out.

The Archon's voice thundered: "Away! Away!"

Then he shrieked in pain as the smoke of the plague dead rasped across his eyes.

He thundered again, but there was fear in his command: "Away! Away!"

The smoke billowed thicker still, blanketing the Archon's great ghostly features. Another howl of pain and anger . . . then he was gone.

I felt weak, drained. I looked down and saw only ordinary water lapping at my knees. Somewhere I heard a bird chirp, and I looked around in wonder and saw a cheerful little fellow on a withered branch. The branch was quite still, and I realized the hot wind had stopped. I stumbled out of the water to Gamelan. He took the Archon's heart from my hand, put it away, and then embraced me.

I heard cheering from the palace and then the Konyans were swarming out, Princess Xia in the lead, tunic flying up over those graceful legs as a cool balmy wind, moist with promised rain, blew across the park.

The spell had been broken.

THE NEXT TIME I stood before the Council of Purity, the nine pairs of eyes staring down at me were not quite so pitiless. They weren't friendly, to be sure, but there was respect in them—a willingness to see what I sought next. I made no preamble, but launched directly to my goal.

"I want freedom for my soldiers and crew," I said. "Return our swords and ships and we will fight with you until peace has been restored."

"How do we know you won't just flee?" Lord Kanara asked. "This is not your fight."

Princess Xia started to protest, but I moved quickly before she could say something unpleasant to her father.

"But it *is* my fight, Lord Kanara," I said. "I've explained it is my people's mortal enemy who has made a bargain with The Sarzana. And it will take more than a few spells to defeat *him* with the Archon as his ally."

"Even then," Lord Kanara said, "he will still be The Sarzana. And he's proven to be enemy enough in the past."

"Then let me kill him for you," I said. "You cannot, because you would be cursed. But I am a stranger, I could not be harmed for taking his life."

Lord Kanara and his fellow nobles had a hasty whispered conference.

He turned back. "What is it exactly that you suggest?"

"I propose to join with you in an expedition against the forces of The Sarzana," I said. "We would be able allies. We Orissans have much experience in warfare."

Another whispered exchange, then: "I'm certain you and your soldiers are brave, Captain," Lord Kanara said. "But there is still the matter of trust. We do not know you. Our experience with you is brief. In one instance, you wronged us. In the other, you helped us. But that was under duress. How do we know which way the dice will fall if we allow a third toss?"

Princess Xia stepped forward. "Please, my lords, may I speak for the youth of Konya?"

Her father was taken aback, but he nodded, go on.

"All suffer in war, my lords," she said. "But is it not the youth who bear the worst of it? And when The Sarzana ruled, was it not to your sons and daughters that he was the most cruel? How many of your children died then, my lords? And how many more die now—as we speak?"

There was muttering among the crowd watching the proceedings, especially among the young nobility.

She put an arm around my shoulder. "You said, Father, that Captain Antero has only been tested twice. I beg your forgiveness for correcting you, but there was one other time she acted—when she rescued me. She could have sailed on. Passed us by. It might even have been the wisest course, for she was in as much danger in that storm as I. But she didn't. She risked her life for me. Her women warriors did the same to save twelve other Konyans from death."

I was afraid she was going to move on to my confrontation with Cholla Yi, when we risked all again. That might speak highly of us, but not of him. I needed that pirate, curse his hide. I was relieved when she skipped past that rock and continued to cross the stream. But I was astounded to see where that next step took her.

"I will prove to you, my lords, how much I trust Captain Antero. I ask—nay, I demand—that I be allowed to go with her when she fights. Her fate will be mine. She will not betray me, my lords. She will not betray the youth—the future—of the Kingdom of Konya."

Her father nearly fell from his seat. His colleagues were equally astounded. The crowd surrounding us, however, thundered its approval. Princess Xia's name was roared to the vaulted ceilings of that great room. Scores surged forward to shout at the Council of Purity, demanding that I be allowed to join in the fight against The Sarzana. With Princess Xia at my side—a hostage to fortune.

The council, led by Lord Kanara, had no choice but to grant permission. As Xia's father hammered for order, the crowd went wild—as if victory had already been won.

I looked at my new lover. Her face was flushed with excitement, eyes dancing with joy. But there was a look about her I had never noticed before: a stubborn tilt to her chin; a squareness to her flung-back shoulders; a regal look in her eyes. By the gods if she didn't look like a queen.

CHAPTER EIGHTEEN

LOVE AND WAR

❖

S ome say the road we all travel in this life has been surveyed and cobble-
stoned by the gods. If so, then the gods must have an unhealthy fond-
ness for strong drink. How else could you account for the madness of
that path—the way it twists and turns, plummeting into muddy holes or rising to breathtaking heights? I'd like to meet the god who mapped my life. I'm
not certain whether I'd cut his throat or buy him another round. In Konya,
one moment I was a most unhappy woman, awaiting my fate in the bowels
of a Konyan dungeon. The next, I was the woman of the hour, my praises
being sung in the greatest halls of the very people who'd locked me away. Is
it too great a stretch, Scribe, to wonder if the god who mapped that route
wasn't drunk?

The days that immediately followed my meeting with the Council of Purity were crazed. We were all released from the dungeon and given most
commodious quarters. Even the meanest sailor, or lowest-ranking Guardswoman, had a room—and plush rooms they were—to him- or herself. They
fed us and clothed us well. So many invitations to entertainments poured in,
I had to refuse them all, rather then end up accidentally insulting some
Konyan noble. It was easy to plead the excuse of being too busy readying for
the coming battle. Mostly, this was true. But there was also ample time for
private pleasures. I had a princess to attend to, after all.

She arranged for me to be given a small villa that overlooked the harbor, and had it staffed with her most discreet servants. The day she showed it to me was warm and the air heavy with the scent of hyacinth. The villa had thick white walls and was roofed with blue tile. Roses climbed the entrance-way, which led into a sunny garden. The pathway cutting through the garden was shaded by an arbor of scented gourds whose flesh was so sweet it drove a colony of wasps quite mad. They darted among the ruby-red fruit, never seeming to be satiated no matter how much they ate. An ancient fountain played in the center of the garden, spilling out under a willow on one side and feeding a soft bed of moss.

The bedroom of the master's quarters was huge, carpeted with thick rugs, upon which were piled pillows of every size and color. The canopied bed was the size of a small practice field, overflowing the largest corner and leaving a pathway between it and the veranda doors, which opened to the most marvel-ous view of the harbor. It was an abode for sunsets and love. We fell into that bed the moment we came into the room. We were as insatiable as those hun-gry wasps, kissing and exploring every inch of sweetness. Shout followed shout, wail followed wail, as we took each other from one height to another.

I see you are red-faced, Scribe; yet the evening is cool. Are you titillated by my descriptions of our lovemaking—or shocked? Ah, I see it's the latter. What could be the cause? You're certainly experienced in memoirs such as these. Is it because they were the adventures of men, doing manly things? Isn't such spicing permissible in a history of a woman? Or is it that same-sex lovemaking offends you? If this is the case, I'm not sorry. I've sworn to tell the truth; and the truth is that love is the same no matter the costume it wears. Passion is the nature of all things that walk, or swim, or crawl. To deny it, to ignore it, is to not fully understand the very life the gods blew into us. In the end, it is your own self you will understand least of all.

Xia and I made love until the sun neared the end of its daily journey. We lolled quietly in each other's arms, enjoying the cool of the early evening winds.

Finally, she broke the silence. "You are not my first," she said, eyes shyly lowered.

I didn't think I was. She was quite experienced for one so young. But that's not what I said. "It's not my business. Your adventures are your own. To share, or to treasure in silence."

"I want to tell you about it," she said. "So you know me."

I kissed her and let her talk.

"I've always felt I was strange, out of place," she said. "It was as if I didn't belong in my family, but was simply left at the door and taken in by my mother, who was certainly a kind enough woman to do such a thing."

"You don't think that's what really happened, do you?" I asked.

She shook her head. "No. Foundlings don't become princesses. Still, the feeling was there. I never liked boys. Not like my girlfriends, who were going on about them even before we all grew breasts and started our monthlies. Actually, it was my *girlfriends* who first attracted me. It was all quite natural, for a time. Even though they talked of boys, we had dalliances. Schoolgirl crushes with one another. Many of which were consummated in bed. No one thought anything of it. Perhaps it's even encouraged a bit in our society. The maidenhead is much prized in Konya, and such innocent play tends to keep it intact until families can negotiate our future—our marriages."

"It's the same in Orissa," I said.

Xia took this in, then continued. "All went well until I reached marrying age, which in Konya is sixteen. Since then my father has become anxious that I wed and bear him grandchildren so our line can continue."

"But you've resisted?" I guessed.

"Absolutely," Xia said. "I want no man to rule me, much less bed me." Again I noted that regal, stubborn look of hers. Xia was not someone I'd like to get on the wrong side of.

She continued: "It has become increasingly difficult to refuse my father. More so because of what happened just before I met you in that storm."

"I've wondered how I came to find you there," I said.

"I was sent to the temple at Selen for purification," she said. "My father learned that I'd become the lover of an older woman. Fiorna's the wife of one of our generals. He was always away, which pleased her, because when he's home he's a brute to her and her children. Also she's like . . . us. Fiorna prefers women to men. Anyway, a scandal was avoided—just. She was sent home to her mother, and her husband was assigned to the outskirts of the kingdom. As for me, my father thought I needed to be purged of my tastes. To undergo purification. Hence, the voyage."

I laughed, stroking her fine breasts. "The purification didn't seem to take," I said.

Xia made a wry face. "Actually, the priestesses there were quite helpful. They taught me how to be more discreet."

She gave me an impish look. Her hand reached and found a place that made me shiver. "They taught me some other things as well." She giggled.

"Lord knows," I said huskily, "I've always been an eager scholar."

Later, as she rose to dress and depart, she said: "Would you do something for me?"

"Anything within my power," I said.

"Would you teach me to fight?"

I rose up, startled. "You're a princess. You have no need for that knowledge."

She shook her head, serious. "I'll be with you when the fight begins. And I refuse to be some helpless flower while other women—your soldiers— risk their lives. I at least want to know how to protect myself. If not more. And don't worry, I won't do something foolish and charge into the fray and be a worry to you. Also, I want to be something other than pretty Princess Xia in the eyes of my people. When this history is written, I intend to be more than a footnote."

I thought over her request. It seemed sensible to me. And then she said: "Besides, we must be discreet, my love. Training with you will be a wonderful excuse for me to come and go as I please."

"Very well," I said. "We'll begin tomorrow."

We did, and she proved as ardent a pupil of battle as she was of love.

MEANWHILE, THE KONYANS prepared for war. The Council of Purity might still have been babbling on about the way to wage that war, but at least there was more than talk in Isolde.

Each day saw more ships arrive off the island. Sometimes there'd be one, sometimes half a dozen, once fleets of over two dozen. Finally, there were nearly four hundred vessels. They'd quickly filled Isolde's harbor from headland to piers, and most lay in the roadstead outside the harbor mouth. They hailed from all over the kingdom—if such a polyglot collection of so many hundreds of islands can be called such a thing, especially since each group seemed to have its own customs and language. Communication was either in Konyan, which most of the ruling classes of the islands knew after a fashion; the Konyan traders' pidgin; or through those Orissans of mine who'd been blessed with the Spell of the Tongues.

The ships were of every variety, from vessels designed only for war, to hastily converted merchantmen and even some sharkish galleys whose crews, I knew, were pirates who'd decided to sail under a known banner for as long as loot was in the offing.

I was impressed by how rapidly the Konyans could turn themselves to battle, and asked Xia if her people had an especial talent for bloodshed. "I don't know about that," she yawned. "But it seems as if someone's always fighting *someone*. If you wish, I'll have one of my servants show you the arsenal."

I did wish, and on the next day I was escorted to a separate part of the harbor, which was fenced and guarded. Inside, I learned the Konyan's secret. The arsenal was a row of wharves, man-made islands, actually, with a long warehouse running the length of each. A narrow strand of water ran between each wharf, and at either end there were wide basins. The wharves swarmed with workmen, who reached them on wide bridges that slid out from the main dockyard. Into the basin at one end an out-of-commission ship would be towed in by lines linked to huge capstans on the shore itself. The ships had been "laid up in ordinary," as it was called, which meant all their stores had been removed, their yards and masts brought down, and the bare hulk anchored to await another crisis.

Big sliding doors opened at each warehouse as the ship was towed down the wharf. From one, masts would be taken—each marked for the ship it had come from. Cranes would restep them and shipwrights lash them into place. At the next warehouse the spars and main yard would be lifted and mounted; following that, coils of lines would appear and the laborious process of rerigging begun. After that, canvas sails would be carried aboard. Xia's servant told me Isolde tried to design their warships uniformly, so supplies could be as common to all as possible.

Now the hulk looked like a ship and was dragged on down the line. The rowers' oars and benches were loaded, then came barrels of salt pork and beef, then bedding, wine and freshwater barrels, and so on—with each warehouse a chandlery with a single specialty. By the time it reached the end of the wharf, the warship was ready to be manned and put out into the roadstead to join its fellows. The process was impressive, but the ships being "launched" I found less so. All of them were huge single-masted galleys, like the one I'd rescued Xia from. The Konyans didn't fancy swift, small galleys such as Cholla Yi, or some of the outer islanders, favored.

I made it my business to inquire how Konyans fought their naval battles, and found it to be even more primitive than the so-called tactics my women had been taught when we sailed after the Archons so long before. A warship would be filled to the gunwales with soldiers—soldiers who knew even less about ships and the sea than I had when we set out from Lycanth. The captain of that warship had simple duties: he was to sail in tight company with the fleet until they encountered the enemy. The order would be given to attack, always in some mass formation designated by the fleet admiral. The captain's final duty was to put his ship alongside that of an enemy. The soldiers would board the ship and take it by storm. All of his weaponry, from catapults to the crow's beaks, which were spiked-end gangplanks meant to embed themselves immovably in an enemy's deck planking, were to produce this single end. Ramming was still considered an innovation, since all too often the ramming ship incurred as much damage as the one being rammed, or else broke free, and the fighting soldiers could not carry the battle to its "proper conclusion." That was sea battle the way it always had been fought, and the way it always would be fought. The Sarzana would be using ships similar to ours, so the day would be carried by numbers, force of arms, sorcery, but most of all, justice. The last, I thought to myself, I'd seldom seen on a battlefield.

I remembered what Stryker and Duban had said during the storm about Xia's galley, and my own thoughts of direwolves bringing down a bear. This time, I did more than just remember. Late in the evenings I began holding very quiet, very private meetings with Corais, Ismet, and Dica, who I welcomed because it's been my experience a complete novice can frequently see a better way more clearly than a veteran. Sometimes Polillo, in spite of her loud protests that she was a fighter, not a planner, took part.

I'd bought a cheap model of one of these monstrous Konyan ships in a bazaar, and the four or five of us would sit around the toy, like so many babes planning the next day's sail in a pond, and think. Sometimes our thoughts were meritorious, mostly foolish or impossible. But I wrote all of them down in a tablet, cursing as I did so and remembering what little talent I have with words. What we were talking about, and what fruits those long hours bore, I'll tell shortly.

DESPITE XIA'S PROTESTS, I left the main part of her training to Ismet. I've learned that such things are best taught by others. A friend will be either too easy or too hard. Besides, there's nothing like the impersonal appraisal of a tough sergeant to see where one really stands; so the princess drilled in the practice yard along with the other Guardswomen. She took to the bow and the spear and sword as if born to it, and flushed with vicious pleasure when she got the upper hand of her drilling partner and gave her a good drubbing with the wooden blade. And when I saw how quickly she learned to fire arrow after arrow into its mark, I was glad I hadn't relented and let her show up the dashing, all-knowing Captain Antero.

Plain exercise was another matter. Every evening we ran along the ring road that circled the humped main section of Isolde. It was a good five miles, beginning at the harbor and ending at a small tavern near my villa. It took me a week to get her built up enough to make that circle once. She was aghast at the end of that week when I told her that our next goal was to make it twice, then three times, then four.

"I doubt we'll make the last goal," I said. "There isn't time to get that much strength into your legs."

"What's wrong with my legs?" she pouted. "You seem to like them well enough when I'm not running on them."

"Oh, I like them fine," I said. "And they're powerful enough when you've got them twined about my neck. But there's more stamina required for fighting than love, thank the gods. A soldier's legs are more important than even her weapons. They must carry her for miles to the fight, then hold her up under the most grueling assaults at that fight, and if it is the whim of her superiors, she might have to march right out again when the battle is over."

"We'll be on ships," she said. "They'll carry us to the fight and back again. So once around the harbor ought to be more than enough."

"Humor me," I said.

"And if I do?" she asked, eyebrows arching up mischievously.

I whispered in her ear. She giggled. "Oh, I *like* that. Are you sure you don't want to start on the next five miles right now?"

ONE DAY a grand meeting of all division captains was called. We were to meet our new fleet admiral. I thought I was well-prepared for this, but as usual when I attempt to predict the thinking of men when it comes to that cheap jade of command, I was wrong.

My women bristled, but I'd known I wouldn't be in overall command of the expedition against The Sarzana, at least not in name. No matter how much the Council of Purity might have praised me, I knew I'd be no more than an adviser at best, a figurehead at worst. Corais and Polillo had growled privately that once again a woman was being forced to kowtow, but I'd asked them if the same situation occurred in Orissa, and I were from distant shores, how many ships and men would our own Magistrates have let me lead to their deaths?

I thought it was a sensible reminder, but both of them looked at each other, and Corais delicately lifted her lip and said, "Rali, my love, of course men will repeat the same stupidity from land to land. We're talking about what an *intelligent* person would do."

That made me laugh, and it was about the only cheeriness the meeting produced.

Cholla Yi and I sat to either side of the new Grand Admiral on the high stage that was framed by a frieze of the gaping bony jaws of some sea monster. The Grand Admiral was named Trahern, and he was awe-inspiring. He was a huge man—nearly as tall as Polillo. His voice rang like a palace bell. He had a great white beard, carefully combed and divided at the chin to sweep to the side in two waves. He must've been in his seventies, but still had a full head of hair, studded with jewels and knotted behind his head. On the breast of his silk and leather tunic he wore many medals—all that a grateful nation could confer on their most celebrated warrior.

Unfortunately, the last war Admiral Trahern had fought was twenty years earlier, a skillful if hardly imaginative campaign against some barbaric outer islanders. Then he'd retired to his huge estates and become a noted historian. His entire career had been one of bravery, honor, and nobility. Now he'd been brought back to lead Konya into what would be its greatest, and his final, triumph.

When he was named, he was cheered and cheered again by the captains. I'd already noticed that too many of the senior captains were natives of Isolde, no matter what other island their ships and crews hailed from. Once again I saw a region whose real rulers hailed from a single area. Perhaps the Sarzana had overly favored men from his native Cevennes, but the barons weren't that different. But while all the men cheered themselves hoarse for Admiral Trahern, what crashed through my own mind was: Hellsfire! It's General Jinnah all over again.

Trahern gave the obligatory heroic address. He said how honored he was to serve the colors once again, how we all were determined to win, how right was on our side, how we could only triumph, how Konya was honored to be given the talents of mighty warriors from the far-distant lands of . . . of, and he paused, trying to remember where the strangers had come from, hastily said Larissa, and continued on and on and on.

After he'd been carried around the room on the shoulders of the exulting officers, he met privately with Cholla Yi and myself. He was full of cheer and reassurances. Of course he knew we were the real leaders of the expedition, being familiar with these damned magicians and so forth, especially this one that hailed from your lands, or so I've heard, although damned if I don't find it hard to believe how someone can be slain and come back to fight again; although certainly no one would slight the powers of a great wizard. He thought he might be of some small assistance to us, since he knew the Konyan waters and, more importantly, the souls of his people, and how they could be roused to fight like the heroes of old; so each Konyan would be as ten, perhaps twenty, soldiers from another land. We would have a high command founded on mutual trust, faith, and determination, united in a common goal of consummate importance to all men and women everywhere.

But to me, all his words were the tapping of the death watch beetle.

ONE EVENING as we were taking an evening stroll in the garden before Xia departed, I asked her if her father was in the least bit suspicious of us.

"He's been so busy with his duties," she said, "that he hasn't had time to think long enough for suspicion to arise. Even if he did, he wouldn't want to make too great a fuss, in fear word would get out to the other members of the Council of Purity."

"I must say, that group hardly looked pure enough to claim such a name," I said.

"Believe me, they are not," she said. "Many a whore would weep at the prospect of poverty if those men were true to their vows. Of course, there'd be an equal amount of cheering among young slaves of both sexes who have been unfortunate enough to join their households."

"Chaste or not," I said, "it seems an odd name for a ruling body."

"It's the fault of one of my more randy ancestors," Xia laughed. "He took decadence to such extremes he even had temples—bawdy houses, actually—built to honor some of our more unsavory gods. He also laid claim to any pretty maid or youth who took his fancy. It got so bad that the barons rose up and forced him to stop. That's when the Council of Purity was formed. Its original job was to make certain the morals of Konya were being upheld. Then, when The Sarzana was defeated, it was the only traditional group under our ancient laws that allowed the barons to take power."

"Do you think the monarchy will ever return to Konya?" I asked.

Xia grew quite serious. She sat at the edge of the fountain and let her fingers trail through the water. "My father certainly hopes so," she finally said. "And perhaps a few of the other nobles who have royal blood in their veins. But if it happened, none of them—even my father—would dare declare themselves king. It would seem too grasping. The kings of Konya, you should know, were deposed by the mobs. The Sarzana came later. And my father and the others fear the masses almost as much as they do The Sarzana. So, no, I don't think that generation will seek the throne. But one of their children might."

"Such as you?" I asked.

"I've never considered it," she said. "It would be foolish for me to do so."

"Has Konya ever had a queen?" I asked.

Xia nodded. "My great-grandmother—who died long before I was born—ruled here. And her husband had no authority. He was merely her consort."

I almost asked her again if she'd really never thought of sitting on the throne. But I could see by the look in her eye that I'd be wise to take her word for it. Royalty never lies. It only changes its mind from time to time.

ONE OF the best things Xia's brave volunteering produced was to make the war into a sacred crusade. It's been my experience that wars are begun by noblemen with paper, and ended by peasants with blood; while those who'll benefit the most from a victory make sure to stay as far as possible away from the battlefield. But following Xia's lead, the young aristocrats of Konya flocked to the colors.

Despite Xia's example, however, I noticed that all the volunteers were men, and reflected that as much as I groused about the treatment of women in Orissa, at least such a thing as the Maranon Guard existed. It wasn't much progress, but it seemed large when measured against the dim-witted policies of other cities and kingdoms.

I hadn't realized how popular Xia was with the others of her class and generation until I saw the long lines of richly dressed men, waiting with a measure of patience at the recruiting booths in the marketplace. Those who'd had some training or experience with sword or sail were easy to fit in, but all too many of them had no developed skills beyond hawking, hunting, and the other indulgences of court. It didn't matter, they said. They would serve in any manner we wanted them to, quartermaster to galley scut. We took them at their word, and for the most part, they served willingly and well. I was surprised, since I thought these soft youths would never be able to handle being chased up a mast by a mate, or bellowed at by Sergeant Ismet or one of the Konyans' own leather lungers.

Still, it was amusing to hear, as I did once, a bosun with his nose and rum breath flush against a pretty lad's face, screaming at the boy as if he were a parade ground distant, "Lord Hilmuth, sir, you ignorant excuse for a six-legged pig with no more gods-damned sense than th' gods gave goats, sir, if I ever see you clew up a sheet like that again, you shitbrain, you prick-ear, I'll have you for my fancy-boy for th' rest of th' cruise, you futtering fool! Beggin' yer pardon, sir."

Two other benefits these noblemen brought: now we could have anything and everything we wanted; and the nobility brought the commoners in as well to serve, and the ships and the men to serve or fight from them were a bottomless barrel. I've often wondered why peasants espouse the most savage hatred for the gentry, but have an abiding fascination for their antics, to the point of relentlessly aping them.

The fleet was beginning to look like the beginnings of a navy, instead of a motley assemblage of ships. We were nearly ready to sail, to confront the Sarzana and his far more dangerous ally and secret master, the Archon.

DURING THOSE LONG WEEKS of preparation, I saw little of Gamelan, even though he was housed in the same villa with me. When I did seek him out for advice on a thorny matter he was maddeningly noncommittal, only saying to do what I thought best. He even refused to attend the morning bone-casting, claiming to be too weary, or sick. What I missed most was our nightly ritual of discussion, where everything under the sun was fair game for debate.

I never saw him smile during that time, and he'd begun to shuffle like an old man—he, who even in blindness, always had a youthful spring to his steps. The women I'd assigned to attend him said he ate little, no matter how

much they tried to tempt him with delicacies, and he drank no spirits at all—
only water. All this from a man who'd previously berated us for losing hope;
who pressed on no matter how difficult the circumstances.

As I watched his spirit shrivel before my eyes, I thought perhaps the experience of the dungeons had been too much for him. I began to fear he
might soon die.

I sought him out one night to ask him what was the matter. I thought
perhaps there was some elixir he could direct me in making that might help
him recover some of his former vigor.

"I'm just old, dammit!" he said, his voice quivering.

"But Gamelan, my friend," I said. "I need you. We need you."

"Your needs are sucking me dry," he shouted. "Now go away and leave
me be."

I left. What else could I do? I did notice however, the closer we came to
being ready, the more despondent he became. If I hadn't been so busy, I
might've found the cause sooner. No, that's not the truth. Hang duty. I
should have made the time; but I was too smitten with Xia to do so.

It was a wondrous spell she wove about me; and I'm vain enough to still
believe I did the same for her. She was meat and drink to me. The more I
bedded her, the more I lusted for our next bedding. She found forbidden
books on sexual tricks and we tried everything, save those that are degrading
or cause pain. We daubed each other with honey and wine and took hours
licking off every speck. We rubbed perfumed oils into every crease in our
bodies, then wrestled until one or the other would pretend to give way. Then
the victor got to choose her pleasure as a reward.

There were also long, languorous afternoons of talk in which we shared
secrets one only tells to lovers. She wept with me with I told her about
Otara. But when I spoke of Tries and our fight, she grew angry and turned
away, and when I attempted to massage her back, she snapped: "Don't touch
me!"

"What have I done?" I said.

"You still love her," she accused.

I sputtered. "Don't be silly. She left me. It's over."

"No, it's not," she said. "I can tell when you speak her name. It's a
game she's playing. The whore! Soon as you return, she'll wrinkle her nose
and you'll be in her arms again."

"I swear, Xia," I protested. "I love only you."

She cried and finally let me comfort her. I whispered her name over and
over, demanding she believe that I loved no other. Eventually we made up.
The sex of forgiveness was hot and violent and Xia was all sweetness and
smiles when she finally left for home. The subject was never raised again. But

I must confess, I certainly thought about her accusation. Did I still love Tries? The remarkable thing was, I couldn't swear to myself that I didn't.

THE TALES OF The Sarzana's latest atrocities came with every fresh arrival to Konya. I imagine his deeds were supposed to send us into paroxysms of panic and either make us battle-foolish or even surrender. But for the most part, they had the opposite effect. Since his ghouls laid waste to every island and port they came across, whether hostile, neutral, or festooned with white flags, resolve actually stiffened. It was very clear to almost everyone that there could be no truce, no compromise, no quarter offered or given. Even those who might've hesitated, or who'd managed to convince themselves The Sarzana's regime wasn't *that* terrible—or even to be preferred to the present rulers—held their tongues and professed patriotism.

I did hear, once or twice, wonderment expressed at how The Sarzana had "changed, darkened." I knew that his alliance with the Archon made his deeds more black-handed, but that the difference between what he was doing now and his past tyranny was only a matter of degrees.

I had a grisly confrontation with his evil one early morning, when the gang watch summoned me on deck. I was maintaining two headquarters— one in the council's palace, for large or formal meetings, the second in Xia's old cabin on board Stryker's galley, for secret or highly important matters. Perhaps I also needed it to remind myself not to become mired in the politics, treacheries, and problems of the Konyans. My duties were simple: first to Orissa, to end the menace of the Archon; and then to my Guardswomen; and finally to Cholla Yi's mercenaries. In the final reckoning, nothing else, beyond my obligation to my own soul, was to be given much weight.

When the deck officer asked if I had time to meet someone, I hurried topside, being bored orry-eyed with lists of lading, duty rosters, and all the rest of a soldier's task the sagas never sing about. Waiting was a slender man in his early fifties. His beard was close-cropped and his hair was tied back in a tiny queue. He wore a plain, loose-fitting tunic and pants. A sword and dagger hung from a belt with a supporting shoulder strap, and I noted both sheaths were dark with age, the hilts of the weapons polished from long us- age. A soldier, then. There was one odd thing. He wore no rings or jewels, but tucked above one ear was a tube perhaps four or five inches long; it was gold, and crusted with jewels.

On the nearby wharf I saw, drawn up in company order, perhaps an- other hundred men dressed similarly, aged from twenty to sixty. I greeted him warmly, hoping his fine body of soldiers had come to join us. Introducing himself as Nor, he assured me they had. He said the men below were only half of those who followed him. I was even more pleased, since I was having great difficulty arranging my own forces for the battle, needing and facing the dismal fact that I had no more than a hundred twenty-five warriors I could truly depend on, my own Guard.

I asked Nor his rank. "I have none," he answered. "And the rank I held before I would be shamed to say."

I looked long into his eyes, and they were stark, burning. I'd seen eyes like that before—from the poor souls we freed from the torture dungeons of the Archon when we took the sea castle in Lycanth. I knew the man had a tale in him, and somehow felt it was not one for all listeners. I saw there were curious ears, both from my own women and from sailors pretending to find tasks nearby. I told Nor he could dismiss his troops and let them find shelter, since it was misting, the mist promising to become a summer rain shortly.

He shook his head. "My men will remain where they are. They don't melt."

I led him to the deserted foredeck, where a tarpaulin had been rigged overhead. I asked if he wished wine, and he said no. Very well, if he wanted to deal with the business at hand, that would be the style of our meeting.

"So you wish to serve," I said. "Why have you come to me, rather than to Admiral Trahern, or one of his generals? Surely men like yours, assuming they can fight as hard as they look, could serve where they wished."

"First, I came to you because I've heard well of you and your women. I don't think you have any interest in the game-playing most Konyans call fighting, with their feints and bluffs and champions and such."

"I do not," I said. "War is what it is, and to be fought as hard and as briefly as I can manage."

He went on as if I'd not interrupted. "Second, though, is that my men are hardly welcome in most ranks."

Shit! I thought. They're probably posers, bandits, or convicts. But I didn't let my disappointment show. Instead, I merely waited.

"These men are my brothers," Nor said. "Once there were a thousand of us. But that was five years and more ago, when we were known as The Sarzana's Own."

Nor caught my shocked reaction. "Yes. We were the bastard's bodyguards. His elite, who surrounded him day and night—in his travels or at his castle. Our lives were his, and his safety and pleasure our only concern."

"Most rulers have such a guard," I said. "But generally they die trying to keep him alive when he's overthrown. Or else they're killed in the aftermath. And seldom have I heard such men, who're generally given great favors by the ruler, unless he's an utter fool, curse his memory."

Nor said nothing, but abruptly lowered his pants. I started back, momentarily sure I was in the presence of the commander of a band of lunatics. Then I saw what he'd meant to show me, and my stomach roiled. He had no penis at all, but rather a small protuberance, less than a finger width. Strangely, underneath that hung a normal-looking scrotum. I'd seen eunuchs before, but they'd always been either completely gelded or with just the testicles cut away.

I nodded—I'd seen. Nor lifted his pants, showing no sign of shame. Now I also knew that jewel-crusted tube was for the men to relieve themselves. I'd heard of such mutilations before; just as I've heard of cruel tribes who mutilate all their girls so they cannot enjoy the pleasure of sex.

"That was the way The Sarzana sealed us to him," Nor said. "He wanted warriors with their manly virtues—and, my pardon for using such trite words to someone who must know better—undamaged. Even better, a man with his seeds intact, but with no way of relieving his desires or needs, would make a deadly fighter, always brimming with blind rage. That was The Sarzana's thinking, and he was quite right. We were terrors and would kill or maim anyone, child, man, or beast, at his slightest whim."

"How could he hold you to him, considering the crime he'd done to you?" I wondered. "Magic?"

"A bit of that," Nor said. "When he was torn from the throne, a veil was lifted that he'd cast on us. But there was something more. He took all of us when we were small children. None of us know who we are, who our parents were, or even where our homes might be. The Sarzana had us kidnapped and . . . cut by a special team of men—although I find it impossible to claim them as human—who also ran his torture chamber; or for such tasks even poor bastards such as we would refuse. None of *them* lived beyond the day The Sarzana fell.

"We were raised and trained separate from the rest of the people; always told we were special and the gods had caused us to be birthed with only one goal—to serve and die for The Sarzana." Nor grimaced. "You tell a child that ten or a thousand times a day from the time he can walk, and you will produce, well, what you see standing out there."

"So you want revenge?"

"Yes," Nor said. "That is the only dream we have. Somehow most of us managed to survive the day the palace fell, and somehow we found each other. That was five years ago, and we had but one goal—to send The Sarzana into the worst hell the gods can design. We called ourselves the Broken Men. I will tell you frankly we were attempting to mount a conspiracy, to find the island where The Sarzana was exiled and seek him there. We'd already purchased five ships for the mission from some Konyan corsairs; ships not very different in design from yours, although I doubt if they're as easily sailed or rowed. We'd spent time teaching ourselves how to sail them as well, both in storm and calm.

"None of us gave, or give, the slightest damn for the curse that comes on he who slays a king of Konya. What curse could be worse than waking each morning and having to piss through this straw"—he touched the jeweled tube in his hair—"and know no woman will look at you, no child will carry your name down the ages, and no one will bother sending your ghost to peace when you lie dead?

"So when The Sarzana used his magic against you Orissans, and found freedom, while most Konyans wept and tore their hair, we celebrated. He was—is—approaching his final doom."

"You think you're that invincible?" I said, not bothering to sound impressed.

"Of course not. I'm a soldier, not a fool. Perhaps he will return and regain the throne. But none of us will be alive on that day. Captain Antero, I know one thing—that if you believe something strongly enough, to the point your own death is meaningless, you have a good chance of reaching that goal."

"True," I said. "So you wish to serve directly under me?"

"That is the only way we'll join this fleet. Otherwise, we'll find a way to fight our own battle. We can buy more ships, or steal them if necessary. And even a sorcerer like The Sarzana can be taken from behind with a dagger at midnight, if there's no other way."

I didn't reply at once, thinking of the problems that could well arise. I decided that since Nor had been brutally honest with me, I would return the favor.

"If I accept your service, you must obey me, and all my officers and sergeants, absolutely in all ways."

"Of course we will! We aren't babes."

"You don't understand me. I mean you must obey any of us if we tell you *not* to fight, *not* to charge, *not* to throw your lives away in some futile attack merely because there is the slightest hope of seeing The Sarzana within bowshot. There's an old soldier's joke that says you must never be shield-companion with someone who's braver than you are. Braver, or more reckless. That is my only condition, Nor, but one you must accept completely. I also shall require your men to swear an oath to do the same, in front of whatever gods you hold most sacred."

Now it was Nor's turn for silence. He grimaced, thinking hard. Finally he looked up.

"I accept. I don't necessarily agree with you—the gods have always blessed those who go mad in battle and care nothing for their own safety.

But ... I accept your conditions." He drew himself rigid and clapped his right hand against his heart.

I returned the salute, while privately wondering whether I believed him or not. The Broken Men were unlikely to hold god-oaths any more sacred than anything else, especially when the fight waged furious. But I decided I could deal with that problem when it arose. Until then, I had twice the number of warriors as I'd had an hour earlier, and the inexorable game of numbers requires many compromises.

THERE IS NEVER any real end when it comes to preparing for battle. No matter how hard you train, it can always be argued more is required. No matter how well you're armed, there's always a newer and better weapon about that someone will want you to carry. And ships can be made more seaworthy until the oceans run dry. But there comes a moment when every soldier knows it's time to face her enemy. From that point on, your enemy can only get stronger and more deadly.

That day finally came for us. The tide was right; the winds were right; and even the soothsayers had their last say.

All of Isolde turned out to see the great fleet depart. There were processions and speeches and wine and incense. Soldiers dallied with maids on the wharf for one last rutting, and even the most prudish smiled and said, isn't that sweet, poor things. Horns blew, drums rolled, and bright clouds of ceremonial kites swooped in fantastic patterns across the sky. Mothers cried out the names of their sons as they boarded; fathers wept in envy for not boarding with them; and sisters wept for not being considered at all. Then pipes were piped and sails were hoisted and soon the entire sea was alive with white-winged ships speeding for their destiny.

As for me—while I watched all the well-wishers on the shore diminish—I recalled another day when we marched from Orissa.

It seemed like such a long, lonely eternity, Scribe, since the prayers of good fortune had been for me and mine.

CHAPTER NINETEEN

WINDRIDER

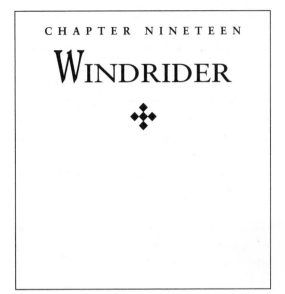

F leet Admiral Trahern may've made all the correct sounds about being equals, but once we were at sea, it was firmly fixed who was in charge, at least in his mind. Both Cholla Yi and I were clear subordinates. Important ones, yes, but certainly not to be taken into Trahern's confidence unless he deemed it fitting. That became obvious when Trahern sent a fast courier boat with his chief aide, carrying orders thinly veiled as a report.

The aide said the Konyan wizards had determined that The Sarzana and his allies were lurking in the Alastors, an island chain about three weeks to the south, where they seemed to have found a base for their battle fleet. Trahern "suggested" we continue scouting as we had been and correct our course so we remained directly in front of his ships. That was all—the aide had no instructions about asking for our observations or ideas.

It was amusing to see Cholla Yi fume and fuss at being treated in such a "shameful" way. Perhaps I shouldn't have, but I couldn't resist quietly mentioning that Trahern's behavior *was* most discourteous, and he should've patterned his style after Cholla Yi's, particularly the way the admiral had treated us when we set forth from Lycanth. All my sarcasm accomplished was to make him angrier.

Xia was even hotter, snarling that she'd been betrayed and this was no way to treat nobility. It was afternoon, in a sleepy midwatch, and all I could hear outside our cabin was the creak of the ship and the boot heels of the watch on deck above us as he walked to and fro. I was sprawled on the bed, and she sat beside me, legs curled under her. I told her she was right, but that was the way of the world, both here and in Orissa. Men appeared to be men wherever I went. Perhaps, I said, she might become queen one day and begin a new way of thinking that'd end the silliness. She looked at me oddly. After a moment she frowned and started to say something further. But I had other thoughts, feeling the warmth in my bones looking at her as she sat in the dim glow from the deadlight. She caught my look and gave a knowing laugh— then all her anger melted in our embrace.

I HADN'T GONE into a rage of my own because I knew in advance that Trahern had no intent of treating us as equals, and I had therefore planned how—and when—I'd deal with it. As long as we weren't in contact with the enemy, I could accept the situation as it was. I concentrated my energies on daily drills to make sure everyone in our small fleet understood the new way I proposed we would fight. The change was great, as great as chalk to cheese.

The greatest change was in attitude. Instead of thinking of ourselves as infantry that happened to be aboard ship instead of on land, we were going to think like cavalry. There's no greater sin a horsewoman can make than to be unhorsed, to become one with the common swine she tramples under her hooves. In our case, our horses were our ships. We were only to "dismount," in other words to board, when we were sure we'd crippled our opponent, just as a cavalrywoman leaves her horse only to administer the final mercy to a fallen enemy.

We were trying to destroy our enemy utterly, not just take the ground he was fighting from, which in a naval fight meant his ship. Burn him, ram him, drive him on the rocks, destroy his sails or oars, and he would be out of the battle.

Naturally, Cholla Yi's captains set up a clamor, again moaning that my ideas meant they'd take no prizes. I told them I understood, secretly cursing and wishing I had seamen under me who fought for the love of their city rather than for gold. But what I had, I had, and so I told them if they obeyed my orders, they might not take a prize *at that moment,* but when the battle was won, there'd be more than enough drifting hulks to claim. Wouldn't it be easier, I asked, to seize such a ship from its demoralized surrendering crew than to have to take it by force of arms? Also, if they didn't close and board a ship unless they had the distinct advantage, their own craft would be less likely to be damaged or sunk. I reminded them these huge galleys of The Sarzana we'd be facing would no doubt have derrick-hung stones that could be dropped straight down from their decks when we tried to grapple them, which would send us straight to the bottom without further ado. They didn't like to admit there could be something new on the sea, let alone ideas produced by greenlings who also were women. So we went over the theory again and again, until little by little it sank in. Anytime one of them said something that mirrored one of our thoughts, I complimented him and told him we'd incorporate it into our thinking.

Eventually it appeared to them they'd had as much to do with this new strategy as we had, and then, with the general idea accepted, we could begin endlessly drilling the specific tactics. Sailors learned how to work their galleys handily in close quarters, practicing one against another, backing, filling, darting in and out like hounds worrying a boar, never holding still long enough for the tusks to slash them down.

We learned how to fight in two- or three-ship elements, striking always for the flanks and where blood showed. We would give no mercy, not expecting any ourselves, nor would we fight a "fair" battle, whatever that means. We had more than enough time to lower sails and turn aside from our course, since our galleys had three or four times as much speed as the hulking Konyan ships behind us.

There was also new weaponry to mount and train on, weapons I'd had built secretly in a small yard and moved onto our galleys under cover of night. They were special catapults, with double troughs set at slightly divergent angles. Somebody'd seen one as we loaded it and asked if we planned on shooting two arrows at once. I just said yes, and didn't explain, assuming The Sarzana had spies thoroughly covering Konya, or else might be observing magically. I'd worried, but Gamelan had reassured me: "Just because someone may be able to look at something doesn't mean he can tell what it is, or what it's intended for, now does it?"

Polillo had been detailed off to train sailors how, and more importantly when, to fire these catapults, which were intended for use deep in the battle.

She'd snarled she had more than enough to do making sure her women were ready, plus keeping herself in shape so that Precious, her axe, would drink deep in the fight. Someone else could worry about those damned sea dogs of Cholla Yi.

Corais laughed, and said she was being innocent. She herself would *never* turn down a chance to teach a man something in his own supposed area of expertise. "It'd be almost as good as showing one of these leap-on, leap-off, drop-a-coin-and-gone oafs how to *really* pleasure a lass."

Polillo had grinned wickedly, then said, dreamily, "Now, *there* is a thought. Perhaps if I'm nice enough, one of them might introduce me to his sister."

"Careful," Corais warned. "Sailors don't have sisters. They only mate with porgies and lighthouse keepers."

I paid little attention to their chatter, deep in my conjectures as to how the Archon had managed to send fire spitting across the waters, and while I'd not been able to come up with a spell that would let me do the same, I thought I might have devised an incantation that could prove a stronger counter than what Gamelan had been able to produce on the instant.

Gamelan was another problem. As much as he tried not to be a burden, and not always be the specter at the feast, he was hardly the picture of cheerfulness. I heard Sergeant Bodilon refer to him once as Evocator Darkness, and I took her aside and asked sharply if she herself would bear up handily should she lose both her arms. Bodilon said if that happened, she'd find the nearest cliff and leap rather than wander about glooming to her once-fellows.

I retorted, "Then it's evident who's got the greater courage, isn't it, since Gamelan soldiers on without giving up." She started at what I said, then bowed her head, apologized, and said I was right.

Maybe I was, but something had to be done about our Evocator. I began to worry that he might, indeed, take Bodilon's way out, and considered warning the two women who were his caretakers.

Then another thought came. I ran it back and forth, and it seemed to have a bit of merit. Or at any rate to be something that would not make matters worse.

The next day was clear and sharp, spray coming off the bow as we made full sail toward where The Sarzana would be waiting. There was a slight haze in the air, just enough to blur the horizon and make it aglow. Gamelan was in his usual daytime post in the bow, staring forward as if he could see. I jerked my head for his two companions to leave us, and greeted him.

"How goes the planning, Rali?" he said, his voice dull and lifeless.

I was surprised at his tone. It'd been days since I'd had time to think about him, and I realized just how much his morale had plunged—like a soldier whose wounds refuse to heal. We talked a bit, and I led the conversation to the predictions of Admiral Trahern's sorcerers that The Sarzana was close.

"I think they're most likely right," he said. "Not because I can feel even a hint of my powers, but out of pure logic from all the years I've lived."

"Go on," I said.

"The Sarzana, or at least so he told us, had his first triumph when he destroyed the fleet the Konyan king sent against him. Wouldn't he want to repeat his triumph?"

"Of course," I said. "That's a trap every soldier must be wary of. If it worked once, it'll work again and again, until one day you walk into an ambush and are slaughtered by an enemy who learned your habits better than you did his."

"Even more to the point," Gamelan went on, "it's in The Sarzana's best interests to break the Council of Purity as rapidly as possible. His bloody ways won't be peaceably accepted for long, if there's an alternative. But if he can shatter the only rule the Konyans know, then they'll most likely accept him rather than risk complete chaos." Gamelan sighed. "So we'll meet them soon, I'm sure.

"Unfortunately, I'm also sure we'll be lured onto ground of The Sarzana's—and the Archon's—choosing. Perhaps I'm being vain, but none of the wizards I've spoken to in Konya impressed me as having half the powers of The Sarzana, let alone the Archon's . . . Gods," he said suddenly, and his voice turned fierce. "This is the battle that'll settle Konya and perhaps the fate of Orissa and I might as well be put at the gate with a bowl to beg! Rali, if you knew how many ways I've prayed and thought and wished for even a touch of my powers to come back!"

"I know," I said. I let the silence hang, then said, as quietly as I knew, "A thought came to me last night, Gamelan, that might be of some help, and perhaps—"

Before I could continue, he'd spun and had me by the arms. His face thrust forward, as if he could *will* sight, could somehow look into my eyes. "Anything, my friend. Anything, please. I cannot continue much longer as I am."

I waited until he calmed, then began. "I don't know very much about wizardry," I said, "in spite of your teachings. By that, I mean I don't know how the Talent comes on you."

"It comes as it went," he said. "Without bidding or whether you wish it. Now I wish it'd never cursed me, but left me as a fisherman on the banks of our river."

"That's what I thought," I said, paying no mind to his bitterness. "And I know it's cheaper in lives if a soldier can figure a way around a defended position, or else take it from the rear, than to shout battle cries and make a frontal charge."

"Which is what I've been doing, trying to force my powers to come back," Gamelan said. "So what is the way around, my cunning friend?"

"You were a fisherman once," I said. "You said that's when people started realizing you had the call to be an Evocator."

"It was."

"Return to that time, or anyway, that manner of thinking. There are hooks and lines here. Maybe you could start fishing. Let your fingers remind you of your thoughts all those years ago, when you always came back with a rich catch."

Gamelan nodded excitedly, and then he smiled, and I realized it was the first time I'd seen him smile for weeks.

He said, "Yes. Yes. You can always tie a knot or splice once your muscles learn how it's done, even though if you try to remember how the line twists, you'll end with a tangle. Maybe . . . maybe . . ." He stopped, and I thought I saw wetness in the corners of his eyes, then he turned away from me.

I motioned for one of the soldiers who companioned him, and told her to get fishing lines and bait and anything else he might need. And when I told Gamelan I must be about my duties, he nodded, barely hearing, his lips moving as they led him into the past.

When I went below that night, he and the two Guardswomen were still up, silhouetted in the bows. I remembered the love of his life, Riana—the woman denied him. I thought of what I'd heard whispered of sex-magic, and how strong a spell that could create. For the briefest instant I wished one of my women, perhaps one of his companions, was of a nature attracted to men, then shook my head. It was foolish. And I'd done the best I could.

IT WAS AFTER evening mess, and I was on deck, helping some of my archers make arrows. I was carefully cutting peacock feathers to the precise angle, and trimming the quill exactly to the instructions of the corporal with the glue pot. Corais was nearby, lapping a bowstring with silk thread. About the time my taskmaster decided we'd made enough arrows to riddle a regiment, Corais finished her own job. I went to the rail with her to enjoy the sunset, one part of seagoing I never tired of.

Corais still had her bow, and as we talked of this and that, she rubbed it up and down, letting the oil from her palm work into the fine yew. I realized she'd had the bow since we were raw recruits, and I'd never known where she'd gotten it. I asked if it was a family treasure, and she shook her head, then looked surprised as she realized that of all the secrets we'd shared, this was something I knew nothing of.

"I made this bow myself," she said. "It took me five years, and I started when I was only ten. There was this man in our village who fascinated me."

"A man *fascinated* you," I joked. "And weren't you the eager young stripling with desires beyond your years? No doubt you were perverted from your true nature not much later, just as so many priests and men would have it."

She wrinkled her nose at me. "As you know, as I've told you time and again, my village was created boring. Beyond midsummer festival, harvest home, and the winter solstice, the most exciting thing was to watch the turnips grow. All we had were farmers, the priest, a cheating shopman, and . . . this fellow. His name was Sollertiana, and he was a bowsmith."

"Now I understand your fascination."

"Not quite," Corais said. "Certainly there were the gleaming lengths of wood in his shop that slowly became singers of death, and the long rows of gray-goose-feathered shafts. But Sollertiana himself held me, not just for the stories he'd tell, nor for the customers that'd ride long distances from the city just to order one of his bows that would require a year or more's wait. I'd just begun to realize I wasn't like the other girls, and couldn't play their little games of squeal and be chased and maybe let a boy put his little pigtail in me and wiggle it. Somehow I knew Sollertiana was different, too. When I was fifteen, after the bow was finished, I knew I'd been right, seeing him look out the scraped-skin window over his bench when a young lad strode past, recognizing the same longing I felt for one or two of the village maids.

"But where I had been able to find a little happiness, even though one claimed she'd been asleep and the other she'd been drunk, Sollertiana knew better than to indulge his passion. Our priest would've raised a mob to burn him and his home if there'd been any suspicion."

She snorted. "Of course, that same priest also gave scant comfort when a woman was beaten by her husband, or even when a man thought he had the right to take all the women of his household, adults or babes, to wife. Priests!" Corais spat overside, then went on.

"Once a year Sollertiana went to Orissa to buy silk and peacock feathers, and I hope he found a measure of comfort there. I always wondered why, since he was what he was, he didn't move to the city. I asked him once, and he just said that he couldn't breathe when he couldn't see the sun's journey from dawn to dark, and in the city the buildings strangled him." Corais shrugged. "I see I've gone astray from my story. But that was why I felt a kinship with Sollertiana. Not only that he was different in his desires, as was I, but he also showed me the way I must take. I knew I couldn't remain in that village and either be an old maid or pretend passion for a man and have to spend my life under his sweaty grunts.

"This bow came from a bunch of three heavy old red-yew trunks that grew close enough to the sacred grove that they'd been permitted to reach great age, yet not close enough so that cutting them was sacrilege. When I told Sollertiana I wanted a bow, he looked at me for a long time. I expected him to just say, 'Go away, child, I've got work to do,' like most of the adults did. Instead, he nodded, and paid me no more mind. A week later he took me to this grove and pointed out the yew trunk. He cut it down with a handsaw, taking over an hour at the task. He sawed the log carefully in two, and kept the half that had grown on the inside of the clump. It had no twigs or pins or knots to it. He took this cutting high in the hills, where a stream ran clear, and he tied the plank securely in the water.

"It sat there for three months, until some of the sap had been washed from it. Then he put it in a damp, dark shed, keeping it in the rafters above the ground for over a year. I wonder if he thought I'd forget about the wood, but I never did. Every day, I visited what would be 'my' bow, and thought I could see it change and dry. I even dreamed only I could see a bow's sleekness hiding there. Little by little, Sollertiana moved it to drier places. The last year before we shaped it was spent in the open wind and air under the eaves of his workshop.

"All the time it was drying, Sollertiana was working with it, tapering it bit by bit after he'd gently peeled off the drying bark. Then he used a succession of rasps, broken glass, pumice stone, and then powder to shape it. As it took form, he trusted me more and more to do the work. Finally, I held what almost looked like a bow in my hands. Then came the most dangerous part. He cut the wood into two billets, and I almost died, sure he'd ruined all our work. But he cleverly shaped, fitted, and then glued the pieces together, and . . . it *was* a bow!

"He waxed and varnished the wood, and fitted these tips I'd carved from the horn of a stag I'd stalked and killed in the heart of the winter with another bow. Then it was mine." Corais regarded the bow lovingly. "It was the first thing I'd really ever owned, besides a couple of dolls my mother'd given me that had been hers as a child.

"Not long after that, Sollertiana died, and I left for Orissa. And that was when we met."

Corais stroked the bow once more. "As much as I let myself dream about the future," she said, so softly that I had to crane to hear her, "which is foolish for a woman who deals in blood, I've always wanted to have a small shop like Sollertiana's one day. Making bows and fitting arrows to them. I'd probably never be as good as Sollertiana, but then I don't need very much. That's one thing soldiering teaches you."

"Where would you live?" I said quietly, not wanting to break into her dream. "In a city?"

"No. I've seen enough of cities, between Orissa and Lycanth. Everybody thinks I'm a great one for the bright lights and all, but really I'm still the barefoot child in a frock with pig shit between her toes. I'd go to the country. Not in that damned village I came from. All I hope for them is a good sacking by three or four sets of barbarians. But somewhere people aren't so quick to look down their damned noses and make judgments."

She sighed. "Maybe it'll be that village you told me about, the one your mother came from where the girl on the panther saved them and they learned better. Maybe I'd be a good reminder of what they'd better not forget."

I'd forgotten I'd once told her where my name came from, and realized yet again how little any of us really knew anyone else, knew what was important to them, what struck the sounding board in their soul.

"Maybe you'd come visit," Corais said. "You and whoever you settle down with, after we've all gotten too creaky-boned to play soldier. Now that'd be something, wouldn't it? The grand Antero lady, who'll probably be a duchess or something by then, coming to this little midden. We'd drink the tavern dry and try to corrupt any virgins still around."

The sea blurred to my eyes a little, and I don't know why. "I think I'd like that," I managed. "I think I'd like that a lot."

"Anyway," Corais said, and her voice went flat, "that was where my bow came from . . . and what I used to dream."

I came back to reality. "Used to?"

Corais didn't say anything at all, but slowly shook her head from side to side. Her hand crept up and touched the bit of The Sarzana's robe she still wore tied around her upper arm. There was a smile, but not of humor, touching her lips.

I might've asked on, but there came a commotion from the bow, and I heard shouts: "I caught one! Gods, I drew him to me!"

It was Gamelan, and a smile nearly split his face in two. I swear I could see a flash of merriment in his unseeing eyes as we hurried to him. One of his companions held a great flapping fish, some kind of cod I thought, high in the air, then dropped it to the deck and killed it.

"I could feel him out there, Rali," and I wondered how he knew it was me standing in front of him, "and I *drew* him, I could *feel* him. He'd come up from the deeps to feed, and I kept telling him the bit of cloth flashing in front of him was the sweetest morsel he could ever dream of, and then he took it in a great rush and he was mine." His smile disappeared. "Rali . . . is it coming back?"

"Yes," I said firmly, forcing conviction into my voice, and trying to feel it in my soul. "Of course it is."

THAT NIGHT, I went to Gamelan in his cabin and told him I thought we were sailing too close to the enemy to be as blind as we were. Like him, I had no great faith in the Konyan wizards and needed more information. He tugged at his beard for a moment, muttered something about the risk being too great, caught himself, and apologized.

He said, "I don't know if the spells will work. Sending your spirit abroad is not the simplest of magics, and one not even a journeyman Evocator is recommended to undertake. But these are parlous times, and who's to say anymore what can or cannot be done? What we need is a creature for you to shape yourself after. I hope you understand that you really don't become that creature—unless one of Janos Greycloak's theories is true, that we are all different manifestations of the same force. That's an idea I've grappled with, but still puzzles me."

"Why not just send my spirit out? That was how the Archon came on us. I'd rather be invisible than in some disguise."

"The problem, my dear friend, with sending you as a pure spirit, assuming the spell would take and hold, is you are extremely vulnerable in such a form. No, it's better to give you the similitude of reality. Perhaps it's safer because the fact you're *real* binds you more closely to our world and gives you strength. I don't know for sure, but that's my theory. It's better to worry about some sharp-eyed sailor spotting you as, say, a dolphin and reaching for a harpoon, than to be sniffed out by a wizard like The Sarzana or the Archon. If they have the proper magical nets set out, your spirit would shine as clearly to them as a rising moon. A master sage—and both of them are that—could then cast a striking spell in seconds and snap that thread between you and your body. Then your doom would be to wander the worlds as if you were a ghost, never finding rest."

I shivered, remembering how my poor brother Halab had been tricked into testing his talents to become an Evocator, and had been trapped and destroyed by Raveline of the Far Kingdoms. There'd been no body for the rites, not ever, and Halab's ghost had been laid to rest finally only after Amalric slew Raveline in a demon-haunted ruin.

I turned my mind away. "What kind of creature, Gamelan? An albatross?"

"Never."

I grinned, pretending injury. "And why not? Wouldn't I make a sleek great bird? I've always fancied them, floating high above the world and the seas, only landing for sleep and to feed."

"You fancy them . . . and so does every other beginning thaumaturge," he said. "Why not pull a banner hooked to your tailfeathers that says 'I am Rali the spy'? We could save the time and trouble casting any protective spells to accompany you."

I saw what he meant. However, after some further talk, we developed a plan that appeared a bit more subtle, and his two companions and I went out to procure the necessary items for the conjuration. I told Xia my intent, and she began to protest, then stopped. She hastily nodded, then could hold firm no more, and darted below to our cabin, sobbing. I didn't follow, for there was nothing I could do. Sometimes it's harder to love a soldier than be one.

I told Corais and Polillo little of what I was intending, but put them in charge of the Guard. It wasn't necessary to say any more about lines of succession. They were soldiers, so they knew. Polillo scowled and started to say something, then clamped her lips closed. I knew she had probably intended to warn me to be careful of sorcery, that art she feared more than a regiment of enemy soldiers.

It was past midnight when we had the necessary bits and pieces together, which Gamelan said was good. That'd put "me," or whatever it was that would be riding the spell, out where The Sarzana's forces were supposed to be near dawn.

Gamelan had his tent set up on the foredeck, and guards surrounding it to keep away the curious. I'll go into some detail on this spell, since it's a good way to show magic sometimes takes damned near as much trouble as doing the job with "real" labor. Part One of our spell was simply getting what Gamelan called my spirit—although he added that wasn't quite what it was, not the elemental soul the word implied—to travel a week or so sail's distance in a few hours.

"There's another thing apprentices don't realize," he said. "Mutter some words, and *pish*, you're a fish. And you promptly expire because you're out of water. Or else you get dumped overside, and then have to swim for two weeks before you reach your goal. Sometimes," he said, taking an injured tone, "it sets my teeth on edge when people think magic can do *anything*.

"The first part of your journey will be made on the wind. You'll be nearly as vulnerable as if you were a pure spirit, but not quite. Once you close on The Sarzana's stronghold, our cunning plan will take effect. Or I hope it's cunning, anyway."

He ordered me to strip bare and coat myself with a salve I'd made earlier under his instructions. It made my skin burn, and Gamelan said that was one of its intents—to make the spirit want to walk free from the body. It was made of certain herbs, including vervain, ginger, and hyssop, and oils from his kit, plus some leather from one of the ship's now-empty magical wind bags that'd been ground to powder, intended to carry the essence of the wind and the spell that snared it. There were other things ground into the oil, things intended to aid the second stage of my journey.

A low fire glowed in Gamelan's brazier, which stank even worse than most incantatory pyres. Gamelan explained a bit of an old sail was the centerpiece of the fire, and would hold the wind and lift me free. Among the herbs burning were peppermint, hemp, and myrrh.

I had prepared the words to recite, and said them as I stood there naked. Gamelan sat silently nearby—I'd wanted him to help, but he was afraid his still-absent Talent might overshadow the spell and ruin it. First I began by reciting over and over the names of ten of the local gods and goddesses who might have power in these circumstances. There was the god of storms, the goddess of the sea, godlets who danced the winds, some zephyr nymph's name remembered from Xia's childhood, and so on. I don't list them here, although I think I could remember them all, because according to most magicians, a minor god's power only extends to lands where he or she is worshiped. Someone wishing to try this spell should use their own deities, or none at all, keeping in mind what I believe is the nature of gods in the first place.

Then I began the spell itself:

"Feel the wind
Touch the wind
Be apart from yourself
The wind is your sister
You must roam free
Float up, float up."

As I spoke, I let bits of paper drift down across the brazier. I'd written the same words on the paper before ripping it apart. The smoke caught and carried them up, and I felt my head swimming, as if a high fever had struck. Then I was lifted *above* myself, and I was looking down at my body. Then the physical *I* slumped down to a sitting position, then sprawled. But I had no mind nor time for that body, because the top of the tent had suddenly opened and I heard the whisper of the cord as Gamelan pulled it away, and above me was the night sky and the stars and I was free.

I was hurled up and on, high into the sky, and I caught a glimpse of a constellation and knew I was being borne south. I was not on the wind, I was the wind, and I felt my heart singing. My body was far below me and far behind me, but my spirit could feel her ghost hair blowing back as I rushed on and on, and the sharp stinging of the night air, just as it feels when one comes from a sauna in the depths of winter and plunges into an icy pool. It was as if I still had a body, but then again, I didn't. I didn't have to turn my "head" to "see" our galleys far behind and below, their masthead lights gleaming against the dark seas, nor farther back to the star dots that were the Konyan ship lights.

Now I understood what sorcery could be, what it could give, instead of being a dark power for death and overpowering another, or a niggling series of words and incantations intended to avoid hard physical work. Maybe I understood and even sympathized for an instant with Janos Greycloak, feeling what had drawn him to magic, the same thing that had destroyed him.

Ahead I sensed land, and then saw it as the gale raced me onward. There were ten, perhaps twenty islands, the smaller ones spread as if they'd been scattered in front of the largest land mass. These were the Alastors, I knew, having seen sketchy maps of the islands the Konyans had named as The Sarzana's refuge. As I swept across the outer skerries, I could sense, down below, men waiting, whose task was to report the first sign of our fleet. The magical part of me was still marveling at being able to see everything, from horizon to horizon, but the cold soldier within was reminding Captain Rali there'd be little likelihood of surprising The Sarzana, since his sentinels were well posted. Not that I'd ever thought we'd be able to anyway, since physical sentries would be the least and most easily fooled of any of The Sarzana's watch guards.

His name crossing my mind made me "feel" ahead, as Gamelan had told me to do, trying to sense if there were any magical traps lying in wait. I could sense none, but wasn't reassured. I was a fresh recruit walking along a path, trying to avoid an ambush that may or may not have been set by a crafty, old warrior.

The main island rose ahead. Now it was time for me to make the second change, into a hopefully less vulnerable form.

The wind that was me did not want to change, did not want to give up its free roaming, but my mind forced the words:

You must change
You must take shape
You are now your cousin
You are the wind's friend
You are flesh
You have shape
You have form
You have flight

And it became so in a dizzying instant. Not only had I taken on physical form, and was tossed by the wind that had been *me* moments earlier, but there were many "*me*s." Gamelan had suggested a less noticeable disguise than that of an albatross, and I'd gone him one better. Why must I be a single bird? One creature could well be a spy, particularly if it behaved oddly. But an entire flock? He lifted his eyebrows in surprise, then chortled and said it was time, indeed, for younger minds to take over magic. There was no reason not to at all.

I was a flock of terns coming in toward the shore. I suppose I ought to call myself "we," but I notice a look of confusion from my scribe, so will try to keep this as simple as I can. It was strange, being many creatures at the same time. I was ten, perhaps fifteen birds, with a common way of thinking, but each with her own eyes. "I" swooped low over a rock that jutted from the sea, flying past on both sides of it, and it was as if I had only one pair of eyes, but eyes that could see the front, sides, and back of something at the same time. Yet everything was quite normal, and I had no feeling of strangeness or of disorientation.

I swooped into the sky as the flock closed on the main island. It was high-mountained, and a long, narrow bay clove the land nearly in two. I could see cities at the tip of that bay, cities guarding the gut's portals. At the bay's end was the island's greatest city, which was named Ticino. Even in this near-dawn hour there were lights gleaming, and I estimated the city to be nearly as large as Isolde's metropolis.

The Sarzana's fleet was anchored in the roadstead, with picket boats around them. I knew he'd have many warships, but was startled by how many there were. I tried to count them, but couldn't, and estimated there were at least four hundred—as many as we had—and most likely more.

I was coming closer to the anchorage and flew perhaps a thousand or so feet overhead. It looked as if most of the ships were huge galleys exactly like those the Konyans sailed, and my soldier's soul felt pleasure. The new battle tactics I'd devised might work well. There were other ships as well, anchored close inshore in another division, and I swooped closer. But somehow I couldn't see them well. My vision was blurred in spots, just as when water's flung unexpectedly into your face before you have time to blink, or, perhaps, when fog swirls in banks through bright sunlight.

Something whispered and said I shouldn't look closer, not yet. And no matter how I tried to "gaze" at them, the fog still hung between us.

There was no sign of alarm below. The few sailors on the decks of the galleys went sleepily about their dawn routine. No one looked up, and if they had, all they would've seen was a flight of swallow-tailed gray-shaded birds overhead, no doubt looking to break their fast.

I determined to fly closer to the city, closer to the danger that was The Sarzana's and the Archon's magics. But once more my "eyes" blurred and I couldn't quite make out details on the ground, although I was quite close and my sharp tern's vision let me make out a single small school of fish as it broke water. Again I felt that whisper, and it became almost a voice, a warning. Reason caught me and sent me banking away, back down the bay.

I'd seen nothing to give me alarm, but felt as if I was bare moments from danger. I flew in three great lazy circles, higher and higher into the sky as the sun glinted on the horizon and the shadows on the land and water below drew in on themselves. I'd had enough for my first scouting.

The Sarzana's fleet was where it'd been predicted, and was clearly ready for battle, as the Konyan Evocators had predicted. But what were these blurry patches?

I didn't know, but felt them to be threats. It didn't matter. I'd done enough for one night.

I would return.

*   *   *

LATER, MY real self took a different and much more pleasant flight—with Xia. I remember coming back from the far place her lips and hands had sent me, knowing nothing, body still echoing to that great roar. I became aware, very dimly, that her head was pillowed on my stomach. I managed a grunt, incapable of more. Xia giggled.

"You went away on me."

"Mmm."

"I'll bet I can send you there again." And her fingers moved. I found energy enough to pull her hand up to cradle my breast.

"No, you can't," I said. "I'm a noodle. I'm a string, I'm a soggy mass of wet silk."

"You *are* silk," she agreed, but left her hand where I'd put it. After a few moments of silence, when I almost went to sleep, she said, "Rali? What comes next?"

"Next I try to get some sleep, you sex-mad animal."

"No. I mean after we kill The Sarzana."

"I love an optimist," I said. "Once we kill the bear, should the roasts be larded or soaked in vinegar? There's a bit of a task to putting this bear on the table, you know."

"We'll kill him. I know that," Xia said. "So answer my question."

I sat up, quite awake now. "I've got to go back to Orissa," I said.

"What about me? What about us? I can't see me going with you as your companion, at least not for very long. I mean, I'm a Kanara. The last one."

"Of course I didn't mean for you to just traipse about after me," I said.

"So then do you want to stay *here*? With me? I don't think your barons or whatever your rulers call themselves would object, considering what you've done for them."

"No," I said. "They wouldn't."

I didn't say anything more, but lay back, thinking. What *did* come next? She was a Kanara, and I was an Antero—and commander of the Maranon Guard, as well. Being an Antero might not be that important—Amalric and our idiot brothers could handle the estates well enough. But was I through with the Guard? Was I through with being a soldier? Even more simply—was I ready to leave Orissa for good?

"What would I do," I wondered, "if I did come back with you?"

"I'll show you," she said, and her fingers tweaked my nipple, and it rose erect. "As often as we can."

"No," I said, "I meant . . ." But I let my words trail off. How odd. Mostly I'd been the person in charge, if that's the right word, of my love affairs. Yet here was this eighteen-year-old starting to plan my future. I didn't know if I liked that. I guessed that was the way royalty reasoned. At least I was being consulted in the matter, I thought wryly. But the idea of being a lap kitten didn't call to me, although I'm sure Xia would find a position for me commanding soldiers if I wished. Noble folks always need a sword to keep their power. But still . . . but still . . .

I took refuge in the old soldier's way of dealing with the morrow: the hell with it. We'll never make it off this battlefield alive anyway.

Not that there was much left to think with. Xia had found the knotted silk cord and was coiling it into place as her other hand swept across, smoothing oil across my stomach.

A DAY OR SO later, just at dawn, I was on deck, letting my body wake up very slowly. Sergeant Ismet was a few feet away, doing a series of muscle-stretching exercises. She finished and joined me at the rail. The day was gorgeous, the sky offering the deepest of blue, the sun bright and welcoming. A breeze touched the crests of the low waves as our galley sped through the waters. Behind us, in our spreading wake, was the rest of our forward element and behind them, bare dots on the horizon, the main fleet.

"Odd," I mused aloud, "here we are, in romantic seas on a day made for a holiday, and we're sailing into battle."

"I don't know about a holiday," Ismet said. "I could never relax seeing that haze ahead of us on the horizon and not knowing what might be hidden in it."

"If you weren't a soldier?"

"If I weren't a soldier," she returned, "I'd never be here, now would I?"

Without waiting for a response, she went on, "If the captain will excuse me, I've some lazy slatterns to roust out of their hammocks who need their exercise." And she was gone.

I was reminded once more what a puzzlement Ismet was. She may, in my tales, sound as if she were stupid, as if she were no more than a beetle-browed goon. But this was far from the case—I'd seen her on occasion match verse with verse with poets when they recited the old lays of battle. But when it came to love songs or tales of the giants and fairies who supposedly walked our land before man, she knew, and wished to know, nothing at all.

Even now, I wish I could say I understood her. But I didn't. None of us did. Perhaps Ismet was one facet of Maranonia incarnate as I'd once fancifully wondered.

THE NEXT morning Gamelan sent for me, and I found him at his favorite fishing spot, positively glowing with excitement.

"Watch," he said, soon as I arrived. He squatted on the deck, and if it wasn't for his robes, he might've been any old fisherman, scowling at the knotted and tangled net piled in front of him.

He reached his hand out, palm down, and touched the net strings, then raised his hand about three inches above the net. He moved it in circles, his fingers twining like cuttlefish. I found it hard to watch them as they moved, then my attention was ripped away as I saw the net strands move of their own volition, nothing touching them, and the net itself curled and dipped and then lay motionless, still a mass, but now with all its skeins untangled.

The handful of sailors and Guardswomen watching cheered, but Gamelan didn't need that to know what'd happened. He was smiling.

"I did it as a child," he said softly, "and I can do it now . . . My Talent *is* returning."

SOME DAYS LATER I made another visit to the stronghold of our enemies. Knowing I needed to get closer, I created a safeguard—if I were forced to flee, it wouldn't be as a comfortable flock of terns. I would be a swifter and more cunning creature. I'd constructed my new unguent in the proximity of two talismans—first I'd taken a bit of The Sarzana's robe Corais had torn off and still wore as a token of her hatred, and second that awful charm that was the heart of the last Archon's brother. Gamelan had protested mightily, but I'd not let him sway me. The mission was important, and I felt if I moved softly, just like a tern, wary of man and jaeger, I could slip in and out without notice.

I gave myself a full extra hour before dawn for my snooping, and there was no stirring as I swept closer to Ticino. Three times I swept over The Sarzana's fortress harbor. But each time, I saw no more than before, except I now realized that the "fog" obscuring my view was magical. Although I could make nothing of the ships close inshore, I could see more of the city itself. It was huge, as I'd thought. It had few streets, but rather canals connecting buildings, villas, and squares. In the center of the city I saw a large squat tower. It was actually a round castle, its rim jagged with turrets and bartizans. The city squares around it were clear except for statuary, and access to the castle was via four causeways that stretched over the walls. This would be a hard fortification to storm, and I hoped we could catch both The Sarzana and the Archon, in whatever form he was in, at sea, and end the long war.

I *had* to see more, and the only way was to increase the power of the spell—knowing if I did so that the danger would increase as well. But it was a risk I had to take. Gathering my strength, I formed an image in my mind of The Sarzana as I'd last seen him—petulant in his silks on the deck of our galley. Wary, I began the incantation. But just as I did so, the mind portrait slipped and I thought of the real and greater enemy.

I lost hold and the image smashed into my mind of the Archon in volcano-ripped seas, blood foaming on his lips and staining his yellowing beard, and then the world spun, spun from under me. I was caught in a maelstrom and I was falling toward that castle.

Then all was calm. I was in a vast, shadowed room, hung with tapestries and lit by tapers. I was no longer a tern, nor my flock of terns, nor was I even a woman. I was a spirit, just a presence, and I was staring at the one man in that room, just as he became aware of me. It was The Sarzana, and he sat at a table, the top of which was a large pool that shone like mercury.

The Sarzana's eyes gleamed. "Antero," he hissed, but it wasn't his voice I heard. Instead, it was that hiss I'd heard from black clouds when we first attempted a feint against Lycanth's sea castle. It was a serpent hiss, and I thought I could smell the same foul breath, the reek of the grave and beyond. The Sarzana stood. He walked toward me, but his motion was strange and unfamiliar. He moved not like the small man we'd rescued from Tristan, but with the long strides of another. And I knew that the flesh before me was inhabited by my greatest enemy—the Archon.

The Sarzana spoke again, with a croak. But I knew it wasn't he who moved those lips and used that throat. He said: "You haven't finished with Lycanth yet, Antero."

And then The Sarzana laughed the laugh of the Archon. "I've learned much," he said, "and had I known what treasures I'd find, I would have taken that journey long ago. There are worlds and worlds beyond, Antero. My brother and I could've seized their fruit and brought it back and made Lycanth a power greater than it ever was, greater than either the real world of the Far Kingdoms or those child's fables we heard before we came on them.

"Even now, the time and the chance may be seized again," he said. The Archon came toward me, and again he howled, as he had on the deck of Symeon's ship, his voice screeching in rage, *"The blood is paid and the battle yet joined,"* and his claws taloned, as had his brother's, but this time there was no armor of steel nor flesh between us.

There was a moment, a bare moment, as the two monsters—for I can't call either the Archon or his now-slave, The Sarzana, men—seemed to hesitate, as if gathering strength, and in that moment I found my own and cast myself, cast my spirit, away and was beyond the walls of the castle, spinning free, with a whirl of images ripping through my mind; a ferret, Gamelan's face, the reliquary holding the Archon's brother's heart, even a flash of Amalric's face, and my mother, my dear mother. As I spun away I could feel the Archon's tentacles stretch out for me.

But for just an instant I was beyond them, and in that instant my mind found the words and cast them forth:

Fly free
Fly fast
To sea
Away
Beyond

My spirit fingers "remembered" that peregrine's feather I'd stroked back aboard ship, and I became that falcon, darting low over the canals, wings flurrying, *away, beyond, to sea.* My peregrine's soul wanted me to climb, to soar high into the sky above danger, but I—the I that was Rali Emilie Antero—knew better, and so I shot through a field of bowmen, hard across the harbor, darting this way and that as I went. I was but seconds beyond the galleys, and I could sense the wrath behind me and the rage boiling forth, like hunting hounds on the scent, but I was gone. I had taken that one moment the Archon and The Sarzana had been too slow to seize.

Near the mouth of the bay I allowed my normal spell to revert, and I was the wind, a wind blowing fast off the island, a sharp gale that was there and then gone. I thought I "saw," far behind me, high in the heavens, a great eagle, the eagle that was the mortal enemy of the peregrine, sweeping, searching—but perhaps not. I couldn't chance either the energy or the possibility of leaving a trail to pay it any mind.

I'd taken the one instant away from the Archon.

He would not give me that luxury again.

GAMELAN WAS ANGRY when I reported what'd happened. "The Archon's marked you yet again, Rali," he said. "When we come to grips with him once more, you'll be his first target."

"He can but try," I said, and immediately felt ashamed of such a sub-altern's bravado, especially when I saw Gamelan's blind eyes fix me and his lip lift scornfully. Before he could tell me what I already knew, that each encounter decreased my odds, I apologized for my foolishness.

"The question now becomes," he went on, "what sort of shield we might be able to give you so that you can meet him on equal ground, at least for a moment. I must think," he said. "I must think."

He may have been the only one interested in thinking, though, after I made my report personally to Admiral Trahern. He ignored any mention I made of the Archon, as if he still had trouble believing magic existed.

"Now we have him trapped," was Trahern's hearty response, and he ordered all sail clapped on and the oars manned. "We'll not let The Sarzana escape us this time."

From our scouting, I knew The Sarzana's ships hadn't made any effort to sail out, and I had to wonder who was being trapped. I also had to wonder why Trahern'd sent the oarsmen to the sweeps. All that would accomplish would be to exhaust his sailors before the day of battle.

But I wasn't consulted, and so held my tongue.

A WEEK LATER we closed on the Alastors. The sail had taken an eternity, even though I was deathly afraid of the battle that would be mounted when we reached them. Was it possible, I dreamed for an instant, that *all* women and men could learn sorcery and be able to send their spirits flying wherever they wished? It was an idle thought, but at least a cheerful one amid the grimness surrounding us.

I'd tried twice more to send my spirit forward, but each time had only stood there naked, dripping oil, and feeling a bit of a fool. The Archon, for so I thought of him regardless of his physical envelope, had firmly bolted that door.

But there was always another way. We took our galley close in, using night and bad weather to shroud us, then I went into the gut with a hand-picked team of sailors in a longboat, past the two portal cities, far enough to be able to see The Sarzana's ships as they waited for battle. No. The Sarzana wasn't running.

Finally the fleet arrived off the islands and assembled into its three battle wings. Fleet Admiral Trahern ordered all ships' captains to assemble on his flagship, the biggest and, I thought, the clumsiest of all the Konyan galleys.

I went across with Gamelan and Cholla Yi. Cholla Yi was already stewing. "I wonder just how," he growled, "that pussel-gutted old man will make sure we'll be denied our fair share of glory?"

I agreed with him that no doubt Trahern would do something stupid. And indeed he did.

He'd had one of his pet aides, who evidently had an artistic bent, draw up a wall-size sketch of the way he proposed to fight the battle. It was quite beautiful, and the aide'd had time to add froth-blowing dragons, mermaids, and even a sea demon or two along the borders, so as not to obscure our complete understanding of Admiral Trahern's brilliance. It fit right in with the gold and imperial velvet decorations of the flag cabin, and with Trahern's ship itself, which made the galley I'd rescued Xia from look like a paragon of subtle decoration and design, with its polished metal and white clay knotwork everywhere, and the sideboys and on-deck watch perfect in blue-striped long-sleeved tunics, white pantaloons, bare feet, and white gloves.

Briefly, Trahern proposed to divide the fleet into three striking elements. One would hold to the left—west—as we entered the gut, and be commanded by Admiral Bhazana, who'd wanted my head when we were captured by the Konyans. He was, at least, a fighter. The wing on the right, the east, would be led by Admiral Bornu, who I'd heard was a complete waste, more concerned by who was rogering his round-heeled but rich wife than the ships under him. The center wing, and command of the entire fleet, would be under the command of Trahern himself.

Trahern's plan was simple—which was its only good point. Our fleet would sail into the bay. It would, somewhere before it reached Ticino, find The Sarzana's fleet. Then all of the Konyan ships would close frontally with The Sarzana's, board, and victory could only be a few hours away. That was the sum total of his "strategy."

I was seething already, having noted there was no mention of our role in the battle. Instead, I forced calm, and asked.

Admiral Trahern, a little nervously, said, "Well, Captain—and damn but I wish we'd arranged to give you a proper title, harder than all blazes realizin' you're more than just a ship's officer—we thought you and your, uh, men, I mean, command, would be our reserve, ready to fling yourselves into the fray at the proper moment."

There'd been a few snickers when he said "men," not only because of my Guards, but because of Nor's unfortunates. I ignored them. "Which will be?" I asked.

"Well," Trahern hedged, "at my signal, of course. Or, once their fleet is broken, perhaps you'll be useful in the mopping up. Yes, that'll be your role."

I was about to explode, and all at once everything came to me, precisely and as crystalline as if I were looking down on a battle miniature under glass. I *knew* what we must do, and, more importantly, realized Admiral Trahern had given us the opportunity. It was just then that Cholla Yi boiled to his feet, sending his chair crashing. I spun, and time froze, just for an instant. Cholla Yi had his mouth open, ready to bellow his frenzy at being left out yet again, and I looked him straight in the eye. I make no claim for working magic at that moment. No spell came, I swear. But somehow what was in my mind must've signaled, because he clamped his mouth shut and, without saying anything, turned and stamped out.

Admiral Trahern was red, about to shout an order for this unruly pirate to be hurled into irons, then regained control. "My apologies for my compatriot," I said smoothly. "He's merely caught up in the desire to destroy this evil, *as are we all.* Isn't that correct?"

Trahern nodded jerkily.

"As long as I'm on my feet," I went on, "I have a question about your strategy. You seem to be forgetting the curse that surrounds those who kill their rulers here in Konya. One of the reasons the Council of Purity listened to me"—and I put emphasis into my voice for this latter—"*and Princess Xia*, was of their wish for me, or my forces, to keep the blood from their hands. Are you saying you propose to defy that curse?"

There were mutters from the other captains, and I saw fear on the faces of more than a few. Trahern harrumphed.

"As to the curse," he said, "well, I must say I've never been entirely comfortable with certain beliefs the masses hold true. I mean, whatever happened to the man, whoever he was, who actually cut the throat of our late king, or however he died? I haven't seen any such ghost being pursued through the streets of Isolde by demons."

He forced a laugh, and was the only one in the room to do so.

"But in fact, Captain Antero, I have taken the curse into account. We have every intent of using your forces to the fullest at the proper time, and have no intent of violating the Council's wishes in any way." Trahern looked a little nervous at *that* thought. "But to be realistic, I must say that if The Sarzana happens to fall in battle at the hands of an unknown soldier or archer, well, whatever penalties might be put on that wight's soul will be balanced by the honors we Konyans will hold his memory in.

"But I do not think that will happen, which is why I've designated your galleys as our reserve. Once we've isolated The Sarzana on his flagship and boarded it, I will signal, either by flag or by magical sign from one of my own wizards, for you and your women to administer the final stroke that will free our lands.

"I'm glad you had the question, Captain, and enabled me to clear up this small misunderstanding."

Misunderstanding, indeed. Trahern was even a bigger ass than I'd dreamed. It was clear he intended that all glory from the death of The Sarzana would cling to him, and would doom all around to make that so. Again I was reminded of General Jinnah—another man who'd rather lose a war than face reality.

I kept a stony face, however, bowed and excused myself, saying I had to order my galleys and I'd be paying close attention to his signals. Trahern knew—or thought he knew—what I was thinking, and was glad to see me leave. I took Gamelan's arm and we left the cabin.

As we came on deck, I saw Cholla Yi pacing back and forth by the railing. He was alone on the deck—none of the Konyans had courage enough to approach this great bear of a man with his spiked hair and face black with rage.

I was about to go to him when Gamelan stopped me. "Rali," he said softly. "Is there anything close at hand that reflects?"

I thought for a moment he had gone mad, then recovered. "Almost everything," I told him. "Admiral Trahern evidently believes that if something moves, it's to be saluted, and if it doesn't, it's to be polished."

"Lead me to something like that. Metal, by preference."

Not three feet away was a decorative shield of some sort, made of bronze and hung from a bulkhead. I obeyed.

"Take out your dagger," he said, "and prick your finger."

"Gamelan—"

"Rali, do as I say!"

I heard the crackle of command and remembered that this man, blind though he was, had ruled all of the Evocators of Orissa, and obeyed.

He said, "Smear a bit of blood on the edge of this thing, whatever it is. Just at the edge, where it'll not be found. And don't let yourself be seen."

Again I obeyed. The Konyans on the deck were intent on their duties—as anyone would be who wishes to survive aboard a ship flying an admiral's flag—or else were gazing in wonderment at Cholla Yi. I touched my finger to the side of the shield.

"Now, collect Cholla Yi and let's away."

"Will you explain?"

"Perhaps. Later."

CHOLLA YI sat in the sternsheets of my longboat, still enraged. We went directly to his galley, and I followed him to his cabin. He started to pour himself a glass of wine, then stopped. He turned, looming over me.

"Well?" was all he said.

I explained my realization. Trahern's plan of attack was impossibly stupid. There was no way I could believe The Sarzana wasn't expecting us. It seemed he was more than pleased to let the Konyans sail right up to him. He must have some sort of an advantage, besides the slight numerical one.

"Of course he has," Cholla Yi put in. "Which is why I wanted to tell that vomit-brained—never mind. Continue."

I did. What was our battle? What was our concern?

"The Archon," Cholla Yi said grudgingly. "Assuming you weren't mind-clouded by a spell, and he, or his ghost or whatever the hell it is, now is one with The Sarzana."

"Right. Once he's dead, or possibly even captured, the war's over. Right?"

"Again."

I went on. I had no interest in sacrificing my women for the Konyans, nor in spending the lives of Cholla Yi's pirates, if it didn't accomplish the goal we'd been assigned by our Orissan leaders. This battle, even if there weren't any nasty surprises prepared by The Sarzana, would be a bloodbath. I assumed Cholla Yi planned to return to Orissan seas with some of his ships and men, or, if he planned to stay in Konya, he'd be wanting something resembling a navy that was floating instead of sitting at the bottom of the Bay of Ticino.

"Again, granted."

So Admiral Trahern could call us what he wished, a mobile reserve or even pink lions. We were after The Sarzana. If we could take him, anything we did after that would be forgiven.

"True. Plus we've got your little birdie the princess along, and she'll be listened to once we get back to Konya."

"Exactly."

What I proposed was that we let the three wings engage the enemy. I'd prepare a spell to find the bastard. When we did, we'd strike directly for his ship, paying no heed to anyone or anything else.

"In the confusion of battle," Cholla Yi said, his rage fading by the word, "such a plan, boldly carried through, stands a good chance of succeeding. If we strike as one, dagger formation perhaps, straight through the melee . . . hmm. And *if* we're the ones who come back with the head of The Sarzana, and whatever the hell it takes to make sure that damned Archon's down in the depths for good and all . . . damn, damn, damn. We'll be able to rename Isolde Yi . . . or Antero, if we wish."

Now he poured wine—two glasses, and he ceremoniously handed the first one to me.

"Captain Antero," he said, "I think you may not only have come up with a plan that'll cover us with glory, which means gold, but also may keep most of us alive to spend it. You're a warrior, Captain."

He started to say something else, stopped himself, and drank. As I sipped, I found it hard to hold back a grin, wondering what words might've slipped out: ". . . for a woman?" ". . . a pity you were born cloven?" ". . . almost a man's man?"

It didn't matter. I finished my wine and returned to my galley.

No one slept that night.

And the next morning we sailed into battle.

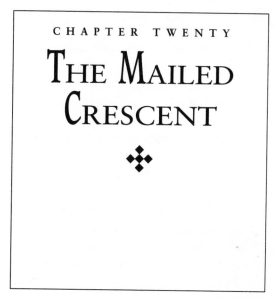

CHAPTER TWENTY

THE MAILED CRESCENT

❖

The Sarzana's ships were waiting. Their battle formation was a huge semicircle blocking the bay, which curved from the eastern shallows of the gut to the steep cliffs on the west. It was a bright morning and I saw the gleam of armor on the enemy ships.

Our galleys sat rolling in the gentle swell, oars at the lift, as the three wings of the Konyan navy went forward to meet the mailed crescent. We hadn't sent our masts down, since we might need full maneuvering speed later in the day. Cholla Yi's galley sat not thirty feet from my own, and I had the morbid thought we were but idle spectators at some great match—with life as the prize. Xia was beside me on the quarterdeck, wearing her new armor and a sword belted about her waist. I'd wanted to assign her a bodyguard, but she'd refused. Corais, Polillo, and Gamelan were also on deck—as were Stryker and Duban. Gamelan was accompanied by his two guards. One of his companions, Pamphylia, had become expert at being the "eyes" for the wizard, and her low drone of narration had become a familiar backdrop to the Evocator's presence.

Oars flashed and feathered on The Sarzana's war fleet as they got under way. The wind blowing up the gut toward Ticino suddenly died. Then another arose, answering the call of our enemy's magic. It blasted south into our faces, and the sails on The Sarzana's ships bellied and filled. The Konyan wizards struck back, and the sails flapped emptily as their counterspell broke

The Sarzana's wind-magic. Winds gusted and swirled from all points of the compass. Cholla Yi bellowed orders, and we, too, began moving, making sure we kept the proper distance behind the Konyan battle line—close enough to give support if summoned, far enough away to avoid entanglement when the fighting began.

I had the sudden impulse to cast my tern-spell and observe the struggle from the skies. Fortunately, I asked Gamelan, and he grimaced. "Rali," he said, "I thought I had taught you better, and I certainly thought you brighter. What do you think would happen if you send yourself spiraling up there, as innocent as any noble booby who takes a picnic to a battlefield to watch the gore splatter, and either of our great enemies happens to sight you, hanging there with no safeguards, no sense, and no cover? Woman, do you *have* to look for the executioner's axe with your neck?" I was properly chastened.

But it didn't matter. I don't know exactly what to call it—more than a vision, less than actual sight—but it was as if I was hanging in the sky overhead or atop one of the cliffs to the west, and could see everything that happened on that dismal day. Just as the Konyans, The Sarzana's forces appeared to be divided into three battle groups. It may have been chance, or perhaps that was a standard tactic in these islands, but to me it boded no good, and suggested there might well have been some spying, magical or otherwise, and The Sarzana had cleverly planned to have his forces capable of responding independently to any equal threat from us.

I tried to look beyond the crescent as it moved forward, back up the bay toward Ticino. Once again I saw that bewildering "mist"—lying low between me and the city, just where The Sarzana's reserve ships should've been. I still couldn't see what lay inside that fog bank, but now knew what it must be—The Sarzana had developed some sort of new magical weapon to be deployed at the proper moment. This was the second ill omen of the day. Then I noted that the clifftops to the west were barren of life. Somehow that made the day even more strange. If a sea battle was being fought close to most cities, the entire populace would turn out to cheer their own warriors, worry about their own fate, or simply gape over the spectacle. I wondered what had happened to the people of Ticino. I had a moment to wonder if we would enter a city emptied save of blood-smeared streets if The Sarzana fell on this day.

"They're firin'," Stryker grunted, and I, too, saw the ranging splashes rise up ahead of the onrushing Konyan galleys.

"Very good," Polillo said, trying to sound optimistic. "We can hope they waste all their weapons killing those waves between us."

I could see war engines on the bows of the enemy ships, and saw trebuchets buck as they lofted boulders through the air. I thought I could hear the thumps as their wooden arms struck the padded crossbars, and I could see them being wound back down for another launching. In Isolde I'd suggested to Admiral Trahern that the Konyan ships appeared underequipped with such gear, but he said there was no place for machinery in their wars: Konyan battles were decided by steel and blood, not wood, rope, and iron. The few devices the Konyan ships had were all that would be necessary for victory, and he had little interest in duplicating any of the special weapons I'd designed. Obviously he'd never learned the truism there's no such thing as too much in battle.

I felt fear crawl up my spine—fear and the certainty of doom, with the added knowledge that I was worse than useless as a captain, more of a danger to my women than the enemy. But this I'd felt before. This was the same spell the Archon had leveled against us so long ago, when we killed his brother at the volcanoes. It still was unsettling, but at least, being familiar, the feeling was endurable. I heard shouts of alarm coming from the Konyan ships and cursed. I'd warned the Konyan Evocators of all the tricks the Archon might try, and they'd assured me that counterspells would be simple. If they'd bothered to prepare any, they obviously weren't working. I remembered one of the frescoes on a wall of our armory in Orissa. It depicted the corpse of a Guardswoman, sprawled on a battlefield, and over it the grim inscription: DESPISE NOT YOUR ENEMY. The Konyans were beginning to learn this lesson themselves, although where they'd gotten such arrogance, forgetting how swiftly The Sarzana had once defeated their best, was beyond me. I suppose victors have even shorter memories than the vanquished.

Now The Sarzana's ships were in range. Another group of machines opened fire—catapults sending long arrows ripping forward to tear through sails, bulwarks, and, often as not, Konyan soldiers. What I'd called "firefingers" rippled out from The Sarzana's forward ships, striking Konyan galleys and sending them roaring into flame. I tried to see if there was a single source for those firestrikes that might give me a clue as to which ship The Sarzana might be aboard, but they seemed to come from everywhere. Evidently the Archon had perfected his spell.

A Konyan ship not far away lost headway, its oars flailing like a water beetle that panics seeing the carp striking up from the depths. Our galleys drew closer and I could see soldiers and sailors fighting desperately on its main deck, as if they'd been boarded by a yet-invisible enemy. Then I saw what they were fighting. The decks were littered with great serpents that thrashed and struck with unnatural energy at the men. I'd seen no trebuchet deliver such a wickedly clever load, and knew the snakes had to have been transported aboard magically.

"The Sarzana has some interesting tricks," Gamelan said when Pamphylia told him what'd happened. "That's one I'd never thought of. Worth noting, too."

"The Sarzana, or maybe the Archon," Corais said quietly. Polillo shivered, and I surreptitiously gripped her hand to reassure her, then let it go before anyone could notice. Polillo recovered in a bare second and was her usual battle-cold self.

"We are forgetting," I agreed, "the Archons ruled Lycanth not just by magic, but by their skills with armies as well."

Xia was looking very worried and not a little frightened, which was natural in her first battle. "What does that mean?" she wanted to know.

I tried to find soothing words, but Stryker spoke first. "Cap'n Antero means we'd best hope th' bull can take th' lancer b'fore his horse dances him out of the way."

The Konyan ships were still going forward, slowly, steadily, bull-like, against the rain of fire that came down. I remembered once being forward of such an attack—I don't even remember in which border skirmish it was—and seeing long lines of infantry advancing against archers. As the shafts struck down from the skies the soldiers hunched their shoulders and bent forward while pushing doggedly onward, exactly like men forcing themselves through a rainstorm. So it was with the Konyan ships.

"Look," Xia said gleefully. "They're breaking!"

So it appeared. The enemy center wing had swung out of line. Signal flags went up from Trahern's warship, but Admiral Bhazana had already seen, and bunting flapped from his own masthead. His ships swung out of the main Konyan formation, away from the shallows and the lagging enemy they'd been expecting to meet, hoping to attack The Sarzana's center on its flank. Such a bold stroke could break the enemy fleet now and end the battle before midday..

"Too soon, too soon," I heard Polillo moan under her breath. "Always wait to make sure the throw is real, not a bluff!"

And so it was. As Bhazana's ships formed their new line, a strong, spell-created wind gusted down the gut toward us, and The Sarzana's waiting ships caught it and shot like bolts against Bhazana's own flank.

"Shit!" Stryker swore. "Caught in th' same net they'd hoped t' cast!"

The threat was to more than just our east wing. Trahern's center was also out of position. Perhaps he'd hoped to help exploit the enemy's mistake, which now was clearly a ruse that we'd fallen for.

The two lines of ships closed and the battle proper began. But it did not open as Trahern and the Konyans had wished. Trahern might've wanted to close and board with the other ships, but The Sarzana's galleys veered, trying to evade contact. Clumsy as they were, there were many instances where they weren't able to turn away, and grapnels went across and Konyan soldiers leapt for the bulwarks. But even when an enemy ship was trapped, the battle still was not joined on Trahern's terms. Another galley would strike the Konyan ship from the rear, keeping just a few yards away, and archers would pelt the ship, trying to divert it. It was just as a well-trained pack of hounds behave, savaging a bear's legs and flanks when he traps one of their brothers.

I heard screams and shouts across the water, and saw flames mount and masts tumble as The Sarzana's ships kept hammering the Konyans. Even boarding wasn't as simple as Trahern had imagined. I saw glints of steel from just above the bulwarks of an enemy ship and stakes protruding out and up at an angle from the rails of the galley—stakes that were so much fence-posting from the sharp strands of steel strung along them. That would be even better than the traditional sagging nets to keep boarders away. Of course, it'd keep The Sarzana's own troops from attacking, but it looked as if he had no intent of fighting a traditional battle this day. Again I knew the Archon's orders had been taken, not only in magic, but in war as well.

We were too close to the fray, and I shouted a warning to Cholla Yi for us to pull back, but to stand by to reinforce Bhazana's wing if it broke. We withdrew to a better position, but still there came no signal for us to join the attack. All we could do was wait. Now it was truly as if I were above the fleets as the battle continued. From the water it appeared as confusing as any land battlefield, with men shouting, bleeding and dying, staggering back and forth, and dust and smoke everywhere, and banners waving and going down, only to rise up once more—except the soldiers were monstrous ships.

Ships were already sinking and there were sailors drowning, clinging to flotsam and shouting for rescue. Some saw our galleys and desperately began swimming toward us. But it was far, too far, and one by one their heads vanished. Other ships drifted back out of battle, some with fighting still raging on their decks, others showing no sign of life at all, still others with their huge deckhouses shattered by boulders. I thought there were more Konyan vessels than enemy ships. Then I saw Konyan ships start to sail back—away from the battle. Some of them were crippled, dragging the ruins of masts overboard, others were smoking and crippled. But all too many of them showed no damage.

Polillo had her axe unsheathed and was holding it in her hand without noticing, slapping its flat hard against her reddening palm, her face mottled in anger and helplessness.

"Weak-gutted sonsabitches," Stryker swore. "Rope-spined bastards are breaking, and the day's not half gone."

I realized with a jolt the sun was now high overhead, and wondered where the hours had gone; then my eyes were torn away, as The Sarzana's sorcerous cloud lifted and his secret weapon broke into the battle. It was a small fleet of ships such as I'd never imagined. They were not much longer than our Orissan ships, if somewhat broader beamed, and single-rowed galleys like ours. But what made them striking and fearsome wasn't just the lurid colors they'd been painted with—the colors of blood and death—but that they were solidly roofed and mastless. They looked like many-legged turtles as they swept forward. There'd be no boarding these craft; small as they were, the hulking Konyan ships would hardly be able to even close with them. I was very glad I wasn't a Konyan captain in the vanguard, because for the moment I had no idea how these invulnerable-looking craft could be destroyed. There were at least thirty of them, and they were attacking in a spearhead formation—striking straight for the ignored and open west side of Trahern's center wing, where a gap lay between it and Admiral Bornu's ships.

Stryker swore, and I heard Duban whine something.

Corais was unbothered. "I don't see how they fight," she observed. "Maybe they're intending to scare us to death."

But in bare seconds we realized the "turtleships" were as deadly in fact as in appearance. They were rams, but I realized once more that The Sarzana's tactics were new, as I saw the first turtleship strike a Konyan vessel and then pull away as if nothing had happened—instead of remaining in a death embrace with its foe. The Konyan ship rolled at the impact, then wallowed to the side as water rushed into the hole the turtleship's beak had torn. In seconds it vanished under the waves. I realized the rams must either be demountable or, more likely, grooved to snap when a certain amount of force was exerted against them. Such a device would be foolhardy on a ship intended to endure hard weather, since it was likely to snap unpredictably and rip the galley's own bows open. Here in the calm waters of the bay, it was an ideal weapon. But that wasn't the only armament the turtleships had. Hatches flipped open on the covering deck and I saw the warheads of huge arrows emerge from one turtleship as it sailed close under a Konyan's stern. Smoke lifted from each arrowhead and then the catapults fired, sending the fire arrows deep into the wooden counter. The hatches banged shut and the gunners began reloading safely out of sight, as flames roared up from the stricken Konyan vessel. The arrows were either pitch-soaked or, more likely, "dressed" with an incantation.

When the first ship burst into flames, I heard Xia hide a tiny shriek of fear, which no one but me could've heard, and I felt a flash of admiration for her courage. She was doing better than most before their first battle, better than I did marching up to my first skirmish, not having learned that the waiting and the thinking are deadlier to bravery than the most brutal foe.

Now the battle's tide was in full flood—and for The Sarzana's forces.

Behind the turtleships came the entire west wing of the fleet, possibly a hundred or more conventional ships. I didn't know what to do. The entire Konyan fleet was breaking. On my left, Admiral Bhazana's ships were reeling back; in the center, Trahern's forces were locked in a smoky melee; and on my right, the turtleships and their reinforcements were driving a wedge through Bornu's wing. As Bornu's forces shattered, I realized there wasn't anything I could've done, unless there were a thousand of me, and a thousand thousand of my Guardswomen and Cholla Yi's galleys. His still-undamaged ships changed course, oars flailing, and set full sail to take advantage of The Sarzana's wind blowing away from the city. Singly and by squadrons they tacked back toward the open sea; on their heels came the turtleships and The Sarzana's large galleys.

The other Konyans must've seen or sensed what had happened, because both Trahern's and Bhazana's wings shattered at the same instant. But not all the ships would be able to retreat. There were many ships still caught in the cauldron of the center; ships that would now be brought to battle and destroyed, one by one. I saw the banner of Bhazana's ship coming away from the shallows, and then spotted Trahern's flagship, its mainsail at full swell, oarsmen pulling for their lives. You bastard, I thought. You led your sailors to this death, and you don't even have the damned courage to stay and share it with them. Whatever courage the admiral had in the past that brought him greatness had vanished with age and ease.

The first ships sailed past and I heard their sailors scream to flee, flee, the battle was lost, and even the dead had risen from the depths to fight us. I wondered for an instant, then nearly retched as a horrible stench rolled over our galley, coming from the first Konyan ships, now not more than three or four hundred yards away.

I made a decision, but Cholla Yi had already made it for me. Flags were at his masthead, and he was crying through his trumpet to retreat, pull back, there was no standing against them.

Xia shouted in blind rage, shouted he was a coward, then spun as I snapped the same orders to Stryker. "You can't!" she cried in her frenzy, nearly in tears. "You're no better than—"

"Silence!" I shouted. "You wanted to be a soldier! Now soldier!" That outcry stopped her for an instant, and in that instant common sense returned and she slumped and turned away from me.

I could see some of The Sarzana's ships clearly now, and gasped. It looked as if the fleeing Konyans were right. On their decks were horrid beings who'd once been men, some rotting from exposure, some dried up into brown wisps by a hot desert wind, others bloated and fish-belly white from their time on the ocean floor. Some were working the sweeps, others methodically served catapults or waited patiently with bow or spear for the range to close. For an instant I remembered my brother's tale of a city of the walking dead far away to the west, almost at the gates of the Far Kingdoms, where even the city's lord was a living cadaver, and how Amalric almost died in that horrid necropolis. But he'd had Greycloak with him . . . and I did not.

The charnel reek was all around us, and even my hardened mercenaries were beginning to show fear, even as they obeyed orders and we turned and fled with the others.

Then I knew what the smell was, and what the corpse-sailors were. I guess I knew this because of my own spell-casting, my own sensitivity to wizardry. Just as I knew what the truth was, I knew the countermeasure. I ordered Xia below and told her to bring up her cosmetics bag. She gaped, and I snapped at her sharply. Puzzled, she obeyed. In a few seconds she'd returned and handed it to me. I found a vial of perfume, unstoppered it, and sniffed. It was ideal—a heavy, strong, flower-based scent.

I cast the bottle into the air and it spun—contents spraying. I chanted, the words coming easily:

"Seek flowers
Seek your foe
Cling to him
Change him
You are the greater
You are on the earth
And of the earth
He comes from the ether
He is not
Take him
Change him
Turn him."

The corpse smell vanished.

"It's just a spell-lie!" I shouted. "Those men're no different than you and I. It's the Archon's magic!"

The words, or possibly just that someone appeared unpanicked, broke the frenzy, even though the men could look behind them and see the onrushing enemy ships still manned by the undead.

"I'll break that spell, too," I shouted, and then stopped short.

The battle was over, but not for all of us. Two galleys were sailing back, back toward The Sarzana's ships! I didn't need to strain my eyes to know who they were. They were two of Nor's galleys, blinded by their rage. I might've felt a bit of admiration for their suicidal attack, having seen and known women who deliberately threw their lives away and charged into the midst of the enemy, shouting their deathsong in joy. But I didn't. There were eight of my women on board those two ships who hadn't chosen that death. Very well, I thought. That'll be another debt to settle, first with Nor, then with The Sarzana and the Archon.

The two ships were surrounded by the turtleships, and their masts vanished and I saw no more of them that day—or ever again.

But there wasn't time for anger.

Just to our west, one of The Sarzana's monster galleys was bearing down on us.

"Polillo!" I shouted, and my legate bounded forward to where her nervous catapult teams waited behind their strange weapons mounted on either side of the foremast. The catapults' prods were wound back to full cock, a shaft in each of the twin troughs, and hanging between them a loose net bag with a coiled chain inside, a thin chain that I'd cast a spell of strength on.

The huge ship rolled down on us, its sail big with The Sarzana's magic wind, and I could hear, dimly, the gleeful shouts of the soldiers aboard the ship, thinking they had us trapped.

Above their shouts I heard Polillo's chant:

"Steady . . . steady . . . left a little . . . steady . . . up . . . a little more . . . steady . . . steady . . ."

"Shoot!" I screamed, and the catapults thwanged like two miscast bells struck with steel mallets. The starboard set of bolts went wide and missed, but the port set sped true. Just as I'd designed, just as I'd tested, the bolts vee-ed out, the net bag snapping and the chain coming taut between them, about to snap or else send the device spinning out of control, and then it struck fair, about halfway up the enemy ship's mast, and snapped it like a twig. The sail billowed back, and stays and yards cascaded down over the ship's deck.

That was the only strike we had time for, and I'd only allowed it so we wouldn't feel completely defeated.

Now it was time to run, before the turtleships could close and destroy us.

Full sail was set, and our rowers pulled for their lives. I thanked Maranonia we hadn't set normal battle order earlier and sent the sails down. Now, with the first part of the Archon's illusion broken, it would be easier to find a counterspell to shatter the rest of it. Perhaps that would be enough to make the fleet turn and at least fight The Sarzana's ships to a standstill.

While one part of my mind sought for the words and ingredients, another was preparing a signal to Trahern. I went to the rail, looking out over the gut, which was now widening to the open sea, and we were almost past the two portal cities. Our ships were scattered across the waters like bits of paper on a flood tide, each trying to escape, none concerned with any but itself and finding safety. Spell or not, there would be no more fighting this day.

It was too late for my magic, mine or anyone else's.

It was fortunate The Sarzana's ships had no greater turn of speed than the Konyans', because if they could've caught them, they would've wiped them out to the man. But they were dropping back now. I saw the turtleships wallow as the first great swells of the ocean struck them, and they turned back to calmer waters, their mission accomplished. A few minutes later the rest of The Sarzana's fleet followed. Now that spell wouldn't be needed. The Sarzana had won his great victory and broken our fleet.

I saw Trahern's galley far to the rear. It might've been one of the first to flee, but was as unhandy as I'd thought, barely making steerage way. Just as my eyes found it, it changed, and became a swelling, building boil of fire and smoke, white streamers soaring high into the heavens as it exploded! Seconds later the shockwave of the blast rolled across the waters and over our galleys.

Before that flameball vanished, an apparition spread across the sky above it.

It was the Archon, seen for just an instant, his filed teeth bared as he howled in glee over his victory. Then the sky was empty and there was nothing but the ashen taste of defeat and death.

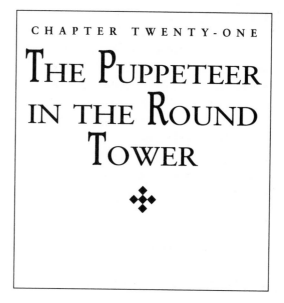

CHAPTER TWENTY-ONE

THE PUPPETEER IN THE ROUND TOWER

❖

Near dusk the Konyans slowed their flight. This wasn't the first battle panic I'd seen, nor would it most likely be the last. Terror-stricken soldiers only run so far and so long. They stop when they can't see the enemy any longer, when they collapse from exhaustion, when they see others slow down, or when they're faced with the unknown—something that's even more frightening than whatever sent them scurrying away from the sound of drums.

Thus it was with the Konyan ships. We were too far away from their homelands, with open seas between us and final safety. Also, some of them might've seen The Sarzana's forces turn back and realized after a while that they were now unpursued. So the ships gathered in little knots around their division leaders or other command ships that'd survived.

This was a grave mistake by The Sarzana. He should've chased us until darkness at least, so that all would "know" the demons were still hot on our trail.

I thought there were two possible reasons. The Sarzana wanted a signal victory, and didn't want to commit his ships to a long series of actions that'd finish us in detail. This is a common mistake with Great Leaders—all of their actions must be marked with boldness and energy, and last no longer than the attention span of those they rule. The grind of small details isn't for them. This is why, when war is waged between a Brilliant General and Scruffy Bandits, it's not entirely foolish to bet on the bandits.

Also, I sensed the killing stroke yet to come would be a storm brewed up by the Archon. This would scatter our ships like sand, so only a few would return to Konya with news of the disaster. I felt magics a-building even as we sailed away from the Gut of Ticino after the fleeing Konyans, making signal after ignored signal. By the time the ships had lowered sails—I swear, as sheepishly as men realizing they're behaving as foolishly as barnyard fowl—the beginnings of the storm were already showing themselves. A chill wind blew up from Ticino; there was a chop to the waves and the glass was falling.

I knew we'd have to deal with that within the next few hours, but there were more important problems at hand.

We closed on Bhazana's galley, which would for the moment be the fleet's flagship, and sent signals requiring him to immediately summon all other ship captains, not just division or element leaders, for a conference. I thought there'd be more than enough room on the flagship—I estimated that less than half of the Konyan ships had survived. I waited, not quite sure what I'd do if my orders were ignored, but saw with relief both flags fluttering and bull's-eye lanterns flashing as the gloom gathered. His signals were received and echoed by other ships as they drew together near the flagship, and I saw small boats being swung out.

I made a signal to Nor's nearby galley that he was not to attend this conference, and that I would require his presence aboard our galley when I summoned him. I wanted to give the Broken Man some time to consider his broken oath. I said I wished Corais, Xia, and Gamelan to accompany me. I told Xia she was to wear her battle garb. She seemed surprised, but I said the reason would become apparent soon.

I left Polillo in charge of the Guard, not only because I wanted someone of her imposing presence to ensure my back was covered, but also because what I intended suited her little. Some of the darker duties of soldiering ill became my legate, and I thought the better of her for it, and secretly despised the part of me that held me firm to distasteful tasks like the one I was almost sure would be required.

I had one longboat launched and sent directly to Admiral Bhazana's flagship. It carried Flag Sergeant Ismet, ten heavily armed Guardswomen, our ship's carpenter, two sailors, and the gear I'd determined necessary. I had another boat launched, and the four of us boarded it. I ordered it rowed to Cholla Yi's ship, and explained to him what I intended at the conference and what *must* be done if we had any hope of survival, let alone recovery from this terrible situation.

I'd had time enough to devise a plan as our galley sped after the others. Surprisingly, Cholla Yi listened closely and grudgingly agreed that most likely I was correct in my thinking and strategy. His only hesitation, I thought, was that the plan wasn't his, nor would he lead it. That gave me one ally, at least for the moment. I was under no illusions as to the pirate's long-term reliability.

As we rowed up to Admiral Bhazana's ship, my anger ebbed when I saw its condition. He hadn't fled at the first hostile shout from The Sarzana. His galley had taken serious damage from The Sarzana's war engines. The upper deckhouse's roof had been torn away, as had one entire railing and part of the hull itself on the starboard side. The main deckhouse was smoke-seared and blackened from fires set by The Sarzana's catapulted arrows, and half his oars had been snapped. Two mainstays had snapped, too, and the ship's mast sagged drunkenly. Men swarmed over the decks making hasty repairs. They tried to avoid looking at the long line of covered bodies on the afterdeck waiting burial.

We boarded and were saluted by the galley's master. I stared at him coldly. "I only accept honors," I said deliberately in a loud voice intended to carry to every seaman within earshot, "from soldiers, not from men who've turned their backs on honor."

He turned red, but didn't meet my eye. That was the first sign I might carry the day—if he'd exploded in anger or reached for a weapon, I would've known the Konyans were truly without courage.

I ordered Yi and the others to wait on deck, and our ship's carpenter and his assistants to set to. I told the ship's master to take me to Admiral Bhazana. He was below, in a cabin nearly as magnificent as that of Admiral Trahern. He had his back to me and was staring out through the round portholes at the afterdeck and the line of corpses.

Without turning, he said, "I'm a fool."

"You are," I agreed. "And worse. You broke."

Now he turned. "First I let myself be drawn in by that childish artifice, then, when the Konyans attacked, I couldn't rally my ships." I just stared at him. "But I swear to you I didn't break," he said. "I swear I saw signals from Trahern's ship ordering me to retreat."

I remained silent, and his shoulders fell. "I cannot expect you to believe me," he went on. "I can only ask your permission to pay for my error."

"How do you propose that?"

"By going to my gods." His fingers touched the shortsword at his waist. "I wanted to do that earlier, but was stopped. Captain Oirot said . . . It doesn't matter what he said."

"You fled once," I said, letting scorn run down my words like blood down a sword, "now you wish to do it again? Your self-indulgence is denied." Bhazana flushed. "You can kill yourself, give yourself medals, or run a mast up your ass when this is over, for all I care, but for the moment you will place yourself under my orders and do exactly as you're told. Is that clear?"

Once a soldier's honor is broken, he's like putty drowned in linseed oil. The trick is to avoid further shaming him, unless you wish to make the ruin complete. This I didn't want.

I said, "Now. Here is what will happen." I went on, closing the subject and giving him very thorough instructions.

An hour later the ship captains were assembled. There were a hundred and seventy-four of them, so they packed not only the foredeck, but the passageways beside the deckhouse as well. Among them was Admiral Bornu, who I noted showed no more battle damage than I'd seen on his ship when it fled toward the open sea. Unlike Bhazana, Bornu was trying to bluster his way out. I paid no attention, but bade him wait on the foredeck with the others. There wasn't much conversation from them, both because of the day's shame and because their attention was fixed by the device I'd had my carpenter set up on the top deck.

I stood just at the top of the companionway that led to the main cabin's top deck. Just behind and beside me were Cholla Yi, Corais, Xia, Gamelan, and Admiral Bhazana. Behind them were my Guardswomen.

We'd come out of the cabin's ruins silently, making no announcement, and stood waiting. Slowly we were noticed, and the buzz of low conversation died. I let the silence build and build until it was intolerable. There was nothing but the whine of the wind as it increased in speed, and the wash of the waves against the galley's sides.

"The Sarzana defeated us today," I said. "And we ran from him like fish flee from the shark pack. Are we to return to Konya with *that* on our souls? Are we going home to tell our loved ones what cowards we were, and for them to prepare to face all of The Sarzana's terror?"

"What else?" It was a voice from the rear. There was a clatter of agreement. Once more I let the words die away into the wind.

"What else? We're going back to Ticino!" I said. "The battle's only begun."

"When?" This was an officer in the front row I didn't recognize. "How long will it take to get reinforcements up from Konya? A month? Two months?"

"We're going back tomorrow. Tomorrow at night," I said.

"That's impossible!" That came from Admiral Bornu.

"Nothing is impossible," I said.

"To blazes with you," he said, and bounded halfway up the companionway and turned to face the other captains. "We were beaten badly this day, beaten by wizardry and the force of arms! There's no way for us to recover, not now, not as outnumbered as we are! This whole damned campaign was doomed! It never should've been fought! We should've waited for The Sarzana to get closer to Isolde and then defeated him on our own grounds, in our own waters!"

I heard agreement building.

"Or maybe," I said, "you think we should have just surrendered without fighting at all?"

Now there was dead silence.

"Maybe we could've struck some kind of arrangement," Bornu said, nearly mumbling. "Maybe if we'd gone to The Sarzana and offered—"

"Offered what?" I asked "Your daughters? Your wives? Your gold? You couldn't have offered your honor, since by your words you possess none!"

Bornu's hand was on his sword. I heard a rustle from behind me and knew Locris or another bow woman was reaching for her quiver. I moved one step closer down the companionway. "Now, Admiral," I said, "*now* you reach for your blade, after letting it rust in its scabbard all day?"

"This is quite mad," he said, but moved his hand off the weapon's grip.

"Is it? Listen, you men. Listen to that wind. Isn't it stronger than it was an hour, two hours ago? Do you really think The Sarzana and his familiar, the Archon, are done with us? Now that they've got us on the open seas, weak of will, bleak of mind and heart, don't you think they'll cast a tempest against us? Do any of you believe they intend for us to return home so we can stand against them once more? If any of you do, *that* I term madness!

"Not that it matters what you believe. You are soldiers and sailors. You swore an oath to defend Konya with your lives. The only ones among you who've kept their oath, who still have their honor, lie back on the stern, sewn into canvas sails with coins in their mouths and a bit of pig iron at their feet to carry them down into the depths.

"The rest of you? What do *you* think of yourselves? How many of you fled the battle with never a shaft being fired, with never a spear being cast? Now, I call on you to obey me. We will attack The Sarzana once more. And this time we'll destroy him!"

"Obey you?" Bornu sneered. "An outlander? A woman?"

I turned to Xia. She stepped forward.

"I am Princess Xia Kanara," she said. "My father sits on the Council of Purity. I claim to speak for him. Are there any of you who will dispute that claim?"

"You're a child," Bornu said. "I swore no oath to obey you."

"But obey me you shall. And I command you to follow the orders to be given by Captain Rali Antero, who was handpicked by the council as one who best knows how to destroy The Sarzana. It is to all our shame this expedition wasn't put in her charge from the beginning."

I was impressed—I'd told Xia some of what I hoped she'd say if the occasion came up, but not this last.

Bornu began to say something, but before he could, Admiral Bhazana was beside Xia.

"Admiral," he said. "Both women are right. This is a day of infamy, and we must make recompense. I know I am not your superior in the naval lists, but you must obey Princess Xia and Captain Antero."

"*I* am Admiral Nepean Bornu, a landed baron," the other man replied, "and my family has served Konya for generations. I have a duty as well, and my duty is to take my ships safely home, where they may help protect Konya in the final battle to come. For me to follow the orders of you, my junior; this foreign sorceress, who may well be in league with The Sarzana himself and who brought this evil on our lands; and this stripling, who's besotted with the outlander . . . No. I refuse."

"I order you once again, Admiral," Xia said, her voice hard beyond her years.

"And I have my duty, a greater duty."

"Princess," I said. "I myself vowed to serve your council to bring down The Sarzana. I must tell you this man's words constitute treason."

There were low outcries from the officers, and I saw heads turn toward the device I'd had erected earlier.

"Not merely treason, but High Treason," I continued, "since he also spoke against the commands of the Council of Purity."

"Treason you call it, and treason it is," Xia said.

Bornu looked around wildly. Before he could move, or anyone could come to his aid, I said, "Sergeant Ismet!"

My women went down the companionway as if they were lionesses attacking, swords whipping out, spears at the rise, and arrows nocking. Ismet and Dacis had Bornu by the arms before his own sword could come out. The officers on deck were shouting now, and I saw the glitter of weapons.

"Sergeant! Hang him!"

Bornu shrieked and struggled, but could do nothing. In a moment he was dragged to the top of the companionway and to my device. It was a gibbet, a simple gallows I'd had constructed aboard our own galley, moved to Bhazana's flagship, and remounted. The rope went around his neck, hanging slackly down to his knees then up to the crossbar, its long knot set just behind his left ear.

I turned to Princess Xia. Her lips set in a firm, thin line.

"Execute the traitor," she said.

Sergeant Ismet swung the gibbet on its axis, and Bornu was sent stumbling out and down, off the deck and falling. The rope came tight, and over the wind's snarl I could hear the sound of his neck snapping. The body flipflopped, then hung limply from the rope's end. Now there was complete stillness.

"I condemned Admiral Bornu as a traitor," I said. "I further condemn all who disobey or disagree with the orders I have issued and am going to issue as traitors, and they will face the same penalty.

"You *will* obey me"—and I let the steel show—"or by the heavens, I will decimate every ship's crew, and then we'll go back into battle with bodies dangling from every yard if it is needed!"

I didn't give them time to recover.

"Now, I want all division and element captains in Admiral Bhazana's cabin immediately, and I'll give you orders to pass along to the others."

I said no more, but strode back into the shadows, and I heard the others behind me. I may've sounded like iron, but inside I felt my stomach turn. I'd dealt with fear and panic before, but never from so many. And while I'd ordered the law many times, up to and including the final penalty, even on one occasion sending a murderous Guardswoman who'd terribly shamed us to the city for sacrifice in the Kissing of the Stones as expiation, I'd never ordered anyone sent to their death out of hand, with no court, no recourse, no appeal.

But I saw then, and see now, nothing else that could've been done. When battle is on the cusp, there cannot be any debate or hesitation, and any weakness must be cut out as swiftly as a poisoned dart, or everything will die.

I note my scribe is intent on his writing and doesn't raise his head to meet my eyes. This is yet another part of war that isn't talked about by anyone, especially by those who wish to forget that killing is the heart of the matter, not battle songs, banners, parades, or armor gleaming in a summer sun. Remember what I said, Scribe, and tell this to your sons and daughters before you allow them to run laughing into the recruiter's embrace.

I was just as stern to the division officers when I gave my orders, although I did give them an explanation, mentioning, and this was the truth, that I'd checked with the shipmaster Oirot, and he'd confirmed that storms in these waters at this time of year were unheard of.

With Bornu's body now unseen, the officers had time to consider. Reluctantly, they agreed with me that it was most unlikely The Sarzana wouldn't attempt to finish us with magic, and that we were as unlikely to escape as if his fleet were still hounding us.

"Of course," one said, "we could always split up and make for home ship by ship, which would really give that bastard a chance to pick us off one by one."

While a bit of understanding hung in the air, I presented my plan. To-morrow I would send representatives to each ship and give the battle plan. Late in the afternoon, we would set sail back to Ticino and sail past the portal cities after full dark, which would mean we'd close on the fleet anchored in the roadstead near Ticino around midnight.

"A night attack," one officer said, and scowled. "My men aren't used to fighting in the dark."

"Do you think The Sarzana's are?"

The officer smiled a bit and shook his head.

"The advantage is always on the side of he who strikes first," I said. "Isn't that true? Isn't the day carried by the boldest?"

"What about magic?" another one asked. "My ships held until they saw those gods-blasted covered ships of theirs, and the ships behind them crewed by the dead."

I said neither the turtleships nor The Sarzana's magics would be as effective, their surprise gone. There would be Orissan magic cast before our attack began, magic that would shatter their spells like thin ice on a pond.

I gave them a flurry of other orders, to make sure the other ships' officers understood the overall plan, to make sure their ships were repaired as best they could manage, and most importantly to feed the sailors and rest them in watches. At dawn the division officers should attempt to reassemble those surviving ships belonging to their elements and stand by for orders.

All this was important, of course, but I wanted the Konyans to be so busy no one would have time to let cowardice creep into his heart again. I further told them that our Orissan galleys had been given special orders—to sail guard around the assembled fleet and ensure no one attempted to flee. "I won't," I said, "even bother putting up a gallows if I seize such a ship, but will send all its crew down to the sea demons unburied, so their ghosts will never rest."

I dismissed them and the others.

The Konyans summoned their boats, which lay just off Bhazana's ship, and one by one disappeared into the night. There were many looks cast back at the dangling corpse of Admiral Bornu.

I waited until the last was gone, then started down the boarding ladder to our longboat. Admiral Bhazana asked me for a private moment, and I stepped away.

"They'll obey now," he said firmly. "And so will I."

I looked at him very long, very hard. But I made no answer as I went down into my boat.

ABOARD OUR own ship, I knew there would be no rest for the remainder of the night for any of us, least of all me. This was the second night I'd go sleepless, so I'd have to force myself to get at least two hours or so of rest during the day, or I'd be as worthless as a toy dagger in battle.

My first tasks weren't those of a war leader, but of an Evocator. First I had to divert the storm that was building, which would most likely strike during the night. But that was where the surprises began.

"We can't cast a spell that directly," Gamelan said.

"Why? I know he's got great powers, greater than ours, but it seems—"

"You don't realize?" Gamelan said, his voice showing surprise.

"Realize what?"

"I thought you knew, and that was where your idea to strike back came from. The Archon believes you dead."

"What? How? Why?" I must've sounded as dumb as I did the first time my watch commander told me my unchecked sentry had taken the opportunity to let two wine sellers into the compound after taking and drinking a full gallon as her share.

"You still are a journeyman," he sighed. "Remember back aboard Trahern's ship, when I smeared a bit of your blood on that shield or whatever the reflecting metal was? I said a few words when I did, hoping some of my powers had come back, since that spell's something a veritable baby Evocator can cast, especially if the seer is looking from afar."

"Oh. The bronze was a mirror, intended to reflect . . . me?" I guessed.

"Just so. When the Archon cast about, in the flurry and frenzy of battle, with wisps of spell and smoke and magic all about, he 'saw' you aboard Trahern's ship. You don't think he gave one tinker's damn about that old bastard, do you? Why would he bother casting whatever spell he sent out to explode that ship like it was a melon dropped from a tower? You were his target, and as far as he knows he succeeded.

"I'd frankly suspect that was why the pursuit turned back and why this storm has taken so long to build. This fleet's destruction may be The Sarzana's ultimate dream, but it's hardly the Archon's. He knows he can destroy Konya when and how he wants, now that you're gone.

"I think we've also solved another puzzle as well. Remember when we wondered just why The Sarzana would allow word to slip out that we'd rescued him, rather than it appearing like some grand miracle all his very own?

"Again, it wasn't his idea, but the Archon's. The Archon must have sent some sort of whispering spell across Konya so that everyone *knew* the Orissans had freed The Sarzana, but none knew where they'd gotten the knowledge.

"He must have your death in hand, and, unlike crude villains such as Nisou Symeon or arrogant men like Raveline of the Far Kingdoms, he's quite content to let others kill his snakes for him."

"He's behaving like I'm some great Evocator, like I was you, with all the powers of the Orissan Evocators' Guild behind me. The man, if that's what he still is, isn't a coward. Am I to believe he's that great a fool?"

"Don't be absurd, Rali. Consider it from his perspective. If you and your brother were great wizards, once in league with even greater magicians to the east, and your plans were first stopped short by someone named Antero, and then your own brother killed by another possibly even more powerful Antero, what actions would you take? It's quite clear that you do have great powers, even if they're still developing."

I was silent, considering. Then I shook my thoughts away. "Be that as it may, Evocator, we have a spell to work out. Let's come up with something that keeps me still dead. I like it a great deal better being out from under that bastard's gimlet gaze."

And so we did, in about an hour. It was a powerful spell, yet a simple one, a spell of delay, not negation. The storm would continue, would still build, but would take at least two days to reach its full fury. Neither of us thought the Archon would sense any opposition, especially since, if Gamelan's reasoning was correct, he had little immediate interest in our scattered warships.

The second spell was more hazardous and chanced exposing the fact I was still alive. But I thought the risk worth taking. I drained a few drops of mercury from the binnacle our compass needle floated on. With that, and a bit of the "flying" unguent, I sat alone in Gamelan's cabin. I lit a single candle, fed it certain herbs, sprinkled an aromatic oil from Gamelan's kit on it, and breathed deeply of the fumes. Next I set a steel mirror beside the candle and concentrated all my attention, my being, on the reflection of that candle. The distance, the remove, would keep "me" safe from being found out, or so I hoped. But I had no concern for the Archon, no thought for The Sarzana as I became the flame, no more than the flame, only the flame.

> *Fire, fire*
> *Elemental fire*
> *There is no other*
> *There is no other*
> *You live alone*
> *You need no other*
> *You are the moment*
> *You are the fire*

The one who was Rali Antero was gone, was absent, and there was only a small flame, looking to illuminate the dark. The fire was fed a trifle of the unguent on a piece of wood, and flared, and became something else, and found new surprise and joy at flying, at flying over water, over land, over its two great enemies. The flame "saw" itself reflected in that tiny drop of mercury, and somehow the fire felt what a human would've known as words:

Now there's another
Now you've a brother
Fire seek
Fire find

Now I was for just a moment that drop of mercury, and again for an instant I "felt" for my brother. In the same moment I found "him," there was ice across my soul, and I could feel darkness gathering, coiling behind me, and in that same instant *I was fire, I was alone,* I was the candle, I was safely back aboard ship, and knew, my drop of mercury having "found" that larger pool of liquid metal that floated atop The Sarzana's table, just where I could find and kill him.

This time we wouldn't be sailing blindly into battle. But it would be a deadly fight—The Sarzana's refuge was the most secure place in Ticino. There'd be much blood shed winkling him out.

It was almost dawn. I spent the last hour before the sun rose drawing an exact map of Ticino and our objectives. Then I cut it into almost two hundred pieces, said a simple duplicating spell, and my table crashed to the deck under the weight of two hundred full-size maps of our target. I could find nothing more to do, so I turned matters over to Corais and collapsed into a dreamless sleep.

WHEN I AWOKE, I had a screen erected on the quarterdeck and took a saltwater shower, dumping buckets of water over my head that one of my privates hauled up and passed to me. It wasn't what I wanted—what I wanted was a long soak in a scented bathtub like the ones in my family's villa: a tub about as large as the entire deck I stood on with water as hot as that cast by a geyser, as soft as a kiss, and perfumed with the most expensive oils and salts. I allowed a moment to dream. A soak, followed by a long massage. The massager would be Xia, although a part of my mind wondered how she had gotten to Orissa, but that wasn't important since we'd both be naked, and she would slowly rub the oil into my skin, her nipples hardening as they caressed my back, and then . . .

. . . and then Corais begged the captain's pardon and said there was a signal from Nor's galley. So I put aside the dreams of what would've come after, the carefully chosen meal, the slow twining of our bodies as we coupled on a silken bed, and then hour after hour of dreamless sleep, to wake once more to the scent of love, and no damned war, sorcerers, or order-giving.

I said to ignore whatever his signal was, but to order him to our galley at once. I dried myself off, feeling the itching start as the salt dried, and put on my battle gear.

I had the quarterdeck cleared of all but the watch officer and helmsman, and had Nor brought to me by two fully armed Guardswomen. I wasn't sure what I'd say to him—he was a hard man, harder than Bhazana or his captains. He knew his officers had broken their oath when they went sailing off to blind destruction, and I saw no point in reminding him. Instead, I told him neither he nor the other two galleys would be needed in this battle, which was why they weren't summoned to the conference on Bhazana's ship. He visibly flinched, then gritted that there was no way of stopping him.

I said there was indeed, and I would have no compunctions about ordering three of Bhazana's ships against each of his. The Broken Men were feared and hated by the others, because they reminded sailors of what could be their fate. Also the other men were eager to prove themselves still warriors, and would leap to my bidding.

He said nothing, and there was nothing to say—he knew I was right. He sagged. "Is there no chance of changing your orders? I will not apologize for what Yanno and Nasby did, but they did break the oath we all swore. I can't expect you to believe any promise I make, but it shall not happen again. All my men saw their brothers die, with no harm at all coming to The Sarzana."

Now I had him. I told him he had only one option, and told him what it was. This was the only way he could fight in the battle and possibly make amends for his men's broken promises. He started to protest, then stopped, realizing I meant what I said, and even though my orders would result in giving up everything they'd planned and the way they'd dreamed of fighting; it was that or nothing.

Reluctantly, he agreed. I told him he had two hours to ready his men to transshipment, and we would have boats standing by at that time.

And so it was. Even as his men were taken off their galleys, their ships were taken in tow by the larger Konyan vessels. Heavy longboats busied themselves around those hulks too badly damaged to return to battle, lifting their stone ballast out of the bilges to provide fresh ammunition for others' trebuchets. Then those ships were abandoned and scuttled.

The fleet set sail for Ticino. We moved slowly, our speed held down by those damaged vessels that would've been abandoned and scuttled if I'd intended using normal tactics, but now, together with Nor's Broken Men, they'd be the opening wedge in my attack.

As we sailed, boats were crossing back and forth from ship to ship, taking certain supplies to the damaged vessels, taking sailors from ship to ship and seeing to other tasks.

I myself was busy. I'd told Bhazana I needed five ships with only the bravest crew, for a special task. He didn't need to think for more than a minute, but said I could take five from Captain Yezo's squadron. They were crewed by men who'd escaped from islands that'd been ravaged by The Sarzana, and Yezo's entire family had been slain by The Sarzana years ago when he held the throne.

I'd heard too much talk of bravery from these people, and seen damned little, so I told Bhazana I'd judge for myself. I had myself rowed to each of the ships whose crews had volunteered. Grudgingly, since at the moment I felt little warmth for these damned Konyans, it appeared they might be capable of what I wanted, although I knew, as always, battle is the only truth. I must take my chances. I wished I had a battalion of Guardswomen, or even enough to provide a stiffening squad on each ship, but of course I didn't.

I made very sure each sailor on each ship knew exactly what he would be required to do, and how unlikely he'd see the sunrise on the morrow. No one stepped back. If the hulks Nor's men now crewed were my opening wedge, these five ships would be the levers to pry the door full open.

I HAD THE MOST skilled whittler on our ship sent to me, and gave him his orders. Surprisingly, it was the murderous Santh, Fyn's compatriot. I began to explain why I wanted what I wanted, but he already knew.

"The son of a poxed whore sent sorcery agin' us," he said. "On'y fair if you c'n use it to turn it back agin him." He tossed the chunk of soft wood in his hand measuringly, then, humming something utterly tuneless to my ears, set to work.

LATER, IN GAMELAN'S CABIN, the old wizard had a chance to put his slowly renewing talent into practice. I remember how pleased I was as he held his hands over me, brow furrowed in concentration as he chanted:

"Turn away
Turn away
Your eyes are bothered
There's naught to see."

He finished the spell, touched my head and either shoulder with a larch twig, and shrugged. "Well, if I've got any powers back, and if I remembered that baby incantation correctly, I've given you some protection from the Archon, at least for a *spell*."

He smiled a little at his feeble joke, and I laughed, not so much at his words, but because it was heartening to see Gamelan's spirits return to what they'd been before Konya. I hoped his powers continued returning apace, and sensed if they didn't, he'd drop back into his former gloom.

His smile faded and he looked anxious. "Can you tell, Rali?"

His spell may have been simple in its execution, but I thought its intent quite clever. It was a subtle variation of the Archon's spell that'd hidden the turtleships under a fog bank, though requiring far less energy and materials to cast. It was intended only for magical "vision," so that further simplified it. If an Evocator happened to be "looking" at an area where I was, his "eyes" would sting slightly, as if water droplets had been flipped in them, as indeed Gamelan had Pamphylia do when he started. It would be simpler and more convenient to look elsewhere, at something else, although that thought should never pass across the conscious mind of the seer.

"Now, how could I tell? I'm not very good yet at 'seeing.' Perhaps we might evoke an Archon or three and ask them?" I said, my own spirits brought up by Gamelan.

"Well, if it works, it works," Gamelan said. "If it doesn't, can I have your grimoire?"

We laughed and moved to the next piece of magic. Before we began, I wondered aloud what it would be like to live in a world where magic never existed.

"Impossible," Gamelan snorted. "That would be like dreaming of a world without water to drink or air to breathe."

My next thought was equally unimportant: "Since mostly battle-magic doesn't work, or doesn't work very well in the confusion of spells and counterspells, what would happen if you'd go into combat without bothering to cast any?"

"Did you ever heat an empty wine jug in a fire, and then, before it could cool, stuff a cork tightly into its mouth?"

"The one time I tried it as a child, the jug shattered across the kitchen and my father sent me to my room for the rest of the day without a meal. But Amalric had better luck, and told me the cork was sucked into the jug with a loud pop."

"Exactly what would happen if you fought a war without Evocators and their spells, even if they are mostly mummery or ineffective. The fire drove something out of that wine jug, and the emptiness was too great, pulling the cork in after it. Your enemy's magic would be drawn over you like a bait net, and you'd be swept up like a school of minnows."

"So it must be then, spell and counterspell and counter-counterspell and counter-counter—"

"Rali, we have to work to do."

We did. But before we went back to alembic and wand, I did have a wistful thought about that world without magic. Gods, but war would be simpler if all you had to rely on was your brain, your muscles, and your sword. In a world like that, there probably wouldn't be any armies, since there would've been no need to develop them, and men and women would settle their differences as our primitive fathers did, in single combat.

Once we had our magics ready, we summoned the surviving Konyan Evocators to our galley. There were only four—the rest had died when the Archon exploded Admiral Trahern's galley. But that gave us four acolytes, since the Konyans were indeed somewhat behind Orissan skills. We'd gathered those few unopened bags of wind from the other ships, and, with those as a base, cast an incantation that would hopefully give the fleet not only a fair wind up the gut toward Ticino, but one we might control as to intensity and even direction.

I'd suggested this last might be achieved by placing one of the small longboat compasses in the mouth of the leather bag, and, as the spell was being chanted by the four Konyans, I snapped the needle with a fingernail so it spun wildly. One of the Konyans said when we were finished that my addition would likely mean the winds would either blow from all directions at once or else we'd have a cyclone. I paid him no attention, knowing better.

As we sailed closer, the Archon's building storm disappeared, and I was reassured—if he was tracking us magically, he certainly would've moved the eye of his storm along with our ships.

It was mid-afternoon when we sighted the first of the offshore islands. I'd become my flock of terns once more and scouted ahead of the fleet. I wasn't in any danger of being discovered, even in this familiar guise, as long as I stayed well away from the mainland. Most of the islands' watching posts had been abandoned, their men recalled to Ticino after they'd seen our ships sail past in disarray, and those still manned had sentries who were hardly at their most alert. Even so, when we approached, another spell was begun. We were taking no chances. It was fortunate the day was cloudy, although I'd thought of an alternative incantation if the skies had been clear. On the open deck we set five braziers on high tripods to mark each point of a pentagram. In each brazier we burnt incense we thought pleasing to the Konyan gods of the air, and—more important—herbs as well, herbs that should bring magical potency whether the gods favored it or not: laurel, mountain star, kalumb root, and monkshood.

In the middle of the pentagram, Gamelan had chalked symbols on the deck where I knelt before a low charcoal fire. Different herbs were cast into the fire, dandelion root and plantain among them, and a pot set to boil atop it. When the pot seethed and the steam billowed, I read certain names I'd written down on a scroll, together with a guide to their pronunciation. I didn't know what language they were in, nor, surprisingly, did Gamelan.

"This is one of those spells that've been handed down from Evocator to Evocator since I do not know when. No one I asked—when it was my time to memorize these words—knew a translation, other than this was a way to call the clouds to cover you, and was mostly used by witches in the farming areas to lessen the effect of a blistering early summer sun on young plants."

We'd modified the spell for our own needs, and, as I said the words, stumbling over their arcane pronunciation, I glanced up and saw that very slowly, very majestically, the clouds were coming down to join their fellow, as we'd bidden them. We stopped the ceremony before the fog became so thick we couldn't see from ship to ship. It would be absurd if the magic intended to conceal so blinded us that we rammed and sank each other, with no necessity for an enemy.

Now magic and magicians were transferred to Admiral Bhazana's flagship. There was no room here on Stryker's galley, nor would it be the safest place when battle was joined. One Konyan was put in charge of maintaining the fog spell and ordered to chant the words if the fog began dissipating; the other three were set to maintaining the wind conjuration. Gamelan wondered if they were to be depended on and thought perhaps he should stay with them. A trace of his former bitterness showed when he said, "At least an old man like me wouldn't get in anyone's way over there."

I was about to retort, but Pamphylia was quicker. "Why sir," she said pertly, "you *must* be with us during the landing. I mean, *someone* has to be in the vanguard who's capable of raping, as they say all soldiers must."

Gamelan snorted, but his good humor came back.

XIA WAS IN OUR cabin when I entered. It was time for me to put on my battle harness. Xia wore the uniform of the Maranon Guard, had her armor nearby, and sat on her clothes chest, looking at the bare sword she'd trained with so hard as if she'd never seen it before.

"Princess," I began, speaking formally, since what I was going to say was an order, not a request and not from a lover; or at least I hoped I'd reached my decision using logic, not love. "When we go into battle—"

Xia interrupted, "When we go into battle, I shall be beside you, Captain."

I stopped. I'd figured she'd object to what I was going to tell her—to transfer to Admiral Bhazana's galley, or at the very least remain aboard Stryker's ship when we landed in Ticino, and had a response ready for that.

But she'd slipped the mat from under me by using my title, just as I'd attempted to start the discussion on more formal ground by doing the same.

"No Kanara has ever fought a battle from the safety of their tent. I shall not shame that tradition," she said.

"All right," I said. "That's quite admirable, Princess. But you are the last Kanara. What if—"

"Then my father will have to legitimize one or another of his bastards, and possibly even marry one of his concubines," she said. "And those weak-bellied sons of his lust'll bring the family heritage crashing down in ten years.

"But what of it?" she said. "I care little about what happened before I was born, unless it affects me, and less about what happens after my death.

"For all I know—or care—when I am taken by the one you call the Seeker, this whole world will flicker and die like a blown-out candle. Perhaps all of this has been put here just for my amusement."

I was about to say something at *this* piece of rather incredible arrogance when I saw she was hiding a grin and that there was a wicked glint to her eye.

She laid the sword down on the deck and stood. "There is another tradition in my family," she said, her voice husky as she came to me. I was wearing only boots, a loose open-necked tunic that ended at mid-thigh, and my own weapons belt. That fell to the deck with a thud, and her hands were on my shoulders, pulling my tunic down to my waist as my nipples rose, and then it, too, was on the deck and she lifted me in her arms and laid me atop it.

Xia never undressed, but took me as a warrior might take a maiden given him as a war prize. Her lips and fingers were everywhere, caressing, stroking, then forcing, and I was thrashing, feeling the deck timbers scrape on my back, trying to keep from crying aloud as she sent me soaring high, higher even than my magic.

Eventually, in a day, a week, or a year, I came back, to see Xia lying on her side next to me, running a fingernail gently across my skin.

"A delightful tradition," I managed. "I think it's one the Anteros should adopt."

I forced energy and turned toward her, but she shook her head.

"After the battle, my Rali. After we've destroyed them. Then there'll be time and more for love."

AT FULL DARK our ships slid past the portal cities. None of the ships showed lights, nor did I hear any shouts from any vessel as we slid along. I wished this had been the way it was two days earlier. There would now be several thousand men still breathing and dreaming of their homes and glory, instead of rotting as silent corpses rolled along the ocean floor by the tides.

We'd arranged the order of battle before entering the gut. Now those half-wrecked hulks manned by Nor's Broken Men and other volunteers were in the vanguard. Our seven galleys were just behind, sailing in close company with Captain Yezo's five Konyan ships. Astern was Admiral Bhazana's flagship and the rest of the fleet. I'd made no suggestions, issued no orders other than that his ships were to close with and destroy any enemy they encountered. I assumed, or at least hoped, the division and ship captains were competent at ordering their own formations. I said it'd be unlikely they'd face the same problems with the enemy evading close battle during this night engagement as they'd had earlier, since we would hopefully have the surprise as an ally. Finally, I ordered that no ship was to withdraw from battle unless specifically ordered by me, and no one else, and that a great spell had been cast to send sea demons up to destroy any ship or sailor who disobeyed.

Not wanting to end my orders with such a lie, I'd thought for a moment, then scribbled, "No man who sets his course toward the sound of battle this night can do wrong. The gods strike for Konya!"

Then there was nothing for me to do for a long while except wait, and pray we weren't discovered.

Corais was beside me in the forepeak. We watched the lights of the portal cities fade behind us as we sailed on toward Ticino. I turned away, to go back to the quarterdeck. She put a hand out to stop me.

"When you are back in Orissa," she said, "on the first day of summer, would you authorize a tournament of archers in my name? And let it be open to all, especially girls who might be drawn to join the Guard?"

I began to say something, then found other words. "I will," I said. "And you'll be the main judge, and make the sacrifice to Maranonia."

"Make it of the early summer flowers. Roses, wisterias, lilacs and such," she said. "Shed no blood in my name."

"Very well," I said. "But there's one condition—you'll have to keep your hands off the archers, at least until their mothers have their backs turned."

Corais smiled, and her fingers touched the bit of The Sarzana's robe tied around her upper arm.

"I thank you," she said, but no more.

TICINO GLIMMERED through the night and haze. Now I'd find out if my strategy would work. My main concerns hadn't been its potential, but whether our attack had been magically discovered and a trap laid for us; plus, of course, the larger worry about whether the Konyans would fight or flee again.

I'd ordered the immediate return to The Sarzana's stronghold not from rage, nor to justify the old saw that a thrown horseman, if he ever wishes to ride without fear, must remount, but because I knew soldiers. After a victory, particularly a victory as smashingly one-sided as theirs, celebration is in order. Soldiers wish to drink, eat, couple, and reaffirm their hold on the world of the living.

Ideally we should've counterattacked the same night we'd been driven out, but that'd been clearly impossible. But when I reflected further, remembering how some of my postbattle hangovers had lingered, even when I'd soddenly attempted to drink them away, attacking The Sarzana on the second day might mean his forces were even less capable. We would know in bare moments. I could see the outline of the anchored Konyan ships against the bright lights of Ticino. I could hear the shouts of celebrants, the clashing music of military marches and drinking songs, and see the flare of torches on gondolas as they wove through the canals that were Ticino's thoroughfares. There were but few lights in the harbor, not even the masthead truck lights most ships set when anchored.

I gave an order, and Sergeant Ismet opened the shutter of her bull's-eye lantern in the long, short, long signal I'd arranged. The Evocators on Bhazana's ship should be obeying and increasing their chants. I felt the wind from the stern freshen, and Gamelan, who was standing beside me, said, "At least they can follow orders. So far, anyway."

"They'd better," Polillo gritted. "Or *I'll* learn magic and cast some sort of spell that'll make what little remains of their cocks shrivel and fall off."

She looked at Corais, expecting some rejoinder, but all she got was a wan smile and silence. Polillo looked concerned, then shrugged and went forward to her station at the catapults.

Our sails filled, and Duban hissed orders to set a reef—the wind was intended to help other, slower craft. It did—the large mainsails on the hulks ahead filled, and the ships groaned as they were forced to speed. Tiny white wavelets appeared beside their bluff bows as they went forward. Captain Yezo's ships also wallowed past at their full speed, their duties to begin before ours.

Thus far my strategy was working perfectly, and I began to worry, remembering the old adage that if your battle plan goes off without a hitch, you're walking into an ambush. A signal light flashed from an enemy picket boat, and a challenge shouted. Seconds later the first of Yezo's ships smashed into the tiny craft and sent its splintered fragments to the bottom. Men's screams drowned as the sea took them. Torches flamed on the Konyan hulks as my plan continued. These crippled ships were sacrifices, fireships, and as we'd sailed back toward Ticino, they'd been loaded with flammables—oil barrels lashed to masts, other barrels below decks with old wax-drenched sails and tarred rigging to feed the flames. When the Konyan sorcerers had fed the wind, Nor's Broken Men and other volunteers aboard the hulks had smashed in the tops of the casks and lit fires.

Flame roared into the night, and I heard screams and shouts as watches on The Sarzana's ships came out of their stupor. In the red and yellow flames, men were outlined on the fireships as they flung their torches into the flammable deck cargo and when the main decks were engulfed, ran for escape, the longboats towed behind each hulk. On one ship they didn't run fast enough, and the fire reached out and took them, screaming, into its embrace. The fireships were glowing like paper lanterns as they bore down on the anchored enemy.

The roadstead was chaos as The Sarzana's sailors tumbled on deck, fuddled by sleep or drink. I imagined the poor bastards trying to decide what to do, which of the many screamed orders to obey. Here and there alert seamen axed mooring lines as the fireships closed, and the wind caught those ships and sent them drifting out of control down on their sisters. One of The Sarzana's galleys wasn't able to float free in time, and a fireship rammed it. Flames roared across to the other ship, and the great torch screamed up at the heavens. Another and then a third of The Sarzana's galleys gouted into firestorms.

Behind us I heard thuds and crashes, as the few war machines on the Konyan ships began launching missiles. They were still at too great a range, and water spouts rose from the dark waters like deadly plants. Then one and another boulder smashed home against the decks of The Sarzana's ships. Fire arrows arced out over the night sky, and here and there more flames flickered on enemy decks.

The lead Konyan ship smashed into an enemy, and grapnels went across, and the storming parties, shouting for blood, swarmed over the bulwarks. Another ship laid alongside it, and a third at its stern. Even these cumbersome Konyan galleys could learn the tactics we'd devised, and worry their prey like packs of hunting beasts.

Our own mast-slashing catapults were firing, from our galley and the other Orissan ships. The masts of The Sarzana's ships were easy targets, outlined black against the flames. But it didn't matter whether my bolts struck true or went on to crash into the city itself—they, like everything else, were intended only to wreak havoc and bring confusion. But from the happy yips and shouts from the foredeck, Polillo was thoroughly enjoying herself after that long day earlier of inaction and defeat.

We had the greatest weapon of all on our side, surprise, and I intended to keep it. All this was diversion for my attack against the Archon. But I had one task before I could go for the kill. Closer to shore lay the turtleships.

They were clearly crewed by more elite or sober seamen; almost half of them had their oars out, had slipped their moorings, and were under way.

I took from its box the small model of the turtleship that Santh had carved so carefully and which I'd treated with a spell and touched with the broadhead of an enemy arrow, to ensure it "knew" its larger brothers and would seek them out. I set the model in a water-filled pan, not so much to further the emulation, but to prevent firing our own ship. I unstopped a vial and dripped lantern oil onto the little ship:

"Oil take life
Oil must grow
Oil take wing
Oil take fire."

I touched a splinter of wood to the illuminating fire in the binnacle until it flickered into life, then held it against the oil-soaked model.

"Now you are fire
Now you have power
You are strong against the night
You end the night
None can stand
All must fall
Reach out and take
All like all
And all is meat
Fire reach out."

The turtleships exploded. I thought grimly that the Archon's weapon I'd first glimpsed in the sea of volcanoes had now flowered and turned back on him. *All* the turtleships were caught by my spell and seared into ruin. The armor plating that'd made them arrow-proof was now a trap. I saw very few sailors scramble out of the ships' hatches before they charred to the water-line, rolled, and went under, the magical fire burning them faster than any earthly flame could've.

The harbor was as light as full day. City lights were blazing on as Ticino stumbled back to alertness, but I didn't have time to worry about that as I began yet another spell. I didn't think this was necessary, but the Konyans had broken once before at an illusion, and I had no intention of losing this battle if that conjuration was used again.

Gamelan had a brazier ready, and onto it I sprinkled, among other dried herbs, wort and rue against sorcery, and rosemary as a guardian against death.

"Eyes, see!
Eyes unblinded
See what is
See what is
See the truth
See through the veil
See beyond the mist
Eyes unfooled."

The tiny cloud of smoke grew and grew, and spread behind us, across the Konyan ships, and then vanished. I'd warned Admiral Bhazana of my incantation to keep the living-dead illusion from taking effect and instructed him to tell his sailors not to take alarm, but even so I heard shouts of fear, and a couple of ships veered from their course. I swore, but had no time for that, either, because Captain Yezo's five ships were closing on their targets. Those were the five sea gates from the ocean into Ticino's canals, normally kept closed to lessen the tide's effect. I saw soldiers running onto the waterfront in fighting order and showering the ships with arrows and spears. But it was far too late.

Now it was time to shed my Evocator's cloak, such as it was, and gladly return to what I knew best. Sword in hand, I pelted off the quarterdeck and forward, along the storming bridge, to where my assault party waited. Xia grinned, a hard humorless smile she probably wasn't even aware of, and now we were closing on the Ticino docks.

Five of Yezo's ships—five seagates . . . I'd ordered him to strike directly in from the sea at the gates, where the water would be deepest. One veered to the side either by accident or perhaps because the helmsman had been hit, and ran aground, hard against the enbankment. But evidently the soldiers didn't recognize the intent of the attack, because some of them broke off firing at the other four and ran to concentrate fire on the stricken ship that had failed in its mission. Yezo's ships were seconds from crashing, and I saw that his men were as disciplined as he'd boasted. Sailors, ignoring the arrow storm, were cutting the ropes that bound anchors to improvised derricks hung over the ships' sterns, as they'd hastily trained to do, and the anchors splashed into the dark harbor waters.

Yezo's four ships struck. I heard the rending crashes loud above the roar of the battle in the roadstead as all four struck fair into the center of the entry ports, sending the sailors aboard sprawling. Then the men came back to their feet as the ships they'd deliberately wrecked lurched and rolled on their beam ends, then back, and were at the crude windlasses we'd had mounted on the quarterdecks, kedging the ships out of our way.

I heard Stryker shouting for full sail, and Duban crying to our oarsmen for speed and more speed, but I was intent on Yezo's craft. Slowly, laboriously, one, two, then three were moving back, freeing the canal mouths. On the fourth I saw a flicker as both anchor cables snapped and whipped back across the decks, cutting men down as they lashed. But three gates were open to the canals, our passage into the heart of the city. Three openings, and on his flagship Cholla Yi was bellowing and I was shouting, and our oars were coming up, feathered, as our galleys, driven by that now high magical wind from the Evocators, shot into their galleys. I heard wood scream and rend as one ship ground along the stone canal banks, but it mattered not how close the fit was as long as we were still moving.

The waterway widened, and we could row, and our ships drove onward. Ticino's planners had laid out their city logically—the canals ran straight from the waterfront and ended around the city's main square. That efficiency would doom the city. Ahead was the empty square overhung by The Sarzana's huge round tower. I had a moment to glance behind, as I heard the din of battle building, and knew what was happening. Yezo's men were coming off their ships as they'd been ordered—swimming, jumping, or hopefully using the long planks we'd put aboard as gangways. Their orders now were simple—to spread panic in the city by fire and sword. They'd been told to spare the citizens and take no loot, but I knew better than to expect that of most of them. Not far behind them, if the battle in the roadstead went as hoped, the other Konyan ships would be landing troops with the same orders.

I wanted chaos, because if Ticino was drowned in rack and ruin, our real enemies might not notice my women and the mercenaries striking for their throats.

I heard Duban shriek pain as "his ship," our galley, slammed into the stone wharf at the edge of the square, but what of that? If we lived, the Konyans would rebuild our galleys a thousand times over before we sailed for home. Gangplanks slammed down and we poured ashore, onto the hard stone square of Ticino. Other men came sliding out of the galleys they'd taken. But there was no time to pause or even look around, and I was running hard for the stairs that curled up to the causeways to the tower. There were five—no, six—sentries, but they were dead, stumbling down with shafts in their chests that'd punched through their armor as if it wasn't there.

The causeways were open, and I could see into the heart of The Sarzana's stronghold, and we were running harder than before, desperate to get inside before the gates that must exist could crash closed. There were archers on the top of the ring wall ahead of us, and an arrow scraped brick next to me and pinwheeled away. Our bows thrummed, and arrows sang away, and those walls were bare.

I heard the battle cries of my women, Corais' yip-yipping like the savage fox she was, and felt a flash of brief joy. This was what I'd built the Guard for, what I'd led them toward. Now they were my shining battle blade, and now I'd strike a deathblow with them. We were united in that moment, in that blood-drenched run down the causeway, past the slumped bodies of soldiers. This was what my life was meant to be, not an endless array of hobbling up and down at sentry-go, or crouching around a fire muttering incantations like some dried-body crone, but even as the red thought came through my blood joy, I knew it was false.

We were a few yards from the short tunnel that led through the tower's ring wall into an inner keep, when rusting metal, long-unused, grated, and I saw the iron spikes of a portcullis slide down from an overhead slot. Then Locris and Polillo slammed into it, keeping it from closing. Four other women—I don't remember three of them, but one was Legate Neustria—leapt past me, and one of them jammed a spear into the groove the second, inner portcullis was supposed to travel down, and jammed it. I stood in the center of that tunnel and saw Polillo impossibly holding the iron grating by herself, and then Locris reappeared, half carrying, half dragging a balk of lumber that she forced up into position, bracing the portcullis open, and the way was open.

Up the causeway ran the rest of my women from the other galleys, and behind them Cholla Yi and his men. Far below, in the square, I saw three figures, and knew they were Gamelan, indomitable even in his blindness, and his two escorts. There were bodies down on the causeway, bodies of my Guardswomen, too many for me to keep my eyes on, and I turned back toward the keep on the other side of this tunnel that led to the tower. From above me, through a murder hole in the center of the tunnel's roof, a crossbow string snapped and a bolt slashed into Locris' side, burying itself nearly to the vanes. She screamed, clawed at the bolt, took two steps, and died. A bow woman sped a shaft back through the slot, but there was no one there, or at least we heard no sound of a hit.

We were running again, out of the tunnel into the lighter darkness of the keep, and now the great round tower rose above us. Its monstrous gates were barred, and in line in front of them was a company of crossbowmen.

I shouted, "Down," and we were flat, just as we'd trained so long in our mock charges, and Xia thudded down beside me as the crossbow strings twanged as loudly as slashed ship cables, and the bolts whined overhead, catching only one or two of Cholla Yi's men, who'd never learned to duck.

Five yards from me, Dica leapt to her feet. "Come on! Before they've time to reload," she shouted, and was running, sword high, no one else on her feet, and before I had a chance to shout warning, the front row of cross-bowmen knelt and the second rank fired, and Dica contorted, hurling her blade high into the night sky, and then she fell.

The night was suddenly red, not the red of fire but of blood, as the Guard came up and charged, screaming rage, and poured across the court-yard like quicksilver, like lightning. Ismet was beside me, snarling like a jungle cat for her once-lover as she ran, and we were among the crossbowmen with sword and axe before any of them had time to cock their pieces, and so they died to a man where they stood. Guardswomen went down with them—in that fierce moment of slaughter Neustria and Jacena went to the Seeker, along with others.

I had a mere second to mourn Dica. Of course she'd erred in rushing the bowmen before she realized they hadn't shot their course, but she died bravely and she died at the head of her troops. I wondered how many Guardswomen might've hesitated before charging, given that front rank time to reload, and died if it hadn't been for Dica's unknowing sacrifice. That's the way all too many of my best have met the Seeker, and why the Maranon Guard has buried as many officers as privates.

The huge gates into the keep were barred, but our sudden bloody rush had left the soldiers without time to close their small sally port, and before anyone within could move, we were inside.

Polillo somehow had gotten in front of me, and there were three soldiers coming at her. I suppose to them, she was a blur, a killing engine, but to me her movements were very precise, very slow and exact as she used the head of her axe to shove one man back into another, then, while they stumbled, recovering, to change her thrust and lunge as if the axe were a halberd, and bury its curved head in the third man's throat. Without changing stance, she recovered, her enormous strength pulling the axe's head free as the other two came at her. She batted the first man's sword out of line like a kitten with a stick, and with the backswing used the bill to hook and snap the neck of the second man. The first man shrieked and tried to flee, but Polillo, still moving as carefully as if she were demonstrating the Art of the Axe to awe-stricken recruits, sent it crashing into the back of his spine and the man flopped away like a gaffed fish.

A man lunged with a long bill, and Xia slashed through the weapon's wooden shaft and the man's arm as well. Spouting gore, he shrieked and fell.

In that instant I "felt" the spell Gamelan had cast vanish, and knew I stood naked to the gaze of the Archon. I "heard" a scream of surprised rage, and we all felt the stone flags under our feet grind and rumble, as if we were in an earthquake, but I knew it was just another sign of the Archon's shock at having been fooled, as he realized I yet lived.

I shouted the charge again, and we dashed down a long, twisting corridor. Squads of soldiers came out of doorways, and arrows flashed past or found a target, spears clattering against stone walls as The Sarzana's guard tried to stop us, tried to rally, but couldn't, and the men were driven back into their cuddies or they died. Then the corridor ended and the roof rose high, and we were in The Sarzana's throne room. The domed ceiling was a hundred feet above, the chamber two hundred feet or more in diameter. The walls were hung with tapestries or battle standards, and there were flaring torches on the walls and a huge fire guttering down at one wall.

The room was empty save for my soldiers and, on a high-raised dais in the center of the room, The Sarzana. That is all any of my women, or Cholla Yi and the handful of men who'd followed us down the corridor, saw.

I saw more.

Standing above The Sarzana, looming like a puppeteer bestride his marionettes, was the Archon! He was huge, maybe thirty feet, and I could see the stones of the far wall through his only partially material body. His arms were coming up, to strike at me.

Corais was beside me, and her bow came up and was full-drawn, broadhead against wood, her fingers holding steady beside her ear. She was as firm and calm as if she were at the butts, and then she loosed and the arrow sped true, straight for The Sarzana. His hand came out, and I swear it was moving as slowly as a fly in honey, but he plucked her shaft from midair and snapped it between two fingers. As he did, I heard a *crack,* and Corais' bow, the one that'd been made so lovingly so long ago, cracked like a twig or like the arrow The Sarzana now tossed aside.

We broke into a run, a desperate charge toward the dais as The Sarzana's right hand lifted, fingers curled like a snake head, and green fire like that I'd seen on the ship's masts during a storm flickered, and then gathered into a ball and flashed toward us. It sent Corais spinning. I thought she was dead, but then she rolled to her feet, her face bloodied as if she'd been beaten. Green fire flickered again on The Sarzana's hand, just as Corais drew her dagger, brushed its blade over the bit of robe she'd tied to her arm, and threw. Corais was no magician, nor claimed any powers of the Evocator, but perhaps that talisman had gathered some of the hate she felt for being nearly shamed by The Sarzana.

Her cast was true, and thudded into The Sarzana's chest, just below his ribs. He screamed, a wailing agony like a gutted roebuck, then his scream became a cry of joy, a screech of "I'm free!"

In that instant I felt the Archon depart.

The Sarzana plucked the dagger from his body and spun it away, back at Corais. The blade darted back toward us like a striking serpent and took her in the chest. I don't know if The Sarzana was already dead or if his great magical powers meant Corais' strike was but a flesh wound, nor did it matter. I was on the dais, sword slashing with all my rage and pain behind it. It struck The Sarzana full on the shoulder, beside his neck, and clove him nearly to the breastbone. Blood fountained, and he fell limply as I yanked my sword free.

But I took no chances and, as Ismet had, slashed and slashed once more and then cast his dripping heart into the dying fireplace. Perhaps I should've saved it for an icon, but I couldn't, not with Corais' life still clinging to it. The flames took the wizard's heart and roared up and out, as if a barrel of oil had been poured on them. The room shimmered, as if seen in summer's heat, and once more the earth shuddered under my boots, and I heard a far-distant wailing as demons took The Sarzana's soul, or what'd been a soul once, and this world would never know him again.

But I wasn't thinking that then, but was going to where Corais lay, her head pillowed on Polillo's knees.

Surprisingly, she still lived, although I could tell the Seeker would embrace her in minutes. She looked at me, tried to smile, but couldn't.

"I would've made a . . . shitty . . . old lady, anyway," she said; then blood runneled from her lips and she was gone.

Polillo looked at me. "Magic killed her," she said in a whisper only I could hear. "Just as it shall take me."

I got to my feet. Xia was beside me, but I didn't want any comfort from her at that moment.

I know we all have to die, and Corais, when she chose a soldier's life, chose a soldier's fate as well. And she had brought down The Sarzana. But just then I would've traded him, and everyone else in those damned Konyan islands, for Corais' return.

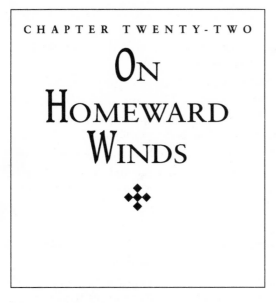

CHAPTER TWENTY-TWO

ON
HOMEWARD
WINDS

❖

I n most lands the god of victory is gloriously winged, its face an image of
fierce nobility. But the idol of victory ought to be a direwolf howling over
its gutted prey. In battle, I've never found victory noble, much less sweet.
Oh, there might be joy for a time—drunken boasting to one's mates about
how you tricked and overcame a particularly canny enemy. But a soldier's joy
soon rings hollow when she fully realizes it was only luck that left her standing, and how many of her comrades had been deserted by luck that day.

There'd been other deaths, besides my Guardswomen. Phocas had been
killed as Cholla Yi's galley swept through the canals, by an arrow launched
by an unseen sniper. Others included Captain Meduduth of our own force,
Admiral Yezo; Nor, who I prayed found some release in death; and many
hundred Konyan soldiers and sailors whose names I knew not. It would be
many a year before this victory lost its mourning banners.

We limped back to Isolde, heroes all. Ships and small boats sailed out
to greet us from every island we passed. Trumpets and horns hailed us. Hill-
tops were alive with Konyans cheering our return. But belowdecks the
wounded groaned; and on the decks, the Evocators blessed corpse after
corpse, and put a coin on their tongues to bribe mercy from the Seeker when
he carried them to his lair. I spoke to no one, not even Gamelan, not even
Xia, but only huddled in my bed mourning Corais and all the women I'd fed

to the demons of war. There were fifty of us now. Fifty! Out of all the hundreds I'd set out with when we marched on Lycanth. I did not weep; I was too frozen with grief. When I awoke in the morning, I waited long moments before I opened my eyes—praying that when I did, another nightmare would have passed and Corais would be looking down on me with that sardonic grin. I missed her. I miss her still. If there is life after this place, I pray we can march together again under the same banner.

Two nights out of Isolde, Xia crept into my arms. Our lovemaking was slow and bittersweet. Afterward, we half dozed in one another's arms, listening to the booming seas. Just before dawn Xia turned to me and looked deep into my eyes. They'd aged—there was pain there, there was knowledge won at much cost.

"I love you, Rali," she said. Before I could answer, she was gone.

I arose, not fresh, or even particularly cheerful, but I did feel somewhat healed. Also, mourning had been replaced by worry. A feeling of dread nagged at me, but of what, I couldn't say.

Gamelan was waiting for me in his cabin. "I was about to send for you, Rali," he said. "I have need of you."

"It's the Archon, isn't it?" I said, guessing immediately what was in his thoughts. "He's not done with us yet. Or we, with him."

"I'm not certain," the wizard said. "I've cast spells in every direction, and he doesn't seem to be about. Admittedly, my conjuring abilities are far from healed. Still, each spell I cast was blocked. No, not blocked—that would be like a wall. This was more like encountering a locked door. That in itself makes me worry."

"How may I help?" I asked, settling by his side. "What can I do that you cannot?"

"I believe there was—or is—a bond between you and the Archon," he said. "It's a bond of hate, to be sure; but there are no stronger chains than can be forged on those fires. Perhaps that bond began when your brother defied the Archons. There were all sorts of black spells about in those days, what with Greycloak and Raveline *and* the Archons burrowing into places few have dared to approach since the ancients. Unwilling though he was, Amalric was at the center of it. Then you came along, and once again an Antero is about when great forces are at work. I knew at Lycanth when Jinnah could not hold—much less cast—the bones that it was to you, and only you, to whom they spoke. Then you slew one of them, confirming the Archons' worst fears about the Anteros. Finally, when the last Archon cursed you with his dying breath—and then managed to defy death by fleeing into the ethers—that curse forged the strongest link of all.

"So, to answer your question, my friend—there is much you can do that I cannot. At least, I pray that it so. Perhaps it is Rali Emilie Antero who holds the key to that barred portal."

"What would you have me do?" I asked.

"Find the Archon," he said. He drew out the box containing the talisman heart.

I didn't argue, but the dread increased to heavy, throbbing pressure as I took the box from his hands.

"Hold it between your palms," he said. "Send your thoughts into it. You must focus as hard as you can. Do not speak or cast about for words for a spell. I will say them for you."

I swallowed. "Give me a moment to prepare myself."

I breathed deeply, emptying my mind as best I could. I rolled my shoulders to loosen them, turned my head from side to side to stretch the muscles. Then I grasped the box firmly between my palms and drew in one last, long breath. I whooshed it out.

"I'm ready," I said.

And Gamelan began:

"Cast wide the net
Mother Fate;
Haul in the catch
Thy daughter seeks;
East to the portals
Where the Old Gods wait;
And sit in judgment
Of he who hates."

I heard a thunderclap and the room darkened. The air became heavy and hot. I smelled sandalwood—my mother's scent. It was stronger than ever before. I heard a voice whisper: "Rali." It was my mother's voice and I wanted to weep, I loved her so, missed her so. Again she whispered my name, and I felt her breath at my ear, delicate as a butterfly's wing. I shivered.

The box gave a hard lurch in my hands. I gripped it tighter. I saw a red glow burn through. It was the twin-headed lion symbol of the Archon's. The lion bared its teeth, then shot away to hover against the far cabin wall. Then I heard a beast hiss and saw a great black panther crouching beneath them. Her teeth were bared in a snarl and her tail lashed furiously. The fiery red lion heads grew larger. Then a mighty body formed to carry them. They roared, heads snaking out on a thick single neck. But it only made the panther angrier. She hissed again and crouched lower to the deck, her claws scything out and her legs tensing to leap. Another thunderclap—and a dark hole opened behind the Archon's beast. The heads gave another roar, and then the beast plunged through the hole. The panther sprang after them.

My mother's voice whispered: "Follow."

Without warning I was in a maelstrom. I was falling from a great height through blackness and swirling lights. My ears were filled with the sounds of howling things, baying things, and things that shrieked in endless pain. I smelled sulfur and blood and fear-voided bowels. I was cold, so cold. Cold as a knife cut in winter seas. Cold as the Seeker's Rain, which comes but once every hundred years and kills forest, field, and folk. Then I was no longer falling, but running through fire-blackened woods. The trail was narrow and rock-sharded, and I nearly lost my footing when I stepped on a huge white worm slithering across the path. I was afraid, but I knew I was the pursuer—not the pursued. Ahead I saw the panther bounding around a turn, and I ran faster still. As I ran I saw demons gibbering in leafless trees. I saw ravens feasting on wounded soldiers who cried out to me as I passed, "Help me, help me, please." But I couldn't stop, dare not stop, but only follow the panther racing along the trail.

I burst out of the dead forest onto a snow-covered, moonlit plain. The path became a ruined road, and I had to leap over crumbling rock and blasted mounds of rubble. There was a battle raging on the plain. Warriors were flailing with swords and axes, and the snow was littered with their corpses and stained red by their blood. In the distance I could see the panther; farther still, the Archon's beast. Framing them was the hump of a black mountain; lightning blasted in its peaks.

The road climbed that mountain; the grade was steep, slippery with ice, and I was tiring. But the panther was beside me instead of in front of me; and she was urging me on. I forced myself forward and soon we were coming out of a pass. A black steel castle crouched where the road died. It looked like a demon's skull, with turrets for horns, battlements for brows, and a torchlit gateway for a mouth. I saw the Archon's beast bolt through the gates, which began to swing closed behind it. The panther leaped ahead, but it was too late and the gates crashed shut. The panther screamed and fought at the bars. Its fury set my own blood to boil, and I railed with it, gripping the ironwork and shouting my battle cry.

I saw the Archon. He was in the courtyard with the twin-headed beast at his side. This time he was no immense visage in a cloud, but man-sized. But he was no less fearful, and when he saw me he jabbed a twisted finger at me and shouted:

"Begone!"

Fire blasted from that finger and struck the bars. I cried out in anger and pain as the hot iron seared my hands. I gripped harder, determined not to let go. I smelled my own flesh begin to burn, and then someone close by shouted in my ear:

"Rali! Rali!" It was Gamelan.

I released the bars and fell back. Then I was in the cabin, still shouting defiance. The talisman box had fallen to the floor where I dropped it. The black husk of a heart lay next to it. Gamelan had an arm about me and was saying:

"It's all right, Rali. It's all right."

I shuddered back to full awareness and said, "I've returned, wizard."

My left hand throbbed with pain. I opened it, and burned on my palm was the Archon's brand—the twin-headed lion.

"Is he still with us?" Gamelan asked. "Does the Archon still threaten?"

"Yes," I said. "He's here."

AFTER I TOLD Gamelan all I'd seen, he said, "This is extremely serious, my friend. The Archon has managed to create a base of power in one of the spirit worlds. He must have become very powerful, indeed."

"But we just defeated him," I said. "He should be less powerful, not more."

"Evil nurtures evil, Rali," the wizard said. "Greycloak unwittingly proved that. The Archon fed on all the spilled blood, all the terror, all the sorrow. The defeat only stopped him from devouring more. And when he ate The Sarzana's soul . . . Ah, that must have been equal to a hundred dead."

"What do you think his purpose is?" I asked.

"That takes no soothsaying at all," Gamelan said. "I know my enemy. First, he wants revenge. He wants to destroy Orissa so not even its memory lingers. Second, he wants even greater power. To create a kingdom in this world. I don't believe Orissa, Lycanth, and even the Far Kingdoms themselves would satisfy him. Think of a dark demigod, and you know what sort of creature we're dealing with."

"How do we stop him?" I asked.

"We must return to Orissa as quickly as possible," he said. "If all our Evocators act in concert, we can defeat him."

His tone was less certain than his words. But I'd worry about how well our Evocators would do when—and if—we reached home.

"About the panther," he said. "It worries me."

"I assumed it was a good omen," I said. "It's undoubtedly the panther from the tale my mother told me. The one my namesake rode to help the villagers."

"Yes, I know," Gamelan said. "Still . . . when I held you . . . just before you . . . returned . . . you screamed."

"Yes," I said. "So?"

And the wizard said: "You sounded just like a panther."

IN ISOLDE, the entire island turned out for our return. The sea was so full of welcoming boats and ships, it was difficult to navigate the bay. Crowds lined the embankment and the streets that led to the docks. Every instrument was employed in joyous noisemaking, every horn, fife, drum, and even pots and pans. The city'd been scoured clean, and banners and flags fluttered from every high place. Bonfires burned in crackling profusion, and the people fed a royal fortune's worth of incense in those fires to perfume the air. Thousands upon thousands of flowers were strewn in our path as we marched off the ships and up the terraced hill to carry official news of our victory to the lords of the Konyans. First in line were all the Konyan officers who'd survived. Then came me and my women, and Cholla Yi and his men. Princess Xia chose to march at my side, and the already hysterical crowd wept when they saw her, and prostrated themselves, calling out her name.

When we reached the Palace of Monarchs, we stood for hours while each member of the Council of Purity—their voices magnified by the wizards—praised us and hailed our victory. Finally, the crowd grew unruly and demanded Princess Xia and I mount the stage so they could see us. They screamed when we did, and I saw men and women alike collapse, they were so overcome.

When they finally wore down, Lord Kanara tugged at my sleeve, motioning. Princess Xia and I slipped away with him. Once in the palace, he led us to a small, richly decorated room. There was a table set with food and drink. He motioned for us to partake. Both of us shook our heads—we were too tired.

"But I'll have a little brandy, Father, if you please," Xia said.

I said I'd like the same. Lord Kanara filled crystal goblets for us, and another for himself. He sat down, and we did the same.

"My daughter," Kanara said, "you have made me very proud."

Xia bowed her head, humble. "I only did my duty, Father," she said. But I could see from the look in her eye that the humility was an act.

"Just the same," her father said, "it was a great thing. You have written your name large in our history, my girl."

I saw Xia shudder when he addressed her as a girl. But she said: "There were others much braver than I, Father. But thank you just the same."

"There will be many honors bestowed on you," he said. "Some, it shall be my pleasure to grant with my own hands."

Xia smiled modestly. "Thank you, Father," she said. And she sounded most sincere. But again I caught that look, and I swear she seemed to be measuring her father. I believe she found him smaller than she once thought.

"And you, Captain Antero," Kanara said. "We owe you much."

"I only ask help with charts and good advice on how we can return home."

"You shall have it," Kanara said. "The charts have already been prepared. The counsel of our best seafarers is at your disposal."

"Thank you, Lord Kanara," I said.

"We also intend a greater reward," he said. "We have agreed your ships will be filled with all the treasure they can hold. When you return home, even your lowest sailor shall be rich."

Once again I thanked him. And he said, "Is there anything else? Any wish we might grant that has not been anticipated?"

I looked at Xia. But I didn't need to see her expression to know not to ask for the first thing that leaped into my mind. So I asked him the second.

"I would beg you to pardon all the men and women in your dungeons, lord," I said. "If you recall, I was your . . . guest there. And I met and befriended many of its inhabitants."

Kanara frowned, and when he did so, he looked remarkably like his daughter. Then he smiled. "It shall be done," he said. He drank his brandy. I could tell he was gathering himself for something else.

Finally: "Now, I have a request of *you*, Captain."

"If it is within my power," I said, "I shall do anything you ask."

"All of you Orissans must leave at once," he said. "And leave quietly."

"Father!" Princess Xia said, shocked. "How could you—"

I raised a hand. "It's all right, your ladyship. I take no offense." Then I turned to her father. "You still fear The Sarzana," I said. "Or at least the curse that has been foretold for she who killed him."

"I think it's a lot of superstitious nonsense," Kanara said. "But others do not. They take it quite seriously. They are afraid of what will happen if you tarry long."

"Then I shall go as quickly as possible," I said. "Besides, I have reasons of my own to get home as swiftly as I can."

Lord Kanara relaxed, quite relieved. He raised his brandy and made a toast. "To Orissa," he said. "May the gods bless her for sending her daughters to us in our time of need."

"To Orissa," I echoed.

As I drank, a feeling of great longing for the city by the river overcame me. Without asking, I refilled my goblet and drank again.

* * *

THE FOLLOWING night I saw Princess Xia for the last time. She came to my villa and we walked quietly in the garden, enjoying the silence and the smell of the blooming hyacinth. Down in the harbor we heard a lyre playing an old sweet melody of love gained and lost. We embraced and I kissed her. Her lips were soft—heady as wine. I drew back, feeling her nipples stir against my breasts. I looked deep into those dark eyes, and at her hair, with its golden tiara glowing in the moonlight.

"I'll miss you," I said.

She pulled away, disturbed. "And I, you," she said.

She walked to the fountain and sat. I rested a boot on the rock facing and waited. "I suppose it's just as well that you're going," she said.

"That has the sound of someone with plans," I said. "Plans my presence might interfere with."

She nodded. "A lot of things have become much clearer to me lately," she said. "I have you—and the example of your Guardswomen—to thank."

I said nothing. She raised her head and looked at me. Her face was a perfect subject for a royal portrait.

"I want you to know this," she said. "In a few years, if any of your people wish to open trade with Konya, they will be welcome. This I promise."

"Is that an influential brat I hear speaking," I said, "or a future queen?"

She laughed. But there was no real humor in it. It was forced, such as when royalty laughs to show it's a good fellow, as able to take a jest as any of us commoners.

Then she said, archly, "You've guessed my secret, O wise Captain."

"That you'll be queen?" I said with a smile. "No wisdom in seeing that. I think I've known it all along. You'll make a good queen. I'd lay money on that. But what about your father?"

"It shouldn't be too difficult to convince him to support me," she said. "And if he is . . . reasonable . . . Well, we shall see. We shall see . . ." She left the remainder of the threat in its sheath. I pitied her father if he stood in her way.

"One other thing, Rali," she said. "I hope this doesn't hurt you . . . I'd never want to cause you pain. But if you should ever take it in your head to return . . . please don't."

"The Sarzana's curse?" I said, knowing that wasn't the reason. But I wanted her to say it.

"I'm my father's daughter in that," she said. "Pure nonsense. However, my plans require that I eventually marry. I'll need a consort to father children. The Kanara line must be continued."

"I can see where I'd get in the way," I said.

She rose from the fountain and took my hand. Her breathing was suddenly heavy. Lust glittered in her eyes.

"I want you, *now*, Rali!" she said. *"Please!"*

And I said harshly: "Take off the crown!"

My words startled her. She hesitated, then nodded. Her hands lifted the tiara free of her curls and she handed it to me. I threw it in the fountain and swept her up into my arms and carried her up the stairs to my bed.

Just as dawn broke she wept. "Oh, Rali," she wailed. "I'm so sorry." It was a long, bone-shuddering fit of tears such as I've rarely seen.

"Don't, my love," I said. "I'll be fine. I'll never forget you . . . but I'll be fine."

She looked at me, tears flooding from those beautiful eyes. "I'm not crying for you, Rali," she sobbed. "I'm crying for me."

WE SET SAIL in a heavy rainstorm, and there was no one on the docks or the hills to say farewell. But the seven ships that were all that was left of our fleet sat low in the water, heavy with golden coin and other riches; the greater gift were the charts in Cholla Yi's stateroom that the Konyan mapmakers and wizards had labored on so we could find our way home.

I'd redisposed my women. There was only a handful left, and I'd gathered them under my command on Stryker's galley. I couldn't chance letting them be dispersed on all seven ships, since I still had no trust in the mercenaries, particularly now they had gold in their purses. I also wanted them close at hand—the butchery had sickened all of us, and it would be best if the Maranon Guard licked its wounds together as it always had.

The rain was cold and made a miserable parting from those enchanting isles, but the east winds blew steady and strong, carrying us swiftly toward Orissa. The rain and wind were unrelenting, but there was no danger in them, and those of us not engaged in sailing fell into a stuporous routine of eating and dreamless sleep. This way many days went by with so little incident that we barely noted them, and before we knew it, we were near the straits the Konyans had marked that would carry us around the fiery reefs.

It was as gray and windy a day as all the others. Visibility was poor, but far to the north there was an eerie glow in the sky and we could hear the distant rumbling of the volcanoes. As predicted, there was land to the south. We'd been advised to hug its shores to make certain we'd avoid the northern reefs. But we'd also been warned not to tarry long—the Konyan wizards said the spells they'd cast to help chart the course encountered much evil in that land. Warily, we crept through the straits, ship by ship, and although we saw nothing, all of us felt a sense of dread. When my ship passed the narrowest part of the passage, my hackles rose as if I were being watched by many eyes. Just at the edge of my vision I thought I saw the panther crouching low on the deck—teeth bared, tail lashing. But when I turned to look, it was gone.

With much relief we made it through without incident. But we stretched sail with haste and flew from that place as fast as we could. That night the skies cleared and we were treated to the sight of more familiar stars. The next day dawned bright and balmy, and although we still had a long way to go, we all felt that now we were truly going home.

Some days later I went to Cholla Yi's ship for a conference. Although we'd sailed these waters before, they were still generally unknown to us, and with our fleet so pared down I thought we ought to be prepared for pirates. There was a small gig tied up beside the gangway. Cholla Yi was having another visitor besides myself. I ordered my boatmen to tie up to the gig and stay in the boat to keep it from swamping as it was towed along by the galley.

I boarded as the watch was changing, and as proof that we'd perhaps become too unwary, no one hailed my coming. The officer in charge seemed startled when he saw me, and saluted. I returned the salute, and when he started to escort me to Cholla Yi's cabin, I told him to stay.

"I'd do a little lookout-skinning if I were you," I said. "If they missed me, who *else* aren't they going to see?" He muttered an apology, and I made my own way along the deck.

I hesitated at the door when I heard the unmistakable rattle of a dice cup, then the throw. Someone cursed at the result. It was Stryker, who must've come over from our galley without my noticing his departure.

"I ain't never seen such luck! If'n we wasn't usin' my dice, I'd ask to check if'n they'd been shaved."

Cholla Yi laughed. "That's six straight passes. Want to put up the rest of your share to see if I can make it seven?"

I smiled. With all the riches on board, Cholla Yi still wasn't satisfied with a share that would please a prince. He was busy skinning his own men for more. He gave new meaning to the phrase "pirate's greed."

Stryker forced a return laugh. "What'd yer go 'n' do, Admiral? Make a bargain with a demon?"

Cholla Yi's voice hardened. "What are you accusing me of?"

Stryker was instantly contrite. "Nothin'. Nothin' t'all, Admiral. I was only cursin' yer infernal good luck."

Cholla Yi relented, chuckling. "You're as bad with a dice cup as you are with a bow. I remember a time when you had a good clean shot, wind just right, and everybody too busy keeping their skin together to notice what you were up to. And then you go and miss."

And Stryker said: "Weren't my fault. And weren't that easy. Deck was pitchin' somethin' fierce. Had half a dozen devils a'ter me hide. 'Sides, we're talkin' luck nobody could match. I mean, yer luck's nothin' next to—"

"Watch your tongue," Cholla Yi cut in. "On a ship you never know who might be listening."

I flushed as the bolt inadvertently hit a guilty target. Wondering if the poor bastard they were referring to ultimately escaped with his life, I knocked.

"Come in," Cholla Yi barked.

When they saw me, both men flushed and rose quickly to their feet. I nearly laughed. On this ship, guilt was as contagious as a summer chill.

Cholla Yi stammered a greeting: "I, uh . . . it's, uh . . . a pleasure to see you, Captain Antero. Stryker and I were, uh . . . just, uh . . ."

"Havin' a bit of a game," Stryker broke in, coming to his admiral's rescue. " 'Course, he's takin' more'n a bit outer me, if yer knows what I mean . . . har har har."

They were acting like schoolboys caught doing something naughty, rather than studying. Now, I *did* laugh.

"Gentlemen, please!" I said. "I'm no stiff-backed prude. In fact, I've been known to shake a dice cup or two to pass the time."

Both men chuckled, but the sound was hollow.

"What can I do for you, Captain?" Cholla Yi asked.

"I thought we might discuss security, Admiral," I said. "These waters have an unfriendly look."

"Good thought," Cholla Yi said. He shot Stryker a look that snapped him to attention, and the rogue quickly made himself scarce.

Cholla Yi and I got down to business over goblets of brandy. He was quick to agree to my suggestions, and soon we were done. Then he refilled our goblets and raised his in salute. "We've had a good run, Captain," he said. "I'm almost sorry to see it coming to an end."

I returned the toast, then drank. "It certainly hasn't turned out the way General Jinnah expected, has it?"

Cholla Yi's face darkened. "What's your point?" he snapped.

I was surprised by his tone. "Why, nothing to take offense at," I said. "I thought it obvious that Jinnah was only trying to get me out of the way so he didn't have to share credit. He never intended, much less envisioned, our success."

"Jinnah cheated me and my men out of our rightful shares of the spoils, is what he did," Cholla Yi snarled. For some reason his old resentments had flown back to roost.

"You'll have the last laugh, then," I said. "We're loaded to the gunwales with gold. Much more than would've been yours if we'd stayed."

But Cholla Yi would not be calmed. "I started out with fifteen good ships of the line," he said. "Now I have seven, and they're so beaten up they're worthless. That's not right, I tell you. I was cheated."

I didn't point out that a mere handful of the Konyan baubles that was his due would replace his lost ships, and more. With so little time left in our voyage, I wanted a happy pirate to sail with. No sense jeopardizing things when we were so close.

"I'll see it's all made right by you," I promised. "If it comes down to it, I'll pay for it out of my share."

"So you think it's just money I'm after, is that it?" Cholla Yi snarled. "What about respect? Pay me off and you've seen the last of me, huh? When they need me, it's Admiral this, and Admiral that, and why don't you go off and die for our cause, sir? But when the war's done, me and my lads are nothing more than common villains in their view."

I'd had enough. He seemed to care little about keeping the peace between us. "You've reminded me many a time, sir, that you are a mercenary. That gold is the only banner you sail for. Fine by me. I've found you gold aplenty. You also have my respect—as a fighter—if that counts for anything. But as for the rest—why, that's the life you've chosen for yourself, my friend."

I swept the dice into the cup and shook. "If you don't like the toss, you have only yourself to blame."

I upended the cup. Cholla Yi reflexively glanced down. He gasped. I looked for myself and saw seven pips—Fortune's favorite—staring up.

Cholla Yi seemed pale, shaken. He gulped brandy. Then he said: "Forgive my temper, Captain Antero." He rubbed his forehead. "I've not slept well of late. And my head has been throbbing so fiercely I'd like to rip it off."

I didn't care, but I didn't want to sound unfeeling. "I'm sorry myself," I said. "I should have seen you weren't well. Is there anything I can do? Perhaps an elixir from our wizard?"

Cholla Yi shook his head—a firm no. Then he smiled, turning on his roguish charm. "This is all the elixir I need," he said, indicating the brandy. He upended the goblet, then wiped his beard. "I'll see to the defense arrangements we discussed," he said, and the interview was at an end. We chatted a few minutes more and then parted company.

Just outside I heard the dice cup rattle, then the clatter of the toss. Cholla Yi cursed. The result must not have been good.

What this all signified, I didn't know.

* * *

POLILLO MOURNED CORAIS even more deeply than I. They'd been constant companions for so many years, it was hard to imagine one without the other. They were as different in temperament as in coloring and size, but each complemented the other. Polillo gave Corais strength and bullheaded courage, while Corais offered speed and sharp-witted cunning. Together they made fearsome adversaries against anyone foolish enough to go up against them on a battlefield, or in a tavern fight. Polillo didn't mope about or weep after Corais died. Instead, she threw herself into her work, constantly drilling the women, teaching them new fighting tricks she'd thought up, or just holding their hands and there-there-ing them when their own troubles spilled over. She'd changed in other ways as well.

One day in practice, as she was dodging the thrust of a wooden sword, I saw her trip over one of the sailors who'd moved too close to watch all the jouncing feminine flesh.

In pain, he pushed at her, shouting, "Get off me, you great cow!"

The deck went to instant hush. Polillo climbed slowly to her feet. She loomed over the sailor, who'd gone white as death itself.

"What did you call me, little man?" Polillo demanded.

The sailor gulped. I knew he was cursing the demons who'd seized command of his tongue.

I also remembered a man who'd made a similar insult at a dockside tavern in Orissa. We'd been peacefully drinking and wenching, and the man had taken offense because the innkeeper's daughter preferred Polillo's company to his. So he'd hit Polillo from behind with a chair, shouting, "Take that, you cow!" Polillo is sensitive about her ample endowments. She took offense. Before we knew it, she'd caught the man and had crushed his face against her breasts, shouting, "Moo, moo, you bastard," as she smothered him. If Corais hadn't intervened, she'd have killed him for sure.

I had visions of the same thing happening here and started to step forward. But to my amazement, Polillo suddenly grinned, and reached down and ruffled the poor sailor's hair. Then she sniffed at him, wrinkling her nose.

"Pissed your breeches, didn't you?" she said.

The man only bobbed his head.

"Better go wash off," she advised. "Nothing worse than a piss rash."

As she turned away, the sailor keeled over in a dead faint.

"Buy you a drink, beautiful?" I said as she dusted off her tunic.

"Best offer I've had all day," she said, looping her arm through mine as we adjourned to my quarters to sample a pale Konyan liquor that had a kick like a warhorse.

"That was an impressive display of mercy," I said after we'd settled into serious drinking.

Polillo shrugged. "Corais always said my hot temper was my worst fault," she said. "Now that's she's gone, I have to keep a lid on it myself." Her eyes misted. "I guess I depended on her for a lot of things. I'm such a moody bitch. Don't know how she put up with me." She gave an angry swipe at a tear.

"She loved you, Polillo," I said. "We all do. And as for your moods, I've always thought they came hand in hand with the great gifts the gods gave you so you wouldn't be too perfect."

She snorted. "Gifts? I'm big and I'm ugly. What kind of gifts are those?"

I was shocked. "Ugly?" I said. "Why, Polillo, there isn't a woman in the world who wouldn't be jealous of your looks."

This was true. As I've said before, Polillo was perfectly formed. Not one ounce of fat spoiled the curve of her figure. Her legs were as graceful as a dancer's, and her face, with those huge, glowing eyes, would make the greatest limner itch for paint and linen.

"I don't break mirrors, at least," she grudged. "But you have to admit I'm of freakish size and strength."

"You've been blessed with the strength of heroes, not freaks," I said. "And someday, when these times are nothing but distant memories, songs will be sung about you, my dearest friend. The ode makers will tell the tale of the beautiful woman who had the strength of ten big men. You might as well face it. You were born to be a woman of legend."

Polillo giggled. "With a bitch of a temper," she said.

"With a bitch of a temper," I agreed.

She took a pull on her drink. "I guess in my time I *have* cracked a few noggins that needed cracking," she allowed.

"Undoubtedly," I said.

"Beginning with my father," she said.

"You've told me he was a bastard," I said. "But you never explained why. He was some kind of innkeeper, wasn't he?"

Polillo nodded. "Part innkeeper, part blacksmith, and all horse's ass. He was a big, strong son of a poxed whore. And if you ever met his mother, you'd know that wasn't an idle insult. My father had a black hole of an inn at the crossroads of our village. Had a forge out back to shoe traveler's horses and such. He drank most of the profits and kept us all in rags and bruises until I got some size. Sometimes I think that's why I grew so big. Ever since I can remember, he was beating on us. Splintered my older brother's arm—and he was such a sweet thing, a gentle soul, it'd break your heart. My mother was always going about with a limp and blackened eyes. He made me so mad that I went after him in his bed with a poker when I was six. He beat the devil out of me, he did. Hurt like the blazes, but I wouldn't cry. Not for him. I decided right then I was going to get so big and strong that he'd be afraid to touch any of us. I started lifting things . . . anything heavy. And running and wrestling. When I was ten I could just manage his anvil. So I waited. But weeks went by before he acted up again. Nearly drove me crazy, waiting. I started worrying that maybe he'd seen the error in his ways. I hated him so much that I prayed he hadn't. That's how badly I wanted to hurt him. But I needed an excuse."

"And he finally gave you one?" I asked.

Polillo gave me a mirthless grin. "Does a dog favor carrion? Sure, he did. He went after my mother. And I stopped him cold." She slammed one big fist into the other. I winced at the bone-breaking sound of it. "One punch. Smashed his ugly jaw. There were teeth all over the place. Even in the soup. Then I drove him out and told my mother that from now on, the tavern was hers."

"You never saw him again?"

Polillo laughed. "Never. How could he show his face with everyone knowing his ten-year-old daughter had flattened him? That's the nice thing about male pride—once broken, never mended."

"Like the sailor who pissed his breeches?" I asked.

Polillo grimaced. "Oh, he's not such a bad sort. I've seen him working— and he puts his back in more'n most of the others. And he's not bad in a fight, either. I just surprised him, that's all. He didn't mean to insult me. It just burst out. When I was looking down at him, I thought, 'Polillo, old girl. How many times have you gotten yourself in a fix by opening your big mouth when you shouldn't?' And then I thought, Corais'd be really angry with me if I killed him. So I didn't."

She started to take another drink, then stopped. Her brow furrowed in worry. "You don't suppose people will think I've gone soft or anything, do you?"

"Do you care?" I asked.

She thought a moment, then: "Not really."

As soon as she realized what she'd said, the most marvelous smile lit her features. "Corais'd really be proud of me, wouldn't she?"

"She would, indeed, my dear," I said.

After that we spent a wondrous night drinking and giggling and telling lies, just like in the old days, when we were young and guiltless and our hopes as bright as the untested steel of our swords.

* * *

AS WE raced east I began making sure I was up before dawn every morning to see the daybreak. It's a sight I never tired of—especially when that pale pink spills across the sky like sugared rose water. Gamelan had the old man's habit of rising early, so he'd join me and I'd describe the view as he fished.

"When I was a boy I favored sunsets," he said one day. "All the day's petty disappointments vanished and the glow of the skies seemed to speak of the fresh possibilities of the morrow. But when I became old, the setting sun seemed so ... well, *final*, dammit! You don't know if there's even going to be a tomorrow. With a sunrise you can lie to yourself that your future stretches to at least the end of the day."

"But you're a wizard," I said. "Don't wizards sense their own departure? I'd think with the Seeker about, a wizard would know it."

Gamelan laughed. "The only wizard I've met who successfully predicted his demise was my old master. But then he swore at the end of every day that we thick-witted acolytes were going to be the death of him. And guess what? That moment eventually arrived when he was ninety-two."

"You'll live longer than him, my friend," I said. "You'd better not disappoint me. I'll speak harshly to you if you do."

Instead of polite laughter at my mild attempt at humor, Gamelan turned serious.

"I dreamed about the panther last night," he said.

"Oh?"

"It was nothing noteworthy," the wizard continued. "In my dream she was in my cabin and wanted out. She was most anxious—pacing up and down. But when I went to the door—I'm sighted in my dreams, you know—I couldn't lift the bar. I called for help, but no one heard me."

"Then?"

"That was all," Gamelan said. "I woke up." Then he asked: "Have you dreamed of the panther, Rali?"

I said, "I haven't dreamed at all. Not since—since I had the vision about the Archon, and first encountered the panther."

"Do you normally dream?" he asked.

"I *always* do," I said. "Even when I don't remember what it was about, I wake up knowing I've dreamed."

Gamelan sighed and shook his head.

"Does it mean anything?" I asked.

"I don't know, Rali," he said. "Greycloak speculated that dreams might be real. That when you dream you're actually in another world. And that world is exactly like your native place, but with some small detail—or even a large one—that is different. Which, as you experience it, becomes the subject of the dream."

"That damned Janos never did shut up about anything," I snarled. "Why does everything have to be weighed, or measured down to the smallest detail? Why can't our dreams just be dreams and to hell with it?"

"Still," the wizard said, "there could be something to it. And I was only wondering because of the panther. You've said you'd imagined you'd seen her sometimes."

"Just at the edge of my vision," I said. "And always in the shadows. Probably my imagination."

"Yes," Gamelan said. "I suppose it is."

That night I tried to force a dream. I thought of Xia—built her image until she seemed almost alive. Then, just as I drifted off, I tried to hold on to that image. It slipped away as soon as I closed my eyes. I roused myself and tried again, with the same result. I attempted fixing other images, both pleasant and the opposite, but no matter how hard I concentrated, they fled as soon as I began to drop off. Then I couldn't sleep at all, tossing and turning and growing hot and cold by turn.

And the whole time I thought I could hear the scrape of a large animal's claws. I knew it was the panther—pacing, pacing, pacing.

Finally, I went on deck. The night was quiet, the seas calm. I went to Gamelan's cabin and pressed my ear against the door. I could hear the click of claws inside.

I tugged at the latch string. It was stuck. I pulled harder, and the bar lifted. I carefully opened the door. The wizard was sleeping peacefully.

I felt a hot rush of air, and I stepped back as something pushed past me. It had no form; in fact, I couldn't swear there was anything there at all. But I distinctly felt fur brush my skin and smelled the powerful odor of a big cat. I looked around and didn't see anything. I checked Gamelan again, then shut the door and returned to my bed. Instantly, I fell asleep.

I dreamed that night. I dreamed of the black panther. She was speeding through a great forest and I was riding on her back.

CHAPTER TWENTY-THREE

THE DEMON SEAS

❖

A s the days passed, the wind held true from the west or west-southwest,
carrying us steadily into what the maps said would be home waters
and eventually to Orissa.

The weather continued balmy, and the tensions of our long chase began
to ebb, and our ships could almost be described as happy. My women sat
yarning, trying to figure out what they'd do with all their riches, even after
the city of Orissa and the Evocators took their legal shares. Two of them
sought me out and wondered, oh so carefully, if someone as honey-tongued
as I might consider appearing before the Council and asking for a boon—
since so many of us had given our all for the city, the least Orissa could do
was forswear its unearned portion of our gold.

I gave them both the same answer: Greed ill becomes a soldier.

One, Pamphylia, said impudently that fighting for gold didn't seem to
slow the sword hand of Cholla Yi or his men. She'd obviously been around
Gamelan too long, and he'd tolerated her flippery. I told her to report to Flag
Sergeant Ismet and ask for a particularly smelly task of Ismet's choice that
suited insubordination. Secretly, though, I was a bit pleased my women still
had spirit left, after the long death lists and months of hardship.

The other, Gerasa, had the same request, but when I answered as I had
to Pamphylia, she looked at me intently and, after asking my permission to

speak, wondered what made me think she had any intent of remaining in the Guard once we returned.

I made no response to that, but dismissed her after saying the law was the law, and it wasn't for her, or me, to question what Orissa did with its gold.

She'd made me wonder, though. I'd never thought much about the future, I realized. I always assumed I'd soldier on with the Guard, eventually be given a medal, a wine-drenched banquet, and promoted to a distinctly honorary—since I was a woman—generalship, and retire to my family's estates. Either that or, more likely, fall in some nameless border skirmish. I'd never much thought of a life beyond the Guard. It'd been my mother, father, lover, and home since I was a girl, as much or sometimes more than anyone named Antero, Otara, Xia, or even Tries, as much as I loved them all.

I tried to set those thoughts aside—it isn't healthy for a soldier to think about the future, because while she's walking her post, dreaming of warm taverns and supple bed partners to come, it's most likely that someone with eyes only on today is slipping up behind her with a bared dagger. But it didn't work.

Besides, I knew very well what would come next. We still had the Archon to deal with. My first duty when I returned home would be to join Gamelan before the Magistrates and Evocators and tell them what we feared.

All this made me feel somewhat bleak, although I tried not to show it. My sleep was uneasy, and I woke often. I was hot, then cold. I know I dreamed, and the dreams were not pleasant, but I couldn't remember them when I woke.

One of those nightmares saved my life.

I'd lurched awake, sitting upright in my hammock, trying to come fully alert, my body wanting me to lie back, and I was resisting, knowing if I didn't get up, pace about and collect my wits, I'd return to that awful dream, whatever it'd been. I vaguely knew it wasn't far from dawn. Over the creaking of the ship's beams and the rush of the sea beyond them, I heard a low rustling, as if someone was trying the slipstring of my door latch. The door opened, and a shadow outlined itself and came forward, sliding across the deck toward me. From its dark bulk emerged an arm, holding a weapon, a long double-edged dagger, and the knife plunged down toward where I lay.

Except I wasn't there.

Before my assassin could grunt surprise, I came up from where I'd knelt in the sheltering darkness and was on him, casting my thrown-off blanket like a fisherman's net, letting it wrap around his body, and then I spun in a full circle, snapping my leg up to waist height as I did. Like a club, it struck the man in the midsection and sent him sprawling.

I dove after him, both of us blind in the darkness, but my muscles and my fists had eyes given them by endless hours of practice, and I hit with the heel of my hand once against his forehead, hammering his head back against the deck; my backhand struck his temple, and then I caught myself before I launched the deathstroke into the softness of his throat. The man gargled pain, sagged, and I was off him and to the gimbaled lantern. I flipped its cover open, blew on the punk that smoldered inside until a flame grew, twisted the valve and let oil feed the flame. I thought of shouting the Guard up, but decided to wait a moment. My attacker was forcing himself up on his hands, trying to shake off his befuddlement. I swept up his dagger, knelt and yanked his head back by the hair.

It was Stryker.

His eyes unglazed and stared at the blade I held just beyond his chin.

"Your idea? Or Cholla Yi's?" I demanded.

His lips clamped shut. I drew the blade's edge across the side of his neck, and blood oozed.

"Cholla Yi," I said, knowing that if it had just been some piece of insane rage from Stryker, he would've instantly pled for an appeal to his superior. "Why?"

Stryker clamped his lips stubbornly, and I started to cut him again.

"You're leadin' us t' our doom," he said hastily. "There's somethin' waitin' out there. Cholla Yi said he c'd feel it, an' I c'n feel somethin', too. An' I know what it is."

"The Archon?"

"Now ain't you th' smart one," he said.

"What'll killing me get you?"

Stryker looked cunning, and once again I cut him.

"Talk, man," I said. "Or I'll hail Polillo in with her axe, and let her trim your fingers one by one until you do."

"So what?" Stryker said. "You'll be killin' me anyways."

"Now's for certain," I said. "A minute or an hour ... that's maybe. What would my death bring?"

"C'n I sit up?"

"You'll talk as you are. Or bleed as you lie."

"Cholla Yi fin'y told me what was happenin'. Tol' me he's been havin' visions. Like he was an Evoc'tor. Said th' Archon come to him, e'en though he di'n't see any face or form, but it hadda be him. Said th' chase wa'n't over, an' there'd be no way we c'd come safe to Orissa wi' his spells opposin' us, an' y'r damned Mag'strates'd ne'er pay what they owes us, anyway. He said those who're wi' him now'll be remembered long, an' those who stand 'gainst him'll be ripped by demons f'r all 'ternity."

"And you . . . or Cholla Yi believed the *Archon*?"

"I know it don't sound like there's sense to it," Stryker said. "But Cholla Yi says we ain't got no choice when a wizard like him talks. 'Specially when he makes promises, an' says he'll be needin' men, real live men, t' help him get his throne back. Throne an' more.

"Now he's got th' real power, Cholla Yi told me. That spell I heard you an' that damn' Gamelan whisperin' 'bout sometime ago, when you thought no one was about.

"Looks to me like th' Archon ain't far from bein' a god," Stryker went on. "Man don't stand 'gainst gods. Best you c'n do is try to make accommodation with 'em. Maybe serve 'em well, an' hope t' get some of th' loot they ain't gonna be wantin'."

Stryker grimaced. "Guess I shoulda known, when I cast death's eyes, back gamin' aboard Cholla Yi's ship, all 'cause you was in th' offin'. Since I first signed on wi' Cholla Yi, weren't for bad luck, I wouldn't a had none at all.

"E'en back th' first time we come on th' Archon, I shoulda knowed I was cursed, when I tried to end matters like I was s'posed to. Back 'fore th' volcanoes went an' spat us int' these waters."

"What does that mean?"

"I'll tell you. Might's well give you all, an' hope that weighs th' scales. When you an' that black bitch went 'cross t' th' Archon's ship, an' up th' foremast?"

It came to me most clear, and I gasped, and without realizing it, slid back, away from Stryker, until I was kneeling about a yard away. I remembered when Ismet and I had clambered to the foretop of the Archon's ship, and an arrow had plunged between us and sliced Ismet's arm, a shaft from an archer neither of us could spot. Of course we couldn't have seen him below, for that arrow had come from our own galley.

"I remember," I said. Stryker pushed himself up into a sitting position. His fingers touched the blood on either side of his neck and he winced. "You shot that arrow?"

"I did. An' missed. Damn near took out th' black bitch, though, which wouldn't of been all bad."

"Cholla Yi ordered it?"

"Nobody *ordered* nothin'," Stryker said. "Cholla Yi jus' told me that Gen'ral Jinnah made it clear that you was his worst enemy, an' when we come back, he'd be sittin' high in th' Magistrates' Council, an' if he didn't have th' bother of dealin' with you, our accounts'd be settled faster an' better, and we was more'n capable of dealin' wi' th' Archon ourselves back then, afore he got all his powers."

"Fools and gods-cursed fools! Why'd you not try again until now?" I asked.

" 'Cause I ain't a pure idjit. A'ter we come over those reefs, int' unknown waters, I figgered, as did Cholla Yi, we'd need all th' swords we c'd muster. He said it'd be time t' worry about Orissa an' Jinnah an' shit like that when, an' if, we closed on its shores agin."

"You're both a pair of stupid bastards," I said. "You *believed* the Archon would find a place for you? Look at The Sarzana. He thought he could cast the dice with him, too. I've never seen—" I broke off, realizing I was about to sound like a fool myself. Of course the Archon's spirit, or demon, or whatever it was, wouldn't have tried to work his wooings without casting a spell of persuasion and belief like some golden cloud around these two scoundrels.

"All right," I began. "We'll deal with matters as they occur. First you, then Cholla Yi."

I did not know what I intended doing with Stryker just then, and had only just turned my mind to considering it. But the ship's captain mistook my words and thought his fate was determined. I hadn't noticed he'd slid his legs back under him, and now he sprang straight for me, one hand grabbing for my knife hand, the other for my eyes.

But again my muscles spoke for me, and I went down, flat on my back, the sharp fang of the dagger sticking up, free hand bracing it, and Stryker impaled himself on his own blade. Blood poured over me, and he moaned shrilly, stiffened and died. I rolled from under his bulk and was on my feet, dropping my tunic over my shoulders and grabbing for my weapons belt. I burst out the door into the lower deck, shouting for the Guard to turn out, turn out, and as my women floundered into wakefulness, I raced up the companion way, onto the main deck and the beginnings of dawn, my blade whipping out of its sheath.

Seventy feet away, Cholla Yi's flagship bore down on us, armed men in its forepeak, gangplanks rigged for boarding. In the forepeak was Cholla Yi himself, in full armor. He saw me, yet alive, and screeched rage. Behind him came two other ships—one was Kidai's, I didn't remember the captain of the other. Evidently he thought he only needed those three to kill us, or else hadn't been able to convince the officers of the other ships to mutiny.

My women poured on deck, pulling on their helmets and buckling their armor. Among them were Stryker's seamen, bewildered by these events. Evidently Cholla Yi, experienced at treachery, had known enough to conspire with as few as necessary. If I'd been murdered below, there would've been time enough for Stryker to rouse his men against my women. But now . . .

"Kill them!" Cholla Yi was shouting. "Kill the bitches! Kill them all! They're in league with the Archon!"

A few sailors looked at us . . . and then at the ready racks of swords.

"Any man who moves against us will die!" I shouted in return. "Cholla Yi's the traitor!" I swore at myself—all I was doing was adding to the confusion, and changed my tactics: "All sailors, fall below! Now! Or you'll die! Stay out of this!"

Some started moving toward the companionways, others were motionless, still amazed. Duban must've been told something, because he snatched a dagger from his belt. Before he could find a target, Ismet cut him down, and sailors shouted anger.

But I hadn't time for them—Cholla Yi's ships were very close.

"Repel boarders," I shouted. "Gerasa! Target the helmsmen and Cholla Yi!" My best bow woman, whom I'd promoted sergeant in spite of her protests, gaped, then shouted her own orders as her section formed up along the rails and opened fire. But it was too late. I saw a shaft take the man standing next to Cholla Yi, grimaced that the archer's aim hadn't been better, and then Cholla Yi's galley crashed into ours, the spiked crow's-feet gangplanks thudded down, and we were tied, ship to ship. Another ship bore alongside to port, but slings hummed and stones spat across the heaving waters between us, and the three men on the quarterdeck fell, chests or skulls splintered, and the helmless ship drifted clear.

The third ship was coming up on our stern, but I had other matters to worry about as Cholla Yi's sailors poured over the gangplanks, and the sea was a milling mass of shouting, fighting men and women.

"Spearhead," Polillo shouted, and four women formed behind her and charged. Sailors screamed fear and tried to get away from that swinging axe. Two sailors ran at me, thinking the odds were theirs, and I jumped to the side, and they were in each other's way. I parried a clumsy stroke from the first, slashed across his upper arm, cutting tendons, and his sword dropped, giving me time to spit his companion, pull free, and finish off the wounded man before another was on me.

"Get the bitches," I heard Cholla Yi bellow. "Kill them! Get their cursed captain first!"

A man rose up in front of me, holding a bloody halberd at half-staff, parried my cut, lunged as I slid aside, and came back to guard. He was a skilled fighter. I bobbed side to side, trying to confuse him, about to lunge, and his eyes widened, and I dropped to my right and rolled, turning as I did, and Santh's sword came down and sent splinters flying from the deck.

He shrieked fear and pulled at the stuck blade as I came up from my crouch, slashing. My sword took off most off his face, and he stumbled back, against the rail, and then fell over the side, but that sailor's halberd darted at me like a snake striking, and its back point seared across my unarmored ribs. Pain flashed, but I paid no heed as my free hand had the staff of the halberd, and I pulled him into me, into me and my sword. His eyes saw no more, and he toppled, and I booted his corpse off my blade.

The brawl was roiling across the decks, and I couldn't tell in whose favor the battle was going. The way to end this was obvious, and I spotted Cholla Yi above the crowd, his sword rising and falling, oiled spiked hair gleaming in the first sunlight, and cut my way toward him.

But Polillo was there first. I saw Cholla Yi aim a cut at her, and Polillo lean back as the sword whispered past, and then smash out with her axe head, like it was the butt of a club. It hit Cholla Yi in the chest and sent him stumbling back. But there was no blood, and his face showed no agony—he was wearing armor beneath his tunic. Now he and Polillo danced back and forth, and somehow all knew this would be the battle's decision, and no one cast spear or stone from the rear, nor sent a shaft thudding home. I don't know why such an absurdity as a duel came to be, on the deck of this heaving pirate ship, between my legate and a renegade turncoat, but it did, for just a moment.

Cholla Yi's blade was huge, double-handed, but perfectly balanced, and he used it both as intended and one-handed, weaving a mesh of steel between him and Polillo's dancing axe as she closed, ever forcing him back and back toward the railing.

Polillo saw a chance, and swung hard. Someone—it might've been me—groaned as she missed, leaving herself open for a killing blow from Cholla Yi. He struck, but impossibly, Polillo stopped her great axe in mid-stroke and brought it back, parrying his blade away, sending Cholla Yi stumbling, off balance. Cholla Yi came back, in a circular return, but again his attack was blocked, and then Polillo struck with all her strength from her short-guard position with as much power as I would've gained with a full swing of the axe, and the blade smashed into Cholla Yi's side, crashing through his armor as if he were naked, and blood and entrails spilled.

Cholla Yi shrilled a howl of agony and fell back, his face black with his last rage.

I came back to myself and struck at a sailor, but he was dropping his sword, hands coming up bare, imploring mercy, and across the deck there were others, and weapons clattered down and there were shouts of surrender. There was still red blood before my eyes as I saw three, no, four of my few remaining women down in death, and perhaps I might've ordered no quarter, but then I saw Gamelan, standing at the edge of the quarterdeck, flanked by Pamphylia and his other companion, faithful to their orders.

"Stop!" he shouted. "He's coming! He's coming! *I can see him!*"

I had a single second to realize what Gamelan was saying, time enough to look and see his eyes were clear, looking at me, at the world, rather than gazing at that inward blankness as they had for so long.

The seas erupted and the Archon attacked.

We never saw him, though, not in the brief moments of that frenzied nightmare, because he attacked not with pure magic, but with sea demons and creatures of the dark ocean depths.

The water darkened to black as if dye had been cast into it, and tentacles writhed out, stretched and took a man, then another, from the ship next to ours, and took them down to where huge lidless eyes stared and a parrot beak gaped and snapped closed, and the screams stopped. There was another creature up from the depths, a scaled salamander three times the size of a man, its scales black with red stripes, and each time its mouth opened, fire spat out. It climbed clumsily up the side of Kidai's galley, and I saw sailors stabbing at it with spears, and then screaming as they flamed into living torches.

Across the waters I saw other creatures, some obvious demons not unlike Elam, if smaller than the Demon Lord, as they boarded ships, talons flashing like swords, or simply grabbing sailors by their midsection and ripping into them with their fangs. Something with tentacles even greater then the kraken I'd seen came out of the sea and took a galley into its embrace and sank back, leaving nothing but some flotsam and a whirling maelstrom.

I suppose all of us went mad in that minute, seeing what no being should ever see, facing deaths no one could imagine in her darkest thoughts. Some of us froze, and died. Others fought bravely, and were taken as well.

The battle wasn't completely one-sided—the fire salamander's mouth opened, and Kidai hurled a spear into it just as flame gouted, and Kidai died as his other seamen did. The salamander roared agony and rolled in its death tangle, crushing men and smashing the galley's masts before it rolled off into the black waters, leaving the galley listing, taking on water and sinking.

A demon clambered over the side of our ship, and met Polillo's axe as it slashed away the top of its head. But the monster didn't die; blinded, it stumbled on across the deck and fell into the sea on the other side.

Another monster slithered out of the depths. It was perhaps twenty feet long and was like a huge, slime-green snake, except there were no eyes, no airholes, and its mouth was round, ringed with fangs, funnel-shaped. It struck at me, and I slid aside, spotted the halberd that'd belonged to the man I'd slain, dropped my sword and had the spear. As the beast, whatever it was, bit at me once more, I struck with all my power, and the blade impaled the monstrosity to the deck. It flailed like a worm impaled on a fishing hook, then lay still.

There was a monstrous sea snake rearing above the prow, fangs gleaming below its horned snout. It darted and took one of my women, then hissed louder than a thousand screams as arrows pin-cushioned its head, and I came from my madness.

Magic had brought this cursed brood up, and only magic would send it down. I sought for words, for a spell, and knew I did not have the time and ran toward Gamelan, just as a demon pounced from the sea onto the quarterdeck. It looked like some impossible kind of water lemur, except streaked like rotting meat, and it had scythes instead of arms. It struck for Gamelan, but he saw it and slipped out of the way. He scrabbled for a marlinspike from a rack, and the demon attacked once more. Pamphylia was between them, serving as she'd been ordered, and took the slash across her body and fell, even as her blade drove deep into the demon's chest.

I came up the companionway, but Gamelan held out his hands.

"No, Rali," he said calmly, as if we were sitting in his tiny room discussing the theory of magic. "Do not come close."

I knew I must obey, and stayed where I was.

Gamelan smiled at me, a friendly, warm smile that welcomed and said farewell at the same time, then his eyes went beyond, to the black sea.

He reached into his robes and took out that black onyx box that contained the Archon's heart. He held it above him in both hands and spoke, very quietly, but his voice rang across the ocean louder than the strongest typhoon:

"Power take power
Black take black
Dark cannot stand
Flame conquers dark
Fire kills night."

"There is all
There is all
There is a finish
Power take power."

His hands moved oddly, in a series of circles, or as if he were scribing invisible symbols as he canted. From nowhere came a roar of pain, and a sound I can only describe as a great *cracking*, like a sheet of ice being smashed.

I don't quite have the words for what came next, but it looked like a fog bank being blown apart by a wind. They were gray wisps, tendrils, and they swept out from Gamelan across the deck, across the sea, swirling toward the demons, and when they struck, the demons shrilled pain and died, or sank beneath the surface. There was the sound of a whirlwind roaring, howling, but our sails hung motionless.

I heard a shout of triumph booming across the heavens and thought it Gamelan's voice, and then all was still.

The sea was as calm as a millpond.

All of the Archon's creatures had vanished.

But the blood and the gore still stained our decks, and the corpses still sprawled, and now the wounded began their cries and moans of agony.

Gamelan stood motionless, and now his hands were empty. I started up toward him, and then he slumped. I caught him before he hit the deck and held him. His eyes were clear, seeing but looking beyond me.

Once more he smiled.

Then he died.

I *felt* him go, *felt* an emptiness in the world that'd been alive, that'd been warm, that'd been good.

I laid him down and stood, not denying my tears.

Gamelan was gone, and in his great sacrifice he'd taken our only talisman, the heart of the Archon.

But I could feel no sign of the Archon's presence.

He'd almost destroyed us through treachery and his wizardry. Of our seven ships, only two were still afloat—ours and Cholla Yi's flagship. The others had been pulled down or sunk.

We bandaged our wounded and buried our dead.

There were many, almost as many as the battle with The Sarzana had cost. Pamphylia. Cliges. Dacis. Others. More sailors than Guardswomen, but what of them? Sometimes we had a body to say the ceremony over, other times nothing except a scrap of their clothing, a jar of scent, a favorite weapon, or in Cliges' case, her well-loved drinking jack, which we could use to keep their ghosts from wandering forever.

We jury-rigged repairs on our ships and set sail once more, limping on, still to the east.

It was two days later that we sighted the ship from Orissa.

BOOK THREE

ORISSA

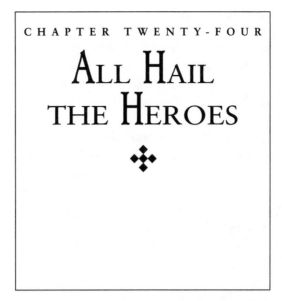

CHAPTER TWENTY-FOUR

ALL HAIL
THE HEROES

❖

The closer the ship came, the more certain we were it wasn't a trick of light or of a battle-weary mind.

"It's from home!" Polillo roared, pounding me on the back.

Some of us cheered, some of us wept; but all of us marveled as the approaching sailors hailed us in our *own* language. Oh, how we loved every inch of that ship—from its familiar shape to the very wood that made it—cut from the fragrant forests outside our city. And the men who hailed us in that lilting, ever-flowing speech of our beloved river were equally as familiar. We knew the weavers' street where their costumes were made; had complained about the smell of the dye vats that gave their clothes all the sunny, Orissan colors. The shape of their beards, the cut of their boots and sandals, even the rings and necklaces they wore—and how they wore them—all sang of home.

Greater joy followed when the captain greeted us and we learned just how far off our charts were—instead of many weeks, we were only a few days from Orissa. A great weight lifted from our shoulders. Now all our burdens, all our worries, all our trials, would be shared by our countrymen. If the Archon threatened us anew, he'd have to contend with Orissans by the tens of thousands. It was no longer solely our burden. We would have the help of our friends, our lovers, and our families.

My steps were buoyant as we boarded, battle fatigue falling away as easily as you might shed a light shift on a hot summer night. Our wounded were tenderly administered to; familiar prayers were said to ease the passage of our dead, as well as to help heal our own grief over their going. Although the ship was crowded, there were only twenty of us left, so there was little trouble finding room. Then, without further ado, we immediately set sail for home. Our two ships, smaller and lighter than the Orissan merchant vessel, were taken in tow; it was easier than transferring all our treasure, although by now I think none of us cared a hang for the gold. Its price had been far too high.

I shared quarters with Polillo, and as soon as we were settled, the captain, whose name was Wazanno, came to make sure we were comfortable.

"You've been gone so long, Captain Antero," he said. "We'd given you up for dead." He poured us each a goblet of the red Orissan wine we'd been without for nearly two years. I could almost taste the sun-drenched vines it came from.

"You were nearly right more times than I like to think," I said.

"The worst fight of all," Polillo said, "was just before you got here. Sea monsters and demons and only the gods know what else attacked us."

"Is that so?" the captain said. "You'll have to tell me about your adventures when you've rested."

Polillo snorted. "Set aside a goodly amount of time and half a dozen bottles of this wine," she said. "There's much to tell. Why, we've sailed nearly half around the world and back. Seen things that'll freeze your pearlies in the telling."

Wazanno rose to go. "I'm most anxious to hear your tale," he said, "if my duties allow it. I'm a captain who likes his own hand at the tiller, so I haven't much time."

Then he yawned. "Forgive me," he said. "I've missed a good deal of sleep on this voyage. We've had a lot of trouble getting the ballast right." He excused himself and was gone.

"That's fellow's got the blood of a fish," Polillo said. "And half the imagination."

I sighed. "He must be one of the new breed my brother's always grousing about," I said. "Since the Far Kingdoms opened up, there's been a shortage of qualified seafarers. He looks competent enough, thank the gods. Amalric has many a horrid tale to tell of the scrapings he's been forced to take."

"At least he left the wine," Polillo said, refilling our goblets.

She toasted me: "Welcome home."

And I echoed: "Welcome home."

A HEROES' GREETING awaited when we docked in Orissa. There was music and dancing in the streets; speeches from the Magistrates and a fiery display of magic from the Evocators. Soldiers dressed in their most dazzling uniforms paraded before us, led by General Jinnah—yes, that damned Jinnah—and wonders of all wonders, he gave a rousing speech telling all what great and noble warriors we were—especially me! As I goggled at this cynical twist of fate that'd ended with me being greeted by my greatest mortal enemy, Jinnah finished his speech and the military musicians trumpeted a stirring hurrah for us all. Then, as quickly as they'd turned out, Jinnah and the soldiers quick-marched away. Then, soon as they'd disappeared from sight, the crowds began to melt away and my fellow Orissans wandered off to resume their daily routine.

The whole thing seemed flat, perfunctory. Apparently, as far as my fellow Orissans were concerned, the war had been over long ago and we were only a bit of not very important unfinished business. I could imagine the tavern talk in a few scant weeks: "Captain Antero, is it? Oh, yes. You're with the Maranon Guard or something. Jinnah's girls. Didn't you do something noble and self-sacrificing? Dashed if I can remember exactly what it was. I'd buy you a glass, but I'm a tad light in the purse just now. Come around another time, my good captain, and I'll treat you to a proper drink." I didn't feel jealous, or sorry for myself, but shrugged it off, chalking it up to the treatment all soldiers have suffered throughout the ages. We're the toast of the land when the war drums sound, but they can't get away from us soon enough when peace is restored. Besides, I was too overwhelmed at being home to dwell on it.

I brought the Guard to attention, and, adhering to protocol, turned the formation over to Flag Sergeant Ismet, eager as any of my women to get away from this clangor of armor and death, and be welcomed home. But as she leather-lunged the dismissal and the Guards stamped their boots twice and broke toward the waiting crowd, I called Ismet to me.

"Sergeant," I said, "you don't have any family that I'm aware of."

"I have the Guard, Captain. What more could a woman want?"

Again, I had that flash of wonderment—could this woman truly be the embodiment of Maranonia? I chose my words carefully.

"I merely thought the barracks might be lonely, with everyone off on leave. Would you care to join me as my guest? There's more than enough room, and we Anteros don't seem happy without at least six or seven friends staying with us."

Ismet looked uncomfortable, and I realized she was having trouble finding words that applied to a situation beyond the military.

"Begging the captain's pardon, but I'm not sure what loneliness is. Being by myself in the barracks, why, I look forward to it. It gives me a chance to relax, a time to remember who I am, and build up my strength. If I need to talk to someone, there's taverns aplenty outside the gate. When I get tired, I can come back and listen to the silence, although there's always the clatter of arms, the chatter of sentries, and the crying of the watch. I wouldn't know what to do, I guess, without that around me.

"The Guard *is* my family. I guess other women need something more. I don't. Maybe . . . maybe it's because of what I came from." Her lips firmed, and I knew that was the only time I'd ever hear Ismet admit there had been a past before the Guard, let alone what it might've been.

I sought for words to end what was becoming embarrassing for both of us. But before I found the right ones, she said, "Thanks, Captain, for the invitation. But you don't need an old soldier hanging about when you've got more important things to take care of. Maybe we'll get together and have some drinks and talk about this campaign, if you want. I've some thoughts as to what went wrong, and what we need to do before they send us out again."

That was Ismet. I said of course I'd see her, and she saluted and was gone.

Polillo and the other Guardswomen were being swept off by friends and relatives to enjoy their long, well-deserved leaves. I searched the melting crowd for my own people, but my heart sank when I couldn't find Amalric. A knot of self-pitying disappointment stuck in my throat. Then I saw Porcemus and my other brothers and their wives coming forward. Dreading their usual cold dislike, I dragged myself to them.

Imagine my surprise when Porcemus threw his arms around me, crying, "Thank the gods you've returned to us, Rali!" Then he kissed me. I pulled back and saw he was so full of emotion, his eyes were welling with tears.

Then the others crowded in, saying I'd made them so proud, and other inanities—all obviously heartfelt just the same. My brothers embraced me and pounded me on the back, and their wives wept and said they'd never known another woman so brave. I was overcome by it all and wept in return, getting all blubbery and snotty.

"Where is Amalric?" I finally managed to get out.

"He'll be so sorry he missed you," Porcemus said. "And Omerye as well. They both set sail once more for the Far Kingdoms not two days ago. We must get a message to them immediately. He's been as worried as the rest of us."

I had more than my own selfish reasons for wanting to see Amalric. Something had to be done about the Archon—immediately! With Gamelan dead, I lacked a sympathetic ear in high places. Then I spotted a familiar, jaunty figure moving down the street away from us. It was Malaren, one of

Amalric's best friends, as well as mine. He'd succeeded his father as a Magistrate not long before I'd marched to Lycanth.

Excusing myself, I broke free of my family's sticky embrace and ran after him. I caught him just before he rounded the corner.

"Malaren," I shouted. "Please wait!"

When he saw me, he stopped. A dim smile twisted one corner of his foppishly handsome face.

"My dear Captain Antero," he said. "What a joy it is to see you safe after all these long months." He stuck out his hand to greet me.

I laughed, brushed it away, and gave him a bear hug. I barely noticed that he seemed startled. "Why all the formality, Malaren?" I said. "Last we spoke, I was the sister you never had, and we plotted to rid me of Porcemus so you could join the family. Of course, we were both drunk at the time, but I thought you made much sense for a fellow lying on the tavern floor."

Malaren gave a nervous titter and returned the embrace—a bit stiffly. "Yes, uh . . . Rali, my dear," he said. "You know that I love you above all others."

"How've you been, you old heartbreaker?" I asked. "Has your wife turned you out yet?"

Another nervous titter. "Oh, you know us, Rali. We might quarrel now and again. But in the end, my dear, all is forgiven."

"That's a load if I ever heard one," I said. "You're just too quick-witted, or she'd have taken a kitchen knife and made you sing high soprano long ago."

More tittering. "How colorful," he said. Then: "Now that you're back, you must come have dinner with us."

"Have you lost your mind as well as your sense of humor?" I said. "You *know* your wife hates me. She thinks I've got a secret yen for you."

"Yes, that's so," he said weakly. "Quite true."

He gave me another stiff embrace. "Excuse my rudeness," he said. "But I really must rush. A Magistrates' meeting, you know."

I stopped him before he could go. "Listen," I said. "There's another reason I wanted to see you—besides missing your handsome face. A much more important reason."

I had a grip on his sleeve and he was trying to tug it away without appearing rude. "Really, my dear," he said, "I must be going."

I was tired and impatient and confused. My temper flared and I wanted to shout at him, tell him that the fate of Orissa hung in the balance. But then my family was catching up to us and I suddenly felt foolish, overly dramatic, and limp as an old bootlace. I said, "Please, Malaren! On our friendship, I beg you. Make the time to see me. It is of vital importance, I promise you."

"Very well," he said with a sigh. "I'll send a litter tomorrow afternoon."

He broke away as Porcemus and the others descended, and once again I was smothered in a mountain of unfamiliar familial love.

MALAREN DIDN'T SEND the promised litter the following day, or the next, or the day after. I sent him several messages, each more pleading then the other. He replied to them all with weak excuses, as if he were trying to avoid me. At the same time, my family doted on me as if I were a prized child. They'd taken up residence in Amalric's villa and they filled my hours with all sorts of events and celebrations. Party after party was given in my honor. Food and wine flowed without end. Odder still, many a tempting young woman was trotted before me. Other than Amalric, my brothers had always been disgusted by my sexual preferences; their wives even more so. But in the spirit of their new love, all that seemed forgotten. I was too weary to be tempted, but went along as best I could, relieved after so many years of being an outcast, that my family finally seemed to accept me for what I was. I didn't bed any of the women—there was no desire in me, especially after I asked about Tries and was told she'd married some fellow and had a child a little less than a year old.

I realize, now, I was an emotional volcano waiting to be set off. Whenever I came close to explosion, I pulled back, fearful that I wouldn't be able to stem the eruption. At the heart of it was Gamelan.

It wasn't just because he'd thrown away his life for me—as if that weren't enough. It had been the greatest bravery I've ever known. Here was an old wizard, blinded and stripped of all his powers. It was unimaginable how deep he'd had to reach to find the strength he needed. I'd seen some of the shadow worlds of magic—if that's what they are. But they were only the depth of a knuckle plunged into a cold, dark sea. He must have gone to the bottom—and beyond—to dredge up the powers to best the Archon. I relived his death and my unworthy salvation night after night, and every quiet moment of each waking hour. Save my mother, I mourned Gamelan as I've mourned for no other, even Otara, or—and I must be honest—my own father.

I tried to drink myself into a stupor, but each time I reached the cliff where sobriety ends, I hesitated, then put the glass down. I was wary of losing control; why, I couldn't say. At times I also felt I was being watched—not by my family, although they hovered over me, making certain all my needs were met—but by some unseen presence. At night I had the oddest feeling I was being probed for weakness. I didn't bother telling my family about the Archon and the threat he still posed; loving as they were, my brothers were a weak lot and overly nervous about magic after the tragedy of Halab so many years ago.

I also pined for my Guardswomen, who'd been my sole company for two years. All of them were on leave, however, and could not be found. I slipped out alone one night to check at our favorite taverns. Although it was early, Orissa was silent and there were only a few lights showing. As you know, ours is a normally boisterous city, with a rich night life. But this particular evening I didn't even see any rats or lizards squabbling in the garbage heaps. The only real activity seemed to be at the Evocators' Palace. A halo of magical light framed the ancient building, more lights blazed on the bottom floor, and there was that odd prickling of the air that comes when the wizards are hard at work. There's the answer, I thought. It must be some religious observance I'd forgotten. That explained why the city was so quiet.

Still, even during holy days, there's always some tavern open. At the Avenue of the Bakers I took a shortcut that led to an inn where a ready drink was more important than any gods. But the alley took an odd twist, and before I knew it, I came out on the same street I'd started at. I looked around, seeing the landmarks I knew so well. There was the Bakers' Guild Hall, and across from it the warehouse where the millers delivered the flour to feed the ovens in the shops lining the street. Once again I struck out down the alley, and once again it curved back to deliver me where I'd started. I started to get frustrated, then shrugged. Amalric has often commented on how false memory can be when you've been gone from home a fair amount of time. Very well, I thought, I'll take the long way.

I set off down the street, turned at Hogshead Lane, where the coopers live and work, and turned a final time at Amalric's favorite chandlery. Three shops down from it I found the tavern just where it was supposed to be. I groaned when I saw it was as silent and dark as the rest of the city. There's a board outside the place where the regulars can post messages to absent friends. I saw several fresh notes pinned to it, and when I checked, I found they were all from my Guardswomen—looking for one another. Among them was one that bore a familiar scrawl.

It read: "Off to see my mother. Back at the full moon. The Captain will stand a round for any Guardswoman who attends . . . Love and sloppy kisses . . . Polillo."

I grinned, knowing the message was for my eyes—and my purse. I noted that the date wasn't far off. It'd be good to see her again. Feeling much better, I returned home.

My good mood, however, didn't last even until dawn. I woke up brooding, with a sense time was running out. I was not kind to my horse as I booted it out of the stable yard and rode to Malaren's house. The closer I got, the more determined I was to have it out with him. I arrived unannounced and pounded on the door. A servant came and tried to say his master wasn't in, but I pushed my way past, calling Malaren's name until he emerged blinking from his study. I didn't bother with his stuttered excuses, but hauled him back into the room, sat him down, and spilled out my story. It took several hours. When I was done, he looked at me as if I were mad.

"You want me to repeat all this to the Magistrates?" he asked. "Tell them that despite all evidence, one of the Archons survives? And that I have the word of a woman who has never previously shown a talent for magic, but claims she's suddenly a great wizard?"

He sighed, shaking his head in despair. "I can't allow it, my dear friend," he said. "It will do your reputation great harm."

"Hang my reputation," I exploded. "I'm sworn to *die* for Orissa if necessary. Now that she's facing a greater threat than ever before, why would I fear mere humiliation? I want a hearing, dammit! I demand a hearing before the Magistrates *and* the Council of Evocators! It is my right and duty as commander of the Maranon Guard to report on my mission. It was by *their* orders that I was sent. And it was by their orders that only twenty of us returned."

He relented. "Very well," he said. "I'll try and see what I can do."

I exploded. "You'll have to do more than try! You don't seem to understand. The Archon is more powerful than ever. By the gods, if Gamelan or Amalric were here, you'd all be jumping right now."

"Yes, yes," he said. "Calm yourself, my dear Rali. I'll see to it immediately."

More time dragged by. Then a message came from Malaren. The Magistrates and Evocators had agreed to a hearing. But first they wanted a written report so they could go over it in detail. "But first," I've noted, is the favorite phrase of the paper-shuffler and small-minded business folk. Only tax collectors do not use it. So I labored over the report for days, drawing and redrawing my argument until it was absolutely clear. The report went out, and, surprisingly, a date was quickly set—the first day of the full moon, which was one week off. During this whole time, my family didn't say a word about my demands. When I warned Porcemus that I'd be stirring things up, he'd only said: "Whatever you think best, Rali." His attitude was so refreshing it was frightening.

The day finally came and I prepared myself with extra care. I took a long, sudsy bath. I trimmed and buffed my nails, had my hair redone in a helmet cut, oiled my harness until it shone, polished every bit of metal, and gave my sword an extra stropping. When I was fully dressed, everything about me gleamed, from the pure white uniform tunic to my burnished boots. Even my legs and arms, which I left bare, glowed a golden sea- and sun-kissed brown.

On the way out of the villa I hesitated, thinking I ought to visit my mother's garden shrine for good luck. As soon as I went through the gate, I knew something was wrong. The garden was usually a pleasant jumble of flowers and trees, but now it was cold perfection. Every stone was white-painted, the grass trimmed nearly to the roots, the trees lined up so exactly that if you stood behind one, the others couldn't be seen; and the plants and flowers were set in an exact pattern, as if put there by a geometer. As I stood there dismayed, wondering if Amalric had lost his mind and dismissed our old family gardener who'd been with us since we were children, I noticed the absence of odor of any kind. The air was balmy, but where was the scent of roses and sandalwood and fruit flowers? Also, where there was usually a flock, only a single bird chirped from the trees, and I heard the buzz of a solitary insect. I saw no other. My steps quickened as I rounded the curve of the path to the shrine. Awaiting me was an even greater mockery. The simple blank stone was gone. As was the rose tree that had framed it, and the charming little musical fountain. Instead, there was a large statue of my mother. Oh, it was exactly like her, and she was a beautiful woman, so I couldn't call it ugly. But there was such an ennobled martyr look about it that I knew she would have hated it, been humiliated by it.

I shouted for Porcemus, and when he came trotting up, I blistered the air. "What have you done?" I demanded.

"Why, what is the matter, Rali?" he asked, startled.

"Mother's shrine is gone," I snapped. "Instead there's this big ugly thing."

Porcemus looked at the statue, gaping stupidly as if seeing it for the first time.

"Does Amalric know about this?" I demanded.

Porcemus recovered and smiled. "Oh, of course, he does. It's his home, after all."

"I can't believe he'd allow such a thing," I said. "You must've done it when he was gone."

"That's it, exactly," Porcemus said. He seemed oddly relieved. "We wanted to surprise him. He quite liked it. I'm sorry you don't."

I didn't listen to another word, but spun on my heel and stalked out, fuming and cursing under my breath. I had the same poor horse as before and expected him to shy away when I stormed into the stable to take him from the groom. Instead he took my angry burden quite placidly, making me madder still. I wanted to boot him into a gallop, but realized I'd only be taking my troubles out on the poor beast, and merely switched his flanks with the reins. He broke into a smooth run and we were soon away from the villa. I calmed myself—there were more important things to face this day. I only hoped the beginning didn't forebode what was going to happen next.

An hour later I was ushered into the main chamber of the Hall of Magistrates and was at rigid attention as our city's rulers came in one by one and took their seats. The hall was otherwise empty—this was to be a private hearing. There were seven of them—the full five who made up the Council of Magistrates, plus two youthful-appearing representatives of the Council of Evocators. I didn't recognize either of them. The Magistrates were all men I knew—especially Malaren, who gave me a friendly smile when he took his seat near the end.

Then my heart sank as I saw a maddeningly familiar figure seat himself in the highest-backed chair in the center, which is reserved for one of the Chief Magistrates. It was Jinnah! By the gods, how could that bastard have risen to such high office? But there was nothing I could do. I could only trust in the good judgment of the other six men. I steeled myself and began the speech I'd assembled with much care.

"My esteemed lords," I said, "I stand before you in great sorrow. The mission you entrusted me with has failed, despite the most extreme efforts of your beloved Maranon Guard. To accomplish the task you charged us with, we sailed far to the west—farther than any man or woman from these parts has ever gone before. We encountered and defeated savages and other hostile forces. In your behalf, and in behalf of Orissa, we befriended the great peoples of the distant Kingdom of Konya, who await your emissaries to begin trade. They are a rich people, a good people, and will make worthy allies as these new lands in the west open to us. But I grieve to tell you that these successes are nothing compared to our ultimate failure to carry out your orders.

"The last Archon of Lycanth eluded us to the very end. Only twenty of us returned, my lords. Twenty of all those who set sail two years ago. The only reason I am able to stand here before you today is because of the blood my sister warriors were willing to shed so I could carry back the warning.

"My lords, Orissa faces the greatest crisis in its existence. As I speak, the Archon is hatching his final plan to humble us, to destroy us. Lord Gamelan himself—the greatest Evocator Orissa has ever bred—gave his life so I might sound the trumpet. I wish the gods had seen it otherwise and it was he who stood before you now, so you could fully realize the peril that faces us. Please, my lords, know that peace is not yet ours. Know that our greatest enemy still stalks us, and there is little time left before he will pounce."

I'd concentrated so hard on my speech, I hadn't noticed the reaction of my leaders. But as I finished and looked into their faces, I was astonished to see such blank looks. It was as if I hadn't said a word.

At long last Jinnah cleared his throat. He gave me that weasel smile of his. "An excellent report, Captain Antero," he said. "You are to be congratulated. Let me be the first to say how much I mourn the noble women who gave their lives for Orissa."

The other members of the group made dull noises of condescension. I could feel my blood rising; anger hammered at my temples. Jinnah raised a copy of the report I'd prepared.

"We've pored over this quite carefully, Captain," he said. "So you needn't go into any additional detail at this time. I must say, we were quite alarmed, weren't we, my lords?"

He turned to the others, who mumbled agreement. Malaren gave a vigorous nod.

"We were so alarmed we didn't wait for this hearing," Jinnah continued. "Rest assured our noble Evocators took immediate action."

I breathed a sigh of relief. Thank Te-Date that something was being done. But my relief was short-lived.

"Spells were cast," Jinnah went on. "Spells, I have been assured, of the utmost sophistication. I'm pleased to report, Captain, there is no basis to your grave fears."

"What?" I roared, forgetting myself. "What are you saying?"

Jinnah only raised his eyebrows. "I'm saying, my brave woman, that contrary to your bleak thinking, your mission was a complete success. Your soldiers did *not* die in vain. Nor did the great Lord Gamelan. The Archon is dead. Thanks to you, Orissa is safer than it has ever been in its history. There is no threat."

Can you imagine the nightmare I was trapped in, Scribe? Here was the man who was proof that cynicism is the real ruler of this world. His motives in sending the Maranon Guard after the Archon were of the meanest, most self-serving kind, and had nothing to do with his concern for Orissa. Those same motives led him to plot against the life of the Guard's commander— threatening the mission itself. This man, this fool, now held the fate of Orissa in his honors-grubbing hands.

"You are making the most terrible error," I shouted. "Lord Gamelan himself confirmed all I have said."

Jinnah smiled, amused. He looked over at the two young Evocators, who had the temerity to giggle. "So you claim, Captain," Jinnah said. "But by your own admission, Lord Gamelan was blinded and had lost his powers. Also—and I hate to malign the dead—Gamelan *was* an old man. Far past his prime, mighty and gloried though that prime might have been." He looked at the Evocators. "Isn't that so, my lords?"

One of the young wizards bobbed his head, still giggling. Then he tried to look mournful, serious. "I fear all you say is true," he said. "Besides being old, poor Lord Gamelan was quite overwhelmed by all the new magical discoveries that have been made since the good captain's brother discovered the Far Kingdoms. He still clung to the old ways of doing things, refused to consider the new theories posed by the late Lord Janos Greycloak—whom he privately denounced. Harsh as it may sound, reason commands us to conclude that Lord Gamelan was no longer competent."

This was absolute nonsense! Gamelan might've feared that age was threatening his wits, but I knew from our many long talks about the philosophy of magic that those fears had only spurred him to think deeper still. How many times had I heard him expound on Greycloak's theories and where they might lead someday? I told them all this; I defended Gamelan to the heavens, but nothing I said would wipe off those damned smiles.

Then Jinnah leaned forward. "That may all be very well, Captain Antero," he said. "But in your report you say it was *you* who cast the spell, not Lord Gamelan. And it was *you* who found evidence of the threat from the Archon. Isn't that so?"

"Yes," I said. "But it was Gamelan who taught me, guided me."

"Ah, so now you claim to be a wizard?" Jinnah said. "Such a great wizard that your magical efforts are to be accepted over the best magical minds in Orissa?" He indicated the two Evocators.

"I can only tell you what I *know*," I said. "I make no claims, except that I speak the truth. Look here on my palm, where the Archon's brand still lingers! Please, my lords. You *must* listen. The Archon must be stopped!"

"Forgive me, Captain Antero," Jinnah said. "But I must call these proceedings to a halt. I, of all people, do not wish to see one of Orissa's greatest heroes humiliate herself. You've been through a great deal. I'm sure you're weary and confused. You should rest awhile, Captain. Then, in the fullness of time, after reflecting on what we said here today, if you still have doubts, come see me. My door is always open to you, Captain. Such is my great respect for your accomplishments."

Then, as I gaped, refusing to believe my own eyes and ears, the seven men rose as one and walked out of the room. A sentry shut the door behind them and took up post in front of it.

I raged out of the hall. There were few people about as I stormed down the street to find a quiet place to think. The river is where all Orissans go to seek peace. She's our comfort when everything else abandons us, so it's no wonder my boots carried me there. There was little ship traffic and only a solitary fisherman far out in the center, tending his nets. I sat on the bank and reviewed all that'd happened. I couldn't see where I should've done anything differently, just as I couldn't see what I ought to do next. I sat there brooding until a chill came into the air and I looked up and saw night closing in. Out on the river, the fisherman rose in his boat and hurled his net. As he did so, I had the most powerful urge to return to the villa. My family would comfort me. I got up, heading for the stable to retrieve my horse. As I neared it, I saw it was the only business open on the street. All the others, including two taverns, were shuttered early against the night. I paid the stablemaster and got my horse. As I mounted outside, the stablemaster's lad barred the door.

This was all very odd. Taverns rarely close on the main streets, and stables *never* do. And, now that I thought of it, the fisherman I'd noticed was nearly as strange. I'd never seen a net caster ply the waters that time of day. Then thoughts of Amalric's peaceful villa drew me and I kicked my horse toward home. But just as I neared the edge of the city, I suddenly remembered Polillo's note. She said she'd be at the tavern near the chandlery when the full moon rose, which was tonight. I turned the horse back into the city and all thoughts of the villa vanished.

Orissa was completely dark by the time I reached the chandlery. The only light, save the bright full moon, was the eerie glow of the Evocators at work in their hilltop palace. I turned the corner and saw the tavern was closed. I was about to dismount and check the message board to see if there was another note from Polillo, when I heard someone shout:

"Watch out, Ismet!"

I barely had time to register that it was Polillo's voice, when I heard the most ghastly roar. I drew my sword and spurred the horse to the mouth of an alley where the sound was coming from.

As I entered it I saw Polillo and Ismet fighting for their lives. A monstrous demon had them cornered against a blank alley wall. It had a squat, toadlike shape, with massive fur-covered legs and long, thick, hairless arms. A demon, here in the heart of Orissa! So much for Jinnah and his Evocators' entrail-stirring!

As I clattered into the alley, the demon turned and saw me. It had a fat man's face, with pouched jaws and lips. It shrieked at me, exposing a yard of filed teeth. My horse reared at the banshee howl and I fell heavily to the ground, barely kicking my feet out of the stirrups in time.

I scrambled up, still gripping my sword. The demon had turned back on Polillo and Ismet. Before I could move forward, the beast gave a mighty kick with one of those massive legs, forcing Polillo and Ismet to dodge apart. The huge foot struck the wall, powdering the rock. Then, as the two women poised for counterattack, sharp talons flicked at Ismet and I saw her roll under them. But it was only a feint, for as she came up, the demon's other arm shot out with amazing speed, slashing across Ismet's belly.

I knew it was a death wound as I charged forward. I didn't have to hear Polillo's shout of grief and fury. I howled my war cry as I sprinted in for the attack. Before I could plunge my sword into the beast, it leaped high into the air and I nearly crashed into the wall. I ran straight up the side and back-flipped over onto my feet. But my guard was open, and the demon roared and sprang toward me, claws scything out.

From nowhere came Ismet, blood pouring from her mouth, holding her guts together with an arm, but all of her killing power in her long sword as it slashed, then slashed again, cutting deep into the demon's leg before it could take me.

The creature screamed . . . and was gone.

"It's up there," Polillo shouted.

The demon was standing on the roof of the tavern, blood gouting from its leg. Polillo and I braced, expecting him to leap back into the fight. The beast peered at me, and I thought I saw a flicker of fear. Then he gave another howl and vanished before our blinking eyes.

Polillo and I ran to Ismet's slumped form. She was still alive—barely. She smiled weakly when she saw me.

"I knew you'd come," she said. Then she died.

We knelt by her body for long moments. This strange warrior woman who had been the spirit of the Guard, more than any banner, any statue of the goddess, was gone.

I knew I would never see her like again. She had been my right arm and, as much as anyone could touch the soul of Ismet, my friend.

I remembered what I'd felt when she became my teammate long ago, against my orders, when I went up the stairs in that sea castle in Lycanth to slay the Archons. *We were a team, and we would die as a team* . . . Instead, she'd died for me.

I'd failed her, although there wasn't anything I could've done. Perhaps I should have insisted she spend her holidays with me. Perhaps . . . perhaps . . . but there wasn't time for those thoughts.

"We'd better go," Polillo said. "He might come back."

I doubted it, but said nothing. My horse was long gone, so we slipped out of the alley on foot and made our way back to the river. Polillo led me to a hiding place under the docks. She whispered fire beads into life and I looked around with surprise when I saw the place had obviously been used for some time. Among other comforts, there was a small mattress, and a jug, which Polillo uncorked. She drank deeply and passed it over. I nearly gagged on the raw brandy, but it was fine once it cleared my gullet.

"You've obviously been here for a while," I said. "Maybe you'd better tell me what's going on."

"I never made it to my mother's house," Polillo said. "If you remember, my brother was waiting to fetch me when we arrived."

I nodded, vaguely recalling the tall, thin young man who'd thrown his arms around Polillo, and then blushed so charmingly when she'd introduced us during the chaos of the homecoming.

"Well, I lost him in the crowd when we were leaving," Polillo continued. "At least that's what I thought at first. I searched for him for nearly an hour, then realized he was probably waiting for me at the crossroads outside of town. I went to the east gate, but there were soldiers there who refused to let me out. I argued, but they were thickheaded louts and wouldn't let me pass. It was the same at the other gates."

"But I've used the west gate several times since we've been back," I said. "And I've never encountered any soldiers at all, much less been refused passage."

Polillo grunted in surprise. "That may be," she said. "But the same thing happened to all the other women I've managed to talk to. None of them were permitted to leave the city."

"Where did you stay?" I asked.

"I spent a few nights in the barracks with Ismet," she said.

I flushed as she said this, again regretting that my invitation to Ismet hadn't been more persuasive.

Polillo sensed my thinking. "Ismet wasn't the only one to die," she said. "Demons have killed three others that I know of." My guts churned. What a wonderful homecoming this was proving to be.

"It wasn't so bad during the day," Polillo said. "You could get a drink at a tavern. A bite to eat at a food stall. But at night everything shuts down, and that's when the demons came after us. None of us knew what was happening at first. I found out by accident when I saw the messages posted outside the tavern."

"I saw your message," I said.

"I was hoping you would," Polillo replied. "I'd been turned back every time I tried to go to your villa and see you. But I figured you'd come back to town *sometime*, and hoped you'd get through where I couldn't. I prayed like a crazed priest you'd look us up in the old haunts and see the message." She managed a small smile. "I never knew you not to stand a round when asked, so I thought I had a pretty good chance you'd show up if you saw it."

"Where are the others?" I asked.

Polillo shrugged. "Hiding all over the city. It'll take a while to round them up, but it could be done."

She went on to say she and Ismet were attacked a few nights after they'd holed up in the barracks. They'd escaped the demon and gradually learned others were being stalked. They decided to stick together and keep in contact with as many of the Guardswomen as they could. They'd been dodging death ever since, waiting for the night when I might appear.

"But I guess that damned demon figured it out," Polillo said. "He was lurking when we got there. Trapped us in the alley."

"That's another strange thing," I said. "Since when did that alley dead-end? Didn't it used to lead to the Avenue of the Bakers?"

"Of course it did," Polillo said. "Drove me mad for a time. But that was nothing. I've wandered all over the city since we got back. There's whole buildings gone. Streets that run straight up to houses and stop. I even tried to look into windows at night, and I swear sometimes I've thought every soul in Orissa sneaks out of the city just to mock us. I mean, you don't hear couples quarreling, kids pissing about going to bed too early, or even any old grandfather snoring the roof off when it gets real late."

She took another pull on the jug. "Now, I'll ask you the same thing you asked me, Captain," she said. "What in the name of any god you'd choose to curse is going on?"

"Whatever it is," I said with a snort, "according to our all wise superiors, it is definitely *not* the Archon."

Polillo gaped. By the time I'd filled her in on my hearing before the Magistrates and Evocators, her jaw was practically dragging through the muck.

"It doesn't take a Janos Greycloak," I said, "to put the sums together and come up with a simple answer. Who else but the Archon could plague us with demons? Who else but the Archon would want to see all the survivors of the expedition dead? I don't know about the other oddities, but whatever is the reason, the Archon *must* be behind it."

"Then why didn't our Evocators sniff him out?" Polillo asked.

"I don't know," I said. "But the only thing that seems awake and alight every night is the Palace of the Evocators. So I propose we take a little moonlit stroll, my fair Polillo. And if chance takes us past the Palace, why, who can say what should happen next?"

Polillo gave me a nasty grin. "Wait a minute, Captain," she said. "Let me get my axe."

She pulled it from under the mattress. It glittered deadly in the light of the fire beads. She gave it a rueful look.

"I thought I was done with her for a while," she said. "*Some* welcome for a soldier home from the wars. All hail the heroes! Bah!"

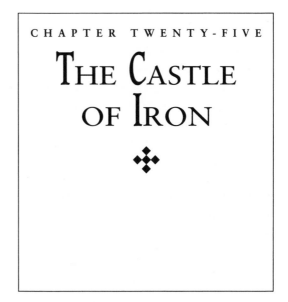

CHAPTER TWENTY-FIVE

THE CASTLE OF IRON

❖

I'm not sure what I expected to find at the Palace of the Evocators that night. As we approached, my nerves were snapping like tightly strung lyre strings. The Palace bulked over us, light glaring through the windows; but it was absent of any other sign of life, save the low, machinelike throbbing of the ground we walked on.

There was little cover on that hill, and as we leaped over naked ground from rock cluster to tree, I began to regret our coming. I'd cast a spell to dull the scent of our auras in case any hunting demons were lurking about, but there was nothing I could do about the bright moonlight menacing overhead. Even when we finally crept into the Palace's dense shadow, I felt no relief. The air stank of sulfurous magic, and my hackles were stiff, hot pins in my flesh. I wasn't comforted when I saw that the big main gate, although closed, was not guarded.

I grew more nervous as we crouched behind a thick clump of rosemary, and I probed ahead with my senses for a magical net and found nothing. Our Evocators have always been a secretive and wary lot, and I think if I'd brushed against the expected alarms, I would've turned back right then. Their very absence, however, heightened my suspicion. Even then I hesitated.

Polillo leaned close to whisper: "What'll they do if they catch us?"

Not long ago—before Amalric tamed them—the Evocators would've put us to death most horribly. They'd once falsely accused my brother,

Halab, of heresy, and they slew him; so the Anteros have more reason than most to be wary. But the new breed of Evocators who reign must abide by the same laws as the rest of us. What could they do to the Hero of Lycanth, the killer of Archons, besides publicly humiliate her? At least that's what I wanted to think. So my answer to Polillo was a shrug—who knows? Still, the dutiful reasoning of a good Orissan citizen nearly prevailed. What I ought to do, I thought, is to confront the Magistrates *and* the Evocators tomorrow. I could show them proof things were not as they believed. There was the blood of Ismet and the other murdered Guardswomen for evidence. Some of us had even witnessed the demons who'd killed them. Yes, I thought, this is a fool's errand I'm on.

It was then I saw the panther. She was crouched by the main gate, peering through the bars. She turned her head and looked at me, eyes glowing in a beam of moonlight that'd escaped the shadows. I felt a tug, as if she were beckoning. Then she turned back, rose to her feet and ghosted through the bars, to disappear on the other side. From Polillo's lack of reaction, I knew she hadn't seen the big cat. I signaled her and we slithered across the grounds to the gate. We knelt by it, checking for a guard, but once again we saw no one about. Then I spotted something clinging to one of the bars. Looking closer, I saw it was a tuft of black fur. It had the powerful odor of cat. I plucked it off and nearly tossed it away. But some instinct intervened and I put it in my pocket instead. Then I motioned to Polillo—it was time.

She boosted me to the top of the gate. As I balanced there, she leaped, grabbed the topmost crossbar and swung over to drop on the other side. Marvel at my friend's great strength steeled my confidence; I jumped, and she caught me in her arms and set me softly down. I grinned at her—just like old times! She buried a laugh, thumped me on the back, and together we slipped down the path to the Palace.

Off to the side I saw the panther again. She was waiting beneath the arch of a small doorway partly hidden by the thick-columned trunk of a poplar. When I turned toward her, she vanished inside. Polillo was as surprised as I was when we came to the arch and found it was nothing more than an empty frame. It was as if the carpenter had built the frame, then became so busy with other things he forgot to mount the door. We waited for a long time to make sure there was no one lurking for us inside. I probed forward with my senses, but found nothing magical to impede us. Polillo unlimbered her axe and I drew my sword. I nodded to her and we entered. As we went inside I had a mad thought: If they do catch us, we can always feign drunkenness. No one ever doubts a soldier when she says liquor made her do it.

We entered a long, dark corridor. Its walls were smooth and blank, made of some kind of black metal. As we cautiously made our way down it and saw the lack of doors or openings on either side, our tension grew, realizing there was no escape but the way we'd come.

The corridor spilled out into an immense chamber, lit only by cold moonlight spilling in through the high windows. As one part of me sniffed for danger, another wondered how the room could be so dark, if from outside we'd seen light pouring through the windows. Then my head was spinning faster as I saw the chamber was entirely empty—not one bench, not one bit of decoration, not even a fireplace to stave off a winter's chill. The only other egress besides the one we stood in was far across the chamber. It gaped like a single dead eye. We slunk toward it, hugging the dark, metallic walls. As we passed one of the windows, Polillo's hand suddenly gripped my shoulder hard. I stopped, bracing for an attack or fast retreat, depending on what was the matter. She jabbed a finger at the window. I could see her eyes were wide with amazement, possibly even fear. I realized she wanted me to look outside. I couldn't—it was too high, coming just to Polillo's chin. She made a stirrup with her hands; I stepped into it and she lifted me up.

At first I didn't know what I was looking at. Then terror bloomed as I saw what it *wasn't*. The view should've been of Orissa sleeping peacefully under the watchful eye of the hilltop Palace of Evocators. Instead, I saw a drear landscape. Across a desolate courtyard were tall, black iron gates. Swooping out from the window I was looking through were high black walls that climbed on either side to frighteningly familiar turrets. I nearly gagged as I realized where we were. This was *not* the Palace of the Evocators—it was a facade, a fake. In fact, we weren't even in Orissa. Instead, we were high on a nightmare mountain—inside the Archon's black iron castle.

I dropped to the floor and sagged against the wall. Polillo was staring at me, wondering what was going on. I had no answer; and even if I had, I was too stunned to speak. Then I heard talons scrape and I jolted up to see the demon rushing at us.

Polillo and I leaped apart. He howled at being denied an easy kill. He turned toward me, pivoting his massive toadlike body as if he carried no weight at all. Polillo came at his back, but the demon lashed behind him with one of his huge, furred feet, catching her in the chest. The blow hurled her clear across the chamber, where she slammed into a wall and slumped to the floor. But her attack gave me a breath of advantage, and I ducked under his taloned blow and slashed at his belly. The blade bit deep and the demon screamed in pain. He leaped back before I could follow through, slashing with his claws at the same time. One talon tip caught my sword with such force that it was ripped from my grasp. He came for me as I scrabbled for my blade. But he moved slowly, blood oozing from the deep wound I'd made. Even so, I was only just scooping up my sword when he came close enough to strike. I was off balance and there was no chance to dodge. Still, I tried—twisting awkwardly away, knowing I hadn't a hope. Before the blow struck, I heard a meaty thud, and without even a gasp the demon crashed to the floor. I rose to see Polillo standing over him. Her axe was buried in the beast's skull. She put her foot on his body for leverage and drew it out, then used his fur to wipe the axe head.

She touched her chest where he'd kicked her and winced. "I'm going to throttle the next woman who says she's jealous of my tits," she said. "All they do is get in the way."

I laughed wildly, not caring how loud it echoed in the steel chamber. Polillo laughed back and we hugged each other. Then we drew apart.

"I *do* love you, Polillo." I giggled.

"Bet you say that to all the demon-whacking girls," she giggled back.

The laughter faded. "*He* knows we're here," I said.

"Good," Polillo answered, hefting her axe. "Let's go find the bastard and kill him."

We walked boldly to the other entryway, boots echoing loudly against the steel floors. The corridor it opened into was as long and dark as the other, but we whispered fire beads to life and held them high to light the way as we advanced. The corridor twisted in wide curves that carried us downward; and the deeper we went, the heavier came the strange machinelike throbbing. Several times I thought I'd glimpsed the shadow of the big cat moving around a bend. Then my sword hand began to burn and I looked at my palm and saw the twin-headed lion scar was swollen and livid with blood. We were getting close. We turned one more corner and I saw light ahead.

I signaled a halt. In a few moments there would be no time to think. The odds on our side were laughably poor—only sword, axe, and muscle against the Archon's magic. And I had no Gamelan beside me with his vast experience of tricks, and trunk of sorcerous powders and vials. In fact, I had no magical implements of any kind. Then I remembered Gamelan saying that Janos Greycloak had disdained such things. He said they only helped you focus your thoughts and energies. Well, *good* for Greycloak, I thought. Good for that back-stabbing, friend-cheating son of a poxed whore. And as I cursed him, and cursed our foul luck, and cursed myself as well for my schoolgirl magical skills, the image of the panther popped into my head. I remembered the fur I'd put in my pocket.

Polillo must've thought I'd gone insane as I grabbed it out and knelt to the floor, muttering to myself as thought swirled about in my brain like litter before a windstorm. Then I had it—prayed I had it—and pressed the fur against my scarred palm.

"Daughter of darkness—
Swift night slayer—
Hunt with me, now;
Hunt the two-head beast,
Who waits in his lair;
Hunt his black wizard master,
Wherever he may flee!"

My palm burned hotter, so hot I almost cried out. I opened my hand and saw the fur and the scar had vanished. But my palm still stung, and I reflexively licked it to soothe pain. In an instant the pain was gone. I rose, my mind clearer than it's ever been. It was as if I'd drunk from a magical spring of clarity. I started toward the light again, strong and confident.

I hadn't gone half a dozen steps when sorcery smashed into me like a wave lifting out of an uneasy sea. But I held my ground against the buffeting and struck back with all my will. The wave retreated, but I knew it was coming again, and in my mind I built a seawall, and this time when it roared down on me again, it burst against that wall. I laughed crazily and turned to urge Polillo to follow me, to rage with me against the Archon.

But she just stood there, her face a mask of pain. She croaked at me: "Rali, I—" Another wave of pain gripped her, cutting off the rest. As I went to help, she suddenly stiffened, rising to her full height. Now, instead of pain, hate mottled her features. She opened her mouth and the Archon's voice burst from her lips: "Now, you shall die, Antero!"

Polillo swung her axe at me with all her incredible strength. I fell back. The axe whiskered past and clanged into the metal wall. Such was the force of her blow that it left a huge ragged hole in the steel as she dragged her axe back to swing again.

"Polillo, don't!" I screamed, although I knew it wasn't Polillo who was attacking me.

I backflipped as the axe came crashing down again, this time splitting the floor. As I came up I saw an opening as she raised that mighty weapon. Even in Polillo's hands an axe is a clumsier weapon than a sword. And I was faster, much faster. I only had to leap inside her guard and run her through. All my training and experience screamed at me to strike. But I could not, would not kill my warrior sister. I'd rather die myself. And I almost did as she swung. I ducked under the axe and scrambled away. Polillo followed me down the corridor, cursing me in the Archon's booming voice, striking at me whenever I was in reach. The metal corridor resounded with the death-dealing music of her axe.

Another opening presented itself, and this time I did jump forward, shifting my sword into my other hand. I hammered at her with my fist, putting all the force I could muster into the punch. But Polillo's ribs were like cabled steel and I nearly broke my wrist. She laughed, but it was the Archon's booming laughter. She lifted me by the back of my neck effortlessly, as if I had no substance at all. I struck out again, not at my friend, but at the laughter, at the Archon. I felt bone crack under my knuckles, and that mouth—Polillo's lovely mouth—became a bloody maw. She spit blood and broken teeth at me. She shook me like a pig killing a snake, and I was helpless against her berserk rage. Then she flung me away and I was sailing through the air, twisting, desperately fighting to land on my feet. But my sword—which I had in a death grip—got in my way and I fell heavily on my knees.

Fear drove me to my feet. I'd landed facing the light at the end of the corridor. I could hear her coming after me, so I sprinted forward, running as fast as I could. But rage made her faster and I knew she was almost on me. Any second and my back would be split by her axe. Then I was out of the corridor, nearly blinded by bright light. Just ahead, a rail blocked my way. I dropped to the floor and heard Polillo grunt in surprise. Then she was falling over me and I heard her slam against the rail.

My head came up and I heard her scream. This time it wasn't the Archon's voice, but Polillo's; my Polillo, screaming in fear. She plunged over the railing and I heard her shout: "Rali!" The shout was cut off. And the only sound I could hear was a great machine, churning, churning, just beyond the rail. I groaned up, limped to it and looked down.

Polillo's body lay broken across a huge toothed gear wheel, part of a monstrous mechanism.

Suspended below her was Orissa!

It was night and I could see the full moon hanging over the city as she slept. I could see the Hall of Magistrates, and the big public square with all the statues of our heroes. There was the Great Amphitheater, with its many rows of stone seats cascading down to the floor of the arena. Beyond were the docks and the river flowing quietly to the sea. Then I saw the whole scene was slowly revolving and I jolted back, realizing I was looking at an immense simulacrum of the city. An image in miniature, revolving, floating over a strange machine that looked like a metal grist wheel turned flat and driven by those huge meshing gears.

As I goggled at the strange device it dawned on me that this was the doom machine we'd feared so long. The Archon had finally gained power enough to build it, and when Gamelan had foiled him in that last battle, the Lycanthian sorcerer had transported me inside it. Everything from the

Orissan ship that'd picked us up after the battle to the lifeless parade that'd greeted us on our arrival was nothing more than an elaborate spell.

Then I noted all the imperfections in the image he'd made of Orissa. Buildings were missing, streets dead-ended where they shouldn't, and everything outside the city's walls was a blank. Well, not all. I could see the road leading to Amalric's villa, with woods and brush sketched about it. As I looked, I realized the Archon's unfamiliarity with my city had resulted in more than just physical imperfections. He'd made Jinnah a Chief Magistrate because that was the enemy he knew—the commander who fought him, however badly, at Lycanth. He also didn't know Malaren was my friend, which was why the automaton who posed as Malaren had behaved so oddly. And, finally, there was the greatest oddity of all—the love of my family. He wouldn't have known how Porcemus and the others truly felt about me. Among the Anteros who live, it is Amalric alone who loves me, and I him. I flushed in shame for the weakness that let those creatures take me in. I'd wanted my family's acceptance so much, I never questioned if their display of affection was false.

Gears suddenly shrieked in protest and the machine jerked to a halt as Polillo's broken body caught in the huge teeth.

I felt a presence and looked up, shielding my eyes against the bright light glaring down from the vaulted iron ceiling. I was standing on a catwalk that circled the edge of the yawning pit that held the Archon's doom machine. On the other side of that pit an open door beckoned. I moved toward it and my boot bumped against something. I looked at my feet and saw Polillo's axe. I sheathed my sword and picked it up. It was heavy, but as I shifted my grip, my fingers curled into the grooves worn by Polillo's fist. I felt the axe lighten until it was no more a burden to me than it had been to my friend.

I whispered to it: *"Avenge us, sister."*

I circled to the door, and when I came to it, I didn't hesitate, but strode into the room. The Archon was waiting.

He was standing by a window and I could see from the bleak view that we were in the iron castle's main turret. His eyes glowed and his lips made a rictus grin through his beard, exposing his long yellow teeth. But this time there was no laughter; there was no curse; there was no obscene mocking of my sex; no pointing with a twisted finger and shouting—begone! I should've been frightened, I should've cowered before this mighty sorcerer. Instead, I let my eyes sweep past him, feeling bold, strong. The turret room was a black wizard's clutter of skulls, demon talons, bottled human parts, and small stone figurines of creatures in pain. It was hot and smelled of sewage and rotting things. There was sinuous motion beside me, but I didn't leap back with alarm. I knew what it was and I looked calmly down to find the panther crouched next to me. She hissed at the Archon.

I scratched behind her ears and looked up at our enemy. "It's over," I said.

Hefting the axe, I stepped forward, the panther moving with me. The Archon made a motion and the air shimmered in front of us; and I came up against an invisible wall. But its surface was yielding and I pushed at it with a spell of my own. It yielded more, then stiffened as the Archon intensified his magic. But I knew it was only a matter of time before it gave.

"Whose demon are you?" he rasped.

I was surprised. "Demon? I'm no demon."

"You are to *me*," he said. "You are the bitch ferret who destroyed my kingdom. You killed my brother and you've hunted me, no matter where I fled."

From his dark view, I suppose he was right. I pushed harder against the wall, felt it shudder. The panther snarled in pleasure. A little more time and I'd be through.

The Archon laughed, his confidence returning. "I'm not done yet, Antero," he said. "You know you are weak against my powers. It's only a trick of your blood that gives you talent. A seed carried forward by your mother, who turned her back on our art. There can be no greatness in such magic."

It was my turn to laugh. "Then why do you fear me?" I said. "How was such a poor weak thing able to foil you?"

"The only mistake I made was when I cursed you," the Archon said. "You were about to slay me, and I thought the curse would be my only revenge. But as I died I saw another way, and escaped into this world. But that damned curse has kept you chained to me. Kept me from winning the greatest dream any wizard could have—the power of the gods themselves."

I sneered at him. "You think *you* could be a god?"

"I am one *now*, bitch ferret," the Archon said. "My battles with you have only made me stronger. I ate your misery. I drank the blood of your dead. And I consumed my slain allies, as well. You would have been wiser to turn back, Antero. You should have heeded the fear I struck in your dreams. You have made me suffer, it is true. But I've made you suffer more. I've killed all your soldiers. I've slain all your friends. I turned the last friend you shall ever have against you. And as she died, I sipped her fear; I nearly grew drunk on her betrayal."

"She didn't betray me, sorcerer," I said. "You possessed her. It was you, not Polillo, who tried to kill me."

The Archon's laughter mocked me. "A hair's difference," he said. "Is it enough to really comfort you?"

Actually, it did. Polillo was no Greycloak, who had turned on my brother. She'd been loyal to the end. I grinned at him, and he could see the truth in that grin. He frowned. It hurt him, not to be of hurt to me. The panther growled as I probed the Archon's defenses, but this time he fought harder, forcing us to retreat a few steps before I managed equilibrium.

The Archon took strength from this. "I admit you have distressed me, bitch ferret," he said. "I've pondered long on what it is about the Anteros that gives me such trouble. That some force is behind your family—especially you—I do not question. That panther, I have no doubt, is his emissary. How else could you have succeeded so long? How else could you have lived? But know this, Rali Antero—whose mother was Emilie. Know that whoever champions you, does it for his purpose, and his purpose alone. He cannot keep you safe much longer.

"Know that I only need to accomplish your death to mount the god's throne I have all but won. When you die, so will Orissa. The machine is set and needs only your blood to oil its works to complete its purpose. With Orissa's fall, the Far Kingdoms will be next. Soon all the known world will be mine. And with that temporal power, the worlds I have entered, escaping death, will fall before me as well."

I was only half listening to his mad babble. As he spoke I remembered Gamelan's musings, built on Greycloak's theorems. "Magic consumes power, Rali," Gamelan had said. "Just as a mill wheel needs an ox to turn it. And the ox needs grain to feed it. And the grain needs seed, which consume the power of the sun to grow. And only the gods know what fires the sun. But even its power may not be endless. And the more that is drawn from it, the less may be its heat."

If this was true, I thought, it'd explain why the Archon stood before me in a weaker, mortal form, instead of an almighty specter in the sky. All his force was being used to contain the odd reality—if that was what it could be called—we stood in. From this turret room, to the iron castle itself, to the false Orissa that waited to be ground up by the doom machine. And the machine itself must be greedily devouring the most power of all.

I stroked the panther and she purred most fearfully. "What happens, sorcerer," I said, "when my sister and I finally burst through your wall? You know it's going to happen. You know you're weakening, while we're getting stronger."

The panther snarled and the Archon's eyes flickered. I hoped it was fear. I raised the axe. "Do you dare face me in that form, sorcerer?" I said.

I swung the axe with all my strength. There was a sound like a potter's furnace exploding. The shimmer of the wall glowed white-hot, then vanished. I stepped forward, the panther at my side.

"To kill me," I said, "you must destroy all else."

I knew by the fire dying in his eyes what I'd said was true. Hate unfroze him and he reared up and the air crackled with magic. I threw the axe. It hit him square in the chest—biting through and carrying him back. He slammed against the wall. He should have been dead then. Or, I should say, dead again—for I had slain him once before. But he struggled up, the axe hanging from the wound. I drew my sword to finish him off, but before I could, red smoke gouted from his body. It boiled up until it filled the room to the high ceiling. And out of that smoke reared the transformed Archon.

The two-headed lion roared at me, twin jaws gnashing teeth as long as spears. But the roar was answered in kind by the panther. She leaped for the beast and sunk her teeth into its forepaw. The lion heads shrieked pain and anger. The beast hurled the panther from it, but as the cat twisted in the air, she grew in size, and by the time she landed and came up again, her head was as high as mine. With a final enraged howl, the beast that was the Archon burst through the walls of the turret, spread its wings and flew away.

The castle shuddered. Molten iron began to run down the walls. Then the entire edifice—castle, machine, simulacrum, and all—began to crumble around and under me. The panther screamed, jolting me out of my shock. Somehow I knew what I had to do. As the floor collapsed, I jumped for her, grabbing great fistfuls of fur. I felt her leap and we were soaring through the gaping hole the Archon had made.

Instead of falling, she soared up and up. I twisted until I was on her back, riding her through the night skies. I looked beneath me and saw the iron castle explode in flame and fury. Then I looked ahead, and far away I saw the red wings of the fleeing Archon.

The panther moved faster, then faster still, until all was a blur of wind stinging my eyes. I clutched her tighter, felt myself blend with those great, rolling muscles. Then those sleek muscles were mine, and the sharp, heavy claws as well. The panther's heart was my heart, and my nerves were afire with quick cat hate, and my mind hungered for the stalk and the kill. I was that panther now, and I howled in joy at all the strength and hate inside me as I pursued the Archon. I leaped from cloud to cloud, disdainful of all winged things, which must be my meat if I commanded it.

I caught him first on a mountaintop. Fire and lightning gouted from the mouths of the beast. But my panther reflexes let me easily slip past those threats, and as I closed, he fled again. I was just on his heels now; but a great black hole yawned in the sky, and the beast shot through it. I followed—knowing I was leaving this world for another, but my panther's heart didn't fear, my panther's brain didn't care—and I found my panther self charging across a great field of ice.

It was translucent blue and shot with thick pink veins. My claws scythed out, gripping the ice, and I scrambled across it, screaming my panther war cry at the lion beast just ahead. I didn't have to think that neither of us could take to the air in this place, I just knew it, accepted it as a law that governed creatures such as ourselves.

Then the world shifted again and I was in another place. A place of fire and thick smoke. I charged blindly ahead, my paws skittering and scorching on the hot path, my lungs searing in the heat. It must have been just as hellish for the Archon, because the fiery world suddenly dissolved around me . . . and I found myself in a narrow ravine.

Poisonous snakes littered the path by the hundreds and they struck at me—a dozen at a time—but I bounded over them, leaping from boulder to great boulder. The ravine, whose walls soared high on either side, twisted like those snakes toward a huge rock face. Far above, sitting on that clifftop, was an emerald-domed palace with columns of gold, which gleamed in the moonlight.

The twin-headed lion was trying to scramble up the rock face to the palace; somehow I knew if he reached it, all would be lost. But the rock was rotten shale, crumbling under his powerful claws.

I screamed and my hunter's cry froze him. The beast turned to confront me. He grew larger and larger and then he transformed into the shape of the Archon again. But this Archon was twenty feet high or more, and he had immense lion claws and huge yellow teeth. He howled a challenge that echoed all along the ravine. I leaped up at him, felt those claws close on me and pierce my flesh.

I slashed at him and bit through his beard; felt his hot, soft throat beneath; and I clamped my strong jaws shut. The blood I lusted for pulsed out. The claws fell away. The Archon collapsed; I didn't loosen my death grip, but only shook and shook until the blood ceased to flow and his heart was still.

I let loose and lifted up my head. I was standing on the Archon's corpse. I saw a small, dark wisp rise from his chest and knew it was what was left of his soul. I slapped it down with my paw as if it were a mouse and crushed it.

The Archon was no more.

My scream of victory resounded from the very moon.

Then Archon, palace, ravine, and moon vanished and I was no longer a panther, but only Rali, an all too mortal woman and soldier.

I was lying on a deck of a ship, bleeding from many wounds. It was *my* ship. And the corpses of my Guardswomen were piled around. Just to one side was Gamelan's body. Next to him was Polillo's. I struggled up and looked out across the rolling seas.

I knew I'd never left that deck—except as a spirit. We'd fought a battle here. And continued the fight in the ethers, where it was finally won. I knelt down on one knee and prayed thanks to Maranonia for gifting her daughters with noble deaths.

I looked at my palm. The lion scar was gone forever.

Then I wept. I wept for Polillo, I wept for Gamelan and Corais and Ismet and all the others. I also wept for me. I still lived, and I knew the guilt of being among the living would not be easy to bear.

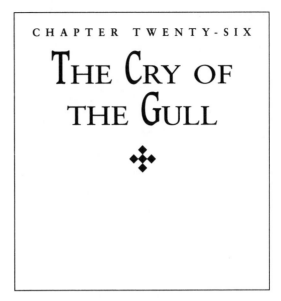

CHAPTER TWENTY-SIX

THE CRY OF THE GULL

❖

I don't remember much about what happened next. It was a long, hard journey home. I think I hungered. I may have suffered from cold and heat. I couldn't say. Somehow I jury-rigged a sail and went on, still to the east, still toward our home. Somehow I must have lashed the tiller. Somehow the winds were kind and didn't rip the sail from the mast. Somehow the seas held their hands. Perhaps the gods saw an end to their jest, and realized there was no more of me to make sport of.

Finally one day I saw a ship, and it was an Orissan ship—a merchantman from Amalric's fleet. This time it was no trick, and the captain who greeted me appeared in awe when he learned who I was and what I had done.

Once home, I got a hero's welcome, as you well know. And it was honest and warm and I was filled with joy to the overflowing. The people of Orissa mobbed me and carried me through the streets to the Great Amphitheater, where my praises were sung and honors heaped on me; and afterward the wine flowed freely in all the homes and taverns in a proper Orissan celebration.

Amalric welcomed me with a hug I thought would crush my ribs. Omerye kissed me and we both cried for being so happy. Porcemus and my brothers were delightfully cold and distant. I treasured the constancy of their dislike almost as much as I valued Amalric's love.

I was even more delighted to learn that Jinnah had never enjoyed any of the honors the Archon envisioned in his false Orissa. When he'd returned from Lycanth, he'd been damned by the Magistrates and Evocators for his misdeeds in the siege, and for sending me after the Archon's fleet with such a puny, ragtag force. He'd been stripped of all rank—condemned even by his family—and banished from the city and all its provinces. When last was heard, he'd been kidnapped by slavers and was pulling an oar on a leaky barge that plies the pirate-infested waters off Jeypur.

While I was gone, a vigil was kept for the whole two years, and many were the prayers and sacrifices for our safe and victorious return. Before I came home, a great earthquake shook Orissa, with its center seemingly the hill the Palace of the Evocators stood on. Fortunately, damage and loss of life was slight. The Evocators have traced that great quake to the time when I fought the Archon in the ethers as a panther.

As for that holy beast itself, I've never seen her again—except in troubled dreams.

My love life could be full, if I wanted. Many women have sought to share my days and nights. As Princess Xia predicted, Tries came running to me as soon as I got back. She hadn't married, of course, but swore she'd kept her love alive all that time. She said it was all a silly misunderstanding, and sometimes I think I might even agree. But other times—well, let's just say I've chosen to remain unattached and chaste for a time.

You ask what will I do next? What does it matter? The book is done, the tale is told, and that should be the end of it.

Oh, very well, Scribe. I'll tell you as best I can.

A week ago Amalric invited me to his villa. We had a lovely time, sipping wine and gossiping while Omerye entertained us on her lyre. The garden was its old, comfortable ramble of overgrown paths slipping by sweet-smelling flowers and fruiting trees. My brother and I strolled through it, taking the wine with us, and found a comfortable seat next to the fountain near my mother's simple stone shrine.

Amalric asked me the same question you just posed: What was I going to do next?

I laughed. "I thought you just wanted me for my company, brother dear," I said. "But now I see you've joined the throng hounding me. No one ever gives a soldier peace when she returns home. She must get busy right away, carve out a life herself. Te-Date forbid, she might become an idler." I raised my goblet. "Right now, all I want is more of this. With a little sun and song as well. What's wrong with that?"

Amalric took my hint and refilled the goblet. Then he said: "They're re-forming the Maranon Guard, you know."

I sighed. "So that's it! Listen—the Magistrates have already been beseeching me to command the new Guard. And I've rejected them as politely as possible."

Amalric blessed me with that boyish grin of his. "So they've told me," he said. "And they asked me to apply a little pressure to get you to change your mind."

I shook my head. "Tell them you pleaded mightily," I said, "but I failed to see reason. And the answer is still no."

"What has changed, Rali?" he asked. "Once, the Maranon Guard was your whole life. Being a soldier was your girlhood dream come true."

I drank more wine. Then: "I grew weary of taking young women out to die," I said. "I've ghosts enough for company as it is. I don't need more."

"Then you're through with soldiering?" he asked.

"I'm not certain," I said. "But as long as Orissa is safe, I doubt I'll take up arms again."

"So what is it that you want?" he pressed.

Unaccountably, tears rose in my eyes. "Just to be left alone," I said, struggling not to weep.

Amalric came to me and put his arms around me. "They won't do that, sister dear," he said. "It's your misfortune to be a hero who lived."

I drove off the self-pity and wiped my eyes. "It's also my misfortune," I said, "that soldiering is all I know."

"That's not true," my brother murmured. "There's more to you than sword and shield. I've known that since I was a hero-worshiping boy pestering his sister to always be in her company."

I looked at the mossy stone that was my mother's shrine. Searching for guidance, I suppose. But none came. There was no sudden, shimmering of an image coming to life. No scent of a sandalwood ghost, or whispered warnings, or advice.

A gentle wind blew up, carrying the smell of the river. And with it came the memory of a hard ship's deck, crackling sails, leaping seas, the smell of salt, the feel of cold spray needling the flesh, and the horizon—teasing like a gossamer-veiled dancing girl—always retreating before your eyes.

"I have an expedition leaving in a month," Amalric said.

And I thought: Yes!

"There's tales of rich trading opportunities," he said, "far to the south where no one has ever been before."

And I thought: Yes . . . yes!

"I won't lie to you that it won't be dangerous," my brother said. "There'll be cold and hunger and only a small chance of success. But there will be adventure, Rali. New lands. New people. New hopes. These things I *can* promise."

And I thought: Please, yes.

"The expedition has need of an Evocator," he said.

My heart dipped. "But they'd never allow it," I said. "No woman has been an expedition Evocator in all the history of Orissa."

Amalric said: "Then it's time we started. After all, you're Rali Emilie Antero. And you can be anything you like. What do you say, sister dear? Will you sail?"

And I said: "Yes!"

So there you have it, Scribe. The tale of a warrior some are fools enough to praise as a hero. You've got most of the journal bundled up now, and soon it'll be ready for the bookstalls.

I wonder what others will think when they read it? Sometimes I imagine a little girl turning the pages, curled up in her bed at night; reading by fire beads under the covers so her nurse won't catch her. I wonder what that little girl will think. Will she want to defy tradition and trade her dolls for a sword? If she does, is that what I desire? To be honest, I'm not certain. What would be best of all, I believe, is that she'd be her own woman; refuse to be anything but equal to any man in whatever life she chooses.

And perhaps, Scribe, when next that child hears a gull cry, she will think of me.

ABOUT THE AUTHORS

Collaborators for more than ten years, and friends for thirty, Chris Bunch and Allan Cole bring their lifelong addiction to distant lands and cultures to *The Warrior's Tale*. Bunch is still haunted by youthful memories of Asian temple bells and snow leopards, and the thousand-year-old tomb of a Korean princess, while Cole recalls hearing *The Tempest* for the first time as a child sitting on an ancient wall in Cyprus—the island Shakespeare had in mind when he penned the play. As adults, their wide travels have taken them from misty gull-haunted isles off Ireland to the frozen wastelands of Antarctica. When not traveling they live in Chinook and Ocean Park, Washington, with their strongest supporters, Karen and Kathryn.